NINETEEN EIGHTY-FOUR

Text
Sources
Criticism

second edition

HARBRACE SOURCEBOOKS

Under the General Editorship of
DAVID LEVIN, Commonwealth Professor of English,
University of Virginia

Orwell's

NINETEEN EIGHTY- FOUR

Text
Sources
Criticism

second edition

edited by
Irving Howe

Hunter College and the Graduate Center
of The City University of New York

 HARCOURT BRACE JOVANOVICH, PUBLISHERS

San Diego   New York   Chicago   Washington, D.C.   Atlanta
London   Sydney   Toronto

ISBN 0-15-565811-5

Library of Congress Catalog Card Number: 81-81897

Printed in the United States of America

Acknowledgments appear on pages 449–50, which constitute
a continuation of the copyright page.

Preface

In 1949, shortly before his death, the English writer George Orwell published his last book, an "anti-utopian" fiction called *Nineteen Eighty-Four*. It soon caught the attention of readers throughout the world, or at least in those parts of the world where people were free to read the books they chose. Even in some of the Communist countries, copies of *Nineteen Eighty-Four* were secretly passed around among intellectuals and read with great interest. The book dramatized an extreme version of certain terrifying possibilities that had been thrown up by the history of the twentieth century—possibilities of a totalitarian state that, going even beyond the regimes of Hitler, Mussolini, and Stalin, but clearly resembling these, would regulate the lives of all its subjects, break every sign of independent thought or feeling, and regiment men and women into machinelike creatures doing the work of the state. Nor was this a mere private nightmare of a disturbed writer. What Orwell made so vivid and frightening in *Nineteen Eighty-Four* troubled the millions of people throughout the world who feared that totalitarianism might be "the wave of the future." That fear is by no means at an end even now, and the issues raised by *Nineteen Eighty-Four* remain as urgent as when Orwell first published his novel.

It was no accident that *Nineteen Eighty-Four* aroused an enormous amount of discussion and debate. A central problem of modern life is involved here, and when individuals grow passionate in writing about it, as some of the essayists in this volume do, they are arguing not merely over the literary merits of a single work but also over such fundamental questions as: What kind of society should we live in? What are the permissible restrictions on liberty that a society may impose? What is the likelihood that the worldwide trends toward bureaucracy, authoritarianism, and regimentation will prevail? The very term "nineteen eighty-four" has entered into the modern vocabulary, and the novel has become a major document of contemporary politics.

The first Sourcebook edition of *Orwell's Nineteen Eighty-Four* appeared in 1963, containing not only the entire text of the novel but also a series of essays and documents that enabled the student to appreciate Orwell's narrative with greater literary and historical depth. A large part of the first edition has been preserved in the second; the continued demand for our critical text persuaded us that the material is considered useful by instructors and students.

The most important material added to the second edition is by Orwell himself—texts taken from the four-volume *Collected Essays, Journalism and Letters of George Orwell* published in 1968. This consists mainly of excerpts from Orwell's letters in which he speaks of getting ready to write his great book, or expresses frustration over the difficult circumstances that prevent him from finishing it, or reflects on problems that spur him to writing it. We have also added one of his major essays, "The Prevention of Literature," which bears significantly on Orwell's creative work. New, too, are a brief section of reviews written when *Nineteen Eighty-Four* was first published and a section called "Personal Responses," in which a number of illustrious literary figures write about Orwell in informal but moving ways. Finally, we conclude with a full-scale reconsideration of *Nineteen Eighty-Four*—one that asks whether the novel still holds up, whether it has been shown to be mistaken by events—that was written especially for the second edition by Michael Harrington, the noted American social critic.

The critical literature on *Nineteen Eighty-Four* written during the recent period has not been as impressive or exciting as that written in the decade or so after the novel first came out. Since we have no wish to burden our new edition with repetitive or tiresome material, we have added only one critical essay, a very interesting piece by the English critic and novelist John Wain.

Otherwise, this book remains largely what it has been these twenty years. In it we have material about the sources used by Orwell, and a selection of essays by critics discussing such matters as the genre of anti-utopian fiction to which *Nineteen Eighty-Four* belongs. We also have essays discussing the special literary problems—the merits and weaknesses—of the novel itself. There are two thoughtful essays, by Hannah Arendt and Richard Lowenthal, examining the phenomenon of totalitarianism, with obvious bearing on *Nineteen Eighty-Four*.

To study this work, therefore, means to become involved with a variety of experiences and issues somewhat greater than is provided by most novels. There are, first, the literary problems: What kind of fiction is it? How good a work is it? By which criteria should we judge it? And how does it compare to similar works? Then there are political and intellectual problems: What kind of light does it throw on totalitarian society? What is the value or significance of writing a book like *Nineteen Eighty-Four?* Finally, there are moral problems concerning the role of individual conscience, personal resistance, and public courage that are raised by the example of Orwell's work and career.

IRVING HOWE
The City University of New York

FOOTNOTE FORM

Those students who write papers based on this book will need a footnote form that simplifies references to material reprinted here. The simplest method of citation, and one that avoids repetition of the title of this volume, would be to cite the author, title, date, and pages of the selection, but not the title of the volume. For example, a footnote that referred to a passage from Lionel Trilling's essay would read:

[1]Lionel Trilling, "George Orwell and the Politics of Truth" (1955), p. 345.

References to works not reprinted in this volume should follow the style established by the Modern Language Association. For information on the MLA style, students should consult their instructors or the *MLA Handbook: For Writers of Research Papers, Theses, and Dissertations.*

About This Book

Readers of *Orwell's Nineteen Eighty-Four,* Second Edition, may be interested in some of the technology used to produce this book. An automated scanner "read" the printed novel and other material from the first edition and transferred it onto magnetic discs. The remaining portions of this edition were typed on a word processor. Then the outputs of both processes were merged onto magnetic discs that generated the printed type you see here.

Contents

Orwell's

NINETEEN EIGHTY-FOUR

Text
Sources
Criticism

second edition

PART ONE

Text

GEORGE ORWELL
Nineteen Eighty-Four

ONE

It was a bright cold day in April, and the clocks were striking thirteen. Winston Smith, his chin nuzzled into his breast in an effort to escape the vile wind, slipped quickly through the glass doors of Victory Mansions, though not quickly enough to prevent a swirl of gritty dust from entering along with him.

The hallway smelt of boiled cabbage and old rag mats. At one end of it a colored poster, too large for indoor display, had been tacked to the wall. It depicted simply an enormous face, more than a meter wide: the face of a man of about forty-five, with a heavy black mustache and ruggedly handsome features. Winston made for the stairs. It was no use trying the lift. Even at the best of times it was seldom working, and at present the electric current was cut off during daylight hours. It was part of the economy drive in preparation for Hate Week. The flat was seven flights up, and Winston, who was thirty-nine and had a varicose ulcer above his right ankle, went slowly, resting several times on the way. On each landing, opposite the lift shaft, the poster with the enormous face gazed from the wall. It was one of those pictures which are so contrived that the eyes follow you about when you move. BIG BROTHER IS WATCHING YOU, the caption beneath it ran.

Inside the flat a fruity voice was reading out a list of figures which had something to do with the production of pig iron. The voice came from an oblong metal plaque like a dulled mirror which formed part of the surface of the right-hand wall. Winston turned a switch and the voice sank somewhat, though the words were still distinguishable. The instrument (the telescreen, it was called) could be dimmed, but there was no way of shutting it off completely. He moved over to the window: a smallish, frail figure, the meagerness of his body merely emphasized by the blue overalls which were the uniform of the Party. His hair was very fair, his face naturally sanguine, his skin roughened by coarse soap and blunt razor blades and the cold of the winter that had just ended.

Outside, even through the shut window pane, the world looked cold. Down in the street little eddies of wind were whirling dust and torn paper

3

into spirals, and though the sun was shining and the sky a harsh blue, there seemed to be no color in anything except the posters that were plastered everywhere. The black-mustachio'd face gazed down from every commanding corner. There was one on the house front immediately opposite. BIG BROTHER IS WATCHING YOU, the caption said, while the dark eyes looked deep into Winston's own. Down at street level another poster, torn at one corner, flapped fitfully in the wind, alternately covering and uncovering the single word INGSOC. In the far distance a helicopter skimmed down between the roofs, hovered for an instant like a bluebottle, and darted away again with a curving flight. It was the Police Patrol, snooping into people's windows. The patrols did not matter, however. Only the Thought Police mattered.

Behind Winston's back the voice from the telescreen was still babbling away about pig iron and the overfulfillment of the Ninth Three-Year Plan. The telescreen received and transmitted simultaneously. Any sound that Winston made, above the level of a very low whisper, would be picked up by it; moreover, so long as he remained within the field of vision which the metal plaque commanded, he could be seen as well as heard. There was of course no way of knowing whether you were being watched at any given moment. How often, or on what system, the Thought Police plugged in on any individual wire was guesswork. It was even conceivable that they watched everybody all the time. But at any rate they could plug in your wire whenever they wanted to. You had to live—did live, from habit that became instinct—in the assumption that every sound you made was overheard, and, except in darkness, every movement scrutinized.

Winston kept his back turned to the telescreen. It was safer; though, as he well knew, even a back can be revealing. A kilometer away the Ministry of Truth, his place of work, towered vast and white above the grimy landscape. This, he thought with a sort of vague distaste—this was London, chief city of Airstrip One, itself the third most populous of the provinces of Oceania. He tried to squeeze out some childhood memory that should tell him whether London had always been quite like this. Were there always these vistas of rotting nineteenth-century houses, their sides shored up with balks of timber, their windows patched with cardboard and their roofs with corrugated iron, their crazy garden walls sagging in all directions? And the bombed sites where the plaster dust swirled in the air and the willow herb straggled over the heaps of rubble; and the places where the bombs had cleared a larger patch and there had sprung up sordid colonies of wooden dwellings like chicken houses? But it was no use, he could not remember: nothing remained of his childhood except a series of bright-lit tableaux, occurring against no background and mostly unintelligible.

The Ministry of Truth—Minitrue, in Newspeak*—was startlingly different from any other object in sight. It was an enormous pyramidal structure of glittering white concrete, soaring up, terrace after terrace, three hundred meters into the air. From where Winston stood it was just possible to read, picked out on its white face in elegant lettering, the three slogans of the Party:

WAR IS PEACE
FREEDOM IS SLAVERY
IGNORANCE IS STRENGTH.

The Ministry of Truth contained, it was said, three thousand rooms above ground level, and corresponding ramifications below. Scattered about London there were just three other buildings of similar appearance and size. So completely did they dwarf the surrounding architecture that from the roof of Victory Mansions you could see all four of them simultaneously. They were the homes of the four Ministries between which the entire apparatus of government was divided: the Ministry of Truth, which concerned itself with news, entertainment, education, and the fine arts; the Ministry of Peace, which concerned itself with war; the Ministry of Love, which maintained law and order; and the Ministry of Plenty, which was responsible for economic affairs. Their names, in Newspeak: Minitrue, Minipax, Miniluv, and Miniplenty.

The Ministry of Love was the really frightening one. There were no windows in it at all. Winston had never been inside the Ministry of Love, nor within half a kilometer of it. It was a place impossible to enter except on official business, and then only by penetrating through a maze of barbed-wire entanglements, steel doors, and hidden machine-gun nests. Even the streets leading up to its outer barriers were roamed by gorilla-faced guards in black uniforms, armed with jointed truncheons.

Winston turned round abruptly. He had set his features into the expression of quiet optimism which it was advisable to wear when facing the telescreen. He crossed the room into the tiny kitchen. By leaving the Ministry at this time of day he had sacrificed his lunch in the canteen, and he was aware that there was no food in the kitchen except a hunk of dark-colored bread which had got to be saved for tomorrow's breakfast. He took down from the shelf a bottle of colorless liquid with a plain white label marked VICTORY GIN. It gave off a sickly, oily smell, as of Chinese rice-spirit. Winston poured out nearly a teacupful, nerved himself for a shock, and gulped it down like a dose of medicine.

Instantly his face turned scarlet and the water ran out of his eyes. The

* Newspeak was the official language of Oceania. For an account of its structure and etymology, see Appendix.

stuff was like nitric acid, and moreover, in swallowing it one had the sensation of being hit on the back of the head with a rubber club. The next moment, however, the burning in his belly died down and the world began to look more cheerful. He took a cigarette from a crumpled packet marked VICTORY CIGARETTES and incautiously held it upright, whereupon the tobacco fell out onto the floor. With the next he was more successful. He went back to the living room and sat down at a small table that stood to the left of the telescreen. From the table drawer he took out a penholder, a bottle of ink, and a thick, quarto-sized blank book with a red back and a marbled cover.

For some reason the telescreen in the living room was in an unusual position. Instead of being placed, as was normal, in the end wall, where it could command the whole room, it was in the longer wall, opposite the window. To one side of it there was a shallow alcove in which Winston was now sitting, and which, when the flats were built, had probably been intended to hold bookshelves. By sitting in the alcove, and keeping well back, Winston was able to remain outside the range of the telescreen, so far as sight went. He could be heard, of course, but so long as he stayed in his present position he could not be seen. It was partly the unusual geography of the room that had suggested to him the thing that he was now about to do.

But it had also been suggested by the book that he had just taken out of the drawer. It was a peculiarly beautiful book. Its smooth creamy paper, a little yellowed by age, was of a kind that had not been manufactured for at least forty years past. He could guess, however, that the book was much older than that. He had seen it lying in the window of a frowsy little junk shop in a slummy quarter of the town (just what quarter he did not now remember) and had been stricken immediately by an overwhelming desire to possess it. Party members were supposed not to go into ordinary shops ("dealing on the free market," it was called), but the rule was not strictly kept, because there were various things such as shoelaces and razor blades which it was impossible to get hold of in any other way. He had given a quick glance up and down the street and then had slipped inside and bought the book for two dollars fifty. At the time he was not conscious of wanting it for any particular purpose. He had carried it guiltily home in his brief case. Even with nothing written in it, it was a compromising possession.

The thing that he was about to do was to open a diary. This was not illegal (nothing was illegal, since there were no longer any laws), but if detected it was reasonably certain that it would be punished by death, or at least by twenty-five years in a forced-labor camp. Winston fitted a nib into the penholder and sucked it to get the grease off. The pen was an archaic instrument, seldom used even for signatures, and he had procured one, furtively and with some difficulty, simply because of a feeling that the beautiful creamy paper deserved to be written on with a real nib instead of being scratched with an ink pencil. Actually he was not used to writing by hand. Apart from very short notes, it was usual to dictate everything into the speakwrite, which was of course impossible for his present purpose. He dipped the pen into the ink and then faltered for just a second. A tremor had gone through his bowels. To mark the paper was the decisive act. In small clumsy letters he wrote:

April 4th, 1984.

He sat back. A sense of complete helplessness had descended upon him. To begin with, he did not know with any certainty that this *was* 1984. It must be round about that date, since he was fairly sure that his age was thirty-nine, and he believed that he had been born in 1944 or 1945; but it was never possible nowadays to pin down any date within a year or two.

For whom, it suddenly occurred to him to wonder, was he writing this diary? For the future, for the unborn. His mind hovered for a moment round the doubtful date on the page, and then fetched up with a bump against the Newspeak word *doublethink*. For the first time the magnitude of what he had undertaken came home to him. How could you communicate with the future? It was of its nature impossible. Either the future would resemble the present, in which case it would not listen to him, or it would be different from it, and his predicament would be meaningless.

For some time he sat gazing stupidly at the paper. The telescreen had changed over to strident military music. It was curious that he seemed not merely to have lost the power of expressing himself, but even to have forgotten what it was that he had originally intended to say. For weeks past he had been making ready for this moment, and it had never crossed his mind that anything would be needed except courage. The actual writing would be easy. All he had to do was to transfer to paper the interminable restless monologue that had been running inside his head, literally for years. At this moment, however, even the monologue had dried up. Moreover, his varicose ulcer had begun itching unbearably. He dared not scratch it, because if he did so it always became inflamed. The seconds were ticking by. He was conscious of nothing except the blankness of the page in front of him, the itching of the skin above his ankle, the blaring of the music, and a slight booziness caused by the gin.

Suddenly he began writing in sheer panic, only imperfectly aware of what he was setting down. His small but childish handwriting straggled up and down the page, shedding first its capital letters and finally even its full stops:

April 4th, 1984. Last night to the flicks. All war films. One very good one of a ship full of refugees being bombed somewhere in the Mediterranean. Audience much amused by shots of a great huge fat man trying to swim away with a helicopter after him. first you saw him wallowing

along in the water like a porpoise, then you saw him through the helicop-
ters gunsights, then he was full of holes and the sea round him turned
pink and he sank as suddenly as though the holes had let in the water.
audience shouting with laughter when he sank. then you saw a lifeboat
full of children with a helicopter hovering over it. there was a middleaged
woman might have been a jewess sitting up in the bow with a little boy
about three years old in her arms. little boy screaming with fright and
hiding his head between her breasts as if he was trying to burrow right
into her and the woman putting her arms round him and comforting him
although she was blue with fright herself. all the time covering him up as
much as possible as if she thought her arms could keep the bullets off him,
then the helicopter planted a 20 kilo bomb in among them terrific flash
and the boat went all to matchwood. then there was a wonderful shot of a
childs arm going up up up right up into the air a helicopter with a camera
in its nose must have followed it up and there was a lot of applause from
the party seats but a woman down in the prole part of the house suddenly
started kicking up a fuss and shouting they didnt oughter of showed it not
in front of kids they didnt it aint right not in front of kids it aint until the
police turned her out i dont suppose anything happened to her nobody
cares what the proles say typical prole reaction they never—

Winston stopped writing, partly because he was suffering from cramp. He did not know what had made him pour out this stream of rubbish. But the curious thing was that while he was doing so a totally different memory had clarified itself in his mind, to the point where he almost felt equal to writing it down. It was, he now realized, because of this other incident that he had suddenly decided to come home and begin the diary today.

It happened that morning at the Ministry, if anything so nebulous could be said to happen.

It was nearly eleven hundred, and in the Records Department, where Winston worked, they were dragging the chairs out of the cubicles and grouping them in the center of the hall, opposite the big telescreen, in preparation for the Two Minutes Hate. Winston was just taking his place in one of the middle rows when two people whom he knew by sight, but had never spoken to, came unexpectedly into the room. One of them was a girl whom he often passed in the corridors. He did not know her name, but he knew that she worked in the Fiction Department. Presumably— since he had sometimes seen her with oily hands and carrying a span- ner—she had some mechanical job on one of the novel-writing machines. She was a bold-looking girl of about twenty-seven, with thick dark hair, a freckled face, and swift, athletic movements. A narrow scarlet sash, em- blem of the Junior Anti-Sex League, was wound several times round the waist of her overalls, just tightly enough to bring out the shapeliness of her hips. Winston had disliked her from the very first moment of seeing her. He knew the reason. It was because of the atmosphere of hockey fields and cold baths and community hikes and general clean-mindedness which she managed to carry about with her. He disliked nearly all women, and especially the young and pretty ones. It was always the women, and above all the young ones, who were the most bigoted adherents of the Party, the swallowers of slogans, the amateur spies and nosers-out of unorthodoxy. But this particular girl gave him the impression of being more dangerous than most. Once when they passed in the corridor she had given him a quick sidelong glance which seemed to pierce right into him and for a moment had filled him with black terror. The idea had even crossed his mind that she might be an agent of the Thought Police. That, it was true, was very unlikely. Still, he continued to feel a peculiar uneasiness, which had fear mixed up in it as well as hostility, whenever she was anywhere near him.

The other person was a man named O'Brien, a member of the Inner Party and holder of some post so important and remote that Winston had only a dim idea of its nature. A momentary hush passed over the group of people round the chairs as they saw the black overalls of an Inner Party member approaching. O'Brien was a large, burly man with a thick neck and a coarse, humorous, brutal face. In spite of his formidable appearance he had a certain charm of manner. He had a trick of resettling his spectacles on his nose which was curiously disarming—in some indefinable way, curiously civilized. It was a gesture which, if anyone had still thought in such terms, might have recalled an eighteenth-century nobleman offering his snuffbox. Winston had seen O'Brien perhaps a dozen times in almost as many years. He felt deeply drawn to him, and not solely because he was intrigued by the contrast between O'Brien's urbane manner and his prizefighter's physique. Much more it was because of a secretly held belief—or perhaps not even a belief, merely a hope—that O'Brien's political orthodoxy was not perfect. Something in his face suggested it irresistibly. And again, perhaps it was not even unorthodoxy that was written in his face, but simply intelligence. But at any rate he had the appearance of being a person that you could talk to, if somehow you could cheat the telescreen and get him alone. Winston had never made the smallest effort to verify this guess; indeed, there was no way of doing so. At this moment O'Brien glanced at his wristwatch, saw that it was nearly eleven hundred, and evidently decided to stay in the Records Department until the Two Minutes Hate was over. He took a chair in the same row as Winston, a couple of places away. A small, sandy-haired woman who worked in the next cubicle to Winston was between them. The girl with dark hair was sitting immediately behind.

The next moment a hideous, grinding screech, as of some monstrous machine running without oil, burst from the big telescreen at the end of the room. It was a noise that set one's teeth on edge and bristled the hair at the back of one's neck. The Hate had started.

As usual, the face of Emmanuel Goldstein, the Enemy of the People, had flashed onto the screen. There were hisses here and there among the audience. The little sandy-haired woman gave a squeak of mingled fear and disgust. Goldstein was the renegade and backslider who once, long ago (how long ago, nobody quite remembered), had been one of the leading figures of the Party, almost on a level with Big Brother himself, and then had engaged in counterrevolutionary activities, had been condemned to death, and had mysteriously escaped and disappeared. The program of the Two Minutes Hate varied from day to day, but there was none in which Goldstein was not the principal figure. He was the primal traitor, the earliest defiler of the Party's purity. All subsequent crimes against the Party, all treacheries, acts of sabotage, heresies, deviations, sprang directly out of his teaching. Somewhere or other he was still alive and hatching his conspiracies: perhaps somewhere beyond the sea, under the protection of his foreign paymasters; perhaps even—so it was occasionally rumored—in some hiding place in Oceania itself.

Winston's diaphragm was constricted. He could never see the face of Goldstein without a painful mixture of emotions. It was a lean Jewish face, with a great fuzzy aureole of white hair and a small goatee beard—a clever face, and yet somehow inherently despicable, with a kind of senile silliness in the long thin nose near the end of which a pair of spectacles was perched. It resembled the face of a sheep, and the voice, too, had a sheeplike quality. Goldstein was delivering his usual venomous attack upon the doctrines of the Party—an attack so exaggerated and perverse that a child should have been able to see through it, and yet just plausible enough to fill one with an alarmed feeling that other people, less level-headed than oneself, might be taken in by it. He was abusing Big Brother, he was denouncing the dictatorship of the Party, he was demanding the immediate conclusion of peace with Eurasia, he was advocating freedom of speech, freedom of the press, freedom of assembly, freedom of thought, he was crying hysterically that the revolution had been betrayed—and all this in rapid polysyllabic speech which was a sort of parody of the habitual style of the orators of the Party, and even contained Newspeak words: more Newspeak words, indeed, than any Party member would normally use in real life. And all the while, lest one should be in any doubt as to the reality which Goldstein's specious claptrap covered, behind his head on the telescreen there marched the endless columns of the Eurasian army—row after row of solid-looking men with expressionless Asiatic faces, who swam up to the surface of the screen and vanished, to be replaced by others exactly similar. The dull, rhythmic tramp of the soldiers' boots formed the background to Goldstein's bleating voice.

Before the Hate had proceeded for thirty seconds, uncontrollable exclamations of rage were breaking out from half the people in the room. The self-satisfied sheeplike face on the screen, and the terrifying power of the Eurasian army behind it, were too much to be borne; besides, the sight or even the thought of Goldstein produced fear and anger automatically. He was an object of hatred more constant than either Eurasia or Eastasia, since when Oceania was at war with one of these powers it was generally at peace with the other. But what was strange was that although Goldstein was hated and despised by everybody, although every day, and a thousand times a day, on platforms, on the telescreen, in newspapers, in books, his theories were refuted, smashed, ridiculed, held up to the general gaze for the pitiful rubbish that they were—in spite of all this, his influence never seemed to grow less. Always there were fresh dupes waiting to be seduced by him. A day never passed when spies and saboteurs acting under his directions were not unmasked by the Thought Police. He was the commander of a vast shadowy army, an underground network of conspirators dedicated to the overthrow of the State. The Brotherhood, its name was supposed to be. There were also whispered stories of a terrible book, a compendium of all the heresies, of which Goldstein was the author and which circulated clandestinely here and there. It was a book without a title. People referred to it, if at all, simply as *the book*. But one knew of such things only through vague rumors. Neither the Brotherhood nor *the book* was a subject that any ordinary Party member would mention if there was a way of avoiding it.

In its second minute the Hate rose to a frenzy. People were leaping up and down in their places and shouting at the tops of their voices in an effort to drown the maddening bleating voice that came from the screen. The little sandy-haired woman had turned bright pink, and her mouth was opening and shutting like that of a landed fish. Even O'Brien's heavy face was flushed. He was sitting very straight in his chair, his powerful chest swelling and quivering as though he were standing up to the assault of a wave. The dark-haired girl behind Winston had begun crying out "Swine! Swine! Swine!" and suddenly she picked up a heavy Newspeak dictionary and flung it at the screen. It struck Goldstein's nose and bounced off; the voice continued inexorably. In a lucid moment Winston found that he was shouting with the others and kicking his heel violently against the rung of his chair. The horrible thing about the Two Minutes Hate was not that one was obliged to act a part, but that it was impossible to avoid joining in. Within thirty seconds any pretense was always unnecessary. A hideous ecstasy of fear and vindictiveness, a desire to kill, to torture, to smash faces in with a sledge hammer, seemed to flow through the whole group of people like an electric current, turning one even against one's will into a grimacing, screaming lunatic. And yet the rage that one felt was an abstract, undirected emotion which could be switched from one object to another like the flame of a blowlamp. Thus, at one moment Winston's hatred was not turned against Goldstein at all, but, on the contrary, against Big Brother, the Party, and the Thought Police; and at such moments his heart went out to the lonely, derided heretic on the screen, sole guardian of truth and sanity in a world of lies. And yet the very next instant he was at one with the people about him, and all that was said of Goldstein seemed to him to be true. At those moments his secret loathing of Big Brother changed into adoration, and Big Brother seemed to tower up, an invincible, fearless protector, standing like a rock against the hordes of Asia, and Goldstein, in spite of his isolation, his helplessness, and the doubt that hung about his very existence, seemed like some sinister enchanter, capable by the mere power of his voice of wrecking the structure of civilization.

It was even possible, at moments, to switch one's hatred this way or that by a voluntary act. Suddenly, by the sort of violent effort with which one wrenches one's head away from the pillow in a nightmare, Winston succeeded in transferring his hatred from the face on the screen to the dark-haired girl behind him. Vivid, beautiful hallucinations flashed through his mind. He would flog her to death with a rubber truncheon. He would tie her naked to a stake and shoot her full of arrows like Saint Sebastian. He would ravish her and cut her throat at the moment of climax. Better than before, moreover, he realized *why* it was that he hated her. He hated her because she was young and pretty and sexless, because he wanted to go to bed with her and would never do so, because round her sweet supple waist, which seemed to ask you to encircle it with your arm, there was only the odious scarlet sash, aggressive symbol of chastity.

The Hate rose to its climax. The voice of Goldstein had become an actual sheep's bleat, and for an instant the face changed into that of a sheep. Then the sheep-face melted into the figure of a Eurasian soldier who seemed to be advancing, huge and terrible, his submachine gun roaring, and seeming to spring out of the surface of the screen, so that some of the people in the front row actually flinched backwards in their seats. But in the same moment, drawing a deep sigh of relief from everybody, the hostile figure melted into the face of Big Brother, black-haired, black mustachio'd, full of power and mysterious calm, and so vast that it almost filled up the screen. Nobody heard what Big Brother was saying. It was merely a few words of encouragement, the sort of words that are uttered in the din of battle, not distinguishable individually but restoring confidence by the fact of being spoken. Then the face of Big Brother faded away again, and instead the three slogans of the Party stood out in bold capitals:

WAR IS PEACE
FREEDOM IS SLAVERY
IGNORANCE IS STRENGTH.

But the face of Big Brother seemed to persist for several seconds on the screen, as though the impact that it had made on everyone's eyeballs were too vivid to wear off immediately. The little sandy-haired woman had flung herself forward over the back of the chair in front of her. With a tremulous murmur that sounded like "My Savior!" she extended her arms toward the screen. Then she buried her face in her hands. It was apparent that she was uttering a prayer.

At this moment the entire group of people broke into a deep, slow, rhythmical chant of "B-B! . . . B-B! . . . B-B!" over and over again, very slowly, with a long pause between the first "B" and the second—a heavy, murmurous sound, somehow curiously savage, in the background of which one seemed to hear the stamp of naked feet and the throbbing of tom-toms. For perhaps as much as thirty seconds they kept it up. It was a refrain that was often heard in moments of overwhelming emotion. Partly it was a sort of hymn to the wisdom and majesty of Big Brother, but still more it was an act of self-hypnosis, a deliberate drowning of consciousness by means of rhythmic noise. Winston's entrails seemed to grow cold. In the Two Minutes Hate he could not help sharing in the general delirium, but this subhuman chanting of "B-B! . . . B-B!" always filled him with horror. Of course he chanted with the rest: it was impossible to do otherwise. To dissemble your feelings, to control your face, to do what everyone else was doing, was an instinctive reaction. But there was a space of a couple of seconds during which the expression in his eyes might conceivably have betrayed him. And it was exactly at this moment that the significant thing happened—if, indeed, it did happen.

Momentarily he caught O'Brien's eye. O'Brien had stood up. He had taken off his spectacles and was in the act of resettling them on his nose with his characteristic gesture. But there was a fraction of a second when their eyes met, and for as long as it took to happen Winston knew—yes, he *knew!*—that O'Brien was thinking the same thing as himself. An unmistakable message had passed. It was as though their two minds had opened and the thoughts were flowing from one into the other through their eyes. "I am with you," O'Brien seemed to be saying to him. "I know precisely what you are feeling. I know all about your contempt, your hatred, your disgust. But don't worry, I am on your side!" And then the flash of intelligence was gone, and O'Brien's face was as inscrutable as everybody else's.

That was all, and he was already uncertain whether it had happened. Such incidents never had any sequel. All that they did was to keep alive in him the belief, or hope, that others besides himself were the enemies of the Party. Perhaps the rumors of vast underground conspiracies were true after all—perhaps the Brotherhood really existed! It was impossible, in spite of the endless arrests and confessions and executions, to be sure that the Brotherhood was not simply a myth. Some days he believed in it, some days not. There was no evidence, only fleeting glimpses that might mean anything or nothing: snatches of overheard conversation, faint scribbles on lavatory walls—once, even, when two strangers met, a small movement of the hands which had looked as though it might be a signal of recognition. It was all guesswork: very likely he had imagined everything. He had gone back to his cubicle without looking at O'Brien again. The idea of following up their momentary contact hardly crossed his mind. It would have been inconceivably dangerous even if he had known how to set about doing it. For a second, two seconds, they had exchanged an equivocal glance, and that was the end of the story. But even that was a memorable event, in the locked loneliness in which one had to live.

Winston roused himself and sat up straighter. He let out a belch. The gin was rising from his stomach.

His eyes refocused on the page. He discovered that while he sat helplessly musing he had also been writing, as though by automatic action. And it was no longer the same cramped awkward handwriting as before. His pen had slid voluptuously over the smooth paper, printing in large neat capitals—

DOWN WITH BIG BROTHER
DOWN WITH BIG BROTHER
DOWN WITH BIG BROTHER
DOWN WITH BIG BROTHER
DOWN WITH BIG BROTHER

over and over again, filling half a page.

He could not help feeling a twinge of panic. It was absurd, since the writing of those particular words was not more dangerous than the initial act of opening the diary; but for a moment he was tempted to tear out the spoiled pages and abandon the enterprise altogether.

He did not do so, however, because he knew that it was useless. Whether he wrote DOWN WITH BIG BROTHER, or whether he refrained from writing it, made no difference. Whether he went on with the diary, or whether he did not go on with it, made no difference. The Thought Police would get him just the same. He had committed—would still have committed, even if he had never set pen to paper—the essential crime that contained all others in itself. Thoughtcrime, they called it. Thoughtcrime was not a thing that could be concealed forever. You might dodge successfully for a while, even for years, but sooner or later they were bound to get you.

It was always at night—the arrests invariably happened at night. The sudden jerk out of sleep, the rough hand shaking your shoulder, the lights glaring in your eyes, the ring of hard faces round the bed. In the vast majority of cases there was no trial, no report of the arrest. People simply disappeared, always during the night. Your name was removed from the registers, every record of everything you had ever done was wiped out, your one-time existence was denied and then forgotten. You were abolished, annihilated: *vaporized* was the usual word.

For a moment he was seized by a kind of hysteria. He began writing in a hurried untidy scrawl:

theyll shoot me i dont care theyll shoot me in the back of the neck i dont care down with big brother they always shoot you in the back of the neck i dont care down with big brother—

He sat back in his chair, slightly ashamed of himself, and laid down the pen. The next moment he started violently. There was a knocking at the door.

Already! He sat as still as a mouse, in the futile hope that whoever it was might go away after a single attempt. But no, the knocking was repeated. The worst thing of all would be to delay. His heart was thumping like a drum, but his face, from long habit, was probably expressionless. He got up and moved heavily toward the door.

II

As he put his hand to the doorknob Winston saw that he had left the diary open on the table. DOWN WITH BIG BROTHER was written all over it, in letters almost big enough to be legible across the room. It was an inconceivably stupid thing to have done. But, he realized, even in his panic he had not wanted to smudge the creamy paper by shutting the book while the ink was wet.

He drew in his breath and opened the door. Instantly a warm wave of relief flowed through him. A colorless, crushed-looking woman, with wispy hair and a lined face, was standing outside.

"Oh, comrade," she began in a dreary, whining sort of voice, "I thought I heard you come in. Do you think you could come across and have a look at our kitchen sink? It's got blocked up and—"

It was Mrs. Parsons, the wife of a neighbor on the same floor. ("Mrs." was a word somewhat discountenanced by the Party—you were supposed to call everyone "comrade"—but with some women one used it instinctively.) She was a woman of about thirty, but looking much older. One had the impression that there was dust in the creases of her face. Winston followed her down the passage. These amateur repair jobs were an almost daily irritation. Victory Mansions were old flats, built in 1930 or thereabouts, and were falling to pieces. The plaster flaked constantly from ceilings and walls, the pipes burst in every hard frost, the roof leaked whenever there was snow, the heating system was usually running at half steam when it was not closed down altogether from motives of economy. Repairs, except what you could do for yourself, had to be sanctioned by remote committees which were liable to hold up even the mending of a window pane for two years.

"Of course it's only because Tom isn't home," said Mrs. Parsons vaguely.

The Parsons's flat was bigger than Winston's, and dingy in a different way. Everything had a battered, trampled-on look, as though the place had just been visited by some large violent animal. Games impedimenta—hockey sticks, boxing gloves, a burst football, a pair of sweaty shorts turned inside out—lay all over the floor, and on the table there was a litter of dirty dishes and dog-eared exercise books. On the walls were scarlet banners of the Youth League and the Spies, and a full-sized poster of Big Brother. There was the usual boiled-cabbage smell, common to the whole building, but it was shot through by a sharper reek of sweat, which—one knew this at the first sniff, though it was hard to say how— was the sweat of some person not present at the moment. In another room someone with a comb and a piece of toilet paper was trying to keep tune with the military music which was still issuing from the telescreen.

"It's the children," said Mrs. Parsons, casting a half-apprehensive glance at the door. "They haven't been out today. And of course—"

She had a habit of breaking off her sentences in the middle. The kitchen sink was full nearly to the brim with filthy greenish water which smelt worse than ever of cabbage. Winston knelt down and examined the angle-joint of the pipe. He hated using his hands, and he hated bending down, which was always liable to start him coughing. Mrs. Parsons looked on helplessly.

"Of course if Tom was home he'd put it right in a moment," she said. "He loves anything like that. He's ever so good with his hands, Tom is."

Parsons was Winston's fellow employee at the Ministry of Truth. He was a fattish but active man of paralyzing stupidity, a mass of imbecile enthusiasms—one of those completely unquestioning, devoted drudges on whom, more even than on the Thought Police, the stability of the Party depended. At thirty-five he had just been unwillingly evicted from the Youth League, and before graduating into the Youth League he had managed to stay on in the Spies for a year beyond the statutory age. At the Ministry he was employed in some subordinate post for which intelligence was not required, but on the other hand he was a leading figure on the Sports Committee and all the other committees engaged in organizing community hikes, spontaneous demonstrations, savings campaigns, and voluntary activities generally. He would inform you with quiet pride, between whiffs of his pipe, that he had put in an appearance at the Community Center every evening for the past four years. An overpowering smell of sweat, a sort of unconscious testimony to the strenuousness of his life, followed him about wherever he went, and even remained behind him after he had gone.

"Have you got a spanner?" said Winston, fiddling with the nut on the angle-joint.

"A spanner," said Mrs. Parsons, immediately becoming invertebrate. "I don't know, I'm sure. Perhaps the children—"

There was a trampling of boots and another blast on the comb as the children charged into the living room. Mrs. Parsons brought the spanner. Winston let out the water and disgustedly removed the clot of human hair that had blocked up the pipe. He cleaned his fingers as best he could in the cold water from the tap and went back into the other room.

"Up with your hands!" yelled a savage voice.

A handsome, tough-looking boy of nine had popped up from behind the table and was menacing him with a toy automatic pistol, while his small sister, about two years younger, made the same gesture with a fragment of wood. Both of them were dressed in the blue shorts, gray shirts, and red neckerchiefs which were the uniform of the Spies. Winston raised his hands above his head, but with an uneasy feeling, so vicious was the boy's demeanor, that it was not altogether a game.

"You're a traitor!" yelled the boy. "You're a thought-criminal! You're a Eurasian spy! I'll shoot you, I'll vaporize you, I'll send you to the salt mines!"

Suddenly they were both leaping round him, shouting "Traitor!" and "Thought-criminal!", the little girl imitating her brother in every movement. It was somehow slightly frightening, like the gamboling of tiger cubs which will soon grow up into man-eaters. There was a sort of calculating ferocity in the boy's eye, a quite evident desire to hit or kick Winston and a consciousness of being very nearly big enough to do so. It was a good job it was not a real pistol he was holding, Winston thought.

Mrs. Parsons's eyes flitted nervously from Winston to the children, and back again. In the better light of the living room he noticed with interest that there actually was dust in the creases of her face.

"They do get so noisy," she said. "They're disappointed because they couldn't go to see the hanging, that's what it is. I'm too busy to take them, and Tom won't be back from work in time."

"Why can't we go and see the hanging?" roared the boy in his huge voice.

"Want to see the hanging! Want to see the hanging!" chanted the little girl, still capering round.

Some Eurasian prisoners, guilty of war crimes, were to be hanged in the Park that evening, Winston remembered. This happened about once a month, and was a popular spectacle. Children always clamored to be taken to see it. He took his leave of Mrs. Parsons and made for the door. But he had not gone six steps down the passage when something hit the back of his neck an agonizingly painful blow. It was as though a red-hot wire had been jabbed into him. He spun round just in time to see Mrs. Parsons dragging her son back into the doorway while the boy pocketed a catapult.

"Goldstein!" bellowed the boy as the door closed on him. But what most struck Winston was the look of helpless fright on the woman's grayish face.

Back in the flat he stepped quickly past the telescreen and sat down at the table again, still rubbing his neck. The music from the telescreen had stopped. Instead, a clipped military voice was reading out, with a sort of brutal relish, a description of the armaments of the new Floating Fortress which had just been anchored between Iceland and the Faroe Islands.

With those children, he thought, that wretched woman must lead a life of terror. Another year, two years, and they would be watching her night and day for symptoms of unorthodoxy. Nearly all children nowadays were horrible. What was worst of all was that by means of such organizations as the Spies they were systematically turned into ungovernable little savages, and yet this produced in them no tendency whatever to rebel against the discipline of the Party. On the contrary, they adored the Party and everything connected with it. The songs, the processions, the banners, the hiking, the drilling with dummy rifles, the yelling of slogans, the worship of Big Brother—it was all a sort of glorious game to them. All their ferocity was turned outwards, against the enemies of the State, against foreigners, traitors, saboteurs, thought-criminals. It was almost normal for people over thirty to be frightened of their own children. And with good reason, for hardly a week passed in which the *Times* did not carry a paragraph describing how some eavesdropping little sneak—"child hero" was the phrase generally used—had overheard some compromising remark and denounced his parents to the Thought Police.

The sting of the catapult bullet had worn off. He picked up his pen half-heartedly, wondering whether he could find something more to write in the diary. Suddenly he began thinking of O'Brien again.

Years ago—how long was it? Seven years it must be—he had dreamed that he was walking through a pitch-dark room. And someone sitting to one side of him had said as he passed: "We shall meet in the place where there is no darkness." It was said very quietly, almost casually—a statement, not a command. He had walked on without pausing. What was curious was that at the time, in the dream, the words had not made much impression on him. It was only later and by degrees that they had seemed to take on significance. He could not now remember whether it was before or after having the dream that he had seen O'Brien for the first time; nor could he remember when he had first identified the voice as O'Brien's. But at any rate the identification existed. It was O'Brien who had spoken to him out of the dark.

Winston had never been able to feel sure—even after this morning's flash of the eyes it was still impossible to be sure—whether O'Brien was a friend or an enemy. Nor did it even seem to matter greatly. There was a link of understanding between them more important than affection or partisanship. "We shall meet in the place where there is no darkness," he had said. Winston did not know what it meant, only that in some way or another it would come true.

The voice from the telescreen paused. A trumpet call, clear and beautiful, floated into the stagnant air. The voice continued raspingly:

"Attention! Your attention, please! A newsflash has this moment arrived from the Malabar front. Our forces in South India have won a glorious victory. I am authorized to say that the action we are now reporting may well bring the war within measurable distance of its end. Here is the newsflash—"

Bad news coming, thought Winston. And sure enough, following on a gory description of the annihilation of a Eurasian army, with stupendous figures of killed and prisoners, came the announcement that, as from next week, the chocolate ration would be reduced from thirty grams to twenty.

Winston belched again. The gin was wearing off, leaving a deflated feeling. The telescreen—perhaps to celebrate the victory, perhaps to drown the memory of the lost chocolate—crashed into "Oceania, 'tis for thee." You were supposed to stand to attention. However, in his present position he was invisible.

"Oceania, 'tis for thee" gave way to lighter music. Winston walked over to the window, keeping his back to the telescreen. The day was still cold and clear. Somewhere far away a rocket bomb exploded with a dull, reverberating roar. About twenty or thirty of them a week were falling on London at present.

Down in the street the wind flapped the torn poster to and fro, and the word INGSOC fitfully appeared and vanished. Ingsoc. The sacred principles of Ingsoc. Newspeak, doublethink, the mutability of the past. He felt as though he were wandering in the forests of the sea bottom, lost in a monstrous world where he himself was the monster. He was alone. The past was dead, the future was unimaginable. What certainty had he that a single human creature now living was on his side? And what way of knowing that the dominion of the Party would not endure *for ever?* Like an answer, the three slogans on the white face of the Ministry of Truth came back at him:

WAR IS PEACE
FREEDOM IS SLAVERY
IGNORANCE IS STRENGTH.

He took a twenty-five-cent piece out of his pocket. There, too, in tiny clear lettering, the same slogans were inscribed, and on the other face of the coin the head of Big Brother. Even from the coin the eyes pursued you. On coins, on stamps, on the covers of books, on banners, on posters, and on the wrapping of a cigarette packet—everywhere. Always the eyes watching you and the voice enveloping you. Asleep or awake, working or eating, indoors or out of doors, in the bath or in bed—no escape. Nothing was your own except the few cubic centimeters inside your skull.

The sun had shifted round, and the myriad windows of the Ministry of Truth, with the light no longer shining on them, looked grim as the loopholes of a fortress. His heart quailed before the enormous pyramidal shape. It was too strong, it could not be stormed. A thousand rocket bombs would not batter it down. He wondered again for whom he was writing the diary. For the future, for the past—for an age that might be imaginary. And in front of him there lay not death but annihilation. The diary would be reduced to ashes and himself to vapor. Only the Thought Police would read what he had written, before they wiped it out of existence and out of memory. How could you make appeal to the future when not a trace of you, not even an anonymous word scribbled on a piece of paper, could physically survive?

The telescreen struck fourteen. He must leave in ten minutes. He had to be back at work by fourteen-thirty.

Curiously, the chiming of the hour seemed to have put new heart into him. He was a lonely ghost uttering a truth that nobody would ever hear. But so long as he uttered it, in some obscure way the continuity was not broken. It was not by making yourself heard but by staying sane that you carried on the human heritage. He went back to the table, dipped his pen, and wrote:

To the future or to the past, to a time when thought is free, when men are different from one another and do not live alone—to a time when truth exists and what is done cannot be undone:

From the age of uniformity, from the age of solitude, from the age of Big Brother, from the age of doublethink—greetings!

He was already dead, he reflected. It seemed to him that it was only now, when he had begun to be able to formulate his thoughts, that he had taken the decisive step. The consequences of every act are included in the act itself. He wrote:

Thoughtcrime does not entail death: thoughtcrime IS death.

Now that he had recognized himself as a dead man it became important to stay alive as long as possible. Two fingers of his right hand were inkstained. It was exactly the kind of detail that might betray you. Some nosing zealot in the Ministry (a woman, probably; someone like the little sandy-haired woman or the dark-haired girl from the Fiction Department) might start wondering why he had been writing during the lunch interval, why he had used an old-fashioned pen, *what* he had been writing—and then drop a hint in the appropriate quarter. He went to the bathroom and carefully scrubbed the ink away with the gritty dark-brown soap which rasped your skin like sandpaper and was therefore well adapted for this purpose.

He put the diary away in the drawer. It was quite useless to think of hiding it, but he could at least make sure whether or not its existence had been discovered. A hair laid across the page-ends was too obvious. With the tip of his finger he picked up an identifiable grain of whitish dust and deposited it on the corner of the cover, where it was bound to be shaken off if the book was moved.

III

Winston was dreaming of his mother.

He must, he thought, have been ten or eleven years old when his mother had disappeared. She was a tall, statuesque, rather silent woman with slow movements and magnificent fair hair. His father he remembered more vaguely as dark and thin, dressed always in neat dark clothes (Winston remembered especially the very thin soles of his father's shoes) and wearing spectacles. The two of them must evidently have been swallowed up in one of the first great purges of the Fifties.

At this moment his mother was sitting in some place deep down beneath him, with his young sister in her arms. He did not remember his sister at all, except as a tiny, feeble baby, always silent, with large, watchful eyes. Both of them were looking up at him. They were down in some subterranean place—the bottom of a well, for instance, or a very deep grave—but it was a place which, already far below him, was itself moving downwards. They were in the saloon of a sinking ship, looking up at him through the darkening water. There was still air in the saloon, they could still see him and he them, but all the while they were sinking down, down into the green waters which in another moment must hide them from sight forever. He was out in the light and air while they were being sucked down to death, and they were down there *because* he was up here. He knew it and they knew it, and he could see the knowledge in their faces. There was no reproach either in their faces or in their hearts, only the knowledge that they must die in order that he might remain alive, and that this was part of the unavoidable order of things.

He could not remember what had happened, but he knew in his dream that in some way the lives of his mother and his sister had been sacrificed to his own. It was one of those dreams which, while retaining the characteristic dream scenery, are a continuation of one's intellectual life, and in which one becomes aware of facts and ideas which still seem new and valuable after one is awake. The thing that now suddenly struck Winston was that his mother's death, nearly thirty years ago, had been tragic and sorrowful in a way that was no longer possible. Tragedy, he perceived, belonged to the ancient time, to a time when there were still privacy, love, and friendship, and when the members of a family stood by one another without needing to know the reason. His mother's memory tore at his heart because she had died loving him, when he was too young and selfish to love her in return, and because somehow, he did not remember how, she had sacrificed herself to a conception of loyalty that was private and unalterable. Such things, he saw, could not happen today. Today there were fear, hatred, and pain, but no dignity of emotion, no deep or complex sorrows. All this he seemed to see in the large eyes of his mother and his sister, looking up at him through the green water, hundreds of fathoms down and still sinking.

Suddenly he was standing on short springy turf, on a summer evening when the slanting rays of the sun gilded the ground. The landscape that he was looking at recurred so often in his dreams that he was never fully certain whether or not he had seen it in the real world. In his waking thoughts he called it the Golden Country. It was an old, rabbit-bitten pasture, with a foot track wandering across it and a molehill here and there. In the ragged hedge on the opposite side of the field the boughs of the elm trees were swaying very faintly in the breeze, their leaves just stirring in dense masses like women's hair. Somewhere near at hand, though out of sight, there was a clear, slow-moving stream where dace were swimming in the pools under the willow trees.

The girl with dark hair was coming toward him across the field. With what seemed a single movement she tore off her clothes and flung them disdainfully aside. Her body was white and smooth, but it aroused no desire in him; indeed, he barely looked at it. What overwhelmed him in the instant was admiration for the gesture with which she had thrown her clothes aside. With its grace and carelessness it seemed to annihilate a whole culture, a whole system of thought, as though Big Brother and the Party and the Thought Police could all be swept into nothingness by a single splendid movement of the arm. That too was a gesture belonging to the ancient time. Winston woke up with the word "Shakespeare" on his lips.

The telescreen was giving forth an ear-splitting whistle which continued on the same note for thirty seconds. It was nought seven fifteen, getting-up time for office workers. Winston wrenched his body out of bed—naked, for a member of the Outer Party received only three thousand clothing coupons annually, and a suit of pajamas was six hundred—and seized a dingy singlet and a pair of shorts that were lying across a chair. The Physical Jerks would begin in three minutes. The next moment he was doubled up by a violent coughing fit which nearly always attacked him soon after waking up. It emptied his lungs so completely that he could only begin breathing again by lying on his back and taking a series of deep gasps. His veins had swelled with the effort of the cough, and the varicose ulcer had started itching.

"Thirty to forty group!" yapped a piercing female voice. "Thirty to forty group! Take your places, please. Thirties to forties!"

Winston sprang to attention in front of the telescreen, upon which the image of a youngish woman, scrawny but muscular, dressed in tunic and gym shoes, had already appeared.

"Arms bending and stretching!" she rapped out. "Take your time by me. *One*, two, three, four! *One*, two, three, four! Come on, comrades, put a bit of life into it! *One*, two, three, four! *One*, two, three, four! . . ."

The pain of the coughing fit had not quite driven out of Winston's mind the impression made by his dream, and the rhythmic movements of the exercise restored it somewhat. As he mechanically shot his arms back and forth, wearing on his face the look of grim enjoyment which was considered proper during the Physical Jerks, he was struggling to think his way backward into the dim period of his early childhood. It was extraordinarily difficult. Beyond the late Fifties everything faded. When there were no external records that you could refer to, even the outline of your own life lost its sharpness. You remembered huge events which had quite probably not happened, you remembered the detail of incidents without being able to recapture their atmosphere, and there were long blank periods to which you could assign nothing. Everything had been different then. Even the names of countries, and their shapes on the map, had been different. Airstrip One, for instance, had not been so called in those days: it had been called England or Britain, though London, he felt fairly certain, had always been called London.

Winston could not definitely remember a time when his country had not been at war, but it was evident that there had been a fairly long interval of peace during his childhood, because one of his early memories was of an air raid which appeared to take everyone by surprise. Perhaps it was the time when the atomic bomb had fallen on Colchester. He did not remember the raid itself, but he did remember his father's hand clutching his own as they hurried down, down, down into some place deep in the earth, round and round a spiral staircase which rang under his feet and which finally so wearied his legs that he began whimpering and they had to stop and rest. His mother, in her slow dreamy way, was following a long way behind them. She was carrying his baby sister—or perhaps it was only a bundle of blankets that she was carrying: he was not certain whether his sister had been born then. Finally they had emerged into a noisy, crowded place which he had realized to be a Tube station.

There were people sitting all over the stone-flagged floor, and other people, packed tightly together, were sitting on metal bunks, one above the other. Winston and his mother and father found themselves a place on the floor, and near them an old man and an old woman were sitting side by side on a bunk. The old man had on a decent dark suit and a black cloth cap pushed back from very white hair; his face was scarlet and his eyes were blue and full of tears. He reeked of gin. It seemed to breathe out of his skin in place of sweat, and one could have fancied that the tears welling from his eyes were pure gin. But though slightly drunk he was also suffering under some grief that was genuine and unbearable. In his childish way Winston grasped that some terrible thing, something that was beyond forgiveness and could never be remedied, had just happened. It also seemed to him that he knew what it was. Someone whom the old man loved, a little granddaughter perhaps, had been killed. Every few minutes the old man kept repeating:

"We didn't ought to 'ave trusted 'em. I said so, Ma, didn't I? That's what come of trusting 'em. I said so all along. We didn't ought to 'ave trusted the buggers."

But which buggers they didn't ought to have trusted Winston could not now remember.

Since about that time, war had been literally continuous, though strictly speaking it had not always been the same war. For several months during his childhood there had been confused street fighting in London itself, some of which he remembered vividly. But to trace out the history of the whole period, to say who was fighting whom at any given moment, would have been utterly impossible, since no written record, and no spoken word, ever made mention of any other alignment than the existing one. At this moment, for example, in 1984 (if it was 1984), Oceania was at war with Eurasia and in alliance with Eastasia. In no public or private utterance was it ever admitted that the three powers had at any time been grouped along different lines. Actually, as Winston well knew, it was only four years since Oceania had been at war with Eastasia and in alliance with Eurasia. But that was merely a piece of furtive knowledge which he happened to possess because his memory was not satisfactorily under control. Officially the change of partners had never happened. Oceania was at war with Eurasia: therefore Oceania had always been at war with Eurasia. The enemy of the moment always represented absolute evil, and it followed that any past or future agreement with him was impossible.

The frightening thing, he reflected for the ten thousandth time as he forced his shoulders painfully backward (with hands on hips, they were gyrating their bodies from the waist, an exercise that was supposed to be good for the back muscles)—the frightening thing was that it might all be true. If the Party could thrust its hand into the past and say of this or that event, *it never happened*—that, surely, was more terrifying than mere torture and death.

The Party said that Oceania had never been in alliance with Eurasia. He, Winston Smith, knew that Oceania had been in alliance with Eurasia as short a time as four years ago. But where did that knowledge exist? Only in his own consciousness, which in any case must soon be annihilated. And if all others accepted the lie which the Party imposed—if all records told the same tale—then the lie passed into history and became truth. "Who controls the past," ran the Party slogan, "controls the future: who controls the present controls the past." And yet the past, though of its nature alterable, never had been altered. Whatever was true now was true from everlasting to everlasting. It was quite simple. All that was needed was an unending series of victories over your own memory. "Reality control," they called it; in Newspeak, "doublethink."

"Stand easy!" barked the instructress, a little more genially.

Winston sank his arms to his sides and slowly refilled his lungs with air. His mind slid away into the labyrinthine world of doublethink. To know and not to know, to be conscious of complete truthfulness while telling carefully constructed lies, to hold simultaneously two opinions which canceled out, knowing them to be contradictory and believing in both of them, to use logic against logic, to repudiate morality while laying claim to it, to believe that democracy was impossible and that the Party was the guardian of democracy, to forget whatever it was necessary to forget, then to draw it back into memory again at the moment when it was needed, and then promptly to forget it again, and above all, to apply the same process to the process itself—that was the ultimate subtlety: consciously to induce unconsciousness, and then, once again, to become unconscious of the act of hypnosis you had just performed. Even to understand the word "doublethink" involved the use of doublethink.

The instructress had called them to attention again. "And now let's see which of us can touch our toes!" she said enthusiastically. "Right over from the hips, please, comrades. *One*-two! *One*-two! . . ."

Winston loathed this exercise, which sent shooting pains all the way from his heels to his buttocks and often ended by bringing on another coughing fit. The half-pleasant quality went out of his meditations. The past, he reflected, had not merely been altered, it had been actually destroyed. For how could you establish even the most obvious fact when there existed no record outside your own memory? He tried to remember in what year he had first heard mention of Big Brother. He thought it must have been at some time in the Sixties, but it was impossible to be certain. In the Party histories, of course, Big Brother figured as the leader and guardian of the Revolution since its very earliest days. His exploits had been gradually pushed backwards in time until already they extended into the fabulous world of the Forties and the Thirties, when the capitalists in their strange cylindrical hats still rode through the streets of London in great gleaming motor cars or horse carriages with glass sides. There was no knowing how much of this legend was true and how much invented. Winston could not even remember at what date the

Party itself had come into existence. He did not believe he had ever heard the word Ingsoc before 1960, but it was possible that in its Oldspeak form—"English Socialism," that is to say—it had been current earlier. Everything melted into mist. Sometimes, indeed, you could put your finger on a definite lie. It was not true, for example, as was claimed in the Party history books, that the Party had invented airplanes. He remembered airplanes since his earliest childhood. But you could prove nothing. There was never any evidence. Just once in his whole life he had held in his hands unmistakable documentary proof of the falsification of a historical fact. And on that occasion—

"Smith!" screamed the shrewish voice from the telescreen. "6079 Smith W! Yes, *you!* Bend lower, please! You can do better than that. You're not trying. Lower, please! *That's* better, comrade. Now stand at ease, the whole squad, and watch me."

A sudden hot sweat had broken out all over Winston's body. His face remained completely inscrutable. Never show dismay! Never show resentment! A single flicker of the eyes could give you away. He stood watching while the instructress raised her arms above her head and— one could not say gracefully, but with remarkable neatness and efficiency—bent over and tucked the first joint of her fingers under her toes.

"There, comrades! *That's* how I want to see you doing it. Watch me again. I'm thirty-nine and I've had four children. Now look." She bent over again. "You see *my* knees aren't bent. You can all do it if you want to," she added as she straightened herself up. "Anyone under forty-five is perfectly capable of touching his toes. We don't all have the privilege of fighting in the front line, but at least we can all keep fit. Remember our boys on the Malabar front! And the sailors in the Floating Fortresses! Just think what *they* have to put up with. Now try again. That's better, comrade, that's *much* better," she added encouragingly as Winston, with a violent lunge, succeeded in touching his toes with knees unbent, for the first time in several years.

IV

With the deep, unconscious sigh which not even the nearness of the telescreen could prevent him from uttering when his day's work started, Winston pulled the speakwrite toward him, blew the dust from its mouthpiece, and put on his spectacles. Then he unrolled and clipped together four small cylinders of paper which had already flopped out of the pneumatic tube on the right-hand side of his desk.

In the walls of the cubicle there were three orifices. To the right of the speakwrite, a small pneumatic tube for written messages; to the left, a larger one for newspapers; and in the side wall, within easy reach of

Winston's arm, a large oblong slit protected by a wire grating. This last was for the disposal of waste paper. Similar slits existed in thousands or tens of thousands throughout the building, not only in every room but at short intervals in every corridor. For some reason they were nicknamed memory holes. When one knew that any document was due for destruction, or even when one saw a scrap of waste paper lying about, it was an automatic action to lift the flap of the nearest memory hole and drop it in, whereupon it would be whirled away on a current of warm air to the enormous furnaces which were hidden somewhere in the recesses of the building.

Winston examined the four slips of paper which he had unrolled. Each contained a message of only one or two lines, in the abbreviated jargon— not actually Newspeak, but consisting largely of Newspeak words— which was used in the Ministry for internal purposes. They ran:

times 17.3.84 bb speech malreported africa rectify
times 19.12.83 forecasts 3 yp 4th quarter 83 misprints verify current issue
times 14.2.84 miniplenty malquoted chocolate rectify
times 3.12.83 reporting bb dayorder doubleplusungood refs unpersons rewrite fullwise upsub antefiling.

With a faint feeling of satisfaction Winston laid the fourth message aside. It was an intricate and responsible job and had better be dealt with last. The other three were routine matters, though the second one would probably mean some tedious wading through lists of figures.

Winston dialed "back numbers" on the telescreen and called for the appropriate issues of the *Times*, which slid out of the pneumatic tube after only a few minutes' delay. The messages he had received referred to articles or news items which for one reason or another it was thought necessary to alter, or, as the official phrase had it, to rectify. For example, it appeared from the *Times* of the seventeenth of March that Big Brother, in his speech of the previous day, had predicted that the South Indian front would remain quiet but that a Eurasian offensive would shortly be launched in North Africa. As it happened, the Eurasian Higher Command had launched its offensive in South India and left North Africa alone. It was therefore necessary to rewrite a paragraph of Big Brother's speech in such a way as to make him predict the thing that had actually happened. Or again, the *Times* of the nineteenth of December had published the official forecasts of the output of various classes of consumption goods in the fourth quarter of 1983, which was also the sixth quarter of the Ninth Three-Year Plan. Today's issue contained a statement of the actual output, from which it appeared that the forecasts were in every instance grossly wrong. Winston's job was to rectify the original figures by making them agree with the later ones. As for the third message, it referred to a very simple error which could be set right in a couple of minutes. As short a time ago as February, the Ministry of Plenty had issued a promise (a "categorical pledge" were the official words) that there would be no reduction of the chocolate ration during 1984. Actually, as Winston was aware, the chocolate ration was to be reduced from thirty grams to twenty at the end of the present week. All that was needed was to substitute for the original promise a warning that it would probably be necessary to reduce the ration at some time in April.

As soon as Winston had dealt with each of the messages, he clipped his speakwritten corrections to the appropriate copy of the *Times* and pushed them into the pneumatic tube. Then, with a movement which was as nearly as possible unconscious, he crumpled up the original message and any notes that he himself had made, and dropped them into the memory hole to be devoured by the flames.

What happened in the unseen labyrinth to which the pneumatic tubes led, he did not know in detail, but he did know in general terms. As soon as all the corrections which happened to be necessary in any particular number of the *Times* had been assembled and collated, that number would be reprinted, the original copy destroyed, and the corrected copy placed on the files in its stead. This process of continuous alteration was applied not only to newspapers, but to books, periodicals, pamphlets, posters, leaflets, films, sound tracks, cartoons, photographs—to every kind of literature or documentation which might conceivably hold any political or ideological significance. Day by day and almost minute by minute the past was brought up to date. In this way every prediction made by the Party could be shown by documentary evidence to have been correct; nor was any item of news, or any expression of opinion, which conflicted with the needs of the moment, ever allowed to remain on record. All history was a palimpsest, scraped clean and reinscribed exactly as often as was necessary. In no case would it have been possible, once the deed was done, to prove that any falsification had taken place. The largest section of the Records Department, far larger than the one in which Winston worked, consisted simply of persons whose duty it was to track down and collect all copies of books, newspapers, and other documents which had been superseded and were due for destruction. A number of the *Times* which might, because of changes in political alignment, or mistaken prophecies uttered by Big Brother, have been rewritten a dozen times still stood on the files bearing its original date, and no other copy existed to contradict it. Books, also, were recalled and rewritten again and again, and were invariably reissued without any admission that any alteration had been made. Even the written instructions which Winston received, and which he invariably got rid of as soon as he had dealt with them, never stated or implied that an act of forgery was to be committed; always the reference was to slips, errors, misprints, or misquotations which it was necessary to put right in the interests of accuracy.

But actually, he thought as he readjusted the Ministry of Plenty's figures, it was not even forgery. It was merely the substitution of one piece of nonsense for another. Most of the material that you were dealing with had no connection with anything in the real world, not even the kind of connection that is contained in a direct lie. Statistics were just as much a fantasy in their original version as in their rectified version. A great deal of the time you were expected to make them up out of your head. For example, the Ministry of Plenty's forecast had estimated the output of boots for the quarter at a hundred and forty-five million pairs. The actual output was given as sixty-two millions. Winston, however, in rewriting the forecast, marked the figure down to fifty-seven millions, so as to allow for the usual claim that the quota had been overfulfilled. In any case, sixty-two millions was no nearer the truth than fifty-seven millions, or than a hundred and forty-five millions. Very likely no boots had been produced at all. Likelier still, nobody knew how many had been produced, much less cared. All one knew was that every quarter astronomical numbers of boots were produced on paper, while perhaps half the population of Oceania went barefoot. And so it was with every class of recorded fact, great or small. Everything faded away into a shadow-world in which, finally, even the date of the year had become uncertain.

Winston glanced across the hall. In the corresponding cubicle on the other side a small, precise-looking, dark-chinned man named Tillotson was working steadily away, with a folded newspaper on his knee and his mouth very close to the mouthpiece of the speakwrite. He had the air of trying to keep what he was saying a secret between himself and the telescreen. He looked up, and his spectacles darted a hostile flash in Winston's direction.

Winston hardly knew Tillotson, and had no idea what work he was employed on. People in the Records Department did not readily talk about their jobs. In the long, windowless hall, with its double row of cubicles and its endless rustle of papers and hum of voices murmuring into speakwrites, there were quite a dozen people whom Winston did not even know by name, though he daily saw them hurrying to and fro in the corridors or gesticulating in the Two Minutes Hate. He knew that in the cubicle next to him the little woman with sandy hair toiled day in, day out, simply at tracking down and deleting from the press the names of people who had been vaporized and were therefore considered never to have existed. There was a certain fitness in this, since her own husband had been vaporized a couple of years earlier. And a few cubicles away a mild, ineffectual, dreamy creature named Ampleforth, with very hairy ears and a surprising talent for juggling with rhymes and meters, was engaged in producing garbled versions—definitive texts, they were called—of poems which had become ideologically offensive but which for one reason or another were to be retained in the anthologies. And this hall, with its fifty workers or thereabouts, was only one sub-section, a single cell, as it were, in the huge complexity of the Records Department. Beyond, above, below, were other swarms of workers engaged in an unimaginable multitude of jobs. There were the huge printing shops with their sub-editors, their typography experts, and their elaborately equipped studios for the faking of photographs. There was the teleprograms section with its engineers, its producers, and its teams of actors specially chosen for their skill in imitating voices. There were the armies of reference clerks whose job was simply to draw up lists of books and periodicals which were due for recall. There were the vast repositories where the corrected documents were stored, and the hidden furnaces where the original copies were destroyed. And somewhere or other, quite anonymous, there were the directing brains who coordinated the whole effort and laid down the lines of policy which made it necessary that this fragment of the past should be preserved, that one falsified, and the other rubbed out of existence.

And the Records Department, after all, was itself only a single branch of the Ministry of Truth, whose primary job was not to reconstruct the past but to supply the citizens of Oceania with newspapers, films, textbooks, telescreen programs, plays, novels—with every conceivable kind of information, instruction, or entertainment, from a statue to a slogan, from a lyric poem to a biological treatise, and from a child's spelling book to a Newspeak dictionary. And the Ministry had not only to supply the multifarious needs of the Party, but also to repeat the whole operation at a lower level for the benefit of the proletariat. There was a whole chain of separate departments dealing with proletarian literature, music, drama, and entertainment generally. Here were produced rubbishy newspapers containing almost nothing except sport, crime, and astrology, sensational five-cent novelettes, films oozing with sex, and sentimental songs which were composed entirely by mechanical means on a special kind of kaleidoscope known as a versificator. There was even a whole sub-section— *Pornosec*, it was called in Newspeak—engaged in producing the lowest kind of pornography, which was sent out in sealed packets and which no Party member, other than those who worked on it, was permitted to look at.

Three messages had slid out of the pneumatic tube while Winston was working; but they were simple matters, and he had disposed of them before the Two Minutes Hate interrupted him. When the Hate was over he returned to his cubicle, took the Newspeak dictionary from the shelf, pushed the speakwrite to one side, cleaned his spectacles, and settled down to his main job of the morning.

Winston's greatest pleasure in life was in his work. Most of it was a tedious routine, but included in it there were also jobs so difficult and intricate that you could lose yourself in them as in the depths of a mathematical problem—delicate pieces of forgery in which you had nothing to guide you except your knowledge of the principles of Ingsoc and your estimate of what the Party wanted you to say. Winston was good at this kind of thing. On occasion he had even been entrusted with the rectification of the *Times* leading articles, which were written entirely in Newspeak. He unrolled the message that he had set aside earlier. It ran:

times 3.12.83 reporting bb dayorder doubleplusungood refs unpersons rewrite fullwise upsub antefiling.

In Oldspeak (or standard English) this might be rendered:

The reporting of Big Brother's Order for the Day in the *Times* of December 3rd 1983 is extremely unsatisfactory and makes references to nonexistent persons. Rewrite it in full and submit your draft to higher authority before filing.

Winston read through the offending article. Big Brother's Order for the Day, it seemed, had been chiefly devoted to praising the work of an organization known as FFCC, which supplied cigarettes and other comforts to the sailors in the Floating Fortresses. A certain Comrade Withers, a prominent member of the Inner Party, had been singled out for special mention and awarded a decoration, the Order of Conspicuous Merit, Second Class.

Three months later FFCC had suddenly been dissolved with no reasons given. One could assume that Withers and his associates were now in disgrace, but there had been no report of the matter in the press or on the telescreen. That was to be expected, since it was unusual for political offenders to be put on trial or even publicly denounced. The great purges involving thousands of people, with public trials of traitors and thought-criminals who made abject confession of their crimes and were afterwards executed, were special showpieces not occurring oftener than once in a couple of years. More commonly, people who had incurred the displeasure of the Party simply disappeared and were never heard of again. One never had the smallest clue as to what had happened to them. In some cases they might not even be dead. Perhaps thirty people personally known to Winston, not counting his parents, had disappeared at one time or another.

Winston stroked his nose gently with a paper clip. In the cubicle across the way Comrade Tillotson was still crouching secretively over his speakwrite. He raised his head for a moment: again the hostile spectacle-flash. Winston wondered whether Comrade Tillotson was engaged on the same job as himself. It was perfectly possible. So tricky a piece of work would never be entrusted to a single person; on the other hand, to turn it over to a committee would be to admit openly that an act of fabrication was taking place. Very likely as many as a dozen people were now working away on rival versions of what Big Brother had actually said. And presently some master brain in the Inner Party would select this version or that, would re-edit it and set in motion the complex processes of cross-referencing that would be required, and then the chosen lie would pass into the permanent records and become truth.

Winston did not know why Withers had been disgraced. Perhaps it was for corruption or incompetence. Perhaps Big Brother was merely getting rid of a too-popular subordinate. Perhaps Withers or someone close to him had been suspected of heretical tendencies. Or perhaps—what was likeliest of all—the thing had simply happened because purges and vaporizations were a necessary part of the mechanics of government. The only real clue lay in the words "refs unpersons," which indicated that Withers was already dead. You could not invariably assume this to be the case when people were arrested. Sometimes they were released and allowed to remain at liberty for as much as a year or two years before being executed. Very occasionally some person whom you had believed dead long since would make a ghostly reappearance at some public trial where he would implicate hundreds of others by his testimony before vanishing, this time forever. Withers, however, was already an *unperson*. He did not exist; he had never existed. Winston decided that it would not be enough simply to reverse the tendency of Big Brother's speech. It was better to make it deal with something totally unconnected with its original subject.

He might turn the speech into the usual denunciation of traitors and thought-criminals, but that was a little too obvious, while to invent a victory at the front, or some triumph of overproduction in the Ninth Three-Year Plan, might complicate the records too much. What was needed was a piece of pure fantasy. Suddenly there sprang into his mind, ready-made as it were, the image of a certain Comrade Ogilvy, who had recently died in battle, in heroic circumstances. There were occasions when Big Brother devoted his Order for the Day to commemorating some humble, rank-and-file Party member whose life and death he held up as an example worthy to be followed. Today he should commemorate Comrade Ogilvy. It was true that there was no such person as Comrade Ogilvy, but a few lines of print and a couple of faked photographs would soon bring him into existence.

Winston thought for a moment, then pulled his speakwrite toward him and began dictating in Big Brother's familiar style: a style at once military and pedantic, and, because of a trick of asking questions and then promptly answering them ("What lessons do we learn from this fact, comrades? The lessons—which is also one of the fundamental principles of Ingsoc—that," etc., etc.), easy to imitate.

At the age of three Comrade Ogilvy had refused all toys except a drum, a submachine gun, and a model helicopter. At six—a year early, by a special relaxation of the rules—he had joined the Spies; at nine he had been a troop leader. At eleven he had denounced his uncle to the Thought Police after overhearing a conversation which appeared to him to have criminal tendencies. At seventeen he had been a district organizer of the Junior Anti-Sex League. At nineteen he had designed a hand grenade which had been adopted by the Ministry of Peace and which, at its first trial, had killed thirty-one Eurasian prisoners in one burst. At twenty-three he had perished in action. Pursued by enemy jet planes while flying over the Indian Ocean with important despatches, he had weighted his body with his machine gun and leapt out of the helicopter into deep water, despatches and all—an end, said Big Brother, which it was impossible to contemplate without feelings of envy. Big Brother added a few remarks on the purity and singlemindedness of Comrade Ogilvy's life. He was a total abstainer and a nonsmoker, had no recreations except a daily hour in the gymnasium, and had taken a vow of celibacy, believing marriage and the care of a family to be incompatible with a twenty-four-hour-a-day devotion to duty. He had no subjects of conversation except the principles of Ingsoc, and no aim in life except the defeat of the Eurasian enemy and the hunting-down of spies, saboteurs, thought-criminals, and traitors generally.

Winston debated with himself whether to award Comrade Ogilvy the Order of Conspicuous Merit; in the end he decided against it because of the unnecessary cross-referencing that it would entail.

Once again he glanced at his rival in the opposite cubicle. Something seemed to tell him with certainty that Tillotson was busy on the same job as himself. There was no way of knowing whose version would finally be adopted, but he felt a profound conviction that it would be his own. Comrade Ogilvy, unimagined an hour ago, was now a fact. It struck him as curious that you could create dead men but not living ones. Comrade Ogilvy, who had never existed in the present, now existed in the past, and when once the act of forgery was forgotten, he would exist just as authentically, and upon the same evidence, as Charlemagne or Julius Caesar.

V

In the low-ceilinged canteen, deep under ground, the lunch queue jerked slowly forward. The room was already very full and deafeningly noisy. From the grille at the counter the steam of stew came pouring forth, with a sour metallic smell which did not quite overcome the fumes of Victory Gin. On the far side of the room there was a small bar, a mere hole in the wall, where gin could be bought at ten cents the large nip.

"Just the man I was looking for," said a voice at Winston's back.

He turned round. It was his friend Syme, who worked in the Research

Department. Perhaps "friend" was not exactly the right word. You did not have friends nowadays, you had comrades; but there were some comrades whose society was pleasanter than that of others. Syme was a philologist, a specialist in Newspeak. Indeed, he was one of the enormous team of experts now engaged in compiling the Eleventh Edition of the Newspeak dictionary. He was a tiny creature, smaller than Winston, with dark hair and large, protuberant eyes, at once mournful and derisive, which seemed to search your face closely while he was speaking to you.

"I wanted to ask you whether you'd got any razor blades," he said.

"Not one!" said Winston with a sort of guilty haste. "I've tried all over the place. They don't exist any longer."

Everyone kept asking you for razor blades. Actually he had two unused ones which he was hoarding up. There had been a famine of them for months past. At any given moment there was some necessary article which the Party shops were unable to supply. Sometimes it was buttons, sometimes it was darning wool, sometimes it was shoelaces; at present it was razor blades. You could only get hold of them, if at all, by scrounging more or less furtively on the "free" market.

"I've been using the same blade for six weeks," he added untruthfully.

The queue gave another jerk forward. As they halted he turned and faced Syme again. Each of them took a greasy metal tray from a pile at the edge of the counter.

"Did you go and see the prisoners hanged yesterday?" said Syme.

"I was working," said Winston indifferently. "I shall see it on the flicks, I suppose."

"A very inadequate substitute," said Syme.

His mocking eyes roved over Winston's face. "I know you," the eyes seemed to say, "I see through you. I know very well why you didn't go to see those prisoners hanged." In an intellectual way, Syme was venomously orthodox. He would talk with a disagreeable gloating satisfaction of helicopter raids on enemy villages, the trials and confessions of thoughtcriminals, the executions in the cellars of the Ministry of Love. Talking to him was largely a matter of getting him away from such subjects and entangling him, if possible, in the technicalities of Newspeak, on which he was authoritative and interesting. Winston turned his head a little aside to avoid the scrutiny of the large dark eyes.

"It was a good hanging," said Syme reminiscently. "I think it spoils it when they tie their feet together. I like to see them kicking. And above all, at the end, the tongue sticking right out, and blue—a quite bright blue. That's the detail that appeals to me."

"Nex', please!" yelled the white-aproned prole with the ladle.

Winston and Syme pushed their trays beneath the grille. Onto each was dumped swiftly the regulation lunch—a metal pannikin of pinkish-gray stew, a hunk of bread, a cube of cheese, a mug of milkless Victory Coffee, and one saccharine tablet.

"There's a table over there, under that telescreen," said Syme. "Let's pick up a gin on the way."

The gin was served out to them in handleless china mugs. They threaded their way across the crowded room and unpacked their trays onto the metal-topped table, on one corner of which someone had left a pool of stew, a filthy liquid mess that had the appearance of vomit. Winston took up his mug of gin, paused for an instant to collect his nerve, and gulped the oily-tasting stuff down. When he had winked the tears out of his eyes he suddenly discovered that he was hungry. He began swallowing spoonfuls of the stew, which, in among its general sloppiness, had cubes of spongy pinkish stuff which was probably a preparation of meat. Neither of them spoke again till they had emptied their pannikins. From the table at Winston's left, a little behind his back, someone was talking rapidly and continuously, a harsh gabble almost like the quacking of a duck, which pierced the general uproar of the room.

"How is the dictionary getting on?" said Winston, raising his voice to overcome the noise.

"Slowly," said Syme. "I'm on the adjectives. It's fascinating."

He had brightened up immediately at the mention of Newspeak. He pushed his pannikin aside, took up his hunk of bread in one delicate hand and his cheese in the other, and leaned across the table so as to be able to speak without shouting.

"The Eleventh Edition is the definitive edition," he said. "We're getting the language into its final shape—the shape it's going to have when nobody speaks anything else. When we've finished with it, people like you will have to learn it all over again. You think, I dare say, that our chief job is inventing new words. But not a bit of it! We're destroying words— scores of them, hundreds of them, every day. We're cutting the language down to the bone. The Eleventh Edition won't contain a single word that will become obsolete before the year 2050."

He bit hungrily into his bread and swallowed a couple of mouthfuls, then continued speaking, with a sort of pedant's passion. His thin dark face had become animated, his eyes had lost their mocking expression and grown almost dreamy.

"It's a beautiful thing, the destruction of words. Of course the great wastage is in the verbs and adjectives, but there are hundreds of nouns that can be got rid of as well. It isn't only the synonyms; there are also the antonyms. After all, what justification is there for a word which is simply the opposite of some other word? A word contains its opposite in itself. Take 'good,' for instance. If you have a word like 'good,' what need is there for a word like 'bad'? 'Ungood' will do just as well—better, because it's an exact opposite, which the other is not. Or again, if you want a stronger version of 'good,' what sense is there in having a whole string of vague useless words like 'excellent' and 'splendid' and all the rest of them? 'Plusgood' covers the meaning, or 'doubleplusgood' if you want something stronger still. Of course we use those forms already, but in the final version of Newspeak there'll be nothing else. In the end the whole notion of goodness and badness will be covered by only six words—in reality, only one word. Don't you see the beauty of that, Winston? It was B.B.'s idea originally, of course," he added as an afterthought.

A sort of vapid eagerness flitted across Winston's face at the mention of Big Brother. Nevertheless Syme immediately detected a certain lack of enthusiasm.

"You haven't a real appreciation of Newspeak, Winston," he said almost sadly. "Even when you write it you're still thinking in Oldspeak. I've read some of those pieces that you write in the *Times* occasionally. They're good enough, but they're translations. In your heart you'd prefer to stick to Oldspeak, with all its vagueness and its useless shades of meaning. You don't grasp the beauty of the destruction of words. Do you know that Newspeak is the only language in the world whose vocabulary gets smaller every year?"

Winston did know that, of course. He smiled, sympathetically he hoped, not trusting himself to speak. Syme bit off another fragment of the dark-colored bread, chewed it briefly, and went on:

"Don't you see that the whole aim of Newspeak is to narrow the range of thought? In the end we shall make thoughtcrime literally impossible, because there will be no words in which to express it. Every concept that can ever be needed will be expressed by exactly *one* word, with its meaning rigidly defined and all its subsidiary meanings rubbed out and forgotten. Already, in the Eleventh Edition, we're not far from that point. But the process will still be continuing long after you and I are dead. Every year fewer and fewer words, and the range of consciousness always a little smaller. Even now, of course, there's no reason or excuse for committing thoughtcrime. It's merely a question of self-discipline, reality-control. But in the end there won't be any need even for that. The Revolution will be complete when the language is perfect. Newspeak is Ingsoc and Ingsoc is Newspeak," he added with a sort of mystical satisfaction. "Has it ever occurred to you, Winston, that by the year 2050, at the very latest, not a single human being will be alive who could understand such a conversation as we are having now?"

"Except—" began Winston doubtfully, and then stopped.

It had been on the tip of his tongue to say "Except the proles," but he checked himself, not feeling fully certain that this remark was not in some way unorthodox. Syme, however, had divined what he was about to say.

"The proles are not human beings," he said carelessly. "By 2050—

earlier, probably—all real knowledge of Oldspeak will have disappeared. The whole literature of the past will have been destroyed. Chaucer, Shakespeare, Milton, Byron—they'll exist only in Newspeak versions, not merely changed into something different, but actually changed into something contradictory of what they used to be. Even the literature of the Party will change. Even the slogans will change. How could you have a slogan like 'freedom is slavery' when the concept of freedom has been abolished? The whole climate of thought will be different. In fact there will *be* no thought, as we understand it now. Orthodoxy means not thinking—not needing to think. Orthodoxy is unconsciousness."

One of these days, thought Winston with sudden deep conviction, Syme will be vaporized. He is too intelligent. He sees too clearly and speaks too plainly. The Party does not like such people. One day he will disappear. It is written in his face.

Winston had finished his bread and cheese. He turned a little sideways in his chair to drink his mug of coffee. At the table on his left the man with the strident voice was still talking remorselessly away. A young woman who was perhaps his secretary, and who was sitting with her back to Winston, was listening to him and seemed to be eagerly agreeing with everything that he said. From time to time Winston caught some such remark as "I think you're *so* right, I do *so* agree with you," uttered in a youthful and rather silly feminine voice. But the other voice never stopped for an instant, even when the girl was speaking. Winston knew the man by sight, though he knew no more about him than that he held some important post in the Fiction Department. He was a man of about thirty, with a muscular throat and a large, mobile mouth. His head was thrown back a little, and because of the angle at which he was sitting, his spectacles caught the light and presented to Winston two blank discs instead of eyes. What was slightly horrible was that from the stream of sound that poured out of his mouth, it was almost impossible to distinguish a single word. Just once Winston caught a phrase—"complete and final elimination of Goldsteinism"—jerked out very rapidly and, as it seemed, all in one piece, like a line of type cast solid. For the rest it was just a noise, a quack-quack-quacking. And yet, though you could not actually hear what the man was saying, you could not be in any doubt about its general nature. He might be denouncing Goldstein and demanding sterner measures against thought-criminals and saboteurs, he might be fulminating against the atrocities of the Eurasian army, he might be praising Big Brother or the heroes on the Malabar front—it made no difference. Whatever it was, you could be certain that every word of it was pure orthodoxy, pure Ingsoc. As he watched the eyeless face with the jaw moving rapidly up and down, Winston had a curious feeling that this was not a real human being but some kind of dummy. It was not the man's brain that was speaking; it was his larynx. The stuff that was coming out of him consisted of words, but it was not speech in the true sense: it was a noise uttered in unconsciousness, like the quacking of a duck.

Syme had fallen silent for a moment, and with the handle of his spoon was tracing patterns in the puddle of stew. The voice from the other table quacked rapidly on, easily audible in spite of the surrounding din.

"There is a word in Newspeak," said Syme. "I don't know whether you know it: *duckspeak,* to quack like a duck. It is one of those interesting words that have two contradictory meanings. Applied to an opponent, it is abuse; applied to someone you agree with, it is praise."

Unquestionably Syme will be vaporized, Winston thought again. He thought it with a kind of sadness, although well knowing that Syme despised him and slightly disliked him, and was fully capable of denouncing him as a thought-criminal if he saw any reason for doing so. There was something subtly wrong with Syme. There was something that he lacked: discretion, aloofness, a sort of saving stupidity. You could not say that he was unorthodox. He believed in the principles of Ingsoc, he venerated Big Brother, he rejoiced over victories, he hated heretics, not merely with sincerity but with a sort of restless zeal, an up-to-dateness of information, which the ordinary Party member did not approach. Yet a faint air of disreputability always clung to him. He said things that would have been better unsaid, he had read too many books, he frequented the Chestnut Tree Café, haunt of painters and musicians. There was no law, not even an unwritten law, against frequenting the Chestnut Tree Café, yet the place was somehow ill-omened. The old, discredited leaders of the Party had been used to gather there before they were finally purged. Goldstein himself, it was said, had sometimes been seen there, years and decades ago. Syme's fate was not difficult to foresee. And yet it was a fact that if Syme grasped, even for three seconds, the nature of his, Winston's, secret opinions, he would betray him instantly to the Thought Police. So would anybody else, for that matter, but Syme more than most. Zeal was not enough. Orthodoxy was unconsciousness.

Syme looked up. "Here comes Parsons," he said.

Something in the tone of his voice seemed to add, "that bloody fool." Parsons, Winston's fellow tenant at Victory Mansions, was in fact threading his way across the room—a tubby, middle-sized man with fair hair and a froglike face. At thirty-five he was already putting on rolls of fat at neck and waistline, but his movements were brisk and boyish. His whole appearance was that of a little boy grown large, so much so that although he was wearing the regulation overalls, it was almost impossible not to think of him as being dressed in the blue shorts, gray shirt, and red neckerchief of the Spies. In visualizing him one saw always a picture of dimpled knees and sleeves rolled back from pudgy forearms. Parsons did, indeed, invariably revert to shorts when a community hike or any other physical activity gave him an excuse for doing so. He greeted them both with a cheery "Hullo, hullo!" and sat down at the table, giving off an intense smell of sweat. Beads of moisture stood out all over his pink face. His powers of sweating were extraordinary. At the Community Center you could always tell when he had been playing table tennis by the dampness of the bat handle. Syme had produced a strip of paper on which there was a long column of words, and was studying it with an ink pencil between his fingers.

"Look at him working away in the lunch hour," said Parsons, nudging Winston. "Keenness, eh? What's that you've got there, old boy? Something a bit too brainy for me, I expect. Smith, old boy, I'll tell you why I'm chasing you. It's that sub you forgot to give me."

"Which sub is that?" said Winston, automatically feeling for money. About a quarter of one's salary had to be earmarked for voluntary subscriptions, which were so numerous that it was difficult to keep track of them.

"For Hate Week. You know—the house-by-house fund. I'm treasurer for our block. We're making an all-out effort—going to put on a tremendous show. I tell you, it won't be my fault if old Victory Mansions doesn't have the biggest outfit of flags in the whole street. Two dollars you promised me."

Winston found and handed over two creased and filthy notes, which Parsons entered in a small notebook, in the neat handwriting of the illiterate.

"By the way, old boy," he said, "I hear that little beggar of mine let fly at you with his catapult yesterday. I gave him a good dressing down for it. In fact I told him I'd take the catapult away if he does it again."

"I think he was a little upset at not going to the execution," said Winston.

"Ah, well—what I mean to say, shows the right spirit, doesn't it? Mischievous little beggars they are, both of them, but talk about keenness! All they think about is the Spies, and the war, of course. D'you know what that little girl of mine did last Saturday, when her troop was on a hike out Berkhampstead way? She got two other girls to go with her, slipped off from the hike, and spent the whole afternoon following a strange man. They kept on his tail for two hours, right through the woods, and then, when they got into Amersham, handed him over to the patrols."

"What did they do that for?" said Winston, somewhat taken aback. Parsons went on triumphantly:

"My kid made sure he was some kind of enemy agent—might have been dropped by parachute, for instance. But here's the point, old boy. What do you think put her onto him in the first place? She spotted he was wearing a funny kind of shoes—said she'd never seen anyone wearing shoes like that before. So the chances were he was a foreigner. Pretty smart for a nipper of seven, eh?"

"What happened to the man?" said Winston.

"Ah, that I couldn't say, of course. But I wouldn't be altogether surprised if—" Parsons made the motion of aiming a rifle, and clicked his tongue for the explosion.

"Good," said Syme abstractedly, without looking up from his strip of paper.

"Of course we can't afford to take chances," agreed Winston dutifully.

"What I mean to say, there is a war on," said Parsons.

As though in confirmation of this, a trumpet call floated from the telescreen just above their heads. However, it was not the proclamation of a military victory this time, but merely an announcement from the Ministry of Plenty.

"Comrades!" cried an eager youthful voice. "Attention, comrades! We have glorious news for you. We have won the battle for production! Returns now completed of the output of all classes of consumption goods show that the standard of living has risen by no less than twenty per cent over the past year. All over Oceania this morning there were irrepressible spontaneous demonstrations when workers marched out of factories and offices and paraded through the streets with banners voicing their gratitude to Big Brother for the new, happy life which his wise leadership has bestowed upon us. Here are some of the completed figures. Foodstuffs—"

The phrase "our new, happy life" recurred several times. It had been a favorite of late with the Ministry of Plenty. Parsons, his attention caught by the trumpet call, sat listening with a sort of gaping solemnity, a sort of edified boredom. He could not follow the figures, but he was aware that they were in some way a cause for satisfaction. He had lugged out a huge and filthy pipe which was already half full of charred tobacco. With the tobacco ration at a hundred grams a week it was seldom possible to fill a pipe up to the top. Winston was smoking a Victory Cigarette which he held carefully horizontal. The new ration did not start till tomorrow and he had only four cigarettes left. For the moment he had shut his ears to the remoter noises and was listening to the stuff that streamed out of the telescreen. It appeared that there had even been demonstrations to thank Big Brother for raising the chocolate ration to twenty grams a week. And only yesterday, he reflected, it had been announced that the ration was to be *reduced* to twenty grams a week. Was it possible that they could swallow that, after only twenty-four hours? Yes, they swallowed it. Parsons swallowed it easily, with the stupidity of an animal. The eyeless creature at the other table swallowed it fanatically, passionately, with a furious desire to track down, denounce, and vaporize anyone who should suggest that last week the ration had been thirty grams. Syme, too—in some more complex way, involving doublethink—Syme swallowed it. Was he, then, *alone* in the possession of a memory?

The fabulous statistics continued to pour out of the telescreen. As compared with last year there was more food, more clothes, more houses, more furniture, more cooking pots, more fuel, more ships, more helicopters, more books, more babies—more of everything except disease, crime, and insanity. Year by year and minute by minute, everybody and everything was whizzing rapidly upwards. As Syme had done earlier, Winston had taken up his spoon and was dabbling in the pale-colored gravy that dribbled across the table, drawing a long streak of it out into a pattern. He meditated resentfully on the physical texture of life. Had it always been like this? Had food always tasted like this? He looked round the canteen. A low-ceilinged, crowded room, its walls grimy from the contact of innumerable bodies; battered metal tables and chairs, placed so close together that you sat with elbows touching; bent spoons, dented trays, coarse white mugs; all surfaces greasy, grime in every crack; and a sourish composite smell of bad gin and bad coffee and metallic stew and dirty clothes. Always in your stomach and in your skin there was a sort of protest, a feeling that you had been cheated of something that you had a right to. It was true that he had no memories of anything greatly different. In any time that he could accurately remember, there had never been quite enough to eat, one had never had socks or underclothes that were not full of holes, furniture had always been battered and rickety, rooms underheated, tube trains crowded, houses falling to pieces, bread dark-colored, tea a rarity, coffee filthy-tasting, cigarettes insufficient— nothing cheap and plentiful except synthetic gin. And though, of course, it grew worse as one's body aged, was it not a sign that this was *not* the natural order of things, if one's heart sickened at the discomfort and dirt and scarcity, the interminable winters, the stickiness of one's socks, the lifts that never worked, the cold water, the gritty soap, the cigarettes that came to pieces, the food with its strange evil tastes? Why should one feel it to be intolerable unless one had some kind of ancestral memory that things had once been different?

He looked round the canteen again. Nearly everyone was ugly, and would still have been ugly even if dressed otherwise than in the uniform blue overalls. On the far side of the room, sitting at a table alone, a small, curiously beetlelike man was drinking a cup of coffee, his little eyes darting suspicious glances from side to side. How easy it was, thought Winston, if you did not look about you, to believe that the physical type set up by the Party as an ideal—tall muscular youths and deep-bosomed maidens, blond-haired, vital, sunburnt, carefree—existed and even predominated. Actually, so far as he could judge, the majority of people in Airstrip One were small, dark, and ill-favored. It was curious how that beetlelike type proliferated in the Ministries: little dumpy men, growing stout very early in life, with short legs, swift scuttling movements, and fat inscrutable faces with very small eyes. It was the type that seemed to flourish best under the dominion of the Party.

The announcement from the Ministry of Plenty ended on another trumpet call and gave way to tinny music. Parsons, stirred to vague enthusiasm by the bombardment of figures, took his pipe out of his mouth.

"The Ministry of Plenty's certainly done a good job this year," he said with a knowing shake of his head. "By the way, Smith old boy, I suppose you haven't got any razor blades you can let me have?"

"Not one," said Winston. "I've been using the same blade for six weeks myself."

"Ah, well—just thought I'd ask you, old boy."

"Sorry," said Winston.

The quacking voice from the next table, temporarily silenced during the Ministry's announcement, had started up again, as loud as ever. For some reason Winston suddenly found himself thinking of Mrs. Parsons, with her wispy hair and the dust in the creases of her face. Within two years those children would be denouncing her to the Thought Police. Mrs. Parsons would be vaporized. Syme would be vaporized. Winston would be vaporized. O'Brien would be vaporized. Parsons, on the other hand, would never be vaporized. The eyeless creature with the quacking voice would never be vaporized. The little beetlelike men who scuttled so nimbly through the labyrinthine corridors of Ministries—they, too, would never be vaporized. And the girl with dark hair, the girl from the Fiction Department—she would never be vaporized either. It seemed to him that he knew instinctively who would survive and who would perish, though just what it was that made for survival, it was not easy to say.

At this moment he was dragged out of his reverie with a violent jerk. The girl at the next table had turned partly round and was looking at him. It was the girl with dark hair. She was looking at him in a sidelong way, but with curious intensity. The instant that she caught his eye she looked away again.

The sweat started out on Winston's backbone. A horrible pang of terror went through him. It was gone almost at once, but it left a sort of nagging uneasiness behind. Why was she watching him? Why did she keep following him about? Unfortunately he could not remember whether she had already been at that table when he arrived, or had come there afterwards. But yesterday, at any rate, during the Two Minutes Hate, she had sat immediately behind him when there was no apparent need to do so. Quite likely her real object had been to listen to him and make sure whether he was shouting loudly enough.

His earlier thought returned to him: probably she was not actually a member of the Thought Police, but then it was precisely the amateur spy who was the greatest danger of all. He did not know how long she had been looking at him, but perhaps for as much as five minutes, and it was possible that his features had not been perfectly under control. It was terribly dangerous to let your thoughts wander when you were in any public place or within range of a telescreen. The smallest thing could give you away. A nervous tic, an unconscious look of anxiety, a habit of muttering to yourself—anything that carried with it the suggestion of abnormality, of having something to hide. In any case, to wear an improper expression on your face (to look incredulous when a victory was announced, for example) was itself a punishable offense. There was even a word for it in Newspeak: *facecrime,* it was called.

The girl had turned her back on him again. Perhaps after all she was not really following him about; perhaps it was coincidence that she had sat so close to him two days running. His cigarette had gone out, and he laid it carefully on the edge of the table. He would finish smoking it after work, if he could keep the tobacco in it. Quite likely the person at the next table was a spy of the Thought Police, and quite likely he would be in the cellars of the Ministry of Love within three days, but a cigarette end must not be wasted. Syme had folded up his strip of paper and stowed it away in his pocket. Parsons had begun talking again.

"Did I ever tell you, old boy," he said, chuckling round the stem of his pipe, "about the time when those two nippers of mine set fire to the old market-woman's skirt because they saw her wrapping up sausages in a poster of B.B.? Sneaked up behind her and set fire to it with a box of matches. Burned her quite badly, I believe. Little beggars, eh? But keen as mustard! That's a first-rate training they give them in the Spies nowadays—better than in my day, even. What d'you think's the latest thing they've served them out with? Ear trumpets for listening through keyholes! My little girl brought one home the other night—tried it out on our sitting room door, and reckoned she could hear twice as much as with her ear to the hole. Of course it's only a toy, mind you. Still, gives 'em the right idea, eh?"

At this moment the telescreen let out a piercing whistle. It was the signal to return to work. All three men sprang to their feet to join in the struggle round the lifts, and the remaining tobacco fell out of Winston's cigarette.

VI

Winston was writing in his diary:

It was three years ago. It was on a dark evening, in a narrow side street near one of the big railway stations. She was standing near a doorway in the wall, under a street lamp that hardly gave any light. She had a young face, painted very thick. It was really the paint that appealed to me, the whiteness of it, like a mask, and the bright red lips. Party women never paint their faces. There was nobody else in the street, and no telescreens. She said two dollars. I—

For the moment it was too difficult to go on. He shut his eyes and pressed his fingers against them, trying to squeeze out the vision that kept recurring. He had an almost overwhelming temptation to shout a string of filthy words at the top of his voice. Or to bang his head against the wall, to kick over the table and hurl the inkpot through the window—to do any violent or noisy or painful thing that might black out the memory that was tormenting him.

Your worst enemy, he reflected, was your own nervous system. At any moment the tension inside you was liable to translate itself into some visible symptom. He thought of a man whom he had passed in the street a few weeks back: a quite ordinary-looking man, a Party member, aged thirty-five or forty, tallish and thin, carrying a brief case. They were a few meters apart when the left side of the man's face was suddenly contorted by a sort of spasm. It happened again just as they were passing one another: it was only a twitch, a quiver, rapid as the clicking of a camera shutter, but obviously habitual. He remembered thinking at the time: that poor devil is done for. And what was frightening was that the action was quite possibly unconscious. The most deadly danger of all was talking in your sleep. There was no way of guarding against that, so far as he could see.

He drew in his breath and went on writing:

I went with her through the doorway and across a backyard into a basement kitchen. There was a bed against the wall, and a lamp on the table, turned down very low. She—

His teeth were set on edge. He would have liked to spit. Simultaneously with the woman in the basement kitchen he thought of Katharine, his wife. Winston was married—had been married, at any rate; probably he still was married, for so far as he knew his wife was not dead. He seemed to breathe again the warm stuffy odor of the basement kitchen, an odor compounded of bugs and dirty clothes and villainous cheap scent, but nevertheless alluring, because no woman of the Party ever used scent, or could be imagined as doing so. Only the proles used scent. In his mind the smell of it was inextricably mixed up with fornication.

When he had gone with that woman it had been his first lapse in two years or thereabouts. Consorting with prostitutes was forbidden, of course, but it was one of those rules that you could occasionally nerve yourself to break. It was dangerous, but it was not a life-and-death matter. To be caught with a prostitute might mean five years in a forced-labor camp: not more, if you had committed no other offense. And it was easy enough, provided that you could avoid being caught in the act. The poorer quarters swarmed with women who were ready to sell themselves. Some could even be purchased for a bottle of gin, which the proles were not supposed to drink. Tacitly the Party was even inclined to encourage prostitution, as an outlet for instincts which could not be altogether suppressed. Mere debauchery did not matter very much, so long as it was furtive and joyless, and only involved the women of a submerged and despised class. The unforgivable crime was promiscuity between Party members. But—though this was one of the crimes that the accused in the great purges invariably confessed to—it was difficult to imagine any such thing actually happening.

The aim of the Party was not merely to prevent men and women from forming loyalties which it might not be able to control. Its real, undeclared purpose was to remove all pleasure from the sexual act. Not love so much as eroticism was the enemy, inside marriage as well as outside it. All marriages between Party members had to be approved by a committee appointed for the purpose, and—though the principle was never clearly stated—permission was always refused if the couple concerned gave the impression of being physically attracted to one another. The only recognized purpose of marriage was to beget children for the service of the Party. Sexual intercourse was to be looked on as a slightly disgusting minor operation, like having an enema. This again was never put into plain words, but in an indirect way it was rubbed into every Party member from childhood onwards. There were even organizations such as the Junior Anti-Sex League which advocated complete celibacy for both sexes. All children were to be begotten by artificial insemination (*artsem*, it was called in Newspeak) and brought up in public institutions. This, Winston was aware, was not meant altogether seriously, but somehow it fitted in with the general ideology of the Party. The Party was trying to kill the sex instinct, or, if it could not be killed, then to distort it and dirty it. He did not know why this was so, but it seemed natural that it should be so. And so far as the women were concerned, the Party's efforts were largely successful.

He thought again of Katharine. It must be nine, ten—nearly eleven years since they had parted. It was curious how seldom he thought of her. For days at a time he was capable of forgetting that he had ever been married. They had only been together for about fifteen months. The Party did not permit divorce, but it rather encouraged separation in cases where there were no children.

Katharine was a tall, fair-haired girl, very straight, with splendid movements. She had a bold, aquiline face, a face that one might have called noble until one discovered that there was as nearly as possible nothing behind it. Very early in their married life he had decided— though perhaps it was only that he knew her more intimately than he knew most people—that she had without exception the most stupid, vulgar, empty mind that he had ever encountered. She had not a thought in her head that was not a slogan, and there was no imbecility, absolutely none, that she was not capable of swallowing if the Party handed it out to her. "The human sound track" he nicknamed her in his own mind. Yet he could have endured living with her if it had not been for just one thing—sex.

As soon as he touched her she seemed to wince and stiffen. To embrace her was like embracing a jointed wooden image. And what was strange was that even when she was clasping him against her he had the feeling that she was simultaneously pushing him away with all her strength. The rigidity of her muscles managed to convey that impression. She would lie there with shut eyes, neither resisting nor co-operating, but *submitting*. It was extraordinarily embarrassing and, after a while, horrible. But even then he could have borne living with her if it had been agreed that they should remain celibate. But curiously enough it was Katharine who refused this. They must, she said, produce a child if they could. So the performance continued to happen, once a week quite regularly, whenever it was not impossible. She used even to remind him of it in the morning, as something which had to be done that evening and which must not be forgotten. She had two names for it. One was "making a baby, " and the other was "our duty to the Party" (yes, she had actually used that phrase). Quite soon he grew to have a feeling of positive dread when the appointed day came round. But luckily no child appeared, and in the end she agreed to give up trying, and soon afterwards they parted.

Winston sighed inaudibly. He picked up his pen again and wrote:

She threw herself down on the bed, and at once, without any kind of preliminary, in the most coarse, horrible way you can imagine, pulled up her skirt. I—

He saw himself standing there in the dim lamplight, with the smell of bugs and cheap scent in his nostrils, and in his heart a feeling of defeat and resentment which even at that moment was mixed up with the thought of Katharine's white body, frozen forever by the hypnotic power of the Party. Why did it always have to be like this? Why could he not have a woman of his own instead of these filthy scuffles at intervals of years? But a real love affair was an almost unthinkable event. The women of the Party were all alike. Chastity was as deeply ingrained in them as Party loyalty. By careful early conditioning, by games and cold water, by the rubbish that was dinned into them at school and in the Spies and the Youth League, by lectures, parades, songs, slogans, and martial music, the natural feeling had been driven out of them. His reason told him that there must be exceptions, but his heart did not believe it. They were all impregnable, as the Party intended that they should be. And what he wanted, more even than to be loved, was to break down that wall of virtue, even if it were only once in his whole life. The sexual act, successfully performed, was rebellion. Desire was thoughtcrime. Even to have awakened Katharine, if he could have achieved it, would have been like a seduction, although she was his wife.

But the rest of the story had got to be written down. He wrote:

I turned up the lamp. When I saw her in the light—

After the darkness, the feeble light of the paraffin lamp had seemed very bright. For the first time he could see the woman properly. He had taken a step toward her and then halted, full of lust and terror. He was painfully conscious of the risk he had taken in coming here. It was perfectly possible that the patrols would catch him on the way out; for that matter they might be waiting outside the door at this moment. If he went away without even doing what he had come here to do—!

It had got to be written down, it had got to be confessed. What he had suddenly seen in the lamplight was that the woman was *old*. The paint was plastered so thick on her face that it looked as though it might crack like a cardboard mask. There were streaks of white in her hair; but the truly dreadful detail was that her mouth had fallen a little open, revealing nothing except a cavernous blackness. She had no teeth at all.

He wrote hurriedly, in scrabbling handwriting:

When I saw her in the light she was quite an old woman, fifty years old at least. But I went ahead and did it just the same.

He pressed his fingers against his eyelids again. He had written it down at last, but it made no difference. The therapy had not worked. The urge to shout filthy words at the top of his voice was as strong as ever.

VII

If there is hope [wrote Winston] it lies in the proles.

If there was hope, it *must* lie in the proles, because only there, in those swarming disregarded masses, eighty-five per cent of the population of Oceania, could the force to destroy the Party ever be generated. The Party could not be overthrown from within. Its enemies, if it had any enemies, had no way of coming together or even of identifying one another. Even if the legendary Brotherhood existed, as just possibly it might, it was inconceivable that its members could ever assemble in larger numbers than twos and threes. Rebellion meant a look in the eyes, an inflection of the voice; at the most, an occasional whispered word. But the proles, if only they could somehow become conscious of their own strength, would have no need to conspire. They needed only to rise up and shake themselves like a horse shaking off flies. If they chose they could blow the Party to pieces tomorrow morning. Surely sooner or later it must occur to them to do it. And yet—!

He remembered how once he had been walking down a crowded street when a tremendous shout of hundreds of voices—women's voices—had burst from a side street a little way ahead. It was a great formidable cry of danger and despair, a deep loud "Oh-o-o-o-oh!" that went humming on like the reverberation of a bell. His heart had leapt. It's started! he had thought. A riot! The proles are breaking loose at last! When he had reached the spot it was to see a mob of two or three hundred women crowding round the stalls of a street market, with faces as tragic as though they had been the doomed passengers on a sinking ship. But at this moment the general despair broke down into a multitude of individual quarrels. It appeared that one of the stalls had been selling tin saucepans. They were wretched, flimsy things, but cooking pots of any kind were always difficult to get. Now the supply had unexpectedly given out. The successful women, bumped and jostled by the rest, were trying to make off with their saucepans while dozens of others clamored round the stall, accusing the stallkeeper of favoritism and of having more saucepans somewhere in reserve. There was a fresh outburst of yells. Two bloated women, one of them with her hair coming down, had got hold of the same saucepan and were trying to tear it out of one another's hands. For a moment they were both tugging, and then the handle came off. Winston watched them disgustedly. And yet, just for a moment, what almost frightening power had sounded in that cry from only a few hundred throats! Why was it that they could never shout like that about anything that mattered?

He wrote:

Until they become conscious they will never rebel, and until after they have rebelled they cannot become conscious.

That, he reflected, might almost have been a transcription from one of the Party textbooks. The Party claimed, of course, to have liberated the proles from bondage. Before the Revolution they had been hideously oppressed by the capitalists, they had been starved and flogged, women had been forced to work in the coal mines (women still did work in the coal mines, as a matter of fact), children had been sold into the factories at the age of six. But simultaneously, true to the principles of doublethink, the Party taught that the proles were natural inferiors who must be kept in subjection, like animals, by the application of a few simple rules. In reality very little was known about the proles. It was not necessary to know much. So long as they continued to work and breed, their other activities were without importance. Left to themselves, like cattle turned loose upon the plains of Argentina, they had reverted to a style of life that appeared to be natural to them, a sort of ancestral pattern. They were born, they grew up in the gutters, they went to work at twelve, they passed through a brief blossoming period of beauty and sexual desire, they married at twenty, they were middle-aged at thirty, they died, for the most part, at sixty. Heavy physical work, the care of home and children, petty quarrels with neighbors, films, football, beer, and, above all, gambling filled up the horizon of their minds. To keep them in control was not difficult. A few agents of the Thought Police moved always among them, spreading false rumors and marking down and eliminating the few individuals who were judged capable of becoming dangerous; but no attempt was made to indoctrinate them with the ideology of the Party. It was not desirable that the proles should have strong political feelings. All that was required of them was a primitive patriotism which could be appealed to whenever it was necessary to make them accept longer working hours or shorter rations. And even when they became discontented, as they sometimes did, their discontent led nowhere, because, being without general ideas, they could only focus it on petty specific grievances. The larger evils invariably escaped their notice. The great majority of proles did not even have telescreens in their homes. Even the civil police interfered with them very little. There was a vast amount of criminality in London, a whole world-within-a-world of thieves, bandits, prostitutes, drug peddlers, and racketeers of every description; but since it all happened among the proles themselves, it was of no importance. In all questions of morals they were allowed to follow their ancestral code. The sexual puritanism of the party was not imposed upon them. Promiscuity went unpunished; divorce was permitted. For that matter, even religious worship would have been permitted if the proles had shown any sign of needing or wanting it. They were beneath suspicion. As the Party slogan put it: "Proles and animals are free."

Winston reached down and cautiously scratched his varicose ulcer. It had begun itching again. The thing you invariably came back to was the impossibility of knowing what life before the Revolution had really been like. He took out of the drawer a copy of a children's history textbook which he had borrowed from Mrs. Parsons, and began copying a passage into the diary:

In the old days [it ran], before the glorious Revolution, London was not the beautiful city that we know today. It was a dark, dirty, miserable place where hardly anybody had enough to eat and where hundreds and thousands of poor people had no boots on their feet and not even a roof to sleep under. Children no older than you are had to work twelve hours a day for cruel masters, who flogged them with whips if they worked too slowly and fed them on nothing but stale breadcrusts and water. But in among all this terrible poverty there were just a few great big beautiful houses that were lived in by rich men who had as many as thirty servants to look after them. These rich men were called capitalists. They were fat, ugly men with wicked faces, like the one in the picture on the opposite page. You can see that he is dressed in a long black coat which was called a frock coat, and a queer, shiny hat shaped like a stovepipe, which was called a top hat. This was the uniform of the capitalists, and no one else was allowed to wear it. The capitalists owned everything in the world, and everyone else was their slave. They owned all the land, all the houses, all the factories, and all the money. If anyone disobeyed them they could throw him into prison, or they could take his job away and starve him to death. When any ordinary person spoke to a capitalist he had to cringe and bow to him, and take off his cap and address him as "Sir." The chief of all the capitalists was called the King, and—

But he knew the rest of the catalogue. There would be mention of the bishops in their lawn sleeves, the judges in their ermine robes, the pillory, the stocks, the treadmill, the cat-o'-nine-tails, the Lord Mayor's Banquet, and the practice of kissing the Pope's toe. There was also something called the *jus primae noctis*, which would probably not be mentioned in a textbook for children. It was the law by which every capitalist had the right to sleep with any woman working in one of his factories.

How could you tell how much of it was lies? It *might* be true that the average human being was better off now than he had been before the Revolution. The only evidence to the contrary was the mute protest in your own bones, the instinctive feeling that the conditions you lived in were intolerable and that at some other time they must have been different. It struck him that the truly characteristic thing about modern life was not its cruelty and insecurity, but simply its bareness, its dinginess, its listlessness. Life, if you looked about you, bore no resemblance not only to the lies that streamed out of the telescreens, but even to the ideals that the Party was trying to achieve. Great areas of it, even for a Party member, were neutral and nonpolitical, a matter of slogging through dreary jobs, fighting for a place on the Tube, darning a worn-out sock, cadging a saccharine tablet, saving a cigarette end. The ideal set up by the Party was something huge, terrible, and glittering—a world of steel and concrete, of monstrous machines and terrifying weapons—a nation of warriors and fanatics, marching forward in perfect unity, all thinking the same thoughts and shouting the same slogans, perpetually working, fighting, triumphing, persecuting—three hundred million people all with the same face. The reality was decaying, dingy cities, where underfed people shuffled to and fro in leaky shoes, in patched-up nineteenth-century houses that smelt always of cabbage and bad lavatories. He seemed to see a vision of London, vast and ruinous, city of a million dust bins, and mixed up with it was a picture of Mrs. Parsons, a woman with lined face and wispy hair, fiddling helplessly with a blocked wastepipe.

He reached down and scratched his ankle again. Day and night the telescreens bruised your ears with statistics proving that people today had more food, more clothes, better houses, better recreations—that they lived longer, worked shorter hours, were bigger, healthier, stronger, happier, more intelligent, better educated, than the people of fifty years ago. Not a word of it could ever be proved or disproved. The Party claimed, for example, that today forty per cent of adult proles were literate; before the Revolution, it was said, the number had only been fifteen per cent. The Party claimed that the infant mortality rate was now only a hundred and sixty per thousand, whereas before the Revolution it had been three hundred—and so it went on. It was like a single equation with two unknowns. It might very well be that literally every word in the history books, even the things that one accepted without question, was pure fantasy. For all he knew there might never have been any such law as the *jus primae noctis*, or any such creature as a capitalist, or any such garment as a top hat.

Everything faded into mist. The past was erased, the erasure was forgotten, the lie became truth. Just once in his life he had possessed—*after* the event: that was what counted—concrete, unmistakable evidence of an act of falsification. He had held it between his fingers for as long as thirty seconds. In 1973, it must have been—at any rate, it was at about the time when he and Katharine had parted. But the really relevant date was seven or eight years earlier.

The story really began in the middle Sixties, the period of the great purges in which the original leaders of the Revolution were wiped out once and for all. By 1970 none of them was left, except Big Brother himself. All the rest had by that time been exposed as traitors and counterrevolutionaries. Goldstein had fled and was hiding, no one knew where, and of the others, a few had simply disappeared, while the majority had been executed after spectacular public trials at which they made confession of their crimes. Among the last survivors were three men named Jones, Aaronson, and Rutherford. It must have been in 1965 that these three had been arrested. As often happened, they had vanished for a year or more, so that one did not know whether they were alive or dead, and then had suddenly been brought forth to incriminate themselves in the usual way. They had confessed to intelligence with the enemy (at that date, too, the enemy was Eurasia), embezzlement of public funds, the murder of various trusted Party members, intrigues against the leadership of Big Brother which had started long before the Revolution happened, and acts of sabotage causing the death of hundreds of thousands of people. After confessing to these things they had been pardoned, reinstated in the Party, and given posts which were in fact sinecures but which sounded important. All three had written long, abject articles in the *Times*, analyzing the reasons for their defection and promising to make amends.

Some time after their release Winston had actually seen all three of them in the Chestnut Tree Café. He remembered the sort of terrified fascination with which he had watched them out of the corner of his eye. They were men far older than himself, relics of the ancient world, almost the last great figures left over from the heroic early days of the Party. The glamor of the underground struggle and the civil war still faintly clung to them. He had the feeling, though already at that time facts and dates were growing blurry, that he had known their names years earlier than he had known that of Big Brother. But also they were outlaws, enemies, untouchables, doomed with absolute certainty to extinction within a year or two. No one who had once fallen into the hands of the Thought Police ever escaped in the end. They were corpses waiting to be sent back to the grave.

There was no one at any of the tables nearest to them. It was not wise even to be seen in the neighborhood of such people. They were sitting in silence before glasses of the gin flavored with cloves which was the speciality of the café. Of the three, it was Rutherford whose appearance had most impressed Winston. Rutherford had once been a famous caricaturist, whose brutal cartoons had helped to inflame popular opinion before and during the Revolution. Even now, at long intervals, his cartoons were appearing in the *Times*. They were simply an imitation of his earlier manner, and curiously lifeless and unconvincing. Always they were a rehashing of the ancient themes—slum tenements, starving children, street battles, capitalists in top hats—even on the barricades the capitalists still seemed to cling to their top hats—an endless, hopeless effort to get back into the past. He was a monstrous man, with a mane of greasy gray hair, his face pouched and seamed, with protuberant lips. At one time he must have been immensely strong; now his great body was sagging, sloping, bulging, falling away in every direction. He seemed to be breaking up before one's eyes, like a mountain crumbling.

It was the lonely hour of fifteen. Winston could not now remember how he had come to be in the café at such a time. The place was almost empty. A tinny music was trickling from the telescreen. The three men sat in their corner almost motionless, never speaking. Uncommanded, the waiter brought fresh glasses of gin. There was a chessboard on the table beside them, with the pieces set out, but no game started. And then, for perhaps half a minute in all, something happened to the telescreens. The tune that they were playing changed, and the tone of the music changed too. There came into it—but it was something hard to describe. It was a peculiar, cracked, braying, jeering note; in his mind Winston called it a yellow note. And then a voice from the telescreen was singing:

> *"Under the spreading chestnut tree*
> *I sold you and you sold me:*
> *There lie they, and here lie we*
> *Under the spreading chestnut tree."*

The three men never stirred. But when Winston glanced again at Rutherford's ruinous face, he saw that his eyes were full of tears. And for the
first time he noticed, with a kind of inward shudder, and yet not knowing
at what he shuddered, that both Aaronson and Rutherford had broken
noses.

A little later all three were rearrested. It appeared that they had engaged in fresh conspiracies from the very moment of their release. At
their second trial they confessed to all their old crimes over again, with a
whole string of new ones. They were executed, and their fate was recorded in the Party histories, a warning to posterity. About five years
after this, in 1973, Winston was unrolling a wad of documents which had
just flopped out of the pneumatic tube onto his desk when he came on a
fragment of paper which had evidently been slipped in among the others
and then forgotten. It was a half-page torn out of the *Times* of about ten
years earlier—the top half of the page, so that it included the date—and
it contained a photograph of the delegates at some Party function in New
York. Prominent in the middle of the group were Jones, Aaronson, and
Rutherford. There was no mistaking them; in any case their names were
in the caption at the bottom.

The point was that at both trials all three men had confessed that on
that date they had been on Eurasian soil. They had flown from a secret
airfield in Canada to a rendezvous somewhere in Siberia, and had con-
ferred with members of the Eurasian General Staff, to whom they had
betrayed important military secrets. The date had stuck in Winston's
memory because it chanced to be Midsummer Day; but the whole story
must be on record in countless other places as well. There was only one
possible conclusion: the confessions were lies.

Of course, this was not in itself a discovery. Even at that time Winston
had not imagined that the people who were wiped out in the purges had
actually committed the crimes that they were accused of. But this was
concrete evidence; it was a fragment of the abolished past, like a fossil
bone which turns up in the wrong stratum and destroys a geological theory. It was enough to blow the Party to atoms, if in some way it could
have been published to the world and its significance made known.

He had gone straight on working. As soon as he saw what the photograph was, and what it meant, he had covered it up with another sheet of
paper. Luckily, when he unrolled it, it had been upside-down from the
point of view of the telescreen.

He took his scribbling pad on his knee and pushed back his chair, so as
to get as far away from the telescreen as possible. To keep your face
expressionless was not difficult, and even your breathing could be controlled, with an effort; but you could not control the beating of your
heart, and the telescreen was quite delicate enough to pick it up. He let
what he judged to be ten minutes go by, tormented all the while by the
fear that some accident—a sudden draught blowing across his desk, for

instance—would betray him. Then, without uncovering it again, he dropped the photograph into the memory hole, along with some other waste papers. Within another minute, perhaps, it would have crumbled into ashes.

That was ten—eleven years ago. Today, probably, he would have kept that photograph. It was curious that the fact of having held it in his fingers seemed to him to make a difference even now, when the photograph itself, as well as the event it recorded, was only memory. Was the Party's hold upon the past less strong, he wondered, because a piece of evidence which existed no longer *had once* existed?

But today, supposing that it could be somehow resurrected from its ashes, the photograph might not even be evidence. Already, at the time when he made his discovery, Oceania was no longer at war with Eurasia, and it must have been to the agents of Eastasia that the three dead men had betrayed their country. Since then there had been other changes—two, three, he could not remember how many. Very likely the confessions had been rewritten and rewritten until the original facts and dates no longer had the smallest significance. The past not only changed, but changed continuously. What most afflicted him with the sense of nightmare was that he had never clearly understood *why* the huge imposture was undertaken. The immediate advantages of falsifying the past were obvious, but the ultimate motive was mysterious. He took up his pen again and wrote:

I understand HOW: I do not understand WHY.

He wondered, as he had many times wondered before, whether he himself was a lunatic. Perhaps a lunatic was simply a minority of one. At one time it had been a sign of madness to believe that the earth goes round the sun; today, to believe that the past is unalterable. He might be *alone* in holding that belief, and if alone, then a lunatic. But the thought of being a lunatic did not greatly trouble him; the horror was that he might also be wrong.

He picked up the children's history book and looked at the portrait of Big Brother which formed its frontispiece. The hypnotic eyes gazed into his own. It was as though some huge force were pressing down upon you—something that penetrated inside your skull, battering against your brain, frightening you out of your beliefs, persuading you, almost, to deny the evidence of your senses. In the end the Party would announce that two and two made five, and you would have to believe it. It was inevitable that they should make that claim sooner or later: the logic of their position demanded it. Not merely the validity of experience, but the very existence of external reality was tacitly denied by their philosophy. The heresy of heresies was common sense. And what was terrifying was not that they would kill you for thinking otherwise, but that they might be right. For, after all, how do we know that two and two make four? Or that the force of gravity works? Or that the past is unchangeable? If both the past and the external world exist only in the mind, and if the mind itself is controllable—what then?

But no! His courage seemed suddenly to stiffen of its own accord. The face of O'Brien, not called up by any obvious association, had floated into his mind. He knew, with more certainty than before, that O'Brien was on his side. He was writing the diary for O'Brien—*to* O'Brien; it was like an interminable letter which no one would ever read, but which was addressed to a particular person and took its color from that fact.

The Party told you to reject the evidence of your eyes and ears. It was their final, most essential command. His heart sank as he thought of the enormous power arrayed against him, the ease with which any Party intellectual would overthrow him in debate, the subtle arguments which he would not be able to understand, much less answer. And yet he was in the right! They were wrong and he was right. The obvious, the silly, and the true had got to be defended. Truisms are true, hold on to that! The solid world exists, its laws do not change. Stones are hard, water is wet, objects unsupported fall toward the earth's center. With the feeling that he was speaking to O'Brien, and also that he was setting forth an important axiom, he wrote:

Freedom is the freedom to say that two plus two make four. If that is granted, all else follows.

VIII

From somewhere at the bottom of a passage the smell of roasting coffee—real coffee, not Victory Coffee—came floating out into the street. Winston paused involuntarily. For perhaps two seconds he was back in the half-forgotten world of his childhood. Then a door banged, seeming to cut off the smell as abruptly as though it had been a sound.

He had walked several kilometers over pavements, and his varicose ulcer was throbbing. This was the second time in three weeks that he had missed an evening at the Community Center: a rash act, since you could be certain that the number of your attendances at the Center were carefully checked. In principle a Party member had no spare time, and was never alone except in bed. It was assumed that when he was not working, eating, or sleeping he would be taking part in some kind of communal recreations; to do anything that suggested a taste for solitude, even to go for a walk by yourself, was always slightly dangerous. There was a word for it in Newspeak: *ownlife*, it was called, meaning individualism and eccentricity. But this evening as he came out of the Ministry the balminess of the April air had tempted him. The sky was a warmer blue than he had seen it that year, and suddenly the long, noisy evening at the

Center, the boring exhausting games, the lectures, the creaking camara-
derie oiled by gin, had seemed intolerable. On impulse he had turned
away from the bus stop and wandered off into the labyrinth of London,
first south, then east, then north again, losing himself along unknown
streets and hardly bothering in which direction he was going.

"If there is hope," he had written in the diary, "it lies in the proles."
The words kept coming back to him, statement of a mystical truth and a
palpable absurdity. He was somewhere in the vague, brown-colored
slums to the north and east of what had once been Saint Pancras Station.
He was walking up a cobbled street of little two-story houses with battered doorways which gave straight on the pavement and which were
somehow curiously suggestive of rat holes. There were puddles of filthy
water here and there among the cobbles. In and out of the dark doorways,
and down narrow alleyways that branched off on either side, people
swarmed in astonishing numbers—girls in full bloom, with crudely lip-
sticked mouths, and youths who chased the girls, and swollen waddling
women who showed you what the girls would be like in ten years time,
and old bent creatures shuffling along on splayed feet, and ragged bare-
footed children who played in the puddles and then scattered at angry
yells from their mothers. Perhaps a quarter of the windows in the street
were broken and boarded up. Most of the people paid no attention to
Winston; a few eyed him with a sort of guarded curiosity. Two monstrous
women with brick-red forearms folded across their aprons were talking
outside a doorway. Winston caught scraps of conversation as he approached.

" 'Yes,' I says to 'er, 'that's all very well,' I says. 'But if you'd of been in
my place you'd of done the same as what I done. It's easy to criticize,' I
says, 'but you ain't got the same problems as what I got.' "

"Ah," said the other, "that's jest it. That's jest where it is."

The strident voices stopped abruptly. The women studied him in hostile
silence as he went past. But it was not hostility, exactly; merely a kind of
wariness, a momentary stiffening, as at the passing of some unfamiliar
animal. The blue overalls of the Party could not be a common sight in a
street like this. Indeed, it was unwise to be seen in such places, unless you
had definite business there. The patrols might stop you if you happened
to run into them. "May I see your papers, comrade? What are you doing
here? What time did you leave work? Is this your usual way home?"—
and so on and so forth. Not that there was any rule against walking home
by an unusual route, but it was enough to draw attention to you if the
Thought Police heard about it.

Suddenly the whole street was in commotion. There were yells of warning from all sides. People were shooting into the doorways like rabbits. A
young woman leapt out of a doorway a little ahead of Winston, grabbed
up a tiny child playing in a puddle, whipped her apron round it, and leapt

back again, all in one movement. At the same instant a man in a concertina-like black suit, who had emerged from a side alley, ran toward Winston, pointing excitedly to the sky.

"Steamer!" he yelled. "Look out, guv'nor! Bang over'ead! Lay down quick!"

"Steamer" was a nickname which, for some reason, the proles applied to rocket bombs. Winston promptly flung himself on his face. The proles were nearly always right when they gave you a warning of this kind. They seemed to possess some kind of instinct which told them several seconds in advance when a rocket was coming, although the rockets supposedly traveled faster than sound. Winston clasped his forearms about his head. There was a roar that seemed to make the pavement heave; a shower of light objects pattered onto his back. When he stood up he found that he was covered with fragments of glass from the nearest window.

He walked on. The bomb had demolished a group of houses two hundred meters up the street. A black plume of smoke hung in the sky, and below it a cloud of plaster dust in which a crowd was already forming round the ruins. There was a little pile of plaster lying on the pavement ahead of him, and in the middle of it he could see a bright red streak. When he got up to it he saw that it was a human hand severed at the wrist. Apart from the bloody stump, the hand was so completely whitened as to resemble a plaster cast.

He kicked the thing into the gutter, and then, to avoid the crowd, turned down a side street to the right. Within three or four minutes he was out of the area which the bomb had affected, and the sordid swarming life of the streets was going on as though nothing had happened. It was nearly twenty hours, and the drinking shops which the proles frequented ("pubs," they called them) were choked with customers. From their grimy swing doors, endlessly opening and shutting, there came forth a smell of urine, sawdust, and sour beer. In an angle formed by a projecting house front three men were standing very close together, the middle one of them holding a folded-up newspaper which the other two were studying over his shoulders. Even before he was near enough to make out the expression on their faces, Winston could see absorption in every line of their bodies. It was obviously some serious piece of news that they were reading. He was a few paces away from them when suddenly the group broke up and two of the men were in violent altercation. For a moment they seemed almost on the point of blows.

"Can't you bleeding well listen to what I say? I tell you no number ending in seven ain't won for over fourteen months!"

"Yes it 'as, then!"

"No, it 'as not! Back 'ome I got the 'ole lot of 'em for over two years wrote down on a piece of paper. I takes 'em down reg'lar as the clock. An' I tell you, no number ending in seven—"

"Yes, a seven 'as won! I could pretty near tell you the bleeding number. Four oh seven, it ended in. It were in February—second week in February."

"February your grandmother! I got it all down in black and white. An' I tell you, no number—"

"Oh, pack it in!" said the third man.

They were talking about the Lottery. Winston looked back when he had gone thirty meters. They were still arguing, with vivid, passionate faces. The Lottery, with its weekly pay-out of enormous prizes, was the one public event to which the proles paid serious attention. It was probable that there were some millions of proles for whom the Lottery was the principal if not the only reason for remaining alive. It was their delight, their folly, their anodyne, their intellectual stimulant. Where the Lottery was concerned, even people who could barely read and write seemed capable of intricate calculations and staggering feats of memory. There was a whole tribe of men who made a living simply by selling systems, forecasts, and lucky amulets. Winston had nothing to do with the running of the Lottery, which was managed by the Ministry of Plenty, but he was aware (indeed everyone in the Party was aware) that the prizes were largely imaginary. Only small sums were actually paid out, the winners of the big prizes being nonexistent persons. In the absence of any real intercommunication between one part of Oceania and another, this was not difficult to arrange.

But if there was hope, it lay in the proles. You had to cling on to that. When you put it in words it sounded reasonable; it was when you looked at the human beings passing you on the pavement that it became an act of faith. The street into which he had turned ran downhill. He had a feeling that he had been in this neighborhood before, and that there was a main thoroughfare not far away. From somewhere ahead there came a din of shouting voices. The street took a sharp turn and then ended in a flight of steps which led down into a sunken alley where a few stall-keepers were selling tired-looking vegetables. At this moment Winston remembered where he was. The alley led out into the main street, and down the next turning, not five minutes away, was the junk shop where he had bought the blank book which was now his diary. And in a small stationer's shop not far away he had bought his penholder and his bottle of ink.

He paused for a moment at the top of the steps. On the opposite side of the alley there was a dingy little pub whose windows appeared to be frosted over but in reality were merely coated with dust. A very old man, bent but active, with white mustaches that bristled forward like those of a prawn, pushed open the swing door and went in. As Winston stood watching it occurred to him that the old man, who must be eighty at the least, had already been middle-aged when the Revolution happened. He and a few others like him were the last links that now existed with the vanished world of capitalism. In the Party itself there were not many people left whose ideas had been formed before the Revolution. The older generation had mostly been wiped out in the great purges of the Fifties and Sixties, and the few who survived had long ago been terrified into complete intellectual surrender. If there was anyone still alive who could give you a truthful account of conditions in the early part of the century, it could only be a prole. Suddenly the passage from the history book that he had copied into his diary came back into Winston's mind, and a lunatic impulse took hold of him. He would go into the pub, he would scrape acquaintance with that old man and question him. He would say: "Tell me about your life when you were a boy. What was it like in those days? Were things better than they are now, or were they worse?"

Hurriedly, lest he should have time to become frightened, he descended the steps and crossed the narrow street. It was madness, of course. As usual, there was no definite rule against talking to proles and frequenting their pubs, but it was far too unusual an action to pass unnoticed. If the patrols appeared he might plead an attack of faintness, but it was not likely that they would believe him. He pushed open the door, and a hideous cheesy smell of sour beer hit him in the face. As he entered, the din of voices dropped to about half its volume. Behind his back he could feel everyone eyeing his blue overalls. A game of darts which was going on at the other end of the room interrupted itself for perhaps as much as thirty seconds. The old man whom he had followed was standing at the bar, having some kind of altercation with the barman, a large, stout, hook-nosed young man with enormous forearms. A knot of others, standing round with glasses in their hands, were watching the scene.

"I arst you civil enough, didn't I?" said the old man, straightening his shoulders pugnaciously. "You telling me you ain't got a pint mug in the 'ole bleeding boozer?"

"And what in hell's name *is* a pint?" said the barman, leaning forward with the tips of his fingers on the counter.

"'Ark at 'im! Calls 'isself a barman and don't know what a pint is! Why, a pint's the 'alf of a quart, and there's four quarts to the gallon. 'Ave to teach you the A, B, C next."

"Never heard of 'em," said the barman shortly. "Liter and half liter—that's all we serve. There's the glasses on the shelf in front of you."

"I likes a pint," persisted the old man. "You could 'a drawed me off a pint easy enough. We didn't 'ave these bleeding liters when I was a young man."

"When you were a young man we were all living in the treetops," said the barman, with a glance at the other customers.

There was a shout of laughter, and the uneasiness caused by Winston's entry seemed to disappear. The old man's white-stubbled face had flushed pink. He turned away, muttering to himself, and bumped into Winston. Winston caught him gently by the arm.

"May I offer you a drink?" he said.

"You're a gent," said the other, straightening his shoulders again. He appeared not to have noticed Winston's blue overalls. "Pint!" he added aggressively to the barman. "Pint of wallop."

The barman swished two half-liters of dark-brown beer into thick glasses which he had rinsed in a bucket under the counter. Beer was the only drink you could get in prole pubs. The proles were supposed not to drink gin, though in practice they could get hold of it easily enough. The game of darts was in full swing again, and the knot of men at the bar had begun talking about lottery tickets. Winston's presence was forgotten for a moment. There was a deal table under the window where he and the old man could talk without fear of being overheard. It was horribly dangerous, but at any rate there was no telescreen in the room, a point he had made sure of as soon as he came in.

" 'E could 'a drawed me off a pint," grumbled the old man as he settled down behind his glass. "A 'alf liter ain't enough. It don't satisfy. And a 'ole liter's too much. It starts my bladder running. Let alone the price."

"You must have seen great changes since you were a young man," said Winston tentatively.

The old man's pale blue eyes moved from the darts board to the bar, and from the bar to the door of the Gents, as though it were in the bar-room that he expected the changes to have occurred.

"The beer was better," he said finally. "And cheaper! When I was a young man, mild beer—wallop, we used to call it—was fourpence a pint. That was before the war, of course."

"Which war was that?" said Winston.

"It's all wars," said the old man vaguely. He took up his glass, and his shoulders straightened again. " 'Ere's wishing you the very best of 'ealth!"

In his lean throat the sharp-pointed Adam's apple made a surprisingly rapid up-and-down movement, and the beer vanished. Winston went to the bar and came back with two more half-liters. The old man appeared to have forgotten his prejudice against drinking a full liter.

"You are very much older than I am," said Winston. "You must have been a grown man before I was born. You can remember what it was like in the old days, before the Revolution. People of my age don't really know anything about those times. We can only read about them in books, and what it says in the books may not be true. I should like your opinion on that. The history books say that life before the Revolution was completely different from what it is now. There was the most terrible oppression, injustice, poverty—worse than anything we can imagine. Here in London, the great mass of the people never had enough to eat from birth to death. Half of them hadn't even boots on their feet. They worked twelve hours a day, they left school at nine, they slept ten in a room. And at the same time there were a very few people, only a few thousands— the capitalists, they were called—who were rich and powerful. They owned everything that there was to own. They lived in great gorgeous houses with thirty servants, they rode about in motor cars and four-horse carriages, they drank champagne, they wore top hats—"

The old man brightened suddenly.

"Top 'ats!" he said. "Funny you should mention 'em. The same thing come into my 'ead only yesterday, I donno why. I was jest thinking, I ain't seen a top 'at in years. Gorn right out, they 'ave. The last time I wore one was at my sister-in-law's funeral. And that was—well, I couldn't give you the date, but it must 'a been fifty years ago. Of course it was only 'ired for the occasion, you understand."

"It isn't very important about the top hats," said Winston patiently. "The point is, these capitalists—they and a few lawyers and priests and so forth who lived on them—were the lords of the earth. Everything existed for their benefit. You—the ordinary people, the workers—were their slaves. They could do what they liked with you. They could ship you off to Canada like cattle. They could sleep with your daughters if they chose. They could order you to be flogged with something called a cat-o'-nine-tails. You had to take your cap off when you passed them. Every capitalist went about with a gang of lackeys who—"

The old man brightened again.

"Lackeys!" he said. "Now there's a word I ain't 'eard since ever so long. Lackeys! That reg'lar takes me back, that does. I recollect—oh, donkey's years ago—I used to sometimes go to 'Yde Park of a Sunday afternoon to 'ear the blokes making speeches. Salvation Army, Roman Catholics, Jews, Indians—all sorts, there was. And there was one bloke—well, I couldn't give you 'is name, but a real powerful speaker, 'e was. 'E didn't 'alf give it 'em! 'Lackeys!' 'e says. 'Lackeys of the bourgeoisie! Flunkies of the ruling class!' Parasites—that was another of them. And 'yenas—'e def'nitely called 'em 'yenas. Of course 'e was referring to the Labour Party, you understand."

Winston had the feeling that they were talking at cross purposes.

"What I really wanted to know was this," he said. "Do you feel that you have more freedom now than you had in those days? Are you treated more like a human being? In the old days, the rich people, the people at the top—"

"The 'Ouse of Lords," put in the old man reminiscently.

"The House of Lords, if you like. What I am asking is, were these people able to treat you as an inferior, simply because they were rich and you were poor? Is it a fact, for instance, that you had to call them 'Sir' and take off your cap when you passed them?"

The old man appeared to think deeply. He drank off about a quarter of his beer before answering.

"Yes," he said. "They liked you to touch your cap to 'em. It showed respect, like. I didn't agree with it, myself, but I done it often enough. Had to, as you might say."

"And was it usual—I'm only quoting what I've read in history books— was it usual for these people and their servants to push you off the pavement into the gutter?"

"One of 'em pushed me once," said the old man. "I recollect it as if it was yesterday. It was Boat Race night—terrible rowdy they used to get on Boat Race night—and I bumps into a young bloke on Shaftesbury Avenue. Quite the gent, 'e was—dress shirt, top 'at, black overcoat. 'E was kind of zigzagging across the pavement, and I bumps into 'im accidental-like. 'E says, 'Why can't you look where you're going?' 'e says. I says, 'Ju think you've bought the bleeding pavement?' 'E says, 'I'll twist your bloody 'ead off if you get fresh with me.' I says, 'You're drunk. I'll give you in charge in 'alf a minute,' I says. 'An if you'll believe me, 'e puts 'is 'and on my chest and gives me a shove as pretty near sent me under the wheels of a bus. Well, I was young in them days, and I was going to 'ave fetched 'im one, only—"

A sense of helplessness took hold of Winston. The old man's memory was nothing but a rubbish heap of details. One could question him all day without getting any real information. The Party histories might still be true, after a fashion; they might even be completely true. He made a last attempt.

"Perhaps I have not made myself clear," he said. "What I'm trying to say is this. You have been alive a very long time; you lived your life before the Revolution. In 1925, for instance, you were already grown up. Would you say, from what you can remember, that life in 1925 was better than it is now, or worse? If you could choose, would you prefer to live then or now?"

The old man looked meditatively at the darts board. He finished up his beer, more slowly than before. When he spoke it was with a tolerant, philosophic air, as though the beer had mellowed him.

"I know what you expect me to say," he said. "You expect me to say as I'd sooner be young again. Most people'd say they'd sooner be young, if you arst 'em. You got your 'ealth and strength when you're young. When you get to my time of life you ain't never well. I suffer something wicked from my feet, and my bladder's jest terrible. Six and seven times a night it 'as me out of bed. On the other 'and there's great advantages in being a old man. You ain't got the same worries. No truck with women, and that's a great thing. I ain't 'ad a woman for near on thirty year, if you'd credit it. Nor wanted to, what's more."

Winston sat back against the window sill. It was no use going on. He was about to buy some more beer when the old man suddenly got up and shuffled rapidly into the stinking urinal at the side of the room. The extra half-liter was already working on him. Winston sat for a minute or two gazing at his empty glass, and hardly noticed when his feet carried him out into the street again. Within twenty years at the most, he reflected, the huge and simple question, "Was life better before the Revolution than it is now?" would have ceased once and for all to be answerable. But in effect it was unanswerable even now, since the few scattered survivors from the ancient world were incapable of comparing one age with another. They remembered a million useless things, a quarrel with a workmate, a hunt for a lost bicycle pump, the expression on a long-dead sister's face, the swirls of dust on a windy morning seventy years ago; but all the relevant facts were outside the range of their vision. They were like the ant, which can see small objects but not large ones. And when memory failed and written records were falsified—when that happened, the claim of the Party to have improved the conditions of human life had got to be accepted, because there did not exist, and never again could exist, any standard against which it could be tested.

At this moment his train of thought stopped abruptly. He halted and looked up. He was in a narrow street, with a few dark little shops interspersed among dwelling houses. Immediately above his head there hung three discolored metal balls which looked as if they had once been gilded. He seemed to know the place. Of course! He was standing outside the junk shop where he had bought the diary.

A twinge of fear went through him. It had been a sufficiently rash act to buy the book in the beginning, and he had sworn never to come near the place again. And yet the instant that he allowed his thoughts to wander, his feet had brought him back here of their own accord. It was precisely against suicidal impulses of this kind that he had hoped to guard himself by opening the diary. At the same time he noticed that although it was nearly twenty-one hours the shop was still open. With the feeling that he would be less conspicuous inside than hanging about on the pavement, he stepped through the doorway. If questioned, he could plausibly say that he was trying to buy razor blades.

The proprietor had just lighted a hanging oil lamp which gave off an unclean but friendly smell. He was a man of perhaps sixty, frail and bowed, with a long, benevolent nose, and mild eyes distorted by thick spectacles. His hair was almost white, but his eyebrows were bushy and still black. His spectacles, his gentle, fussy movements, and the fact that he was wearing an aged jacket of black velvet, gave him a vague air of intellectuality, as though he had been some kind of literary man, or perhaps a musician. His voice was soft, as though faded, and his accent less debased than that of the majority of proles.

"I recognized you on the pavement," he said immediately. "You're the gentleman that bought the young lady's keepsake album. That was a beautiful bit of paper, that was. Cream laid, it used to be called. There's been no paper like that made for—oh, I dare say fifty years." He peered at Winston over the top of his spectacles. "Is there anything special I can do for you? Or did you just want to look round?"

"I was passing," said Winston vaguely. "I just looked in. I don't want anything in particular."

"It's just as well," said the other, "because I don't suppose I could have satisfied you." He made an apologetic gesture with his soft-palmed hand. "You see how it is; an empty shop, you might say. Between you and me, the antique trade's just about finished. No demand any longer, and no stock either. Furniture, china, glass—it's all been broken up by degrees. And of course the metal stuff's mostly been melted down. I haven't seen a brass candlestick in years."

The tiny interior of the shop was in fact uncomfortably full, but there was almost nothing in it of the slightest value. The floor space was very restricted, because all round the walls were stacked innumerable dusty picture frames. In the window there were trays of nuts and bolts, worn-out chisels, penknives with broken blades, tarnished watches that did not even pretend to be in going order, and other miscellaneous rubbish. Only on a small table in the corner was there a litter of odds and ends—lacquered snuffboxes, agate brooches, and the like—which looked as though they might include something interesting. As Winston wandered toward the table his eye was caught by a round, smooth thing that gleamed softly in the lamplight, and he picked it up.

It was a heavy lump of glass, curved on one side, flat on the other, making almost a hemisphere. There was a peculiar softness, as of rainwater, in both the color and the texture of the glass. At the heart of it, magnified by the curved surface, there was a strange, pink, convoluted object that recalled a rose or a sea anemone.

"What is it?" said Winston, fascinated.

"That's coral, that is," said the old man. "It must have come from the Indian Ocean. They used to kind of embed it in the glass. That wasn't made less than a hundred years ago. More, by the look of it."

"It's a beautiful thing," said Winston.

"It is a beautiful thing," said the other appreciatively. "But there's not many that'd say so nowadays." He coughed. "Now, if it so happened that you wanted to buy it, that'd cost you four dollars. I can remember when a thing like that would have fetched eight pounds, and eight pounds was— well, I can't work it out, but it was a lot of money. But who cares about genuine antiques nowadays—even the few that's left?"

Winston immediately paid over the four dollars and slid the coveted thing into his pocket. What appealed to him about it was not so much its beauty as the air it seemed to possess of belonging to an age quite different from the present one. The soft, rainwatery glass was not like any glass that he had ever seen. The thing was doubly attractive because of its apparent uselessness, though he could guess that it must once have been intended as a paperweight. It was very heavy in his pocket, but fortunately it did not make much of a bulge. It was a queer thing, even a compromising thing, for a Party member to have in his possession. Anything old, and for that matter anything beautiful, was always vaguely suspect. The old man had grown noticeably more cheerful after receiving the four dollars. Winston realized that he would have accepted three or even two.

"There's another room upstairs that you might care to take a look at," he said. "There's not much in it. Just a few pieces. We'll do with a light if we're going upstairs."

He lit another lamp and, with bowed back, led the way slowly up the steep and worn stairs and along a tiny passage, into a room which did not give on the street but looked out on a cobbled yard and a forest of chimney pots. Winston noticed that the furniture was still arranged as though the room were meant to be lived in. There was a strip of carpet on the floor, a picture or two on the walls, and a deep, slatternly armchair drawn up to the fireplace. An old-fashioned glass clock with a twelve-hour face was ticking away on the mantelpiece. Under the window, and occupying nearly a quarter of the room, was an enormous bed with the mattress still on it.

"We lived here till my wife died," said the old man half apologetically. "I'm selling the furniture off by little and little. Now that's a beautiful mahogany bed, or at least it would be if you could get the bugs out of it. But I dare say you'd find it a little bit cumbersome."

He was holding the lamp high up, so as to illumine the whole room, and in the warm dim light the place looked curiously inviting. The thought flitted through Winston's mind that it would probably be quite easy to rent the room for a few dollars a week, if he dared to take the risk. It was a wild, impossible notion, to be abandoned as soon as thought of; but the room had awakened in him a sort of nostalgia, a sort of ancestral memory. It seemed to him that he knew exactly what it felt like to sit in a room like this, in an armchair beside an open fire with your feet in the fender and a kettle on the hob, utterly alone, utterly secure, with nobody watching you, no voice pursuing you, no sound except the singing of the kettle and the friendly ticking of the clock.

"There's no telescreen!" he could not help murmuring.

"Ah," said the old man, "I never had one of those things. Too expensive. And I never seemed to feel the need of it, somehow. Now that's a nice gateleg table in the corner there. Though of course you'd have to put new hinges on it if you wanted to use the flaps."

There was a small bookcase in the other corner, and Winston had already gravitated toward it. It contained nothing but rubbish. The hunting-down and destruction of books had been done with the same thoroughness in the prole quarters as everywhere else. It was very unlikely that there existed anywhere in Oceania a copy of a book printed earlier than 1960. The old man, still carrying the lamp, was standing in front of a picture in a rosewood frame which hung on the other side of the fireplace, opposite the bed.

"Now, if you happen to be interested in old prints at all—" he began delicately.

Winston came across to examine the picture. It was a steel engraving of an oval building with rectangular windows, and a small tower in front. There was a railing running round the building, and at the rear end there was what appeared to be a statue. Winston gazed at it for some moments. It seemed vaguely familiar, though he did not remember the statue.

"The frame's fixed to the wall," said the old man, "but I could unscrew it for you, I dare say."

"I know that building," said Winston finally. "It's a ruin now. It's in the middle of the street outside the Palace of Justice."

"That's right. Outside the Law Courts. It was bombed in—oh, many years ago. It was a church at one time. St. Clement's Dane, its name was." He smiled apologetically, as though conscious of saying something slightly ridiculous, and added: *"Oranges and lemons, say the bells of St. Clement's!"*

"What's that?" said Winston.

"Oh—*Oranges and lemons, say the bells of St. Clement's*. That was a rhyme we had when I was a little boy. How it goes on I don't remember, but I do know it ended up, *Here comes a candle to light you to bed, Here comes a chopper to chop off your head*. It was a kind of a dance. They held out their arms for you to pass under, and when they came to *Here comes a chopper to chop off your head* they brought their arms down and caught you. It was just names of churches. All the London churches were in it—all the principal ones, that is."

Winston wondered vaguely to what century the church belonged. It was always difficult to determine the age of a London building. Anything large and impressive, if it was reasonably new in appearance, was automatically claimed as having been built since the Revolution, while anything that was obviously of earlier date was ascribed to some dim period called the Middle Ages. The centuries of capitalism were held to have produced nothing of any value. One could not learn history from architecture any more than one could learn it from books. Statues, inscriptions, memorial stones, the names of streets—anything that might throw light upon the past had been systematically altered.

"I never knew it had been a church," he said.

"There's a lot of them left, really," said the old man, "though they've been put to other uses. Now, how did that rhyme go? Ah! I've got it!

Oranges and lemons, say the bells of St. Clement's,
You owe me three farthings, say the bells of St. Martin's—

there, now, that's as far as I can get. A farthing, that was a small copper coin, looked something like a cent."

"Where was St. Martin's?" said Winston.

"St. Martin's? That's still standing. It's in Victory Square, alongside the picture gallery. A building with a kind of a triangular porch and pillars in front, and a big flight of steps."

Winston knew the place well. It was a museum used for propaganda displays of various kinds—scale models of rocket bombs and Floating Fortresses, waxwork tableaux illustrating enemy atrocities, and the like.

"St. Martin's in the Fields it used to be called," supplemented the old man, "though I don't recollect any fields anywhere in those parts."

Winston did not buy the picture. It would have been an even more incongruous possession than the glass paperweight, and impossible to carry home, unless it were taken out of its frame. But he lingered for some minutes more, talking to the old man, whose name, he discovered, was not Weeks—as one might have gathered from the inscription over the shopfront—but Charrington. Mr. Charrington, it seemed, was a widower aged sixty-three and had inhabited this shop for thirty years. Throughout that time he had been intending to alter the name over the window, but had never quite got to the point of doing it. All the while that they were talking the half-remembered rhyme kept running through Winston's head: *Oranges and lemons, say the bells of St. Clement's, You owe me three farthings, say the bells of St. Martin's!* It was curious, but when you said it to yourself you had the illusion of actually hearing bells, the bells of a lost London that still existed somewhere or other, disguised and forgotten. From one ghostly steeple after another he seemed to hear them pealing forth. Yet so far as he could remember he had never in real life heard church bells ringing.

He got away from Mr. Charrington and went down the stairs alone, so as not to let the old man see him reconnoitering the street before stepping out of the door. He had already made up his mind that after a suitable interval—a month, say—he would take the risk of visiting the shop again. It was perhaps not more dangerous than shirking an evening at the Center. The serious piece of folly had been to come back here in the first place, after buying the diary and without knowing whether the proprietor of the shop could be trusted. However—!

Yes, he thought again, he would come back. He would buy further scraps of beautiful rubbish. He would buy the engraving of St. Clement's Dane, take it out of its frame, and carry it home concealed under the jacket of his overalls. He would drag the rest of that poem out of Mr.

Charrington's memory. Even the lunatic project of renting the room upstairs flashed momentarily through his mind again. For perhaps five seconds exaltation made him careless, and he stepped out onto the pavement without so much as a preliminary glance through the window. He
had even started humming to an improvised tune—

Oranges and lemons, say the bells of St. Clement's,
You owe me three farthings, say the–

Suddenly his heart seemed to turn to ice and his bowels to water. A figure
in blue overalls was coming down the pavement, not ten meters away. It
was the girl from the Fiction Department, the girl with dark hair. The
light was failing, but there was no difficulty in recognizing her. She
looked him straight in the face, then walked quickly on as though she had
not seen him.

For a few seconds Winston was too paralyzed to move. Then he turned
to the right and walked heavily away, not noticing for the moment that
he was going in the wrong direction. At any rate, one question was settled. There was no doubting any longer that the girl was spying on him.
She must have followed him here, because it was not credible that by
pure chance she should have happened to be walking on the same evening up the same obscure back street, kilometers distant from any quarter where Party members lived. It was too great a coincidence. Whether
she was really an agent of the Thought Police, or simply an amateur spy
actuated by officiousness, hardly mattered. It was enough that she was
watching him. Probably she had seen him go into the pub as well.

It was an effort to walk. The lump of glass in his pocket banged against
his thigh at each step, and he was half minded to take it out and throw it
away. The worst thing was the pain in his belly. For a couple of minutes
he had the feeling that he would die if he did not reach a lavatory soon.
But there would be no public lavatories in a quarter like this. Then the
spasm passed, leaving a dull ache behind.

The street was a blind alley. Winston halted, stood for several seconds
wondering vaguely what to do, then turned round and began to retrace
his steps. As he turned it occurred to him that the girl had only passed
him three minutes ago and that by running he could probably catch up
with her. He could keep on her track till they were in some quiet place,
and then smash her skull in with a cobblestone. The piece of glass in his
pocket would be heavy enough for the job. But he abandoned the idea
immediately, because even the thought of making any physical effort was
unbearable. He could not run, he could not strike a blow. Besides, she was
young and lusty and would defend herself. He thought also of hurrying to
the Community Center and staying there till the place closed, so as to
establish a partial alibi for the evening. But that too was impossible. A

deadly lassitude had taken hold of him. All he wanted was to get home quickly and then sit down and be quiet.

It was after twenty-two hours when he got back to the flat. The lights would be switched off at the main at twenty-three thirty. He went into the kitchen and swallowed nearly a teacupful of Victory Gin. Then he went to the table in the alcove, sat down, and took the diary out of the drawer. But he did not open it at once. From the telescreen a brassy female voice was squalling a patriotic song. He sat staring at the marbled cover of the book, trying without success to shut the voice out of his consciousness.

It was at night that they came for you, always at night. The proper thing was to kill yourself before they got you. Undoubtedly some people did so. Many of the disappearances were actually suicides. But it needed desperate courage to kill yourself in a world where firearms, or any quick and certain poison, were completely unprocurable. He thought with a kind of astonishment of the biological uselessness of pain and fear, the treachery of the human body which always freezes into inertia at exactly the moment when a special effort is needed. He might have silenced the dark-haired girl if only he had acted quickly enough; but precisely because of the extremity of his danger he had lost the power to act. It struck him that in moments of crisis one is never fighting against an external enemy but always against one's own body. Even now, in spite of the gin, the dull ache in his belly made consecutive thought impossible. And it is the same, he perceived, in all seemingly heroic or tragic situations. On the battlefield, in the torture chamber, on a sinking ship, the issues that you are fighting for are always forgotten, because the body swells up until it fills the universe, and even when you are not paralyzed by fright or screaming with pain, life is a moment-to-moment struggle against hunger or cold or sleeplessness, against a sour stomach or an aching tooth.

He opened the diary. It was important to write something down. The woman on the telescreen had started a new song. Her voice seemed to stick into his brain like jagged splinters of glass. He tried to think of O'Brien, for whom, or to whom, the diary was written, but instead he began thinking of the things that would happen to him after the Thought Police took him away. It would not matter if they killed you at once. To be killed was what you expected. But before death (nobody spoke of such things, yet everybody knew of them) there was the routine of confession that had to be gone through: the groveling on the floor and screaming for mercy, the crack of broken bones, the smashed teeth and bloody clots of hair. Why did you have to endure it, since the end was always the same? Why was it not possible to cut a few days or weeks out of your life? Nobody ever escaped detection, and nobody ever failed to confess. When once you had succumbed to thoughtcrime it was certain that by a given

date you would be dead. Why then did that horror, which altered nothing, have to lie embedded in future time?

He tried with a little more success than before to summon up the image
of O'Brien. "We shall meet in the place where there is no darkness,"
O'Brien had said to him. He knew what it meant, or thought he knew.
The place where there is no darkness was the imagined future, which one
would never see; but which, by foreknowledge, one could mystically share
in. But with the voice from the telescreen nagging at his ears he could not
follow the train of thought further. He put a cigarette in his mouth. Half
the tobacco promptly fell out on to his tongue, a bitter dust which was
difficult to spit out again. The face of Big Brother swam into his mind,
displacing that of O'Brien. Just as he had done a few days earlier, he slid
a coin out of his pocket and looked at it. The face gazed up at him, heavy,
calm, protecting, but what kind of smile was hidden beneath the dark
mustache? Like a leaden knell the words came back at him:

WAR IS PEACE
FREEDOM IS SLAVERY
IGNORANCE IS STRENGTH.

TWO

It was the middle of the morning, and Winston had left his cubicle to go to
the lavatory.

A solitary figure was coming toward him from the other end of the
long, brightly lit corridor. It was the girl with dark hair. Four days had
gone past since the evening when he had run into her outside the junk
shop. As she came nearer he saw that her right arm was in a sling, not
noticeable at a distance because it was of the same color as her overalls.
Probably she had crushed her hand while swinging round one of the big
kaleidoscopes on which the plots of novels were "roughed in." It was a
common accident in the Fiction Department.

They were perhaps four meters apart when the girl stumbled and fell
almost flat on her face. A sharp cry of pain was wrung out of her. She
must have fallen right on the injured arm. Winston stopped short. The
girl had risen to her knees. Her face had turned a milky yellow color
against which her mouth stood out redder than ever. Her eyes were fixed
on his, with an appealing expression that looked more like fear than
pain.

A curious emotion stirred in Winston's heart. In front of him was an
enemy who was trying to kill him; in front of him, also, was a human
creature, in pain and perhaps with a broken bone. Already he had instinctively started forward to help her. In the moment when he had seen
her fall on the bandaged arm, it had been as though he felt the pain in his
own body.

"You're hurt?" he said.

"It's nothing. My arm. It'll be all right in a second."

She spoke as though her heart were fluttering. She had certainly turned very pale.

"You haven't broken anything?"

"No, I'm all right. It hurt for a moment, that's all."

She held out her free hand to him, and he helped her up. She had regained some of her color, and appeared very much better.

"It's nothing," she repeated shortly. "I only gave my wrist a bit of a bang. Thanks, comrade!"

And with that she walked on in the direction in which she had been going, as briskly as though it had really been nothing. The whole incident could not have taken as much as half a minute. Not to let one's feelings appear in one's face was a habit that had acquired the status of an instinct, and in any case they had been standing straight in front of a telescreen when the thing happened. Nevertheless it had been very difficult not to betray a momentary surprise, for in the two or three seconds while he was helping her up the girl had slipped something into his hand. There was no question that she had done it intentionally. It was something small and flat. As he passed through the lavatory door he transferred it to his pocket and felt it with the tips of his fingers. It was a scrap of paper folded into a square.

While he stood at the urinal he managed, with a little more fingering, to get it unfolded. Obviously there must be a message of some kind written on it. For a moment he was tempted to take it into one of the water closets and read it at once. But that would be shocking folly, as he well knew. There was no place where you could be more certain that the telescreens were watched continuously.

He went back to his cubicle, sat down, threw the fragment of paper casually among the other papers on the desk, put on his spectacles and hitched the speakwrite toward him. "Five minutes," he told himself, "five minutes at the very least!" His heart bumped in his breast with frightening loudness. Fortunately the piece of work he was engaged on was mere routine, the rectification of a long list of figures, not needing close attention.

Whatever was written on the paper, it must have some kind of political meaning. So far as he could see there were two possibilities. One, much the more likely, was that the girl was an agent of the Thought Police, just as he had feared. He did not know why the Thought Police should choose to deliver their messages in such a fashion, but perhaps they had their reasons. The thing that was written on the paper might be a threat, a summons, an order to commit suicide, a trap of some description. But there was another, wilder possibility that kept raising its head, though he tried vainly to suppress it. This was, that the message did not come from the Thought Police at all, but from some kind of underground organization. Perhaps the Brotherhood existed after all! Perhaps the girl was part of it! No doubt the idea was absurd, but it had sprung into his mind in the very instant of feeling the scrap of paper in his hand. It was not till a couple of minutes later that the other, more probable explanation had occurred to him. And even now, though his intellect told him that the message probably meant death—still, that was not what he believed, and the unreasonable hope persisted, and his heart banged, and it was with difficulty that he kept his voice from trembling as he murmured his figures into the speakwrite.

He rolled up the completed bundle of work and slid it into the pneumatic tube. Eight minutes had gone by. He readjusted his spectacles on his nose, sighed, and drew the next batch of work toward him, with the scrap of paper on top of it. He flattened it out. On it was written, in a large unformed handwriting:

I love you.

For several seconds he was too stunned even to throw the incriminating thing into the memory hole. When he did so, although he knew very well the danger of showing too much interest, he could not resist reading it once again, just to make sure that the words were really there.

For the rest of the morning it was very difficult to work. What was even worse than having to focus his mind on a series of niggling jobs was the need to conceal his agitation from the telescreen. He felt as though a fire were burning in his belly. Lunch in the hot, crowded, noise-filled canteen was torment. He had hoped to be alone for a little while during the lunch hour, but as bad luck would have it the imbecile Parsons flopped down beside him, the tang of his sweat almost defeating the tinny smell of stew, and kept up a stream of talk about the preparations for Hate Week. He was particularly enthusiastic about a papier-mâché model of Big Brother's head, two meters wide, which was being made for the occasion by his daughter's troop of Spies. The irritating thing was that in the racket of voices Winston could hardly hear what Parsons was saying, and was constantly having to ask for some fatuous remark to be repeated. Just once he caught a glimpse of the girl, at a table with two other girls at the far end of the room. She appeared not to have seen him, and he did not look in that direction again.

The afternoon was more bearable. Immediately after lunch there arrived a delicate, difficult piece of work which would take several hours and necessitated putting everything else aside. It consisted in falsifying a series of production reports of two years ago in such a way as to cast discredit on a prominent member of the Inner Party who was now under a cloud. This was the kind of thing that Winston was good at, and for more than two hours he succeeded in shutting the girl out of his mind altogether. Then the memory of her face came back, and with it a raging, intolerable desire to be alone. Until he could be alone it was impossible to think this new development out. Tonight was one of his nights at the Community Center. He wolfed another tasteless meal in the canteen, hurried off to the Center, took part in the solemn foolery of a "discussion group," played two games of table tennis, swallowed several glasses of gin, and sat for half an hour through a lecture entitled "Ingsoc in relation to chess." His soul writhed with boredom, but for once he had had no impulse to shirk his evening at the Center. At the sight of the words *I love you* the desire to stay alive had welled up in him, and the taking of minor risks suddenly seemed stupid. It was not till twenty-three hours, when he was home and in bed—in the darkness, where you were safe even from the telescreen so long as you kept silent—that he was able to think continuously.

It was a physical problem that had to be solved: how to get in touch with the girl and arrange a meeting. He did not consider any longer the possibility that she might be laying some kind of trap for him. He knew that it was not so, because of her unmistakable agitation when she handed him the note. Obviously she had been frightened out of her wits, as well she might be. Nor did the idea of refusing her advances even cross his mind. Only five nights ago he had contemplated smashing her skull in with a cobblestone; but that was of no importance. He thought of her naked, youthful body, as he had seen it in his dream. He had imagined her a fool like all the rest of them, her head stuffed with lies and hatred, her belly full of ice. A kind of fever seized him at the thought that he might lose her, the white youthful body might slip away from him! What he feared more than anything else was that she would simply change her mind if he did not get in touch with her quickly. But the physical difficulty of meeting was enormous. It was like trying to make a move at chess when you were already mated. Whichever way you turned, the telescreen faced you. Actually, all the possible ways of communicating with her had occurred to him within five minutes of reading the note; but now, with time to think, he went over them one by one, as though laying out a row of instruments on a table.

Obviously the kind of encounter that had happened this morning could not be repeated. If she had worked in the Records Department it might have been comparatively simple, but he had only a very dim idea whereabouts in the building the Fiction Department lay, and he had no pretext for going there. If he had known where she lived, and at what time she left work, he could have contrived to meet her somewhere on her way home; but to try to follow her home was not safe, because it would mean loitering about outside the Ministry, which was bound to be noticed. As for sending a letter through the mails, it was out of the question. By a routine that was not even secret, all letters were opened in transit. Actu-

ally, few people ever wrote letters. For the messages that it was occasionally necessary to send, there were printed postcards with long lists of
phrases, and you struck out the ones that were inapplicable. In any case
he did not know the girl's name, let alone her address. Finally he decided
that the safest place was the canteen. If he could get her at a table by
herself, somewhere in the middle of the room, not too near the telescreens, and with a sufficient buzz of conversation all round—if these
conditions endured for, say, thirty seconds, it might be possible to exchange a few words.

For a week after this, life was like a restless dream. On the next day she
did not appear in the canteen until he was leaving it, the whistle having
already blown. Presumably she had been changed onto a later shift. They
passed each other without a glance. On the day after that she was in the
canteen at the usual time, but with three other girls and immediately
under a telescreen. Then for three dreadful days she did not appear at all.
His whole mind and body seemed to be afflicted with an unbearable sensitivity, a sort of transparency, which made every movement, every sound,
every contact, every word that he had to speak or listen to, an agony.
Even in sleep he could not altogether escape from her image. He did not
touch the diary during those days. If there was any relief, it was in his
work, in which he could sometimes forget himself for ten minutes at a
stretch. He had absolutely no clue as to what happened to her. There was
no inquiry he could make. She might have been vaporized, she might
have committed suicide, she might have been transferred to the other
end of Oceania—worst and likeliest of all, she might simply have
changed her mind and decided to avoid him.

The next day she reappeared. Her arm was out of the sling and she had
a band of sticking plaster round her wrist. The relief of seeing her was so
great that he could not resist staring directly at her for several seconds.
On the following day he very nearly succeeded in speaking to her. When
he came into the canteen she was sitting at a table well out from the wall,
and was quite alone. It was early, and the place was not very full. The
queue edged forward till Winston was almost at the counter, then was
held up for two minutes because someone in front was complaining that
he had not received his tablet of saccharine. But the girl was still alone
when Winston secured his tray and began to make for her table. He
walked casually toward her, his eyes searching for a place at some table
beyond her. She was perhaps three meters away from him. Another two
seconds would do it. Then a voice behind him called, "Smith!" He pretended not to hear. "Smith!" repeated the voice, more loudly. It was no
use. He turned round. A blond-headed, silly-faced young man named Wil-
sher, whom he barely knew, was inviting him with a smile to a vacant
place at his table. It was not safe to refuse. After having been recognized,
he could not go and sit at a table with an unattended girl. It was too

noticeable. He sat down with a friendly smile. The silly blond face beamed into his. Winston had a hallucination of himself smashing a pickax right into the middle of it. The girl's table filled up a few minutes later.

But she must have seen him coming toward her, and perhaps she would take the hint. Next day he took care to arrive early. Sure enough, she was at a table in about the same place, and again alone. The person immediately ahead of him in the queue was a small, swiftly moving, beetlelike man with a flat face and tiny, suspicious eyes. As Winston turned away from the counter with his tray, he saw that the little man was making straight for the girl's table. His hopes sank again. There was a vacant place at a table further away, but something in the little man's appearance suggested that he would be sufficiently attentive to his own comfort to choose the emptiest table. With ice at his heart Winston followed. It was no use unless he could get the girl alone. At this moment there was a tremendous crash. The little man was sprawling on all fours, his tray had gone flying, two streams of soup and coffee were flowing across the floor. He started to his feet with a malignant glance at Winston, whom he evidently suspected of having tripped him up. But it was all right. Five seconds later, with a thundering heart, Winston was sitting at the girl's table.

He did not look at her. He unpacked his tray and promptly began eating. It was all-important to speak at once, before anyone else came, but now a terrible fear had taken possession of him. A week had gone by since she had first approached. She would have changed her mind, she must have changed her mind! It was impossible that this affair should end successfully; such things did not happen in real life. He might have flinched altogether from speaking if at this moment he had not seen Ampleforth, the hairy-eared poet, wandering limply round the room with a tray, looking for a place to sit down. In his vague way Ampleforth was attached to Winston, and would certainly sit down at his table if he caught sight of him. There was perhaps a minute in which to act. Both Winston and the girl were eating steadily. The stuff they were eating was a thin stew, actually a soup, of haricot beans. In a low murmur Winston began speaking. Neither of them looked up; steadily they spooned the watery stuff into their mouths, and between spoonfuls exchanged the few necessary words in low expressionless voices.

"What time do you leave work?"

"Eighteen thirty."

"Where can we meet?"

"Victory Square, near the monument."

"It's full of telescreens."

"It doesn't matter if there's a crowd."

"Any signal?"

"No. Don't come up to me until you see me among a lot of people. And
don't look at me. Just keep somewhere near me."

"What time?"

"Nineteen hours."

"All right."

Ampleforth failed to see Winston and sat down at another table. The
girl finished her lunch quickly and made off, while Winston stayed to
smoke a cigarette. They did not speak again, and, so far as it was possible
for two people sitting on opposite sides of the same table, they did not look
at one another.

Winston was in Victory Square before the appointed time. He wandered round the base of the enormous fluted column, at the top of which
Big Brother's statue gazed southward toward the skies where he had
vanquished the Eurasian airplanes (the Eastasian airplanes, it had been,
a few years ago) in the Battle of Airstrip One. In the street in front of it
there was a statue of a man on horseback which was supposed to represent Oliver Cromwell. At five minutes past the hour the girl had still not
appeared. Again the terrible fear seized upon Winston. She was not coming, she had changed her mind! He walked slowly up to the north side of
the square and got a sort of pale-colored pleasure from identifying St.
Martin's church, whose bells, when it had bells, had chimed "You owe me
three farthings." Then he saw the girl standing at the base of the monument, reading or pretending to read a poster which ran spirally up the
column. It was not safe to go near her until some more people had accu-
mulated. There were telescreens all round the pediment. But at this
moment there was a din of shouting and a zoom of heavy vehicles from
somewhere to the left. Suddenly everyone seemed to be running across
the square. The girl nipped nimbly round the lions at the base of the
monument and joined in the rush. Winston followed. As he ran, he gathered from some shouted remarks that a convoy of Eurasian prisoners was
passing.

Already a dense mass of people was blocking the south side of the
square. Winston, at normal times the kind of person who gravitates to
the outer edge of any kind of scrimmage, shoved, butted, squirmed his
way forward into the heart of the crowd. Soon he was within arm's length
of the girl, but the way was blocked by an enormous prole and an almost
equally enormous woman, presumably his wife, who seemed to form an
impenetrable wall of flesh. Winston wriggled himself sideways, and with
a violent lunge managed to drive his shoulder between them. For a moment it felt as though his entrails were being ground to pulp between the
two muscular hips, then he had broken through, sweating a little. He was
next to the girl. They were shoulder to shoulder, both staring fixedly in
front of them.

A long line of trucks, with wooden-faced guards armed with submachine guns standing upright in each corner, was passing slowly down the street. In the trucks little yellow men in shabby greenish uniforms were squatting, jammed close together. Their sad Mongolian faces gazed out over the sides of the trucks, utterly incurious. Occasionally when a truck jolted there was a clank-clank of metal: all the prisoners were wearing leg irons. Truckload after truckload of the sad faces passed. Winston knew they were there, but he saw them only intermittently. The girl's shoulder, and her arm right down to the elbow, were pressed against his. Her cheek was almost near enough for him to feel its warmth. She had immediately taken charge of the situation, just as she had done in the canteen. She began speaking in the same expressionless voice as before, with lips barely moving, a mere murmur easily drowned by the din of voices and the rumbling of the trucks.

"Can you hear me?"

"Yes."

"Can you get Sunday afternoon off?"

"Yes."

"Then listen carefully. You'll have to remember this. Go to Paddington Station—"

With a sort of military precision that astonished him, she outlined the route that he was to follow. A half-hour railway journey; turn left outside the station; two kilometers along the road; a gate with the top bar missing; a path across a field; a grass-grown lane; a track between bushes; a dead tree with moss on it. It was as though she had a map inside her head. "Can you remember all that?" she murmured finally.

"Yes."

"You turn left, then right, then left again. And the gate's got no top bar."

"Yes. What time?"

"About fifteen. You may have to wait. I'll get there by another way. Are you sure you remember everything?"

"Yes."

"Then get away from me as quick as you can."

She need not have told him that. But for the moment they could not extricate themselves from the crowd. The trucks were still filing past, the people still insatiably gaping. At the start there had been a few boos and hisses, but it came only from the Party members among the crowd, and had soon stopped. The prevailing emotion was simply curiosity. Foreigners, whether from Eurasia or from Eastasia, were a kind of strange animal. One literally never saw them except in the guise of prisoners, and even as prisoners one never got more than a momentary glimpse of them. Nor did one know what became of them, apart from the few who were hanged as war criminals; the others simply vanished, presumably into forced-labor camps. The round Mongol faces had given way to faces of a more European type, dirty, bearded, and exhausted. From over scrubby cheekbones eyes looked into Winston's, sometimes with strange intensity, and flashed away again. The convoy was drawing to an end. In the last truck he could see an aged man, his face a mass of grizzled hair, standing upright with wrists crossed in front of him, as though he were used to having them bound together. It was almost time for Winston and the girl to part. But at the last moment, while the crowd still hemmed them in, her hand felt for his and gave it a fleeting squeeze.

It could not have been ten seconds, and yet it seemed a long time that their hands were clasped together. He had time to learn every detail of her hand. He explored the long fingers, the shapely nails, the work-hardened palm with its row of calluses, the smooth flesh under the wrist. Merely from feeling it he would have known it by sight. In the same instant it occurred to him that he did not know what color the girl's eyes were. They were probably brown, but people with dark hair sometimes had blue eyes. To turn his head and look at her would have been inconceivable folly. With hands locked together, invisible among the press of bodies, they stared steadily in front of them, and instead of the eyes of the girl, the eyes of the aged prisoner gazed mournfully at Winston out of nests of hair.

II

Winston picked his way up the lane through dappled light and shade, stepping out into pools of gold wherever the boughs parted. Under the trees to the left of them the ground was misty with bluebells. The air seemed to kiss one's skin. It was the second of May. From somewhere deeper in the heart of the wood came the droning of ring doves.

He was a bit early. There had been no difficulties about the journey, and the girl was so evidently experienced that he was less frightened than he would normally have been. Presumably she could be trusted to find a safe place. In general you could not assume that you were much safer in the country than in London. There were no telescreens, of course, but there was always the danger of concealed microphones by which your voice might be picked up and recognized; besides, it was not easy to make a journey by yourself without attracting attention. For distances of less than a hundred kilometers it was not necessary to get your passport endorsed, but sometimes there were patrols hanging about the railway stations, who examined the papers of any Party member they found there and asked awkward questions. However, no patrols had appeared, and on the walk from the station he had made sure by cautious backward glances that he was not being followed. The train was full of proles, in holiday mood because of the summery weather. The wooden-seated carriage in which he traveled was filled to overflowing by a single enormous family, ranging from a toothless great-grandmother to a month-old baby, going out to spend an afternoon with "in-laws" in the country, and, as they freely explained to Winston, to get hold of a little black-market butter.

The lane widened, and in a minute he came to the footpath she had told him of, a mere cattle track which plunged between the bushes. He had no watch, but it could not be fifteen yet. The bluebells were so thick underfoot that it was impossible not to tread on them. He knelt down and began picking some, partly to pass the time away, but also from a vague idea that he would like to have a bunch of flowers to offer to the girl when they met. He had got together a big bunch and was smelling their faint sickly scent when a sound at his back froze him, the unmistakable crackle of a foot on twigs. He went on picking bluebells. It was the best thing to do. It might be the girl, or he might have been followed after all. To look round was to show guilt. He picked another and another. A hand fell lightly on his shoulder.

He looked up. It was the girl. She shook her head, evidently as a warning that he must keep silent, then parted the bushes and quickly led the way along the narrow track into the wood. Obviously she had been that way before, for she dodged the boggy bits as though by habit. Winston followed, still clasping his bunch of flowers. His first feeling was relief, but as he watched the strong slender body moving in front of him, with the scarlet sash that was just tight enough to bring out the curve of her hips, the sense of his own inferiority was heavy upon him. Even now it seemed quite likely that when she turned round and looked at him she would draw back after all. The sweetness of the air and the greenness of the leaves daunted him. Already, on the walk from the station, the May sunshine had made him feel dirty and etiolated, a creature of indoors, with the sooty dust of London in the pores of his skin. It occurred to him that till now she had probably never seen him in broad daylight in the open. They came to the fallen tree that she had spoken of. The girl hopped over and forced apart the bushes, in which there did not seem to be an opening. When Winston followed her, he found that they were in a natural clearing, a tiny grassy knoll surrounded by tall saplings that shut it in completely. The girl stopped and turned.

"Here we are," she said.

He was facing her at several paces' distance. As yet he did not dare move nearer to her.

"I didn't want to say anything in the lane," she went on, "in case there's a mike hidden there. I don't suppose there is, but there could be. There's always the chance of one of those swine recognizing your voice. We're all right here."

He still had not the courage to approach her. "We're all right here?" he repeated stupidly.

"Yes. Look at the trees." They were small ashes, which at some time had been cut down and had sprouted up again into a forest of poles, none of them thicker than one's wrist. "There's nothing big enough to hide a mike in. Besides, I've been here before."

They were only making conversation. He had managed to move closer to her now. She stood before him very upright, with a smile on her face that looked faintly ironical, as though she were wondering why he was so slow to act. The bluebells had cascaded on to the ground. They seemed to have fallen of their own accord. He took her hand.

"Would you believe," he said, "that till this moment I didn't know what color your eyes were?" They were brown, he noted, a rather light shade of brown, with dark lashes. "Now that you've seen what I'm really like, can you still bear to look at me?"

"Yes, easily."

"I'm thirty-nine years old. I've got a wife that I can't get rid of. I've got varicose veins. I've got five false teeth."

"I couldn't care less," said the girl.

The next moment, it was hard to say by whose act, she was in his arms. At the beginning he had no feeling except sheer incredulity. The youthful body was strained against his own, the mass of dark hair was against his face, and yes! actually she had turned her face up and he was kissing the wide red mouth. She had clasped her arms about his neck, she was calling him darling, precious one, loved one. He had pulled her down on to the ground, she was utterly unresisting, he could do what he liked with her. But the truth was that he had no physical sensation except that of mere contact. All he felt was incredulity and pride. He was glad that this was happening, but he had no physical desire. It was too soon, her youth and prettiness had frightened him, he was too much used to living without women—he did not know the reason. The girl picked herself up and pulled a bluebell out of her hair. She sat against him, putting her arm round his waist.

"Never mind, dear. There's no hurry. We've got the whole afternoon. Isn't this a splendid hide-out? I found it when I got lost once on a community hike. If anyone was coming you could hear them a hundred meters away."

"What is your name?" said Winston.

"Julia. I know yours. It's Winston—Winston Smith."

"How did you find that out?"

"I expect I'm better at finding things out than you are, dear. Tell me, what did you think of me before that day I gave you the note?"

He did not feel any temptation to tell lies to her. It was even a sort of love offering to start off by telling the worst.

"I hated the sight of you," he said. "I wanted to rape you and then murder you afterwards. Two weeks ago I thought seriously of smashing your head in with a cobblestone. If you really want to know, I imagined that you had something to do with the Thought Police."

The girl laughed delightedly, evidently taking this as a tribute to the excellence of her disguise.

"Not the Thought Police! You didn't honestly think that?"

"Well, perhaps not exactly that. But from your general appearance— merely because you're young and fresh and healthy, you understand—I thought that probably—"

"You thought I was a good Party member. Pure in word and deed. Banners, processions, slogans, games, community hikes—all that stuff. And you thought that if I had a quarter of a chance I'd denounce you as a thought-criminal and get you killed off?"

"Yes, something of that kind. A great many young girls are like that, you know."

"It's this bloody thing that does it," she said, ripping off the scarlet sash of the Junior Anti-Sex League and flinging it onto a bough. Then, as though touching her waist had reminded her of something, she felt in the pocket of her overalls and produced a small slab of chocolate. She broke it in half and gave one of the pieces to Winston. Even before he had taken it he knew by the smell that it was very unusual chocolate. It was dark and shiny, and was wrapped in silver paper. Chocolate normally was dull-brown crumbly stuff that tasted, as nearly as one could describe it, like the smoke of a rubbish fire. But at some time or another he had tasted chocolate like the piece she had given him. The first whiff of its scent had stirred up some memory which he could not pin down, but which was powerful and troubling.

"Where did you get this stuff?" he said.

"Black market," she said indifferently. "Actually I am that sort of girl, to look at. I'm good at games. I was a troop leader in the Spies. I do voluntary work three evenings a week for the Junior Anti-Sex League. Hours and hours I've spent pasting their bloody rot all over London. I always carry one end of a banner in the processions. I always look cheerful and I never shirk anything. Always yell with the crowd, that's what I say. It's the only way to be safe."

The first fragment of chocolate had melted on Winston's tongue. The taste was delightful. But there was still that memory moving round the edges of his consciousness, something strongly felt but not reducible to definite shape, like an object seen out of the corner of one's eye. He pushed it away from him, aware only that it was the memory of some action which he would have liked to undo but could not.

"You are very young," he said. "You are ten or fifteen years younger than I am. What could you see to attract you in a man like me?"

"It was something in your face. I thought I'd take a chance. I'm good at spotting people who don't belong. As soon as I saw you I knew you were against *them*."

Them, it appeared, meant the Party, and above all the Inner Party, about whom she talked with an open jeering hatred which made Winston feel uneasy, although he knew that they were safe here if they could be safe anywhere. A thing that astonished him about her was the coarseness of her language. Party members were supposed not to swear, and Winston himself very seldom did swear, aloud, at any rate. Julia, however, seemed unable to mention the Party, and especially the Inner Party, without using the kind of words that you saw chalked up in dripping alleyways. He did not dislike it. It was merely one symptom of her revolt against the Party and all its ways, and somehow it seemed natural and healthy, like the sneeze of a horse that smells bad hay. They had left the clearing and were wandering again through the checkered shade, with their arms round each other's waists whenever it was wide enough to walk two abreast. He noticed how much softer her waist seemed to feel now that the sash was gone. They did not speak above a whisper. Outside the clearing, Julia said, it was better to go quietly. Presently they had reached the edge of the little wood. She stopped him.

"Don't go out into the open. There might be someone watching. We're all right if we keep behind the boughs."

They were standing in the shade of hazel bushes. The sunlight, filtering through innumerable leaves, was still hot on their faces. Winston looked out into the field beyond, and underwent a curious, slow shock of recognition. He knew it by sight. An old, close-bitten pasture, with a footpath wandering across it and a molehill here and there. In the ragged hedge on the opposite side the boughs of the elm trees swayed just perceptibly in the breeze, and their leaves stirred faintly in dense masses like women's hair. Surely somewhere near by, but out of sight, there must be a stream with green pools where dace were swimming.

"Isn't there a stream somewhere near here?" he whispered.

"That's right, there is a stream. It's at the edge of the next field, actually. There are fish in it, great big ones. You can watch them lying in the pools under the willow trees, waving their tails."

"It's the Golden Country—almost," he murmured.

"The Golden Country?"

"It's nothing, really. A landscape I've seen sometimes in a dream."

"Look!" whispered Julia.

A thrush had alighted on a bough not five meters away, almost at the level of their faces. Perhaps it had not seen them. It was in the sun, they in the shade. It spread out its wings, fitted them carefully into place again, ducked its head for a moment, as though making a sort of obeisance to the sun, and then began to pour forth a torrent of song. In the afternoon hush the volume of sound was startling. Winston and Julia clung together, fascinated. The music went on and on, minute after minute, with astonishing variations, never once repeating itself, almost as though the bird were deliberately showing off its virtuosity. Sometimes it stopped for a few seconds, spread out and resettled its wings, then swelled its speckled breast and again burst into song. Winston watched it with a sort of vague reverence. For whom, for what, was that bird singing? No mate, no rival was watching it. What made it sit at the edge of the lonely wood and pour its music into nothingness? He wondered whether after all there was a microphone hidden somewhere near. He and Julia had only spoken in low whispers, and it would not pick up what they had said, but it would pick up the thrush. Perhaps at the other end of the instrument some small, beetlelike man was listening intently—listening to *that*. But by degrees the flood of music drove all speculations out of his mind. It was as though it were a liquid stuff that poured all over him and got mixed up with the sunlight that filtered through the leaves. He stopped thinking and merely felt. The girl's waist in the bend of his arm was soft and warm. He pulled her round so that they were breast to breast; her body seemed to melt into his. Wherever his hands moved it was all as yielding as water. Their mouths clung together; it was quite different from the hard kisses they had exchanged earlier. When they moved their faces apart again both of them sighed deeply. The bird took fright and fled with a clatter of wings.

Winston put his lips against her ear. *"Now,"* he whispered.

"Not here," she whispered back. "Come back to the hide-out. It's safer."

Quickly, with an occasional crackle of twigs, they threaded their way back to the clearing. When they were once inside the ring of saplings she turned and faced him. They were both breathing fast, but the smile had reappeared round the corners of her mouth. She stood looking at him for an instant, then felt at the zipper of her overalls. And, yes! It was almost as in his dream. Almost as swiftly as he had imagined it, she had torn her clothes off, and when she flung them aside it was with that same magnificent gesture by which a whole civilization seemed to be annihilated. Her body gleamed white in the sun. But for a moment he did not look at her body; his eyes were anchored by the freckled face with its faint, bold smile. He knelt down before her and took her hands in his.

"Have you done this before?"

"Of course. Hundreds of times—well, scores of times, anyway."

"With Party members?"

"Yes, always with Party members."

"With members of the Inner Party?"

"Not with those swine, no. But there's plenty that *would* if they got half a chance. They're not so holy as they make out."

His heart leapt. Scores of times she had done it; he wished it had been hundreds—thousands. Anything that hinted at corruption always filled him with a wild hope. Who knew? Perhaps the Party was rotten under the surface, its cult of strenuousness and self-denial simply a sham concealing iniquity. If he could have infected the whole lot of them with leprosy or syphilis, how gladly he would have done so! Anything to rot, to weaken, to undermine! He pulled her down so that they were kneeling face to face.

"Listen. The more men you've had, the more I love you. Do you understand that?"

"Yes, perfectly."

"I hate purity, I hate goodness. I don't want any virtue to exist anywhere. I want everyone to be corrupt to the bones."

"Well then, I ought to suit you, dear. I'm corrupt to the bones."

"You like doing this? I don't mean simply me; I mean the thing in itself?"

"I adore it."

That was above all what he wanted to hear. Not merely the love of one person, but the animal instinct, the simple undifferentiated desire: that was the force that would tear the Party to pieces. He pressed her down upon the grass, among the fallen bluebells. This time there was no difficulty. Presently the rising and falling of their breasts slowed to normal speed, and in a sort of pleasant helplessness they fell apart. The sun seemed to have grown hotter. They were both sleepy. He reached out for the discarded overalls and pulled them partly over her. Almost immediately they fell asleep and slept for about half an hour.

Winston woke first. He sat up and watched the freckled face, still peacefully asleep, pillowed on the palm of her hand. Except for her mouth, you could not call her beautiful. There was a line or two round the eyes, if you looked closely. The short dark hair was extraordinarily thick and soft. It occurred to him that he still did not know her surname or where she lived.

The young, strong body, now helpless in sleep, awoke in him a pitying, protecting feeling. But the mindless tenderness that he had felt under the hazel tree, while the thrush was singing, had not quite come back. He pulled the overalls aside and studied her smooth white flank. In the old days, he thought, a man looked at a girl's body and saw that it was desirable, and that was the end of the story. But you could not have pure love or pure lust nowadays. No emotion was pure, because everything was mixed up with fear and hatred. Their embrace had been a battle, the climax a victory. It was a blow struck against the Party. It was a political act.

III

"We can come here once again," said Julia. "It's generally safe to use any hide-out twice. But not for another month or two, of course."

As soon as she woke up her demeanor had changed. She became alert and businesslike, put her clothes on, knotted the scarlet sash about her waist, and began arranging the details of the journey home. It seemed natural to leave this to her. She obviously had a practical cunning which Winston lacked, and she seemed also to have an exhaustive knowledge of the countryside round London, stored away from innumerable community hikes. The route she gave him was quite different from the one by which he had come, and brought him out at a different railway station. "Never go home the same way as you went out," she said, as though enunciating an important general principle. She would leave first, and Winston was to wait half an hour before following her.

She had named a place where they could meet after work, four evenings hence. It was a street in one of the poorer quarters, where there was an open market which was generally crowded and noisy. She would be hanging about among the stalls, pretending to be in search of shoelaces or sewing thread. If she judged that the coast was clear she would blow her nose when he approached; otherwise he was to walk past her without recognition. But with luck, in the middle of the crowd, it would be safe to talk for a quarter of an hour and arrange another meeting.

"And now I must go," she said as soon as he had mastered his instructions. "I'm due back at nineteen-thirty. I've got to put in two hours for the Junior Anti-Sex League, handing out leaflets, or something. Isn't it bloody? Give me a brush-down, would you. Have I got any twigs in my hair? Are you sure? Then good-by, my love, good-by!"

She flung herself into his arms, kissed him almost violently, and a moment later pushed her way through the saplings and disappeared into the wood with very little noise. Even now he had not found out her surname or her address. However, it made no difference, for it was inconceivable that they could ever meet indoors or exchange any kind of written communication.

As it happened they never went back to the clearing in the wood. During the month of May there was only one further occasion on which they actually succeeded in making love. That was in another hiding place known to Julia, the belfry of a ruined church in an almost-deserted stretch of country where an atomic bomb had fallen thirty years earlier. It was a good hiding place when once you got there, but the getting there was very dangerous. For the rest they could meet only in the streets, in a different place every evening and never for more than half an hour at a time. In the street it was usually possible to talk, after a fashion. As they drifted down the crowded pavements, not quite abreast and never looking at one another, they carried on a curious, intermittent conversation which flicked on and off like the beams of a lighthouse, suddenly nipped into silence by the approach of a Party uniform or the proximity of a telescreen, then taken up again minutes later in the middle of a sentence, then abruptly cut short as they parted at the agreed spot, then continued almost without introduction on the following day. Julia appeared to be quite used to this kind of conversation, which she called "talking by installments." She was also surprisingly adept at speaking without moving her lips. Just once in almost a month of nightly meetings they managed to exchange a kiss. They were passing in silence down a side street (Julia would never speak when they were away from the main streets) when there was a deafening roar, the earth heaved and the air darkened, and Winston found himself lying on his side, bruised and terrified. A rocket bomb must have dropped quite near at hand. Suddenly he became aware of Julia's face a few centimeters from his own, deathly white, as white as chalk. Even her lips were white. She was dead! He clasped her against him, and found that he was kissing a live warm face. But there was some powdery stuff that got in the way of his lips. Both of their faces were thickly coated with plaster.

There were evenings when they reached their rendezvous and then had to walk past one another without a sign, because a patrol had just come round the corner or a helicopter was hovering overhead. Even if it had been less dangerous, it would still have been difficult to find time to meet. Winston's working week was sixty hours, Julia's was even longer, and their free days varied according to the pressure of work and did not often coincide. Julia, in any case, seldom had an evening completely free. She spent an astonishing amount of time in attending lectures and demonstrations, distributing literature for the Junior Anti-Sex League, preparing banners for Hate Week, making collections for the savings campaign, and suchlike activities. It paid, she said; it was camouflage. If you kept the small rules you could break the big ones. She even induced Winston to mortgage yet another of his evenings by enrolling himself for the part-time munition work which was done voluntarily by zealous Party members. So, one evening every week, Winston spent four hours of paralyzing boredom, screwing together small bits of metal which were probably parts of bomb fuses, in a draughty ill-lit workshop where the knocking of hammers mingled drearily with the music of the telescreens.

When they met in the church tower the gaps in their fragmentary conversation were filled up. It was a blazing afternoon. The air in the little square chamber above the bells was hot and stagnant, and smelt overpoweringly of pigeon dung. They sat talking for hours on the dusty, twig-littered floor, one or other of them getting up from time to time to cast a glance through the arrow slits and make sure that no one was coming.

Julia was twenty-six years old. She lived in a hostel with thirty other girls ("Always in the stink of women! How I hate women!" she said parenthetically), and she worked, as he had guessed, on the novel-writing machines in the Fiction Department. She enjoyed her work, which consisted chiefly in running and servicing a powerful but tricky electric motor. She was "not clever," but was fond of using her hands and felt at home with machinery. She could describe the whole process of composing a novel, from the general directive issued by the Planning Committee down to the final touching-up by the Rewrite Squad. But she was not interested in the finished product. She "didn't much care for reading," she said. Books were just a commodity that had to be produced, like jam or bootlaces.

She had no memories of anything before the early Sixties, and the only person she had ever known who talked frequently of the days before the Revolution was a grandfather who had disappeared when she was eight. At school she had been captain of the hockey team and had won the gymnastics trophy two years running. She had been a troop leader in the Spies and a branch secretary in the Youth League before joining the Junior Anti-Sex League. She had always borne an excellent character. She had even (an infallible mark of good reputation) been picked out to work in Pornosec, the sub-section of the Fiction Department which turned out cheap pornography for distribution among the proles. It was nicknamed Muck House by the people who worked in it, she remarked. There she had remained for a year, helping to produce booklets in sealed packets with titles like *Spanking Stories* or *One Night in a Girls' School,* to be bought furtively by proletarian youths who were under the impression that they were buying something illegal.

"What are these books like?" said Winston curiously.

"Oh, ghastly rubbish. They're boring, really. They only have six plots, but they swap them round a bit. Of course I was only on the kaleidoscopes. I was never in the Rewrite Squad. I'm not literary, dear—not even enough for that."

He learned with astonishment that all the workers in Pornosec, except the head of the department, were girls. The theory was that men, whose sex instincts were less controllable than those of women, were in greater danger of being corrupted by the filth they handled.

"They don't even like having married women there," she added. "Girls are always supposed to be so pure. Here's one who isn't, anyway."

She had had her first love affair when she was sixteen, with a Party member of sixty who later committed suicide to avoid arrest. "And a good job too," said Julia. "Otherwise they'd have had my name out of him when he confessed." Since then there had been various others. Life as she saw it was quite simple. You wanted a good time; "they," meaning the Party, wanted to stop you having it; you broke the rules as best you could. She seemed to think it just as natural that "they" should want to rob you of your pleasures as that you should want to avoid being caught. She hated the Party, and said so in the crudest words, but she made no general criticism of it. Except where it touched upon her own life she had no interest in Party doctrine. He noticed that she never used Newspeak words, except the ones that had passed into everyday use. She had never heard of the Brotherhood, and refused to believe in its existence. Any kind of organized revolt against the Party, which was bound to be a failure, struck her as stupid. The clever thing was to break the rules and stay alive all the same. He wondered vaguely how many others like her there might be in the younger generation—people who had grown up in the world of the Revolution, knowing nothing else, accepting the Party as something unalterable, like the sky, not rebelling against its authority but simply evading it, as a rabbit dodges a dog.

They did not discuss the possibility of getting married. It was too remote to be worth thinking about. No imaginable committee would ever sanction such a marriage even if Katharine, Winston's wife, could somehow have been got rid of. It was hopeless even as a daydream.

"What was she like, your wife?" said Julia.

"She was—do you know the Newspeak word *goodthinkful?* Meaning naturally orthodox, incapable of thinking a bad thought?"

"No, I didn't know the word, but I know the kind of person, right enough."

He began telling her the story of his married life, but curiously enough she appeared to know the essential parts of it already. She described to him, almost as though she had seen or felt it, the stiffening of Katharine's body as soon as he touched her, the way in which she still seemed to be pushing him from her with all her strength, even when her arms were clasped tightly round him. With Julia he felt no difficulty in talking about such things; Katharine, in any case, had long ceased to be a painful memory and become merely a distasteful one.

"I could have stood it if it hadn't been for one thing," he said. He told her about the frigid little ceremony that Katharine had forced him to go through on the same night every week. "She hated it, but nothing would make her stop doing it. She used to call it—but you'll never guess."

"Our duty to the Party," said Julia promptly.

"How did you know that?"

"I've been at school too, dear. Sex talks once a month for the over-sixteens. And in the Youth Movement. They rub it into you for years. I dare say it works in a lot of cases. But of course you can never tell; people are such hypocrites."

She began to enlarge upon the subject. With Julia, everything came back to her own sexuality. As soon as this was touched upon in any way she was capable of great acuteness. Unlike Winston, she had grasped the inner meaning of the Party's sexual puritanism. It was not merely that the sex instinct created a world of its own which was outside the Party's control and which therefore had to be destroyed if possible. What was more important was that sexual privation induced hysteria, which was desirable because it could be transformed into war fever and leader worship. The way she put it was:

"When you make love you're using up energy; and afterwards you feel happy and don't give a damn for anything. They can't bear you to feel like that. They want you to be bursting with energy all the time. All this marching up and down and cheering and waving flags is simply sex gone sour. If you're happy inside yourself, why should you get excited about Big Brother and the Three-Year Plans and the Two Minutes Hate and all the rest of their bloody rot?"

That was very true, he thought. There was a direct, intimate connection between chastity and political orthodoxy. For how could the fear, the hatred, and the lunatic credulity which the Party needed in its members be kept at the right pitch except by bottling down some powerful instinct and using it as a driving force? The sex impulse was dangerous to the Party, and the Party had turned it to account. They had played a similar trick with the instinct of parenthood. The family could not actually be abolished, and, indeed, people were encouraged to be fond of their children in almost the old-fashioned way. The children, on the other hand, were systematically turned against their parents and taught to spy on them and report their deviations. The family had become in effect an extension of the Thought Police. It was a device by means of which everyone could be surrounded night and day by informers who knew him intimately.

Abruptly his mind went back to Katharine. Katharine would unquestionably have denounced him to the Thought Police if she had not happened to be too stupid to detect the unorthodoxy of his opinions. But what really recalled her to him at this moment was the stifling heat of the afternoon, which had brought the sweat out on his forehead. He began telling Julia of something that had happened, or rather had failed to happen, on another sweltering summer afternoon, eleven years ago.

It was three or four months after they were married. They had lost their way on a community hike somewhere in Kent. They had only lagged behind the others for a couple of minutes, but they took a wrong turning, and presently found themselves pulled up short by the edge of an old chalk quarry. It was a sheer drop of ten or twenty meters, with boulders at the bottom. There was nobody of whom they could ask the way. As soon as she realized that they were lost Katharine became very uneasy. To be away from the noisy mob of hikers even for a moment gave her a feeling of wrongdoing. She wanted to hurry back by the way they had come and start searching in the other direction. But at this moment Winston noticed some tufts of loosestrife growing in the cracks of the cliff beneath them. One tuft was of two colors, magenta and brick red, apparently growing on the same root. He had never seen anything of the kind before, and he called to Katharine to come and look at it.

"Look, Katharine! Look at those flowers. That clump down near the bottom. Do you see they're two different colors?"

She had already turned to go, but she did rather fretfully come back for a moment. She even leaned out over the cliff face to see where he was pointing. He was standing a little behind her, and he put his hand on her waist to steady her. At this moment it suddenly occurred to him how completely alone they were. There was not a human creature anywhere, not a leaf stirring, not even a bird awake. In a place like this the danger that there would be a hidden microphone was very small, and even if there was a microphone it would only pick up sounds. It was the hottest, sleepiest hour of the afternoon. The sun blazed down upon them, the sweat tickled his face. And the thought struck him. . . .

"Why didn't you give her a good shove?" said Julia. "I would have."

"Yes, dear, you would have. I would have, if I'd been the same person then as I am now. Or perhaps I would—I'm not certain."

"Are you sorry you didn't?"

"Yes. On the whole I'm sorry I didn't."

They were sitting side by side on the dusty floor. He pulled her closer against him. Her head rested on his shoulder, the pleasant smell of her hair conquering the pigeon dung. She was very young, he thought, she still expected something from life, she did not understand that to push an inconvenient person over a cliff solves nothing.

"Actually it would have made no difference," he said.

"Then why are you sorry you didn't do it?"

"Only because I prefer a positive to a negative. In this game that we're playing, we can't win. Some kinds of failure are better than other kinds, that's all."

He felt her shoulders give a wriggle of dissent. She always contradicted him when he said anything of this kind. She would not accept it as a law of nature that the individual is always defeated. In a way she realized that she herself was doomed, that sooner or later the Thought Police would catch her and kill her, but with another part of her mind she believed that it was somehow possible to construct a secret world in which you could live as you chose. All you needed was luck and cunning and boldness. She did not understand that there was no such thing as happiness, that the only victory lay in the far future, long after you were dead, that from the moment of declaring war on the Party it was better to think of yourself as a corpse.

"We are the dead," he said.

"We're not dead yet," said Julia prosaically.

"Not physically. Six months, a year—five years, conceivably. I am afraid of death. You are young, so presumably you're more afraid of it than I am. Obviously we shall put it off as long as we can. But it makes very little difference. So long as human beings stay human, death and life are the same thing."

"Oh, rubbish! Which would you sooner sleep with, me or a skeleton?

Don't you enjoy being alive? Don't you like feeling: This is me, this is my hand, this my leg, I'm real, I'm solid, I'm alive! Don't you like *this?*"

She twisted herself round and pressed her bosom against him. He could feel her breasts, ripe yet firm, through her overalls. Her body seemed to be pouring some of its youth and vigor into his.

"Yes, I like that," he said.

"Then stop talking about dying. And now listen, dear, we've got to fix up about the next time we meet. We may as well go back to the place in the wood. We've given it a good long rest. But you must get there by a different way this time. I've got it all planned out. You take the train—but look, I'll draw it out for you."

And in her practical way she scraped together a small square of dust, and with a twig from a pigeon's nest began drawing a map on the floor.

IV

Winston looked round the shabby little room above Mr. Charrington's shop. Beside the window the enormous bed was made up, with ragged blankets and a coverless bolster. The old-fashioned clock with the twelve-hour face was ticking away on the mantelpiece. In the corner, on the gateleg table, the glass paperweight which he had bought on his last visit gleamed softly out of the half-darkness.

In the fender was a battered tin oilstove, a saucepan and two cups, provided by Mr. Charrington. Winston lit the burner and set a pan of water to boil. He had brought an envelope full of Victory Coffee and some saccharine tablets. The clock's hands said seven-twenty; it was nineteen-twenty really. She was coming at nineteen-thirty.

Folly, folly, his heart kept saying: conscious, gratuitous, suicidal folly! Of all the crimes that a Party member could commit, this one was the least possible to conceal. Actually the idea had first floated into his head in the form of a vision of the glass paperweight mirrored by the surface of the gateleg. As he had foreseen, Mr. Charrington had made no diffi-culty about letting the room. He was obviously glad of the few dollars that it would bring him. Nor did he seem shocked or become offensively knowing when it was made clear that Winston wanted the room for the purpose of a love affair. Instead he looked into the middle distance and spoke in generalities, with so delicate an air as to give the impression that he had become partly invisible. Privacy, he said, was a very valuable thing. Everyone wanted a place where they could be alone occasionally. And when they had such a place, it was only common courtesy in anyone else who knew of it to keep his knowledge to himself. He even, seeming almost to fade out of existence as he did so, added that there were two entries to the house, one of them through the backyard, which gave on an alley.

Under the window somebody was singing. Winston peeped out, secure in the protection of the muslin curtain. The June sun was still high in the sky, and in the sun-filled court below a monstrous woman, solid as a Norman pillar, with brawny red forearms and a sacking apron strapped about her middle, was stumping to and fro between a washtub and a clothesline, pegging out a series of square white things which Winston recognized as babies' diapers. Whenever her mouth was not corked with clothes pegs she was singing in a powerful contralto:

> "It was only an 'opeless fancy,
> It passed like an Ipril dye,
> But a look an' a word an' the dreams they stirred
> They 'ave stolen my 'eart awaye!"

The tune had been haunting London for weeks past. It was one of countless similar songs published for the benefit of the proles by a sub-section of the Music Department. The words of these songs were composed without any human intervention whatever on an instrument known as a versificator. But the woman sang so tunefully as to turn the dreadful rubbish into an almost pleasant sound. He could hear the woman singing and the scrape of her shoes on the flagstones, and the cries of the children in the street, and somewhere in the far distance a faint roar of traffic, and yet the room seemed curiously silent, thanks to the absence of a telescreen.

Folly, folly, folly! he thought again. It was inconceivable that they could frequent this place for more than a few weeks without being caught. But the temptation of having a hiding place that was truly their own, indoors and near at hand, had been too much for both of them. For some time after their visit to the church belfry it had been impossible to arrange meetings. Working hours had been drastically increased in anticipation of Hate Week. It was more than a month distant, but the enormous complex preparations that it entailed were throwing extra work onto everybody. Finally both of them managed to secure a free afternoon on the same day. They had agreed to go back to the clearing in the wood. On the evening beforehand they met briefly in the street. As usual Winston hardly looked at Julia as they drifted toward one another in the crowd, but from the short glance he gave her it seemed to him that she was paler than usual.

"It's all off," she murmured as soon as she judged it safe to speak. "Tomorrow, I mean."

"What?"

"Tomorrow afternoon. I can't come."

"Why not?"

"Oh, the usual reason. It's started early this time."

For a moment he was violently angry. During the month that he had known her the nature of his desire for her had changed. At the beginning there had been little true sensuality in it. Their first love-making had been simply an act of the will. But after the second time it was different. The smell of her hair, the taste of her mouth, the feeling of her skin seemed to have got inside him, or into the air all round him. She had become a physical necessity, something that he not only wanted but felt that he had a right to. When she said that she could not come, he had the feeling that she was cheating him. But just at this moment the crowd pressed them together and their hands accidentally met. She gave the tips of his fingers a quick squeeze that seemed to invite not desire but affection. It struck him that when one lived with a woman this particular disappointment must be a normal, recurring event; and a deep tenderness, such as he had not felt for her before, suddenly took hold of him. He wished that they were a married couple of ten years' standing. He wished that he were walking through the streets with her just as they were doing now, but openly and without fear, talking of trivialities and buying odds and ends for the household. He wished above all that they had some place where they could be alone together without feeling the obligation to make love every time they met. It was not actually at that moment, but at some time on the following day, that the idea of renting Mr. Charrington's room had occurred to him. When he suggested it to Julia she had agreed with unexpected readiness. Both of them knew that it was lunacy. It was as though they were intentionally stepping nearer to their graves. As he sat waiting on the edge of the bed he thought again of the cellars of the Ministry of Love. It was curious how that predestined horror moved in and out of one's consciousness. There it lay, fixed in future time, preceding death as surely as 99 precedes 100. One could not avoid it, but one could perhaps postpone it; and yet instead, every now and again, by a conscious, willful act, one chose to shorten the interval before it happened.

At this moment there was a quick step on the stairs. Julia burst into the room. She was carrying a tool bag of coarse brown canvas, such as he had sometimes seen her carrying to and fro at the Ministry. He started forward to take her in his arms, but she disengaged herself rather hurriedly, partly because she was still holding the tool bag.

"Half a second," she said. "Just let me show you what I've brought. Did you bring some of that filthy Victory Coffee? I thought you would. You can chuck it away again, because we shan't be needing it. Look here."

She fell on her knees, threw open the bag, and tumbled out some spanners and a screwdriver that filled the top part of it. Underneath was a number of neat paper packets. The first packet that she passed to Winston had a strange and yet vaguely familiar feeling. It was filled with some kind of heavy, sandlike stuff which yielded wherever you touched it.

"It isn't sugar?" he said.

"Real sugar. Not saccharine, sugar. And here's a loaf of bread—proper white bread, not our bloody stuff—and a little pot of jam. And here's a tin of milk—but look! This is the one I'm really proud of. I had to wrap a bit of sacking round it, because—"

But she did not need to tell him why she had wrapped it up. The smell was already filling the room, a rich hot smell which seemed like an emanation from his early childhood, but which one did occasionally meet with even now, blowing down a passageway before a door slammed, or diffusing itself mysteriously in a crowded street, sniffed for an instant and then lost again.

"It's coffee," he murmured, "real coffee."

"It's Inner Party coffee. There's a whole kilo here," she said.

"How did you manage to get hold of all these things?"

"It's all Inner Party stuff. There's nothing those swine don't have, nothing. But of course waiters and servants and people pinch things, and—look, I got a little packet of tea as well."

Winston had squatted down beside her. He tore open a corner of the packet.

"It's real tea. Not blackberry leaves."

"There's been a lot of tea about lately. They've captured India, or something," she said vaguely. "But listen, dear. I want you to turn your back on me for three minutes. Go and sit on the other side of the bed. Don't go too near the window. And don't turn round till I tell you."

Winston gazed abstractedly through the muslin curtain. Down in the yard the red-armed woman was still marching to and fro between the washtub and the line. She took two more pegs out of her mouth and sang with deep feeling:

> *"They sye that time 'eals all things,*
> *They sye you can always forget;*
> *But the smiles an' the tears acrorss the years*
> *They twist my 'eartstrings yet!"*

She knew the whole driveling song by heart, it seemed. Her voice floated upward with the sweet summer air, very tuneful, charged with a sort of happy melancholy. One had the feeling that she would have been perfectly content if the June evening had been endless and the supply of clothes inexhaustible, to remain there for a thousand years, pegging out diapers and singing rubbish. It struck him as a curious fact that he had never heard a member of the Party singing alone and spontaneously. It would even have seemed slightly unorthodox, a dangerous eccentricity, like talking to oneself. Perhaps it was only when people were somewhere near the starvation level that they had anything to sing about.

"You can turn round now," said Julia.

He turned round, and for a second almost failed to recognize her. What he had actually expected was to see her naked. But she was not naked. The transformation that had happened was much more surprising than that. She had painted her face.

She must have slipped into some shop in the proletarian quarters and bought herself a complete set of make-up materials. Her lips were deeply reddened, her cheeks rouged, her nose powdered; there was even a touch of something under the eyes to make them brighter. It was not very skillfully done, but Winston's standards in such matters were not high. He had never before seen or imagined a woman of the Party with cosmetics on her face. The improvement in her appearance was startling. With just a few dabs of color in the right places she had become not only very much prettier, but, above all, far more feminine. Her short hair and boyish overalls merely added to the effect. As he took her in his arms a wave of synthetic violets flooded his nostrils. He remembered the half-darkness of a basement kitchen and a woman's cavernous mouth. It was the very same scent that she had used; but at the moment it did not seem to matter.

"Scent, too!" he said.

"Yes, dear, scent, too. And do you know what I'm going to do next? I'm going to get hold of a real woman's frock from somewhere and wear it instead of these bloody trousers. I'll wear silk stockings and high-heeled shoes! In this room I'm going to be a woman, not a Party comrade."

They flung their clothes off and climbed into the huge mahogany bed. It was the first time that he had stripped himself naked in her presence. Until now he had been too much ashamed of his pale and meager body, with the varicose veins standing out on his calves and the discolored patch over his ankle. There were no sheets, but the blanket they lay on was threadbare and smooth, and the size and springiness of the bed astonished both of them. "It's sure to be full of bugs, but who cares?" said Julia. One never saw a double bed nowadays except in the homes of the proles. Winston had occasionally slept in one in his boyhood; Julia had never been in one before, so far as she could remember.

Presently they fell asleep for a little while. When Winston woke up the hands of the clock had crept round to nearly nine. He did not stir, because Julia was sleeping with her head in the crook of his arm. Most of her make-up had transferred itself to his own face or the bolster, but a light stain of rouge still brought out the beauty of her cheekbone. A yellow ray from the sinking sun fell across the foot of the bed and lighted up the fireplace, where the water in the pan was boiling fast. Down in the yard the woman had stopped singing, but the faint shouts of children floated in from the street. He wondered vaguely whether in the abolished past it had been a normal experience to lie in bed like this, in the cool of a summer evening, a man and a woman with no clothes on, making love when they chose, talking of what they chose, not feeling any compulsion to get up, simply lying there and listening to peaceful sounds outside. Surely there could never have been a time when that seemed ordinary. Julia woke up, rubbed her eyes, and raised herself on her elbow to look at the oilstove.

"Half that water's boiled away," she said. "I'll get up and make some coffee in another moment. We've got an hour. What time do they cut the lights off at your flats?"

"Twenty-three thirty."

"It's twenty-three at the hostel. But you have to get in earlier than that, because—Hi! Get out, you filthy brute!"

She suddenly twisted herself over in the bed, seized a shoe from the floor, and sent it hurtling into the corner with a boyish jerk of her arm, exactly as he had seen her fling the dictionary at Goldstein, that morning during the Two Minutes Hate.

"What was it?" he said in surprise.

"A rat. I saw him stick his beastly nose out of the wainscoting. There's a hole down there, I gave him a good fright, anyway."

"Rats!" murmured Winston. "In this room!"

"They're all over the place," said Julia indifferently as she lay down again. "We've even got them in the kitchen at the hostel. Some parts of London are swarming with them. Did you know they attack children? Yes, they do. In some of these streets a woman daren't leave a baby alone for two minutes. It's the great huge brown ones that do it. And the nasty thing is that the brutes always—"

"Don't go on!" said Winston, with his eyes tightly shut.

"Dearest! You've gone quite pale. What's the matter? Do they make you feel sick?"

"Of all horrors in the world—a rat!"

She pressed herself against him and wound her limbs round him, as though to reassure him with the warmth of her body. He did not reopen his eyes immediately. For several moments he had had the feeling of being back in a nightmare which had recurred from time to time throughout his life. It was always very much the same. He was standing in front of a wall of darkness, and on the other side of it there was something unendurable, something too dreadful to be faced. In the dream his deepest feeling was always one of self-deception, because he did in fact know what was behind the wall of darkness. With a deadly effort, like wrenching a piece out of his own brain, he could even have dragged the thing into the open. He always woke up without discovering what it was, but somehow it was connected with what Julia had been saying when he cut her short.

"I'm sorry," he said. "It's nothing. I don't like rats, that's all."

"Don't worry, dear, we're not going to have the filthy brutes in here. I'll stuff the hole with a bit of sacking before we go. And next time we come here I'll bring some plaster and bung it up properly."

Already the black instant of panic was half-forgotten. Feeling slightly ashamed of himself, he sat up against the bedhead. Julia got out of bed, pulled on her overalls, and made the coffee. The smell that rose from the saucepan was so powerful and exciting that they shut the window lest anybody outside should notice it and become inquisitive. What was even better than the taste of the coffee was the silky texture given to it by the sugar, a thing Winston had almost forgotten after years of saccharine. With one hand in her pocket and a piece of bread and jam in the other, Julia wandered about the room, glancing indifferently at the bookcase, pointing out the best way of repairing the gateleg table, plumping herself down in the ragged armchair to see if it was comfortable, and examining the absurd twelve-hour clock with a sort of tolerant amusement. She brought the glass paperweight over to the bed to have a look at it in a better light. He took it out of her hand, fascinated as always by the soft, rainwatery appearance of the glass.

"What is it, do you think?" said Julia.

"I don't think it's anything—I mean, I don't think it was ever put to any use. That's what I like about it. It's a little chunk of history that they've forgotten to alter. It's a message from a hundred years ago, if one knew how to read it."

"And that picture over there—" she nodded at the engraving on the opposite wall—"would that be a hundred years old?"

"More. Two hundred, I dare say. One can't tell. It's impossible to discover the age of anything nowadays."

She went over to look at it. "Here's where that brute stuck his nose out," she said, kicking the wainscoting immediately below the picture. "What is this place? I've seen it before somewhere."

"It's a church, or at least it used to be. St. Clement's Dane its name was." The fragment of rhyme that Mr. Charrington had taught him came back into his head, and he added half-nostalgically: *"Oranges and lemons, say the bells of St. Clement's!"*

To his astonishment she capped the line:

"You owe me three farthings, say the bells of St. Martin's,
When will you pay me? say the bells of Old Bailey–

"I can't remember how it goes on after that. But anyway I remember it ends up, *Here comes a candle to light you to bed, here comes a chopper to chop off your head!"*

It was like the two halves of a countersign. But there must be another line after *the bells of Old Bailey.* Perhaps it could be dug out of Mr. Charrington's memory, if he were suitably prompted.

"Who taught you that?" he said.

"My grandfather. He used to say it to me when I was a little girl. He was vaporized when I was eight—at any rate, he disappeared. I wonder what a lemon was," she added inconsequently. "I've seen oranges. They're a kind of round yellow fruit with a thick skin."

"I can remember lemons," said Winston. "They were quite common in the Fifties. They were so sour that it set your teeth on edge even to smell them."

"I bet that picture's got bugs behind it," said Julia. "I'll take it down and give it a good clean some day. I suppose it's almost time we were leaving. I must start washing this paint off. What a bore! I'll get the lipstick off your face afterwards."

Winston did not get up for a few minutes more. The room was darkening. He turned over toward the light and lay gazing into the glass paperweight. The inexhaustibly interesting thing was not the fragment of coral but the interior of the glass itself. There was such a depth of it, and yet it was almost as transparent as air. It was as though the surface of the glass had been the arch of the sky, enclosing a tiny world with its atmosphere complete. He had the feeling that he could get inside it, and that in fact he was inside it, along with the mahogany bed and the gateleg table and the clock and the steel engraving and the paperweight itself. The paperweight was the room he was in, and the coral was Julia's life and his own, fixed in a sort of eternity at the heart of the crystal.

V

Syme had vanished. A morning came, and he was missing from work; a few thoughtless people commented on his absence. On the next day nobody mentioned him. On the third day Winston went into the vestibule of the Records Department to look at the notice board. One of the notices carried a printed list of the members of the Chess Committee, of whom Syme had been one. It looked almost exactly as it had looked before—nothing had been crossed out—but it was one name shorter. It was enough. Syme had ceased to exist; he had never existed.

The weather was baking hot. In the labyrinthine Ministry the windowless, air-conditioned rooms kept their normal temperature, but outside the pavements scorched one's feet and the stench of the Tubes at the rush hours was a horror. The preparations for Hate Week were in full swing, and the staffs of all the Ministries were working overtime. Processions, meetings, military parades, lectures, waxwork displays, film shows, telescreen programs all had to be organized; stands had to be erected, effigies built, slogans coined, songs written, rumors circulated, photographs faked. Julia's unit in the Fiction Department had been taken off the production of novels and was rushing out a series of atrocity pamphlets.

Winston, in addition to his regular work, spent long periods every day in going through back files of the *Times* and altering and embellishing news items which were to be quoted in speeches. Late at night, when crowds of rowdy proles roamed the streets, the town had a curiously febrile air. The rocket bombs crashed oftener than ever, and sometimes in the far distance there were enormous explosions which no one could explain and about which there were wild rumors.

The new tune which was to be the theme song of Hate Week (the "Hate Song," it was called) had already been composed and was being endlessly plugged on the telescreens. It had a savage, barking rhythm which could not exactly be called music, but resembled the beating of a drum. Roared out by hundreds of voices to the tramp of marching feet, it was terrifying. The proles had taken a fancy to it, and in the midnight streets it competed with the still-popular "It Was Only a Hopeless Fancy." The Parsons children played it at all hours of the night and day, unbearably, on a comb and a piece of toilet paper. Winston's evenings were fuller than ever. Squads of volunteers, organized by Parsons, were preparing the street for Hate Week, stitching banners, painting posters, erecting flagstaffs on the roofs, and perilously slinging wires across the street for the reception of streamers. Parsons boasted that Victory Mansions alone would display four hundred meters of bunting. He was in his native element and as happy as a lark. The heat and the manual work had even given him a pretext for reverting to shorts and an open shirt in the evenings. He was everywhere at once, pushing, pulling, sawing, hammering, improvising, jollying everyone along with comradely exhortations and giving out from every fold of his body what seemed an inexhaustible supply of acrid-smelling sweat.

A new poster had suddenly appeared all over London. It had no caption, and represented simply the monstrous figure of a Eurasian soldier, three or four meters high, striding forward with expressionless Mongolian face and enormous boots, a submachine gun pointed from his hip. From whatever angle you looked at the poster, the muzzle of the gun, magnified by the foreshortening, seemed to be pointed straight at you. The thing had been plastered on every blank space on every wall, even outnumbering the portraits of Big Brother. The proles, normally apathetic about the war, were being lashed into one of their periodical frenzies of patriotism. As though to harmonize with the general mood, the rocket bombs had been killing larger numbers of people than usual. One fell on a crowded film theater in Stepney, burying several hundred victims among the ruins. The whole population of the neighborhood turned out for a long, trailing funeral which went on for hours and was in effect an indignation meeting. Another bomb fell on a piece of waste ground which was used as a playground, and several dozen children were blown to pieces. There were further angry demonstrations, Goldstein was burned in effigy, hundreds of copies of the poster of the Eurasian soldier were torn down and added to the flames, and a number of shops were looted in the turmoil; then a rumor flew round that spies were directing the rocket bombs by means of wireless waves, and an old couple who were suspected of being of foreign extraction had their house set on fire and perished of suffocation.

In the room over Mr. Charrington's shop, when they could get there, Julia and Winston lay side by side on a stripped bed under the open window, naked for the sake of coolness. The rat had never come back, but the bugs had multiplied hideously in the heat. It did not seem to matter. Dirty or clean, the room was paradise. As soon as they arrived they would sprinkle everything with pepper bought on the black market, tear off their clothes and make love with sweating bodies, then fall asleep and wake to find that the bugs had rallied and were massing for the counter-attack.

Four, five, six—seven times they met during the month of June. Winston had dropped his habit of drinking gin at all hours. He seemed to have lost the need for it. He had grown fatter, his varicose ulcer had subsided, leaving only a brown stain on the skin above his ankle, his fits of coughing in the early morning had stopped. The process of life had ceased to be intolerable, he had no longer any impulse to make faces at the telescreen or shout curses at the top of his voice. Now that they had a secure hiding place, almost a home, it did not even seem a hardship that they could only meet infrequently and for a couple of hours at a time. What mattered was that the room over the junk shop should exist. To know that it was there, inviolate, was almost the same as being in it. The room was a world, a pocket of the past where extinct animals could walk. Mr. Charrington, thought Winston, was another extinct animal. He usually stopped to talk with Mr. Charrington for a few minutes on his way upstairs. The old man seemed seldom or never to go out of doors, and on the other hand to have almost no customers. He led a ghostlike existence between the tiny, dark shop and an even tinier back kitchen where he prepared his meals and which contained, among other things, an unbelievably ancient gramophone with an enormous horn. He seemed glad of the opportunity to talk. Wandering about among his worthless stock, with his long nose and thick spectacles and his bowed shoulders in the velvet jacket, he had always vaguely the air of being a collector rather than a tradesman. With a sort of faded enthusiasm he would finger this scrap of rubbish or that—a china bottle-stopper, the painted lid of a broken snuffbox, a pinchbeck locket containing a strand of some long-dead baby's hair—never asking that Winston should buy it, merely that he should admire it. To talk to him was like listening to the tinkling of a worn-out musical box. He had dragged out from the corners of his memory some more fragments of forgotten rhymes. There was one about four and twenty blackbirds, and another about a cow with a crumpled horn, and another about the death of poor Cock Robin. "It just occurred to me you might be interested," he would say with a deprecating little laugh whenever he produced a new fragment. But he could never recall more than a few lines of any one rhyme.

Both of them knew—in a way, it was never out of their minds—that what was now happening could not last long. There were times when the fact of impending death seemed as palpable as the bed they lay on, and they would cling together with a sort of despairing sensuality, like a damned soul grasping at his last morsel of pleasure when the clock is within five minutes of striking. But there were also times when they had the illusion not only of safety but of permanence. So long as they were actually in this room, they both felt, no harm could come to them. Getting there was difficult and dangerous, but the room itself was sanctuary. It was as when Winston had gazed into the heart of the paperweight, with the feeling that it would be possible to get inside that glassy world, and that once inside it time could be arrested. Often they gave themselves up to daydreams of escape. Their luck would hold indefinitely, and they would carry on their intrigue, just like this, for the remainder of their natural lives. Or Katharine would die, and by subtle maneuverings Winston and Julia would succeed in getting married. Or they would commit suicide together. Or they would disappear, alter themselves out of recognition, learn to speak with proletarian accents, get jobs in a factory, and live out their lives undetected in a back street. It was all nonsense, as they both knew. In reality there was no escape. Even the one plan that was practicable, suicide, they had no intention of carrying out. To hang on from day to day and from week to week, spinning out a present that had no future, seemed an unconquerable instinct, just as one's lungs will always draw the next breath so long as there is air available.

Sometimes, too, they talked of engaging in active rebellion against the Party, but with no notion of how to take the first step. Even if the fabulous Brotherhood was a reality, there still remained the difficulty of finding one's way into it. He told her of the strange intimacy that existed, or seemed to exist, between himself and O'Brien, and of the impulse he sometimes felt simply to walk into O'Brien's presence, announce that he was the enemy of the Party, and demand his help. Curiously enough this did not strike her as an impossibly rash thing to do. She was used to judging people by their faces, and it seemed natural to her that Winston should believe O'Brien to be trustworthy on the strength of a single flash of the eyes. Moreover she took it for granted that everyone, or nearly everyone, secretly hated the Party and would break the rules if he thought it safe to do so. But she refused to believe that widespread, organized opposition existed or could exist. The tales about Goldstein and his underground army, she said, were simply a lot of rubbish which the

Party had invented for its own purposes and which you had to pretend to believe in. Times beyond number, at Party rallies and spontaneous demonstrations, she had shouted at the top of her voice for the execution of people whose names she had never heard and in whose supposed crimes she had not the faintest belief. When public trials were happening she had taken her place in the detachments from the Youth League who surrounded the courts from morning to night, chanting at intervals "Death to the traitors!" During the Two Minutes Hate she always excelled all others in shouting insults at Goldstein. Yet she had only the dimmest idea of who Goldstein was and what doctrines he was supposed to represent. She had grown up since the Revolution and was too young to remember the ideological battles of the Fifties and Sixties. Such a thing as an independent political movement was outside her imagination; and in any case the Party was invincible. It would always exist, and it would always be the same. You could only rebel against it by secret disobedience or, at most, by isolated acts of violence such as killing somebody or blowing something up.

In some ways she was far more acute than Winston, and far less susceptible to Party propaganda. Once when he happened in some connection to mention the war against Eurasia, she startled him by saying casually that in her opinion the war was not happening. The rocket bombs which fell daily on London were probably fired by the Government of Oceania itself, "just to keep people frightened." This was an idea that had literally never occurred to him. She also stirred a sort of envy in him by telling him that during the Two Minutes Hate her great difficulty was to avoid bursting out laughing. But she only questioned the teachings of the Party when they in some way touched upon her own life. Often she was ready to accept the official mythology, simply because the difference between truth and falsehood did not seem important to her. She believed, for instance, having learnt it at school, that the Party had invented airplanes. (In his own schooldays, Winston remembered, in the late Fifties, it was only the helicopter that the Party claimed to have invented; a dozen years later, when Julia was at school, it was already claiming the airplane; one generation more, and it would be claiming the steam engine.) And when he told her that airplanes had been in existence before he was born, and long before the Revolution, the fact struck her as totally uninteresting. After all, what did it matter who had invented airplanes? It was rather more of a shock to him when he discovered from some chance remark that she did not remember that Oceania, four years ago, had been at war with Eastasia and at peace with Eurasia. It was true that she regarded the whole war as a sham; but apparently she had not even noticed that the name of the enemy had changed. "I thought we'd always been at war with Eurasia," she said vaguely. It frightened him a little. The invention of airplanes dated from long before her birth, but the switch-over in the war had happened only four years ago, well after she was grown up. He argued with her about it for perhaps a quarter of an hour. In the end he succeeded in forcing her memory back until she did dimly recall that at one time Eastasia and not Eurasia had been the enemy. But the issue still struck her as unimportant. "Who cares?" she said impatiently. "It's always one bloody war after another, and one knows the news is all lies anyway."

Sometimes he talked to her of the Records Department and the impudent forgeries that he committed there. Such things did not appear to horrify her. She did not feel the abyss opening beneath her feet at the thought of lies becoming truths. He told her the story of Jones, Aaronson, and Rutherford and the momentous slip of paper which he had once held between his fingers. It did not make much impression on her. At first, indeed, she failed to grasp the point of the story.

"Were they friends of yours?" she said.

"No, I never knew them. They were Inner Party members. Besides, they were far older men than I was. They belonged to the old days, before the Revolution. I barely knew them by sight."

"Then what was there to worry about? People are being killed off all the time, aren't they?"

He tried to make her understand. "This was an exceptional case. It wasn't just a question of somebody being killed. Do you realize that the past, starting from yesterday, has been actually abolished? If it survives anywhere, it's in a few solid objects with no words attached to them, like that lump of glass there. Already we know almost literally nothing about the Revolution and the years before the Revolution. Every record has been destroyed or falsified, every book has been rewritten, every picture has been repainted, every statue and street and building has been renamed, every date has been altered. And that process is continuing day by day and minute by minute. History has stopped. Nothing exists except an endless present in which the Party is always right. I *know*, of course, that the past is falsified, but it would never be possible for me to prove it, even when I did the falsification myself. After the thing is done, no evidence ever remains. The only evidence is inside my own mind, and I don't know with any certainty that any other human being shares my memories. Just in that one instance, in my whole life, I did possess actual concrete evidence *after* the event—years after it."

"And what good was that?"

"It was no good, because I threw it away a few minutes later. But if the same thing happened today, I should keep it."

"Well, I wouldn't!" said Julia. "I'm quite ready to take risks, but only for something worth while, not for bits of old newspapers. What could you have done with it even if you had kept it?"

"Not much, perhaps. But it was evidence. It might have planted a few doubts here and there, supposing that I'd dared to show it to anybody. I don't imagine that we can alter anything in our own lifetime. But one can imagine little knots of resistance springing up here and there—small groups of people banding themselves together, and gradually growing, and even leaving a few records behind, so that the next generation can carry on where we leave off."

"I'm not interested in the next generation, dear, I'm interested in *us*."

"You're only a rebel from the waist downwards," he told her.

She thought this brilliantly witty and flung her arms round him in delight.

In the ramifications of Party doctrine she had not the faintest interest. Whenever he began to talk of the principles of Ingsoc, doublethink, the mutability of the past and the denial of objective reality, and to use Newspeak words, she became bored and confused and said that she never paid any attention to that kind of thing. One knew that it was all rubbish, so why let oneself be worried by it? She knew when to cheer and when to boo, and that was all one needed. If he persisted in talking of such subjects, she had a disconcerting habit of falling asleep. She was one of those people who can go to sleep at any hour and in any position. Talking to her, he realized how easy it was to present an appearance of orthodoxy while having no grasp whatever of what orthodoxy meant. In a way, the world-view of the Party imposed itself most successfully on people incapable of understanding it. They could be made to accept the most flagrant violations of reality, because they never fully grasped the enormity of what was demanded of them, and were not sufficiently interested in public events to notice what was happening. By lack of understanding they remained sane. They simply swallowed everything, and what they swallowed did them no harm, because it left no residue behind, just as a grain of corn will pass undigested through the body of a bird.

VI

It had happened at last. The expected message had come. All his life, it seemed to him, he had been waiting for this to happen.

He was walking down the long corridor at the Ministry, and he was almost at the spot where Julia had slipped the note into his hand when he became aware that someone larger than himself was walking just behind him. The person, whoever it was, gave a small cough, evidently as a prelude to speaking. Winston stopped abruptly and turned. It was O'Brien.

At last they were face to face, and it seemed that his only impulse was to run away. His heart bounded violently. He would have been incapable of speaking. O'Brien, however, had continued forward in the same movement, laying a friendly hand for a moment on Winston's arm, so that the two of them were walking side by side. He began speaking with the peculiar grave courtesy that differentiated him from the majority of Inner Party members.

"I had been hoping for an opportunity of talking to you," he said. "I was reading one of your Newspeak articles in the *Times* the other day. You take a scholarly interest in Newspeak, I believe?"

Winston had recovered part of his self-possession. "Hardly scholarly," he said. "I'm only an amateur. It's not my subject. I have never had anything to do with the actual construction of the language."

"But you write it very elegantly," said O'Brien. "That is not only my own opinion. I was talking recently to a friend of yours who is certainly an expert. His name has slipped my memory for the moment."

Again Winston's heart stirred painfully. It was inconceivable that this was anything other than a reference to Syme. But Syme was not only dead, he was abolished, an *unperson.* Any identifiable reference to him would have been mortally dangerous. O'Brien's remark must obviously have been intended as a signal, a code word. By sharing a small act of thoughtcrime he had turned the two of them into accomplices. They had continued to stroll slowly down the corridor, but now O'Brien halted. With the curious, disarming friendliness that he always managed to put into the gesture, he resettled his spectacles on his nose. Then he went on:

"What I had really intended to say was that in your article I noticed you had used two words which have become obsolete. But they have only become so very recently. Have you seen the tenth edition of the Newspeak dictionary?"

"No," said Winston. "I didn't think it had been issued yet. We are still using the ninth in the Records Department."

"The tenth edition is not due to appear for some months, I believe. But a few advance copies have been circulated. I have one myself. It might interest you to look at it, perhaps?"

"Very much so," said Winston, immediately seeing where this tended.

"Some of the new developments are most ingenious. The reduction in the number of verbs—that is the point that will appeal to you, I think. Let me see, shall I send a messenger to you with the dictionary? But I am afraid I invariably forget anything of that kind. Perhaps you could pick it up at my flat some time that suited you? Wait. Let me give you my address."

They were standing in front of a telescreen. Somewhat absent-mindedly O'Brien felt two of his pockets and then produced a small leather-covered notebook and a gold ink pencil. Immediately beneath the telescreen, in such a position that anyone who was watching at the other end of the instrument could read what he was writing, he scribbled an address, tore out the page, and handed it to Winston.

"I am usually at home in the evenings," he said. "If not, my servant will give you the dictionary."

He was gone, leaving Winston holding the scrap of paper, which this time there was no need to conceal. Nevertheless he carefully memorized what was written on it, and some hours later dropped it into the memory hole along with a mass of other papers.

They had been talking to one another for a couple of minutes at the most. There was only one meaning that the episode could possibly have. It had been contrived as a way of letting Winston know O'Brien's address. This was necessary, because except by direct inquiry it was never possible to discover where anyone lived. There were no directories of any kind. "If you ever want to see me, this is where I can be found," was what O'Brien had been saying to him. Perhaps there would even be a message concealed somewhere in the dictionary. But at any rate, one thing was certain. The conspiracy that he had dreamed of did exist, and he had reached the outer edges of it.

He knew that sooner or later he would obey O'Brien's summons. Perhaps tomorrow, perhaps after a long delay—he was not certain. What was happening was only the working-out of a process that had started years ago. The first step had been a secret, involuntary thought; the second had been the opening of the diary. He had moved from thoughts to words, and now from words to actions. The last step was something that would happen in the Ministry of Love. He had accepted it. The end was contained in the beginning. But it was frightening; or, more exactly, it was like a foretaste of death, like being a little less alive. Even while he was speaking to O'Brien, when the meaning of the words had sunk in, a chilly shuddering feeling had taken possession of his body. He had the sensation of stepping into the dampness of a grave, and it was not much better because he had always known that the grave was there and waiting for him.

VII

Winston had woken up with his eyes full of tears. Julia rolled sleepily against him, murmuring something that might have been "What's the matter?"

"I dreamt—" he began, and stopped short. It was too complex to be put into words. There was the dream itself, and there was a memory connected with it that had swum into his mind in the few seconds after waking.

He lay back with his eyes shut, still sodden in the atmosphere of the dream. It was a vast, luminous dream in which his whole life seemed to stretch out before him like a landscape on a summer evening after rain. It had all occurred inside the glass paperweight, but the surface of the glass was the dome of the sky, and inside the dome everything was flooded with clear soft light in which one could see into interminable distances. The dream had also been comprehended by—indeed, in some sense it had consisted in—a gesture of the arm made by his mother, and made again thirty years later by the Jewish woman he had seen on the news film, trying to shelter the small boy from the bullets, before the helicopters blew them both to pieces.

"Do you know," he said, "that until this moment I believed I had murdered my mother?"

"Why did you murder her?" said Julia, almost asleep.

"I didn't murder her. Not physically."

In the dream he had remembered his last glimpse of his mother, and within a few moments of waking the cluster of small events surrounding it had all come back. It was a memory that he must have deliberately pushed out of his consciousness over many years. He was not certain of the date, but he could not have been less than ten years old, possibly twelve, when it had happened.

His father had disappeared some time earlier; how much earlier, he could not remember. He remembered better the rackety, uneasy circumstances of the time: the periodical panics about air raids and the sheltering in Tube stations, the piles of rubble everywhere, the unintelligible proclamations posted at street corners, the gangs of youths in shirts all the same color, the enormous queues outside the bakeries, the intermittent machine-gun fire in the distance—above all, the fact that there was never enough to eat. He remembered long afternoons spent with other boys in scrounging round dustbins and rubbish heaps, picking out the ribs of cabbage leaves, potato peelings, sometimes even scraps of stale breadcrust from which they carefully scraped away the cinders; and also in waiting for the passing of trucks which traveled over a certain route and were known to carry cattle feed, and which, when they jolted over the bad patches in the road, sometimes spilt a few fragments of oilcake.

When his father disappeared, his mother did not show any surprise or any violent grief, but a sudden change came over her. She seemed to have become completely spiritless. It was evident even to Winston that she was waiting for something that she knew must happen. She did everything that was needed—cooked, washed, mended, made the bed, swept the floor, dusted the mantelpiece—always very slowly and with a curious lack of superfluous motion like an artist's lay-figure moving of its own accord. Her large shapely body seemed to relapse naturally into stillness. For hours at a time she would sit almost immobile on the bed, nursing his young sister, a tiny, ailing, very silent child of two or three, with a face made simian by thinness.

Very occasionally she would take Winston in her arms and press him against her for a long time without saying anything. He was aware, in spite of his youthfulness and selfishness, that this was somehow connected with the never-mentioned thing that was about to happen.

He remembered the room where they lived, a dark, close-smelling room that seemed half filled by a bed with a white counterpane. There was a gas ring in the fender, and a shelf where food was kept, and on the landing outside there was a brown earthenware sink, common to several rooms. He remembered his mother's statuesque body bending over the gas ring to stir at something in a saucepan. Above all he remembered his continuous hunger, and the fierce sordid battles at mealtimes. He would ask his mother naggingly, over and over again, why there was not more food, he would shout and storm at her (he even remembered the tones of his voice, which was beginning to break prematurely and sometimes boomed in a peculiar way), or he would attempt a sniveling note of pathos in his efforts to get more than his share. His mother was quite ready to give him more than his share. She took it for granted that he, "the boy," should have the biggest portion; but however much she gave him he invariably demanded more. At every meal she would beseech him not to be selfish and to remember that his little sister was sick and also needed food, but it was no use. He would cry out with rage when she stopped ladling, he would try to wrench the saucepan and spoon out of her hands, he would grab bits from his sister's plate. He knew that he was starving the other two, but he could not help it; he even felt that he had a right to do it. The clamorous hunger in his belly seemed to justify him. Between meals, if his mother did not stand guard, he was constantly pilfering at the wretched store of food on the shelf.

One day a chocolate ration was issued. There had been no such issue for weeks or months past. He remembered quite clearly that precious little morsel of chocolate. It was a two-ounce slab (they still talked about ounces in those days) between the three of them. It was obvious that it ought to be divided into three equal parts. Suddenly, as though he were listening to somebody else, Winston heard himself demanding in a loud booming voice that he should be given the whole piece. His mother told him not to be greedy. There was a long, nagging argument that went round and round, with shouts, whines, tears, remonstrances, bargainings. His tiny sister, clinging to her mother with both hands, exactly like a baby monkey, sat looking over her shoulders at him with large mournful eyes. In the end his mother broke off three-quarters of the chocolate and gave it to Winston, giving the other quarter to his sister. The little girl took hold of it and looked at it dully, perhaps not knowing what it was. Winston stood watching her for a moment. Then with a sudden swift spring he had snatched the piece of chocolate out of his sister's hand and was fleeing for the door.

"Winston, Winston!" his mother called after him. "Come back! Give your sister back her chocolate!"

He stopped, but he did not come back. His mother's anxious eyes were fixed on his face. Even now she was thinking about the thing, he did not know what it was, that was on the point of happening. His sister, conscious of having been robbed of something, had set up a feeble wail. His mother drew her arm round the child and pressed its face against her breast. Something in the gesture told him that his sister was dying. He turned and fled down the stairs, with the chocolate growing sticky in his hand.

He never saw his mother again. After he had devoured the chocolate he felt somewhat ashamed of himself and hung about in the streets for several hours, until hunger drove him home. When he came back his mother had disappeared. This was already becoming normal at that time. Nothing was gone from the room except his mother and his sister. They had not taken any clothes, not even his mother's overcoat. To this day he did not know with any certainty that his mother was dead. It was perfectly possible that she had merely been sent to a forced-labor camp. As for his sister, she might have been removed, like Winston himself, to one of the colonies for homeless children (Reclamation Centers, they were called) which had grown up as a result of the civil war; or she might have been sent to the labor camp along with his mother, or simply left somewhere or other to die.

The dream was still vivid in his mind, especially the enveloping, protecting gesture of the arm in which its whole meaning seemed to be contained. His mind went back to another dream of two months ago. Exactly as his mother had sat on the dingy white-quilted bed, with the child clinging to her, so she had sat in the sunken ship, far underneath him and drowning deeper every minute, but still looking up at him through the darkening water.

He told Julia the story of his mother's disappearance. Without opening her eyes she rolled over and settled herself into a more comfortable position.

"I expect you were a beastly little swine in those days," she said indistinctly. "All children are swine."

"Yes. But the real point of the story—"

From her breathing it was evident that she was going off to sleep again. He would have liked to continue talking about his mother. He did not suppose, from what he could remember of her, that she had been an unusual woman, still less an intelligent one; and yet she had possessed a kind of nobility, a kind of purity, simply because the standards that she obeyed were private ones. Her feelings were her own, and could not be altered from outside. It would not have occurred to her that an action which is ineffectual thereby becomes meaningless. If you loved someone, you loved him, and when you had nothing else to give, you still gave him love. When the last of the chocolate was gone, his mother had clasped the child in her arms. It was no use, it changed nothing, it did not produce more chocolate, it did not avert the child's death or her own; but it seemed natural to her to do it. The refugee woman in the boat had also covered the little boy with her arm, which was no more use against the bullets than a sheet of paper. The terrible thing that the Party had done was to persuade you that mere impulses, mere feelings, were of no account, while at the same time robbing you of all power over the material world. When once you were in the grip of the Party, what you felt or did not feel, what you did or refrained from doing, made literally no difference. Whatever happened you vanished, and neither you nor your actions were ever heard of again. You were lifted clean out of the stream of history. And yet to the people of only two generations ago, this would not have seemed all-important, because they were not attempting to alter history. They were governed by private loyalties which they did not question. What mattered were individual relationships, and a completely helpless gesture, an embrace, a tear, a word spoken to a dying man, could have value in itself. The proles, it suddenly occurred to him, had remained in this condition. They were not loyal to a party or a country or an idea, they were loyal to one another. For the first time in his life he did not despise the proles or think of them merely as an inert force which would one day spring to life and regenerate the world. The proles had stayed human. They had not become hardened inside. They had held onto the primitive emotions which he himself had to relearn by conscious effort. And in thinking this he remembered, without apparent relevance, how a few weeks ago he had seen a severed hand lying on the pavement and had kicked it into the gutter as though it had been a cabbage stalk.

"The proles are human beings," he said aloud. "We are not human."

"Why not?" said Julia, who had woken up again.

He thought for a little while. "Has it ever occurred to you," he said, "that the best thing for us to do would be simply to walk out of here before it's too late, and never see each other again?"

"Yes, dear, it has occurred to me, several times. But I'm not going to do it, all the same."

"We've been lucky," he said, "but it can't last much longer. You're young. You look normal and innocent. If you keep clear of people like me, you might stay alive for another fifty years."

"No. I've thought it all out. What you do, I'm going to do. And don't be too downhearted. I'm rather good at staying alive."

"We may be together for another six months—a year—there's no knowing. At the end we're certain to be apart. Do you realize how utterly alone we shall be? When once they get hold of us there will be nothing, literally nothing, that either of us can do for the other. If I confess, they'll shoot you, and if I refuse to confess they'll shoot you just the same. Nothing that I can do or say, or stop myself from saying, will put off your death for as much as five minutes. Neither of us will even know whether the other is alive or dead. We shall be utterly without power of any kind. The one thing that matters is that we shouldn't betray one another, although even that can't make the slightest difference."

"If you mean confessing," she said, "we shall do that, right enough. Everybody always confesses. You can't help it. They torture you."

"I don't mean confessing. Confession is not betrayal. What you say or do doesn't matter; only feelings matter. If they could make me stop loving you—that would be the real betrayal."

She thought it over. "They can't do that," she said finally. "It's the one thing they can't do. They can make you say anything—*anything*—but they can't make you believe it. They can't get inside you."

"No," he said a little more hopefully, "no; that's quite true. They can't get inside you. If you can *feel* that staying human is worth while, even when it can't have any result whatever, you've beaten them."

He thought of the telescreen with its never-sleeping ear. They could spy upon you night and day, but if you kept your head you could still outwit them. With all their cleverness they had never mastered the secret of finding out what another human being was thinking. Perhaps that was less true when you were actually in their hands. One did not know what happened inside the Ministry of Love, but it was possible to guess: tortures, drugs, delicate instruments that registered your nervous reactions, gradual wearing-down by sleeplessness and solitude and persistent questioning. Facts, at any rate, could not be kept hidden. They could be tracked down by inquiry, they could be squeezed out of you by torture. But if the object was not to stay alive but to stay human, what difference did it ultimately make? They could not alter your feelings; for that matter you could not alter them yourself, even if you wanted to. They could lay bare in the utmost detail everything that you had done or said or thought; but the inner heart, whose workings were mysterious even to yourself, remained impregnable.

VIII

They had done it, they had done it at last!

The room they were standing in was long-shaped and softly lit. The telescreen was dimmed to a low murmur; the richness of the dark-blue carpet gave one the impression of treading on velvet. At the far end of the room O'Brien was sitting at a table under a green-shaded lamp, with a mass of papers on either side of him. He had not bothered to look up when the servant showed Julia and Winston in.

Winston's heart was thumping so hard that he doubted whether he would be able to speak. They had done it, they had done it at last, was all he could think. It had been a rash act to come here at all, and sheer folly to arrive together; though it was true that they had come by different routes and only met on O'Brien's doorstep. But merely to walk into such a place needed an effort of the nerve. It was only on very rare occasions that one saw inside the dwelling places of the Inner Party, or even penetrated into the quarter of the town where they lived. The whole atmos-

phere of the huge block of flats, the richness and spaciousness of everything, the unfamiliar smells of good food and good tobacco, the silent and
incredibly rapid lifts sliding up and down, the white-jacketed servants
hurrying to and fro—everything was intimidating. Although he had a
good pretext for coming here, he was haunted at every step by the fear
that a black-uniformed guard would suddenly appear from round the
corner, demand his papers, and order him to get out. O'Brien's servant,
however, had admitted the two of them without demur. He was a small,
dark-haired man in a white jacket, with a diamond-shaped, completely
expressionless face which might have been that of a Chinese. The passage
down which he led them was softly carpeted, with cream-papered walls
and white wainscoting, all exquisitely clean. That too was intimidating.
Winston could not remember ever to have seen a passageway whose walls
were not grimy from the contact of human bodies.

O'Brien had a slip of paper between his fingers and seemed to be studying it intently. His heavy face, bent down so that one could see the line of
the nose, looked both formidable and intelligent. For perhaps twenty seconds he sat without stirring. Then he pulled the speakwrite toward him
and rapped out a message in the hybrid jargon of the Ministries:

"Items one comma five comma seven approved fullwise stop suggestion
contained item six doubleplus ridiculous verging crimethink cancel stop
unproceed constructionwise antegetting plusful estimates machinery
overheads stop end message."

He rose deliberately from his chair and came toward them across the
soundless carpet. A little of the official atmosphere seemed to have fallen
away from him with the Newspeak words, but his expression was grim-
mer than usual, as though he were not pleased at being disturbed. The
terror that Winston already felt was suddenly shot through by a streak of
ordinary embarrassment. It seemed to him quite possible that he had
simply made a stupid mistake. For what evidence had he in reality that
O'Brien was any kind of political conspirator? Nothing but a flash of the
eyes and a single equivocal remark; beyond that, only his own secret
imaginings, founded on a dream. He could not even fall back on the pretense that he had come to borrow the dictionary, because in that case
Julia's presence was impossible to explain. As O'Brien passed the telescreen a thought seemed to strike him. He stopped, turned aside, and
pressed a switch on the wall. There was a sharp snap. The voice had
stopped.

Julia uttered a tiny sound, a sort of squeak of surprise. Even in the
midst of his panic, Winston was too much taken aback to be able to hold
his tongue.

"You can turn it off!" he said.

"Yes," said O'Brien, "we can turn it off. We have that privilege."

He was opposite them now. His solid form towered over the pair of them, and the expression on his face was still indecipherable. He was waiting, somewhat sternly, for Winston to speak, but about what? Even now it was quite conceivable that he was simply a busy man wondering irritably why he had been interrupted. Nobody spoke. After the stopping of the telescreen the room seemed deadly silent. The seconds marched past, enormous. With difficulty Winston continued to keep his eyes fixed on O'Brien's. Then suddenly the grim face broke down into what might have been the beginnings of a smile. With his characteristic gesture O'Brien resettled his spectacles on his nose.

"Shall I say it, or will you?" he said.

"I will say it," said Winston promptly. "That thing is really turned off?"

"Yes, everything is turned off. We are alone."

"We have come here because—"

He paused, realizing for the first time the vagueness of his own motives. Since he did not in fact know what kind of help he expected from O'Brien, it was not easy to say why he had come here. He went on, conscious that what he was saying must sound both feeble and pretentious:

"We believe that there is some kind of conspiracy, some kind of secret organization working against the Party, and that you are involved in it. We want to join it and work for it. We are enemies of the Party. We disbelieve in the principles of Ingsoc. We are thought-criminals. We are also adulterers. I tell you this because we want to put ourselves at your mercy. If you want us to incriminate ourselves in any other way, we are ready."

He stopped and glanced over his shoulder, with the feeling that the door had opened. Sure enough, the little yellow-faced servant had come in without knocking. Winston saw that he was carrying a tray with a decanter and glasses.

"Martin is one of us," said O'Brien impassively. "Bring the drinks over here, Martin. Put them on the round table. Have we enough chairs? Then we may as well sit down and talk in comfort. Bring a chair for yourself, Martin. This is business. You can stop being a servant for the next ten minutes."

The little man sat down, quite at his ease, and yet still with a servant-like air, the air of a valet enjoying a privilege. Winston regarded him out of the corner of his eye. It struck him that the man's whole life was playing a part, and that he felt it to be dangerous to drop his assumed personality even for a moment. O'Brien took the decanter by the neck and filled up the glasses with a dark-red liquid. It aroused in Winston dim memories of something seen long ago on a wall or a hoarding—a vast bottle composed of electric lights which seemed to move up and down and pour its contents into a glass. Seen from the top the stuff looked almost black, but in the decanter it gleamed like a ruby. It had a sour-sweet smell. He saw Julia pick up her glass and sniff at it with frank curiosity.

"It is called wine," said O'Brien with a faint smile. "You will have read about it in books, no doubt. Not much of it gets to the Outer Party, I am afraid." His face grew solemn again, and he raised his glass: "I think it is fitting that we should begin by drinking a health. To our Leader: To Emmanuel Goldstein."

Winston took up his glass with a certain eagerness. Wine was a thing he had read and dreamed about. Like the glass paperweight or Mr. Charrington's half-remembered rhymes, it belonged to the vanished, romantic past, the olden time as he liked to call it in his secret thoughts. For some reason he had always thought of wine as having an intensely sweet taste, like that of blackberry jam, and an immediate intoxicating effect. Actually, when he came to swallow it, the stuff was distinctly disappointing. The truth was that after years of gin drinking he could barely taste it. He set down the empty glass.

"Then there is such a person as Goldstein?" he said.

"Yes, there is such a person, and he is alive. Where, I do not know."

"And the conspiracy—the organization? It is real? It is not simply an invention of the Thought Police?"

"No, it is real. The Brotherhood, we call it. You will never learn much more about the Brotherhood than that it exists and that you belong to it. I will come back to that presently." He looked at his wristwatch. "It is unwise even for members of the Inner Party to turn off the telescreen for more than half an hour. You ought not to have come here together, and you will have to leave separately. You, comrade—" he bowed his head to Julia— "will leave first. We have about twenty minutes at our disposal. You will understand that I must start by asking you certain questions. In general terms, what are you prepared to do?"

"Anything that we are capable of," said Winston.

O'Brien had turned himself a little in his chair so that he was facing Winston. He almost ignored Julia, seeming to take it for granted that Winston could speak for her. For a moment the lids flitted down over his eyes. He began asking his questions in a low, expressionless voice, as though this were a routine, a sort of catechism, most of whose answers were known to him already.

"You are prepared to give your lives?"

" Yes."

"You are prepared to commit murder?"

"Yes."

"To commit acts of sabotage which may cause the death of hundreds of innocent people?"

"Yes."

"To betray your country to foreign powers?"

"Yes."

"You are prepared to cheat, to forge, to blackmail, to corrupt the minds of children, to distribute habit-forming drugs, to encourage prostitution, to disseminate venereal diseases—to do anything which is likely to cause demoralization and weaken the power of the Party?"

"Yes."

"If, for example, it would somehow serve our interests to throw sulphuric acid in a child's face—are you prepared to do that?"

"Yes."

"You are prepared to lose your identity and live out the rest of your life as a waiter or a dock worker?"

"Yes."

"You are prepared to commit suicide, if and when we order you to do so?"

"Yes."

"You are prepared, the two of you, to separate and never see one another again?"

"No!" broke in Julia.

It appeared to Winston that a long time passed before he answered. For a moment he seemed even to have been deprived of the power of speech. His tongue worked soundlessly, forming the opening syllables first of one word, then of the other, over and over again. Until he had said it, he did not know which word he was going to say. "No," he said finally.

"You did well to tell me," said O'Brien. "It is necessary for us to know everything."

He turned himself toward Julia and added in a voice with somewhat more expression in it:

"Do you understand that even if he survives, it may be as a different person? We may be obliged to give him a new identity. His face, his movements, the shape of his hands, the color of his hair—even his voice would be different. And you yourself might have become a different person. Our surgeons can alter people beyond recognition. Sometimes it is necessary. Sometimes we even amputate a limb."

Winston could not help snatching another sidelong glance at Martin's Mongolian face. There were no scars that he could see. Julia had turned a shade paler, so that her freckles were showing, but she faced O'Brien boldly. She murmured something that seemed to be assent.

"Good. Then that is settled."

There was a silver box of cigarettes on the table. With a rather absent-minded air O'Brien pushed them toward the others, took one himself, then stood up and began to pace slowly to and fro, as though he could think better standing. They were very good cigarettes, very thick and well-packed, with an unfamiliar silkiness in the paper. O'Brien looked at his wristwatch again.

"You had better go back to your pantry, Martin," he said. "I shall switch on in a quarter of an hour. Take a good look at these comrades' faces before you go. You will be seeing them again. I may not."

Exactly as they had done at the front door, the little man's dark eyes flickered over their faces. There was not a trace of friendliness in his manner. He was memorizing their appearance, but he felt no interest in them, or appeared to feel none. It occurred to Winston that a synthetic face was perhaps incapable of changing its expression. Without speaking or giving any kind of salutation, Martin went out, closing the door silently behind him. O'Brien was strolling up and down, one hand in the pocket of his black overalls, the other holding his cigarette.

"You understand," he said, "that you will be fighting in the dark. You will always be in the dark. You will receive orders and you will obey them, without knowing why. Later I shall send you a book from which you will learn the true nature of the society we live in, and the strategy by which we shall destroy it. When you have read the book, you will be full members of the Brotherhood. But between the general aims that we are fighting for, and the immediate tasks of the moment, you will never know anything. I tell you that the Brotherhood exists but I cannot tell you whether it numbers a hundred members, or ten million. From your personal knowledge you will never be able to say that it numbers even as many as a dozen. You will have three or four contacts, who will be renewed from time to time as they disappear. As this was your first contact, it will be preserved. When you receive orders, they will come from me. If we find it necessary to communicate with you, it will be through Martin. When you are finally caught, you will confess. That is unavoidable. But you will have very little to confess, other than your own actions. You will not be able to betray more than a handful of unimportant people. Probably you will not even betray me. By that time I may be dead, or I shall have become a different person, with a different face."

He continued to move to and fro over the soft carpet. In spite of the bulkiness of his body there was a remarkable grace in his movements. It came out even in the gesture with which he thrust a hand into his pocket, or manipulated a cigarette. More even than of strength, he gave an impression of confidence and of an understanding tinged by irony. However much in earnest he might be, he had nothing of the single-mindedness that belongs to a fanatic. When he spoke of murder, suicide, venereal disease, amputated limbs, and altered faces, it was with a faint air of persiflage. "This is unavoidable," his voice seemed to say; "this is what we have got to do, unflinchingly. But this is not what we shall be doing when life is worth living again." A wave of admiration, almost of worship, flowed out from Winston toward O'Brien. For the moment he had forgotten the shadowy figure of Goldstein. When you looked at O'Brien's powerful shoulders and his blunt-featured face, so ugly and yet so civilized, it was impossible to believe that he could be defeated. There was no stratagem that he was not equal to, no danger that he could not foresee. Even Julia seemed to be impressed. She had let her cigarette go out and was listening intently. O'Brien went on:

"You will have heard rumors of the existence of the Brotherhood. No doubt you have formed your own picture of it. You have imagined, probably, a huge underworld of conspirators, meeting secretly in cellars, scribbling messages on walls, recognizing one another by code words or by special movements of the hand. Nothing of the kind exists. The members of the Brotherhood have no way of recognizing one another, and it is impossible for any one member to be aware of the identity of more than a very few others. Goldstein himself, if he fell into the hands of the Thought Police, could not give them a complete list of members, or any information that would lead them to a complete list. No such list exists. The Brotherhood cannot be wiped out because it is not an organization in the ordinary sense. Nothing holds it together except an idea which is indestructible. You will never have anything to sustain you except the idea. You will get no comradeship and no encouragement. When finally you are caught, you will get no help. We never help our members. At most, when it is absolutely necessary that someone should be silenced, we are occasionally able to smuggle a razor blade into a prisoner's cell. You will have to get used to living without results and without hope. You will work for a while, you will be caught, you will confess, and then you will die. Those are the only results that you will ever see. There is no possibility that any perceptible change will happen within our own lifetime. We are the dead. Our only true life is in the future. We shall take part in it as handfuls of dust and splinters of bone. But how far away that future may be, there is no knowing. It might be a thousand years. At present nothing is possible except to extend the area of sanity little by little. We cannot act collectively. We can only spread our knowledge outwards from individual to individual, generation after generation. In the face of the Thought Police, there is no other way."

He halted and looked for the third time at his wristwatch.

"It is almost time for you to leave, comrade," he said to Julia. "Wait. The decanter is still half full."

He filled the glasses and raised his own glass by the stem.

"What shall it be this time?" he said, still with the same faint suggestion of irony. "To the confusion of the Thought Police? To the death of Big Brother? To humanity? To the future?"

"To the past," said Winston.

"The past is more important," agreed O'Brien gravely. They emptied their glasses, and a moment later Julia stood up to go. O'Brien took a small box from the top of a cabinet and handed her a flat white tablet which he told her to place on her tongue. It was important, he said, not to go out smelling of wine: the lift attendants were very observant. As soon as the door had shut behind her he appeared to forget her existence. He took another pace or two up and down, then stopped.

"There are details to be settled," he said. "I assume that you have a hiding place of some kind?"

Winston explained about the room over Mr. Charrington's shop.

"That will do for the moment. Later we will arrange something else for you. It is important to change one's hiding place frequently. Meanwhile I shall send you a copy of *the book*—" even O'Brien, Winston noticed, seemed to pronounce the words as though they were in italics— "Goldstein's book, you understand, as soon as possible. It may be some days before I can get hold of one. There are not many in existence, as you can imagine. The Thought Police hunts them down and destroys them almost as fast as we can produce them. It makes very little difference. The book is indestructible. If the last copy were gone, we could reproduce it almost word for word. Do you carry a brief case to work with you?" he added.

"As a rule, yes."

"What is it like?"

"Black, very shabby. With two straps."

"Black, two straps, very shabby—good. One day in the fairly near future—I cannot give a date—one of the messages among your morning's work will contain a misprinted word, and you will have to ask for a repeat. On the following day you will go to work without your brief case. At some time during the day, in the street, a man will touch you on the arm and say, 'I think you have dropped your brief case.' The one he gives you will contain a copy of Goldstein's book. You will return it within fourteen days."

They were silent for a moment.

"There are a couple of minutes before you need go," said O'Brien. "We shall meet again—if we do meet again—"

Winston looked up at him. "In the place where there is no darkness?" he said hesitantly.

O'Brien nodded without appearance of surprise. "In the place where there is no darkness," he said, as though he had recognized the allusion. "And in the meantime, is there anything that you wish to say before you leave? Any message? Any question?"

Winston thought. There did not seem to be any further question that he wanted to ask; still less did he feel any impulse to utter high-sounding generalities. Instead of anything directly connected with O'Brien or the Brotherhood, there came into his mind a sort of composite picture of the dark bedroom where his mother had spent her last days, and the little room over Mr. Charrington's shop, and the glass paperweight, and the steel engraving in its rosewood frame. Almost at random he said:

"Did you ever happen to hear an old rhyme that begins *Oranges and lemons, say the bells of St. Clement's?*"

Again O'Brien nodded. With a sort of grave courtesy he completed the stanza:

"Oranges and lemons, say the bells of St. Clement's,
You owe me three farthings, say the bells of St. Martin's,
When will you pay me? say the bells of Old Bailey,
When I grow rich, say the bells of Shoreditch."

"You knew the last line!" said Winston.

"Yes, I knew the last line. And now, I am afraid, it is time for you to go. But wait. You had better let me give you one of these tablets."

As Winston stood up O'Brien held out a hand. His powerful grip crushed the bones of Winston's palm. At the door Winston looked back, but O'Brien seemed already to be in process of putting him out of mind. He was waiting with his hand on the switch that controlled the tele-screen. Beyond him Winston could see the writing table with its green-shaded lamp and the speakwrite and the wire baskets deep-laden with papers. The incident was closed. Within thirty seconds, it occurred to him, O'Brien would be back at his interrupted and important work on behalf of the Party.

IX

Winston was gelatinous with fatigue. Gelatinous was the right word. It had come into his head spontaneously. His body seemed to have not only the weakness of a jelly, but its translucency. He felt that if he held up his hand he would be able to see the light through it. All the blood and lymph had been drained out of him by an enormous debauch of work, leaving only a frail structure of nerves, bones, and skin. All sensations seemed to be magnified. His overalls fretted his shoulders, the pavement tickled his feet, even the opening and closing of a hand was an effort that made his joints creak.

He had worked more than ninety hours in five days. So had everyone else in the Ministry. Now it was all over, and he had literally nothing to do, no Party work of any description, until tomorrow morning. He could spend six hours in the hiding place and another nine in his own bed. Slowly, in mild afternoon sunshine, he walked up a dingy street in the direction of Mr. Charrington's shop, keeping one eye open for the patrols, but irrationally convinced that this afternoon there was no danger of anyone interfering with him. The heavy brief case that he was carrying bumped against his knees at each step, sending a tingling sensation up and down the skin of his leg. Inside it was *the book*, which he had now had in his possession for six days and had not yet opened, nor even looked at.

On the sixth day of Hate Week, after the processions, the speeches, the shouting, the singing, the banners, the posters, the films, the waxworks, the rolling of drums and squealing of trumpets, the tramp of marching feet, the grinding of the caterpillars of tanks, the roar of massed planes, the booming of guns—after six days of this, when the great orgasm was quivering to its climax and the general hatred of Eurasia had boiled up into such delirium that if the crowd could have got their hands on the two thousand Eurasian war criminals who were to be publicly hanged on the last day of the proceedings, they would unquestionably have torn them to pieces—at just this moment it had been announced that Oceania was not after all at war with Eurasia. Oceania was at war with Eastasia. Eurasia was an ally.

There was, of course, no admission that any change had taken place. Merely it became known, with extreme suddenness and everywhere at once, that Eastasia and not Eurasia was the enemy. Winston was taking part in a demonstration in one of the central London squares at the moment when it happened. It was night, and the white faces and the scarlet banners were luridly floodlit. The square was packed with several thousand people, including a block of about a thousand schoolchildren in the uniform of the Spies. On a scarlet-draped platform an orator of the Inner Party, a small lean man with disproportionately long arms and a large, bald skull over which a few lank locks straggled, was haranguing the crowd. A little Rumpelstiltskin figure, contorted with hatred, he gripped the neck of the microphone with one hand while the other, enormous at the end of a bony arm, clawed the air menacingly above his head. His voice, made metallic by the amplifiers, boomed forth an endless catalogue of atrocities, massacres, deportations, lootings, rapings, torture of prisoners, bombing of civilians, lying propaganda, unjust aggressions, broken treaties. It was almost impossible to listen to him without being first convinced and then maddened. At every few moments the fury of the crowd boiled over and the voice of the speaker was drowned by a wild beastlike roaring that rose uncontrollably from thousands of throats. The most savage yells of all came from the schoolchildren. The speech had been proceeding for perhaps twenty minutes when a messenger hurried onto the platform and a scrap of paper was slipped into the speaker's hand. He unrolled and read it without pausing in his speech. Nothing altered in his voice or manner, or in the content of what he was saying, but suddenly the names were different. Without words said, a wave of understanding rippled through the crowd. Oceania was at war with Eastasia! The next moment there was a tremendous commotion. The banners and posters with which the square was decorated were all wrong! Quite half of them had the wrong faces on them. It was sabotage! The agents of Goldstein had been at work! There was a riotous interlude while posters were ripped from the walls, banners torn to shreds and trampled underfoot. The Spies performed prodigies of activity in clambering over the rooftops and cutting the streamers that fluttered from the chimneys. But within two or three minutes it was all over. The orator, still gripping the neck of the microphone, his shoulders hunched forward, his free hand clawing at the air, had gone straight on with his speech. One minute more, and the feral roars of rage were again bursting from the crowd. The Hate continued exactly as before, except that the target had been changed.

The thing that impressed Winston in looking back was that the speaker had switched from one line to the other actually in mid-sentence, not only without a pause, but without even breaking the syntax. But at the moment he had other things to preoccupy him. It was during the moment of disorder while the posters were being torn down that a man whose face he did not see had tapped him on the shoulder and said, "Excuse me, I think you've dropped your brief case." He took the brief case abstractedly, without speaking. He knew that it would be days before he had an opportunity to look inside it. The instant that the demonstration was over he went straight to the Ministry of Truth, though the time was now nearly twenty-three hours. The entire staff of the Ministry had done likewise. The orders already issuing from the telescreens, recalling them to their posts, were hardly necessary.

Oceania was at war with Eastasia: Oceania had always been at war with Eastasia. A large part of the political literature of five years was now completely obsolete. Reports and records of all kinds, newspapers, books, pamphlets, films, sound tracks, photographs—all had to be rectified at lightning speed. Although no directive was ever issued, it was known that the chiefs of the Department intended that within one week no reference to the war with Eurasia, or the alliance with Eastasia, should remain in existence anywhere. The work was overwhelming, all the more so because the processes that it involved could not be called by their true names. Everyone in the Records Department worked eighteen hours in the twenty-four, with two three-hour snatches of sleep. Mattresses were brought up from the cellars and pitched all over the corridors; meals consisted of sandwiches and Victory Coffee wheeled round on trolleys by attendants from the canteen. Each time that Winston broke off for one of his spells of sleep he tried to leave his desk clear of work, and each time that he crawled back, sticky-eyed and aching, it was to find that another shower of paper cylinders had covered the desk like a snow-drift, half burying the speakwrite and overflowing onto the floor, so that the first job was always to stack them into a neat-enough pile to give him room to work. What was worst of all was that the work was by no means purely mechanical. Often it was enough merely to substitute one name for another, but any detailed report of events demanded care and imagination. Even the geographical knowledge that one needed in transferring the war from one part of the world to another was considerable.

By the third day his eyes ached unbearably and his spectacles needed wiping every few minutes. It was like struggling with some crushing physical task, something which one had the right to refuse and which one was nevertheless neurotically anxious to accomplish. In so far as he had time to remember it, he was not troubled by the fact that every word he murmured into the speakwrite, every stroke of his ink pencil, was a deliberate lie. He was as anxious as anyone else in the Department that the forgery should be perfect. On the morning of the sixth day the dribble of cylinders slowed down. For as much as half an hour nothing came out of the tube; then one more cylinder, then nothing. Everywhere at about the same time the work was easing off. A deep and as it were secret sigh went through the Department. A mighty deed, which could never be mentioned, had been achieved. It was now impossible for any human being to prove by documentary evidence that the war with Eurasia had ever happened. At twelve hundred it was unexpectedly announced that all workers in the Ministry were free till tomorrow morning. Winston, still carrying the brief case containing *the book,* which had remained between his feet while he worked and under his body while he slept, went home, shaved himself, and almost fell asleep in his bath, although the water was barely more than tepid.

With a sort of voluptuous creaking in his joints he climbed the stair above Mr. Charrington's shop. He was tired, but not sleepy any longer. He opened the window, lit the dirty little oilstove, and put on a pan of water for coffee. Julia would arrive presently; meanwhile there was *the book.* He sat down in the sluttish armchair and undid the straps of the brief case.

A heavy black volume, amateurishly bound, with no name or title on the cover. The print also looked slightly irregular. The pages were worn at the edges, and fell apart easily, as though the book had passed through many hands. The inscription on the title page ran:

THE THEORY AND PRACTICE
OF OLIGARCHICAL COLLECTIVISM
by
EMMANUEL GOLDSTEIN

[Winston began reading.]

Chapter 1.

IGNORANCE IS STRENGTH.

Throughout recorded time, and probably since the end of the Neolithic Age, there have been three kinds of people in the world, the High, the Middle, and the Low. They have been subdivided in many ways, they have borne countless different names, and their relative numbers, as well as their attitude toward one another, have varied from age to age; but the essential structure of society has never altered. Even after enormous upheavals and seemingly irrevocable changes, the same pattern has always reasserted itself, just as a gyroscope will always return to equilibrium, however far it is pushed one way or the other.

The aims of these three groups are entirely irreconcilable. . . .

Winston stopped reading, chiefly in order to appreciate the fact that he *was* reading, in comfort and safety. He was alone: no telescreen, no ear at the keyhole, no nervous impulse to glance over his shoulder or cover the page with his hand. The sweet summer air played against his cheek. From somewhere far away there floated the faint shouts of children; in the room itself there was no sound except the insect voice of the clock. He settled deeper into the armchair and put his feet up on the fender. It was bliss, it was eternity. Suddenly, as one sometimes does with a book of which one knows that one will ultimately read and reread every word, he opened it at a different place and found himself at the third chapter. He went on reading:

Chapter 3.

WAR IS PEACE.

The splitting-up of the world into three great superstates was an event which could be and indeed was foreseen before the middle of the twentieth century. With the absorption of Europe by Russia and of the British Empire by the United States, two of the three existing powers, Eurasia and Oceania, were already effectively in being. The third, Eastasia, only emerged as a distinct unit after another decade of confused fighting. The frontiers between the three superstates are in some places arbitrary, and in others they fluctuate according to the fortunes of war, but in general they follow geographical lines. Eurasia comprises the whole of the northern part of the European and Asiatic land-mass, from Portugal to the Bering Strait. Oceania comprises the Americas, the Atlantic islands including the British Isles, Australasia, and the southern portion of Africa. Eastasia, smaller than the others and with a less definite western frontier, comprises China and the countries to the south of it, the Japanese islands and a large but fluctuating portion of Manchuria, Mongolia, and Tibet.

In one combination or another, these three superstates are permanently at war, and have been so for the past twenty-five years. War, however, is no longer the desperate, annihilating struggle that it was in the early decades of the twentieth century. It is a warfare of limited aims between combatants who are unable to destroy one another, have no material cause for fighting, and are not divided by any genuine ideological difference. This is not to say that either the conduct of war, or the prevailing attitude toward it, has become less bloodthirsty or more chivalrous. On the contrary, war hysteria is continuous and universal in all countries, and such acts as raping, looting, the slaughter of children, the reduction of whole populations to slavery, and reprisals against prisoners which extend even to boiling and burying alive, are looked upon as normal, and, when they are committed by one's own side and not by the enemy, meritorious. But in a physical sense war involves very small numbers of people, mostly highly trained specialists, and causes comparatively few casualties. The fighting, when there is any, takes place on the vague frontiers whose whereabouts the average man can only guess at, or round the Floating Fortresses which guard strategic spots on the sea lanes. In the centers of civilization war means no more than a continuous shortage of consumption goods, and the occasional crash of a rocket bomb which may cause a few scores of deaths. War has in fact changed its character. More exactly, the reasons for which war is waged have changed in their order of importance. Motives which were already present to some small extent in the great wars of the early twentieth century have now become dominant and are consciously recognized and acted upon.

To understand the nature of the present war—for in spite of the regrouping which occurs every few years, it is always the same war—one must realize in the first place that it is impossible for it to be decisive. None of the three superstates could be definitely conquered even by the other two in combination. They are too evenly matched, and their natural defenses are too formidable. Eurasia is protected by its vast land spaces, Oceania by the width of the Atlantic and the Pacific, Eastasia by the fecundity and industriousness of its inhabitants. Secondly, there is no longer, in a material sense, anything to fight about. With the establishment of self-contained economies, in which production and consumption are geared to one another, the scramble for markets which was a main cause of previous wars has come to an end, while the competition for raw materials is no longer a matter of life and death. In any case, each of the three superstates is so vast that it can obtain almost all the materials that it needs within its own boundaries. In so far as the war has a direct economic purpose, it is a war for labor power. Between the frontiers of the superstates, and not permanently in the possession of any of them, there lies a rough quadrilateral with its corners at Tangier, Brazzaville, Darwin, and Hong Kong, containing within it about a fifth of the population of the earth. It is for the possession of these thickly populated regions, and of the northern ice cap, that the three powers are constantly struggling. In practice no one power ever controls the whole of the disputed area. Portions of it are constantly changing hands, and it is the chance of seizing this or that fragment by a sudden stroke of treachery that dictates the endless changes of alignment.

All of the disputed territories contain valuable minerals, and some of them yield important vegetable products such as rubber which in colder climates it is necessary to synthesize by comparatively expensive methods. But above all they contain a bottomless reserve of cheap labor. Whichever power controls equatorial Africa, or the countries of the Middle East, or Southern India, or the Indonesian Archipelago, disposes also of the bodies of scores or hundreds of millions of ill-paid and hardworking coolies. The inhabitants of these areas, reduced more or less openly to the status of slaves, pass continually from conqueror to conqueror, and are expended like so much coal or oil in the race to turn out more armaments, to capture more territory, to control more labor power, to turn out more armaments, to capture more territory, and so on indefinitely. It should be noted that the fighting never really moves beyond the edges of the disputed areas. The frontiers of Eurasia flow back and forth between the basin of the Congo and the northern shore of the Mediterranean; the islands of the Indian Ocean and the Pacific are constantly being captured and recaptured by Oceania or by Eastasia; in Mongolia the dividing line between Eurasia and Eastasia is never stable; round the Pole all three powers lay claim to enormous territories which in fact are largely uninhabited and unexplored; but the balance of power always remains roughly even, and the territory which forms the heartland of each superstate always remains inviolate. Moreover, the labor of the exploited peoples round the Equator is not really necessary to the world's economy. They add nothing to the wealth of the world, since whatever they produce is used for purposes of war, and the object of waging a war is always to be in a better position in which to wage another war. By their labor the slave populations allow the tempo of continuous warfare to be speeded up. But if they did not exist, the structure of world society, and the process by which it maintains itself, would not be essentially different.

The primary aim of modern warfare (in accordance with the principles of *doublethink*, this aim is simultaneously recognized and not recognized by the directing brains of the Inner Party) is to use up the products of the machine without raising the general standard of living. Ever since the end of the nineteenth century, the problem of what to do with the surplus of consumption goods has been latent in industrial society. At present, when few human beings even have enough to eat, this problem is obviously not urgent, and it might not have become so, even if no artificial processes of destruction had been at work. The world of today is a bare, hungry, dilapidated place compared with the world that existed before 1914, and still more so if compared with the imaginary future to which the people of that period looked forward. In the early twentieth century, the vision of a future society unbelievably rich, leisured, orderly and efficient—a glittering antiseptic world of glass and steel and snow-white concrete—was part of the consciousness of nearly every literate person. Science and technology were developing at a prodigious speed, and it seemed natural to assume that they would go on developing. This failed to happen, partly because of the impoverishment caused by a long series of wars and revolutions, partly because scientific and technical progress depended on the empirical habit of thought, which could not survive in a strictly regimented society. As a whole the world is more primitive today than it was fifty years ago. Certain backward areas have advanced, and various devices, always in some way connected with warfare and police espionage, have been developed, but experiment and invention have largely stopped, and the ravages of the atomic war of the Nineteen-fifties have never been fully repaired. Nevertheless the dangers inherent in the machine are still there. From the moment when the machine first made its appearance it was clear to all thinking people that the need for human drudgery, and therefore to a great extent for human inequality, had disappeared. If the machine were used deliberately for that end, hunger, overwork, dirt, illiteracy, and disease could be eliminated within a few generations. And in fact, without being used for any such purpose, but by a sort of automatic process—by producing wealth which it was sometimes impossible not to distribute—the machine did raise the living standards of the average human being very greatly over a period of about fifty years at the end of the nineteenth and the beginning of the twentieth centuries.

But it was also clear that an all-round increase in wealth threatened the destruction—indeed, in some sense was the destruction—of a hierarchical society. In a world in which everyone worked short hours, had enough to eat, lived in a house with a bathroom and a refrigerator, and possessed a motorcar or even an airplane, the most obvious and perhaps the most important form of inequality would already have disappeared. If it once became general, wealth would confer no distinction. It was possible, no doubt, to imagine a society in which *wealth*, in the sense of personal possessions and luxuries, should be evenly distributed, while *power* remained in the hands of a small privileged caste. But in practice such a society could not long remain stable. For if leisure and security were enjoyed by all alike, the great mass of human beings who are normally stupefied by poverty would become literate and would learn to think for themselves; and when once they had done this, they would sooner or later realize that the privileged minority had no function, and they would sweep it away. In the long run, a hierarchical society was only possible on a basis of poverty and ignorance. To return to the agricultural past, as some thinkers about the beginning of the twentieth century dreamed of doing, was not a practicable solution. It conflicted with the tendency toward mechanization which had become quasi-instinctive throughout almost the whole world, and moreover, any country which remained industrially backward was helpless in a military sense and was bound to be dominated, directly or indirectly, by its more advanced rivals.

Nor was it a satisfactory solution to keep the masses in poverty by restricting the output of goods. This happened to a great extent during the final phase of capitalism, roughly between 1920 and 1940. The economy of many countries was allowed to stagnate, land went out of cultivation, capital equipment was not added to, great blocks of the population were prevented from working and kept half alive by State charity. But this, too, entailed military weakness, and since the privations it inflicted were obviously unnecessary, it made opposition inevitable. The problem was how to keep the wheels of industry turning without increasing the real wealth of the world. Goods must be produced, but they must not be distributed. And in practice the only way of achieving this was by continuous warfare.

The essential act of war is destruction, not necessarily of human lives, but of the products of human labor. War is a way of shattering to pieces, or pouring into the stratosphere, or sinking in the depths of the sea, materials which might otherwise be used to make the masses too comfortable, and hence, in the long run, too intelligent. Even when weapons of war are not actually destroyed, their manufacture is still a convenient way of expending labor power without producing anything that can be consumed. A Floating Fortress, for example, has locked up in it the labor that would build several hundred cargo ships. Ultimately it is scrapped as obsolete, never having brought any material benefit to anybody, and with further enormous labors another Floating Fortress is built. In principle the war effort is always so planned as to eat up any surplus that might exist after meeting the bare needs of the population. In practice the needs of the population are always underestimated, with the result that there is a chronic shortage of half the necessities of life; but this is looked on as an advantage. It is deliberate policy to keep even the favored groups somewhere near the brink of hardship, because a general state of scarcity increases the importance of small privileges and thus magnifies the distinction between one group and another. By the standards of the early twentieth century, even a member of the Inner Party lives an austere, laborious kind of life. Nevertheless, the few luxuries that he does enjoy—his large well-appointed flat, the better texture of his clothes, the better quality of his food and drink and tobacco, his two or three servants, his private motorcar or helicopter—set him in a different world from a member of the Outer Party, and the members of the Outer Party have a similar advantage in comparison with the submerged masses whom we call "the proles." The social atmosphere is that of a besieged city, where the possession of a lump of horseflesh makes the difference between wealth and poverty. And at the same time the consciousness of being at war, and therefore in danger, makes the handing-over of all power to a small caste seem the natural, unavoidable condition of survival.

War, it will be seen, not only accomplishes the necessary destruction, but accomplishes it in a psychologically acceptable way. In principle it would be quite simple to waste the surplus labor of the world by building temples and pyramids, by digging holes and filling them up again, or even by producing vast quantities of goods and then setting fire to them. But this would provide only the economic and not the emotional basis for a hierarchical society. What is concerned here is not the morale of the masses, whose attitude is unimportant so long as they are kept steadily at work, but the morale of the Party itself. Even the humblest Party member is expected to be competent, industrious, and even intelligent within narrow limits, but it is also necessary that he should be a credulous and ignorant fanatic whose prevailing moods are fear, hatred, adulation, and orgiastic triumph. In other words it is necessary that he should have the mentality appropriate to a state of war. It does not matter whether the war is actually happening, and, since no decisive victory is possible, it does not matter whether the war is going well or badly. All that is needed is that a state of war should exist. The splitting of the intelligence which the Party requires of its members, and which is more easily achieved in an atmosphere of war, is now almost universal, but the higher up the ranks one goes, the more marked it becomes. It is precisely in the Inner Party that war hysteria and hatred of the enemy are strongest. In his capacity as an administrator, it is often necessary for a member of the Inner Party to know that this or that item of war news is untruthful, and he may often be aware that the entire war is spurious and is either not happening or is being waged for purposes quite other than the declared ones; but such knowledge is easily neutralized by the technique of *doublethink*. Meanwhile no Inner Party member wavers for an instant in his mystical belief that the war *is* real, and that it is bound to end victoriously, with Oceania the undisputed master of the entire world.

All members of the Inner Party believe in this coming conquest as an article of faith. It is to be achieved either by gradually acquiring more and more territory and so building up an overwhelming preponderance of power, or by the discovery of some new and unanswerable weapon. The search for new weapons continues unceasingly, and is one of the very few remaining activities in which the inventive or speculative type of mind can find any outlet. In Oceania at the present day, Science, in the old sense, has almost ceased to exist. In Newspeak there is no word for "Science." The empirical method of thought, on which all the scientific achievements of the past were founded, is opposed to the most fundamental principles of Ingsoc. And even technological progress only happens when its products can in some way be used for the diminution of human liberty. In all the useful arts the world is either standing still or going backwards. The fields are cultivated with horse plows while books are written by machinery. But in matters of vital importance—meaning, in effect, war and police espionage—the empirical approach is still encouraged, or at least tolerated. The two aims of the Party are to conquer the whole surface of the earth and to extinguish once and for all the possibility of independent thought. There are therefore two great problems which the Party is concerned to solve. One is how to discover, against his will, what another human being is thinking, and the other is how to kill several hundred million people in a few seconds without giving warning beforehand. In so far as scientific research still continues, this is its subject matter. The scientist of today is either a mixture of psychologist and inquisitor, studying with extraordinary minuteness the meaning of facial expressions, gestures, and tones of voice, and testing the truth-producing effects of drugs, shock therapy, hypnosis, and physical torture; or he is a chemist, physicist, or biologist concerned only with such branches of his special subject as are relevant to the taking of life. In the vast laboratories of the Ministry of Peace, and in the experimental stations hidden in the Brazilian forests, or in the Australian desert, or on lost islands of the Antarctic, the teams of experts are indefatigably at work. Some are concerned simply with planning the logistics of future wars; others devise larger and larger rocket bombs, more and more powerful explosives, and more and more impenetrable armor-plating; others search for new and deadlier gases, or for soluble poisons capable of being produced in such quantities as to destroy the vegetation of whole continents, or for breeds of disease germs immunized against all possible antibodies; others strive to produce a vehicle that shall bore its way under the soil like a submarine under the water, or an airplane as independent of its base as a sailing ship; others explore even remoter possibilities such as focusing the sun's rays through lenses suspended thousands of kilometers away in space, or producing artificial earthquakes and tidal waves by tapping the heat at the earth's center.

But none of these projects ever comes anywhere near realization, and none of the three superstates ever gains a significant lead on the others. What is more remarkable is that all three powers already possess, in the atomic bomb, a weapon far more powerful than any that their present researches are likely to discover. Although the Party, according to its habit, claims the invention for itself, atomic bombs first appeared as early as the Nineteen-forties, and were first used on a large scale about ten years later. At that time some hundreds of bombs were dropped on industrial centers, chiefly in European Russia, Western Europe, and North America. The effect was to convince the ruling groups of all countries that a few more atomic bombs would mean the end of organized society, and hence of their own power. Thereafter, although no formal agreement was ever made or hinted at, no more bombs were dropped. All three powers merely continue to produce atomic bombs and store them up against the decisive opportunity which they all believe will come sooner or later. And meanwhile the art of war has remained almost stationary for thirty or forty years. Helicopters are more used than they were formerly, bombing planes have been largely superseded by self-propelled projectiles, and the fragile movable battleship has given way to the almost unsinkable Floating Fortress; but otherwise there has been little development. The tank, the submarine, the torpedo, the machine gun, even the rifle and the hand grenade are still in use. And in spite of the endless slaughters reported in the press and on the telescreens, the desperate battles of earlier wars, in which hundreds of thousands or even millions of men were often killed in a few weeks, have never been repeated.

None of the three superstates ever attempts any maneuver which involves the risk of serious defeat. When any large operation is undertaken, it is usually a surprise attack against an ally. The strategy that all three powers are following, or pretend to themselves that they are following, is the same. The plan is, by a combination of fighting, bargaining, and well-timed strokes of treachery, to acquire a ring of bases completely encircling one or other of the rival states, and then to sign a pact of friendship with that rival and remain on peaceful terms for so many years as to lull suspicion to sleep. During this time rockets loaded with atomic bombs can be assembled at all the strategic spots; finally they will all be fired simultaneously, with effects so devastating as to make retaliation impossible. It will then be time to sign a pact of friendship with the remaining world power, in preparation for another attack. This scheme, it is hardly necessary to say, is a mere daydream, impossible of realization. Moreover, no fighting ever occurs except in the disputed areas round the Equator and the Pole; no invasion of enemy territory is ever undertaken. This explains the fact that in some places the frontiers between the superstates are arbitrary. Eurasia, for example, could easily conquer the British Isles, which are geographically part of Europe, or on the other hand it would be possible for Oceania to push its frontiers to the Rhine or even to the Vistula. But this would violate the principle, followed on all sides though never formulated, of cultural integrity. If Oceania were to conquer the areas that used once to be known as France and Germany, it would be necessary either to exterminate the inhabitants, a task of great physical difficulty, or to assimilate a population of about a hundred million people, who, so far as technical development goes, are roughly on the Oceanic level. The problem is the same for all three superstates. It is absolutely necessary to their structure that there should be no contact with foreigners except, to a limited extent, with war prisoners and colored slaves. Even the official ally of the moment is always regarded with the darkest suspicion. War prisoners apart, the average citizen of Oceania never sets eyes on a citizen of either Eurasia or Eastasia, and he is forbidden the knowledge of foreign languages. If he were allowed contact with foreigners he would discover that they are creatures similar to himself and that most of what he has been told about them is lies. The sealed world in which he lives would be broken, and the fear, hatred, and self-righteousness on which his morale depends might evaporate. It is therefore realized on all sides that however often Persia, or Egypt, or Java, or Ceylon may change hands, the main frontiers must never be crossed by anything except bombs.

Under this lies a fact never mentioned aloud, but tacitly understood and acted upon: namely, that the conditions of life in all three superstates are very much the same. In Oceania the prevailing philosophy is called Ingsoc, in Eurasia it is called Neo-Bolshevism, and in Eastasia it is called by a Chinese name usually translated as Death-worship, but perhaps better rendered as Obliteration of the Self. The citizen of Oceania is not allowed to know anything of the tenets of the other two philosophies, but he is taught to execrate them as barbarous outrages upon morality and common sense. Actually the three philosophies are barely distinguishable, and the social systems which they support are not distinguishable at all. Everywhere there is the same pyramidal structure, the same worship of a semi-divine leader, the same economy existing by and for continuous warfare. It follows that the three superstates not only cannot conquer one another, but would gain no advantage by doing so. On the contrary, so long as they remain in conflict they prop one another up, like three sheaves of corn. And, as usual, the ruling groups of all three powers are simultaneously aware and unaware of what they are doing. Their lives are dedicated to world conquest, but they also know that it is necessary that the war should continue everlastingly and without victory. Meanwhile the fact that there *is* no danger of conquest makes possible the denial of reality which is the special feature of Ingsoc and its rival systems of thought. Here it is necessary to repeat what has been said earlier, that by becoming continuous war has fundamentally changed its character.

In past ages, a war, almost by definition, was something that sooner or later came to an end, usually in unmistakable victory or defeat. In the past, also, war was one of the main instruments by which human societies were kept in touch with physical reality. All rulers in all ages have tried to impose a false view of the world upon their followers, but they could not afford to encourage any illusion that tended to impair military efficiency. So long as defeat meant the loss of independence, or some other result generally held to be undesirable, the precautions against defeat had to be serious. Physical facts could not be ignored. In philosophy, or religion, or ethics, or politics, two and two might make five, but when one was designing a gun or an airplane they had to make four. Inefficient nations were always conquered sooner or later, and the struggle for efficiency was inimical to illusions. Moreover, to be efficient it was necessary to be able to learn from the past, which meant having a fairly accurate idea of what had happened in the past. Newspapers and history books were, of course, always colored and biased, but falsification of the kind that is practiced today would have been impossible. War was a sure safeguard of sanity, and so far as the ruling classes were concerned it was probably the most important of all safeguards. While wars could be won or lost, no ruling class could be completely irresponsible.

But when war becomes literally continuous, it also ceases to be dangerous. When war is continuous there is no such thing as military necessity. Technical progress can cease and the most palpable facts can be denied or disregarded. As we have seen, researches that could be called scientific are still carried out for the purposes of war, but they are essentially a kind of daydreaming, and their failure to show results is not important. Efficiency, even military efficiency, is no longer needed. Nothing is efficient in Oceania except the Thought Police. Since each of the three super-states is unconquerable, each is in effect a separate universe within which almost any perversion of thought can be safely practiced. Reality only exerts its pressure through the needs of everyday life—the need to eat and drink, to get shelter and clothing, to avoid swallowing poison or stepping out of top-story windows, and the like. Between life and death, and between physical pleasure and physical pain, there is still a distinction, but that is all. Cut off from contact with the outer world, and with the past, the citizen of Oceania is like a man in interstellar space, who has no way of knowing which direction is up and which is down. The rulers of such a state are absolute, as the Pharaohs or the Caesars could not be. They are obliged to prevent their followers from starving to death in numbers large enough to be inconvenient, and they are obliged to remain at the same low level of military technique as their rivals; but once that minimum is achieved, they can twist reality into whatever shape they choose.

The war, therefore, if we judge it by the standards of previous wars, is merely an imposture. It is like the battles between certain ruminant animals whose horns are set at such an angle that they are incapable of hurting one another. But though it is unreal it is not meaningless. It eats up the surplus of consumable goods, and it helps to preserve the special mental atmosphere that a hierarchical society needs. War, it will be seen, is now a purely internal affair. In the past, the ruling groups of all countries, although they might recognize their common interest and therefore limit the destructiveness of war, did fight against one another, and the victor always plundered the vanquished. In our own day they are not fighting against one another at all. The war is waged by each ruling group against its own subjects, and the object of the war is not to make or prevent conquests of territory, but to keep the structure of society intact. The very word "war," therefore, has become misleading. It would probably be accurate to say that by becoming continuous war has ceased to exist. The peculiar pressure that it exerted on human beings between the Neolithic Age and the early twentieth century has disappeared and been replaced by something quite different. The effect would be much the same if the three superstates, instead of fighting one another, should agree to live in perpetual peace, each inviolate within its own boundaries. For in that case each would still be a self-contained universe, freed forever from the sobering influence of external danger. A peace that was truly permanent would be the same as a permanent war. This—although the vast majority of Party members understand it only in a shallower sense—is the inner meaning of the Party slogan: WAR IS PEACE.

Winston stopped reading for a moment. Somewhere in remote distance a rocket bomb thundered. The blissful feeling of being alone with the forbidden book, in a room with no telescreen, had not worn off. Solitude and safety were physical sensations, mixed up somehow with the tiredness of his body, the softness of the chair, the touch of the faint breeze from the window that played upon his cheek. The book fascinated him, or more exactly it reassured him. In a sense it told him nothing that was new, but that was part of the attraction. It said what he would have said, if it had been possible for him to set his scattered thoughts in order. It was the product of a mind similar to his own, but enormously more powerful, more systematic, less fear-ridden. The best books, he perceived, are those that tell you what you know already. He had just turned back to Chapter 1 when he heard Julia's footstep on the stair and started out of his chair to meet her. She dumped her brown tool bag on the floor and flung herself into his arms. It was more than a week since they had seen one another.

"I've got *the book*," he said as they disentangled themselves.

"Oh, you've got it? Good," she said without much interest, and almost immediately knelt down beside the oilstove to make the coffee.

They did not return to the subject until they had been in bed for half an hour. The evening was just cool enough to make it worth while to pull up the counterpane. From below came the familiar sound of singing and the scrape of boots on the flagstones. The brawny red-armed woman whom Winston had seen there on his first visit was almost a fixture in the yard. There seemed to be no hour of daylight when she was not marching to and fro between the washtub and the line, alternately gagging herself with clothes pegs and breaking forth into lusty song. Julia had settled down on her side and seemed to be already on the point of falling asleep.

He reached out for the book, which was lying on the floor, and sat up against the bedhead.

"We must read it," he said. "You too. All members of the Brotherhood have to read it."

"You read it," she said with her eyes shut. "Read it aloud. That's the best way. Then you can explain it to me as you go."

The clock's hands said six, meaning eighteen. They had three or four hours ahead of them. He propped the book against his knees and began reading:

Chapter 1.

IGNORANCE IS STRENGTH.

Throughout recorded time, and probably since the end of the Neolithic Age, there have been three kinds of people in the world, the High, the Middle, and the Low. They have been subdivided in many ways, they have borne countless different names, and their relative numbers, as well as their attitude toward one another, have varied from age to age; but the essential structure of society has never altered. Even after enormous upheavals and seemingly irrevocable changes, the same pattern has always reasserted itself, just as a gyroscope will always return to equilibrium, however far it is pushed one way or the other.

"Julia, are you awake?" said Winston.

"Yes, my love, I'm listening. Go on. It's marvelous."

He continued reading:

The aims of these three groups are entirely irreconcilable. The aim of the High is to remain where they are. The aim of the Middle is to change places with the High. The aim of the Low, when they have an aim —for it is an abiding characteristic of the Low that they are too much crushed by drudgery to be more than intermittently conscious of anything outside their daily lives—is to abolish all distinctions and create a society in which all men shall be equal. Thus throughout history a struggle which is the same in its main outlines recurs over and over again. For long periods the High seem to be securely in power, but sooner or later there always comes a moment when they lose either their belief in themselves, or their capacity to govern efficiently, or both. They are then overthrown by the Middle, who enlist the Low on their side by pretending to them that they are fighting for liberty and justice. As soon as they have reached their objective, the Middle thrust the Low back into their old position of servitude, and themselves become the High. Presently a new Middle group splits off from one of the other groups, or from both of them, and the struggle begins over again. Of the three groups, only the Low are never even temporarily successful in achieving their aims. It would be an exaggeration to say that throughout history there has been no progress of a material kind. Even today, in a period of decline, the average human being is physically better off than he was a few centuries ago. But no advance in wealth, no softening of manners, no reform or revolution has ever brought human equality a millimeter nearer. From the point of view of the Low, no historic change has ever meant much more than a change in the name of their masters.

By the late nineteenth century the recurrence of this pattern had become obvious to many observers. There then arose schools of thinkers who interpreted history as a cyclical process and claimed to show that inequality was the unalterable law of human life. This doctrine, of course, had always had its adherents, but in the manner in which it was now put forward there was a significant change. In the past the need for a hierarchical form of society had been the doctrine specifically of the High. It had been preached by kings and aristocrats and by the priests, lawyers, and the like who were parasitical upon them, and it had generally been softened by promises of compensation in an imaginary world beyond the grave. The Middle, so long as it was struggling for power, had always made use of such terms as freedom, justice, and fraternity. Now, however, the concept of human brotherhood began to be assailed by people who were not yet in positions of command, but merely hoped to be so before long. In the past the Middle had made revolutions under the banner of equality, and then had established a fresh tyranny as soon as the old one was overthrown. The new Middle groups in effect proclaimed their tyranny beforehand. Socialism, a theory which appeared in the early nineteenth century and was the last link in a chain of thought stretching back to the slave rebellions of antiquity, was still deeply infected by the Utopianism of past ages. But in each variant of Socialism that appeared from about 1900 onwards the aim of establishing liberty and equality was more and more openly abandoned. The new movements which appeared in the middle years of the century, Ingsoc in Oceania, Neo-Bolshevism in Eurasia, Death-worship, as it is commonly called, in Eastasia, had the conscious aim of perpetuating *un*freedom and *in*equality. These new movements, of course, grew out of the old ones and tended to keep their names and pay lip-service to their ideology. But the purpose of all of them was to arrest progress and freeze history at a chosen moment. The familiar pendulum swing was to happen once more, and then stop. As usual, the High were to be turned out by the Middle, who would then become the High; but this time, by conscious strategy, the High would be able to maintain their position permanently.

The new doctrines arose partly because of the accumulation of historical knowledge, and the growth of the historical sense, which had hardly existed before the nineteenth century. The cyclical movement of history was now intelligible, or appeared to be so; and if it was intelligible, then it was alterable. But the principal, underlying cause was that, as early as the beginning of the twentieth century, human equality had become technically possible. It was still true that men were not equal in their native talents and that functions had to be specialized in ways that favored some individuals against others; but there was no longer any real need for class distinctions or for large differences of wealth. In earlier ages, class distinctions had been not only inevitable but desirable. Inequality was the price of civilization. With the development of machine production, however, the case was altered. Even if it was still necessary for human beings to do different kinds of work, it was no longer necessary for them to live at different social or economic levels. Therefore, from the point of view of the new groups who were on the point of seizing power, human equality was no longer an ideal to be striven after, but a danger to be averted. In more primitive ages, when a just and peaceful society was in fact not possible, it had been fairly easy to believe in it. The idea of an earthly paradise in which men should live together in a state of brotherhood, without laws and without brute labor, had haunted the human imagination for thousands of years. And this vision had had a certain hold even on the groups who actually profited by each historic change. The heirs of the French, English, and American revolutions had partly believed in their own phrases about the rights of man, freedom of speech, equality before the law, and the like, and had even allowed their conduct to be influenced by them to some extent. But by the fourth decade of the twentieth century all the main currents of political thought were authoritarian. The earthly paradise had been discredited at exactly the moment when it became realizable. Every new political theory, by whatever name it called itself, led back to hierarchy and regimentation. And in the general hardening of outlook that set in round about 1930, practices which had been long abandoned, in some cases for hundreds of years— imprisonment without trial, the use of war prisoners as slaves, public executions, torture to extract confessions, the use of hostages and the deportation of whole populations—not only became common again, but were tolerated and even defended by people who considered themselves enlightened and progressive.

It was only after a decade of national wars, civil wars, revolutions and counterrevolutions in all parts of the world that Ingsoc and its rivals emerged as fully worked-out political theories. But they had been foreshadowed by the various systems, generally called totalitarian, which had appeared earlier in the century, and the main outlines of the world which would emerge from the prevailing chaos had long been obvious. What kind of people would control this world had been equally obvious. The new aristocracy was made up for the most part of bureaucrats, scientists, technicians, trade-union organizers, publicity experts, sociologists, teachers, journalists, and professional politicians. These people, whose origins lay in the salaried middle class and the upper grades of the working class, had been shaped and brought together by the barren world of monopoly industry and centralized government. As compared with their opposite numbers in past ages, they were less avaricious, less tempted by luxury, hungrier for pure power, and, above all, more conscious of what they were doing and more intent on crushing opposition. This last difference was cardinal. By comparison with that existing today, all the tyrannies of the past were half-hearted and inefficient. The ruling groups were always infected to some extent by liberal ideas, and were content to leave loose ends everywhere, to regard only the overt act, and to be uninterested in what their subjects were thinking. Even the Catholic Church of the Middle Ages was tolerant by modern standards. Part of the reason for this was that in the past no government had the power to keep its citizens under constant surveillance. The invention of print, however, made it easier to manipulate public opinion, and the film and the radio carried the process further. With the development of television, and the technical advance which made it possible to receive and transmit simultaneously on the same instrument, private life came to an end. Every citizen, or at least every citizen important enough to be worth watching, could be kept for twenty-four hours a day under the eyes of the police and in the sound of official propaganda, with all other channels of communication closed. The possibility of enforcing not only complete obedience to the will of the State, but complete uniformity of opinion on all subjects, now existed for the first time.

After the revolutionary period of the Fifties and Sixties, society regrouped itself, as always, into High, Middle, and Low. But the new High group, unlike all its forerunners, did not act upon instinct but knew what was needed to safeguard its position. It had long been realized that the only secure basis for oligarchy is collectivism. Wealth and privilege are most easily defended when they are possessed jointly. The so-called "abolition of private property" which took place in the middle years of the century meant, in effect, the concentration of property in far fewer hands than before; but with this difference, that the new owners were a group instead of a mass of individuals. Individually, no member of the Party owns anything, except petty personal belongings. Collectively, the Party owns everything in Oceania, because it controls everything and disposes of the products as it thinks fit. In the years following the Revolution it was able to step into this commanding position almost unopposed, because the whole process was represented as an act of collectivization. It had always been assumed that if the capitalist class were expropriated, Socialism must follow; and unquestionably the capitalists had been expropriated. Factories, mines, land, houses, transport—everything had been taken away from them; and since these things were no longer private property, it followed that they must be public property. Ingsoc, which grew out of the earlier Socialist movement and inherited its phraseology, has in fact carried out the main item in the Socialist program, with the result, foreseen and intended beforehand, that economic inequality has been made permanent.

But the problems of perpetuating a hierarchical society go deeper than this. There are only four ways in which a ruling group can fall from power. Either it is conquered from without, or it governs so inefficiently that the masses are stirred to revolt, or it allows a strong and discontented Middle Group to come into being, or it loses its own self-confidence and willingness to govern. These causes do not operate singly, and as a rule all four of them are present in some degree. A ruling class which could guard against all of them would remain in power permanently. Ultimately the determining factor is the mental attitude of the ruling class itself.

After the middle of the present century, the first danger had in reality disappeared. Each of the three powers which now divide the world is in fact unconquerable, and could only become conquerable through slow demographic changes which a government with wide powers can easily avert. The second danger, also, is only a theoretical one. The masses never revolt of their own accord, and they never revolt merely because they are oppressed. Indeed, so long as they are not permitted to have standards of comparison, they never even become aware that they are oppressed. The recurrent economic crises of past times were totally unnecessary and are not now permitted to happen, but other and equally large dislocations can and do happen without having political results, because there is no way in which discontent can become articulate. As for the problem of overproduction, which has been latent in our society since the development of machine technique, it is solved by the device of continuous warfare (*see* Chapter 3), which is also useful in keying up public morale to the necessary pitch. From the point of view of our present rulers, therefore, the only genuine dangers are the splitting-off of a new group of able, underemployed, power-hungry people, and the growth of liberalism and skepticism in their own ranks. The problem, that is to say, is educational. It is a problem of continuously molding the consciousness both of the directing group and of the larger executive group that lies immediately below it. The consciousness of the masses needs only to be influenced in a negative way.

Given this background, one could infer, if one did not know it already, the general structure of Oceanic society. At the apex of the pyramid comes Big Brother. Big Brother is infallible and all-powerful. Every success, every achievement, every victory, every scientific discovery, all knowledge, all wisdom, all happiness, all virtue, are held to issue directly from his leadership and inspiration. Nobody has ever seen Big Brother. He is a face on the hoardings, a voice on the telescreen. We may be reasonably sure that he will never die, and there is already considerable uncertainty as to when he was born. Big Brother is the guise in which the Party chooses to exhibit itself to the world. His function is to act as a focusing point for love, fear, and reverence, emotions which are more easily felt toward an individual than toward an organization. Below Big Brother comes the Inner Party, its numbers limited to six millions, or something less than two per cent of the population of Oceania. Below the Inner Party comes the Outer Party, which, if the Inner Party is described as the brain of the State, may be justly likened to the hands. Below that come the dumb masses whom we habitually refer to as "the proles," numbering perhaps eighty-five per cent of the population. In the terms of our earlier classification, the proles are the Low, for the slave populations of the equatorial lands, who pass constantly from conqueror to conqueror, are not a permanent or necessary part of the structure.

In principle, membership in these three groups is not hereditary. The child of Inner Party parents is in theory not born into the Inner Party. Admission to either branch of the Party is by examination, taken at the age of sixteen. Nor is there any racial discrimination, or any marked domination of one province by another. Jews, Negroes, South Americans of pure Indian blood are to be found in the highest ranks of the Party, and the administrators of any area are always drawn from the inhabitants of that area. In no part of Oceania do the inhabitants have the feeling that they are a colonial population ruled from a distant capital. Oceania has no capital, and its titular head is a person whose whereabouts nobody knows. Except that English is its chief lingua franca and Newspeak its official language, it is not centralized in any way. Its rulers are not held together by blood ties but by adherence to a common doctrine. It is true that our society is stratified, and very rigidly stratified, on what at first appear to be hereditary lines. There is far less to-and-fro movement between the different groups than happened under capitalism or even in the pre-industrial ages. Between the two branches of the Party there is a certain amount of interchange, but only so much as will ensure that weaklings are excluded from the Inner Party and that ambitious members of the Outer Party are made harmless by allowing them to rise. Proletarians, in practice, are not allowed to graduate into the Party. The most gifted among them, who might possibly become nuclei of discontent, are simply marked down by the Thought Police and eliminated. But this state of affairs is not necessarily permanent, nor is it a matter of principle. The Party is not a class in the old sense of the word. It does not aim at transmitting power to its own children, as such; and if there were no other way of keeping the ablest people at the top, it would be perfectly prepared to recruit an entire new generation from the ranks of the proletariat. In the crucial years, the fact that the Party was not a hereditary body did a great deal to neutralize opposition. The older kind of Socialist, who had been trained to fight against something called "class privilege," assumed that what is not hereditary cannot be permanent. He did not see that the continuity of an oligarchy need not be physical, nor did he pause to reflect that hereditary aristocracies have always been short-lived, whereas adoptive organizations such as the Catholic Church have sometimes lasted for hundreds or thousands of years. The essence of oligarchical rule is not father-to-son inheritance, but the persistence of a certain world-view and a certain way of life, imposed by the dead upon the living. A ruling group is a ruling group so long as it can nominate its successors. The Party is not concerned with perpetuating its blood but with perpetuating itself. *Who* wields power is not important, provided that the hierarchical structure remains always the same.

All the beliefs, habits, tastes, emotions, mental attitudes that characterize our time are really designed to sustain the mystique of the Party and prevent the true nature of present-day society from being perceived. Physical rebellion, or any preliminary move toward rebellion, is at present not possible. From the proletarians nothing is to be feared. Left to themselves, they will continue from generation to generation and from century to century, working, breeding, and dying, not only without any impulse to rebel, but without the power of grasping that the world could be other than it is. They could only become dangerous if the advance of industrial technique made it necessary to educate them more highly; but, since military and commercial rivalry are no longer important, the level of popular education is actually declining. What opinions the masses hold, or do not hold, is looked on as a matter of indifference. They can be granted intellectual liberty because they have no intellect. In a Party member, on the other hand, not even the smallest deviation of opinion on the most unimportant subject can be tolerated.

A Party member lives from birth to death under the eye of the Thought Police. Even when he is alone he can never be sure that he is alone. Wherever he may be, asleep or awake, working or resting, in his bath or in bed, he can be inspected without warning and without knowing that he is being inspected. Nothing that he does is indifferent. His friendships, his relaxations, his behavior toward his wife and children, the expression of his face when he is alone, the words he mutters in sleep, even the characteristic movements of his body, are all jealously scrutinized. Not only any actual misdemeanor, but any eccentricity, however small, any change of habits, any nervous mannerism that could possibly be the symptom of an inner struggle, is certain to be detected. He has no freedom of choice in any direction whatever. On the other hand, his actions are not regulated by law or by any clearly formulated code of behavior. In Oceania there is no law. Thoughts and actions which, when detected, mean certain death are not formally forbidden, and the endless purges, arrests, tortures, imprisonments, and vaporizations are not inflicted as punishment for crimes which have actually been committed, but are merely the wiping-out of persons who might perhaps commit a crime at some time in the future. A Party member is required to have not only the right opinions, but the right instincts. Many of the beliefs and attitudes demanded of him are never plainly stated, and could not be stated without laying bare the contradictions inherent in Ingsoc. If he is a person naturally orthodox (in Newspeak, a *goodthinker*), he will in all circumstances know, without taking thought, what is the true belief or the desirable emotion. But in any case an elaborate mental training, undergone in childhood and grouping itself round the Newspeak words *crimestop, blackwhite,* and *doublethink,* makes him unwilling and unable to think too deeply on any subject whatever.

A Party member is expected to have no private emotions and no res-pites from enthusiasm. He is supposed to live in a continuous frenzy of hatred of foreign enemies and internal traitors, triumph over victories, and self-abasement before the power and wisdom of the Party. The dis-contents produced by his bare, unsatisfying life are deliberately turned outwards and dissipated by such devices as the Two Minutes Hate, and the speculations which might possibly induce a skeptical or rebellious attitude are killed in advance by his early acquired inner discipline. The first and simplest stage in the discipline, which can be taught even to young children, is called, in Newspeak, *crimestop. Crimestop* means the faculty of stopping short, as though by instinct, at the threshold of any dangerous thought. It includes the power of not grasping analogies, of failing to perceive logical errors, of misunderstanding the simplest argu-ments if they are inimical to Ingsoc, and of being bored or repelled by any train of thought which is capable of leading in a heretical direction. *Crimestop,* in short, means protective stupidity. But stupidity is not enough. On the contrary, orthodoxy in the full sense demands a control over one's own mental processes as complete as that of a contortionist over his body. Oceanic society rests ultimately on the belief that Big Brother is omnipotent and that the Party is infallible. But since in reality Big Brother is not omnipotent and the Party is not infallible, there is need for an unwearying, moment-to-moment flexibility in the treatment of facts. The key word here is *blackwhite.* Like so many Newspeak words, this word has two mutually contradictory meanings. Applied to an oppo-nent, it means the habit of impudently claiming that black is white, in contradiction of the plain facts. Applied to a Party member, it means a loyal willingness to say that black is white when Party discipline de-mands this. But it means also the ability to *believe* that black is white, and more, to *know* that black is white, and to forget that one has ever believed the contrary. This demands a continuous alteration of the past, made possible by the system of thought which really embraces all the rest, and which is known in Newspeak as *doublethink.*

The alteration of the past is necessary for two reasons, one of which is subsidiary and, so to speak, precautionary. The subsidiary reason is that the Party member, like the proletarian, tolerates present-day conditions partly because he has no standards of comparison. He must be cut off from the past, just as he must be cut off from foreign countries, because it is necessary for him to believe that he is better off than his ancestors and that the average level of material comfort is constantly rising. But by far the more important reason for the readjustment of the past is the need to safeguard the infallibility of the Party. It is not merely that speeches, statistics, and records of every kind must be constantly brought up to date in order to show that the predictions of the Party were in all cases right. It is also that no change in doctrine or in political alignment can ever be admitted. For to change one's mind, or even one's policy, is a confession of weakness. If, for example, Eurasia or Eastasia (whichever it may be) is the enemy today, then that country must always have been the enemy. And if the facts say otherwise, then the facts must be altered. Thus history is continuously rewritten. This day-to-day falsification of the past, carried out by the Ministry of Truth, is as necessary to the stability of the regime as the work of repression and espionage carried out by the Ministry of Love.

The mutability of the past is the central tenet of Ingsoc. Past events, it is argued, have no objective existence, but survive only in written records and in human memories. The past is whatever the records and the memories agree upon. And since the Party is in full control of all records, and in equally full control of the minds of its members, it follows that the past is whatever the Party chooses to make it. It also follows that though the past is alterable, it never has been altered in any specific instance. For when it has been recreated in whatever shape is needed at the moment, then this new version *is* the past, and no different past can ever have existed. This holds good even when, as often happens, the same event has to be altered out of recognition several times in the course of a year. At all times the Party is in possession of absolute truth, and clearly the absolute can never have been different from what it is now. It will be seen that the control of the past depends above all on the training of memory. To make sure that all written records agree with the orthodoxy of the moment is merely a mechanical act. But it is also necessary to *remember* that events happened in the desired manner. And if it is necessary to rearrange one's memories or to tamper with written records, then it is necessary to *forget* that one has done so. The trick of doing this can be learned like any other mental technique. It *is* learned by the majority of Party members, and certainly by all who are intelligent as well as ortho-dox. In Oldspeak it is called, quite frankly, "reality control." In Newspeak it is called *doublethink*, though *doublethink* comprises much else as well.

Doublethink means the power of holding two contradictory beliefs in one's mind simultaneously, and accepting both of them. The Party intellectual knows in which direction his memories must be altered; he therefore knows that he is playing tricks with reality; but by the exercise of *doublethink* he also satisfies himself that reality is not violated. The process has to be conscious, or it would not be carried out with sufficient precision, but it also has to be unconscious, or it would bring with it a feeling of falsity and hence of guilt. *Doublethink* lies at the very heart of Ingsoc, since the essential act of the Party is to use conscious deception while retaining the firmness of purpose that goes with complete honesty. To tell deliberate lies while genuinely believing in them, to forget any fact that has become inconvenient, and then, when it becomes necessary again, to draw it back from oblivion for just so long as it is needed, to deny the existence of objective reality and all the while to take account of the reality which one denies—all this is indispensably necessary. Even in using the word *doublethink* it is necessary to exercise *doublethink*. For by using the word one admits that one is tampering with reality; by a fresh act of *doublethink* one erases this knowledge; and so on indefinitely, with the lie always one leap ahead of the truth. Ultimately it is by means of *doublethink* that the Party has been able—and may, for all we know, continue to be able for thousands of years—to arrest the course of history.

All past oligarchies have fallen from power either because they ossified or because they grew soft. Either they became stupid and arrogant, failed to adjust themselves to changing circumstances, and were overthrown, or they became liberal and cowardly, made concessions when they should have used force, and once again were overthrown. They fell, that is to say, either through consciousness or through unconsciousness. It is the achievement of the Party to have produced a system of thought in which both conditions can exist simultaneously. And upon no other intellectual basis could the dominion of the Party be made permanent. If one is to rule, and to continue ruling, one must be able to dislocate the sense of reality. For the secret of rulership is to combine a belief in one's own infallibility with the power to learn from past mistakes.

It need hardly be said that the subtlest practitioners of *doublethink* are those who invented *doublethink* and know that it is a vast system of mental cheating. In our society, those who have the best knowledge of what is happening are also those who are furthest from seeing the world as it is. In general, the greater the understanding, the greater the delusion: the more intelligent, the less sane. One clear illustration of this is the fact that war hysteria increases in intensity as one rises in the social scale. Those whose attitude toward the war is most nearly rational are the subject peoples of the disputed territories. To these people the war is simply a continuous calamity which sweeps to and fro over their bodies like a tidal wave. Which side is winning is a matter of complete indiffer-

ence to them. They are aware that a change of overlordship means simply that they will be doing the same work as before for new masters who
treat them in the same manner as the old ones. The slightly more favored
workers whom we call "the proles" are only intermittently conscious of
the war. When it is necessary they can be prodded into frenzies of fear
and hatred, but when left to themselves they are capable of forgetting for
long periods that the war is happening. It is in the ranks of the Party, and
above all of the Inner Party, that the true war enthusiasm is found.
World-conquest is believed in most firmly by those who know it to be
impossible. This peculiar linking-together of opposites—knowledge with
ignorance, cynicism with fanaticism—is one of the chief distinguishing
marks of Oceanic society. The official ideology abounds with contradictions even where there is no practical reason for them. Thus, the Party
rejects and vilifies every principle for which the Socialist movement originally stood, and it chooses to do this in the name of Socialism. It preaches
a contempt for the working class unexampled for centuries past, and it
dresses its members in a uniform which was at one time peculiar to manual workers and was adopted for that reason. It systematically under-
mines the solidarity of the family, and it calls its leader by a name which
is a direct appeal to the sentiment of family loyalty. Even the names of
the four Ministries by which we are governed exhibit a sort of impudence
in their deliberate reversal of the facts. The Ministry of Peace concerns
itself with war, the Ministry of Truth with lies, the Ministry of Love with
torture, and the Ministry of Plenty with starvation. These contradictions
are not accidental, nor do they result from ordinary hypocrisy: they are
deliberate exercises in *doublethink*. For it is only by reconciling contradictions that power can be retained indefinitely. In no other way could
the ancient cycle be broken. If human equality is to be forever averted—
if the High, as we have called them, are to keep their places permanently—then the prevailing mental condition must be controlled insanity.

But there is one question which until this moment we have almost
ignored. It is: *why* should human equality be averted? Supposing that the
mechanics of the process have been rightly described, what is the motive
for this huge, accurately planned effort to freeze history at a particular
moment of time?

Here we reach the central secret. As we have seen, the mystique of the
Party, and above all of the Inner Party, depends upon *doublethink*. But
deeper than this lies the original motive, the never-questioned instinct
that first led to the seizure of power and brought *doublethink*, the
Thought Police, continuous warfare, and all the other necessary para-
phernalia into existence afterwards. This motive really consists . . .

Winston became aware of silence, as one becomes aware of a new
sound. It seemed to him that Julia had been very still for some time past.

She was lying on her side, naked from the waist upwards, with her cheek pillowed on her hand and one dark lock tumbling across her eyes. Her breast rose and fell slowly and regularly.

"Julia."

No answer.

"Julia, are you awake?"

No answer. She was asleep. He shut the book, put it carefully on the floor, lay down, and pulled the coverlet over both of them.

He had still, he reflected, not learned the ultimate secret. He understood *how;* he did not understand *why.* Chapter 1, like Chapter 3, had not actually told him anything that he did not know; it had merely systematized the knowledge that he possessed already. But after reading it he knew better than before that he was not mad. Being in a minority, even a minority of one, did not make you mad. There was truth and there was untruth, and if you clung to the truth even against the whole world, you were not mad. A yellow beam from the sinking sun slanted in through the window and fell across the pillow. He shut his eyes. The sun on his face and the girl's smooth body touching his own gave him a strong, sleepy, confident feeling. He was safe, everything was all right. He fell asleep murmuring "Sanity is not statistical," with the feeling that this remark contained in it a profound wisdom.

X

When he woke it was with the sensation of having slept for a long time, but a glance at the old-fashioned clock told him that it was only twenty-thirty. He lay dozing for a little while; then the usual deep-lunged singing struck up from the yard below:

> *"It was only an 'opeless fancy,*
> *It passed like an Ipril dye,*
> *But a look an' a word an' the dreams they stirred*
> *They 'ave stolen my 'eart awye!"*

The driveling song seemed to have kept its popularity. You still heard it all over the place. It had outlived the "Hate Song." Julia woke at the sound, stretched herself luxuriously, and got out of bed.

"I'm hungry," she said. "Let's make some more coffee. Damn! The stove's gone out and the water's cold." She picked the stove up and shook it. "There's no oil in it."

"We can get some from old Charrington, I expect."

"The funny thing is I made sure it was full. I'm going to put my clothes on," she added. "It seems to have got colder."

Winston also got up and dressed himself. The indefatigable voice sang on:

"They sye that time 'eals all things,
They sye you can always forget;
But the smiles an' the tears across the years
They twist my 'eartstrings yet!"

As he fastened the belt of his overalls he strolled across to the window. The sun must have gone down behind the houses; it was not shining into the yard any longer. The flagstones were wet as though they had just been washed, and he had the feeling that the sky had been washed too, so fresh and pale was the blue between the chimney pots. Tirelessly the woman marched to and fro, corking and uncorking herself, singing and falling silent, and pegging out more diapers, and more and yet more. He wondered whether she took in washing for a living, or was merely the slave of twenty or thirty grandchildren. Julia had come across to his side; together they gazed down with a sort of fascination at the sturdy figure below. As he looked at the woman in her characteristic attitude, her thick arms reaching up for the line, her powerful marelike buttocks protruded, it struck him for the first time that she was beautiful. It had never before occurred to him that the body of a woman of fifty, blown up to monstrous dimensions by childbearing, then hardened, roughened by work till it was coarse in the grain like an overripe turnip, could be beautiful. But it was so, and after all, he thought, why not? The solid, contourless body, like a block of granite, and the rasping red skin, bore the same relation to the body of a girl as the rose hip to the rose. Why should the fruit be held inferior to the flower?

"She's beautiful," he murmured.

"She's a meter across the hips, easily," said Julia.

"That is her style of beauty," said Winston. He held Julia's supple waist easily encircled by his arm. From the hip to the knee her flank was against his. Out of their bodies no child would ever come. That was the one thing they could never do. Only by word of mouth, from mind to mind, could they pass on the secret. The woman down there had no mind, she had only strong arms, a warm heart, and a fertile belly. He wondered how many children she had given birth to. It might easily be fifteen. She had had her momentary flowering, a year, perhaps, of wildrose beauty, and then she had suddenly swollen like a fertilized fruit and grown hard and red and coarse, and then her life had been laundering, scrubbing, darning, cooking, sweeping, polishing, mending, scrubbing, laundering, first for children, then for grandchildren, over thirty unbroken years. At the end of it she was still singing. The mystical reverence that he felt for her was somehow mixed up with the aspect of the pale, cloudless sky, stretching away behind the chimney pots into interminable distances. It was curious to think that the sky was the same for everybody, in Eurasia or Eastasia as well as here. And the people under the sky were also very much the same—everywhere, all over the world, hundreds or thousands of millions of people just like this, people ignorant of one another's existence, held apart by walls of hatred and lies, and yet almost exactly the same—people who had never learned to think but who were storing up in their hearts and bellies and muscles the power that would one day overturn the world. If there was hope, it lay in the proles! Without having read to the end of *the book*, he knew that that must be Goldstein's final message. The future belonged to the proles. And could he be sure that when their time came, the world they constructed would not be just as alien to him, Winston Smith, as the world of the Party? Yes, because at the least it would be a world of sanity. Where there is equality there can be sanity. Sooner or later it would happen: strength would change into consciousness. The proles were immortal; you could not doubt it when you looked at that valiant figure in the yard. In the end their awakening would come. And until that happened, though it might be a thousand years, they would stay alive against all the odds, like birds, passing on from body to body the vitality which the Party did not share and could not kill.

"Do you remember," he said, "the thrush that sang to us, that first day, at the edge of the wood?"

"He wasn't singing to us," said Julia. "He was singing to please himself. Not even that. He was just singing."

The birds sang, the proles sang, the Party did not sing. All round the world, in London and New York, in Africa and Brazil and in the mysterious, forbidden lands beyond the frontiers, in the streets of Paris and Berlin, in the villages of the endless Russian plain, in the bazaars of China and Japan—everywhere stood the same solid unconquerable figure, made monstrous by work and childbearing, toiling from birth to death and still singing. Out of those mighty loins a race of conscious beings must one day come. You were the dead; theirs was the future. But you could share in that future if you kept alive the mind as they kept alive the body, and passed on the secret doctrine that two plus two make four.

"We are the dead," he said.

"We are the dead," echoed Julia dutifully.

"You are the dead," said an iron voice behind them.

They sprang apart. Winston's entrails seemed to have turned into ice. He could see the white all round the irises of Julia's eyes. Her face had turned a milky yellow. The smear of rouge that was still on each cheekbone stood out sharply, almost as though unconnected with the skin beneath.

"You are the dead," repeated the iron voice.

"It was behind the picture," breathed Julia.

"It was behind the picture," said the voice. "Remain exactly where you are. Make no movement until you are ordered."

It was starting, it was starting at last! They could do nothing except stand gazing into one another's eyes. To run for life, to get out of the house before it was too late—no such thought occurred to them. Unthinkable to disobey the iron voice from the wall. There was a snap as though a catch had been turned back, and a crash of breaking glass. The picture had fallen to the floor, uncovering the telescreen behind it.

"Now they can see us," said Julia.

"Now we can see you," said the voice. "Stand out in the middle of the room. Stand back to back. Clasp your hands behind your heads. Do not touch one another."

They were not touching, but it seemed to him that he could feel Julia's body shaking. Or perhaps it was merely the shaking of his own. He could just stop his teeth from chattering, but his knees were beyond his control. There was a sound of trampling boots below, inside the house and outside. The yard seemed to be full of men. Something was being dragged across the stones. The woman's singing had stopped abruptly. There was a long, rolling clang, as though the washtub had been flung across the yard, and then a confusion of angry shouts which ended in a yell of pain.

"The house is surrounded," said Winston.

"The house is surrounded," said the voice.

He heard Julia snap her teeth together. "I suppose we may as well say good-by," she said.

"You may as well say good-by," said the voice. And then another quite different voice, a thin, cultivated voice which Winston had the impression of having heard before, struck in: "And by the way, while we are on the subject, *Here comes a candle to light you to bed, here comes a chopper to chop off your head!*"

Something crashed on to the bed behind Winston's back. The head of a ladder had been thrust through the window and had burst in the frame. Someone was climbing through the window. There was a stampede of boots up the stairs. The room was full of solid men in black uniforms, with ironshod boots on their feet and truncheons in their hands.

Winston was not trembling any longer. Even his eyes he barely moved. One thing alone mattered: to keep still, to keep still and not give them an excuse to hit you! A man with a smooth prizefighter's jowl in which the mouth was only a slit paused opposite him, balancing his truncheon meditatively between thumb and forefinger. Winston met his eyes. The feeling of nakedness, with one's hands behind one's head and one's face and body all exposed, was almost unbearable. The man protruded the tip of a white tongue, licked the place where his lips should have been, and then passed on. There was another crash. Someone had picked up the glass paperweight from the table and smashed it to pieces on the hearth-stone.

The fragment of coral, a tiny crinkle of pink like a sugar rosebud from a cake, rolled across the mat. How small, thought Winston, how small it always was! There was a gasp and a thump behind him, and he received a violent kick on the ankle which nearly flung him off his balance. One of the men had smashed his fist into Julia's solar plexus, doubling her up like a pocket ruler. She was thrashing about on the floor, fighting for breath. Winston dared not turn his head even by a millimeter, but sometimes her livid, gasping face came within the angle of his vision. Even in his terror it was as though he could feel the pain in his own body, the deadly pain which nevertheless was less urgent than the struggle to get back her breath. He knew what it was like: the terrible, agonizing pain which was there all the while but could not be suffered yet, because before all else it was necessary to be able to breathe. Then two of the men hoisted her up by knees and shoulders and carried her out of the room like a sack. Winston had a glimpse of her face, upside down, yellow and contorted, with the eyes shut, and still with a smear of rouge on either cheek; and that was the last he saw of her.

He stood dead still. No one had hit him yet. Thoughts which came of their own accord but seemed totally uninteresting began to flit through his mind. He wondered whether they had got Mr. Charrington. He wondered what they had done to the woman in the yard. He noticed that he badly wanted to urinate, and felt a faint surprise, because he had done so only two or three hours ago. He noticed that the clock on the mantelpiece said nine, meaning twenty-one. But the light seemed too strong. Would not the light be fading at twenty-one hours on an August evening? He wondered whether after all he and Julia had mistaken the time—had slept the clock round and thought it was twenty-thirty when really it was nought eight-thirty on the following morning. But he did not pursue the thought further. It was not interesting.

There was another, lighter step in the passage. Mr. Charrington came into the room. The demeanor of the black-uniformed men suddenly became more subdued. Something had also changed in Mr. Charrington's appearance. His eye fell on the fragments of the glass paperweight.

"Pick up those pieces," he said sharply.

A man stooped to obey. The cockney accent had disappeared; Winston suddenly realized whose voice it was that he had heard a few moments ago on the telescreen. Mr. Charrington was still wearing his old velvet jacket, but his hair, which had been almost white, had turned black. Also he was not wearing his spectacles. He gave Winston a single sharp glance, as though verifying his identity, and then paid no more attention to him. He was still recognizable, but he was not the same person any longer. His body had straightened, and seemed to have grown bigger. His face had undergone only tiny changes that had nevertheless worked a complete transformation. The black eyebrows were less bushy, the wrinkles were gone, the whole lines of the face seemed to have altered; even the nose seemed shorter. It was the alert, cold face of a man of about five-and-thirty. It occurred to Winston that for the first time in his life he was looking, with knowledge, at a member of the Thought Police.

THREE

He did not know where he was. Presumably he was in the Ministry of Love; but there was no way of making certain.

He was in a high-ceilinged windowless cell with walls of glittering white porcelain. Concealed lamps flooded it with cold light, and there was a low, steady humming sound which he supposed had something to do with the air supply. A bench, or shelf, just wide enough to sit on ran round the wall, broken only by the door and, at the end opposite the door, a lavatory pan with no wooden seat. There were four telescreens, one in each wall.

There was a dull aching in his belly. It had been there ever since they had bundled him into the closed van and driven him away. But he was also hungry, with a gnawing, unwholesome kind of hunger. It might be twenty-four hours since he had eaten, it might be thirty-six. He still did not know, probably never would know, whether it had been morning or evening when they arrested him. Since he was arrested he had not been fed.

He sat as still as he could on the narrow bench, with his hands crossed on his knee. He had already learned to sit still. If you made unexpected movements they yelled at you from the telescreen. But the craving for food was growing upon him. What he longed for above all was a piece of bread. He had an idea that there were a few breadcrumbs in the pocket of his overalls. It was even possible—he thought this because from time to time something seemed to tickle his leg—that there might be a sizable bit of crust there. In the end the temptation to find out overcame his fear; he slipped a hand into his pocket.

"Smith!" yelled a voice from the telescreen. "6079 Smith W! Hands out of pockets in the cells!"

He sat still again, his hands crossed on his knee. Before being brought here he had been taken to another place which must have been an ordinary prison or a temporary lock-up used by the patrols. He did not know how long he had been there; some hours, at any rate; with no clocks and no daylight it was hard to gauge the time. It was a noisy, evil-smelling place. They had put him into a cell similar to the one he was now in, but filthily dirty and at all times crowded by ten or fifteen people. The majority of them were common criminals, but there were a few political prisoners among them. He had sat silent against the wall, jostled by dirty bodies, too preoccupied by fear and the pain in his belly to take much interest in his surroundings, but still noticing the astonishing difference in demeanor between the Party prisoners and the others. The Party prisoners were always silent and terrified, but the ordinary criminals seemed to care nothing for anybody. They yelled insults at the guards, fought back fiercely when their belongings were impounded, wrote obscene words on the floor, ate smuggled food which they produced from mysterious hiding places in their clothes, and even shouted down the telescreen when it tried to restore order. On the other hand, some of them seemed to be on good terms with the guards, called them by nicknames, and tried to wheedle cigarettes through the spy-hole in the door. The guards, too, treated the common criminals with a certain forbearance, even when they had to handle them roughly. There was much talk about the forced-labor camps to which most of the prisoners expected to be sent. It was "all right" in the camps, he gathered, so long as you had good contacts and knew the ropes. There were bribery, favoritism, and racketeering of every kind, there were homosexuality and prostitution, there was even illicit alcohol distilled from potatoes. The positions of trust were given only to the common criminals, especially the gangsters and the murderers, who formed a sort of aristocracy. All the dirty jobs were done by the politicals.

There was a constant come-and-go of prisoners of every description: drug peddlers, thieves, bandits, black marketeers, drunks, prostitutes. Some of the drunks were so violent that the other prisoners had to combine to suppress them. An enormous wreck of a woman, aged about sixty, with great tumbling breasts and thick coils of white hair which had come down in her struggles, was carried in, kicking and shouting, by four guards who had hold of her one at each corner. They wrenched off the boots with which she had been trying to kick them and dumped her down across Winston's lap, almost breaking his thighbones. The woman hoisted herself upright and followed them out with a yell of "F———bastards!" Then, noticing that she was sitting on something uneven, she slid off Winston's knees onto the bench.

"Beg pardon, dearie," she said. "I wouldn't 'a sat on you, only the buggers put me there. They dono 'ow to treat a lady, do they?" She paused, patted her breast, and belched. "Pardon," she said, "I ain't meself, quite."

She leant forward and vomited copiously on the floor.

"Thass better," she said, leaning back with closed eyes. "Never keep it down, thass what I say. Get it up while it's fresh on your stomach, like."

She revived, turned to have another look at Winston, and seemed immediately to take a fancy to him. She put a vast arm round his shoulder and drew him toward her, breathing beer and vomit into his face.

"Wass your name, dearie?" she said.

"Smith," said Winston.

"Smith?" said the woman. "Thass funny. My name's Smith too. Why," she added sentimentally, "I might be your mother!"

She might, thought Winston, be his mother. She was about the right age and physique, and it was probable that people changed somewhat after twenty years in a forced-labor camp.

No one else had spoken to him. To a surprising extent the ordinary criminals ignored the Party prisoners. "The pol*its*," they called them, with a sort of uninterested contempt. The Party prisoners seemed terrified of speaking to anybody, and above all of speaking to one another. Only once, when two Party members, both women, were pressed close together on the bench, he overheard amid the din of voices a few hurriedly whispered words; and in particular a reference to something called "room one-oh-one," which he did not understand.

It might be two or three hours ago that they had brought him here. The dull pain in his belly never went away, but sometimes it grew better and sometimes worse, and his thoughts expanded or contracted accordingly. When it grew worse he thought only of the pain itself, and of his desire for food. When it grew better, panic took hold of him. There were moments when he foresaw the things that would happen to him with such actuality that his heart galloped and his breath stopped. He felt the smash of truncheons on his elbows and iron-shod boots on his shins; he saw himself groveling on the floor, screaming for mercy through broken teeth. He hardly thought of Julia. He could not fix his mind on her. He loved her and would not betray her; but that was only a fact, known as he knew the rules of arithmetic. He felt no love for her, and he hardly even wondered what was happening to her. He thought oftener of O'Brien, with a flickering hope. O'Brien must know that he had been arrested. The Brotherhood, he had said, never tried to save its members. But there was the razor blade; they would send the razor blade if they could. There would be perhaps five seconds before the guards could rush into the cell. The blade would bite into him with a sort of burning coldness, and even the fingers that held it would be cut to the bone. Everything came back to his sick body, which shrank trembling from the smallest pain. He was not certain that he would use the razor blade even if he got the chance. It was more natural to exist from moment to moment, accepting another ten minutes' life even with the certainty that there was torture at the end of it.

Sometimes he tried to calculate the number of porcelain bricks in the walls of the cell. It should have been easy, but he always lost count at some point or another. More often he wondered where he was, and what time of day it was. At one moment he felt certain that it was broad daylight outside, and at the next equally certain that it was pitch darkness. In this place, he knew instinctively, the lights would never be turned out. It was the place with no darkness: he saw now why O'Brien had seemed to recognize the allusion. In the Ministry of Love there were no windows. His cell might be at the heart of the building or against its outer wall; it might be ten floors below ground, or thirty above it. He moved himself mentally from place to place, and tried to determine by the feeling of his body whether he was perched high in the air or buried deep underground.

There was a sound of marching boots outside. The steel door opened with a clang. A young officer, a trim black-uniformed figure who seemed to glitter all over with polished leather and whose pale, straight-featured face was like a wax mask, stepped smartly through the doorway. He motioned to the guards outside to bring in the prisoner they were leading. The poet Ampleforth shambled into the cell. The door clanged shut again.

Ampleforth made one or two uncertain movements from side to side, as though having some idea that there was another door to go out of, and then began to wander up and down the cell. He had not yet noticed Winston's presence. His troubled eyes were gazing at the wall about a meter above the level of Winston's head. He was shoeless; large, dirty toes were sticking out of the holes in his socks. He was also several days away from a shave. A scrubby beard covered his face to the cheekbones, giving him an air of ruffianism that went oddly with his large weak frame and nervous movements.

Winston roused himself a little from his lethargy. He must speak to Ampleforth, and risk the yell from the telescreen. It was even conceivable that Ampleforth was the bearer of the razor blade.

"Ampleforth," he said.

There was no yell from the telescreen. Ampleforth paused, mildly startled. His eyes focused themselves slowly on Winston.

"Ah, Smith!" he said. "You, too!"

"What are you in for?"

"To tell you the truth—" He sat down awkwardly on the bench opposite Winston. "There is only one offense, is there not?" he said.

"And have you committed it?"

"Apparently I have."

He put a hand to his forehead and pressed his temples for a moment, as though trying to remember something.

"These things happen," he began vaguely. "I have been able to recall one instance—a possible instance. It was an indiscretion, undoubtedly. We were producing a definitive edition of the poems of Kipling. I allowed the word 'God' to remain at the end of a line. I could not help it!" he added almost indignantly, raising his face to look at Winston. "It was impossible to change the line. The rhyme was 'rod.' Do you realize that there are only twelve rhymes to 'rod' in the entire language? For days I had racked my brains. There *was* no other rhyme."

The expression on his face changed. The annoyance passed out of it and for a moment he looked almost pleased. A sort of intellectual warmth, the joy of the pedant who has found out some useless fact, shone through the dirt and scrubby hair.

"Has it ever occurred to you," he said, "that the whole history of English poetry has been determined by the fact that the English language lacks rhymes?"

No, that particular thought had never occurred to Winston. Nor, in the circumstances, did it strike him as very important or interesting.

"Do you know what time of day it is?" he said.

Ampleforth looked startled again. "I had hardly thought about it. They arrested me—it could be two days ago—perhaps three." His eyes flitted round the walls, as though he half expected to find a window somewhere. "There is no difference between night and day in this place. I do not see how one can calculate the time."

They talked desultorily for some minutes, then, without apparent reason, a yell from the telescreen bade them be silent. Winston sat quietly, his hands crossed. Ampleforth, too large to sit in comfort on the narrow bench, fidgeted from side to side, clasping his lank hands first round one knee, then round the other. The telescreen barked at him to keep still. Time passed. Twenty minutes, an hour—it was difficult to judge. Once more there was a sound of boots outside. Winston's entrails contracted. Soon, very soon, perhaps in five minutes, perhaps now, the tramp of boots would mean that his own turn had come.

The door opened. The cold-faced young officer stepped into the cell. With a brief movement of the hand he indicated Ampleforth.

"Room 101," he said.

Ampleforth marched clumsily out between the guards, his face vaguely perturbed, but uncomprehending.

What seemed like a long time passed. The pain in Winston's belly had revived. His mind sagged round and round on the same track, like a ball falling again and again into the same series of slots. He had only six thoughts. The pain in his belly; a piece of bread; the blood and the screaming; O'Brien; Julia; the razor blade. There was another spasm in his entrails; the heavy boots were approaching. As the door opened, the wave of air that it created brought in a powerful smell of cold sweat. Parsons walked into the cell. He was wearing khaki shorts and a sports shirt.

This time Winston was startled into self-forgetfulness.

"*You* here!" he said.

Parsons gave Winston a glance in which there was neither interest nor surprise, but only misery. He began walking jerkily up and down, evidently unable to keep still. Each time he straightened his pudgy knees it was apparent that they were trembling. His eyes had a wide-open, staring look, as though he could not prevent himself from gazing at something in the middle distance.

"What are you in for?" said Winston.

"Thoughtcrime!" said Parsons, almost blubbering. The tone of his voice implied at once a complete admission of his guilt and a sort of incredulous horror that such a word could be applied to himself. He paused opposite Winston and began eagerly appealing to him: "You don't think they'll shoot me, do you, old chap? They don't shoot you if you haven't actually done anything—only thoughts, which you can't help? I know they give you a fair hearing. Oh, I trust them for that! They'll know my record, won't they? *You* know what kind of a chap I was. Not a bad chap in my way. Not brainy, of course, but keen. I tried to do my best for the Party, didn't I? I'll get off with five years, don't you think? Or even ten years? A chap like me could make himself pretty useful in a labor camp. They wouldn't shoot me for going off the rails just once?"

"Are you guilty?" said Winston.

"Of course I'm guilty!" cried Parsons with a servile glance at the telescreen. "You don't think the Party would arrest an innocent man, do you?" His froglike face grew calmer, and even took on a slightly sanctimonious expression. "Thoughtcrime is a dreadful thing, old man," he said sententiously. "It's insidious. It can get hold of you without your even knowing it. Do you know how it got hold of me? In my sleep! Yes, that's a fact. There I was, working away, trying to do my bit—never knew I had any bad stuff in my mind at all. And then I started talking in my sleep. Do you know what they heard me saying?"

He sank his voice, like someone who is obliged for medical reasons to utter an obscenity.

" 'Down with Big Brother!' Yes, I said that! Said it over and over again, it seems. Between you and me, old man, I'm glad they got me before it went any further. Do you know what I'm going to say to them when I go up before the tribunal? 'Thank you,' I'm going to say, 'thank you for saving me before it was too late.' "

"Who denounced you?" said Winston.

"It was my little daughter," said Parsons with a sort of doleful pride. "She listened at the keyhole. Heard what I was saying, and nipped off to the patrols the very next day. Pretty smart for a nipper of seven, eh? I don't bear her any grudge for it. In fact I'm proud of her. It shows I brought her up in the right spirit, anyway."

He made a few more jerky movements up and down, several times casting a longing glance at the lavatory pan. Then he suddenly ripped down his shorts.

"Excuse me, old man," he said. "I can't help it. It's the waiting."

He plumped his large posteriors onto the lavatory pan. Winston covered his face with his hands.

"Smith!" yelled the voice from the telescreen. "6079 Smith W! Uncover your face. No faces covered in the cells."

Winston uncovered his face. Parsons used the lavatory, loudly and abundantly. It then turned out that the plug was defective, and the cell stank abominably for hours afterwards.

Parsons was removed. More prisoners came and went mysteriously. One, a woman, was consigned to "Room 101," and, Winston noticed, seemed to shrivel and turn a different color when she heard the words. A time came when, if it had been morning when he was brought here, it would be afternoon; or if it had been afternoon, then it would be midnight. There were six prisoners in the cell, men and women. All sat very still. Opposite Winston there sat a man with a chinless, toothy face exactly like that of some large, harmless rodent. His fat, mottled cheeks were so pouched at the bottom that it was difficult not to believe that he had little stores of food tucked away there. His pale-gray eyes flitted timorously from face to face, and turned quickly away again when he caught anyone's eye.

The door opened, and another prisoner was brought in whose appearance sent a momentary chill through Winston. He was a commonplace, mean-looking man who might have been an engineer or technician of some kind. But what was startling was the emaciation of his face. It was like a skull. Because of its thinness the mouth and eyes looked disproportionately large, and the eyes seemed filled with a murderous, unappeasable hatred of somebody or something.

The man sat down on the bench at a little distance from Winston. Winston did not look at him again, but the tormented, skull-like face was as vivid in his mind as though it had been straight in front of his eyes. Suddenly he realized what was the matter. The man was dying of starvation. The same thought seemed to occur almost simultaneously to everyone in the cell. There was a very faint stirring all the way round the bench. The eyes of the chinless man kept flitting toward the skull-faced man, then turning guiltily away, then being dragged back by an irresistible attraction. Presently he began to fidget on his seat. At last he stood up, waddled clumsily across the cell, dug down into the pocket of his overalls, and, with an abashed air, held out a grimy piece of bread to the skull-faced man.

There was a furious, deafening roar from the telescreen. The chinless man jumped in his tracks. The skull-faced man had quickly thrust his hands behind his back, as though demonstrating to all the world that he refused the gift.

"Bumstead!" roared the voice. "2713 Bumstead J! Let fall that piece of bread."

The chinless man dropped the piece of bread on the floor.

"Remain standing where you are," said the voice. "Face the door. Make no movement."

The chinless man obeyed. His large pouchy cheeks were quivering uncontrollably. The door clanged open. As the young officer entered and stepped aside, there emerged from behind him a short stumpy guard with enormous arms and shoulders. He took his stand opposite the chinless man, and then, at a signal from the officer, let free a frightful blow, with all the weight of his body behind it, full in the chinless man's mouth. The force of it seemed almost to knock him clear of the floor. His body was flung across the cell and fetched up against the base of the lavatory seat. For a moment he lay as though stunned, with dark blood oozing from his mouth and nose. A very faint whimpering or squeaking, which seemed unconscious, came out of him. Then he rolled over and raised himself unsteadily on hands and knees. Amid a stream of blood and saliva, the two halves of a dental plate fell out of his mouth.

The prisoners sat very still, their hands crossed on their knees. The chinless man climbed back into his place. Down one side of his face the flesh was darkening. His mouth had swollen into a shapeless cherry-colored mass with a black hole in the middle of it. From time to time a little blood dripped onto the breast of his overalls. His gray eyes still flitted from face to face, more guiltily than ever, as though he were trying to discover how much the others despised him for his humiliation.

The door opened. With a small gesture the officer indicated the skull-faced man.

"Room 101," he said.

There was a gasp and a flurry at Winston's side. The man had actually flung himself on his knees on the floor, with his hands clasped together.

"Comrade! Officer!" he cried. "You don't have to take me to that place! Haven't I told you everything already? What else is it you want to know? There's nothing I wouldn't confess, nothing! Just tell me what it is and I'll confess it straight off. Write it down and I'll sign it—anything! Not room 101!"

"Room 101," said the officer.

The man's face, already very pale, turned a color Winston would not have believed possible. It was definitely, unmistakably, a shade of green.

"Do anything to me!" he yelled. "You've been starving me for weeks. Finish it off and let me die. Shoot me. Hang me. Sentence me to twenty-five years. Is there somebody else you want me to give away? Just say who it is and I'll tell you anything you want. I don't care who it is or what you do to them. I've got a wife and three children. The biggest of them isn't six years old. You can take the whole lot of them and cut their throats in front of my eyes, and I'll stand by and watch it. But not room 101!"

"Room 101," said the officer.

The man looked frantically round at the other prisoners, as though with some idea that he could put another victim in his own place. His eyes settled on the smashed face of the chinless man. He flung out a lean arm.

"That's the one you ought to be taking, not me!" he shouted. "You didn't hear what he was saying after they bashed his face. Give me a chance and I'll tell you every word of it. *He's* the one that's against the Party, not me." The guards stepped forward. The man's voice rose to a shriek. "You didn't hear him!" he repeated. "Something went wrong with the telescreen. *He's* the one you want. Take him, not me!"

The two sturdy guards had stooped to take him by the arms. But just at this moment he flung himself across the floor of the cell and grabbed one of the iron legs that supported the bench. He had set up a wordless howling, like an animal. The guards took hold of him to wrench him loose, but he clung on with astonishing strength. For perhaps twenty seconds they were hauling at him. The prisoners sat quiet, their hands crossed on their knees, looking straight in front of them. The howling stopped; the man had no breath left for anything except hanging on. Then there was a different kind of cry. A kick from a guard's boot had broken the fingers of one of his hands. They dragged him to his feet.

"Room 101," said the officer.

The man was led out, walking unsteadily, with head sunken, nursing his crushed hand, all the fight gone out of him.

A long time passed. If it had been midnight when the skull-faced man was taken away, it was morning; if morning, it was afternoon. Winston was alone, and had been alone for hours. The pain of sitting on the narrow bench was such that often he got up and walked about, unreproved by the telescreen. The piece of bread still lay where the chinless man had dropped it. At the beginning it needed a hard effort not to look at it, but presently hunger gave way to thirst. His mouth was sticky and evil-tasting. The humming sound and the unvarying white light induced a sort of faintness, an empty feeling inside his head. He would get up because the ache in his bones was no longer bearable, and then would sit down again almost at once because he was too dizzy to make sure of staying on his feet. Whenever his physical sensations were a little under control the terror returned. Sometimes with a fading hope he thought of O'Brien and the razor blade. It was thinkable that the razor blade might arrive concealed in his food, if he were ever fed. More dimly he thought of Julia. Somewhere or other she was suffering, perhaps far worse than he. She might be screaming with pain at this moment. He thought: "If I could save Julia by doubling my own pain, would I do it? Yes, I would." But that was merely an intellectual decision, taken because he knew that he ought to take it. He did not feel it. In this place you could not feel anything, except pain and the foreknowledge of pain. Besides, was it possible, when you were actually suffering it, to wish for any reason whatever that your own pain should increase? But that question was not answerable yet.

The boots were approaching again. The door opened. O'Brien came in.

Winston started to his feet. The shock of the sight had driven all caution out of him. For the first time in many years he forgot the presence of the telescreen.

"They've got you too!" he cried.

"They got me a long time ago," said O'Brien with a mild, almost regretful irony. He stepped aside. From behind him there emerged a broadchested guard with a long black truncheon in his hand.

"You knew this, Winston," said O'Brien. "Don't deceive yourself. You did know it—you have always known it."

Yes, he saw now, he had always known it. But there was no time to think of that. All he had eyes for was the truncheon in the guard's hand. It might fall anywhere: on the crown, on the tip of the ear, on the upper arm, on the elbow—

The elbow! He had slumped to his knees, almost paralyzed, clasping the stricken elbow with his other hand. Everything had exploded into yellow light. Inconceivable, inconceivable that one blow could cause such pain! The light cleared and he could see the other two looking down at him. The guard was laughing at his contortions. One question at any rate was answered. Never, for any reason on earth, could you wish for an increase of pain. Of pain you could wish only one thing: that it should stop. Nothing in the world was so bad as physical pain. In the face of pain there are no heroes, no heroes, he thought over and over as he writhed on the floor, clutching uselessly at his disabled left arm.

II

He was lying on something that felt like a camp bed, except that it was higher off the ground and that he was fixed down in some way so that he could not move. Light that seemed stronger than usual was falling on his face. O'Brien was standing at his side, looking down at him intently. At the other side of him stood a man in a white coat, holding a hypodermic syringe.

Even after his eyes were open he took in his surroundings only gradually. He had the impression of swimming up into this room from some quite different world, a sort of underwater world far beneath it. How long he had been down there he did not know. Since the moment when they arrested him he had not seen darkness or daylight. Besides, his memories were not continuous. There had been times when consciousness, even the sort of consciousness that one has in sleep, had stopped dead and started again after a blank interval. But whether the intervals were of days or weeks or only seconds, there was no way of knowing.

With that first blow on the elbow the nightmare had started. Later he was to realize that all that then happened was merely a preliminary, a routine interrogation to which nearly all prisoners were subjected. There was a long range of crimes—espionage, sabotage, and the like—to which everyone had to confess as a matter of course. The confession was a formality, though the torture was real. How many times he had been beaten, how long the beatings had continued, he could not remember. Always there were five or six men in black uniforms at him simultaneously. Sometimes it was fists, sometimes it was truncheons, sometimes it was steel rods, sometimes it was boots. There were times when he rolled about the floor, as shameless as an animal, writhing his body this way and that in an endless, hopeless effort to dodge the kicks, and simply inviting more and yet more kicks, in his ribs, in his belly, on his elbows, on his shins, in his groin, in his testicles, on the bone at the base of his spine. There were times when it went on and on until the cruel, wicked, unforgivable thing seemed to him not that the guards continued to beat him but that he could not force himself into losing consciousness. There were times when his nerve so forsook him that he began shouting for mercy even before the beating began, when the mere sight of a fist drawn back for a blow was enough to make him pour forth a confession of real and imaginary crimes. There were other times when he started out with the resolve of confessing nothing, when every word had to be forced out of him between gasps of pain, and there were times when he feebly tried to compromise, when he said to himself: "I will confess, but not yet. I must hold out till the pain becomes unbearable. Three more kicks, two more kicks, and then I will tell them what they want." Sometimes he was beaten till he could hardly stand, then flung like a sack of potatoes onto the stone floor of a cell, left to recuperate for a few hours, and then taken out and beaten again. There were also longer periods of recovery. He remembered them dimly, because they were spent chiefly in sleep or stupor. He remembered a cell with a plank bed, a sort of shelf sticking out from the wall, and a tin washbasin, and meals of hot soup and bread and sometimes coffee. He remembered a surly barber arriving to scrape his chin and crop his hair, and businesslike, unsympathetic men in white coats feeling his pulse, tapping his reflexes, turning up his eyelids, running harsh fingers over him in search of broken bones, and shooting needles into his arm to make him sleep.

The beatings grew less frequent, and became mainly a threat, a horror to which he could be sent back at any moment when his answers were unsatisfactory. His questioners now were not ruffians in black uniforms but party intellectuals, little rotund men with quick movements and flashing spectacles, who worked on him in relays over periods which lasted—he thought, he could not be sure—ten or twelve hours at a stretch. These other questioners saw to it that he was in constant slight pain, but it was not chiefly pain that they relied on. They slapped his face, wrung his ears, pulled his hair, made him stand on one leg, refused him leave to urinate, shone glaring lights in his face until his eyes ran with water; but the aim of this was simply to humiliate him and destroy his power of arguing and reasoning. Their real weapon was the merciless questioning that went on and on hour after hour, tripping him up, laying traps for him, twisting everything that he said, convicting him at every step of lies and self-contradiction, until he began weeping as much from shame as from nervous fatigue. Sometimes he would weep half a dozen times in a single session. Most of the time they screamed abuse at him and threatened at every hesitation to deliver him over to the guards again; but sometimes they would suddenly change their tune, call him comrade, appeal to him in the name of Ingsoc and Big Brother, and ask him sorrowfully whether even now he had not enough loyalty to the Party left to make him wish to undo the evil he had done. When his nerves were in rags after hours of questioning, even this appeal could reduce him to sniveling tears. In the end the nagging voices broke him down more completely than the boots and fists of the guards. He became simply a mouth that uttered, a hand that signed whatever was demanded of him. His sole concern was to find out what they wanted him to confess, and then confess it quickly, before the bullying started anew. He confessed to the assassination of eminent Party members, the distribution of seditious pamphlets, embezzlement of public funds, sale of military secrets, sabotage of every kind. He confessed that he had been a spy in the pay of the Eastasian government as far back as 1968. He confessed that he was a religious believer, an admirer of capitalism, and a sexual pervert. He confessed that he had murdered his wife, although he knew, and his questioners must have known, that his wife was still alive. He confessed that for years he had been in personal touch with Goldstein and had been a member of an underground organization which had included almost every human being he had ever known. It was easier to confess everything and implicate everybody. Besides, in a sense it was all true. It was true that he had been the enemy of the Party, and in the eyes of the Party there was no distinction between the thought and the deed.

There were also memories of another kind. They stood out in his mind disconnectedly, like pictures with blackness all round them.

He was in a cell which might have been either dark or light, because he could see nothing except a pair of eyes. Near at hand some kind of instrument was ticking slowly and regularly. The eyes grew larger and more luminous. Suddenly he floated out of his seat, dived into the eyes, and was swallowed up.

He was strapped into a chair surrounded by dials, under dazzling lights. A man in a white coat was reading the dials. There was a tramp of heavy boots outside. The door clanged open. The waxen-faced officer marched in, followed by two guards.

"Room 101," said the officer.

The man in the white coat did not turn round. He did not look at Winston either; he was looking only at the dials.

He was rolling down a mighty corridor, a kilometer wide, full of glorious, golden light, roaring with laughter and shouting out confessions at the top of his voice. He was confessing everything, even the things he had succeeded in holding back under the torture. He was relating the entire history of his life to an audience who knew it already. With him were the guards, the other questioners, the men in white coats, O'Brien, Julia, Mr. Charrington, all rolling down the corridor together and shouting with laughter. Some dreadful thing which had lain embedded in the future had somehow been skipped over and had not happened. Everything was all right, there was no more pain, the last detail of his life was laid bare, understood, forgiven.

He was starting up from the plank bed in the half-certainty that he had heard O'Brien's voice. All through his interrogation, although he had never seen him, he had had the feeling that O'Brien was at his elbow, just out of sight. It was O'Brien who was directing everything. It was he who set the guards onto Winston and who prevented them from killing him. It was he who decided when Winston should scream with pain, when he should have a respite, when he should be fed, when he should sleep, when the drugs should be pumped into his arm. It was he who asked the questions and suggested the answers. He was the tormentor, he was the protector, he was the inquisitor, he was the friend. And once—Winston could not remember whether it was in drugged sleep, or in normal sleep, or even in a moment of wakefulness—a voice murmured in his ear: "Don't worry, Winston; you are in my keeping. For seven years I have watched over you. Now the turning point has come. I shall save you, I shall make you perfect." He was not sure whether it was O'Brien's voice; but it was the same voice that had said to him, "We shall meet in the place where there is no darkness," in that other dream, seven years ago.

He did not remember any ending to his interrogation. There was a period of blackness and then the cell, or room, in which he now was had gradually materialized round him. He was almost flat on his back, and unable to move. His body was held down at every essential point. Even the back of his head was gripped in some manner. O'Brien was looking down at him gravely and rather sadly. His face, seen from below, looked coarse and worn, with pouches under the eyes and tired lines from nose to chin. He was older than Winston had thought him; he was perhaps forty-eight or fifty. Under his hand there was a dial with a lever on top and figures running round the face.

"I told you," said O'Brien, "that if we met again it would be here."

"Yes," said Winston.

Without any warning except a slight movement of O'Brien's hand, a wave of pain flooded his body. It was a frightening pain, because he could not see what was happening, and he had the feeling that some mortal injury was being done to him. He did not know whether the thing was really happening, or whether the effect was electrically produced; but his body was being wrenched out of shape, the joints were being slowly torn apart. Although the pain had brought the sweat out on his forehead, the worst of all was the fear that his backbone was about to snap. He set his teeth and breathed hard through his nose, trying to keep silent as long as possible.

"You are afraid," said O'Brien, watching his face, "that in another moment something is going to break. Your especial fear is that it will be your backbone. You have a vivid mental picture of the vertebrae snapping apart and the spinal fluid dripping out of them. That is what you are thinking, is it not, Winston?"

Winston did not answer. O'Brien drew back the lever on the dial. The wave of pain receded almost as quickly as it had come.

"That was forty," said O'Brien. "You can see that the numbers on this dial run up to a hundred. Will you please remember, throughout our conversation, that I have it in my power to inflict pain on you at any moment and to whatever degree I choose. If you tell me any lies, or attempt to prevaricate in any way, or even fall below your usual level of intelligence, you will cry out with pain, instantly. Do you understand that?"

"Yes," said Winston.

O'Brien's manner became less severe. He resettled his spectacles thoughtfully, and took a pace or two up and down. When he spoke his voice was gentle and patient. He had the air of a doctor, a teacher, even a priest, anxious to explain and persuade rather than to punish.

"I am taking trouble with you, Winston," he said, "because you are worth trouble. You know perfectly well what is the matter with you. You have known it for years, though you have fought against the knowledge. You are mentally deranged. You suffer from a defective memory. You are unable to remember real events, and you persuade yourself that you remember other events which never happened. Fortunately it is curable. You have never cured yourself of it, because you did not choose to. There was a small effort of the will that you were not ready to make. Even now, I am well aware, you are clinging to your disease under the impression that it is a virtue. Now we will take an example. At this moment, which power is Oceania at war with?"

"When I was arrested, Oceania was at war with Eastasia."

"With Eastasia. Good. And Oceania has always been at war with Eastasia, has it not?"

Winston drew in his breath. He opened his mouth to speak and then did not speak. He could not take his eyes away from the dial.

"The truth, please, Winston. *Your* truth. Tell me what you think you remember."

"I remember that until only a week before I was arrested, we were not at war with Eastasia at all. We were in alliance with them. The war was against Eurasia. That had lasted for four years. Before that—"

O'Brien stopped him with a movement of the hand.

"Another example," he said. "Some years ago you had a very serious delusion indeed. You believed that three men, three one-time Party members named Jones, Aaronson, and Rutherford—men who were executed for treachery and sabotage after making the fullest possible confession— were not guilty of the crimes they were charged with. You believed that you had seen unmistakable documentary evidence proving that their confessions were false. There was a certain photograph about which you had a hallucination. You believed that you had actually held it in your hands. It was a photograph something like this."

An oblong slip of newspaper had appeared between O'Brien's fingers. For perhaps five seconds it was within the angle of Winston's vision. It was a photograph, and there was no question of its identity. It was *the* photograph. It was another copy of the photograph of Jones, Aaronson, and Rutherford at the Party function in New York, which he had chanced upon eleven years ago and promptly destroyed. For only an instant it was before his eyes, then it was out of sight again. But he had seen it, unquestionably he had seen it! He made a desperate, agonizing effort to wrench the top half of his body free. It was impossible to move so much as a centimeter in any direction. For the moment he had even forgotten the dial. All he wanted was to hold the photograph in his fingers again, or at least to see it.

"It exists!" he cried.

"No," said O'Brien.

He stepped across the room. There was a memory hole in the opposite wall. O'Brien lifted the grating. Unseen, the frail slip of paper was whirling away on the current of warm air; it was vanishing in a flash of flame. O'Brien turned away from the wall.

"Ashes," he said. "Not even identifiable ashes. Dust. It does not exist. It never existed."

"But it did exist! It does exist! It exists in memory. I remember it. You remember it."

"I do not remember it," said O'Brien.

Winston's heart sank. That was doublethink. He had a feeling of deadly helplessness. If he could have been certain that O'Brien was lying, it would not have seemed to matter. But it was perfectly possible that O'Brien had really forgotten the photograph. And if so, then already he would have forgotten his denial of remembering it, and forgotten the act of forgetting. How could one be sure that it was simply trickery? Perhaps that lunatic dislocation in the mind could really happen: that was the thought that defeated him.

O'Brien was looking down at him speculatively. More than ever he had the air of a teacher taking pains with a wayward but promising child.

"There is a party slogan dealing with the control of the past," he said. "Repeat it, if you please."

" 'Who controls the past controls the future; who controls the present controls the past,' " repeated Winston obediently.

" 'Who controls the present controls the past,' " said O'Brien, nodding his head with slow approval. "Is it your opinion, Winston, that the past has real existence?"

Again the feeling of helplessness descended upon Winston. His eyes flitted toward the dial. He not only did not know whether "yes" or "no" was the answer that would save him from pain; he did not even know which answer he believed to be the true one.

O'Brien smiled faintly. "You are no metaphysician, Winston," he said. "Until this moment you had never considered what is meant by existence. I will put it more precisely. Does the past exist concretely, in space? Is there somewhere or other a place, a world of solid objects, where the past is still happening?"

"No."

"Then where does the past exist, if at all?"

"In records. It is written down."

"In records. And—?"

"In the mind. In human memories."

"In memory. Very well, then. We, the Party, control all records, and we control all memories. Then we control the past, do we not?"

"But how can you stop people remembering things?" cried Winston, again momentarily forgetting the dial. "It is involuntary. It is outside oneself. How can you control memory? You have not controlled mine!"

O'Brien's manner grew stern again. He laid his hand on the dial.

"On the contrary," he said, "*you* have not controlled it. That is what has brought you here. You are here because you have failed in humility, in self-discipline. You would not make the act of submission which is the price of sanity. You preferred to be a lunatic, a minority of one. Only the disciplined mind can see reality, Winston. You believe that reality is something objective, external, existing in its own right. You also believe that the nature of reality is self-evident. When you delude yourself into thinking that you see something, you assume that everyone else sees the same thing as you. But I tell you, Winston, that reality is not external. Reality exists in the human mind, and nowhere else. Not in the individual mind, which can make mistakes, and in any case soon perishes; only in the mind of the Party, which is collective and immortal. Whatever the Party holds to be truth is truth. It is impossible to see reality except by looking through the eyes of the Party. That is the fact that you have got to relearn, Winston. It needs an act of self-destruction, an effort of the will. You must humble yourself before you can become sane."

He paused for a few moments, as though to allow what he had been saying to sink in.

"Do you remember," he went on, "writing in your diary, 'Freedom is the freedom to say that two plus two make four'?"

"Yes," said Winston.

O'Brien held up his left hand, its back toward Winston, with the thumb hidden and the four fingers extended.

"How many fingers am I holding up, Winston?"

"Four."

"And if the Party says that it is not four but five—then how many?"

"Four."

The word ended in a gasp of pain. The needle of the dial had shot up to fifty-five. The sweat had sprung out all over Winston's body. The air tore into his lungs and issued again in deep groans which even by clenching his teeth he could not stop. O'Brien watched him, the four fingers still extended. He drew back the lever. This time the pain was only slightly eased.

"How many fingers, Winston?"

"Four."

The needle went up to sixty.

"How many fingers, Winston?"

"Four! Four! What else can I say? Four!"

The needle must have risen again, but he did not look at it. The heavy, stern face and the four fingers filled his vision. The fingers stood up before his eyes like pillars, enormous, blurry, and seeming to vibrate, but unmistakably four.

"How many fingers, Winston?"

"Four! Stop it, stop it! How can you go on? Four! Four!"

"How many fingers, Winston?"

"Five! Five! Five!"

"No, Winston, that is no use. You are lying. You still think there are four. How many fingers, please?"

"Four! Five! Four! Anything you like. Only stop it, stop the pain!"

Abruptly he was sitting up with O'Brien's arm round his shoulders. He had perhaps lost consciousness for a few seconds. The bonds that had held his body down were loosened. He felt very cold, he was shaking uncontrollably, his teeth were chattering, the tears were rolling down his cheeks. For a moment he clung to O'Brien like a baby, curiously comforted by the heavy arm round his shoulders. He had the feeling that O'Brien was his protector, that the pain was something that came from outside, from some other source, and that it was O'Brien who would save him from it.

"You are a slow learner, Winston," said O'Brien gently.

"How can I help it?" he blubbered. "How can I help seeing what is in front of my eyes? Two and two are four."

"Sometimes, Winston. Sometimes they are five. Sometimes they are three. Sometimes they are all of them at once. You must try harder. It is not easy to become sane."

He laid Winston down on the bed. The grip on his limbs tightened again, but the pain had ebbed away and the trembling had stopped, leaving him merely weak and cold. O'Brien motioned with his head to the man in the white coat, who had stood immobile throughout the proceedings. The man in the white coat bent down and looked closely into Winston's eyes, felt his pulse, laid an ear against his chest, tapped here and there; then he nodded to O'Brien.

"Again," said O'Brien.

The pain flowed into Winston's body. The needle must be at seventy, seventy-five. He had shut his eyes this time. He knew that the fingers were still there, and still four. All that mattered was somehow to stay alive until the spasm was over. He had ceased to notice whether he was crying out or not. The pain lessened again. He opened his eyes. O'Brien had drawn back the lever.

"How many fingers, Winston?"

"Four. I suppose there are four. I would see five if I could. I am trying to see five."

"Which do you wish: to persuade me that you see five, or really to see them?"

"Really to see them."

"Again," said O'Brien.

Perhaps the needle was at eighty—ninety. Winston could only intermittently remember why the pain was happening. Behind his screwed-up eyelids a forest of fingers seemed to be moving in a sort of dance, weaving in and out, disappearing behind one another and reappearing again. He was trying to count them, he could not remember why. He knew only that it was impossible to count them, and that this was somehow due to the mysterious identity between five and four. The pain died down again. When he opened his eyes it was to find that he was still seeing the same thing. Innumerable fingers, like moving trees, were still streaming past in either direction, crossing and recrossing. He shut his eyes again.

"How many fingers am I holding up, Winston?"

"I don't know. I don't know. You will kill me if you do that again. Four, five, six—in all honesty I don't know."

"Better," said O'Brien.

A needle slid into Winston's arm. Almost in the same instant a blissful, healing warmth spread all through his body. The pain was already half-forgotten. He opened his eyes and looked up gratefully at O'Brien. At sight of the heavy, lined face, so ugly and so intelligent, his heart seemed to turn over. If he could have moved he would have stretched out a hand and laid it on O'Brien's arm. He had never loved him so deeply as at this moment, and not merely because he had stopped the pain. The old feeling, that at bottom it did not matter whether O'Brien was a friend or an enemy, had come back. O'Brien was a person who could be talked to.

Perhaps one did not want to be loved so much as to be understood. O'Brien had tortured him to the edge of lunacy, and in a little while, it was certain, he would send him to his death. It made no difference. In some sense that went deeper than friendship, they were intimates; somewhere or other, although the actual words might never be spoken, there was a place where they could meet and talk. O'Brien was looking down at him with an expression which suggested that the same thought might be in his own mind. When he spoke it was in an easy, conversational tone.

"Do you know where you are, Winston?" he said.

"I don't know. I can guess. In the Ministry of Love."

"Do you know how long you have been here?"

"I don't know. Days, weeks, months—I think it is months."

"And why do you imagine that we bring people to this place?"

"To make them confess."

"No, that is not the reason. Try again."

"To punish them."

"No!" exclaimed O'Brien. His voice had changed extraordinarily, and his face had suddenly become both stern and animated. "No! Not merely to extract your confession, nor to punish you. Shall I tell you why we have brought you here? To cure you! To make you sane! Will you understand, Winston, that no one whom we bring to this place ever leaves our hands uncured? We are not interested in those stupid crimes that you have committed. The Party is not interested in the overt act; the thought is all we care about. We do not merely destroy our enemies; we change them. Do you understand what I mean by that?"

He was bending over Winston. His face looked enormous because of its nearness, and hideously ugly because it was seen from below. Moreover it was filled with a sort of exaltation, a lunatic intensity. Again Winston's heart shrank. If it had been possible he would have cowered deeper into the bed. He felt certain that O'Brien was about to twist the dial out of sheer wantonness. At this moment, however, O'Brien turned away. He took a pace or two up and down. Then he continued less vehemently:

"The first thing for you to understand is that in this place there are no martyrdoms. You have read of the religious persecutions of the past. In the Middle Ages there was the Inquisition. It was a failure. It set out to eradicate heresy, and ended by perpetuating it. For every heretic it burned at the stake, thousands of others rose up. Why was that? Because the Inquisition killed its enemies in the open, and killed them while they were still unrepentant; in fact, it killed them because they were unrepentant. Men were dying because they would not abandon their true beliefs. Naturally all the glory belonged to the victim and all the shame to the Inquisitor who burned him. Later, in the twentieth century, there were the totalitarians, as they were called. There were the German Nazis and the Russian Communists. The Russians persecuted heresy more cruelly than the Inquisition had done. And they imagined that they had learned from the mistakes of the past; they knew, at any rate, that one must not make martyrs. Before they exposed their victims to public trial, they deliberately set themselves to destroy their dignity. They wore them down by torture and solitude until they were despicable, cringing wretches, confessing whatever was put into their mouths, covering themselves with abuse, accusing and sheltering behind one another, whimpering for mercy. And yet after only a few years the same thing had happened over again. The dead men had become martyrs and their degradation was forgotten. Once again, why was it? In the first place, because the confessions that they had made were obviously extorted and untrue. We do not make mistakes of that kind. All the confessions that are uttered here are true. We make them true. And, above all, we do not allow the dead to rise up against us. You must stop imagining that posterity will vindicate you, Winston. Posterity will never hear of you. You will be lifted clean out from the stream of history. We shall turn you into gas and pour you into the stratosphere. Nothing will remain of you: not a name in a register, not a memory in a living brain. You will be annihilated in the past as well as in the future. You will never have existed."

Then why bother to torture me? thought Winston, with a momentary bitterness. O'Brien checked his step as though Winston had uttered the thought aloud. His large ugly face came nearer, with the eyes a little narrowed.

"You are thinking," he said, "that since we intend to destroy you utterly, so that nothing that you say or do can make the smallest difference—in that case, why do we go to the trouble of interrogating you first? That is what you were thinking, was it not?"

"Yes," said Winston.

O'Brien smiled slightly. "You are a flaw in the pattern, Winston. You are a stain that must be wiped out. Did I not tell you just now that we are different from the persecutors of the past? We are not content with negative obedience, nor even with the most abject submission. When finally you surrender to us, it must be of your own free will. We do not destroy the heretic because he resists us; so long as he resists us we never destroy him. We convert him, we capture his inner mind, we reshape him. We burn all evil and all illusion out of him; we bring him over to our side, not in appearance, but genuinely, heart and soul. We make him one of ourselves before we kill him. It is intolerable to us that an erroneous thought should exist anywhere in the world, however secret and powerless it may be. Even in the instant of death we cannot permit any deviation. In the old days the heretic walked to the stake still a heretic, proclaiming his heresy, exulting in it. Even the victim of the Russian purges could carry rebellion locked up in his skull as he walked down the passage waiting for the bullet. But we make the brain perfect before we blow it out. The command of the old despotisms was 'Thou shalt not.' The command of the totalitarians was 'Thou shalt.' Our command is *'Thou art.'* No one whom we bring to this place ever stands out against us. Everyone is washed clean. Even those three miserable traitors in whose innocence you once believed—Jones, Aaronson, and Rutherford—in the end we broke them down. I took part in their interrogation myself. I saw them gradually worn down, whimpering, groveling, weeping—and in the end it was not with pain or fear, only with penitence. By the time we had finished with them they were only the shells of men. There was nothing left in them except sorrow for what they had done, and love of Big Brother. It was touching to see how they loved him. They begged to be shot quickly, so that they could die while their minds were still clean."

His voice had grown almost dreamy. The exaltation, the lunatic enthusiasm, was still in his face. He is not pretending, thought Winston; he is not a hypocrite; he believes every word he says. What most oppressed him was the consciousness of his own intellectual inferiority. He watched the heavy yet graceful form strolling to and fro, in and out of the range of his vision. O'Brien was a being in all ways larger than himself. There was no idea that he had ever had, or could have, that O'Brien had not long ago known, examined, and rejected. His mind *contained* Winston's mind. But in that case how could it be true that O'Brien was mad? It must be he, Winston, who was mad. O'Brien halted and looked down at him. His voice had grown stern again.

"Do not imagine that you will save yourself, Winston, however completely you surrender to us. No one who has once gone astray is ever spared. And even if we chose to let you live out the natural term of your life, still you would never escape from us. What happens to you here is forever. Understand that in advance. We shall crush you down to the point from which there is no coming back. Things will happen to you from which you could not recover, if you lived a thousand years. Never again will you be capable of ordinary human feeling. Everything will be dead inside you. Never again will you be capable of love, or friendship, or joy of living, or laughter, or curiosity, or courage, or integrity. You will be hollow. We shall squeeze you empty, and then we shall fill you with ourselves."

He paused and signed to the man in the white coat. Winston was aware of some heavy piece of apparatus being pushed into place behind his head. O'Brien had sat down beside the bed, so that his face was almost on a level with Winston's.

"Three thousand," he said, speaking over Winston's head to the man in the white coat. Two soft pads, which felt slightly moist, clamped themselves against Winston's temples. He quailed. There was pain coming, a new kind of pain. O'Brien laid a hand reassuringly, almost kindly, on his.

"This time it will not hurt," he said. "Keep your eyes fixed on mine."

At this moment there was a devastating explosion, or what seemed like
an explosion, though it was not certain whether there was any noise.
There was undoubtedly a blinding flash of light. Winston was not hurt,
only prostrated. Although he had already been lying on his back when
the thing happened, he had a curious feeling that he had been knocked
into that position. A terrific, painless blow had flattened him out. Also
something had happened inside his head. As his eyes regained their focus
he remembered who he was, and where he was, and recognized the face
that was gazing into his own; but somewhere or other there was a large
patch of emptiness, as though a piece had been taken out of his brain.

"It will not last," said O'Brien. "Look me in the eyes. What country is
Oceania at war with?"

Winston thought. He knew what was meant by Oceania, and that he
himself was a citizen of Oceania. He also remembered Eurasia and Eastasia; but who was at war with whom he did not know. In fact he had not
been aware that there was any war.

"I don't remember."

"Oceania is at war with Eastasia. Do you remember that now?"

"Yes."

"Oceania has always been at war with Eastasia. Since the beginning of
your life, since the beginning of the Party, since the beginning of history,
the war has continued without a break, always the same war. Do you
remember that?"

"Yes."

"Eleven years ago you created a legend about three men who had been
condemned to death for treachery. You pretended that you had seen a
piece of paper which proved them innocent. No such piece of paper ever
existed. You invented it, and later you grew to believe in it. You remember now the very moment at which you first invented it. Do you remember that?"

"Yes."

"Just now I held up the fingers of my hand to you. You saw five fingers.
Do you remember that?"

"Yes."

O'Brien held up the fingers of his left hand, with the thumb concealed.

"There are five fingers there. Do you see five fingers?"

"Yes."

And he did see them, for a fleeting instant, before the scenery of his
mind changed. He saw five fingers, and there was no deformity. Then
everything was normal again, and the old fear, the hatred, and the bewil-
derment came crowding back again. But there had been a moment—he
did not know how long, thirty seconds, perhaps—of luminous certainty,
when each new suggestion of O'Brien's had filled up a patch of emptiness
and become absolute truth, and when two and two could have been three

as easily as five, if that were what was needed. It had faded out before O'Brien had dropped his hand; but though he could not recapture it, he could remember it, as one remembers a vivid experience at some remote period of one's life when one was in effect a different person.

"You see now," said O'Brien, "that it is at any rate possible."

"Yes," said Winston.

O'Brien stood up with a satisfied air. Over to his left Winston saw the man in the white coat break an ampoule and draw back the plunger of a syringe. O'Brien turned to Winston with a smile. In almost the old manner he resettled his spectacles on his nose.

"Do you remember writing in your diary," he said, "that it did not matter whether I was a friend or an enemy, since I was at least a person who understood you and could be talked to? You were right. I enjoy talking to you. Your mind appeals to me. It resembles my own mind except that you happen to be insane. Before we bring the session to an end you can ask me a few questions, if you choose."

"Any question I like?"

"Anything." He saw that Winston's eyes were upon the dial. "It is switched off. What is your first question?"

"What have you done with Julia?" said Winston.

O'Brien smiled again. "She betrayed you, Winston. Immediately—unreservedly. I have seldom seen anyone come over to us so promptly. You would hardly recognize her if you saw her. All her rebelliousness, her deceit, her folly, her dirty-mindedness—everything has been burned out of her. It was a perfect conversion, a textbook case."

"You tortured her."

O'Brien left this unanswered. "Next question," he said.

"Does Big Brother exist?"

"Of course he exists. The Party exists. Big Brother is the embodiment of the Party."

"Does he exist in the same way as I exist?"

"You do not exist," said O'Brien.

Once again the sense of helplessness assailed him. He knew, or he could imagine, the arguments which proved his own nonexistence; but they were nonsense, they were only a play on words. Did not the statement, "You do not exist," contain a logical absurdity? But what use was it to say so? His mind shriveled as he thought of the unanswerable, mad arguments with which O'Brien would demolish him.

"I think I exist," he said wearily. "I am conscious of my own identity. I was born, and I shall die. I have arms and legs. I occupy a particular point in space. No other solid object can occupy the same point simultaneously. In that sense, does Big Brother exist?"

"It is of no importance. He exists."

"Will Big Brother ever die?"

"Of course not. How could he die? Next question."

"Does the Brotherhood exist?"

"That, Winston, you will never know. If we choose to set you free when we have finished with you, and if you live to be ninety years old, still you will never learn whether the answer to that question is Yes or No. As long as you live, it will be an unsolved riddle in your mind."

Winston lay silent. His breast rose and fell a little faster. He still had not asked the question that had come into his mind the first. He had got to ask it, and yet it was as though his tongue would not utter it. There was a trace of amusement in O'Brien's face. Even his spectacles seemed to wear an ironical gleam. He knows, thought Winston suddenly, he knows what I am going to ask! At the thought the words burst out of him:

"What is in Room 101?"

The expression on O'Brien's face did not change. He answered drily:

"You know what is in Room 101, Winston. Everyone knows what is in Room 101."

He raised a finger to the man in the white coat. Evidently the session was at an end. A needle jerked into Winston's arm. He sank almost instantly into deep sleep.

III

"There are three stages in your reintegration," said O'Brien. "There is learning, there is understanding, and there is acceptance. It is time for you to enter upon the second stage."

As always, Winston was lying flat on his back. But of late his bonds were looser. They still held him to the bed, but he could move his knees a little and could turn his head from side to side and raise his arms from the elbow. The dial, also, had grown to be less of a terror. He could evade its pangs if he was quick-witted enough; it was chiefly when he showed stupidity that O'Brien pulled the lever. Sometimes they got through a whole session without use of the dial. He could not remember how many sessions there had been. The whole process seemed to stretch out over a long, indefinite time—weeks, possibly—and the intervals between the sessions might sometimes have been days, sometimes only an hour or two.

"As you lie there," said O'Brien, "you have often wondered—you have even asked me—why the Ministry of Love should expend so much time and trouble on you. And when you were free you were puzzled by what was essentially the same question. You could grasp the mechanics of the society you lived in, but not its underlying motives. Do you remember writing in your diary, 'I understand *how*; I do not understand *why*'? It was when you thought about 'why' that you doubted your own sanity. You have read *the book*, Goldstein's book, or parts of it, at least. Did it tell you anything that you did not know already?"

"You have read it?" said Winston.

"I wrote it. That is to say, I collaborated in writing it. No book is produced individually, as you know."

"Is it true, what it says?"

"As description, yes. The program it sets forth is nonsense. The secret accumulation of knowledge—a gradual spread of enlightenment—ultimately a proletarian rebellion—the overthrow of the Party. You foresaw yourself that that was what it would say. It is all nonsense. The proletarians will never revolt, not in a thousand years or a million. They cannot. I do not have to tell you the reason; you know it already. If you have ever cherished any dreams of violent insurrection, you must abandon them. There is no way in which the Party can be overthrown. The rule of the Party is forever. Make that the starting point of your thoughts."

He came closer to the bed. "Forever!" he repeated. "And now let us get back to the question of 'how' and 'why.' You understand well enough *how* the Party maintains itself in power. Now tell me *why* we cling to power. What is our motive? Why should we want power? Go on, speak," he added as Winston remained silent.

Nevertheless Winston did not speak for another moment or two. A feeling of weariness had overwhelmed him. The faint, mad gleam of enthusiasm had come back into O'Brien's face. He knew in advance what O'Brien would say: that the Party did not seek power for its own ends, but only for the good of the majority. That it sought power because men in the mass were frail, cowardly creatures who could not endure liberty or face the truth, and must be ruled over and systematically deceived by others who were stronger than themselves. That the choice for mankind lay between freedom and happiness, and that, for the great bulk of mankind, happiness was better. That the Party was the eternal guardian of the weak, a dedicated sect doing evil that good might come, sacrificing its own happiness to that of others. The terrible thing, thought Winston, the terrible thing was that when O'Brien said this he would believe it. You could see it in his face. O'Brien knew everything. A thousand times better than Winston, he knew what the world was really like, in what degradation the mass of human beings lived and by what lies and barbarities the Party kept them there. He had understood it all, weighed it all, and it made no difference: all was justified by the ultimate purpose. What can you do, thought Winston, against the lunatic who is more intelligent than yourself, who gives your arguments a fair hearing and then simply persists in his lunacy?

"You are ruling over us for our own good," he said feebly. "You believe that human beings are not fit to govern themselves, and therefore—"

He started and almost cried out. A pang of pain had shot through his body. O'Brien had pushed the lever of the dial up to thirty-five.

"That was stupid, Winston, stupid!" he said. "You should know better than to say a thing like that."

He pulled the lever back and continued:

"Now I will tell you the answer to my question. It is this. The Party seeks power entirely for its own sake. We are not interested in the good of others; we are interested solely in power. Not wealth or luxury or long life or happiness; only power, pure power. What pure power means you will understand presently. We are different from all the oligarchies of the past in that we know what we are doing. All the others, even those who resembled ourselves, were cowards and hypocrites. The German Nazis and the Russian Communists came very close to us in their methods, but they never had the courage to recognize their own motives. They pretended, perhaps they even believed, that they had seized power unwillingly and for a limited time, and that just round the corner there lay a paradise where human beings would be free and equal. We are not like that. We know that no one ever seizes power with the intention of relinquishing it. Power is not a means; it is an end. One does not establish a dictatorship in order to safeguard a revolution; one makes the revolution in order to establish the dictatorship. The object of persecution is persecution. The object of torture is torture. The object of power is power. Now do you begin to understand me?"

Winston was struck, as he had been struck before, by the tiredness of O'Brien's face. It was strong and fleshy and brutal, it was full of intelligence and a sort of controlled passion before which he felt himself helpless; but it was tired. There were pouches under the eyes, the skin sagged from the cheekbones. O'Brien leaned over him, deliberately bringing the worn face nearer.

"You are thinking," he said, "that my face is old and tired. You are thinking that I talk of power, and yet I am not even able to prevent the decay of my own body. Can you not understand, Winston, that the individual is only a cell? The weariness of the cell is the vigor of the organism. Do you die when you cut your fingernails?"

He turned away from the bed and began strolling up and down again, one hand in his pocket.

"We are the priests of power," he said. "God is power. But at present power is only a word so far as you are concerned. It is time for you to gather some idea of what power means. The first thing you must realize is that power is collective. The individual only has power in so far as he ceases to be an individual. You know the Party slogan: 'Freedom is Slavery.' Has it ever occurred to you that it is reversible? Slavery is freedom. Alone—free—the human being is always defeated. It must be so, because every human being is doomed to die, which is the greatest of all failures. But if he can make complete, utter submission, if he can escape from his identity, if he can merge himself in the Party so that he *is* the Party, then he is all-powerful and immortal. The second thing for you to realize is that power is power over human beings. Over the body—but, above all, over the mind. Power over matter—external reality, as you would call it—is not important. Already our control over matter is absolute."

For a moment Winston ignored the dial. He made a violent effort to raise himself into a sitting position, and merely succeeded in wrenching his body painfully.

"But how can you control matter?" he burst out. "You don't even control the climate or the law of gravity. And there are disease, pain, death—"

O'Brien silenced him by a movement of the hand. "We control matter because we control the mind. Reality is inside the skull. You will learn by degrees, Winston. There is nothing that we could not do. Invisibility, levitation—anything. I could float off this floor like a soap bubble if I wished to. I do not wish to, because the Party does not wish it. You must get rid of those nineteenth-century ideas about the laws of nature. We make the laws of nature."

"But you do not! You are not even masters of this planet. What about Eurasia and Eastasia? You have not conquered them yet."

"Unimportant. We shall conquer them when it suits us. And if we did not, what difference would it make? We can shut them out of existence. Oceania is the world."

"But the world itself is only a speck of dust. And man is tiny—helpless! How long has he been in existence? For millions of years the earth was uninhabited."

"Nonsense. The earth is as old as we are, no older. How could it be older? Nothing exists except through human consciousness."

"But the rocks are full of the bones of extinct animals—mammoths and mastodons and enormous reptiles which lived here long before man was ever heard of."

"Have you ever seen those bones, Winston? Of course not. Nineteenth-century biologists invented them. Before man there was nothing. After man, if he could come to an end, there would be nothing. Outside man there is nothing."

"But the whole universe is outside us. Look at the stars! Some of them are a million light-years away. They are out of our reach forever."

"What are the stars?" said O'Brien indifferently. "They are bits of fire a few kilometers away. We could reach them if we wanted to. Or we could blot them out. The earth is the center of the universe. The sun and the stars go round it."

Winston made another convulsive movement. This time he did not say anything. O'Brien continued as though answering a spoken objection:

"For certain purposes, of course, that is not true. When we navigate the ocean, or when we predict an eclipse, we often find it convenient to assume that the earth goes round the sun and that the stars are millions upon millions of kilometers away. But what of it? Do you suppose it is beyond us to produce a dual system of astronomy? The stars can be near or distant, according as we need them. Do you suppose our mathematicians are unequal to that? Have you forgotten doublethink?"

Winston shrank back upon the bed. Whatever he said, the swift answer crushed him like a bludgeon. And yet he knew, he *knew*, that he was in the right. The belief that nothing exists outside your own mind—surely there must be some way of demonstrating that it was false. Had it not been exposed long ago as a fallacy? There was even a name for it, which he had forgotten. A faint smile twitched the corners of O'Brien's mouth as he looked down at him.

"I told you, Winston," he said, "that metaphysics is not your strong point. The word you are trying to think of is solipsism. But you are mistaken. This is not solipsism. Collective solipsism, if you like. But that is a different thing; in fact, the opposite thing. All this is a digression," he added in a different tone. "The real power, the power we have to fight for night and day, is not power over things, but over men." He paused, and for a moment assumed again his air of a schoolmaster questioning a promising pupil:

"How does one man assert his power over another, Winston?"

Winston thought. "By making him suffer," he said.

"Exactly. By making him suffer. Obedience is not enough. Unless he is suffering, how can you be sure that he is obeying your will and not his own? Power is in inflicting pain and humiliation. Power is in tearing human minds to pieces and putting them together again in new shapes of your own choosing. Do you begin to see, then, what kind of world we are creating? It is the exact opposite of the stupid hedonistic Utopias that the old reformers imagined. A world of fear and treachery and torment, a world of trampling and being trampled upon, a world which will grow not less but *more* merciless as it refines itself. Progress in our world will be progress toward more pain. The old civilizations claimed that they were founded on love or justice. Ours is founded upon hatred. In our world there will be no emotions except fear, rage, triumph, and self-abasement. Everything else we shall destroy—everything. Already we are breaking down the habits of thought which have survived from before the Revolution. We have cut the links between child and parent, and between man and man, and between man and woman. No one dares trust a wife or a child or a friend any longer. But in the future there will be no wives and no friends. Children will be taken from their mothers at birth, as one takes eggs from a hen. The sex instinct will be eradicated. Procreation will be an annual formality like the renewal of a ration card. We shall abolish the orgasm. Our neurologists are at work upon it now. There will be no loyalty, except toward the Party. There will be no love, except the love of Big Brother. There will be no laughter, except the laugh of triumph over a defeated enemy. There will be no art, no literature, no science. When we are omnipotent we shall have no more need of science. There will be no distinction between beauty and ugliness. There will be no curiosity, no enjoyment of the process of life. All competing pleasures will be destroyed. But always—do not forget this, Winston—always there will be the intoxication of power, constantly increasing and constantly growing subtler. Always, at every moment, there will be the thrill of victory, the sensation of trampling on an enemy who is helpless. If you want a picture of the future, imagine a boot stamping on a human face—forever."

He paused as though he expected Winston to speak. Winston had tried to shrink back into the surface of the bed again. He could not say anything. His heart seemed to be frozen. O'Brien went on:

"And remember that it is forever. The face will always be there to be stamped upon. The heretic, the enemy of society, will always be there, so that he can be defeated and humiliated over again. Everything that you have undergone since you have been in our hands—all that will continue, and worse. The espionage, the betrayals, the arrests, the tortures, the executions, the disappearances will never cease. It will be a world of terror as much as a world of triumph. The more the Party is powerful, the less it will be tolerant; the weaker the opposition, the tighter the despotism. Goldstein and his heresies will live forever. Every day, at every moment, they will be defeated, discredited, ridiculed, spat upon—and yet they will always survive. This drama that I have played out with you during seven years will be played out over and over again, generation after generation, always in subtler forms. Always we shall have the heretic here at our mercy, screaming with pain, broken up, contemptible—and in the end utterly penitent, saved from himself, crawling to our feet of his own accord. That is the world that we are preparing, Winston. A world of victory after victory, triumph after triumph after triumph: an endless pressing, pressing, pressing upon the nerve of power. You are beginning, I can see, to realize what that world will be like. But in the end you will do more than understand it. You will accept it, welcome it, become part of it."

Winston had recovered himself sufficiently to speak. "You can't!" he said weakly.

"What do you mean by that remark, Winston?"

"You could not create such a world as you have just described. It is a dream. It is impossible."

"Why?"

"It is impossible to found a civilization on fear and hatred and cruelty. It would never endure."

"Why not?"

"It would have no vitality. It would disintegrate. It would commit suicide."

"Nonsense. You are under the impression that hatred is more exhausting than love. Why should it be? And if it were, what difference would that make? Suppose that we choose to wear ourselves out faster. Suppose that we quicken the tempo of human life till men are senile at thirty. Still what difference would it make? Can you not understand that the death of the individual is not death? The Party is immortal."

As usual, the voice had battered Winston into helplessness. Moreover he was in dread that if he persisted in his disagreement O'Brien would twist the dial again. And yet he could not keep silent. Feebly, without arguments, with nothing to support him except his inarticulate horror of what O'Brien had said, he returned to the attack.

"I don't know—I don't care. Somehow you will fail. Something will defeat you. Life will defeat you."

"We control life, Winston, at all its levels. You are imagining that there is something called human nature which will be outraged by what we do and will turn against us. But we create human nature. Men are infinitely malleable. Or perhaps you have returned to your old idea that the proletarians or the slaves will arise and overthrow us. Put it out of your mind. They are helpless, like the animals. Humanity is the Party. The others are outside—irrelevant. "

"I don't care. In the end they will beat you. Sooner or later they will see you for what you are, and then they will tear you to pieces."

"Do you see any evidence that that is happening? Or any reason why it should?"

"No. I believe it. I *know* that you will fail. There is something in the universe—I don't know, some spirit, some principle—that you will never overcome."

"Do you believe in God, Winston?"

"No."

"Then what is it, this principle that will defeat us?"

"I don't know. The spirit of Man."

"And do you consider yourself a man?"

"Yes."

"If you are a man, Winston, you are the last man. Your kind is extinct; we are the inheritors. Do you understand that you are *alone*? You are outside history, you are nonexistent." His manner changed and he said more harshly: "And you consider yourself morally superior to us, with our lies and our cruelty?"

"Yes, I consider myself superior."

O'Brien did not speak. Two other voices were speaking. After a moment Winston recognized one of them as his own. It was a sound track of the conversation he had had with O'Brien, on the night when he had enrolled himself in the Brotherhood. He heard himself promising to lie, to steal, to forge, to murder, to encourage drug taking and prostitution, to disseminate venereal diseases, to throw vitriol in a child's face. O'Brien made a small impatient gesture, as though to say that the demonstration was hardly worth making. Then he turned a switch and the voices stopped.

"Get up from the bed," he said.

The bonds had loosened themselves. Winston lowered himself to the floor and stood up unsteadily.

"You are the last man," said O'Brien. "You are the guardian of the human spirit. You shall see yourself as you are. Take off your clothes."

Winston undid the bit of string that held his overalls together. The zip fastener had long since been wrenched out of them. He could not remember whether at any time since his arrest he had taken off all his clothes at one time. Beneath the overalls his body was looped with filthy yellowish rags, just recognizable as the remnants of underclothes. As he slid them to the ground he saw that there was a three-sided mirror at the far end of the room. He approached it, then stopped short. An involuntary cry had broken out of him.

"Go on," said O'Brien. "Stand between the wings of the mirror. You shall see the side view as well."

He had stopped because he was frightened. A bowed, gray-colored, skeletonlike thing was coming toward him. Its actual appearance was frightening, and not merely the fact that he knew it to be himself. He moved closer to the glass. The creature's face seemed to be protruded, because of its bent carriage. A forlorn, jailbird's face with a nobby forehead running back into a bald scalp, a crooked nose and battered-looking cheekbones above which the eyes were fierce and watchful. The cheeks were seamed, the mouth had a drawn-in look. Certainly it was his own face, but it seemed to him that it had changed more than he had changed inside. The emotions it registered would be different from the ones he felt. He had gone partially bald. For the first moment he had thought that he had gone gray as well, but it was only the scalp that was gray. Except for his hands and a circle of his face, his body was gray all over with ancient, ingrained dirt. Here and there under the dirt there were the red scars of wounds, and near the ankle the varicose ulcer was an inflamed mass with flakes of skin peeling off it. But the truly frightening thing was the emaciation of his body. The barrel of the ribs was as narrow as that of a skeleton; the legs had shrunk so that the knees were thicker than the thighs. He saw now what O'Brien had meant about seeing the side view. The curvature of the spine was astonishing. The thin shoulders were hunched forward so as to make a cavity of the chest, the scraggy neck seemed to be bending double under the weight of the skull. At a guess he would have said that it was the body of a man of sixty, suffering from some malignant disease.

"You have thought sometimes," said O'Brien, "that my face—the face of a member of the Inner Party—looks old and worn. What do you think of your own face?"

He seized Winston's shoulder and spun him round so that he was facing him.

"Look at the condition you are in!" he said. "Look at this filthy grime all over your body. Look at the dirt between your toes. Look at that disgusting running sore on your leg. Do you know that you stink like a goat? Probably you have ceased to notice it. Look at your emaciation. Do you see? I can make my thumb and forefinger meet around your bicep. I could snap your neck like a carrot. Do you know that you have lost twenty-five kilograms since you have been in our hands? Even your hair is coming out in handfuls. Look!" He plucked at Winston's head and brought away a tuft of hair. "Open your mouth. Nine, ten, eleven teeth left. How many had you when you came to us? And the few you have left are dropping out of your head. Look here!"

He seized one of Winston's remaining front teeth between his powerful thumb and forefinger. A twinge of pain shot through Winston's jaw. O'Brien had wrenched the loose tooth out by the roots. He tossed it across the cell.

"You are rotting away," he said; "you are falling to pieces. What are you? A bag of filth. Now turn round and look into that mirror again. Do you see that thing facing you? That is the last man. If you are human, that is humanity. Now put your clothes on again."

Winston began to dress himself with slow stiff movements. Until now he had not seemed to notice how thin and weak he was. Only one thought stirred in his mind: that he must have been in this place longer than he had imagined. Then suddenly as he fixed the miserable rags round himself a feeling of pity for his ruined body overcame him. Before he knew what he was doing he had collapsed onto a small stool that stood beside the bed and burst into tears. He was aware of his ugliness, his gracelessness, a bundle of bones in filthy underclothes sitting weeping in the harsh white light; but he could not stop himself. O'Brien laid a hand on his shoulder, almost kindly.

"It will not last forever," he said. "You can escape from it whenever you choose. Everything depends on yourself."

"You did it!" sobbed Winston. "You reduced me to this state."

"No, Winston, you reduced yourself to it. This is what you accepted when you set yourself up against the Party. It was all contained in that first act. Nothing has happened that you did not foresee."

He paused, and then went on:

"We have beaten you, Winston. We have broken you up. You have seen what your body is like. Your mind is in the same state. I do not think there can be much pride left in you. You have been kicked and flogged and insulted, you have screamed with pain, you have rolled on the floor in your own blood and vomit. You have whimpered for mercy, you have betrayed everybody and everything. Can you think of a single degradation that has not happened to you?"

Winston had stopped weeping, though the tears were still oozing out of his eyes. He looked up at O'Brien.

"I have not betrayed Julia," he said.

O'Brien looked down at him thoughtfully. "No," he said, "no; that is perfectly true. You have not betrayed Julia."

The peculiar reverence for O'Brien, which nothing seemed able to destroy, flooded Winston's heart again. How intelligent, he thought, how intelligent! Never did O'Brien fail to understand what was said to him. Anyone else on earth would have answered promptly that he *had* betrayed Julia. For what was there that they had not screwed out of him under the torture? He had told them everything he knew about her, her habits, her character, her past life; he had confessed in the most trivial detail everything that had happened at their meetings, all that he had said to her and she to him, their black-market meals, their adulteries, their vague plottings against the Party—everything. And yet, in the sense in which he intended the word, he had not betrayed her. He had not stopped loving her; his feeling toward her had remained the same. O'Brien had seen what he meant without the need for explanation.

"Tell me," he said, "how soon will they shoot me?"

"It might be a long time," said O'Brien. "You are a difficult case. But don't give up hope. Everyone is cured sooner or later. In the end we shall shoot you."

IV

He was much better. He was growing fatter and stronger every day, if it was proper to speak of days.

The white light and the humming sound were the same as ever, but the cell was a little more comfortable than the others he had been in. There were a pillow and a mattress on the plank bed, and a stool to sit on. They had given him a bath, and they allowed him to wash himself fairly frequently in a tin basin. They even gave him warm water to wash with. They had given him new underclothes and a clean suit of overalls. They had dressed his varicose ulcer with soothing ointment. They had pulled out the remnants of his teeth and given him a new set of dentures.

Weeks or months must have passed. It would have been possible now to keep count of the passage of time, if he had felt any interest in doing so, since he was being fed at what appeared to be regular intervals. He was getting, he judged, three meals in the twenty-four hours; sometimes he wondered dimly whether he was getting them by night or by day. The food was surprisingly good, with meat at every third meal. Once there was even a packet of cigarettes. He had no matches, but the never-speaking guard who brought his food would give him a light. The first time he tried to smoke it made him sick, but he persevered, and spun the packet out for a long time, smoking half a cigarette after each meal.

They had given him a white slate with a stump of pencil tied to the corner. At first he made no use of it. Even when he was awake he was completely torpid. Often he would lie from one meal to the next almost without stirring, sometimes asleep, sometimes waking into vague reveries in which it was too much trouble to open his eyes. He had long grown used to sleeping with a strong light on his face. It seemed to make no difference, except that one's dreams were more coherent. He dreamed a great deal all through this time, and they were always happy dreams. He was in the Golden Country, or he was sitting among enormous, glorious, sunlit ruins, with his mother, with Julia, with O'Brien—not doing anything, merely sitting in the sun, talking of peaceful things. Such thoughts as he had when he was awake were mostly about his dreams. He seemed to have lost the power of intellectual effort, now that the stimulus of pain had been removed. He was not bored; he had no desire for conversation or distraction. Merely to be alone, not to be beaten or questioned, to have enough to eat, and to be clean all over, was completely satisfying.

By degrees he came to spend less time in sleep, but he still felt no impulse to get off the bed. All he cared for was to lie quiet and feel the strength gathering in his body. He would finger himself here and there, trying to make sure that it was not an illusion that his muscles were growing rounder and his skin tauter. Finally it was established beyond a doubt that he was growing fatter; his thighs were now definitely thicker than his knees. After that, reluctantly at first, he began exercising himself regularly. In a little while he could walk three kilometers, measured by pacing the cell, and his bowed shoulders were growing straighter. He attempted more elaborate exercises, and was astonished and humiliated to find what things he could not do. He could not move out of a walk, he could not hold his stool out at arm's length, he could not stand on one leg without falling over. He squatted down on his heels, and found that with agonizing pains in thigh and calf he could just lift himself to a standing position. He lay flat on his belly and tried to lift his weight by his hands. It was hopeless; he could not raise himself a centimeter. But after a few more days—a few more mealtimes—even that feat was accomplished. A time came when he could do it six times running. He began to grow actually proud of his body, and to cherish an intermittent belief that his face was growing back to normal. Only when he chanced to put his hand on his bald scalp did he remember the seamed, ruined face that had looked back at him out of the mirror.

His mind grew more active. He sat down on the plank bed, his back against the wall and the slate on his knees, and set to work deliberately at the task of re-educating himself.

He had capitulated; that was agreed. In reality, as he saw now, he had been ready to capitulate long before he had taken the decision. From the moment when he was inside the Ministry of Love—and yes, even during those minutes when he and Julia had stood helpless while the iron voice from the telescreen told them what to do—he had grasped the frivolity, the shallowness of his attempt to set himself up against the power of the Party. He knew now that for seven years the Thought Police had watched him like a beetle under a magnifying glass. There was no physical act, no word spoken aloud, that they had not noticed, no train of thought that they had not been able to infer. Even the speck of whitish dust on the cover of his diary they had carefully replaced. They had played sound tracks to him, shown him photographs. Some of them were photographs of Julia and himself. Yes, even . . . He could not fight against the Party any longer. Besides, the Party was in the right. It must be so: how could the immortal, collective brain be mistaken? By what external standard could you check its judgments? Sanity was statistical. It was merely a question of learning to think as they thought. Only—!

The pencil felt thick and awkward in his fingers. He began to write down the thoughts that came into his head. He wrote first in large clumsy capitals:

FREEDOM IS SLAVERY.

Then almost without a pause he wrote beneath it:

TWO AND TWO MAKE FIVE.

But then there came a sort of check. His mind, as though shying away from something, seemed unable to concentrate. He knew that he knew what came next, but for the moment he could not recall it. When he did recall it, it was only by consciously reasoning out what it must be; it did not come of its own accord. He wrote:

GOD IS POWER.

He accepted everything. The past was alterable. The past never had been altered. Oceania was at war with Eastasia. Oceania had always been at war with Eastasia. Jones, Aaronson, and Rutherford were guilty of the crimes they were charged with. He had never seen the photograph that disproved their guilt. It had never existed; he had invented it. He remembered remembering contrary things, but those were false memories, products of self-deception. How easy it all was! Only surrender, and everything else followed. It was like swimming against a current that swept you backwards however hard you struggled, and then suddenly deciding to turn round and go with the current instead of opposing it. Nothing had changed except your own attitude; the predestined thing happened in any case. He hardly knew why he had ever rebelled. Everything was easy, except—!

Anything could be true. The so-called laws of nature were nonsense.

The law of gravity was nonsense. "If I wished," O'Brien had said, "I could float off this floor like a soap bubble." Winston worked it out. "If he *thinks* he floats off the floor, and if I simultaneously *think* I see him do it, then the thing happens." Suddenly, like a lump of submerged wreckage breaking the surface of water, the thought burst into his mind: "It doesn't really happen. We imagine it. It is hallucination." He pushed the thought under instantly. The fallacy was obvious. It presupposed that somewhere or other, outside oneself, there was a "real" world where "real" things happened. But how could there be such a world? What knowledge have we of anything, save through our own minds? All happenings are in the mind. Whatever happens in all minds, truly happens.

He had no difficulty in disposing of the fallacy, and he was in no danger of succumbing to it. He realized, nevertheless, that it ought never to have occurred to him. The mind should develop a blind spot whenever a dangerous thought presented itself. The process should be automatic, instinctive. *Crimestop,* they called it in Newspeak.

He set to work to exercise himself in crimestop. He presented himself with propositions—"the Party says the earth is flat," "the Party says that ice is heavier than water"—and trained himself in not seeing or not understanding the arguments that contradicted them. It was not easy. It needed great powers of reasoning and improvisation. The arithmetical problems raised, for instance, by such a statement as "two and two make five" were beyond his intellectual grasp. It needed also a sort of athleticism of mind, an ability at one moment to make the most delicate use of logic and at the next to be unconscious of the crudest logical errors. Stupidity was as necessary as intelligence, and as difficult to attain.

All the while, with one part of his mind, he wondered how soon they would shoot him. "Everything depends on yourself," O'Brien had said; but he knew that there was no conscious act by which he could bring it nearer. It might be ten minutes hence, or ten years. They might keep him for years in solitary confinement; they might send him to a labor camp; they might release him for a while, as they sometimes did. It was perfectly possible that before he was shot the whole drama of his arrest and interrogation would be enacted all over again. The one certain thing was that death never came at an expected moment. The tradition—the unspoken tradition: somehow you knew it, though you never heard it said—was that they shot you from behind, always in the back of the head, without warning, as you walked down a corridor from cell to cell.

One day—but "one day" was not the right expression; just as probably it was in the middle of the night: once—he fell into a strange, blissful reverie. He was walking down the corridor, waiting for the bullet. He knew that it was coming in another moment. Everything was settled, smoothed out, reconciled. There were no more doubts, no more arguments, no more pain, no more fear. His body was healthy and strong. He walked easily, with a joy of movement and with a feeling of walking in sunlight. He was not any longer in the narrow white corridors of the Ministry of Love; he was in the enormous sunlit passage, a kilometer wide, down which he had seemed to walk in the delirium induced by drugs. He was in the Golden Country, following the foot track across the old rabbit-cropped pasture. He could feel the short springy turf under his feet and the gentle sunshine on his face. At the edge of the field were the elm trees, faintly stirring, and somewhere beyond that was the stream where the dace lay in the green pools under the willows.

Suddenly he started up with a shock of horror. The sweat broke out on his backbone. He had heard himself cry aloud:

"Julia! Julia! Julia, my love! Julia!"

For a moment he had had an overwhelming hallucination of her presence. She had seemed to be not merely with him, but inside him. It was as though she had got into the texture of his skin. In that moment he had loved her far more than he had ever done when they were together and free. Also he knew that somewhere or other she was still alive and needed his help.

He lay back on the bed and tried to compose himself. What had he done? How many years had he added to his servitude by that moment of weakness?

In another moment he would hear the tramp of boots outside. They could not let such an outburst go unpunished. They would know now, if they had not known before, that he was breaking the agreement he had made with them. He obeyed the Party, but he still hated the Party. In the old days he had hidden a heretical mind beneath an appearance of conformity. Now he had retreated a step further: in the mind he had surrendered, but he had hoped to keep the inner heart inviolate. He knew that he was in the wrong, but he preferred to be in the wrong. They would understand that—O'Brien would understand it. It was all confessed in that single foolish cry.

He would have to start all over again. It might take years. He ran a hand over his face, trying to familiarize himself with the new shape. There were deep furrows in the cheeks, the cheekbones felt sharp, the nose flattened. Besides, since last seeing himself in the glass he had been given a complete new set of teeth. It was not easy to preserve inscrutability when you did not know what your face looked like. In any case, mere control of the features was not enough. For the first time he perceived that if you want to keep a secret you must also hide it from yourself. You must know all the while that it is there, but until it is needed you must never let it emerge into your consciousness in any shape that could be given a name. From now onwards he must not only think right; he must feel right, dream right. And all the while he must keep his hatred locked up inside him like a ball of matter which was part of himself and yet unconnected with the rest of him, a kind of cyst.

One day they would decide to shoot him. You could not tell when it would happen, but a few seconds beforehand it should be possible to guess. It was always from behind, walking down a corridor. Ten seconds would be enough. In that time the world inside him could turn over. And then suddenly, without a word uttered, without a check in his step, without the changing of a line in his face—suddenly the camouflage would be down and bang! would go the batteries of his hatred. Hatred would fill him like an enormous roaring flame. And almost in the same instant bang! would go the bullet, too late, or too early. They would have blown his brain to pieces before they could reclaim it. The heretical thought would be unpunished, unrepented, out of their reach forever. They would have blown a hole in their own perfection. To die hating them, that was freedom. He shut his eyes. It was more difficult than accepting an intellectual discipline. It was a question of degrading himself, mutilating himself. He had got to plunge into the filthiest of filth. What was the most horrible, sickening thing of all? He thought of Big Brother. The enormous face (because of constantly seeing it on posters he always thought of it as being a meter wide), with its heavy black mustache and the eyes that followed you to and fro, seemed to float into his mind of its own accord. What were his true feelings toward Big Brother?

There was a heavy tramp of boots in the passage. The steel door swung open with a clang. O'Brien walked into the cell. Behind him were the waxen-faced officer and the black-uniformed guards.

"Get up," said O'Brien. "Come here."

Winston stood opposite him. O'Brien took Winston's shoulders between his strong hands and looked at him closely.

"You have had thoughts of deceiving me," he said. "That was stupid. Stand up straighter. Look me in the face."

He paused, and went on in a gentler tone:

"You are improving. Intellectually there is very little wrong with you. It is only emotionally that you have failed to make progress. Tell me, Winston—and remember, no lies; you know that I am always able to detect a lie—tell me, what are your true feelings toward Big Brother?"

"I hate him."

"You hate him. Good. Then the time has come for you to take the last step. You must love Big Brother. It is not enough to obey him; you must love him."

He released Winston with a little push toward the guards.

"Room 101," he said.

V

At each stage of his imprisonment he had known, or seemed to know, whereabouts he was in the windowless building. Possibly there were slight differences in the air pressure. The cells where the guards had beaten him were below ground level. The room where he had been interrogated by O'Brien was high up near the roof. This place was many meters underground, as deep down as it was possible to go.

It was bigger than most of the cells he had been in. But he hardly noticed his surroundings. All he noticed was that there were two small tables straight in front of him, each covered with green baize. One was only a meter or two from him; the other was further away, near the door. He was strapped upright in a chair, so tightly that he could move nothing, not even his head. A sort of pad gripped his head from behind, forcing him to look straight in front of him.

For a moment he was alone, then the door opened and O'Brien came in.

"You asked me once," said O'Brien, "what was in Room 101. I told you that you knew the answer already. Everyone knows it. The thing that is in Room 101 is the worst thing in the world."

The door opened again. A guard came in, carrying something made of wire, a box or basket of some kind. He set it down on the further table. Because of the position in which O'Brien was standing, Winston could not see what the thing was.

"The worst thing in the world," said O'Brien, "varies from individual to individual. It may be burial alive, or death by fire, or by drowning, or by impalement, or fifty other deaths. There are cases where it is some quite trivial thing, not even fatal."

He had moved a little to one side, so that Winston had a better view of the thing on the table. It was an oblong wire cage with a handle on top for carrying it by. Fixed to the front of it was something that looked like a fencing mask, with the concave side outwards. Although it was three or four meters away from him, he could see that the cage was divided lengthways into two compartments, and that there was some kind of creature in each. They were rats.

"In your case," said O'Brien, "the worst thing in the world happens to be rats."

A sort of premonitory tremor, a fear of he was not certain what, had passed through Winston as soon as he caught his first glimpse of the cage. But at this moment the meaning of the masklike attachment in front of it suddenly sank into him. His bowels seemed to turn to water.

"You can't do that!" he cried out in a high cracked voice. "You couldn't, you couldn't! It's impossible."

"Do you remember," said O'Brien, "the moment of panic that used to occur in your dreams? There was a wall of blackness in front of you, and a roaring sound in your ears. There was something terrible on the other side of the wall. You knew that you knew what it was, but you dared not drag it into the open. It was the rats that were on the other side of the wall."

"O'Brien!" said Winston, making an effort to control his voice. "You know this is not necessary. What is it that you want me to do?"

O'Brien made no direct answer. When he spoke it was in the school-masterish manner that he sometimes affected. He looked thoughtfully into the distance, as though he were addressing an audience somewhere behind Winston's back.

"By itself," he said, "pain is not always enough. There are occasions when a human being will stand out against pain, even to the point of death. But for everyone there is something unendurable—something that cannot be contemplated. Courage and cowardice are not involved. If you are falling from a height it is not cowardly to clutch at a rope. If you have come up from deep water it is not cowardly to fill your lungs with air. It is merely an instinct which cannot be disobeyed. It is the same with the rats. For you, they are unendurable. They are a form of pressure that you cannot withstand, even if you wished to. You will do what is required of you."

"But what is it, what is it? How can I do it if I don't know what it is?"

O'Brien picked up the cage and brought it across to the nearer table. He set it down carefully on the baize cloth. Winston could hear the blood singing in his ears. He had the feeling of sitting in utter loneliness. He was in the middle of a great empty plain, a flat desert drenched with sunlight, across which all sounds came to him out of immense distances. Yet the cage with the rats was not two meters away from him. They were enormous rats. They were at the age when a rat's muzzle grows blunt and fierce and his fur brown instead of gray.

"The rat," said O'Brien, still addressing his invisible audience, "although a rodent, is carnivorous. You are aware of that. You will have heard of the things that happen in the poor quarters of this town. In some streets a woman dare not leave her baby alone in the house, even for five minutes. The rats are certain to attack it. Within quite a small time they will strip it to the bones. They also attack sick or dying people. They show astonishing intelligence in knowing when a human being is helpless."

There was an outburst of squeals from the cage. It seemed to reach Winston from far away. The rats were fighting; they were trying to get at each other through the partition. He heard also a deep groan of despair. That, too, seemed to come from outside himself.

O'Brien picked up the cage, and, as he did so, pressed something in it. There was a sharp click. Winston made a frantic effort to tear himself loose from the chair. It was hopeless: every part of him, even his head, was held immovably. O'Brien moved the cage nearer. It was less than a meter from Winston's face.

"I have pressed the first lever," said O'Brien. "You understand the construction of this cage. The mask will fit over your head, leaving no exit. When I press this other lever, the door of the cage will slide up. These starving brutes will shoot out of it like bullets. Have you ever seen a rat leap through the air? They will leap onto your face and bore straight into it. Sometimes they attack the eyes first. Sometimes they burrow through the cheeks and devour the tongue."

The cage was nearer; it was closing in. Winston heard a succession of shrill cries which appeared to be occurring in the air above his head. But he fought furiously against his panic. To think, to think, even with a split second left—to think was the only hope. Suddenly the foul musty odor of the brutes struck his nostrils. There was a violent convulsion of nausea inside him, and he almost lost consciousness. Everything had gone black. For an instant he was insane, a screaming animal. Yet he came out of the blackness clutching an idea. There was one and only one way to save himself. He must interpose another human being, the *body* of another human being, between himself and the rats.

The circle of the mask was large enough now to shut out the vision of anything else. The wire door was a couple of hand-spans from his face. The rats knew what was coming now. One of them was leaping up and down; the other, an old scaly grandfather of the sewers, stood up, with his pink hands against the bars, and fiercely snuffed the air. Winston could see the whiskers and the yellow teeth. Again the black panic took hold of him. He was blind, helpless, mindless.

"It was a common punishment in Imperial China," said O'Brien as didactically as ever.

The mask was closing on his face. The wire brushed his cheek. And then—no, it was not relief, only hope, a tiny fragment of hope. Too late, perhaps too late. But he had suddenly understood that in the whole world there was just *one* person to whom he could transfer his punishment— *one* body that he could thrust between himself and the rats. And he was shouting frantically, over and over:

"Do it to Julia! Do it to Julia! Not me! Julia! I don't care what you do to her. Tear her face off, strip her to the bones. Not me! Julia! Not me!"

He was falling backwards, into enormous depths, away from the rats. He was still strapped in the chair, but he had fallen through the floor, through the walls of the building, through the earth, through the oceans, through the atmosphere, into outer space, into the gulfs between the stars—always away, away, away from the rats. He was light-years distant, but O'Brien was still standing at his side. There was still the cold touch of a wire against his cheek. But through the darkness that enveloped him he heard another metallic click, and knew that the cage door had clicked shut and not open.

VI

The Chestnut Tree was almost empty. A ray of sunlight slanting through a window fell yellow on dusty tabletops. It was the lonely hour of fifteen. A tinny music trickled from the telescreens.

Winston sat in his usual corner, gazing into an empty glass. Now and again he glanced up at a vast face which eyed him from the opposite wall. BIG BROTHER IS WATCHING YOU, the caption said. Unbidden, a waiter came and filled his glass up with Victory Gin, shaking into it a few drops from another bottle with a quill through the cork. It was saccharine flavored with cloves, the speciality of the café.

Winston was listening to the telescreen. At present only music was coming out of it, but there was a possibility that at any moment there might be a special bulletin from the Ministry of Peace. The news from the African front was disquieting in the extreme. On and off he had been worrying about it all day. A Eurasian army (Oceania was at war with Eurasia: Oceania had always been at war with Eurasia) was moving southward at terrifying speed. The midday bulletin had not mentioned any definite area, but it was probable that already the mouth of the Congo was a battlefield. Brazzaville and Leopoldville were in danger. One did not have to look at the map to see what it meant. It was not merely a question of losing Central Africa; for the first time in the whole war, the territory of Oceania itself was menaced.

A violent emotion, not fear exactly but a sort of undifferentiated excitement, flared up in him, then faded again. He stopped thinking about the war. In these days he could never fix his mind on any one subject for more than a few moments at a time. He picked up his glass and drained it at a gulp. As always, it made him shudder and even retch slightly. The stuff was horrible. The cloves and saccharine, themselves disgusting enough in their sickly way, could not disguise the flat oily smell; and what was worst of all was that the smell of gin, which dwelt with him night and day, was inextricably mixed up in his mind with the smell of those——

He never named them, even in his thoughts, and so far as it was possible he never visualized them. They were something that he was half aware of, hovering close to his face, a smell that clung to his nostrils. As the gin rose in him he belched through purple lips. He had grown fatter since they released him, and had regained his old color—indeed, more than regained it. His features had thickened, the skin on nose and cheekbones was coarsely red, even the bald scalp was too deep a pink. A waiter, again unbidden, brought the chessboard and the current issue of the *Times,* with the page turned down at the chess problem. Then, seeing that Winston's glass was empty, he brought the gin bottle and filled it. There was no need to give orders. They knew his habits. The chessboard was always waiting for him, his corner table was always reserved; even when the place was full he had it to himself, since nobody cared to be seen sitting too close to him. He never even bothered to count his drinks. At irregular intervals they presented him with a dirty slip of paper which they said was the bill, but he had the impression that they always undercharged him. It would have made no difference if it had been the other way about. He had always plenty of money nowadays. He even had a job, a sinecure, more highly paid than his old job had been.

The music from the telescreen stopped and a voice took over. Winston raised his head to listen. No bulletin from the front, however. It was merely a brief announcement from the Ministry of Plenty. In the preceding quarter, it appeared, the Tenth Three-Year Plan's quota for bootlaces had been overfulfilled by ninety-eight per cent.

He examined the chess problem and set out the pieces. It was a tricky ending, involving a couple of knights. "White to play and mate in two moves." Winston looked up at the portrait of Big Brother. White always mates, he thought with a sort of cloudy mysticism. Always, without exception, it is so arranged. In no chess problem since the beginning of the world has black ever won. Did it not symbolize the eternal, unvarying triumph of Good over Evil? The huge face gazed back at him, full of calm power. White always mates.

The voice from the telescreen paused and added in a different and much graver tone: "You are warned to stand by for an important announcement at fifteen-thirty. Fifteen-thirty! This is news of the highest importance. Take care not to miss it. Fifteen-thirty!" The tinkling music struck up again.

Winston's heart stirred. That was the bulletin from the front; instinct told him that it was bad news that was coming. All day, with little spurts of excitement, the thought of a smashing defeat in Africa had been in and out of his mind. He seemed actually to see the Eurasian army swarming across the never-broken frontier and pouring down into the tip of Africa like a column of ants. Why had it not been possible to outflank them in some way? The outline of the West African coast stood out vividly in his mind. He picked up the white knight and moved it across the board. *There* was the proper spot. Even while he saw the black horde racing southward he saw another force, mysteriously assembled, suddenly planted in their rear, cutting their communications by land and sea. He felt that by willing it he was bringing that other force into existence. But it was necessary to act quickly. If they could get control of the whole of Africa, if they had airfields and submarine bases at the Cape, it would cut Oceania in two. It might mean anything: defeat, breakdown, the redivision of the world, the destruction of the Party! He drew a deep breath. An extraordinary medley of feelings—but it was not a medley, exactly; rather it was successive layers of feeling, in which one could not say which layer was undermost—struggled inside him.

The spasm passed. He put the white knight back in its place, but for the moment he could not settle down to serious study of the chess problem. His thoughts wandered again. Almost unconsciously he traced with his finger in the dust on the table:

$$2 + 2 = 5.$$

"They can't get inside you," she had said. But they could get inside you. "What happens to you here is *forever,*" O'Brien had said. That was a true word. There were things, your own acts, from which you could not recover. Something was killed in your breast; burnt out, cauterized out.

He had seen her; he had even spoken to her. There was no danger in it. He knew as though instinctively that they now took almost no interest in his doings. He could have arranged to meet her a second time if either of them had wanted to. Actually it was by chance that they had met. It was in the Park, on a vile, biting day in March, when the earth was like iron and all the grass seemed dead and there was not a bud anywhere except a few crocuses which had pushed themselves up to be dismembered by the wind. He was hurrying along with frozen hands and watering eyes when he saw her not ten meters away from him. It struck him at once that she had changed in some ill-defined way. They almost passed one another without a sign; then he turned and followed her, not very eagerly. He knew that there was no danger, nobody would take any interest in them. She did not speak. She walked obliquely away across the grass as though trying to get rid of him, then seemed to resign herself to having him at her side. Presently they were in among a clump of ragged leafless shrubs, useless either for concealment or as protection from the wind. They halted. It was vilely cold. The wind whistled through the twigs and fretted the occasional, dirty-looking crocuses. He put his arm round her waist.

There was no telescreen, but there must be hidden microphones; besides, they could be seen. It did not matter, nothing mattered. They could have lain down on the ground and done *that* if they had wanted to. His flesh froze with horror at the thought of it. She made no response whatever to the clasp of his arm; she did not even try to disengage herself. He knew now what had changed in her. Her face was sallower, and there was a long scar, partly hidden by the hair, across her forehead and temple; but that was not the change. It was that her waist had grown thicker and, in a surprising way, had stiffened. He remembered how once, after the explosion of a rocket bomb, he had helped to drag a corpse out of some ruins, and had been astonished not only by the incredible weight of the thing, but by its rigidity and awkwardness to handle, which made it seem more like stone than flesh. Her body felt like that. It occurred to him that the texture of her skin would be quite different from what it had once been.

He did not attempt to kiss her, nor did they speak. As they walked back across the grass she looked directly at him for the first time. It was only a momentary glance, full of contempt and dislike. He wondered whether it was a dislike that came purely out of the past or whether it was inspired also by his bloated face and the water that the wind kept squeezing from his eyes. They sat down on two iron chairs, side by side but not too close together. He saw that she was about to speak. She moved her clumsy shoe a few centimeters and deliberately crushed a twig. Her feet seemed to have grown broader, he noticed.

"I betrayed you," she said baldly.

"I betrayed you," he said.

She gave him another quick look of dislike.

"Sometimes," she said, "they threaten you with something—something you can't stand up to, can't even think about. And then you say, 'Don't do it to me, do it to somebody else, do it to so-and-so.' And perhaps you might pretend, afterwards, that it was only a trick and that you just said it to make them stop and didn't really mean it. But that isn't true. At the time when it happens you do mean it. You think there's no other way of saving yourself, and you're quite ready to save yourself that way. You *want* it to happen to the other person. You don't give a damn what they suffer. All you care about is yourself."

"All you care about is yourself," he echoed.

"And after that, you don't feel the same toward the other person any longer."

"No," he said, "you don't feel the same."

There did not seem to be anything more to say. The wind plastered their thin overalls against their bodies. Almost at once it became embarrassing to sit there in silence; besides it was too cold to keep still. She said something about catching her Tube and stood up to go.

"We must meet again," he said.

"Yes," she said, "we must meet again."

He followed irresolutely for a little distance, half a pace behind her. They did not speak again. She did not actually try to shake him off, but walked at just such a speed as to prevent his keeping abreast of her. He had made up his mind that he would accompany her as far as the Tube station, but suddenly this process of trailing along in the cold seemed pointless and unbearable. He was overwhelmed by a desire not so much to get away from Julia as to get back to the Chestnut Tree Café, which had never seemed so attractive as at this moment. He had a nostalgic vision of his corner table, with the newspaper and the chessboard and the ever-flowing gin. Above all, it would be warm in there. The next moment, not altogether by accident, he allowed himself to become separated from her by a small knot of people. He made a halfhearted attempt to catch up, then slowed down, turned and made off in the opposite direction. When he had gone fifty meters he looked back. The street was not crowded, but already he could not distinguish her. Any one of a dozen hurrying figures might have been hers. Perhaps her thickened, stiffened body was no longer recognizable from behind.

"At the time when it happens," she had said, "you do mean it." He had meant it. He had not merely said it, he had wished it. He had wished that she and not he should be delivered over to the——

Something changed in the music that trickled from the telescreen. A cracked and jeering note, a yellow note, came into it. And then—perhaps it was not happening, perhaps it was only a memory taking on the semblance of sound—a voice was singing:

> *"Under the spreading chestnut tree*
> *I sold you and you sold me—"*

The tears welled up in his eyes. A passing waiter noticed that his glass was empty and came back with the gin bottle.

He took up his glass and sniffed at it. The stuff grew not less but more horrible with every mouthful he drank. But it had become the element he swam in. It was his life, his death, and his resurrection. It was gin that sank him into stupor every night, and gin that revived him every morning. When he woke, seldom before eleven hundred, with gummed-up eyelids and fiery mouth and a back that seemed to be broken, it would have been impossible even to rise from the horizontal if it had not been for the bottle and teacup placed beside the bed overnight. Through the midday hours he sat with glazed face, the bottle handy, listening to the telescreen. From fifteen to closing time he was a fixture in the Chestnut Tree. No one cared what he did any longer, no whistle woke him, no telescreen admonished him. Occasionally, perhaps twice a week, he went to a dusty, forgotten-looking office in the Ministry of Truth and did a little work, or what was called work. He had been appointed to a sub-committee of a sub-committee which had sprouted from one of the innumerable committees dealing with minor difficulties that arose in the compilation of the Eleventh Edition of the Newspeak dictionary. They were engaged in producing something called an Interim Report, but what it was that they were reporting on he had never definitely found out. It was something to do with the question of whether commas should be placed inside brackets, or outside. There were four others on the committee, all of them persons similar to himself. There were days when they assembled and then promptly dispersed again, frankly admitting to one another that there was not really anything to be done. But there were other days when they settled down to their work almost eagerly, making a tremendous show of entering up their minutes and drafting long memoranda which were never finished—when the argument as to what they were supposedly arguing about grew extraordinarily involved and abstruse, with subtle hagglings over definitions, enormous digressions, quarrels—threats, even, to appeal to higher authority. And then suddenly the life would go out of them and they would sit round the table looking at one another with extinct eyes, like ghosts fading at cock-crow.

The telescreen was silent for a moment. Winston raised his head again. The bulletin! But no, they were merely changing the music. He had the map of Africa behind his eyelids. The movement of the armies was a diagram: a black arrow tearing vertically southward, and a white arrow tearing horizontally eastward, across the tail of the first. As though for reassurance he looked up at the imperturbable face in the portrait. Was it conceivable that the second arrow did not even exist?

His interest flagged again. He drank another mouthful of gin, picked up the white knight, and made a tentative move. Check. But it was evidently not the right move, because—

Uncalled, a memory floated into his mind. He saw a candle-lit room with a vast white-counterpaned bed, and himself, a boy of nine or ten, sitting on the floor, shaking a dice box and laughing excitedly. His mother was sitting opposite him and also laughing.

It must have been about a month before she disappeared. It was a moment of reconciliation, when the nagging hunger in his belly was forgotten and his earlier affection for her had temporarily revived. He remembered the day well, a pelting, drenching day when the water streamed down the window pane and the light indoors was too dull to read by. The boredom of the two children in the dark, cramped bedroom became unbearable. Winston whined and grizzled, made futile demands for food, fretted about the room, pulling everything out of place and kicking the wainscoting until the neighbors banged on the wall, while the younger child wailed intermittently. In the end his mother had said, "Now be good, and I'll buy you a toy. A lovely toy—you'll love it"; and then she had gone out in the rain, to a little general shop which was still sporadically open near by, and come back with a cardboard box containing an outfit of Snakes and Ladders. He could still remember the smell of the damp cardboard. It was a miserable outfit. The board was cracked and the tiny wooden dice were so ill-cut that they would hardly lie on their sides. Winston looked at the thing sulkily and without interest. But then his mother lit a piece of candle and they sat down on the floor to play. Soon he was wildly excited and shouting with laughter as the tiddly-winks climbed hopefully up the ladders and then came slithering down the snakes again, almost back to the starting point. They played eight games, winning four each. His tiny sister, too young to understand what the game was about, had sat propped up against a bolster, laughing because the others were laughing. For a whole afternoon they had all been happy together, as in his earlier childhood.

He pushed the picture out of his mind. It was a false memory. He was troubled by false memories occasionally. They did not matter so long as one knew them for what they were. Some things had happened, others had not happened. He turned back to the chessboard and picked up the white knight again. Almost in the same instant it dropped onto the board with a clatter. He had started as though a pin had run into him.

A shrill trumpet call had pierced the air. It was the bulletin! Victory! It always meant victory when a trumpet call preceded the news. A sort of electric thrill ran through the café. Even the waiters had started and pricked up their ears.

The trumpet call had let loose an enormous volume of noise. Already an excited voice was gabbling from the telescreen, but even as it started it was almost drowned by a roar of cheering from outside. The news had run round the streets like magic. He could hear just enough of what was issuing from the telescreen to realize that it had all happened as he had foreseen: a vast seaborne armada secretly assembled, a sudden blow in the enemy's rear, the white arrow tearing across the tail of the black. Fragments of triumphant phrases pushed themselves through the din: "Vast strategic maneuver—perfect co-ordination—utter rout—half a million prisoners—complete demoralization—control of the whole of Africa—bring the war within measurable distance of its end—victory— greatest victory in human history—victory, victory, victory!"

Under the table Winston's feet made convulsive movements. He had not stirred from his seat, but in his mind he was running, swiftly running, he was with the crowds outside, cheering himself deaf. He looked up again at the portrait of Big Brother. The colossus that bestrode the world! The rock against which the hordes of Asia dashed themselves in vain! He thought how ten minutes ago—yes, only ten minutes—there had still been equivocation in his heart as he wondered whether the news from the front would be of victory or defeat. Ah, it was more than a Eurasian army that had perished! Much had changed in him since that first day in the Ministry of Love, but the final, indispensable, healing change had never happened, until this moment.

The voice from the telescreen was still pouring forth its tale of prisoners and booty and slaughter, but the shouting outside had died down a little. The waiters were turning back to their work. One of them approached with the gin bottle. Winston, sitting in a blissful dream, paid no attention as his glass was filled up. He was not running or cheering any longer. He was back in the Ministry of Love, with everything forgiven, his soul white as snow. He was in the public dock, confessing everything, implicating everybody. He was walking down the white-tiled corridor, with the feeling of walking in sunlight, and an armed guard at his back. The long-hoped-for bullet was entering his brain.

He gazed up at the enormous face. Forty years it had taken him to learn what kind of smile was hidden beneath the dark mustache. O cruel, needless misunderstanding! O stubborn, self-willed exile from the loving breast! Two gin-scented tears trickled down the sides of his nose. But it was all right, everything was all right, the struggle was finished. He had won the victory over himself. He loved Big Brother.

THE END

Appendix

THE PRINCIPLES OF NEWSPEAK

Newspeak was the official language of Oceania and had been devised to meet the ideological needs of Ingsoc, or English Socialism. In the year 1984 there was not as yet anyone who used Newspeak as his sole means of communication, either in speech or writing. The leading articles in the *Times* were written in it, but this was a tour de force which could only be carried out by a specialist. It was expected that Newspeak would have finally superseded Oldspeak (or Standard English, as we should call it) by about the year 2050. Meanwhile it gained ground steadily, all Party members tending to use Newspeak words and grammatical constructions more and more in their everyday speech. The version in use in 1984, and embodied in the Ninth and Tenth Editions of the Newspeak dictionary, was a provisional one, and contained many superfluous words and archaic formations which were due to be suppressed later. It is with the final, perfected version, as embodied in the Eleventh Edition of the dictionary, that we are concerned here.

The purpose of Newspeak was not only to provide a medium of expression for the world-view and mental habits proper to the devotees of Ingsoc, but to make all other modes of thought impossible. It was intended that when Newspeak had been adopted once and for all and Oldspeak forgotten, a heretical thought—that is, a thought diverging from the principles of Ingsoc—should be literally unthinkable, at least so far as thought is dependent on words. Its vocabulary was so constructed as to give exact and often very subtle expression to every meaning that a Party member could properly wish to express, while excluding all other meanings and also the possibility of arriving at them by indirect methods. This was done partly by the invention of new words, but chiefly by eliminating undesirable words and by stripping such words as remained of unorthodox meanings, and so far as possible of all secondary meanings whatever. To give a simple example. The word *free* still existed in Newspeak, but it could only be used in such statements as "This dog is free from lice" or "This field is free from weeds." It could not be used in its old sense of "politically free" or "intellectually free," since political and intellectual freedom no longer existed even as concepts, and were therefore of necessity nameless. Quite apart from the suppression of definitely heretical words, reduction of vocabulary was regarded as an end in itself, and no word that could be dispensed with was allowed to survive. Newspeak was designated not to extend but to *diminish* the range of thought, and this purpose was indirectly assisted by cutting the choice of words down to a minimum.

Newspeak was founded on the English language as we now know it, though many Newspeak sentences, even when not containing newly created words, would be barely intelligible to an English-speaker of our own day. Newspeak words were divided into three distinct classes, known as the A vocabulary, the B vocabulary (also called compound words), and the C vocabulary. It will be simpler to discuss each class separately, but the grammatical peculiarities of the language can be dealt with in the section devoted to the A vocabulary, since the same rules held good for all three categories.

The A vocabulary. The A vocabulary consisted of the words needed for the business of everyday life—for such things as eating, drinking, working, putting on one's clothes, going up and down stairs, riding in vehicles, gardening, cooking, and the like. It was composed almost entirely of words that we already possess—words like *hit, run, dog, tree, sugar, house, field*—but in comparison with the present-day English vocabulary, their number was extremely small, while their meanings were far more rigidly defined. All ambiguities and shades of meaning had been purged out of them. So far as it could be achieved, a Newspeak word of this class was simply a staccato sound expressing one clearly understood concept. It would have been quite impossible to use the A vocabulary for literary purposes or for political or philosophical discussion. It was intended only to express simple, purposive thoughts, usually involving concrete objects or physical actions.

The grammar of Newspeak had two outstanding peculiarities. The first of these was an almost complete interchangeability between different parts of speech. Any word in the language (in principle this applied even to very abstract words such as *if* or *when*) could be used either as verb, noun, adjective, or adverb. Between the verb and the noun form, when they were of the same root, there was never any variation, this rule of itself involving the destruction of many archaic forms. The word *thought,* for example, did not exist in Newspeak. Its place was taken by *think,* which did duty for both noun and verb. No etymological principle was followed here; in some cases it was the original noun that was chosen for retention, in other cases the verb. Even where a noun and verb of kindred meaning were not etymologically connected, one or other of them was frequently suppressed. There was, for example, no such word as *cut,* its meaning being sufficiently covered by the noun-verb *knife.* Adjectives were formed by adding the suffix *-ful* to the noun-verb, and adverbs by adding *-wise.* Thus, for example, *speedful* meant "rapid" and *speedwise* meant "quickly." Certain of our present-day adjectives, such as *good, strong, big, black, soft,* were retained, but their total number was very small. There was little need for them, since almost any adjectival meaning could be arrived at by adding *-ful* to a noun-verb. None of the now-existing adverbs was retained, except for a very few already ending in *-wise;* the *-wise* termination was invariable. The word *well,* for example, was replaced by *goodwise.*

In addition, any word—this again applied in principle to every word in the language—could be negatived by adding the affix *un-,* or could be strengthened by the affix *plus-,* or, for still greater emphasis, *doubleplus-.* Thus, for example, *uncold* meant "warm," while *pluscold* and *doublepluscold* meant, respectively, "very cold" and "superlatively cold." It was also possible, as in present-day English, to modify the meaning of almost any word by prepositional affixes such as *ante-, post-, up-, down-,* etc. By such methods it was found possible to bring about an enormous diminution of vocabulary. Given, for instance, the word *good,* there was no need for such a word as *bad,* since the required meaning was equally well—indeed, better—expressed by *ungood.* All that was necessary, in any case where two words formed a natural pair of opposites, was to decide which of them to suppress. *Dark,* for example, could be replaced by *unlight,* or *light* by *undark,* according to preference.

The second distinguishing mark of Newspeak grammar was its regularity. Subject to a few exceptions which are mentioned below, all inflections followed the same rules. Thus, in all verbs the preterite and the past participle were the same and ended in *-ed*. The preterite of *steal* was *stealed*, the preterite of *think* was *thinked*, and so on throughout the language, all such forms as *swam, gave, brought, spoke, taken*, etc., being abolished. All plurals were made by adding *-s* or *-es* as the case might be. The plurals of *man, ox, life* were *mans, oxes, lifes*. Comparison of adjectives was invariably made by adding *-er, -est (good, gooder, goodest)*, irregular forms and the *more, most* formation being suppressed. *The only classes of words that were still allowed to inflect irregularly were the pronouns, the relatives, the demonstrative adjectives, and the auxiliary verbs. All of these followed their ancient usage, except that whom* had been scrapped as unnecessary, and the *shall, should* tenses had been dropped, all their uses being covered by *will* and *would*. There were also certain irregularities in word-forming arising out of the need for rapid and easy speech. A word which was difficult to utter, or was liable to be incorrectly heard, was held to be ipso facto a bad word; occasionally therefore, for the sake of euphony, extra letters were inserted into a word or an archaic formation was retained. But this need made itself felt chiefly in connection with the B vocabulary. *Why* so great an importance was attached to ease of pronunciation will be made clear later in this essay.

The B vocabulary. The B vocabulary consisted of words which had been deliberately constructed for political purposes: words, that is to say, which not only had in every case a political implication, but were intended to impose a desirable mental attitude upon the person using them. Without a full understanding of the principles of Ingsoc it was difficult to use these words correctly. In some cases they could be translated into Oldspeak, or even into words taken from the A vocabulary, but this usually demanded a long paraphrase and always involved the loss of certain overtones. The B words were a sort of verbal shorthand, often packing whole ranges of ideas into a few syllables, and at the same time more accurate and forcible than ordinary language.

The B words were in all cases compound words.* They consisted of two or more words, or portions of words, welded together in an easily pronounceable form. The resulting amalgam was always a noun-verb, and inflected according to the ordinary rules. To take a single example: the word *goodthink*, meaning, very roughly, "orthodoxy," or, if one chose to regard it as a verb, "to think in an orthodox manner." This inflected as follows: noun-verb, *goodthink;* past tense and past participle, *goodthinked;* present participle, *goodthinking;* adjective, *goodthinkful;* adverb, *goodthinkwise;* verbal noun, *goodthinker.*

The B words were not constructed on any etymological plan. The words of which they were made up could be any parts of speech, and could be placed in any order and mutilated in any way which made them easy to pronounce while indicating their derivation. In the word *crimethink* (thoughtcrime), for instance, the *think* came second, whereas in *thinkpol* (Thought Police) it came first, and in the latter word *police* had lost its second syllable. Because of the greater difficulty in securing euphony, irregular formations were commoner in the B vocabulary than in the A vocabulary. For example, the adjectival forms of *Minitrue, Minipax*, and *Miniluv* were, respectively, *Minitruthful, Minipeaceful*, and *Minilovely*,

---

* Compound words, such as *speakwrite*, were of course to be found in the A vocabulary, but these were merely convenient abbreviations and had no special ideological color.

simply because -*trueful*, -*paxful*, and -*loveful* were slightly awkward to pronounce. In principle, however, all B words could inflect, and all inflected in exactly the same way.

Some of the B words had highly subtilized meanings, barely intelligible to anyone who had not mastered the language as a whole. Consider, for example, such a typical sentence from a *Times* leading article as *Oldthinkers unbellyfeel Ingsoc*. The shortest rendering that one could make of this in Oldspeak would be: "Those whose ideas were formed before the Revolution cannot have a full emotional understanding of the principles of English Socialism." But this is not an adequate translation. To begin with, in order to grasp the full meaning of the Newspeak sentence quoted above, one would have to have a clear idea of what is meant by *Ingsoc*. And, in addition, only a person thoroughly grounded in Ingsoc could appreciate the full force of the word *bellyfeel*, which implied a blind, enthusiastic acceptance difficult to imagine today; or of the word *oldthink*, which was inextricably mixed up with the idea of wickedness and decadence. But the special function of certain Newspeak words, of which *oldthink* was one, was not so much to express meanings as to destroy them. These words, necessarily few in number, had had their meanings extended until they contained within themselves whole batteries of words which, as they were sufficiently covered by a single comprehensive term, could now be scrapped and forgotten. The greatest difficulty facing the compilers of the Newspeak dictionary was not to invent new words, but, having invented them, to make sure what they meant: to make sure, that is to say, what ranges of words they canceled by their existence.

As we have already seen in the case of the word *free*, words which had once borne a heretical meaning were sometimes retained for the sake of convenience, but only with the undesirable meanings purged out of them. Countless other words such as *honor, justice, morality, internationalism, democracy, science,* and *religion* had simply ceased to exist. A few blanket words covered them, and, in covering them, abolished them. All words grouping themselves round the concepts of liberty and equality, for instance, were contained in the single word *crimethink*, while all words grouping themselves round the concepts of objectivity and rationalism were contained in the single word *oldthink*. Greater precision would have been dangerous. What was required in a Party member was an outlook similar to that of the ancient Hebrew who knew, without knowing much else, that all nations other than his own worshiped "false gods." He did not need to know that these gods were called Baal, Osiris, Moloch, Ashtaroth, and the like; probably the less he knew about them the better for his orthodoxy. He knew Jehovah and the commandments of Jehovah; he knew, therefore, that all gods with other names or other attributes were false gods. In somewhat the same way, the Party member knew what constituted right conduct, and in exceedingly vague, generalized terms he knew what kinds of departure from it were possible. His sexual life, for example, was entirely regulated by the two Newspeak words *sexcrime* (sexual immorality) and *goodsex* (chastity). *Sexcrime* covered all sexual misdeeds whatever. It covered fornication, adultery, homosexuality, and other perversions, and, in addition, normal intercourse practiced for its own sake. There was no need to enumerate them separately, since they were all equally culpable, and, in principle, all punishable by death. In the C vocabulary, which consisted of scientific and technical words, it might be necessary to give specialized names to certain sexual aberrations, but the ordinary citizen had no need of them. He knew what was meant by *goodsex*—that is to say, normal intercourse between man and wife, for the sole purpose of begetting children, and without physical pleasure on the part of the woman; all else was *sexcrime*. In Newspeak it was seldom possible to follow a heretical thought further than the perception that it *was* heretical; beyond that point the necessary words were nonexistent.

No word in the B vocabulary was ideologically neutral. A great many were euphemisms. Such words, for instance, as *joycamp* (forced-labor camp) or *Minipax* (Ministry of Peace, i.e., Ministry of War) meant almost the exact opposite of what they appeared to mean. Some words, on the other hand, displayed a frank and contemptuous understanding of the real nature of Oceanic society. An example was *prolefeed,* meaning the rubbishy entertainment and spurious news which the party handed out to the masses. Other words, again, were ambivalent, having the connotation "good" when applied to the Party and "bad" when applied to its enemies. But in addition there were great numbers of words which at first sight appeared to be mere abbreviations and which derived their ideological color not from their meaning but from their structure.

So far as it could be contrived, everything that had or might have political significance of any kind was fitted into the B vocabulary. The name of every organization, or body of people, or doctrine, or country, or institution, or public building, was invariably cut down into the familiar shape; that is, a single easily pronounced word with the smallest number of syllables that would preserve the original derivation. In the Ministry of Truth, for example, the Records Department, in which Winston Smith worked, was called *Recdep,* the Fiction Department was called *Ficdep,* the Teleprograms Department was called *Teledep,* and so on. This was not done solely with the object of saving time. Even in the early decades of the twentieth century, telescoped words and phrases had been one of the characteristic features of political language; and it had been noticed that the tendency to use abbreviations of this kind was most marked in totalitarian countries and totalitarian organizations. Examples were such words as *Nazi, Gestapo, Comintern, Inprecorr, Agitprop.* In the beginning the practice had been adopted as it were instinctively, but in Newspeak it was used with a conscious purpose. It was perceived that in thus abbreviating a name one narrowed and subtly altered its meaning, by cutting out most of the associations that would otherwise cling to it. The words *Communist International,* for instance, call up a composite picture of universal human brotherhood, red flags, barricades, Karl Marx, and the Paris Commune. The word *Comintern,* on the other hand, suggests merely a tightly knit organization and a well-defined body of doctrine. It refers to something almost as easily recognized, and as limited in purpose, as a chair or a table. *Comintern* is a word that can be uttered almost without taking thought, whereas *Communist International* is a phrase over which one is obliged to linger at least momentarily. In the same way, the associations called up by a word like *Minitrue* are fewer and more controllable than those called up by *Ministry of Truth.* This accounted not only for the habit of abbreviating whenever possible, but also for the almost exaggerated care that was taken to make every word easily pronounceable.

In Newspeak, euphony outweighed every consideration other than exactitude of meaning. Regularity of grammar was always sacrificed to it when it seemed necessary. And rightly so, since what was required, above all for political purposes, were short clipped words of unmistakable meaning which could be uttered rapidly and which roused the minimum of echoes in the speaker's mind. The words of the B vocabulary even gained in force from the fact that nearly all of them were very much alike. Almost invariably these words—*goodthink, Minipax, prolefeed, sexcrime, joycamp, Ingsoc, bellyfeel, thinkpol,* and countless others—were words of two or three syllables, with the stress distributed equally between the first syllable and the last. The use of them encouraged a gabbling style of speech, at once staccato and monotonous. And this was exactly what was aimed at. The intention was to make speech, and especially speech on any subject not ideologically neutral, as nearly as possible independent of consciousness. For the purposes of everyday life it was no doubt necessary, or sometimes necessary, to reflect before speaking, but a Party member called upon to make a political or ethical judgment should be able to spray forth the correct opinions as automatically as a machine gun spraying forth bullets. His training fitted him to do this, the language gave him an almost foolproof instrument, and the texture of the words, with their harsh sound and a certain willful ugliness which was in accord with the spirit of Ingsoc, assisted the process still further.

So did the fact of having very few words to choose from. Relative to our own, the Newspeak vocabulary was tiny, and new ways of reducing it were constantly being devised. Newspeak, indeed, differed from almost all other languages in that its vocabulary grew smaller instead of larger every year. Each reduction was a gain, since the smaller the area of choice, the smaller the temptation to take thought. Ultimately it was hoped to make articulate speech issue from the larynx without involving the higher brain centers at all. This aim was frankly admitted in the Newspeak word *duckspeak,* meaning "to quack like a duck." Like various other words in the B vocabulary, *duckspeak* was ambivalent in meaning. Provided that the opinions which were quacked out were orthodox ones, it implied nothing but praise, and when the *Times* referred to one of the orators of the Party as a *doubleplusgood duckspeaker* it was paying a warm and valued compliment.

The C vocabulary. The C vocabulary was supplementary to the others and consisted entirely of scientific and technical terms. These resembled the scientific terms in use today, and were constructed from the same roots, but the usual care was taken to define them rigidly and strip them of undesirable meanings. They followed the same grammatical rules as the words in the other two vocabularies. Very few of the C words had any currency either in everyday speech or in political speech. Any scientific worker or technician could find all the words he needed in the list devoted to his own speciality, but he seldom had more than a smattering of the words occurring in the other lists. Only a very few words were common to all lists, and there was no vocabulary expressing the function of Science as a habit of mind, or a method of thought, irrespective of its particular branches. There was, indeed, no word for "Science," any meaning that it could possibly bear being already sufficiently covered by the word *Ingsoc.*

From the foregoing account it will be seen that in Newspeak the expression of unorthodox opinions, above a very low level, was well-nigh impossible. It was of course possible to utter heresies of a very crude kind, a species of blasphemy. It would have been possible, for example, to say *Big Brother is ungood.* But this statement, which to an orthodox ear merely conveyed a self-evident absurdity, could not have been sustained by reasoned argument, because the necessary words were not available. Ideas inimical to Ingsoc could only be entertained in a vague wordless form, and could only be named in very broad terms which lumped together and condemned whole groups of heresies without defining them in doing so. One could, in fact, only use Newspeak for unorthodox purposes by illegitimately translating some of the words back into Oldspeak. For example, *All mans are equal* was a possible Newspeak sentence, but only in the same sense in which *All men are redhaired* is a possible Oldspeak sentence. It did not contain a grammatical error, but it expressed a palpable untruth, i.e., that all men are of equal size, weight, or strength. The concept of political equality no longer existed, and this secondary meaning had accordingly been purged out of the word *equal*. In 1984, when Oldspeak was still the normal means of communication, the danger theoretically existed that in using Newspeak words one might remember their original meanings. In practice it was not difficult for any person well grounded in *doublethink* to avoid doing this, but within a couple of generations even the possibility of such a lapse would have vanished. A person growing up with Newspeak as his sole language would no more know that *equal* had once had the secondary meaning of "politically equal," or that *free* had once meant "intellectually free," than, for instance, a person who had never heard of chess would be aware of the secondary meanings attaching to *queen* and *rook*. There would be many crimes and errors which it would be beyond his power to commit, simply because they were nameless and therefore unimaginable. And it was to be foreseen that with the passage of time the distinguishing characteristics of Newspeak would become more and more pronounced—its words growing fewer and fewer, their meanings more and more rigid, and the chance of putting them to improper uses always diminishing.

When Oldspeak had been once and for all superseded, the last link with the past would have been severed. History had already been rewritten, but fragments of the literature of the past survived here and there, imperfectly censored, and so long as one retained one's knowledge of Oldspeak it was possible to read them. In the future such fragments, even if they chanced to survive, would be unintelligible and untranslatable. It was impossible to translate any passage of Oldspeak into Newspeak unless it either referred to some technical process or some very simple everyday action, or was already orthodox (*goodthinkful* would be the Newspeak expression) in tendency. In practice this meant that no book written before approximately 1960 could be translated as a whole. Prerevolutionary literature could only be subjected to ideological translation—that is, alteration in sense as well as language. Take for example the well-known passage from the Declaration of Independence:

We hold these truths to be self-evident, that all men are created equal, that they are endowed by their Creator with certain inalienable rights, that among these are life, liberty and the pursuit of happiness. That to secure these rights, Governments are instituted among men, deriving their powers from the consent of the governed. That whenever any form of Government becomes destructive of those ends, it is the right of the People to alter or abolish it, and to institute new Government . . .

It would have been quite impossible to render this into Newspeak while keeping to the sense of the original. The nearest one could come to doing so would be to swallow the whole passage up in the single word *crimethink*. A full translation could only be an ideological translation, whereby Jefferson's words would be changed into a panegyric on absolute government.

A good deal of the literature of the past was, indeed, already being transformed in this way. Considerations of prestige made it desirable to preserve the memory of certain historical figures, while at the same time bringing their achievements into line with the philosophy of Ingsoc. Various writers, such as Shakespeare, Milton, Swift, Byron, Dickens, and some others were therefore in process of translation; when the task had been completed, their original writings, with all else that survived of the literature of the past, would be destroyed. These translations were a slow and difficult business, and it was not expected that they would be finished before the first or second decade of the twenty-first century. There were also large quantities of merely utilitarian literature—indispensable technical manuals and the like—that had to be treated in the same way. It was chiefly in order to allow time for the preliminary work of translation that the final adoption of Newspeak had been fixed for so late a date as 2050.

1949

PART TWO

Sources

The four items in this section can be regarded as possible sources for or "influences" upon *Nineteen Eighty-Four*. Aldous Huxley's *Brave New World*, first published in 1932, is a fictional satire of a soulless and mechanized utopia; the book was extremely influential throughout the thirties and forties in the Western world, coming as a kind of intellectual shock to many persons of liberal and left-wing persuasions. Eugene Zamiatin's *We*, which is discussed both in Orwell's "Freedom and Happiness" and Irving Howe's "The Fiction of Anti-Utopia," is another anti-utopian fiction, this one written in Russia in the early 1920s by a gifted Russian novelist who opposed the increasing authoritarianism of the Communist regime and spent his later years in Paris as an exile. Zamiatin's book was translated into English in 1924 but soon forgotten; Orwell, preparing to write *Nineteen Eighty-Four*, turned to it with great fascination. Cyril Connolly's "Year Nine" is a sketch that may also have interested Orwell. Finally, there is a brief selection from Leon Trotsky's *The Revolution Betrayed*. A major leader of the Russian Revolution, head of the Red Army during the civil war in Russia, and a central figure in the early Bolshevik regime, Leon Trotsky became in 1923 a critic of the "bureaucratization" of the Russian Revolution, and in 1929 was exiled by the Stalin dictatorship. He devoted the rest of his life to the writing of books and articles sharply critical of totalitarian rule in Russia. He was murdered in his Mexican refuge in 1940 by an agent of the Stalin regime. One of his most famous books, *The Revolution Betrayed*, which first appeared in 1937, served as a model for the pamphlet that Emmanuel Goldstein writes against the dictatorship of Big Brother in *Nineteen Eighty-Four*.

ALDOUS HUXLEY

from Brave New World

Chapter I

A squat grey building of only thirty-four stories. Over the main entrance the words, CENTRAL LONDON HATCHERY AND CONDITIONING CENTRE, and, in a shield, the World State's motto, COMMUNITY, IDENTITY, STABILITY.

The enormous room on the ground floor faced towards the north. Cold for all the summer beyond the panes, for all the tropical heat of the room itself, a harsh thin light glared through the windows, hungrily seeking some draped lay figure, some pallid shape of academic goose-flesh, but finding only the glass and nickel and bleakly shining porcelain of a laboratory. Wintriness responded to wintriness. The overalls of the workers were white, their hands gloved with a pale corpse-coloured rubber. The light was frozen, dead, a ghost. Only from the yellow barrels of the microscopes did it borrow a certain rich and living substance, lying along the polished tubes like butter, streak after luscious streak in long recession down the work tables.

"And this," said the Director opening the door, "is the Fertilizing Room."

Bent over their instruments, three hundred Fertilizers were plunged, as the Director of Hatcheries and Conditioning entered the room, in the scarcely breathing silence, the absent-minded, soliloquizing hum or whistle, of absorbed concentration. A troop of newly arrived students, very young, pink and callow, followed nervously, rather abjectly, at the Director's heels. Each of them carried a notebook, in which, whenever the great man spoke, he desperately scribbled. Straight from the horse's mouth. It was a rare privilege. The D.H.C. for Central London always made a point of personally conducting his new students round the various departments.

"Just to give you a general idea," he would explain to them. For of course some sort of general idea they must have, if they were to do their work intelligently—though as little of one, if they were to be good and happy members of society, as possible. For particulars, as every one knows, make for virtue and happiness; generalities are intellectually necessary evils. Not philosophers but fret-sawyers and stamp collectors compose the backbone of society.

"To-morrow," he would add, smiling at them with a slightly menacing geniality, "you'll be settling down to serious work. You won't have time for generalities. Meanwhile . . ."

Meanwhile, it was a privilege. Straight from the horse's mouth into the notebook. The boys scribbled like mad.

Tall and rather thin but upright, the Director advanced into the room. He had a long chin and big, rather prominent teeth, just covered, when he was not talking, by his full, floridly curved lips. Old, young? Thirty? Fifty? Fifty-five? It was hard to say. And anyhow the question didn't arise; in this year of stability, A.F. 632, it didn't occur to you to ask it.

"I shall begin at the beginning," said the D.H.C. and the more zealous students recorded his intention in their notebooks: *Begin at the beginning*. "These," he waved his hand, "are the incubators." And opening an insulated door he showed them racks upon racks of numbered test-tubes. "The week's supply of ova. Kept," he explained, "at blood heat; whereas the male gametes," and here he opened another door, "they have to be kept at thirty-five instead of thirty-seven. Full blood heat sterilizes." Rams wrapped in theremogene beget no lambs.

Still leaning against the incubators he gave them, while the pencils scurried illegibly across the pages, a brief description of the modern fertilizing process; spoke first, of course, of its surgical introduction—"the operation undergone voluntarily for the good of Society, not to mention the fact that it carries a bonus amounting to six months' salary"; continued with some account of the technique for preserving the excised ovary alive and actively developing; passed on to a consideration of optimum temperature, salinity, viscosity; referred to the liquor in which the detached and ripened eggs were kept; and, leading his charges to the work tables, actually showed them how this liquor was drawn off from the test-tubes; how it was let out drop by drop onto the specially warmed slides of the microscopes; how the eggs which it contained were inspected for abnormalities, counted and transferred to a porous receptacle; how (and he now took them to watch the operation) this receptacle was immersed in a warm bouillon containing free-swimming spermatozoa—at a minimum concentration of one hundred thousand per cubic centimetre, he insisted; and how, after ten minutes, the container was lifted out of the liquor and its contents re-examined; how, if any of the eggs remained unfertilized, it was again immersed, and, if necessary, yet again; how the fertilized ova went back to the incubators; where the Alphas and Betas remained until definitely bottled; while the Gammas, Deltas and Epsilons were brought out again, after only thirty-six hours, to undergo Bokanovsky's Process.

"Bokanovsky's Process," repeated the Director, and the students underlined the words in their little notebooks.

One egg, one embryo, one adult—normality. But a bokanovskified egg will bud, will proliferate, will divide. From eight to ninety-six buds, and every bud will grow into a perfectly formed embryo, and every embryo into a full-sized adult. Making ninety-six human beings grow where only one grew before. Progress.

"Essentially," the D.H.C. concluded, "bokanovskification consists of a series of arrests of development. We check the normal growth and, paradoxically enough, the egg responds by budding."

Responds by budding. The pencils were busy.

He pointed. On a very slowly moving band a rack-full of test-tubes was entering a large metal box, another rack-full was emerging. Machinery faintly purred. It took eight minutes for the tubes to go through, he told them. Eight minutes of hard X-rays being about as much as an egg can stand. A few died; of the rest, the least susceptible divided into two; most put out four buds; some eight; all were returned to the incubators, where the buds began to develop; then, after two days, were suddenly chilled, chilled and checked. Two, four, eight, the buds in their turn budded; and having budded were dosed almost to death with alcohol; consequently burgeoned again and having budded—bud out of bud out of bud—were thereafter—further arrest being generally fatal—left to develop in peace. By which time the original egg was in a fair way to becoming anything from eight to ninety-six embryos—a prodigious improvement, you will agree, on nature. Identical twins—but not in piddling twos and threes as in the old viviparous days, when an egg would sometimes accidentally divide; actually by dozens, by scores at a time.

"Scores," the Director repeated and flung out his arms, as though he were distributing largesse. "Scores."

But one of the students was fool enough to ask where the advantage lay.

"My good boy!" The Director wheeled sharply round on him. "Can't you see? Can't you *see*?" He raised a hand; his expression was solemn. "Bokanovsky's Process is one of the major instruments of social stability!"

Major instruments of social stability.

Standard men and women; in uniform batches. The whole of a small factory staffed with the products of a single bokanovskified egg.

"Ninety-six identical twins working ninety-six identical machines!" The voice was almost tremulous with enthusiasm. "You really know where you are. For the first time in history." He quoted the planetary motto. "Community, Identity, Stability." Grand words. "If we could bokanovskify indefinitely the whole problem would be solved."

Solved by standard Gammas, unvarying Deltas, uniform Epsilons. Millions of identical twins. The principle of mass production at last applied to biology.

"But, alas," the Director shook his head, "we *can't* bokanovskify indefinitely."

Ninety-six seemed to be the limit; seventy-two a good average. From the same ovary and with gametes of the same male to manufacture as many batches of identical twins as possible—that was the best (sadly a second best) that they could do. And even that was difficult.

"For in nature it takes thirty years for two hundred eggs to reach maturity. But our business is to stabilize the population at this moment, here and now. Dribbling out twins over a quarter of a century—what would be the use of that?"

Obviously, no use at all. But Podsnap's Technique had immensely accelerated the process of ripening. They could make sure of at least a hundred and fifty mature eggs within two years. Fertilize and bokanovskify—in other words, multiply by seventy-two—and you get an average of nearly eleven thousand brothers and sisters in a hundred and fifty batches of identical twins, all within two years of the same age.

"And in exceptional cases we can make one ovary yield us over fifteen thousand adult individuals."

Beckoning to a fair-haired, ruddy young man who happened to be passing at the moment, "Mr. Foster," he called. The ruddy young man approached. "Can you tell us the record for a single ovary, Mr. Foster?"

"Sixteen thousand and twelve in this Centre," Mr. Foster replied without hesitation. He spoke very quickly, had a vivacious blue eye, and took an evident pleasure in quoting figures. "Sixteen thousand and twelve; in one hundred and eighty-nine batches of identicals. But of course they've done much better," he rattled on, "in some of the tropical Centres. Singapore has often produced over sixteen thousand five hundred; and Mombasa has actually touched the seventeen thousand mark. But then they have unfair advantages. You should see the way a negro ovary responds to pituitary! It's quite astonishing, when you're used to working with European material. Still," he added, with a laugh (but the light of combat was in his eyes and the lift of his chin was challenging), "still, we mean to beat them if we can. I'm working on a wonderful Delta-Minus ovary at this moment. Only just eighteen months old. Over twelve thousand seven hundred children already, either decanted or in embryo. And still going strong. We'll beat them yet."

"That's the spirit I like!" cried the Director, and clapped Mr. Foster on the shoulder. "Come along with us and give these boys the benefit of your expert knowledge."

Mr. Foster smiled modestly. "With pleasure." They went.

In the Bottling Room all was harmonious bustle and ordered activity. Flaps of fresh sow's peritoneum ready cut to the proper size came shooting up in little lifts from the Organ Store in the sub-basement. Whizz and then, click! the lift-hatches flew open; the bottle-liner had only to reach out a hand, take the flap, insert, smooth-down, and before the lined bottle had had time to travel out of reach along the endless band, whizz, click! another flap of peritoneum had shot up from the depths, ready to be slipped into yet another bottle, the next of that slow interminable procession on the band.

Next to the Liners stood the Matriculators. The procession advanced; one by one the eggs were transferred from their test-tubes to the larger containers; deftly the peritoneal lining was slit, the morula dropped into place, the saline solution poured in . . . and already the bottle had passed, and it was the turn of the labellers. Heredity, date of fertilization, membership of Bokanovsky Group—details were transferred from test-tube to bottle. No longer anonymous, but named, identified, the procession marched slowly on; on through an opening in the wall, slowly on into the Social Predestination Room.

"Eighty-eight cubic metres of card-index," said Mr. Foster with relish, as they entered.

"Containing *all* the relevant information," added the Director.

"Brought up to date every morning."

"And co-ordinated every afternoon."

"On the basis of which they make their calculations."

"So many individuals, of such and such quality," said Mr. Foster.

"Distributed in such and such quantities."

"The optimum Decanting Rate at any given moment."

"Unforeseen wastages promptly made good."

"Promptly," repeated Mr. Foster. "If you knew the amount of overtime I had to put in after the last Japanese earthquake!" He laughed good-humouredly and shook his head.

"The Predestinators send in their figures to the Fertilizers."

"Who give them the embryos they ask for."

"And the bottles come in here to be predestinated in detail."

"After which they are sent down to the Embryo Store."

"Where we now proceed ourselves."

And opening a door Mr. Foster led the way down a staircase into the basement.

The temperature was still tropical. They descended into a thickening twilight. Two doors and a passage with a double turn insured the cellar against any possible infiltration of the day.

"Embryos are like photograph film," said Mr. Foster waggishly, as he pushed open the second door. "They can only stand red light."

And in effect the sultry darkness into which the students now followed him was visible and crimson, like the darkness of closed eyes on a summer's afternoon. The bulging flanks of row on receding row and tier above tier of bottles glinted with innumerable rubies, and among the rubies moved the dim red spectres of men and women with purple eyes and all the symptoms of lupus. The hum and rattle of machinery faintly stirred the air.

"Give them a few figures, Mr. Foster," said the Director, who was tired of talking.

Mr. Foster was only too happy to give them a few figures.

Two hundred and twenty metres long, two hundred wide, ten high. He pointed upwards. Like chickens drinking, the students lifted their eyes towards the distant ceiling.

Three tiers of racks: ground floor level, first gallery, second gallery.

The spidery steel-work of gallery above gallery faded away in all directions into the dark. Near them three red ghosts were busily unloading demi-johns from a moving staircase.

The escalator from the Social Predestination Room.

Each bottle could be placed on one of fifteen racks, each rack, though you couldn't see it, was a conveyor travelling at the rate of thirty-three and a third centimetres an hour. Two hundred and sixty-seven days at eight metres a day. Two thousand one hundred and thirty-six metres in all. One circuit of the cellar at ground level, one on the first gallery, half on the second, and on the two hundred and sixty-seventh morning, daylight in the Decanting Room. Independent existence—so called.

"But in the interval," Mr. Foster concluded, "we've managed to do a lot to them. Oh, a very great deal." His laugh was knowing and triumphant.

"That's the spirit I like," said the Director once more. "Let's walk round. You tell them everything, Mr. Foster."

Mr. Foster duly told them.

Told them of the growing embryo on its bed of peritoneum. Made them taste the rich blood surrogate on which it fed. Explained why it had to be stimulated with placentin and thyroxin. Told them of the *corpus luteum* extract. Showed them the jets through which at every twelfth metre from zero to 2040 it was automatically injected. Spoke of those gradually increasing doses of pituitary administered during the final ninety-six metres of their course. Described the artificial maternal circulation installed on every bottle at Metre 112; showed them the reservoir of blood-surrogate, the centrifugal pump that kept the liquid moving over the placenta and drove it through the synthetic lung and waste-product filter. Referred to the embryo's troublesome tendency to anaemia, to the massive doses of hog's stomach extract and foetal foal's liver with which, in consequence, it had to be supplied.

Showed them the simple mechanism by means of which, during the last two metres out of every eight, all the embryos were simultaneously shaken into familiarity with movement. Hinted at the gravity of the so-called "trauma of decanting," and enumerated the precautions taken to minimize, by a suitable training of the bottled embryo, that dangerous shock. Told them of the tests for sex carried out in the neighbourhood of

Metre 200. Explained the system of labelling—a T for the males, a circle for the females and for those who were destined to become freemartins a question mark, black on a white ground.

"For of course," said Mr. Foster, "in the vast majority of cases, fertility is merely a nuisance. One fertile ovary in twelve hundred—that would really be quite sufficient for our purposes. But we want to have a good choice. And of course one must always leave an enormous margin of safety. So we allow as many as thirty per cent. of the female embryos to develop normally. The others get a dose of male sex-hormone every twenty-four metres for the rest of the course. Result: they're decanted as freemartins—structurally quite normal (except," he had to admit, "that they *do* have just the slightest tendency to grow beards), but sterile. Guaranteed sterile. Which brings us at last," continued Mr. Foster, "out of the realm of mere slavish imitation of nature into the much more interesting world of human invention."

He rubbed his hands. For of course, they didn't content themselves with merely hatching out embryos: any cow could do that.

"We also predestine and condition. We decant our babies as socialized human beings, as Alphas or Epsilons, as future sewage workers or future . . ." He was going to say "future World controllers," but correcting himself, said "future Directors of Hatcheries," instead. The D.H.C. acknowledged the compliment with a smile.

They were passing Metre 320 on Rack 11. A young Beta-Minus mechanic was busy with screwdriver and spanner on the blood-surrogate pump of a passing bottle. The hum of the electric motor deepened by fractions of a tone as he turned the nuts. Down, down . . . A final twist, a glance at the revolution counter, and he was done. He moved two paces down the line and began the same process on the next pump.

"Reducing the number of revolutions per minute," Mr. Foster explained. "The surrogate goes round slower; therefore passes through the lung at longer intervals; therefore gives the embryo less oxygen. Nothing like oxygen-shortage for keeping an embryo below par." Again he rubbed his hands.

"But why do you want to keep the embryo below par?" asked an ingenuous student.

"Ass!" said the Director, breaking a long silence. "Hasn't it occurred to you that an Epsilon embryo must have an Epsilon environment as well as an Epsilon heredity?"

It evidently hadn't occurred to him. He was covered with confusion.

"The lower the caste," said Mr. Foster, "the shorter the oxygen." The first organ affected was the brain. After that the skeleton. At seventy per cent. of normal oxygen you got dwarfs. At less than seventy eyeless monsters.

"Who are no use at all," concluded Mr. Foster.

Whereas (his voice became confidential and eager), if they could discover a technique for shortening the period of maturation what a triumph, what a benefaction to Society!

"Consider the horse."

They considered it.

Mature at six; the elephant at ten. While at thirteen a man is not yet sexually mature; and is only full-grown at twenty. Hence, of course, that fruit of delayed development, the human intelligence.

"But in Epsilons," said Mr. Foster very justly, "we don't need human intelligence."

Didn't need and didn't get it. But though the Epsilon mind was mature at ten, the Epsilon body was not fit to work till eighteen. Long years of superfluous and wasted immaturity. If the physical development could be speeded up till it was as quick, say, as a cow's, what an enormous saving to the Community!

"Enormous!" murmured the students. Mr. Foster's enthusiasm was infectious.

He became rather technical; spoke of the abnormal endocrine co-ordination which made men grow so slowly; postulated a germinal mutation to account for it. Could the effects of this germinal mutation be undone? Could the individual Epsilon embryo be made to revert, by a suitable technique, to the normality of dogs and cows? That was the problem. And it was all but solved.

Pilkington, at Mombasa, had produced individuals who were sexually mature at four and full-grown at six and a half. A scientific triumph. But socially useless. Six-year-old men and women were too stupid to do even Epsilon work. And the process was an all-or-nothing one; either you failed to modify at all, or else you modified the whole way. They were still trying to find the ideal compromise between adults of twenty and adults of six. So far without success. Mr. Foster sighed and shook his head.

Their wanderings through the crimson twilight had brought them to the neighbourhood of Metre 170 on Rack 9. From this point onwards Rack 9 was enclosed and the bottles performed the remainder of their journey in a kind of tunnel, interrupted here and there by openings two or three metres wide.

"Heat conditioning," said Mr. Foster.

Hot tunnels alternated with cool tunnels. Coolness was wedded to discomfort in the form of hard X-rays. By the time they were decanted the embryos had a horror of cold. They were predestined to emigrate to the tropics, to be miners and acetate silk spinners and steel workers. Later on their minds would be made to endorse the judgment of their bodies. "We condition them to thrive on heat," concluded Mr. Foster. "Our colleagues upstairs will teach them to love it."

"And that," put in the Director sententiously, "that is the secret of happiness and virtue—liking what you've *got* to do. All conditioning aims at that: making people like their unescapable social destiny."

In a gap between two tunnels, a nurse was delicately probing with a long fine syringe into the gelatinous contents of a passing bottle. The students and their guides stood watching her for a few moments in silence.

"Well, Lenina," said Mr. Foster, when at last she withdrew the syringe and straightened herself up.

The girl turned with a start. One could see that for all the lupus and the purple eyes, she was uncommonly pretty.

"Henry!" Her smile flashed redly at him—a row of coral teeth.

"Charming, charming," murmured the Director and, giving her two or three little pats, received in exchange a rather deferential smile for himself.

"What are you giving them?" asked Mr. Foster, making his tone very professional.

"Oh, the usual typhoid and sleeping sickness."

"Tropical workers start being inoculated at Metre 150," Mr. Foster explained to the students. "The embryos still have gills. We immunize the fish against the future man's diseases." Then, turning back to Lenina, "Ten to five on the roof this afternoon," he said, "as usual."

"Charming," said the Director once more, and, with a final pat, moved away after the others.

On Rack 10 rows of next generation's chemical workers were being trained in the toleration of lead, caustic soda, tar, chlorine. The first of a batch of two hundred and fifty embryonic rocket-plane engineers was just passing the eleven hundred metre mark on Rack 3. A special mechanism kept their containers in constant rotation. "To improve their sense of balance," Mr. Foster explained. "Doing repairs on the outside of a rocket in mid-air is a ticklish job. We slacken off the circulation when they're right way up, so that they're half starved, and double the flow of surrogate when they're upside down. They learn to associate topsy-turvydom with well-being; in fact, they're only truly happy when they're standing on their heads.

"And now," Mr. Foster went on, "I'd like to show you some very interesting conditioning for Alpha Plus Intellectuals. We have a big batch of them on Rack 5. First Gallery level," he called to two boys who had started to go down to the ground floor.

"They're round about Metre 900," he explained. "You can't really do any useful intellectual conditioning till the foetuses have lost their tails. Follow me."

But the Director had looked at his watch. "Ten to three," he said. "No time for the intellectual embryos, I'm afraid. We must go up to the Nurseries before the children have finished their afternoon sleep."

Mr. Foster was disappointed. "At least one glance at the Decanting Room," he pleaded.

"Very well then." The Director smiled indulgently. "Just one glance."

Chapter II

Mr. Foster was left in the Decanting Room. The D.H.C. and his students stepped into the nearest lift and were carried up to the fifth floor.

INFANT NURSERIES. NEO-PAVLOVIAN CONDITIONING ROOMS, announced the notice board.

The Director opened a door. They were in a large bare room, very bright and sunny; for the whole of the southern wall was a single window. Half a dozen nurses, trousered and jacketed in the regulation white viscose-linen uniform, their hair aseptically hidden under white caps, were engaged in setting out bowls of roses in a long row across the floor. Big bowls, packed tight with blossom. Thousands of petals, ripe-blown and silkily smooth, like the cheeks of innumerable little cherubs, but of cherubs, in that bright light, not exclusively pink and Aryan, but also luminously Chinese, also Mexican, also apoplectic with too much blowing of celestial trumpets, also pale as death, pale with the posthumous whiteness of marble.

The nurses stiffened to attention as the D.H.C. came in.

"Set out the books," he said curtly.

In silence the nurses obeyed his command. Between the rose bowls the books were duly set out—a row of nursery quartos opened invitingly each at some gaily coloured image of beast or fish or bird.

"Now bring in the children."

They hurried out of the room and returned in a minute or two, each pushing a kind of tall dumb-waiter laden, on all its four wire-netted shelves, with eight-month-old babies, all exactly alike (a Bokanovsky Group, it was evident) and all (since their caste was Delta) dressed in khaki.

"Put them down on the floor."

The infants were unloaded.

"Now turn them so that they can see the flowers and books."

Turned, the babies at once fell silent, then began to crawl towards those clusters of sleek colours, those shapes so gay and brilliant on the white pages. As they approached, the sun came out of a momentary eclipse behind a cloud. The roses flamed up as though with a sudden passion from within; a new and profound significance seemed to suffuse the shining pages of the books. From the ranks of the crawling babies came little squeals of excitement, gurgles and twitterings of pleasure.

The Director rubbed his hands. "Excellent!" he said. "It might almost have been done on purpose."

The swiftest crawlers were already at their goal. Small hands reached out uncertainly, touched, grasped, unpetaling the transfigured roses, crumpling the illuminated pages of the books. The Director waited until all were happily busy. Then, "Watch carefully," he said. And, lifting his hand, he gave the signal.

The Head Nurse, who was standing by a switchboard at the other end of the room, pressed down a little lever.

There was a violent explosion. Shriller and ever shriller, a siren shrieked. Alarm bells maddeningly sounded.

The children started, screamed; their faces were distorted with terror.

"And now," the Director shouted (for the noise was deafening), "now we proceed to rub in the lesson with a mild electric shock."

He waved his hand again, and the Head Nurse pressed a second lever. The screaming of the babies suddenly changed its tone. There was something desperate, almost insane, about the sharp spasmodic yelps to which they now gave utterance. Their little bodies twitched and stiffened; their limbs moved jerkily as if to the tug of unseen wires.

"We can electrify that whole strip of floor," bawled the Director in explanation. "But that's enough," he signalled to the nurse.

The explosions ceased, the bells stopped ringing, the shriek of the siren died down from tone to tone into silence. The stiffly twitching bodies relaxed, and what had become the sob and yelp of infant maniacs broadened out once more into a normal howl of ordinary terror.

"Offer them the flowers and the books again."

The nurses obeyed; but at the approach of the roses, at the mere sight of those gaily-coloured images of pussy and cock-a-doodle-doo and baa-baa black sheep, the infants shrank away in horror; the volume of their howling suddenly increased.

"Observe," said the Director triumphantly, "observe."

Books and loud noises, flowers and electric shocks—already in the infant mind these couples were compromisingly linked; and after two hundred repetitions of the same or a similar lesson would be wedded indissolubly. What man has joined, nature is powerless to put asunder.

"They'll grow up with what the psychologists used to call an 'instinctive' hatred of books and flowers. Reflexes unalterably conditioned. They'll be safe from books and botany all their lives." The Director turned to his nurses. "Take them away again."

Still yelling, the khaki babies were loaded on to their dumb-waiters and wheeled out, leaving behind them the smell of sour milk and a most welcome silence.

One of the students held up his hand; and though he could see quite well why you couldn't have lower-caste people wasting the Community's time over books, and that there was always the risk of their reading something which might undesirably decondition one of their reflexes, yet . . . well, he couldn't understand about the flowers. Why go to the trouble of making it psychologically impossible for Deltas to like flowers?

Patiently the D.H.C. explained. If the children were made to scream at the sight of a rose, that was on grounds of high economic policy. Not so very long ago (a century or thereabouts), Gammas, Deltas, even Epsilons, had been conditioned to like flowers—flowers in particular and wild nature in general. The idea was to make them want to be going out into the country at every available opportunity, and so compel them to consume transport.

"And didn't they consume transport?" asked the student.

"Quite a lot," the D.H.C. replied. "But nothing else."

Primroses and landscapes, he pointed out, have one grave defect: they are gratuitous. A love of nature keeps no factories busy. It was decided to abolish the love of nature, at any rate among the lower classes; to abolish the love of nature, but *not* the tendency to consume transport. For of course it was essential that they should keep on going to the country, even though they hated it. The problem was to find an economically sounder reason for consuming transport than a mere affection for primroses and landscapes. It was duly found.

"We condition the masses to hate the country," concluded the Director. "But simultaneously we condition them to love all country sports. At the same time, we see to it that all country sports shall entail the use of elaborate apparatus. So that they consume manufactured articles as well as transport. Hence those electric shocks."

"I see," said the student, and was silent, lost in admiration.

There was a silence; then, clearing his throat, "Once upon a time," the Director began, "while our Ford was still on earth, there was a little boy called Reuben Rabinovitch. Reuben was the child of Polish-speaking parents." The Director interrupted himself. "You know what Polish is, I suppose?"

"A dead language."

"Like French and German," added another student, officiously showing off his learning.

"And 'parent'?" questioned the D.H.C.

There was an uneasy silence. Several of the boys blushed. They had not yet learned to draw the significant but often very fine distinction between smut and pure science. One, at last, had the courage to raise a hand.

"Human beings used to be . . ." he hesitated; the blood rushed to his cheeks. "Well, they used to be viviparous."

"Quite right." The Director nodded approvingly.

"And when the babies were decanted . . ."

" 'Born'," came the correction.

"Well, then they were the parents—I mean, not the babies, of course; the other ones." The poor boy was overwhelmed with confusion.

"In brief," the Director summed up, "the parents were the father and the mother." The smut that was really science fell with a crash into the boys' eye-avoiding silence. "Mother," he repeated loudly rubbing in the science; and, leaning back in his chair, "These," he said gravely, "are unpleasant facts; I know it. But then most historical facts *are* unpleasant."

He returned to Little Reuben—to Little Reuben, in whose room, one evening, by an oversight, his father and mother (crash, crash!) happened to leave the radio turned on.

("For you must remember that in those days of gross viviparous reproduction, children were always brought up by their parents and not in State Conditioning Centres.")

While the child was asleep, a broadcast programme from London suddenly started to come through; and the next morning, to the astonishment of his crash and crash (the more daring of the boys ventured to grin at one another), Little Reuben woke up repeating word for word a long lecture by that curious old writer ("one of the very few whose works have been permitted to come down to us"), George Bernard Shaw, who was speaking, according to a well-authenticated tradition, about his own genius. To Little Reuben's wink and snigger, this lecture was, of course, perfectly incomprehensible and, imagining that their child had suddenly gone mad, they sent for a doctor. He, fortunately, understood English, recognized the discourse as that which Shaw had broadcasted the previous evening, realized the significance of what had happened, and sent a letter to the medical press about it.

"The principle of sleep-teaching, or hypnopaedia, had been discovered." The D.H.C. made an impressive pause.

The principle had been discovered; but many, many years were to elapse before the principle was usefully applied.

"The case of Little Reuben occurred only twenty-three years after Our Ford's first T-Model was put on the market." (Here the Director made a sign of the T on his stomach and all the students reverently followed suit.) "And yet . . ."

Furiously the students scribbled. "*Hypnopaedia, first used officially in A.F. 214. Why not before? Two reasons. (a) . . .*"

"These early experimenters," the D.H.C. was saying, "were on the wrong track. They thought that hypnopaedia could be made an instrument of intellectual education . . ."

(A small boy asleep on his right side, the right arm stuck out, the right hand hanging limp over the edge of the bed. Through a round grating in the side of a box a voice speaks softly.

"The Nile is the longest river in Africa and the second in length of all rivers of the globe. Although falling short of the length of the Mississippi-Missouri, the Nile is at the head of all rivers as regards the length of its basin which extends through 35 degrees of latitude . . ."

At breakfast the next morning, "Tommy," some one says, "do you know which is the longest river in Africa?" A shaking of the head. "But don't you remember something that begins: The Nile is the . . ."

"The - Nile - is - the - longest - river - in - Africa - and - the - second - in - length - of - all - the - rivers - of - the - globe . . ." The words come rushing out. "Although - falling - short - of . . ."

"Well now, which is the longest river in Africa?"

The eyes are blank. "I don't know."

"But the Nile, Tommy."

"The - Nile - is - the - longest - river - in - Africa - and - second . . ."

"Then which river is the longest, Tommy?"

Tommy bursts into tears. "I don't know," he howls.)

That howl, the Director made it plain, discouraged the earliest investigators. The experiments were abandoned. No further attempt was made to teach children the length of the Nile in their sleep. Quite rightly. You can't learn a science unless you know what it's all about.

"Whereas, if they'd only started on *moral* education," said the Director, leading the way towards the door. The students followed him, desperately scribbling as they walked and all the way up in the lift. "Moral education, which ought never, in any circumstances, to be rational."

"Silence, silence," whispered a loud speaker as they stepped out on the fourteenth floor, and "Silence, silence," the trumpet mouths indefatigably repeated at intervals down every corridor. The students and even the Director himself rose automatically to the tips of their toes. They were Alphas, of course; but even Alphas have been well conditioned. "Silence, silence." All the air of the fourteenth floor was sibilant with the categorical imperative.

Fifty yards of tiptoeing brought them to a door which the Director cautiously opened. They stepped over the threshold into the twilight of a shuttered dormitory. Eighty cots stood in a row against the wall. There was a sound of light regular breathing and a continuous murmur, as of very faint voices remotely whispering.

A nurse rose as they entered and came to attention before the Director.

"What's the lesson this afternoon?" he asked.

"We had Elementary Sex for the first forty minutes," she answered. "But now it's switched over to Elementary Class Consciousness."

The Director walked slowly down the long line of cots. Rosy and relaxed with sleep, eighty little boys and girls lay softly breathing. There was a whisper under every pillow. The D.H.C. halted and, bending over one of the little beds, listened attentively.

"Elementary Class Consciousness, did you say? Let's have it repeated a little louder by the trumpet."

At the end of the room a loud speaker projected from the wall. The Director walked up to it and pressed a switch.

". . . all wear green," said a soft but very distinct voice, beginning in the middle of a sentence, "and Delta Children wear khaki. Oh no, I don't want to play with Delta children. And Epsilons are still worse. They're too stupid to be able to read or write. Besides they wear black, which is such a beastly colour. I'm *so* glad I'm a Beta."

There was a pause; then the voice began again.

"Alpha children wear grey. They work much harder than we do, because they're so frightfully clever. I'm really awfully glad I'm a Beta because I don't work so hard. And then we are much better than the Gammas and Deltas. Gammas are stupid. They all wear green; and Delta children wear khaki. Oh no, I *don't* want to play with Delta children. And Epsilons are still worse. They're too stupid to be able . . ."

The Director pushed back the switch. The voice was silent. Only its thin ghost continued to mutter from beneath the eighty pillows.

"They'll have that repeated forty or fifty times more before they wake; then again on Thursday, and again on Saturday. A hundred and twenty times three times a week for thirty months. After which they go on to a more advanced lesson."

Roses and electric shocks, the khaki of Deltas and a whiff of asafoetida—wedded indissolubly before the child can speak. But wordless conditioning is crude and wholesale; cannot bring home the finer distinctions, cannot inculcate the more complex courses of behaviour. For that there must be words, but words without reason. In brief, hypnopaedia.

"The greatest moralizing and socializing force of all time."

The students took it down in their little books. Straight from the horse's mouth.

Once more the Director touched the switch.

". . . so frightfully clever," the soft, insinuating, indefatigable voice was saying. "I'm really awfully glad I'm a Beta, because . . ."

Not so much like drops of water, though water, it is true, can wear holes in the hardest granite; rather, drops of liquid sealing-wax, drops that adhere, incrust, incorporate themselves with what they fall on, till finally the rock is all one scarlet blob.

"Till at last the child's mind *is* these suggestions, and the sum of the suggestions *is* the child's mind. And not the child's mind only. The adult's mind too—all his life long. The mind that judges and desires and decides—made up of these suggestions. But all these suggestions are *our* suggestions!" The Director almost shouted in his triumph. "Suggestions from the State." He banged the nearest table. "It therefore follows . . ."

A noise made him turn round.

"Oh, Ford!" he said in another tone, "I've gone and woken the children."

                                                                                    1932

EUGENE ZAMIATIN
from We

The following excerpts are taken from Eugene Zamiatin's *We*, a novel discussed elsewhere in this book (see Orwell's "Freedom and Happiness" and Howe's "The Fiction of Anti-Utopia"). *We* is written in the form of a series of meditations or "records" composed by D-503, a mathematician living in the "United State," a totalitarian utopia obviously anticipating Orwell's Oceania. Employed in the construction of the *Integral*, a spaceship intended to subjugate other planets to the power of the United State, D-503 suffers from heretical thoughts and urges to individuality: "I know that I have imagination: that is what my illness consists of." In "Record Thirty-One" D-503 learns that the state has now perfected an operation that will cure men of their "fancy," which is to say, of human desire and restlessness. He encounters the woman U-, who feels that he will now be cured of his "illness," and then the woman I-330, a secret heretic who has shown him the possibilities of human existence, both joyous and tragic, from which the operation would forever remove him. At the end of "Record Thirty-One" D-503 faces the choice between the inhuman happiness promised by the operation that will remove "fancy" from men's minds, and the personal relationship, with all its troubles and uncertainties, represented by I-330.

RECORD FIFTEEN

The Bell
The Mirror-like Sea
I Am to Burn Eternally

I was walking on the dock where the *Integral* is being built, when the Second Builder came to meet me. His face, as usual, was round and white, a porcelain plate. When he speaks it seems as if he serves you a plate of something unbearably tasty.

"You chose to be ill, and without the Chief we had sort of an accident yesterday."

"An accident?"

"Yes, sir. We finished the bell and started to let it down, and imagine; the men caught a male without a number. How he got in I can't make out. They took him to the Operation Department. Oh, they'll get the answers out of the fellow there; 'why' and 'how,' etc. . . ." He smiled delightedly.

Our best and most experienced physicians work in the Operation Department under the direct supervision of the Well-Doer himself. They have all kinds of instruments, but the best of all is the Gas Bell. The procedure is taken from an ancient experiment of elementary physics: they used to put a rat under a gas bell and gradually pump out the air; the air becomes more and more rarefied, and . . . you know the rest.

But our Gas Bell is certainly a more perfect apparatus, and it is used in combination with different gases. Furthermore, we don't torture a defenseless animal as the ancients did. We use it for a higher purpose: to guard the security of the United State—in other words, the happiness of millions. About five centuries ago, when the work of the Operation Department was only beginning, there were yet to be found some fools who compared our Operation Department with the ancient Inquisition. But this is as absurd as to compare a surgeon performing a tracheotomy with a highway cutthroat. Both use a knife, perhaps the same kind of knife, both do the same thing, viz., cut the throat of a living man; yet one is a well-doer, the other is a murderer; one is marked plus, the other minus. . . . All this becomes perfectly clear in one second, in one turn of our wheel of logic, the teeth of which engage that *minus*, turn it upward, and thus change its aspect.

One other matter is somewhat different: the ring in the door was still oscillating, apparently the door had just closed, yet she, I-330, had disappeared, she was not there! The wheel of logic could not turn this fact. A dream? But even now I still feel in my right shoulder that incomprehensibly sweet pain of I-330 near me in the fog, pressing herself against me. "Thou lovest fog?" Yes, I love the fog, too. I love everything, and everything appears to me wonderful, new, tense; everything is so good! . . .

"So good," I said aloud.

"Good?" The porcelain eyes bulged out. "What good do you find in that? If that man without a number contrived to sneak in, it means that there are others around here, everywhere, all the time, here around the *Integral*, they—"

"Whom do you mean by 'they'?"

"How do I know who? But I sense them, all the time."

"Have you heard about the new operation which has been invented? I mean the surgical removal of fancy?" (There really were rumors of late about something of the sort.)

"No, I haven't. What has that to do with it?"

"Merely this: if I were you, I should go and ask to have this operation performed upon me."

The plate distinctly expressed something lemonlike, sour. Poor fellow! He took offense if one even hinted that he might possess imagination. Well, a week ago I, too, would have taken offense at such a hint. Not now though, for I know that I have imagination; that is what my illness consists of. And more than that: I know that it is a wonderful illness—one does not want to be cured, simply does not want to!

We ascended the glass steps; the world spread itself below us like the palm of a hand.

You, readers of these records, whoever you may be, you have the sun above you. And if you ever were ill, as I am now, then you know what kind of sun there is or may be in the morning; you know that pinkish, lucid, warm gold; the air itself looks a little pinkish; everything seems permeated by the tender blood of the sun; everything is alive; the stones seem soft and living, iron living and warm, people full of life and smiles. Perhaps in a short while all this will disappear, in an hour the pinkish blood of the sun will be drained out; but in the meantime everything is alive. And I see how something flows and pulsates in the sides of the *Integral*; I see the *Integral*; I think of its great and lofty future, of the heavy cargo of inevitable happiness which it is to carry up there into the heights, to you, unseen ones, to you who seek eternally and who never find. You shall find! You shall be happy! You must be happy, and now you have not very long to wait!

The body of the *Integral* is almost ready; it is an exquisite, oblong ellipsoid, made of our glass, which is everlasting like gold and flexible like steel. I watched them within, fixing its transverse ribs and its longitudinal stringers; in the stern they were erecting the base of the gigantic motor. Every three seconds the powerful tail of the *Integral* will eject flame and gases into universal space, and the *Integral* will soar higher and higher, like a flaming Tamerlane of happiness! I watched how the workers, true to the Taylor system, would bend down, then unbend and turn around swiftly and rhythmically like levers of an enormous engine. In their hands they held glittering glass pipes which emitted bluish streaks of flame; the glass walls were being cut into with flame; with flame were being welded the angles, the ribs, the bars. I watched the monstrous glass cranes easily rolling over the glass rails; like the workers themselves, they would obediently turn, bend down, and bring their loads inward into the bowels of the *Integral*. All seemed one: humanized machine and mechanized humans. It was the most magnificent, most stirring beauty, harmony, music!

Quick! Down! To them and with them! And I descended and mingled with them, fused with their mass, caught in the rhythm of steel and glass. Their movements were measured, tense and round. Their cheeks were colored with health, their mirrorlike foreheads unclouded by the insanity of thinking. I was floating upon a mirror-like sea. I was resting. . . . Suddenly one of them turned his carefree face toward me.

"Well, better today?"

"What, better?"

"You were not here yesterday. And we thought something serious . . ."
His forehead was shining—a childish and innocent smile.

My blood rushed to my face. No, I could not lie, facing those eyes. I remained silent; I was drowning. . . . Above, a shiny, round, white porcelain face appeared in the hatchway.

"Hey! D-503! Come up here! Something is wrong with a frame and brackets here, and . . ."

Not waiting until he had finished, I rushed to him, upstairs; I was shamefully saving myself by flight. I had not the power to raise my eyes. I was dazed by the sparkling glass steps under my feet, and with every step I felt more and more hopeless. I, a corrupted man, a criminal, was out of place here. No, I shall probably never again be able to fuse myself into this mechanical rhythm, nor float over this mirror-like, untroubled sea. I am to burn eternally from now on, running from place to place, seeking a nook where I may hide my eyes, eternally, until I . . . A spark cold as ice pierced me. "I myself, I matter little, but is it necessary that *she* also . . . ? I must see that she . . ."

I crawled through the hatchway to the deck and stood there; where was I to go now? I did not know what I had come for! I looked aloft. The midday sun, exhausted by its march, was fuming dimly. Below was the *Integral*, a gray mass of glass—dead. The pink blood was drained out! It was obvious to me that all this was my imagination and that everything was the same as before; yet it was also clear to me that . . .

"What is the matter with you, D-503? Are you deaf? I call and call you. What is the matter with you?" It was the Second Builder yelling directly into my ear; he must have been yelling that way for quite a while.

What was the matter with me? I had lost my rudder; the motor was groaning as before, the aero was quivering and rushing on, but it had no rudder. I did not even know where I was rushing, down to the earth or up to the sun, to its flame. . . .

RECORD THIRTY-ONE

The Great Operation
I Forgave Everything
The Collision of Trains

Saved! At the very last moment, when it seemed that there was nothing to hold on to, that it was the end! . . .

It was as if you already ascended the steps toward the threatening machine of the Well-Doer, or as if the great glass Bell with a heavy thud had already covered you, and for the last time in life you looked at the blue sky to devour it with your eyes . . . when suddenly, it was only a dream! The sun is pink and cheerful and the wall . . . What happiness to be able to touch the cold wall! And the pillow! To delight endlessly in the little cavity formed by your own head in the white pillow! . . . This is approximately what I felt, when I read the *State Journal* this morning. It has all been a terrible dream, and the dream is over. And I was so feeble, so unfaithful, that I thought of selfish, voluntary death! I am ashamed now to reread yesterday's last lines. But let them remain as a memory of that incredible what-might-have-happened, which will not happen! On the front page of the *State Journal* the following gleamed:

REJOICE!

For from now on we are *perfect*!
Until today your own creation, engines, were more perfect than you.

WHY?

For every spark from a dynamo is a spark of pure reason; each motion of a piston, a pure syllogism. Is it not true that the same faultless reason is within you?

The philosophy of the cranes, presses, and pumps is complete and clear like a circle. But is your philosophy less circular? The beauty of a mechanism lies in its immutable, precise rhythm, like that of a pendulum. But have you not become as precise as a pendulum, you who are brought up on the system of Taylor?

Yes, but there is one difference:

MECHANISMS HAVE NO FANCY.

Did you ever notice a pump cylinder with a wide, distant, sensuously dreaming smile upon its face while it was working? Did you ever hear cranes that were restless, tossing about and sighing at night during the hours designed for rest?

NO!

Yet on your faces (you may well blush with shame!) the Guardians have more and more frequently seen those smiles, and they have heard your sighs. And (you should hide your eyes for shame!) the historians of the United State have all tendered their resignations so as to be relieved from having to record such shameful occurrences.

It is not your fault; you are ill. And the name of your illness is:

FANCY.

It is a worm that gnaws black wrinkles on one's forehead. It is a fever that drives one to run further and further, even though "further" may begin where happiness ends. It is the last barricade on our road to happiness.

Rejoice! This Barricade Has Been Blasted at Last! The Road Is Open!

The latest discovery of our State science is that there is a center for fancy—a miserable little nervous knot in the lower region of the frontal lobe of the brain. A triple treatment of this knot with X-rays will cure you of fancy.

Forever!

You are perfect; you are mechanized; the road to one-hundred-per-cent happiness is open! Hasten then all of you, young and old, hasten to undergo the Great Operation! Hasten to the auditoriums where the Great Operation is being performed! Long live the Great Operation! Long live the United State! Long live the Well-Doer!

You, had you not read all this in my records—which look like an ancient, strange novel—had you, like me, held in your trembling hands the newspaper, smelling of typographic ink . . . if you knew, as I do, that all this is a most certain reality—if not the reality of today, then that of tomorrow—would you not feel the very things I feel? Would your head not whirl as mine does? Would there not run over your back and arms those strange, sweet, icy needles? Would you not feel that you were a giant, an Atlas?—that if you only stood up and straightened out you would reach the ceiling with your head?

I snatched the telephone receiver.

"I-330. Yes . . . Yes. Yes . . . 330!" And then, swallowing my own words, I shouted, "Are you at home? Yes? Have you read? You are reading now? Isn't it, isn't it stupendous?"

"Yes. . . ." A long, dark silence. The wires buzzed almost imperceptibly. She was thinking.

"I must see you today without fail. Yes, in my room, after sixteen, without fail!"

Dear . . . she is such a dear! . . . "Without fail!" I was smiling, and I could not stop! I felt I would carry that smile with me into the street like a light above my head.

Outside the wind ran over me, whirling, whistling, whipping, but I felt even more cheerful. "All right, go on, go on moaning and groaning! The Walls cannot be torn down." Flying leaden clouds broke over my head . . . well, let them! They could not eclipse the sun! We chained it to the zenith like so many Joshuas, sons of Nun!

At the corner a group of such Joshuas, sons of Nun, were standing with their foreheads pasted to the glass of the wall. Inside, on a dazzling white table, a Number already lay. You could see two naked soles emerging from under the sheet in a yellow angle. . . . White medics bent over his head—a white hand, a stretched-out hand holding a syringe filled with something. . . .

"And you, what are you waiting for?" I asked nobody in particular, or rather all of them.

"And you?" Someone's round head turned to me.

"I? Oh, afterward! I must first . . ." Somewhat confused, I left the place. I really had to see I-330 first. But why first? I could not explain to myself. . . .

The docks. The *Integral*, bluish like ice, was glistening and sparkling. The engine was caressingly grumbling, repeating some one word, as if it were my word, a familiar one. I bent down and stroked the long, cold tube of the motor. "Dear! What a dear tube! Tomorrow it will come to life, tomorrow for the first time it will tremble with burning, flaming streams in its bowels."

With what eyes would I have looked at the glass monster had everything remained as it was yesterday? If I knew that tomorrow at twelve I should betray it, yes, betray. . . . Someone behind cautiously touched my elbow. I turned around. The plate-like, flat face of the Second Builder.

"Do you know already?" he asked.

"What? About the Operation? Yes. How everything, everything . . . suddenly . . ."

"No, not that. The trial flight is put off until day after tomorrow, on account of that Operation. They rushed us for nothing; we hurried . . ."

"On account of that Operation!" Funny, limited man. He could see no further than his own platter! If only he knew that, but for the Operation, tomorrow at twelve he would have been locked up in a glass cage, tossing about, trying to climb the walls!

At twelve-thirty when I came into my room I saw U-. She was sitting at my table, firm, straight, bone-like, resting her right cheek on her hand. She must have been waiting for a long while, because when she rose brusquely to meet me the five white imprints of her fingers remained on her cheek.

For a second that terrible morning came back to me: she beside I-330, indignant. But for a second only. All that was at once washed away by today's sun—as happens sometimes when you enter your room on a bright day and absent-mindedly turn on the light, and the bulb shines but is out of place, comical, unnecessary.

Without hesitation I held out my hand to her; I forgave her everything. She firmly grasped both my hands and pressed them till they hurt. Her cheeks quivering and hanging down like ancient precious ornaments, she said with emotion:

"I was waiting. . . . I want only one moment. . . . I only wanted to say . . . how happy, how joyous I am for you! You realize, of course, that tomorrow or day after tomorrow you will be healthy again, as if born anew."

I noticed my papers on the table; the last two pages of my record of yesterday were in the place where I had left them the night before. If only she knew what I had written there! But I didn't really care. Now it was only history; it was a ridiculously far-off distance, like an image seen through a reversed opera glass.

"Yes," I said. "A while ago, while passing along the avenue, I saw a man walking ahead of me. His shadow stretched along the pavement— and think of it! His shadow was luminous! I think—more than that, I am absolutely certain—that tomorrow all shadows will disappear. Not a shadow from any person or any thing! The sun will be shining through everything."

She, gently and earnestly:

"You are a dreamer! I would not allow my children in school to talk that way."

She told me something about the children: that they were all led in one herd to the Operation; that it was necessary to bind them afterward with ropes; that one must love pitilessly, "yes, pitilessly," and that she thought she might finally decide to . . .

She smoothed out the grayish-blue fold of the unif that fell between her knees, swiftly pasted her smiles all over me, and went out.

Fortunately the sun did not stop today. The sun was running. It was already sixteen o'clock. . . . I was knocking at the door, my heart was knocking. . . .

"Come in!"

I threw myself upon the floor near her chair, to embrace her limbs, to lift my head upward and look into her eyes, first into one, then into the other, and in each of them to see the reflection of myself in wonderful captivity. . . .

There beyond the wall it looked stormy, there the clouds were leaden—let them be! My head was overcrowded with impetuous words, and I was speaking aloud, and flying with the sun I knew not where. . . . No, now we knew where we were flying; planets were following me, planets sparkling with flame and populated with fiery, singing flowers, and mute planets, blue ones where rational stones were unified into one organized society, and planets which like our own earth had already reached the apex of one-hundred-per-cent happiness.

Suddenly, from above:

"And don't you think that at the apex are, precisely, *stones* unified into an organized society?" The triangle grew sharper and sharper, darker and darker.

"Happiness . . . well? . . . Desires are tortures, aren't they? It is clear, therefore, that happiness is when there are no longer any desires, not a single desire any more. What an error, what an absurd prejudice it was, that we used to mark happiness with the sign 'plus'! No, absolute happiness must be marked 'minus'—divine minus!"

I remember I stammered unintelligibly:

"Absolute zero!—minus 273° C."

"Minus 273°—exactly! A somewhat cool temperature. But doesn't it prove that we are at the summit?"

As before she seemed somehow to speak for me and through me, developing my own thoughts to the end. But there was something so morbid in her tone that I could not refrain . . . with an effort I drew out a "No."

"No," I said. "You, you are mocking. . . ."

She burst out laughing loudly, too loudly. Swiftly, in a second, she laughed herself to some unseen edge, stumbled, and fell over. . . . Silence.

She stood up, put her hands upon my shoulders, and looked into me for a long while. Then she pulled me toward her and everything seemed to have disappeared save her sharp, hot lips. . . .

"Good-by."

"The words came from afar, from above, and reached me not at once but only after a minute, perhaps two minutes later.

"Why . . . why 'good-by'?"

"You have been ill, have you not? Because of me you have committed crimes. Hasn't all this tormented you? And now you have the Operation to look forward to. You will be cured of me. And that means—good-by."

"No!" I cried.

A pitilessly sharp black triangle on a white background.

"What? Do you mean that you don't want happiness?"

My head was breaking into pieces; two logical trains collided and crawled upon each other, rattling and smothering. . . .

"Well, I am waiting. You must choose; the Operation and one-hundred-per-cent happiness, or . . ."

"I cannot . . . without you . . . I must not . . . without you . . ." I said, or perhaps I only thought—I am not sure which—but I-330 heard.

"Yes, I know," she said. Then, her hands still on my shoulders and her eyes not letting my eyes go, "Then . . . until tomorrow. Tomorrow at twelve. You remember?"

"No, it was postponed for a day. Day after tomorrow!"

"So much the better for us. At twelve, day after tomorrow!"

I walked alone in the dusty street. The wind was whirling, carrying, driving me like a piece of paper; fragments of the leaden sky were soaring, soaring—they had to soar through the infinite for another day or two. . . .

Unifs of Numbers were brushing my sides—yet I was walking alone. It was clear to me that all were being saved but that there was no salvation for me. For I *do not want* salvation. . . .

1924

CYRIL CONNOLLY
Year Nine

Cyril Connolly, a leading English literary critic, first published his sketch "Year Nine" in 1938. It appears to anticipate Orwell's book, particularly in its suggestion that the victim of the totalitarian state not only can be made to confess

imaginary "crimes" but also can come to believe in the rightness of the punishment he must suffer. At various points Connolly's sketch seems to refer to both
the Nazi and Stalinist dictatorships, especially to the Moscow Trials of the mid-
thirties, in which a number of old Bolsheviks, once leading figures in the Communist regime, were forced by the Stalin dictatorship, through torture and psychological pressure, to confess to a series of preposterous crimes.

Whether Orwell read Connolly's sketch at the time of its appearance is not
known for certain, but since the two men were friends, it seems quite likely.

Augur's Prison—Year IX. I have been treated with great kindness, with a
consideration utterly out of keeping with the gravity of my offence, yet
typical of the high conception of justice implicit in our state. Justice in
sentence, celerity in execution in the words of Our Leader. Excuse my
fatal impediment. I call attention to it, as eagerly as in Tintoretto's
plague hospital they point to bleeding bubos on the legs and shoulders.
Let me tell you how it all happened. With a friend, a young woman, I
arranged to spend last Leaderday evening. We met under the clock outside the Youngleaderboys building. Having some minutes to spare before
the Commonmeal and because it was raining slightly, we took shelter in
the glorious Artshouse. There were the ineffable misterpasses of our glorious culture, the pastermieces of titalitorian tra, the magnificent
Leadersequence, the superstatues of Comradeship, Blatherhood, and
Botherly Love, the 73 Martyrs of the Defence of the Bourse, the Leader as
a simple special constable. There they were so familiar that my sinful
feet were doubly to be blamed for straying—for they strayed not only
beyond the radius of divine beauty but beyond the sphere of ever-loving
Authority, creeping with their putrid freight down the stairs to the forgotten basement. There, breeding filth in the filth that gravitates around
it, glows the stagnant rottenness called Degenerate Art, though only perfect Leadercourtesy could bestow the term Art on such Degeneration!
There are the vile pustules of the rotting Demos, on canvases his sores
have hideously excoriated. Still Lives—as if life could be ever still! Plates
of food, bowls of fruit; under the old regime the last deplorable night-
dreams and imaginations of starving millions, the prurient lucubrations
of the unsterilized—bathing coves of womblike obscenity, phallic church
towers and monoliths, lighthouses and pyramids, trees even painted singly in their stark suggestiveness, instead of in the official groups; all hideous and perverted symbols of an age of private love, ignorant of the harmony of our Commonmeals, and the State administration of
Sheepthinkers Groupbegettingday. There were illicit couples, depicted in
articulo amoris, women who had never heard of the three K's, whose
so-called clothes were gaudy dishrags, whose mouths were painted offal.
Engrossed in disgust and mental anguish I thoughtlessly began to mark
on my official catalogue the names of the most detestable fartists. This

was partly to hold them up to ridicule at Commonmeals, partly to use in articles which would refute the pseudocriticism of our enemies, but above all unconsciously—a tic expressive of my odious habit, for *I only chose names that were easily or interestingly reversible*. That is my only justification. Nacnud Tnarg; Sutsugua Nhoj; Ossacip. Repip. The filthy anti-Fascists who dared to oppose our glorious fishynazists! Hurriedly we made for the clean outdoors, the welcoming statues of the great upstairs, and outside where the supreme spectae streams on the filament—the neon Leaderface. In my haste I dropped my catalog by the turnstyle. The rest of the evening passed as usual. We attended Commonmeal in seats 7111037 and 7111038 respectively, and after the digestive drill and the documentaries went to our dormitories. The young woman on departing blew me a kiss and I called out merrily yet admonishingly: "None of that stuff, 7111038, otherwise we shall never be allowed to produce a little 7111037-8. ♂ on Groupbegettingday."

During the next week nothing happened. But some four days after that, having occasion to telephone the young woman, and while speaking to her in a spirit of party badinage, I was astounded to hear a playful repartee of mine answered by a male eructation. "Was that you?" I said—but no answer came. On picking up the receiver again to ask the janitor for ten minutes' extra light, I heard—above the ringing noise—for he had not yet answered—an impatient yawn. These two noises made an enormous impression, for I realized that I was an object of attention (although unwelcome attention) to a member of a class far above my own, a superior with the broad chest and masculine virility of a Stoop Trauma!

The next morning my paper bore the dreaded headline, "Who are the Censors Looking for?" At the office we were lined up at 10.10 and some officials from the censor's department, in their camouflaged uniforms, carrying the white-hot Tongs, symbol of Truth, the Thumbcaps of Enquiry, and the Head on the Dish, emblem of Justice, passed down the line. As the hot breath of the tongs approached, many of us confessed involuntarily to grave peccadilloes. A man on my left screamed that he had stayed too long in the lavatory. But the glorious department disdained force. We were each given three photographs to consider, and told to arrange them in order of aesthetic merit. The first was a reproduction of a steel helmet, the second of a sack of potatoes, the third of some couples with their arms round their necks in an attitude of illicit sexual groupactivity. I arranged them in that order. One of the inspectors looked for a long time at me. We were then asked to write down the names of any infamous poets or painters we could remember from the old regime. "Badshaw, Deadwells, Staleworthy, Baldpole," I wrote. Then, in an emotion, a veritable paroxysm stronger than me, with the eyes of the examiner upon me, my hands bearing the pen downwards as ineluctably as the State diviner bears down on his twig, I added: "Toilet, Red Neps." And once more: "Nacnud Tnarg, Sutsugua Nhoj, Ossacip. *Jewlysses. Winagains Fake.*" The censors this time did not look at me, but passing down the line made an ever more and more perfunctory examination, towards the end simply gathering the papers from the willing outstretched hands of the workers and carelessly tearing them up. They then swept out of the room, escorted by the foreman, the political and industrial commissars of our office, and Mr. Abject, the Ownerslave. We were instructed to continue our duties. As the envelopes came by on the belt I seized them with trembling hand, and vainly tried to perform my task as if nothing had happened. It was my business to lick the top flap of the envelope, whose bottom flap would then be licked by my neighbour, the one beyond him sticking the flaps together—for all sponges and rollers were needed for munitions. At the same time I used my free hand to inscribe on the corner of the envelope my contribution to the address (for all envelopes were addressed to the censor's headquarters) the letters S.W.3. Alas how many illegible S.W.3's that morning betrayed my trepidation, and when I came to licking the outer flap my tongue was either so parched by terror as to be unable to wet the corner at all, or so drowned in nervous salivation as to spread small bubbles of spittle over the whole surface, causing the flap to curl upwards and producing in my near neighbours many a sign of their indignant impatience and true party horror of bad work. Shortly before leaderbreak the commissars, followed by Mr. Abject, returned down the line. My companions on the belt, now feeling that I manifested emotional abnormality, were doing everything to attract attention to me by causing me to fail in my work, kicking me on the ankles as they received my envelopes, and one of them, seizing a ruler, made a vicious jab upwards with it as I was adding S.W.3, causing acute agony to my public parts. As the commissars came near me they began to joke, smiling across at my neighbours and grunting: "As long as you can spit, man, the State will have a use for you," and "Don't try and find out where the gum you lick comes from, my boyo." Friendly condescensions which seemed designed to render more pregnant and miserable the silence with which they came to me. At last, with a terrible downward look, the commissar paused before me. The smile had faded from his face, his eyes flashed lightning, his mouth was thin as a backsight, his nose was a hairtrigger. Mr. Abject looked at me with profound commiseration till he received a nudge from the other commissar, and said in a loud voice: "This is your man." I was marched out between them while the serried ranks of my old beltmates sang the Leaderchorus and cried: "Show mercy to us by showing no mercy to him, the dog and the traitor." Outside the newsboys were screaming: "Long live the Censor. Gum-licking wrecker discovered."

Our justice is swift: our trials are fair: hardly was the preliminary bone-breaking over than my case came up. I was tried by the secret censor's tribunal in a pitchdark circular room. My silly old legs were no use to me now and I was allowed the privilege of wheeling myself in on a kind of invalid's chair. In the darkness I could just see the aperture high up in the wall from whence I should be cross-examined, for it is part of our new justice that no prejudicial view is obtained of the personal forces at work between accused and accuser. The charge was read out and I was asked if I had anything to say. I explained the circumstances as I have related them to you, and made my defence. Since an early initiation accident I have never been considered sound of mind, hence my trick of reversing words—quite automatically and without the intention of seeking hidden and antinomian meanings, hence my subordinate position in the Spit-shop. My action, I repeated, was purely involuntary. The voice of my chief witness-accuser-judge replied from the orifice:

"Involuntary! But don't you see, that makes it so much worse! For what we voluntarily do, voluntarily we may undo, but what we do not of our own free will, we lack the will to revoke. What sort of a person are you, whose feet carry you helplessly to the forbidden basement? Yet not forbidden, for that basement is an open trap. Poor flies walk down it as down the gummy sides of a pitcher plant; a metronome marks the time they spend there, a radioactive plate interprets the pulsations which those works inspire, a pulsemeter projects them on a luminous screen which is perpetually under observation in the censor's office. It was at once known that you were there and what you felt there. But instead of being followed to your Blokery in the normal way you eluded your pursuers by dropping your catalog. They decided it was their duty to carry it immediately to the cipher department and thus allowed you to escape. Your crime is fivefold:

" 'That you of your own impulse visited the basement of degenerate art and were aesthetically stimulated thereby.'

" 'That you attempted to convince a young woman, 7111038, of the merit of the daubs you found there, thereby being guilty of treason—for Our Leader is a painter too, and thereby being guilty of the far worse sin of inciting to treason a member of the nonrational (and therefore not responsible for her actions) sex.'

" 'That you made notes on the daubs in question with a view to perverting your fellow-workers.'

" 'That you caused deliberate inconvenience to the board of censors, attempting to throw them off your trail, thus making improper use of them.'

" 'That you did not confess before your offence was notified, or even at the time of your examination.'

"The penalty, as you know, for all these crimes is death. But there has interceded on your behalf the young woman whose denunciation helped us to find you. To reward her we have commuted your crime to that of coprophagy—for that is what your bestial appreciation of the faeces of so-called democratic art amounts to. Your plea of involuntary compulsion forces me to proclaim the full sentence. For which such a subconscious libido there must surely be a cancerous ego! I therefore proclaim that you will be cut open by a qualified surgeon in the presence of the State Augur. You will be able to observe the operation, and if the Augur decides the entrails are favourable they will be put back. If not, not. You may congratulate yourself on being of more use to your leader in your end than your beginning. For on this augury an important decision on foreign policy will be taken. Annexation or Annihilation? Be worthy of your responsibility. Should the worst befall, you will be sent to the gumfactory, and part of you may even form the flap of an envelope which your successor on the belt, Miss 7111038, may lick! You lucky dog."

Yes, I have been treated with great kindness.

1938

LEON TROTSKY
from The Revolution Betrayed

THE SOVIET THERMIDOR*

Parallel with the political degeneration of the party, there occurred a moral decay of the uncontrolled apparatus. The word "sovbour"—soviet bourgeois—as applied to a privileged dignitary appeared very early in the workers' vocabulary. With the transfer to the NEP bourgeois tendencies received a more copious field of action. At the 11th Congress of the party, in March 1922, Lenin gave warning of the danger of a degeneration of the ruling stratum. It has occurred more than once in history, he said, that the conqueror took over the culture of the conquered, when the latter stood on a higher level. The culture of the Russian bourgeoisie and the old bureaucracy was, to be sure, miserable, but alas the new ruling stratum must often take off its hat to that culture. "Four thousand seven hundred responsible communists" in Moscow administer the state machine. "Who is leading whom? I doubt very much whether you can say that the communists are in the lead. . . ." In subsequent congresses, Lenin could not speak. But all his thoughts in the last months of his

---

* Thermidor is the month of the French revolutionary calendar during which Robespierre was assassinated and the counterrevolution was begun. By analogy Trotsky used "Thermidor" to describe the period in which Stalin consolidated his personal dictatorship, destroying the remnants of opposition within the Bolshevik Party and deviating from the equalitarian ideals proclaimed at the outset of the Russian Revolution.—Editor

active life were of warning and arming the workers against the oppression, caprice and decay of the bureaucracy. He, however, saw only the first symptoms of the disease.

Christian Rakovsky, former president of the Soviet of People's Commissars of the Ukraine, and later Soviet Ambassador in London and Paris, sent to his friends in 1928, when already in exile, a brief inquiry into the Soviet bureaucracy, which we have quoted above several times, for it still remains the best that has been written on this subject. "In the mind of Lenin, and in all our minds," says Rakovsky, "the task of the party leadership was to protect both the party and the working class from the corrupting action of privilege, place and patronage on the part of those in power, from *rapprochement* with the relics of the old nobility and burgherdom, from the corrupting influence of the NEP, from the temptation of bourgeois morals and ideologies. . . . We must say frankly, definitely and loudly that the party apparatus has not fulfilled this task, that it has revealed a complete incapacity for its double role of protector and educator. It has failed. It is bankrupt."

It is true that Rakovsky himself, broken by the bureaucratic repressions, subsequently repudiated his own critical judgments. But the seventy-year-old Galileo too, caught in the vise of the Holy Inquisition, found himself compelled to repudiate the system of Copernicus—which did not prevent the earth from continuing to revolve around the sun. We do not believe in the recantation of the sixty-year-old Rakovsky, for he himself has more than once made a withering analysis of such recantations. As to his political criticisms, they have found in the facts of the objective development a far more reliable support than in the subjective stout-heartedness of their author.

The conquest of power changes not only the relations of the proletariat to other classes, but also its own inner structure. The wielding of power becomes the specialty of a definite social group, which is the more impatient to solve its own "social problem," the higher its opinion of its own mission. "In a proletarian state, where capitalist accumulation is forbidden to the members of the ruling party, the differentiation is at first functional, but afterward becomes social. I do not say it becomes a class differentiation, but a social one. . . ." Rakovsky further explains: "The social situation of the communist who has at his disposition an automobile, a good apartment, regular vacations, and receives the party maximum of salary, differs from the situation of the communist who works in the coal mines, where he receives from fifty to sixty rubles a month." Counting over the causes of the degeneration of the Jacobins when in power—the chase after wealth, participation in government contracts, supplies, etc., Rakovsky cites a curious remark of Babeuf to the effect that the degeneration of the new ruling stratum was helped along not a little by the former young ladies of the aristocracy toward whom the Jacobins were very friendly. "What are you doing, small-hearted plebeian?" cries Babeuf. "Today they are embracing you and tomorrow they will strangle you." A census of the wives of the ruling stratum in the Soviet Union would show a similar picture. The well-known Soviet journalist, Sosnovsky, pointed out the special role played by the "automobile-harem factor" in forming the morals of the Soviet bureaucracy. It is true that Sosnovsky, too, following Rakovsky, recanted and was returned from Siberia. But that did not improve the morals of the bureaucracy. On the contrary, that very recantation is proof of a progressing demoralization.

The old articles of Sosnovsky, passed about in manuscript from hand to hand, were sprinkled with unforgettable episodes from the life of the new ruling stratum, plainly showing to what vast degree the conquerors have assimilated the morals of the conquered. Not to return, however, to past years—for Sosnovsky finally exchanged his whip for a lyre in 1934—we will confine ourselves to wholly fresh examples from the Soviet press. And we will not select the abuses and so-called "excesses," either, but everyday phenomena legalized by official social opinion.

The director of a Moscow factory, a prominent communist, boasts in *Pravda* of the cultural growth of the enterprise directed by him. "A mechanic telephones: 'What is your order, sir, check the furnace immediately or wait?' I answer: 'Wait.' "* The mechanic addresses the director with extreme respect, using the second person plural, while the director answers him in the second person singular. And this disgraceful dialogue, impossible in any cultured capitalist country, is related by the director himself on the pages of *Pravda* as something entirely normal! The editor does not object because he does not notice it. The readers do not object because they are accustomed to it. We also are not surprised, for at solemn sessions in the Kremlin, the "leaders" and People's Commissars address in the second person singular directors of factories subordinate to them, presidents of collective farms, shop foremen and working women, especially invited to receive decorations. How can they fail to remember that one of the most popular revolutionary slogans in tzarist Russia was the demand for the abolition of the use of the second person singular by bosses in addressing their subordinates!

These Kremlin dialogues of the authorities with "the people," astonishing in their lordly ungraciousness, unmistakably testify that, in spite of the October revolution, the nationalization of the means of production, collectivization, and "the liquidation of the kulaks as a class," the relations among men, and that at the very heights of the Soviet pyramid, have not only not yet risen to socialism, but in many respects are still lagging behind a cultured capitalism. In recent years enormous back-

---

* It is impossible to convey the flavor of this dialogue in English. The second person singular is used either with intimates in token of affection, or with children, servants and animals in token of superiority.

ward steps have been taken in this very important sphere. And the source of this revival of genuine Russian barbarism is indubitably the Soviet Thermidor, which has given complete independence and freedom from control to a bureaucracy possessing little culture, and has given to the masses the well-known gospel of obedience and silence.

We are far from intending to contrast the abstraction of dictatorship with the abstraction of democracy, and weigh their merits on the scales of pure reason. Everything is relative in this world, where change alone endures. The dictatorship of the Bolshevik party proved one of the most powerful instruments of progress in history. But here too, in the words of the poet, "Reason becomes unreason, kindness a pest." The prohibition of oppositional parties brought after it the prohibition of factions. The prohibition of factions ended in a prohibition to think otherwise than the infallible leaders. The police-manufactured monolithism of the party resulted in a bureaucratic impunity which has become the source of all kinds of wantonness and corruption.

1937

PART THREE

Orwell's Ideas

This section provides a sample of George Orwell's remarkable gifts as an essayist. The four essays here included are of great interest in their own right, but you will probably also want to see how various ideas touched upon in these short pieces contribute to the unfolding of *Nineteen Eighty-Four*. "Politics and the English Language" shows Orwell's passion for clarity of thought, modesty and precision in the use of language—all the very opposite of "Newspeak." "Why I Write" is a personal credo with a bearing upon his last novel that the student will want to work out for himself. "Freedom and Happiness" shows Orwell expressing his interest in *We*, the remarkable Russian novel by Eugene Zamiatin at a time when it was barely known in the English-speaking world. And "The Prevention of Literature" finds Orwell in an especially incisive and combative mood, talking about various kinds of censorship which would destroy the writer's freedom to think and speak independently—almost as if he were anticipating the kind of world he would later portray in *Nineteen Eighty-Four*.

GEORGE ORWELL
Why I Write

From a very early age, perhaps the age of five or six, I knew that when I grew up I should be a writer. Between the ages of about seventeen and twenty-four I tried to abandon this idea, but I did so with the consciousness that I was outraging my true nature and that sooner or later I should have to settle down and write books.

I was the middle child of three, but there was a gap of five years on either side, and I barely saw my father before I was eight. For this and other reasons I was somewhat lonely, and I soon developed disagreeable mannerisms which made me unpopular throughout my schooldays. I had the lonely child's habit of making up stories and holding conversations with imaginary persons, and I think from the very start my literary ambitions were mixed up with the feeling of being isolated and undervalued. I knew that I had a facility with words and a power of facing unpleasant facts, and I felt that this created a sort of private world in which I could get my own back for my failure in everyday life. Nevertheless the volume of serious—*i.e.* seriously intended—writing which I produced all through my childhood and boyhood would not amount to half a dozen pages. I wrote my first poem at the age of four or five, my mother taking it down to dictation. I cannot remember anything about it except that it was about a tiger and the tiger had "chair-like teeth"—a good enough phrase, but I fancy the poem was a plagiarism of Blake's "Tiger, Tiger." At eleven, when the war of 1914–18 broke out, I wrote a patriotic poem which was printed in the local newspaper, as was another, two years later, on the death of Kitchener. From time to time, when I was a bit older, I wrote bad and usually unfinished "nature poems" in the Georgian style. I also, about twice, attempted a short story which was a ghastly failure. That was the total of the would-be serious work that I actually set down on paper during all those years.

However, throughout this time I did in a sense engage in literary activities. To begin with there was the made-to-order stuff which I produced quickly, easily and without much pleasure to myself. Apart from school work, I wrote *vers d'occasion*, semi-comic poems which I could turn out at what now seems to me astonishing speed—at fourteen I wrote a whole rhyming play, in imitation of Aristophanes, in about a week—and helped to edit school magazines, both printed and in manuscript. These magazines were the most pitiful burlesque stuff that you could imagine, and I took far less trouble with them than I now would with the cheapest journalism. But side by side with all this, for fifteen years or more, I was carrying out a literary exercise of a quite different kind: this was the making up of a continuous "story" about myself, a sort of diary existing only in the mind. I believe this is a common habit of children and adolescents. As a very small child I used to imagine that I was, say, Robin Hood, and picture myself as the hero of thrilling adventures, but quite soon my "story" ceased to be narcissistic in a crude way and became more and more a mere description of what I was doing and the things I saw. For minutes at a time this kind of thing would be running through my head: "He pushed the door open and entered the room. A yellow beam of sunlight, filtering through the muslin curtains, slanted on to the table, where a match-box, half open, lay beside the inkpot. With his right hand in his pocket he moved across to the window. Down in the street a tortoiseshell cat was chasing a dead leaf," etc., etc. This habit continued till I was about twenty-five, right through my non-literary years. Although I had to search, and did search, for the right words, I seemed to be making this descriptive effort almost against my will, under a kind of compulsion from outside. The "story" must, I suppose, have reflected the styles of the various writers I admired at different ages, but so far as I remember it always had the same meticulous descriptive quality.

When I was about sixteen I suddenly discovered the joy of mere words, *i.e.* the sounds and associations of words. The lines from *Paradise Lost*—

> So hee with difficulty and labour hard
> Moved on: with difficulty and labour hee,

which do not now seem to me so very wonderful, sent shivers down my backbone; and the spelling "hee" for "he" was an added pleasure. As for the need to describe things, I knew all about it already. So it is clear what kind of books I wanted to write, in so far as I could be said to want to write books at that time. I wanted to write enormous naturalistic novels with unhappy endings, full of detailed descriptions and arresting similes, and also full of purple passages in which words were used partly for the sake of their sound. And in fact my first completed novel, *Burmese Days*, which I wrote when I was thirty but projected much earlier, is rather that kind of book.

I give all this background information because I do not think one can assess a writer's motives without knowing something of his early development. His subject matter will be determined by the age he lives in—at least this is true in tumultuous, revolutionary ages like our own—but before he ever begins to write he will have acquired an emotional attitude from which he will never completely escape. It is his job, no doubt, to discipline his temperament and avoid getting stuck at some immature stage, or in some perverse mood: but if he escapes from his early influences altogether, he will have killed his impulse to write. Putting aside the need to earn a living, I think there are four great motives for writing, at any rate for writing prose. They exist in different degrees in every writer, and in any one writer the proportions will vary from time to time, according to the atmosphere in which he is living. They are:

(1) Sheer egoism. Desire to seem clever, to be talked about, to be remembered after death, to get your own back on grown-ups who snubbed you in childhood, etc., etc. It is humbug to pretend that this is not a motive, and a strong one. Writers share this characteristic with scientists, artists, politicians, lawyers, soldiers, successful businessmen—in short, with the whole top crust of humanity. The great mass of human beings are not acutely selfish. After the age of about thirty they abandon individual ambition—in many cases, indeed, they almost abandon the sense of being individuals at all—and live chiefly for others, or are simply smothered under drudgery. But there is also the minority of gifted, wilful people who are determined to live their own lives to the end, and writers belong in this class. Serious writers, I should say, are on the whole more vain and self-centered than journalists, though less interested in money.

(2) Aesthetic enthusiasm. Perception of beauty in the external world, or, on the other hand, in words and their right arrangement. Pleasure in the impact of one sound on another, in the firmness of good prose or the rhythm of a good story. Desire to share an experience which one feels is valuable and ought not to be missed. The aesthetic motive is very feeble in a lot of writers, but even a pamphleteer or a writer of textbooks will have pet words and phrases which appeal to him for non-utilitarian reasons; or he may feel strongly about typography, width of margins, etc. Above the level of a railway guide, no book is quite free from aesthetic considerations.

(3) Historical impulse. Desire to see things as they are, to find out true facts and store them up for the use of posterity.

(4) Political purpose—using the word "political" in the widest possible sense. Desire to push the world in a certain direction, to alter other people's idea of the kind of society that they should strive after. Once again, no book is genuinely free from political bias. The opinion that art should have nothing to do with politics is itself a political attitude.

It can be seen how these various impulses must war against one another, and how they must fluctuate from person to person and from time to time. By nature—taking your "nature" to be the state you have attained when you are first adult—I am a person in whom the first three motives would outweigh the fourth. In a peaceful age I might have written ornate or merely descriptive books, and might have remained almost unaware of my political loyalties. As it is I have been forced into becoming a sort of pamphleteer. First I spent five years in an unsuitable profession (the Indian Imperial Police, in Burma), and then I underwent poverty and the sense of failure. This increased my natural hatred of authority and made me for the first time fully aware of the existence of the working classes, and the job in Burma had given me some understanding of the nature of imperialism: but these experiences were not enough to give me an accurate political orientation. Then came Hitler, the Spanish civil war, etc. By the end of 1935 I had still failed to reach a firm decision. I remember a little poem that I wrote at that date, expressing my dilemma:

> A happy vicar I might have been
> Two hundred years ago,
> To preach upon eternal doom
> And watch my walnuts grow;
>
> But born, alas, in an evil time,
> I missed that pleasant haven,
> For the hair has grown on my upper lip
> And the clergy are all clean-shaven.
>
> And later still the times were good,
> We were so easy to please,
> We rocked our troubled thoughts to sleep
> On the bosoms of the trees.
>
> All ignorant we dared to own
> The joys we now dissemble;
> The greenfinch on the apple bough
> Could make my enemies tremble.
>
> But girls' bellies and apricots,
> Roach in a shaded stream,
> Horses, ducks in flight at dawn,
> All these are a dream.
>
> It is forbidden to dream again;
> We maim our joys or hide them;
> Horses are made of chromium steel
> And little fat men shall ride them.
>
> I am the worm who never turned,
> The eunuch without a harem;
> Between the priest and the commissar
> I walk like Eugene Aram;
>
> And the commissar is telling my fortune
> While the radio plays,
> But the priest has promised an Austin Seven,
> For Duggie always pays.

I dreamed I dwelt in marble halls,
And woke to find it true;
I wasn't born for an age like this;
Was Smith? Was Jones? Were you?

The Spanish war and other events in 1936–7 turned the scale and thereafter I knew where I stood. Every line of serious work that I have written since 1936 has been written, directly or indirectly, *against* totalitarianism and *for* democratic socialism, as I understand it. It seems to me nonsense, in a period like our own, to think that one can avoid writing of such subjects. Everyone writes of them in one guise or another. It is simply a question of which side one takes and what approach one follows. And the more one is conscious of one's political bias, the more chance one has of acting politically without sacrificing one's aesthetic and intellectual integrity.

What I have most wanted to do throughout the past ten years is to make political writing into an art. My starting point is always a feeling of partisanship, a sense of injustice. When I sit down to write a book, I do not say to myself, "I am going to produce a work of art." I write it because there is some lie that I want to expose, some fact to which I want to draw attention, and my initial concern is to get a hearing. But I could not do the work of writing a book, or even a long magazine article, if it were not also an aesthetic experience. Anyone who cares to examine my work will see that even when it is downright propaganda it contains much that a full-time politician would consider irrelevant. I am not able, and I do not want, completely to abandon the world view that I acquired in childhood. So long as I remain alive and well I shall continue to feel strongly about prose style, to love the surface of the earth, and to take a pleasure in solid objects and scraps of useless information. It is no use trying to suppress that side of myself. The job is to reconcile my ingrained likes and dislikes with the essentially public, non-individual activities that this age forces on all of us.

It is not easy. It raises problems of construction and of language, and it raises in a new way the problem of truthfulness. Let me give just one example of the cruder kind of difficulty that arises. My book about the Spanish civil war, *Homage to Catalonia*, is, of course, a frankly political book, but in the main it is written with a certain detachment and regard for form. I did try very hard in it to tell the whole truth without violating my literary instincts. But among other things it contains a long chapter, full of newspaper quotations and the like, defending the Trotskyists who were accused of plotting with Franco. Clearly such a chapter, which after a year or two would lose its interest for any ordinary reader, must ruin the book. A critic whom I respect read me a lecture about it. "Why did you put in all that stuff?" he said. "You've turned what might have been a good book into journalism." What he said was true, but I could not have done otherwise. I happened to know, what very few people in England had been allowed to know, that innocent men were being falsely accused. If I had not been angry about that I should never have written the book.

In one form or another this problem comes up again. The problem of language is subtler and would take too long to discuss. I will only say that of late years I have tried to write less picturesquely and more exactly. In any case I find that by the time you have perfected any style of writing, you have always outgrown it. *Animal Farm* was the first book in which I tried, with full consciousness of what I was doing, to fuse political purpose and artistic purpose into one whole. I have not written a novel for seven years, but I hope to write another fairly soon. It is bound to be a failure, every book is a failure, but I do know with some clarity what kind of book I want to write. Looking back through the last page or two, I see that I have made it appear as though my motives in writing were wholly public-spirited. I don't want to leave that as the final impression. All writers are vain, selfish, and lazy, and at the very bottom of their motives there lies a mystery. Writing a book is a horrible, exhausting struggle, like a long bout of some painful illness. One would never undertake such a thing if one were not driven on by some demon whom one can neither resist nor understand. For all one knows that demon is simply the same instinct that makes a baby squall for attention. And yet it is also true that one can write nothing readable unless one constantly struggles to efface one's own personality. Good prose is like a windowpane. I cannot say with certainty which of my motives are the strongest, but I know which of them deserve to be followed. And looking back through my work, I see that it is invariably where I lacked a *political* purpose that I wrote lifeless books and was betrayed into purple passages, sentences without meaning, decorative adjectives and humbug generally.

1947

GEORGE ORWELL
Politics and the English Language

Most people who bother with the matter at all would admit that the English language is in a bad way, but it is generally assumed that we cannot by conscious action do anything about it. Our civilization is decadent and our language—so the argument runs—must inevitably share in the general collapse. It follows that any struggle against the abuse of language is a sentimental archaism, like preferring candles to electric light or hansom cabs to aeroplanes. Underneath this lies the half-conscious belief that language is a natural growth and not an instrument which we shape for our own purposes.

Now, it is clear that the decline of a language must ultimately have political and economic causes: it is not due simply to the bad influence of this or that individual writer. But an effect can become a cause, reinforcing the original cause and producing the same effect in an intensified form, and so on indefinitely. A man may take to drink because he feels himself to be a failure, and then fail all the more completely because he drinks. It is rather the same thing that is happening to the English language. It becomes ugly and inaccurate because our thoughts are foolish, but the slovenliness of our language makes it easier for us to have foolish thoughts. The point is that the process is reversible. Modern English, especially written English, is full of bad habits which spread by imitation and which can be avoided if one is willing to take the necessary trouble. If one gets rid of these habits one can think more clearly, and to think clearly is a necessary first step toward political regeneration: so that the fight against bad English is not frivolous and is not the exclusive concern of professional writers. I will come back to this presently, and I hope that by that time the meaning of what I have said here will have become clearer. Meanwhile, here are five specimens of the English language as it is now habitually written.

These five passages have not been picked out because they are especially bad—I could have quoted far worse if I had chosen—but because they illustrate various of the mental vices from which we now suffer. They are a little below the average, but are fairly representative samples. I number them so that I can refer back to them when necessary:

(1) I am not, indeed, sure whether it is not true to say that the Milton who once seemed not unlike a seventeenth-century Shelley had not become, out of an experience ever more bitter in each year, more alien [*sic*] to the founder of that Jesuit sect which nothing could induce him to tolerate.

> Professor Harold Laski
> (Essay in *Freedom of Expression*)

(2) Above all, we cannot play ducks and drakes with a native battery of idioms which prescribes such egregious collocations of vocables as the Basic *put up with* for *tolerate* or *put at a loss* for *bewilder*.

> Professor Lancelot Hogben (*Interglossa*)

(3) On the one side we have the free personality: by definition it is not neurotic, for it has neither conflict nor dream. Its desires, such as they are, are transparent, for they are just what institutional approval keeps in the forefront of

consciousness; another institutional pattern would alter their number and intensity; there is little in them that is natural, irreducible, or culturally dangerous. But *on the other side*, the social bond itself is nothing but the mutual reflection of these self-secure integrities. Recall the definition of love. Is not this the very picture of a small academic? Where is there a place in this hall of mirrors for either personality or fraternity?

Essay on psychology in *Politics* (New York)

(4) All the "best people" from the gentlemen's clubs, and all the frantic fascist captains, united in common hatred of Socialism and bestial horror of the rising tide of the mass revolutionary movement, have turned to acts of provocation, to foul incendiarism, to medieval legends of poisoned wells, to legalize their own destruction of proletarian organizations, and rouse the agitated petty-bourgeoisie to chauvinistic fervor on behalf of the fight against the revolutionary way out of the crisis.

Communist pamphlet

(5) If a new spirit *is* to be infused into this old country, there is one thorny and contentious reform which must be tackled, and that is the humanization and galvanization of the B.B.C. Timidity here will bespeak canker and atrophy of the soul. The heart of Britain may be sound and of strong beat, for instance, but the British lion's roar at present is like that of Bottom in Shakespeare's *Midsummer Night's Dream*—as gentle as any sucking dove. A virile new Britain cannot continue indefinitely to be traduced in the eyes or rather ears, of the world by the effete languors of Langham Place, brazenly masquerading as "standard English." When the Voice of Britain is heard at nine o'clock, better far and infinitely less ludicrous to hear aitches honestly dropped than the present priggish, inflated, inhibited, school-ma'amish arch braying of blameless bashful mewing maidens!

Letter in *Tribune*

Each of these passages has faults of its own, but, quite apart from avoidable ugliness, two qualities are common to all of them. The first is staleness of imagery; the other is lack of precision. The writer either has a meaning and cannot express it, or he inadvertently says something else, or he is almost indifferent as to whether his words mean anything or not. This mixture of vagueness and sheer incompetence is the most marked characteristic of modern English prose, and especially of any kind of political writing. As soon as certain topics are raised, the concrete melts into the abstract and no one seems able to think of turns of speech that are not hackneyed: prose consists less and less of *words* chosen for the sake of their meaning, and more and more of *phrases* tacked together like the sections of a prefabricated henhouse. I list below, with notes and examples, various of the tricks by means of which the work of prose-construction is habitually dodged:

Dying metaphors. A newly invented metaphor assists thought by evoking a visual image, while on the other hand a metaphor which is technically "dead" (e.g. *iron resolution*) has in effect reverted to being an ordinary word and can generally be used without loss of vividness. But in between these two classes there is a huge dump of worn-out metaphors which have lost all evocative power and are merely used because they save people the trouble of inventing phrases for themselves. Examples are: *Ring the changes on, take up the cudgels for, toe the line, ride roughshod over, stand shoulder to shoulder with, play into the hands of, no axe to grind, grist to the mill, fishing in troubled waters, on the order of the day, Achilles' heel, swan song, hotbed.* Many of these are used without knowledge of their meaning (what is a "rift," for instance?), and incompatible metaphors are frequently mixed, a sure sign that the writer is not interested in what he is saying. Some metaphors now current have been twisted out of their original meaning without those who use them even being aware of the fact. For example, *toe the line* is sometimes written *tow the line.* Another example is *the hammer and the anvil,* now always used with the implication that the anvil gets the worst of it. In real life it is always the anvil that breaks the hammer, never the other way about: a writer who stopped to think what he was saying would be aware of this, and would avoid perverting the original phrase.

Operators or *verbal false limbs.* These save the trouble of picking out appropriate verbs and nouns, and at the same time pad each sentence with extra syllables which give it an appearance of symmetry. Characteristic phrases are *render inoperative, militate against, make contact with, be subjected to, give rise to, give grounds for, have the effect of, play a leading part (role) in, make itself felt, take effect, exhibit a tendency to, serve the purpose of, etc., etc.* The keynote is the elimination of simple verbs. Instead of being a single word, such as *break, stop, spoil, mend, kill,* a verb becomes a *phrase,* made up of a noun or adjective tacked on to some general-purpose verb such as *prove, serve, form, play, render.* In addition, the passive voice is wherever possible used in preference to the active, and noun constructions are used instead of gerunds (*by examination of* instead of *by examining*). The range of verbs is further cut down by means of the *-ize* and *de-* formations, and the banal statements are given an appearance of profundity by means of the *not un-* formation. Simple conjunctions and prepositions are replaced by such phrases as *with respect to, having regard to, the fact that, by dint of, in view of, in the interests of, on the hypothesis that;* and the ends of sentences are saved from anticlimax by such resounding commonplaces as *greatly to be desired, cannot be left out of account, a development to be expected in the* *near future, deserving of serious consideration, brought to a satisfactory conclusion,* and so on and so forth.

Pretentious diction. Words like *phenomenon, element, individual* (as noun), *objective, categorical, effective, virtual, basic, primary, promote, constitute, exhibit, exploit, utilize, eliminate, liquidate,* are used to dress up simple statement and give an air of scientific impartiality to biased judgments. Adjectives like *epoch-making, epic, historic, unforgettable, triumphant, age-old, inevitable, inexorable, veritable,* are used to dignify the sordid processes of international politics, while writing that aims at glorifying war usually takes on an archaic color, its characteristic words being: *realm, throne, chariot, mailed fist, trident, sword, shield, buckler, banner, jackboot, clarion.* Foreign words and expressions such as *cul de sac, ancien régime, deus ex machina, mutatis mutandis, status quo, gleichschaltung, weltanschauung,* are used to give an air of culture and elegance. Except for the useful abbreviations *i.e., e.g.,* and *etc.,* there is no real need for any of the hundreds of foreign phrases now current in English. Bad writers, and especially scientific, political, and sociological writers, are nearly always haunted by the notion that Latin or Greek words are grander than Saxon ones, and unnecessary words like *expedite, ameliorate, predict, extraneous, deracinated, clandestine, subaqueous,* and hundreds of others constantly gain ground from their Anglo-Saxon opposite numbers.* The jargon peculiar to Marxist writing (*hyena, hangman, cannibal, petty bourgeois, these gentry, lackey, flunkey, mad dog, White Guard, etc.*) consists largely of words and phrases translated from Russian, German, or French; but the normal way of coining a new word is to use the Latin or Greek root with the appropriate affix and, where necessary, the size formation. It is often easier to make up words of this kind (*deregionalize, impermissible, extramarital, nonfragmentary* and so forth) than to think up the English words that will cover one's meaning. The result, in general, is an increase in slovenliness and vagueness.

Meaningless words. In certain kinds of writing, particularly in art criticism and literary criticism, it is normal to come across long passages which are almost completely lacking in meaning.† Words like *romantic, plastic, values, human, dead, sentimental, natural, vitality,* as used in art

* An interesting illustration of this is the way in which the English flower names which were in use till very recently are being ousted by Greek ones, *snapdragon* becoming *antirrhinum, forget-me-not* becoming *myosotis,* etc. It is hard to see any practical reason for this change of fashion: it is probably due to an instinctive turning away from the more homely word and a vague feeling that the Greek word is scientific.

† Example: "Comfort's catholicity of perception and image, strangely Whitmanesque in range, almost the exact opposite in aesthetic compulsion, continues to evoke that trembling atmospheric accumulative hinting at a cruel, an inexorably serene timelessness. . . . Wrey Gardiner scores by aiming at simple bull's-eyes with precision. Only they are not so simple, and through this contented sadness runs more than the surface bittersweet of resignation." *(Poetry Quarterly.)*

criticism, are strictly meaningless, in the sense that they not only do not point to any discoverable object, but are hardly ever expected to do so by the reader. When one critic writes, "The outstanding feature of Mr. X's work is its living quality," while another writes, "The immediately striking thing about Mr. X's work is its peculiar deadness," the reader accepts this as a simple difference of opinion. If words like *black* and *white* were involved, instead of the jargon words *dead* and *living*, he would see at once that language was being used in an improper way. Many political words are similarly abused. The word *Fascism* has now no meaning except in so far as it signifies "something not desirable." The words *democracy, socialism, freedom, patriotic, realistic, justice,* have each of them several different meanings which cannot be reconciled with one another. In the case of a word like *democracy,* not only is there no agreed definition, but the attempt to make one is resisted from all sides. It is almost universally felt that when we call a country democratic we are praising it: consequently the defenders of every kind of régime claim that it is a democracy, and fear that they might have to stop using the word if it were tied down to any one meaning. Words of this kind are often used in a consciously dishonest way. That is, the person who uses them has his own private definition, but allows his hearer to think he means something quite different. Statements like *Marshal Pétain was a true patriot, The Soviet Press is the freest in the world, The Catholic Church is opposed to persecution,* are almost always made with intent to deceive. Other words used in variable meanings, in most cases more or less dishonestly, are: *class, totalitarian, science, progressive, reactionary, bourgeois, equality.*

Now that I have made this catalogue of swindles and perversions, let me give another example of the kind of writing that they lead to. This time it must of its nature be an imaginary one. I am going to translate a passage of good English into modern English of the worst sort. Here is a well-known verse from *Ecclesiastes:*

> I returned and saw under the sun, that the race is not to the swift, nor the battle to the strong, neither yet bread to the wise, nor yet riches to men of understanding, nor yet favour to men of skill; but time and chance happeneth to them all.

Here it is in modern English:

> Objective considerations of contemporary phenomena compel the conclusion that success or failure in competitive activities exhibits no tendency to be commensurate with innate capacity, but that a considerable element of the unpredictable must invariably be taken into account.

This is a parody, but not a very gross one. Exhibit (3), above, for instance, contains several patches of the same kind of English. It will be

seen that I have not made a full translation. The beginning and ending of
the sentence follow the original meaning fairly closely, but in the middle
the concrete illustrations—race, battle, bread—dissolve into the vague
phrase "success or failure in competitive activities." This had to be so,
because no modern writer of the kind I am discussing—no one capable of
using phrases like "objective consideration of contemporary phenomena"
—would ever tabulate his thoughts in that precise and detailed way. The
whole tendency of modern prose is away from concreteness. Now analyze
these two sentences a little more closely. The first contains forty-nine
words but only sixty syllables, and all its words are those of everyday life.
The second contains thirty-eight words of ninety syllables: eighteen of its
words are from Latin roots, and one from Greek. The first sentence contains six vivid images, and only one phrase ("time and chance") that
could be called vague. The second contains not a single fresh, arresting
phrase, and in spite of its ninety syllables it gives only a shortened version of the meaning contained in the first. Yet without a doubt it is the
second kind of sentence that is gaining ground in modern English. I do
not want to exaggerate. This kind of writing is not yet universal, and
outcrops of simplicity will occur here and there in the worst-written page.
Still, if you or I were told to write a few lines on the uncertainty of human
fortunes, we should probably come much nearer to my imaginary sentence than to the one from *Ecclesiastes*.

  As I have tried to show, modern writing at its worst does not consist in
picking out words for the sake of their meaning and inventing images in
order to make the meaning clearer. It consists in gumming together long
strips of words which have already been set in order by someone else, and
making the results presentable by sheer humbug. The attraction of this
way of writing is that it is easy. It is easier—even quicker, once you have
the habit—to say *In my opinion it is not an unjustifiable assumption that*
than to say *I think*. If you use ready-made phrases, you not only don't
have to hunt about for words; you also don't have to bother with the
rhythms of your sentences, since these phrases are generally so arranged
as to be more or less euphonious. When you are composing in a hurry—
when you are dictating to a stenographer, for instance, or making a public speech—it is natural to fall into a pretentious, Latinized style. Tags
like *a consideration which we should do well to bear in mind* or *a conclusion to which all of us would readily assent* will save many a sentence
from coming down with a bump. By using stale metaphors, similes, and
idioms, you save much mental effort, at the cost of leaving your meaning
vague, not only for your reader but for yourself. This is the significance of
mixed metaphors. The sole aim of a metaphor is to call up a visual image.
When these images clash—as in *The Fascist octopus has sung its swan
song, the jackboot is thrown into the melting pot*—it can be taken as
certain that the writer is not seeing a mental image of the objects he is

naming; in other words he is not really thinking. Look again at the examples I gave at the beginning of this essay. Professor Laski (1) uses five negatives in fifty-three words. One of these is superfluous, making nonsense of the whole passage, and in addition there is the slip—*alien* for akin—making further nonsense, and several avoidable pieces of clumsiness which increase the general vagueness. Professor Hogben (2) plays ducks and drakes with a battery which is able to write prescriptions, and, while disapproving of the everyday phrase *put up with*, is unwilling to look *egregious* up in the dictionary and see what it means; (3), if one takes an uncharitable attitude towards it, is simply meaningless: probably one could work out its intended meaning by reading the whole of the article in which it occurs. In (4), the writer knows more or less what he wants to say, but an accumulation of stale phrases chokes him like tea leaves blocking a sink. In (5), words and meaning have almost parted company. People who write in this manner usually have a general emotional meaning—they dislike one thing and want to express solidarity with another—but they are not interested in the detail of what they are saying. A scrupulous writer, in every sentence that he writes, will ask himself at least four questions, thus: What am I trying to say? What words will express it? What image or idiom will make it clearer? Is this image fresh enough to have an effect? And he will probably ask himself two more: Could I put it more shortly? Have I said anything that is avoidably ugly? But you are not obliged to go to all this trouble. You can shirk it by simply throwing your mind open and letting the ready-made phrases come crowding in. They will construct your sentences for you—even think your thoughts for you, to a certain extent—and at need they will perform the important service of partially concealing your meaning even from yourself. It is at this point that the special connection between politics and the debasement of language becomes clear.

In our time it is broadly true that political writing is bad writing. Where it is not true, it will generally be found that the writer is some kind of rebel, expressing his private opinions and not a "party line." Orthodoxy, of whatever color, seems to demand a lifeless, imitative style. The political dialects to be found in pamphlets, leading articles, manifestoes, White papers and the speeches of undersecretaries do, of course, vary from party to party, but they are all alike in that one almost never finds in them a fresh, vivid, homemade turn of speech. When one watches some tired hack on the platform mechanically repeating the familiar phrases—*bestial atrocities, iron heel, bloodstained tyranny, free peoples of the world, stand shoulder to shoulder*—one often has a curious feeling that one is not watching a live human being but some kind of dummy: a feeling which suddenly becomes stronger at moments when the light catches the speaker's spectacles and turns them into blank d'scs which seem to have no eyes behind them. And this is not altogether fanciful. A

speaker who uses that kind of phraseology has gone some distance toward turning himself into a machine. The appropriate noises are coming
out of his larynx, but his brain is not involved as it would be if he were
choosing his words for himself. If the speech he is making is one that he is
accustomed to make over and over again, he may be almost unconscious
of what he is saying, as one is when one utters the responses in church.
And this reduced state of consciousness, if not indispensable, is at any
rate favorable to political conformity.

In our time, political speech and writing are largely the defense of the
indefensible. Things like the continuance of British rule in India, the
Russian purges and deportations, the dropping of the atom bombs on
Japan, can indeed be defended, but only by arguments which are too
brutal for most people to face, and which do not square with the professed
aims of political parties. Thus political language has to consist largely of
euphemism, question-begging and sheer cloudy vagueness. Defenseless
villages are bombarded from the air, the inhabitants driven out into the
countryside, the cattle machine-gunned, the huts set on fire with incendiary bullets: this is called *pacification*. Millions of peasants are robbed of
their farms and sent trudging along the roads with no more than they
can carry: this is called *transfer of population* or *rectification of frontiers*.
People are imprisoned for years without trial, or shot in the back of the
neck or sent to die of scurvy in Arctic lumber camps: this is called
elimination of undesirable elements. Such phraseology is needed if one
wants to name things without calling up mental pictures of them. Consider for instance some comfortable English professor defending Russian
totalitarianism. He cannot say outright, "I believe in killing off your opponents when you can get good results by doing so." Probably, therefore,
he will say something like this:

"While freely conceding that the Soviet régime exhibits certain features which the humanitarian may be inclined to deplore, we must, I
think, agree that a certain curtailment of the right to political opposition
is an unavoidable concomitant of transitional periods, and that the rigors
which the Russian people have been called upon to undergo have been
amply justified in the sphere of concrete achievement."

The inflated style is itself a kind of euphemism. A mass of Latin words
falls upon the facts like soft snow, blurring the outlines and covering up
all the details. The great enemy of clear language is insincerity. When
there is a gap between one's real and one's declared aims, one turns as it
were instinctively to long words and exhausted idioms, like a cuttlefish
squirting out ink. In our age there is no such thing as "keeping out of
politics." All issues are political issues, and politics itself is a mass of lies,
evasions, folly, hatred, and schizophrenia. When the general atmosphere
is bad, language must suffer. I should expect to find—this is a guess
which I have not sufficient knowledge to verify—that the German, Rus-

sian and Italian languages have all deteriorated in the last ten or fifteen years, as a result of dictatorship.

But if thought corrupts language, language can also corrupt thought. A bad usage can spread by tradition and imitation, even among people who should and do know better. The debased language that I have been discussing is in some ways very convenient. Phrases like *a not unjustifiable assumption, leaves much to be desired, would serve no good purpose, a consideration which we should do well to bear in mind,* are a continuous temptation, a packet of aspirins always at one's elbow. Look back through this essay, and for certain you will find that I have again and again committed the very faults I am protesting against. By this morning's post I have received a pamphlet dealing with conditions in Germany. The author tells me that he "felt impelled" to write it. I open it at random, and here is almost the first sentence that I see: "[The Allies] have an opportunity not only of achieving a radical transformation of Germany's social and political structure in such a way as to avoid a nationalistic reaction in Germany itself, but at the same time of laying the foundations of a co-operative and unified Europe." You see, he "feels impelled" to write—feels, presumably, that he has something new to say—and yet his words, like cavalry horses answering the bugle, group themselves automatically into the familiar dreary pattern. This invasion of one's mind by ready-made phrases *(lay the foundations, achieve a radical transformation)* can only be prevented if one is constantly on guard against them, and every such phrase anaesthetizes a portion of one's brain.

I said earlier that the decadence of our language is probably curable. Those who deny this would argue, if they produced an argument at all, that language merely reflects existing social conditions, and that we cannot influence its development by any direct tinkering with words and constructions. So far as the general tone or spirit of a language goes, this may be true, but it is not true in detail. Silly words and expressions have often disappeared, not through any evolutionary process but owing to the conscious action of a minority. Two recent examples were *explore every avenue* and *leave no stone unturned,* which were killed by the jeers of a few journalists. There is a long list of flyblown metaphors which could similarly be got rid of if enough people would interest themselves in the job; and it should also be possible to laugh the *not un-* formation out of existence,* to reduce the amount of Latin and Greek in the average sentence, to drive out foreign phrases and strayed scientific words, and, in general, to make pretentiousness unfashionable. But all these are minor points. The defense of the English language implies more than this, and perhaps it is best to start by saying what it does *not* imply.

---

* One can cure oneself of the *not un-* formation by memorizing this sentence: *A not unblack dog was chasing a not unsmall rabbit across a not ungreen field.*

To begin with it has nothing to do with archaism, with the salvaging of obsolete words and turns of speech, or with the setting up of a "standard English" which must never be departed from. On the contrary, it is especially concerned with the scrapping of every word or idiom which has outworn its usefulness. It has nothing to do with correct grammar and syntax, which are of no importance so long as one makes one's meaning clear, or with the avoidance of Americanisms, or with having what is called a "good prose style." On the other hand it is not concerned with fake simplicity and the attempt to make written English colloquial. Nor does it even imply in every case preferring the Saxon word to the Latin one, though it does imply using the fewest and shortest words that will cover one's meaning. What is above all needed is to let the meaning choose the word, and not the other way about. In prose, the worst thing one can do with words is to surrender to them. When you think of a concrete object, you think wordlessly, and then, if you want to describe the thing you have been visualizing you probably hunt about till you find the exact words that seem to fit it. When you think of something abstract you are more inclined to use words from the start, and unless you make a conscious effort to prevent it, the existing dialect will come rushing in and do the job for you, at the expense of blurring or even changing your meaning. Probably it is better to put off using words as long as possible and get one's meaning as clear as one can through pictures or sensations. Afterward one can choose—not simply *accept*—the phrases that will best cover the meaning, and then switch round and decide what impressions one's words are likely to make on another person. This last effort of the mind cuts out all stale or mixed images, all prefabricated phrases, needless repetitions, and humbug and vagueness generally. But one can often be in doubt about the effect of a word or a phrase, and one needs rules that one can rely on when instinct fails. I think the following rules will cover most cases:

(i) Never use a metaphor, simile, or other figure of speech which you are used to seeing in print.

(ii) Never use a long word where a short one will do.

(iii) If it is possible to cut a word out, always cut it out.

(iv) Never use the passive where you can use the active.

(v) Never use a foreign phrase, a scientific word, or a jargon word if you can think of an everyday English equivalent.

(vi) Break any of these rules sooner than say anything outright barbarous.

These rules sound elementary, and so they are, but they demand a deep change of attitude in anyone who has grown used to writing in the style now fashionable. One could keep all of them and still write bad English, but one could not write the kind of stuff that I quoted in those five specimens at the beginning of this article.

I have not here been considering the literary use of language, but merely language as an instrument for expressing and not for concealing or preventing thought. Stuart Chase and others have come near to claiming that all abstract words are meaningless, and have used this as a pretext for advocating a kind of political quietism. Since you don't know what Fascism is, how can you struggle against Fascism? One need not swallow such absurdities as this, but one ought to recognize that the present political chaos is connected with the decay of language, and that one can probably bring about some improvement by starting at the verbal end. If you simplify your English, you are freed from the worst follies of orthodoxy. You cannot speak any of the necessary dialects, and when you make a stupid remark its stupidity will be obvious, even to yourself. Political language—and with variations this is true of all political parties, from Conservatives to Anarchists—is designed to make lies sound truthful and murder respectable, and to give an appearance of solidity to pure wind. One cannot change this all in a moment, but one can at least change one's own habits, and from time to time one can even, if one jeers loudly enough, send some worn-out and useless phrase—some *jackboot, Achilles' heel, hotbed, melting pot, acid test, veritable inferno,* or other lump of verbal refuse—into the dustbin where it belongs.

1946

GEORGE ORWELL
Freedom and Happiness

Several years after hearing of its existence I have at last got my hands on a copy of Zamiatin's *We,* which is one of the literary curiosities of this book-burning age. Looking it up in Gleb Struve's *25 Years of Soviet Russian Literature,* I find its history to have been this:

Zamiatin, who died in Paris in 1937, was a Russian novelist and critic who published a number of books both before and after the Revolution. *We* was written about 1923, and though it is not about Russia and has no direct connection with contemporary politics—it is a fantasy dealing with the twenty-sixth century A.D.—it was refused publication on the ground that it was ideologically undesirable. A copy of the manuscript found its way out of the country, and the book has appeared in English, French and Czech translations, but never in Russian. The English translation was published in the United States, and I have never been able to procure a copy: but copies of the French translation (the title is *Nous Autres*) do exist, and I have at last succeeded in borrowing one. So far as I can judge it is not a book of the first order, but it is certainly an unusual one, and it is astonishing that no English publisher has been enterprising enough to re-issue it.

The first thing anyone would notice about *We* is the fact—never pointed out, I believe—that Aldous Huxley's *Brave New World* must be partly derived from it. Both books deal with the rebellion of the primitive human spirit against a rationalised, mechanised, painless world, and both stories are supposed to take place about six hundred years hence. The atmosphere of the two books is similar, and it is roughly speaking the same kind of society that is being described, though Huxley's book shows less political awareness and is more influenced by recent biological and psychological theories.

In the twenty-sixth century, in Zamiatin's vision of it, the inhabitants of Utopia have so completely lost their individuality as to be known only by numbers. They live in glass houses (this was written before television was invented), which enables the political police, known as the "Guardians," to supervise them more easily. They all wear identical uniforms, and a human being is commonly referred to either as "a number" or "a unif" (uniform). They live on synthetic food, and their usual recreation is to march in fours while the anthem of the Single State is played through loudspeakers. At stated intervals they are allowed for one hour (known as "the sex hour") to lower the curtains round their glass apartments. There is, of course, no marriage, though sex life does not appear to be completely promiscuous. For purposes of lovemaking everyone has a sort of ration book of pink tickets, and the partner with whom he spends one of his allotted sex hours signs the counterfoil. The Single State is ruled over by a personage known as The Benefactor, who is annually re-elected by the entire population, the vote being always unanimous. The guiding principle of the State is that happiness and freedom are incompatible. In the Garden of Eden man was happy, but in his folly he demanded freedom and was driven out into the wilderness. Now the Single State has restored his happiness by removing his freedom.

So far the resemblance with *Brave New World* is striking. But though Zamiatin's book is less well put together—it has a rather weak and episodic plot which is too complex to summarize—it has a political point which the other lacks. In Huxley's book the problem of "human nature" is in a sense solved, because it assumes that by pre-natal treatment, drugs and hypnotic suggestion the human organism can be specialized in any way that is desired. A first-rate scientific worker is as easily produced as an Epsilon semi-moron, and in either case the vestiges of primitive instincts, such as maternal feeling or the desire for liberty, are easily dealt with. At the same time no clear reason is given why society should be stratified in the elaborate way that is described. The aim is not economic exploitation, but the desire to bully and dominate does not seem to be a motive either. There is no power-hunger, no sadism, no hardness of any kind. Those at the top have no strong motive for staying at the top, and though everyone is happy in a vacuous way, life has become so pointless that it is difficult to believe that such a society could endure.

Zamiatin's book is on the whole more relevant to our own situation. In spite of education and the vigilance of the Guardians, many of the ancient human instincts are still there. The teller of the story, D-503, who, though a gifted engineer, is a poor conventional creature, a sort of Utopian Billy Brown of London Town, is constantly horrified by the atavistic impulses which seize upon him. He falls in love (this is a crime, of course) with a certain I-330 who is a member of an underground resistance movement and succeeds for a while in leading him into rebellion. When the rebellion breaks out it appears that the enemies of the Benefactor are in fact fairly numerous, and these people, apart from plotting the overthrow of the State, even indulge, at the moment when their curtains are down, in such vices as smoking cigarettes and drinking alcohol. D-503 is ultimately saved from the consequences of his own folly. The authorities announce that they have discovered the cause of the recent disorders: it is that some human beings suffer from a disease called imagination. The nerve-centre responsible for imagination has now been located, and the disease can be cured by X-ray treatment. D-503 undergoes the operation, after which it is easy for him to do what he has known all along that he ought to do—that is, betray his confederates to the police. With complete equanimity he watches I-330 tortured by means of compressed air under a glass bell.

> She looked at me, her hands clasping the arms of the chair, until her eyes were completely shut. They took her out, brought her to herself by means of an electric shock, and put her under the bell again. This operation was repeated three times, and not a word issued from her lips.
>
> The others who had been brought along with her showed themselves more honest. Many of them confessed after one application. Tomorrow they will all be sent to the Machine of the Benefactor.

The Machine of the Benefactor is the guillotine. There are many executions in Zamiatin's Utopia. They take place publicly, in the presence of the Benefactor, and are accompanied by triumphal odes recited by the official poets. The guillotine, of course, is not the old crude instrument but a much improved model which literally liquidates its victim, reducing him in an instant to a puff of smoke and a pool of clear water. The execution is, in fact, a human sacrifice, and the scene describing it is given deliberately the colour of the sinister slave civilisations of the ancient world. It is this intuitive grasp of the irrational side of totalitarianism—human sacrifice, cruelty as an end in itself, the worship of a Leader who is credited with divine attributes—that makes Zamiatin's book superior to Huxley's.

It is easy to see why the book was refused publication. The following conversation (I abridge it slightly) between D-503 and I-330 would have been quite enough to set the blue pencils working:

"Do you realize that what you are suggesting is revolution?"

"Of course, it's revolution. Why not?"

"Because there can't *be* a revolution. Our revolution was the last and there can never be another. Everybody knows that."

"My dear, you're a mathematician: tell me, which is the last number?"

"What do you mean, the last number?"

"Well, then, the biggest number!"

"But that's absurd. Numbers are infinite. There can't be a last one."

"Then why do you talk about the last revolution?"

There are other similar passages. It may well be, however, that Zamiatin did not intend the Soviet regime to be the special target of his satire. Writing at about the time of Lenin's death, he cannot have had the Stalin dictatorship in mind, and conditions in Russia in 1923 were not such that anyone would revolt against them on the ground that life was becoming too safe and comfortable. What Zamiatin seems to be aiming at is not any particular country but the implied aims of industrial civilization. I have not read any of his other books, but I learn from Gleb Struve that he had spent several years in England and had written some blistering satires on English life. It is evident from *We* that he had a strong leaning towards primitivism. Imprisoned by the Czarist Government in 1906, and then imprisoned by the Bolsheviks in 1922 in the same corridor of the same prison, he had cause to dislike the political regime he had lived under, but his book is not simply the expression of a grievance. It is in effect a study of the Machine, the genie that man has thoughtlessly let out of its bottle and cannot put back again. This is a book to look out for when an English version appears.

1946

GEORGE ORWELL
The Prevention of Literature

About a year ago I attended a meeting of the PEN Club, the occasion being the tercentenary of Milton's *Areopagitica*—a pamphlet, it may be remembered, in defence of freedom of the press. Milton's famous phrase about the sin of 'killing' a book was printed on the leaflets, advertising the meeting, which had been circulated beforehand.

There were four speakers on the platform. One of them delivered a speech which did deal with the freedom of the press, but only in relation to India; another said, hesitantly, and in very general terms, that liberty was a good thing; a third delivered an attack on the laws relating to obscenity in literature. The fourth devoted most of his speech to a defence of the Russian purges. Of the speeches from the body of the hall, some reverted to the question of obscenity and the laws that deal with it, others were simply eulogies of Soviet Russia. Moral liberty—the liberty to discuss sex questions frankly in print—seemed to be generally approved, but political liberty was not mentioned. Out of this concourse of several hundred people, perhaps half of whom were directly connected with the writing trade, there was not a single one who could point out that freedom of the press, if it means anything at all, means the freedom to criticize and oppose. Significantly, no speaker quoted from the pamphlet which was ostensibly being commemorated. Nor was there any mention of the various books that have been 'killed' in this country and the United States during the war. In its net effect the meeting was a demonstration in favour of censorship.*

There was nothing particularly surprising in this. In our age, the idea of intellectual liberty is under attack from two directions. On the one side are its theoretical enemies, the apologists of totalitarianism, and on the other its immediate, practical enemies, monopoly and bureaucracy. Any writer or journalist who wants to retain his integrity finds himself thwarted by the general drift of society rather than by active persecution. The sort of things that are working against him are the concentration of the press in the hands of a few rich men, the grip of monopoly on radio and the films, the unwillingness of the public to spend money on books, making it necessary for nearly every writer to earn part of his living by hack work, the encroachment of official bodies like the M.O.I.†and the British Council, which help the writer to keep alive but also waste his time and dictate his opinions, and the continuous war atmosphere of the past ten years, whose distorting effects no one has been able to escape. Everything in our age conspires to turn the writer, and every other kind of artist as well, into a minor official, working on themes handed to him from above and never telling what seems to him the whole of the truth. But in struggling against this fate he gets no help from his own side: that is, there is no large body of opinion which will assure him that he is in the right. In the past, at any rate throughout the Protestant centuries, the idea of rebellion and the idea of intellectual integrity were

* It is fair to say that the PEN Club celebrations, which lasted a week or more, did not always stick at quite the same level. I happened to strike a bad day. But an examination of the speeches (printed under the title *Freedom of Expression*) shows that almost nobody in our own day is able to speak out as roundly in favour of intellectual liberty as Milton could do three hundred years ago—and this in spite of the fact Milton was writing in a period of civil war. [Orwell's footnote.]

† Ministry of Information.

mixed up. A heretic—political, moral, religious, or aesthetic—was one who refused to outrage his own conscience. His outlook was summed up in the words of the Revivalist hymn:

> Dare to be a Daniel,
> Dare to stand alone;
> Dare to have a purpose firm,
> Dare to make it known.

To bring this hymn up to date one would have to add a 'Don't' at the beginning of each line. For it is the peculiarity of our age that the rebels against the existing order, at any rate the most numerous and character-istic of them, are also rebelling against the idea of individual integrity. 'Daring to stand alone' is ideologically criminal as well as practically dangerous. The independence of the writer and the artist is eaten away by vague economic forces, and at the same time it is undermined by those who should be its defenders. It is with the second process that I am con-cerned here.

Freedom of thought and of the press are usually attacked by argu-ments which are not worth bothering about. Anyone who has experience of lecturing and debating knows them off backwards. Here I am not try-ing to deal with the familiar claim that freedom is an illusion, or with the claim that there is more freedom in totalitarian countries than in demo-cratic ones, but with the much more tenable and dangerous proposition that freedom is undesirable and that intellectual honesty is a form of antisocial selfishness. Although other aspects of the question are usually in the foreground the controversy over freedom of speech and of the press is at the bottom a controversy over the desirability, or otherwise, of tell-ing lies. What is really at issue is the right to report contemporary events truthfully, or as truthfully as is consistent with the ignorance, bias and self-deception from which every observer necessarily suffers. In saying this I may seem to be saying that straightforward 'reportage' is the only branch of literature that matters: but I will try to show later that at every literary level, and probably in every one of the arts, the same issue arises in more or less subtilized forms. Meanwhile, it is necessary to strip away the irrelevancies in which this controversy is usually wrapped up.

The enemies of intellectual liberty always try to present their case as a plea for discipline versus individualism. The issue truth-versus-untruth is as far as possible kept in the background. Although the point of emphasis may vary, the writer who refuses to sell his opinions is always branded as a mere egoist. He is accused, that is, either of wanting to shut himself up in an ivory tower, or of making an exhibitionist display of his own person-ality, or of resisting the inevitable current of history in an attempt to cling to unjustified privileges. The Catholic and the Communist are alike in assuming that an opponent cannot be both honest and intelligent. Each of them tacitly claims that 'the truth' has already been revealed, and that the heretic, if he is not simply a fool, is secretly aware of 'the truth' and merely resists it out of selfish motives. In Communist literature the attack on intellectual liberty is usually masked by oratory about 'petty-bourgeois individualism', 'the illusions of nineteenth-century liberalism', etc., and backed up by words of abuse such as 'romantic' and 'sentimental', which, since they do not have any agreed meaning, are difficult to answer. In this way the controversy is manoeuvred away from its real issue. One can accept, and most enlightened people would accept, the Communist thesis that pure freedom will only exist in a classless society, and that one is most nearly free when one is working to bring such a society about. But slipped in with this is the quite unfounded claim that the Communist Party is itself aiming at the establishment of the classless society, and that in the U.S.S.R. this aim is actually on the way to being realized. If the first claim is allowed to entail the second, there is almost no assault on common sense and common decency that cannot be justified. But meanwhile, the real point has been dodged. Freedom of the intellect means the freedom to report what one has seen, heard, and felt, and not to be obliged to fabricate imaginary facts and feelings. The familiar tirades against 'escapism', 'individualism', 'romanticism' and so forth, are merely a forensic device, the aim of which is to make the perversion of history seem respectable.

Fifteen years ago, when one defended the freedom of the intellect, one had to defend it against Conservatives, against Catholics, and to some extent—for they were not of great importance in England—against Fascists. Today one has to defend it against Communists and 'fellow-travellers'. One ought not to exaggerate the direct influence of the small English Communist Party, but there can be no question about the poisonous effect of the Russian *mythos* on English intellectual life. Because of it, known facts are suppressed and distorted to such an extent as to make it doubtful whether a true history of our times can ever be written. Let me give just one instance out of hundreds that could be cited. When Germany collapsed, it was found that very large numbers of Soviet Russians— mostly, no doubt, from non-political motives—had changed sides and were fighting for the Germans. Also, a small but not negligible proportion of the Russian prisoners and Displaced Persons refused to go back to the U.S.S.R., and some of them, at least, were repatriated against their will. These facts, known to many journalists on the spot, went almost unmentioned in the British press, while at the same time russophile publicists in England continued to justify the purges and deportations of 1936–8 by claiming that the U.S.S.R. 'had no quislings'. The fog of lies and misinformation that surrounds such subjects as the Ukraine famine, the Spanish Civil War, Russian policy in Poland, and so forth, is not due entirely to conscious dishonesty, but any writer or journalist who is fully sympathetic to the U.S.S.R.—sympathetic, that is, in the way the Russians themselves would want him to be—does have to acquiesce in deliberate falsification on important issues. I have before me what must be a very rare pamphlet, written by Maxim Litvinov in 1918 and outlining the recent events in the Russian Revolution. It makes no mention of Stalin, but gives high praise to Trotsky, and also to Zinoviev, Kamenev and others. What could be the attitude of even the most intellectually scrupulous Communist towards such a pamphlet? At best, the obscurantist attitude of saying that it is an undesirable document and better suppressed. And if for some reason it were decided to issue a garbled version of the pamphlet, denigrating Trotsky and inserting references to Stalin, no Communist who remained faithful to his Party could protest. Forgeries almost as gross as this have been committed in recent years. But the significant thing is not that they happen, but that even when they are known about they provoke no reaction from the left-wing intelligentsia as a whole. The argument that to tell the truth would be 'inopportune' or would 'play into the hands of' somebody or other is felt to be unanswerable, and few people are bothered by the prospect of the lies which they condone getting out of the newspapers and into the history books.

The organized lying practised by totalitarian states is not, as is sometimes claimed, a temporary expedient of the same nature as military deception. It is something integral to totalitarianism, something that would still continue even if concentration camps and secret police forces had ceased to be necessary. Among intelligent Communists there is an underground legend to the effect that although the Russian Government is obliged now to deal in lying propaganda, frame-up trials, and so forth, it is secretly recording the true facts and will publish them at some future time. We can, I believe, be quite certain that this is not the case, because the mentality implied by such an action is that of a liberal historian who believes that the past cannot be altered and that a correct knowledge of history is valuable as a matter of course. From the totalitarian point of view history is something to be created rather than learned. A totalitarian state is in effect a theocracy, and its ruling caste, in order to keep its position, has to be thought of as infallible. But since, in practice, no one is infallible, it is frequently necessary to rearrange past events in order to show that this or that mistake was not made, or that this or that imaginary triumph actually happened. Then, again, every major change in policy demands a corresponding change of doctrine and a revaluation of prominent historical figures. This kind of thing happens everywhere, but is clearly likelier to lead to outright falsification in societies where only one opinion is permissible at any given moment. Totalitarianism demands, in fact, the continuous alteration of the past, and in the long run probably demands a disbelief in the very existence of objective truth. The friends of totalitarianism in this country tend to argue that since absolute truth is not attainable, a big lie is no worse than a little lie. It is pointed out that all historical records are biassed and inaccurate, or, on the other hand, that modern physics has proved that what seems to us the real world is an illusion, so that to believe in the evidence of one's senses is simply vulgar philistinism. A totalitarian society which succeeded in perpetuating itself would probably set up a schizophrenic system of thought, in which the laws of common sense held good in everyday life and in certain exact sciences, but could be disregarded by the politician, the historian, and the sociologist. Already there are countless people who would think it scandalous to falsify a scientific text-book, but would see nothing wrong in falsifying an historical fact. It is at the point where literature and politics cross that totalitarianism exerts its greatest pressure on the intellectual. The exact sciences are not, at this date, menaced to anything like the same extent. This partly accounts for the fact that in all countries it is easier for the scientists than for the writers to line up behind their respective governments.

To keep the matter in perspective, let me repeat what I said at the beginning of this essay: that in England the immediate enemies of truthfulness, and hence of freedom of thought, are the press lords, the film magnates, and the bureaucrats, but that on a long view the weakening of the desire for liberty among the intellectuals themselves is the most serious symptom of all. It may seem that all this time I have been talking about the effects of censorship, not on literature as a whole, but merely on one department of political journalism. Granted that Soviet Russia constitutes a sort of forbidden area in the British press, granted that issues like Poland, the Spanish Civil War, the Russo-German Pact, and so forth, are debarred from serious discussion, and that if you possess information that conflicts with the prevailing orthodoxy you are expected to distort it or to keep quiet about it—granted all this, why should literature in the wider sense be affected? Is every writer a politician, and is every book necessarily a work of straightforward 'reportage'? Even under the tightest dictatorship, cannot the individual writer remain free inside his own mind and distil or disguise his unorthodox ideas in such a way that the authorities will be too stupid to recognize them? And in any case, if the writer himself is in agreement with the prevailing orthodoxy, why should it have a cramping effect on him? Is not literature, or any of the arts, likeliest to flourish in societies in which there are no major conflicts of opinion and no sharp distinction between the artist and his audience? Does one have to assume that every writer is a rebel, or even that a writer as such is an exceptional person?

Whenever one attempts to defend intellectual liberty against the claims of totalitarianism, one meets with these arguments in one form or another. They are based on a complete misunderstanding of what literature is, and how—one should perhaps rather say why—it comes into being. They assume that a writer is either a mere entertainer or else a venal hack who can switch from one line of propaganda to another as easily as an organ-grinder changing tunes. But after all, how is it that books ever come to be written? Above a quite low level, literature is an attempt to influence the viewpoint of one's contemporaries by recording experience. And so far as freedom of expression is concerned, there is not much difference between a mere journalist and the most 'unpolitical' imaginative writer. The journalist is unfree, and is conscious of unfreedom, when he is forced to write lies or suppress what seems to him important news: the imaginative writer is unfree when he has to falsify his subjective feelings, which from his point of view are facts. He may distort and caricature reality in order to make his meaning clearer, but he cannot misrepresent the scenery of his own mind: he cannot say with any conviction that he likes what he dislikes, or believes what he disbelieves. If he is forced to do so, the only result is that his creative faculties dry up. Nor can he solve the problem by keeping away from controversial topics. There is no such thing as genuinely non-political literature, and least of all in an age like our own, where fears, hatreds, and loyalties of a directly political kind are near to the surface of everyone's consciousness. Even a single taboo can have an all-round crippling effect upon the mind, because there is always the danger that any thought which is freely followed up may lead to the forbidden thought. It follows that the atmosphere of totalitarianism is deadly to any kind of prose writer, though a poet, at any rate a lyric poet, might possibly find it breathable. And in any totalitarian society that survives for more than a couple of generations, it is probable that prose literature, of the kind that has existed during the past four hundred years, must actually come to an end.

Literature has sometimes flourished under despotic régimes, but, as has often been pointed out, the despotisms of the past were not totalitarian. Their repressive apparatus was always inefficient, their ruling classes were usually either corrupt or apathetic or half-liberal in outlook, and the prevailing religious doctrines usually worked against perfectionism and the notion of human infallibility. Even so it is broadly true that prose literature has reached its highest levels in periods of democracy and free speculation. What is new in totalitarianism is that its doctrines are not only unchallengeable but also unstable. They have to be accepted on pain of damnation, but on the other hand they are always liable to be altered at a moment's notice. Consider, for example, the various attitudes, completely incompatible with one another, which an English Communist or 'fellow-traveller' has had to adopt towards the war between Britain and Germany. For years before September 1939 he was expected to be in a continuous stew about 'the horrors of Nazism' and to twist everything he wrote into a denunciation of Hitler: after September 1939, for twenty months, he had to believe that Germany was more sinned against than sinning, and the word 'Nazi', at least so far as print went, had to drop right out of his vocabulary. Immediately after hearing the 8 o'clock news bulletin on the morning of 22 June 1941, he had to start believing once again that Nazism was the most hideous evil the world had ever seen. Now, it is easy for a politician to make such changes: for a writer the case is somewhat different. If he is to switch his allegiance at exactly the right moment, he must either tell lies about his subjective feelings, or else suppress them altogether. In either case he has destroyed his dynamo. Not only will ideas refuse to come to him, but the very words he uses will seem to stiffen under his touch. Political writing in our time consists almost entirely of prefabricated phrases bolted together like the pieces of a child's Meccano set. It is the unavoidable result of self-censorship. To write in plain, vigorous language one has to think fearlessly, and if one thinks fearlessly one cannot be politically orthodox. It might be otherwise in an 'age of faith', when the prevailing orthodoxy has been long established and is not taken too seriously. In that case it would be possible, or might be possible, for large areas of one's mind to remain unaffected by what one officially believed. Even so, it is worth noticing that prose literature almost disappeared during the only age of faith that Europe has ever enjoyed. Throughout the whole of the Middle Ages there was almost no imaginative prose literature and very little in the way of historical writing: and the intellectual leaders of society expressed their most serious thoughts in a dead language which barely altered during a thousand years.

Totalitarianism, however, does not so much promise an age of faith as an age of schizophrenia. A society becomes totalitarian when its structure becomes flagrantly artificial: that is, when its ruling class has lost its function but succeeds in clinging to power by force or fraud. Such a society, no matter how long it persists, can never afford to become either tolerant or intellectually stable. It can never permit either the truthful recording of facts, or the emotional sincerity, that literary creation demands. But to be corrupted by totalitarianism one does not have to live in a totalitarian country. The mere prevalence of certain ideas can spread a kind of poison that makes one subject after another impossible for literary purposes. Wherever there is an enforced orthodoxy—or even two orthodoxies, as often happens—good writing stops. This was well illustrated by the Spanish Civil War. To many English intellectuals the war was a deeply moving experience, but not an experience about which they could write sincerely. There were only two things that you were allowed to say, and both of them were palpable lies: as a result, the war produced acres of print but almost nothing worth reading.

It is not certain whether the effects of totalitarianism upon verse need be so deadly as its effects on prose. There is a whole series of converging reasons why it is somewhat easier for a poet than for a prose writer to feel at home in an authoritarian society. To begin with, bureaucrats and other 'practical' men usually despise the poet too deeply to be much interested in what he is saying. Secondly, what the poet is saying—that is, what his poem 'means' if translated into prose—is relatively unimportant even to himself. The thought contained in a poem is always simple, and is no more the primary purpose of the poem than the anecdote is the primary purpose of a picture. A poem is an arrangement of sounds and associations, as a painting is an arrangement of brush-marks. For short snatches, indeed, as in the refrain of a song, poetry can even dispense with meaning altogether. It is therefore fairly easy for a poet to keep away from dangerous subjects and avoid uttering heresies: and even when he does utter them, they may escape notice. But above all, good verse, unlike good prose, is not necessarily an individual product. Certain kinds of poems, such as ballads, or, on the other hand, very artificial verse forms, can be composed co-operatively by groups of people. Whether the ancient English and Scottish ballads were originally produced by individuals, or by the people at large, is disputed; but at any rate they are non-individual in the sense that they constantly change in passing from mouth to mouth. Even in print no two versions of a ballad are ever quite the same. Many primitive peoples compose verse communally. Someone begins to improvise, probably accompanying himself on a musical instrument, somebody else chips in with a line or a rhyme when the first singer breaks down, and so the process continues until there exists a whole song or ballad which has no identifiable author.

In prose, this kind of intimate collaboration is quite impossible. Serious prose, in any case, has to be composed in solitude, whereas the excitement of being part of a group is actually an aid to certain kinds of versification. Verse—and perhaps good verse of its kind, though it would not be the highest kind—might survive under even the most inquisitorial régime. Even in a society where liberty and individuality had been extinguished, there would still be need either for patriotic songs and heroic ballads celebrating victories, or for elaborate exercises in flattery: and these are the kinds of poem that can be written to order, or composed communally, without necessarily lacking artistic value. Prose is a different matter, since the prose writer cannot narrow the range of his thoughts without killing his inventiveness. But the history of totalitarian societies, or of groups of people who have adopted the totalitarian outlook, suggests that loss of liberty is inimical to all forms of literature. German literature almost disappeared during the Hitler régime, and the case was not much better in Italy. Russian literature, so far as one can judge by translations, has deteriorated markedly since the early days of the Revolution, though some of the verse appears to be better than the prose. Few if any Russian novels that it is possible to take seriously have been translated for about fifteen years. In western Europe and America large sections of the literary intelligentsia have either passed through the Communist Party or been warmly sympathetic to it, but this whole leftward movement has produced extraordinarily few books worth reading. Orthodox Catholicism, again, seems to have a crushing effect upon certain literary forms, especially the novel. During a period of three hundred years, how many people have been at once good novelists and good Catholics? The fact is that certain themes cannot be celebrated in words, and tyranny is one of them. No one ever wrote a good book in praise of the Inquisition. Poetry might survive, in a totalitarian age, and certain arts or half-arts, such as architecture, might even find tyranny beneficial, but the prose writer would have no choice between silence and death. Prose literature as we know it is the product of rationalism, of the Protestant centuries, of the autonomous individual. And the destruction of intellectual liberty cripples the journalist, the sociological writer, the historian, the novelist, the critic and the poet, in that order. In the future it is possible that a new kind of literature, not involving individual feeling or truthful observation, may arise, but no such thing is at present imaginable. It seems much likelier that if the liberal culture that we have lived in since the Renaissance actually comes to an end, the literary art will perish with it.

Of course, print will continue to be used, and it is interesting to speculate what kinds of reading matter would survive in a rigidly totalitarian society. Newspapers will presumably continue until television technique reaches a higher level, but apart from newspapers it is doubtful even now whether the great mass of people in the industrialized countries feel the need for any kind of literature. They are unwilling, at any rate, to spend anywhere near as much on reading matter as they spend on several other recreations. Probably novels and stories will be completely superseded by film and radio productions. Or perhaps some kind of low-grade sensational fiction will survive, produced by a sort of conveyor-belt process that reduces human initiative to the minimum.

It would probably not be beyond human ingenuity to write books by machinery. But a sort of mechanizing process can already be seen at work in the film and radio, in publicity and propaganda, and in the lower reaches of journalism. The Disney films, for instance, are produced by what is essentially a factory process, the work being done partly mechanically and partly by teams of artists who have to subordinate their individual style. Radio features are commonly written by tired hacks to whom the subject and the manner of treatment are dictated beforehand: even so, what they write is merely a kind of raw material to be chopped into shape by producers and censors. So also with the innumerable books and pamphlets commissioned by government departments. Even more machine-like is the production of short stories, serials, and poems for the

very cheap magazines. Papers such as the *Writer* abound with advertise-
ments of Literary Schools, all of them offering you ready-made plots at a
few shillings a time. Some, together with the plot, supply the opening and
closing sentences of each chapter. Others furnish you with a sort of alge-
braical formula by the use of which you can construct your plots for
yourself. Others offer packs of cards marked with characters and situations, which have only to be shuffled and dealt in order to produce ingenious stories automatically. It is probably in some such way that the
literature of a totalitarian society would be produced, if literature were
still felt to be necessary. Imagination—even consciousness, so far as possible—would be eliminated from the process of writing. Books would be
planned in their broad lines by bureaucrats, and would pass through so
many hands that when finished they would be no more an individual
product than a Ford car at the end of the assembly line. It goes without
saying that anything so produced would be rubbish; but anything that
was not rubbish would endanger the structure of the State. As for the
surviving literature of the past, it would have to be suppressed or at least
elaborately rewritten.

Meanwhile totalitarianism has not fully triumphed everywhere. Our
own society is still, broadly speaking, liberal. To exercise your right of
free speech you have to fight against economic pressure and against
strong sections of public opinion, but not, as yet, against a secret police
force. You can say or print almost anything so long as you are willing to
do it in a hole-and-corner way. But what is sinister, as I said at the beginning of this essay, is that the conscious enemies of liberty are those to
whom liberty ought to mean most. The big public do not care about the
matter one way or the other. They are not in favour of persecuting the
heretic, and they will not exert themselves to defend him. They are at
once too sane and too stupid to acquire the totalitarian outlook. The direct, conscious attack on intellectual decency comes from the intellectuals themselves.

It is possible that the russophile intelligentsia, if they had not succumbed to that particular myth, would have succumbed to another of
much the same kind. But at any rate the Russian myth is there, and the
corruption it causes stinks. When one sees highly educated men looking
on indifferently at oppression and persecution, one wonders which to
despise more, their cynicism or their shortsightedness. Many scientists,
for example, are the uncritical admirers of the U.S.S.R. They appear to
think that the destruction of liberty is of no importance so long as their
own line of work is for the moment unaffected. The U.S.S.R. is a large,
rapidly developing country which has acute need of scientific workers
and, consequently, treats them generously. Provided that they steer clear
of dangerous subjects such as psychology, scientists are privileged persons. Writers, on the other hand, are viciously persecuted. It is true that

literary prostitutes like Ilya Ehrenburg or Alexei Tolstoy are paid huge sums of money, but the only thing which is of any value to the writer as such—his freedom of expression—is taken away from him. Some, at least, of the English scientists who speak so enthusiastically of the opportunities enjoyed by scientists in Russia are capable of understanding this. But their reflection appears to be: 'Writers are persecuted in Russia. So what? I am not a writer.' They do not see that any attack on intellectual liberty, and on the concept of objective truth, threatens in the long run every department of thought.

For the moment the totalitarian state tolerates the scientist because it needs him. Even in Nazi Germany, scientists, other than Jews, were relatively well treated, and the German scientific community, as a whole, offered no resistance to Hitler. At this stage of history, even the most autocratic ruler is forced to take account of physical reality, partly because of the lingering-on of liberal habits of thought, partly because of the need to prepare for war. So long as physical reality cannot be altogether ignored, so long as two and two have to make four when you are, for example, drawing the blue-print of an aeroplane, the scientist has his function, and can even be allowed a measure of liberty. His awakening will come later, when the totalitarian state is firmly established. Meanwhile, if he wants to safeguard the integrity of science, it is his job to develop some kind of solidarity with his literary colleagues and not regard it as a matter of indifference when writers are silenced or driven to suicide, and newspapers systematically falsified.

But however it may be with the physical sciences, or with music, painting, and architecture, it is—as I have tried to show—certain that literature is doomed if liberty of thought perishes. Not only is it doomed in any country which retains a totalitarian structure; but any writer who adopts the totalitarian outlook, who finds excuses for persecution and the falsification of reality, thereby destroys himself as a writer. There is no way out of this. No tirades against 'individualism' and 'the ivory tower', no pious platitudes to the effect that 'true individuality is only attained through identification with the community', can get over the fact that a bought mind is a spoiled mind. Unless spontaneity enters at some point or another, literary creation is impossible, and language itself becomes ossified. At some time in the future, if the human mind becomes something totally different from what it now is, we may learn to separate literary creation from intellectual honesty. At present we know only that the imagination, like certain wild animals, will not breed in captivity. Any writer or journalist who denies that fact—and nearly all the current praise of the Soviet Union contains or implies such a denial—is, in effect, demanding his own destruction.

1946

PART
FOUR

Orwell on
Nineteen Eighty-Four:
Letters and Essays

When *The Collected Essays, Journalism and Letters of George Orwell* was published in 1968, a great deal of useful information was brought together for the study of *Nineteen Eighty-Four*. This material is of a miscellaneous sort—paragraphs from essays, occasional reviews, and letters—but it illuminates many aspects of the novel. We learn, for instance, that Orwell had been intrigued by the idea of anti-utopian fiction for some time before beginning *Nineteen Eighty-Four*. From his letters to his English publisher, we also learn how Orwell thought his book should be read and interpreted.

A vivid picture of Orwell the writer emerges from his letters, as he fights for time and money to write *Nineteen Eighty-Four*. More tragically, we can also read of his tuberculosis, until he dies of that disease in 1950 at the age of forty-seven.

Most of the selections that follow are excerpts from larger pieces or letters. All of the selections are from *The Collected Essays, Journalism and Letters of George Orwell*, Vols. 2–4.

from Prophecies of Fascism—July 12, 1940

The reprinting of Jack London's *The Iron Heel* brings within general reach a book which has been much sought after during the years of Fascist aggression. Like others of Jack London's books it has been widely read in Germany, and it has had the reputation of being an accurate forecast of the coming of Hitler. In reality it is not that. It is merely a tale of capitalist oppression, and it was written at a time when various things that have made Fascism possible—for instance, the tremendous revival of nationalism—were not easy to foresee.

Where London did show special insight, however, was in realizing that the transition to Socialism was not going to be automatic or even easy. The capitalist class was not going to 'perish of its own contradictions' like a flower dying at the end of the season. The capitalist class was quite clever enough to see what was happening, to sink its own differences and counterattack against the workers; and the resulting struggle would be the most bloody and unscrupulous the world had ever seen.

It is worth comparing *The Iron Heel* with another imaginative novel of the future which was written somewhat earlier and to which it owes something, H. G. Wells's *The Sleeper Wakes*. By doing so one can see both London's limitations and also the advantage to be enjoyed in not being, like Wells, a fully civilized man. As a book, *The Iron Heel* is hugely inferior. It is clumsily written, it shows no grasp of scientific possibilities, and the hero is the kind of human gramophone who is now disappearing even from Socialist tracts. But because of his own streak of savagery London could grasp something that Wells apparently could not, and that is that hedonistic societies do not endure.

Everyone who has ever read *The Sleeper Wakes* remembers it. It is a vision of a glittering, sinister world in which society has hardened into a caste system and the workers are permanently enslaved. It is also a world without purpose in which the upper castes for whom the workers toil are completely soft, cynical and faithless. There is no consciousness of any object in life, nothing corresponding to the fervour of the revolutionary or the religious martyr.

In Aldous Huxley's *Brave New World*, a sort of post-war parody of the Wellsian Utopia, these tendencies are immensely exaggerated. Here the hedonistic principle is pushed to its utmost, the whole world has turned into a Riviera hotel. But though *Brave New World* was a brilliant caricature of the present (the present of 1930), it probably casts no light on the future. No society of that kind would last more than a couple of generations, because the ruling class which thought princi-

277

pally in terms of a 'good time' would soon lose its vitality. A ruling class has got to have a strict morality, a quasi-religious belief in itself, a mystique. London was aware of this, and though he describes the caste of plutocrats who rule the world for seven centuries as inhuman monsters, he does not describe them as idlers or sensualists. They can only maintain their position while they honestly believe that civilization depends on themselves alone, and therefore in a different way they are just as brave, able and devoted as the revolutionaries who oppose them.

In an intellectual way London accepted the conclusions of Marxism, and he imagined that the 'contradictions' of capitalism, the unconsumable surplus and so forth, would persist even after the capitalist class had organized themselves into a single corporate body. But temperamentally he was very different from the majority of Marxists. With his love of violence and physical strength, his belief in 'natural aristocracy', his animal-worship and exaltation of the primitive, he had in him what one might fairly call a Fascist strain. This probably helped him to understand just how the possessing class would behave when once they were seriously menaced.

It is just here that Marxian Socialists have usually fallen short. Their interpretation of history has been so mechanistic that they have failed to foresee dangers that were obvious to people who had never heard the name of Marx. It is sometimes urged against Marx that he failed to predict the rise of Fascism. I do not know whether he predicted it or not—at that date he could only have done so in very general terms—but it is at any rate certain that his followers failed to see any danger in Fascism until they themselves were at the gate of the concentration camp. A year or more *after* Hitler had risen to power official Marxism was still proclaiming that Hitler was of no importance and 'Social Fascism' (i.e. democracy) was the real enemy. London would probably not have made this mistake. His instincts would have warned him that Hitler was dangerous. He knew that economic laws do not operate in the same way as the law of gravity, that they can be held up (for long periods) by people who, like Hitler, believe in their own destiny. *(Vol. 2, Item 11)*

from Letter to Gleb Struve[1]—February 17, 1944

Please forgive me for not writing earlier to thank you for the very kind gift of *25 Years of Soviet Russian Literature*, with its still more kind inscription. I am afraid I know very little about Russian literature and

[1] Professor of Russian Literature at the University of California at Berkeley; author of the book on Russian literature mentioned by Orwell. For an excerpt from *We*, see p. 224; for Orwell's review of *We*, see p. 259.—Editor

I hope your book will fill up some of the many gaps in my knowledge. It has already roused my interest in Zamiatin's *We*, which I had not heard of before. I am interested in that kind of book, and even keep making notes for one myself that may get written sooner or later. *(Vol. 3, Item 21)*

from The English People—May 1944

Nations do not often die out, and the English people will still be in existence a hundred years hence, whatever has happened in the meantime. But if Britain is to survive as what is called a 'great' nation, playing an important and useful part in the world's affairs, one must take certain things as assured. One must assume that Britain will remain on good terms with Russia and Europe, will keep its special links with America and the Dominions, and will solve the problem of India in some amicable way. That is perhaps a great deal to assume, but without it there is not much hope for civilization as a whole, and still less for Britain itself. If the savage international struggle of the last twenty years continues, there will only be room in the world for two or three great powers, and in the long run Britain will not be one of them. It has not either the population or the resources. In a world of power politics the English would ultimately dwindle to a satellite people, and the special thing that it is in their power to contribute might be lost. *(Vol. 3, Item 1)*

Letter to H. J. Willmett[2]—May 18, 1944

Many thanks for your letter. You ask whether totalitarianism, leader worship, etc., are really on the up-grade and instance the fact that they are not apparently growing in this country and the U.S.A.

I must say I believe, or fear, that taking the world as a whole these things are on the increase. Hitler, no doubt, will soon disappear, but only at the expense of strengthening (a) Stalin, (b) the Anglo-American millionaires and (c) all sorts of petty fuehrers of the type of de Gaulle. All the national movements everywhere, even those that originate in resistance to German domination, seem to take non-democratic forms, to group themselves round some superhuman fuehrer (Hitler, Stalin, Salazar, Franco, Gandhi, De Valera are all varying examples) and to adopt the theory that the end justifies the means. Everywhere the world movement seems to be in the direction of centralized economies

[2] Not identified.—Editor

which can be made to 'work' in an economic sense but which are not democratically organized and which tend to establish a caste system. With this go the horrors of emotional nationalism and a tendency to disbelieve in the existence of objective truth because all the facts have to fit in with the words and prophecies of some infallible fuehrer. Already history has in a sense ceased to exist, i.e. there is no such thing as a history of our own times which could be universally accepted, and the exact sciences are endangered as soon as military necessity ceases to keep people up to the mark. Hitler can say that the Jews started the war, and if he survives that will become official history. He can't say that two and two are five, because for the purposes of, say, ballistics, they have to make four. But if the sort of world that I am afraid of arrives, a world of two or three great superstates which are unable to conquer one another, two and two could become five if the fuehrer wished it. That, so far as I can see, is the direction in which we are actually moving, though, of course, the process is reversible.

As to the comparative immunity of Britain and the U.S.A. Whatever the pacifists, etc., may say, we have *not* gone totalitarian yet and this is a very hopeful symptom. I believe very deeply, as I explained in my book *The Lion and the Unicorn*, in the English *people* and in their capacity to centralize their economy without destroying freedom in doing so. But one must remember that Britain and the U.S.A. haven't been really tried, they haven't known defeat or severe suffering, and there are some bad symptoms to balance the good ones. To begin with there is the general indifference to the decay of democracy. Do you realize, for instance, that no one in England under 26 now has a vote and that so far as one can see the great mass of people of that age don't give a damn for this? Secondly there is the fact that the intellectuals are more totalitarian in outlook than the common people. On the whole the English intelligentsia have opposed Hitler, but only at the price of accepting Stalin. Most of them are perfectly ready for dictatorial methods, secret police, systematic falsifications of history, etc., so long as they feel that it is on 'our' side. Indeed the statement that we haven't a Fascist movement in England largely means that the young, at this moment, look for their fuehrer elsewhere. One can't be sure that that won't change, nor can one be sure that the common people won't think ten years hence as the intellectuals do now. I *hope* they won't, I even trust they won't, but if so it will be at the cost of a struggle. If one simply proclaims that all is for the best and doesn't point to the sinister symptoms, one is merely helping to bring totalitarianism nearer.

You also ask, if I think the world tendency is towards Fascism, why do I support the war. It is a choice of evils—I fancy nearly every war is that. I know enough of British imperialism not to like it, but I would support it against Nazism or Japanese imperialism, as the lesser evil. Similarly I would support the U.S.S.R. against Germany because I think the U.S.S.R. cannot altogether escape its past and retains enough of the original ideas of the Revolution to make it a more hopeful phenomenon than Nazi Germany. I think and have thought ever since the war began, in 1936 or thereabouts, that our cause is the better, but we have to keep on making it the better, which involves constant criticism.

Yours sincerely
Geo. Orwell
(Vol. 3, Item 39)

from As I Please—February 2, 1945

A not-too-distant explosion shakes the house, the windows rattle in their sockets, and in the next room the 1964 class wakes up and lets out a yell or two. Each time this happens I find myself thinking, 'Is it possible that human beings can continue with this lunacy very much longer?' You know the answer, of course. Indeed, the difficulty nowadays is to find anyone who thinks that there will *not* be another war in the fairly near future.

Germany, I suppose, will be defeated this year, and when Germany is out of the way Japan will not be able to stand up to the combined power of Britain and the U.S.A. Then there will be a peace of exhaustion, with only minor and unofficial wars raging all over the place, and perhaps this so-called peace may last for decades. But after that, by the way the world is actually shaping, it may well be that war will *become permanent*. Already, quite visibly and more or less with the acquiescence of all of us, the world is splitting up into the two or three huge superstates forecast in James Burnham's *Managerial Revolution*. One cannot draw their exact boundaries as yet, but one can see more or less what areas they will comprise. And if the world does settle down into this pattern, it is likely that these vast states will be permanently at war with one another, though it will not necessarily be a very intensive or bloody kind of war. Their problems, both economic and psychological, will be a lot simpler if the doodlebugs are more or less constantly whizzing to and fro.

If these two or three super-states do establish themselves, not only will each of them be too big to be conquered, but they will be under no necessity to trade with one another, and in a position to prevent all contact between their nationals. Already, for a dozen years or so, large areas of the earth have been cut off from one another, although technically at peace. *(Vol. 3, Item 92)*

from Letter to Geoffrey Gorer[3]—January 22, 1946

I have definitely arranged I am going to stop doing the *Evening Standard* stuff and most other journalism in May, and take six months off to write another novel. *(Vol. 4, Item 21)*

from Letter to A. S. F. Gow[4]—April 13, 1946

. . . I am just on the point of dropping all journalism and other casual work for six months. I may start another book during the period, but I have resolved to stop hackwork for a bit, because I have been writing three articles a week for two years and for two years previous to that had been in the B.B.C. where I wrote enough rubbish (news commentaries and so on) to fill a shelf of books. I have become more and more like a sucked orange and I am going to get out of it and go to Scotland for six months to a place where there is no telephone and not much of a postal service. *(Vol. 4, Item 42)*

from Letter to F. J. Warburg[5]—May 31, 1947

Many thanks for your letter. I have made a fairly good start on the book and I think I must have written nearly a third of the rough draft. I have got as far as I had hoped to do by this time, because I have really been in most wretched health this year ever since about January (my chest as usual) and can't quite shake it off. However I keep pegging away, and I hope that when I leave here in October I shall either have finished the rough draft or at any rate broken its back. Of course the rough draft is always a ghastly mess having very little relation to the finished result, but all the same it is the main part of the job. So if I do finish the rough draft by October I might get the book done fairly early in 1948, barring illness. I don't like talking about books before they are written, but I will tell you now that this is a novel about the future—

---

[3] Social anthropologist and friend of Orwell's since the early 1930s. This letter contains the first mention of *Nineteen Eighty-Four*.—Editor
[4] Orwell's classical tutor at Eton College; later Fellow of Trinity College, Cambridge.—Editor
[5] Orwell's publisher in England.—Editor

that is, it is in a sense a fantasy, but in the form of a naturalistic novel. That is what makes it a difficult job—of course as a book of anticipations it would be comparatively simple to write. *(Vol. 4, Item 85)*

from Letter to George Woodcock[6]—August 9, 1947

I am struggling with this novel which I hope to finish early in 1948. I don't even expect to finish the rough draft before about October, then I must come to London for about a month to see to various things and do one or two articles I have promised, then I shall get down to the rewriting of the book which will probably take me 4 or 5 months. It always takes me a hell of a time to write a book even if I am doing nothing else, and I can't help doing an occasional article, usually for some American magazine, because one must earn some money occasionally. *(Vol. 4, Item 89)*

from Letter to Roger Senhouse[7]—October 22, 1947

I *hope* before I arrive to have finished the rough draft of my novel, which I'm on the last lap of now. But it's a most dreadful mess and about two thirds of it will have to be rewritten entirely besides the usual touching up. I don't know how long that will take—I hope only 4 or 5 months but it might well be longer. I've been in such wretched health all this year that I never seem to have much spare energy. *(Vol. 4, Item 93)*

from Letter to F. J. Warburg—February 4, 1948

I can't attempt any serious work while I am like this (1½ stone under weight) but I like to do a little to keep my hand in and incidentally earn some money. I've been definitely ill since abt October, and really, I think, since the beginning of 1947. I believe that frightful winter in London started it off. I didn't really feel well all last year except during the hot period in the summer. Before taking to my bed I had finished the rough draft of my novel all save the last few hundred words, and if I had been well I might have finished it by abt May. If I'm well and out of here by June, I might finish it by the end of the year—I don't know.

---

[6] A writer who was a close friend of Orwell's.—Editor
[7] A director of Secker & Warburg, Orwell's publisher in England.—Editor

It is just a ghastly mess as it stands, but the idea is so good that I could not possibly abandon it. If anything should happen to me I've instructed Richard Rees, my literary executor, to destroy the MS. without showing it to anybody, but it's unlikely that anything like that would happen. This disease isn't dangerous at my age, and they say the cure is going on quite well, though slowly. . . . We are now sending for some new American drug called streptomycin which they say will speed up the cure. *(Vol. 4, Item 105)*

from Letter to F. J. Warburg—October 22, 1948

You will have had my wire by now, and if anything crossed your mind I dare say I shall have had a return wire from you by the time this goes off. I shall finish the book, D.V., early in November, and I am rather flinching from the job of typing it, because it is a very awkward thing to do in bed, where I still have to spend half the time. Also there will have to be carbon copies, a thing which always fidgets me, and the book is fearfully long, I should think well over 100,000 words, possibly 125,000. I can't send it away because it is an unbelievably bad MS. and no one could make head or tail of it without explanation. On the other hand a skilled typist under my eye could do it easily enough. If you can think of anybody who would be willing to come, I will send money for the journey and full instructions. I think we could make her quite comfortable. There is always plenty to eat and I will see that she has a comfortable warm place to work in.

I am not pleased with the book but I am not absolutely dissatisfied. I first thought of it in 1943. I think it is a good idea but the execution would have been better if I had not written it under the influence of T.B. I haven't definitely fixed on the title but I am hesitating between 'Nineteen Eighty-Four' and 'The Last Man in Europe'. *(Vol. 4, Item 125)*

from Letter to Anthony Powell[8]—November 15, 1948

I am just on the grisly job of typing out my novel. I can't type much because it tires me too much to sit up at table, and I asked Roger Senhouse to try and send me a stenog for a fortnight, but of course it's not so easy to get people for short periods like that. It's awful to think

---

[8] English novelist and friend of Orwell's.—Editor

I've been mucking about with this book since June 1947, and it's a ghastly mess now, a good idea ruined, but of course I was seriously ill for 7 or 8 months of the time. *(Vol. 4, Item 128)*

from Letter to F. J. Warburg—December 21, 1948

I'm glad you liked the book. It isn't a book I would gamble on for a big sale, but I suppose one could be sure of 10,000 anyway. *(Vol. 4, Item 131)*

from Letter to Roger Senhouse—December 26, 1948

What it is really meant to do is to discuss the implications of dividing the world up into 'Zones of influence' (I thought of it in 1944 as a result of the Teheran Conference), & in addition to indicate by parodying them the intellectual implications of totalitarianism. It has always seemed to me that people have not faced up to these & that, e.g. the persecution of scientists in Russia, is simply part of a logical process which should have been foreseeable 10–20 years ago. When you get to the proof stage, how would it be to get some eminent person who might be interested, e.g. Bertrand Russell or Lancelot Hogben, to give his opinions abt the book, & (if he consented) use a piece of that as the blurb? There are a number of people one might choose from. *(Vol. 4, Item 132)*

Letter to Leonard Moore[9]—March 17, 1949

You will have had Robert Giroux's letter, of which he sent me a duplicate.

I can't possibly agree to the kind of alteration and abbreviation suggested. It would alter the whole colour of the book and leave out a good deal that is essential. I think it would also—though the judges, having read the parts that it is proposed to cut out, may not appreciate this— make the story unintelligible. There would also be something visibly

[9] Orwell's literary agent. Robert Giroux, referred to in this letter, was Orwell's editor at Harcourt, Brace & World, which published the American edition of *Nineteen Eighty-Four.*—Editor

wrong with the structure of the book if about a fifth or a quarter were cut out and the last chapter then tacked on to the abbreviated trunk. A book is built up as a balanced structure and one cannot simply remove large chunks here and there unless one is ready to recast the whole thing. In any case, merely to cut out the suggested chapters and abridge the passages from the 'book within the book' would mean a lot of rewriting which I simply do not feel equal to at present.

The only terms on which I could agree to any such arrangement would be if the book were published definitely as an abridged version and if it were clearly stated that the English edition contained several chapters which had been omitted. But obviously the Book of the Month people couldn't be expected to agree to any such thing. As Robert Giroux says in his letter, they have not promised to select the book in any case, but he evidently hopes they might, and I suppose it will be disappointing to Harcourt Brace if I reject the suggestion. I suppose you, too, stand to lose a good deal· of commission. But I really cannot allow my work to be mucked about beyond a certain point, and I doubt whether it even pays in the long run. I should be much obliged if you would make my point of view clear to them. *(Vol. 4, Item 144)*

from Letter to Richard Rees[10]—April 8, 1949

I thought you'd all like to know that I have just had a cable saying that the Book of the Month Club have selected my novel after all, in spite of my refusing to make the changes they demanded. So that shows that virtue is its own reward, or honesty is the best policy, I forget which. I don't know whether I shall ultimately end up with a net profit, but at any rate this should pay off my arrears of income tax. *(Vol. 4, Item 148)*

from Letter to Francis A. Henson—June 1949

[Part of a letter, since lost, written on 16 June 1949 by Orwell to Francis A. Henson of the United Automobile Workers answering questions about *Nineteen Eighty-Four*. Excerpts from the letter were published in *Life*, 25 July 1949, and the *New York Times Book Review*, 31 July 1949; the following is an amalgam of these.]

My recent novel is NOT intended as an attack on Socialism or on the British Labour Party (of which I am a supporter) but as a show-up of the perversions to which a centralized economy is liable and which

[10] English author and critic; friend and supporter of Orwell for many years.—Editor

have already been partly realized in Communism and Fascism. I do not believe that the kind of society I describe necessarily *will* arrive, but I believe (allowing of course for the fact that the book is a satire) that something resembling it *could* arrive. I believe also that totalitarian ideas have taken root in the minds of intellectuals everywhere, and I have tried to draw these ideas out to their logical consequences. The scene of the book is laid in Britain in order to emphasize that the English-speaking races are not innately better than anyone else and that totalitarianism, *if not fought against*, could triumph anywhere. *(Vol. 4, Item 158)*

from Letter to Julian Symons[11]—June 16, 1949

I think it was you who reviewed *1984* in the *T.L.S.* I must thank you for such a brilliant as well as generous review. I don't think you could have brought out the sense of the book better in so short a space. You are of course right abt the vulgarity of the 'Room 101' business. I was aware of this while writing it, but I didn't know another way of getting somewhere near the effect I wanted. *(Vol. 4, Item 159)*

from Letter to Vernon Richards[12]—June 22, 1949

I had a lot of fuss with *Life*, who wanted to send interviewers here etc., but I put them off because that kind of thing tires me too much. I am afraid some of the U.S. Republican papers have tried to use *1984* as propaganda against the Labour Party, but I have issued a sort of démenti which I hope will be printed. *(Vol. 4, Item 160)*

[11] English author and critic; his review of *Nineteen Eighty-Four* is reprinted on p. 293.—Editor
[12] English journalist and anarchist. For the "démenti" referred to by Orwell, see his letter to Francis A. Henson, p. 286.—Editor

PART
FIVE

From the Early Reviews

This section contains five of the more interesting early reviews of *Nineteen Eighty-Four*. They illustrate the varied responses evoked by the novel when it was first published. In their diversity, these reviews suggest some of the reactions and problems you are likely to have as a reader. (Some of the reviews have been edited; the reviewer's opinions have been retained, but paraphrases of the novel's plot omitted.)

V. S. PRITCHETT
Review of *1984*

Nineteen Eighty-Four is a book that goes through the reader like an east wind, cracking the skin, opening the sores; hope has died in Mr. Orwell's wintry mind, and only pain is known. I do not think I have ever read a novel more frightening and depressing; and yet, such are the originality, the suspense, the speed of writing and withering indignation that it is impossible to put the book down. The faults of Orwell as a writer— monotony, nagging, the lonely schoolboy shambling down the one dispiriting track—are transformed now he rises to a large subject. He is the most devastating pamphleteer alive because he is the plainest and most individual—there is none of Koestler's lurid journalism—and because, with steady misanthropy, he knows exactly where on the new Jesuitism to apply the Protestant whip. . . .

Mr. Orwell's book is a satirical pamphlet. I notice that some critics have said that his prophecy is not probable. Neither was Swift's *Modest Proposal* nor Wells's *Island of Dr. Moreau*. Probability is not a necessary condition of satire which, when it pretends to draw the future, is, in fact, scourging the present. The purges in Russia and, later, in the Russian satellites, the dreary seediness of London in the worst days of the war, the pockets of 19th-century life in decaying England, the sordidness of bad flats, bad food, the native and whining streak of domestic sluttishness which have sickened English satirists since Smollett, all these have given Mr. Orwell his material. The duty of the satirist is to go one worse than reality; and it might be objected that Mr. Orwell is too literal, that he is too oppressed by what he sees, to exceed it. In one or two incidents where he does exceed, notably in the torture scenes, he is merely melodramatic: he introduces those rather grotesque machines which used to appear in terror stories for boys. In one place—I mean the moment when Winston's Inquisitor drives him to call out for the death of his girl, by threatening to set a cageful of famished rats on him—we reach a peak of imaginative excess in terror, but it is superfluous because mental terrorism is his real subject.

Until our time, irony and unnatural laughter were thought to be the duty of the satirist: in *Candide* the more atrocious the fact—and a large number of Voltaire's facts were true—the gayer the laugh. More strikingly than in any other genre, it is indispensable for satire to sound "untrue," an effect Voltaire obtained by running a large number of true things together in a natural manner. The laughter of Voltaire, the hatred of Swift were assertions of vitality and the instinct to live in us, which continually struggles not only against evil but against the daily environment.

But disgust, the power to make pain sickening, the taste for punishment, exceed irony and laughter in the modern satirist. Neither Winston Smith nor the author laughs when he discovers that the women of the new State are practised hypocrites and make fools of the Party members. For Mr. Orwell, the most honest writer alive, hypocrisy is too dreadful for laughter: it feeds his despair.

As a pamphleteer Orwell may be right in his choice of means. The life-instinct rebels against the grey tyrannies that, like the Jehovah of the Old Testament, can rule only as long as they create guilt. The heart sinks, but the spirit rebels as one reads Mr. Orwell's ruthless opening page, even though we have met that boiled cabbage in all his books before:

> It was a bright, cold day in April, and the clocks were striking thirteen. Winston Smith, his chin nuzzled into his breast in an effort to escape the vile wind, slipped quickly through the glass doors of Victory Mansions, though not quickly enough to prevent a swirl of gritty dust from entering along with him.
>
> The hallway smelt of boiled cabbage and old rag mats. . . . It was no use trying the lift. Even at the best of times it was seldom working, and at present the electricity current was cut off during daylight hours. It was part of the economy drive in preparation for Hate Week. The flat was seven flights up, and Winston, who was 39 and had a varicose ulcer above his right ankle, went slowly, resting several times on the way. On each landing, opposite the lift shaft, the poster with the enormous face gazed from the wall. It was one of those pictures which are so contrived that the eyes follow you about when you move. Big Brother IS WATCHING YOU, the caption beneath it ran.

But though the indignation of *Nineteen Eighty-Four* is singeing, the book does suffer from a division of purpose. Is it an account of present hysteria, is it a satire on propaganda, or is it a world that sees itself entirely in inhuman terms? Is Mr. Orwell saying, not that there is no hope, but that there is no hope for man in the political conception of man? We have come to the end of a movement. He is like some dour Protestant or Jansenist who sees his faith corrupted by the "doublethink" of the Roman Catholic Church, and who fiercely rejects the corrupt civilisations that appear to be able to flourish even under that dispensation.

1949

JULIAN SYMONS
George Orwell's Utopia

The picture of society in *Nineteen Eighty-Four* has an awful plausibility which is not present in other modern projections of our future. In some ways life does not differ very much from the life we live today. The pannikin of pinkish-grey stew, the hunk of bread and cube of cheese, the mug of milkless Victory coffee with its accompanying saccharine tablet—that is the kind of meal we very well remember; and the pleasures of recognition are roused, too, by the description of Victory gin (reserved for the privileged—the 'proles' drink beer), which has 'a sickly oily smell, as of Chinese rice-spirit' and gives to those who drink it 'the sensation of being hit on the back of the head with a rubber club.' We can generally view projections of the future with detachment because they seem to refer to people altogether unlike ourselves. By creating a world in which the 'proles' still have their sentimental songs and their beer, and the privileged consume their Victory gin, Orwell involves us most skillfully and uncomfortably in his story, and obtains more readily our belief in the fantasy of thought-domination that occupies the foreground of his book. . . .

The corrosion of the will through which human freedom is worn away has always fascinated Orwell; *Nineteen Eighty-Four* elaborates a theme which was touched on in *Burmese Days*. Flory's criticism of Burma might be Winston Smith's view of Oceania: 'It is a stifling, stultifying world in which every word and every thought is censored. . . . Free speech is unthinkable.' And Flory's bitter words: 'Be as degenerate as you can. It all postpones Utopia', is a prevision of Winston saying to Julia in his revolt against Party asceticism: 'I hate purity, I hate goodness! I don't want any virtue to exist anywhere.' But in *Nineteen Eighty-Four* the case for the Party is put with a high degree of sophistical skill in argument. O'Brien is able easily to dispose of Winston in their discussions, on the basis that power is the reality of life. The arrests, the tortures, the executions, he says, will never cease. The heresies of Goldstein will live on the endless intoxication of power. 'If you want a picture of the future, imagine a boot stamping on a human face—for ever.'

Mr. Orwell's book is less an examination of any kind of Utopia than an argument, carried on at a very high intellectual level, about power and corruption. And here again we are offered the doubtful pleasure of recognition. Goldstein resembles Trotsky in appearance and even uses Trotsky's phrase, 'the revolution betrayed'; and the censorship of Oceania does not greatly exceed that which has been practised in the Soviet Union, by the suppression of Trotsky's works and the creation of 'Trotskyism' as an evil principle. 'Doublethink', also, has been a familiar feature of political and social life in more than one country for a quarter of a century.

The sobriety and subtlety of the argument, however, is marred by a schoolboyish sensationalism of approach. Considered as a story *Nineteen Eighty-Four* has other faults (some thirty pages are occupied by extracts from Goldstein's book, *The Theory and Practice of Oligarchical Collectivism*), but none so damaging as this inveterate schoolboyishness. The melodramatic idea of the Brotherhood is one example of it; the use of a nursery rhyme to symbolize the unattainable and desirable past is another; but the most serious of these errors in taste is the nature of the torture which breaks the last fragments of Winston's resistance. He is taken, as many others have been taken before him, to 'Room 101'. In Room 101, O'Brien tells him, is 'the worst thing in the world'. The worst thing in the world varies in every case; but for Winston, we learn, it is rats. The rats are brought into the room in a wire cage, and under threat of attack by them Winston abandons the love for Julia which is his last link with ordinary humanity. This kind of crudity (we may say with Lord Jeffrey) will never do. However great the pains expended upon it, the idea of Room 101 and the rats will always remain comic rather than horrific.

But the last word about this book must be one of thanks, rather than of criticism: thanks for a writer who deals with the problems of the world rather than the ingrowing pains of individuals, and who is able to speak seriously and with originality of the nature of reality and the terrors of power.

1949

MARK SCHORER
An Indignant and Prophetic Novel

. . . George Orwell's new novel, *Nineteen Eighty-Four*, is a great work of kinetic art. This may mean that its greatness is only immediate, its power for us alone, now, in this generation, this decade, this year, that it is doomed to be the pawn of time. Nevertheless, it is probable that no other work of this generation has made us desire freedom more earnestly or loathe tyranny with such fulness.

Nineteen Eighty-Four appears at first glance to fall into that long-established tradition of satirical fiction, set either in future times or in imagined places or both, that contains works so diverse as *Gulliver's Travels* itself, Butler's *Erewhon,* and Huxley's *Brave New World.* Yet before one has finished reading the nearly bemused first page, it is evident that this is fiction of another order, and presently one makes the distinctly unpleasant discovery that it is not to be satire at all.

In the excesses of satire one may take a certain comfort. . . . But *Nineteen Eighty-Four* is a work of pure horror, and the horror is crushingly immediate. . . .

Such physical details, even as the outlines of the horrendous moral world that Smith inhabits becomes clear, create the texture, the immediate reality of the novel, and as the dust of the broken plaster settles into the pores of [Winston Smith's] skin, as he eats his dispirited way through many tasteless, sodden, public meals, as he drinks the raw, burning stimulant called Victory Gin, he is seen in one area after another of his lonely and never private life more and more deeply submerged in the gray squalor of a world which is without joy or love and in which desultory but still destructive war is the permanent condition. It is always the atmosphere created by these details that heightens and intensifies, that signifies, indeed, the appalling moral facts. . . .

No real reader can neglect this experience with impunity. He will be moved by Smith's wistful attempts to remember a different kind of life from his. He will make a whole new discovery of the beauty of love between man and woman, and of the strange beauty of landscape in a totally mechanized world. He will be asked to read through pages of sustained physical and psychological pain that have seldom been equaled and never in such quiet, sober prose. And he will return to his own life from Smith's escape into living death with a resolution to resist power wherever it means to deny him his individuality, and to resist for himself the poisonous lures of power.

Nineteen Eighty-Four, the most contemporary novel of this year and who knows of how many past and to come, is a great examination of Lord Acton's famous apothegm, "Power tends to corrupt and absolute power corrupts absolutely."

1949

LIONEL TRILLING
Orwell on the Future

Nineteen Eighty-Four is a profound, terrifying, and wholly fascinating book. It is a fantasy of the political future, and like any such fantasy, serves its author as a magnifying device for an examination of the present. Despite the impression it may give at first, it is not an attack on the Labour Government. The shabby London of the Super-State of the future, the bad food, the dull clothing, the fusty housing, the infinite ennui—all these certainly reflect the English life of today, but they are not meant to represent the outcome of the utopian pretensions of Labourism or of any socialism. Indeed, it is exactly one of the cruel essential points of the book that utopianism is no longer a living issue. For Orwell, the day has gone by when we could afford the luxury of making our flesh creep with the spiritual horrors of a successful hedonistic society; grim years have intervened since Aldous Huxley, in *Brave New World,* rigged out the welfare state of Ivan Karamazov's Grand Inquisitor in the knickknacks of modern science and amusement, and said what Dosteovski and all the other critics of the utopian ideal had said before— that men might actually gain a life of security, adjustment, and fun, but only at the cost of their spiritual freedom, which is to say, of their humanity. Orwell agrees that the State of the future will establish its power by destroying souls. But he believes that men will be coerced, not cosseted, into soullessness. They will be dehumanized not by sex, massage, and private helicopters but by a marginal life of deprivation, dullness, and fear of pain. . . .

Orwell's theory of power is developed brilliantly, at considerable length. And the social system that it postulates is described with magnificent circumstantiality: the three orders of the population—Inner Party, Outer Party, and proletarians; the complete surveillance of the citizenry by the Thought Police, the only really efficient arm of the government; the total negation of the personal life; the directed emotions of hatred and patriotism; the deified Leader, omnipresent but invisible, wonderfully named Big Brother; the children who spy on their parents; and the total destruction of culture. Orwell is particularly successful in his exposition of the official mode of thought, Doublethink, which gives one "the power of holding two contradictory beliefs in one's mind simultaneously, and accepting both of them." This intellectual safeguard of the State is reinforced by a language, Newspeak, the goal of which is to purge itself of all words in which a free thought might be formulated. The systematic obliteration of the past further protects the citizen from Crimethink, and nothing could be more touching, or more suggestive of what history means to the mind, than the efforts of poor Winston Smith to think about the condition of man without knowledge of what others have thought before him. . . .

The whole effort of the culture of the last hundred years has been directed toward teaching us to understand the economic motive as the irrational road to death, and to seek salvation in the rational and the planned. Orwell marks a turn in thought; he asks us to consider whether the triumph of certain forces of the mind, in their naked pride and excess, may not produce a state of things far worse than any we have ever known. He is not the first to raise the question, but he is the first to raise it on truly liberal or radical grounds, with no intention of abating the demand for a just society, and with an overwhelming intensity and passion. This priority makes his book a momentous one.

1949

SAMUEL SILLEN
Maggot-of-the-Month

The following item has been taken from a now defunct Communist magazine, *Masses and Mainstream,* published in the United States. It illustrates something of the anger and ferocity with which Orwell's book was met in Communist circles.

Like his previous diatribe against the human race, *Animal Farm,* George Orwell's new book has received an ovation in the capitalist press. The gush of comparisons with Swift and Dostoyevsky has washed away the few remaining pebbles of literary probity. Not even the robots of Orwell's dyspeptic vision of the world in 1984 seem as solidly regimented as the freedom-shouters who chose it for the Book of the Month Club, serialized it in *Reader's Digest,* illustrated it in eight pages of *Life,* and wrote pious homilies on it in *Partisan Review* and the New York *Times.* Indeed the response is far more significant than the book itself; it demonstrates that Orwell's sickness is epidemic.

The premise of the fable is that capitalism has ceased to exist in 1984; and the moral is that if capitalism departs the world will go to pot. The earth is divided into three "socialist" areas, Oceania, Eurasia and Eastasia, which unlike the good old days of free enterprise are in perpetual warfare. The hero, Winston Smith, lives on Airstrip One (England) and balks at the power-crazed regime. He is nabbed by the Thought Police, tortured with fiendish devices, and finally he wins the privilege of being shot when he learns to love the invisible dictator.

Orwell's nightmare is also inhabited by the "proles," who constitute a mere 85 per cent of Oceania and who are described with fear and loathing as ignorant, servile, brutish. A critic of Orwell's earlier novel in the *Saturday Review of Literature* expressed a profound insight when he noted: "The message of *Animal Farm* seems to be . . . *that people are no damn good.*"

"People are no damn good"—that is precisely the message of this plodding tale as well. For Orwell, life is a dunghill, and after a while the "animals" look "from pig to man, and from man to pig, and from pig to man again; but already it was impossible to say which was which."

As a piece of fiction this is threadbare stuff with a tasteless sex angle which has been rhapsodically interpreted by Mark Schorer in the New York *Times* as a "new discovery of the beauty of love between man and woman." This new discovery is well illustrated by the following scene in which Winston Smith makes love to Julia, a fellow-rebel against the dictatorial regime:

> "Listen. The more men you've had, the more I love you. Do you understand that?"
> "Yes, perfectly."
> "I hate purity, I hate goodness. I don't want any virtue to exist anywhere. I want everyone to be corrupt to the bones."
> "Well, then, I ought to suit you, dear. I'm corrupt to the bones."
> "You like doing this? I don't mean simply me; I mean the thing in itself?"
> "I adore it."
> That was above all what he wanted to hear. Not merely the love of one person, but the animal instinct, the simple undifferentiated desire: that was the force that would tear the party to pieces.

According to *Life* magazine this is "one of the most furtive and pathetic little love affairs in all literature."

Or consider this: Orwell's hero, who is supposed to awaken what the reviewers call "compassion," is interviewed by a man whom he believes to be the leader of the underground resistance to the tyrannical regime:

> "You are prepared to cheat, to forge, to blackmail, to corrupt the minds of children, to distribute habit-forming drugs, to encourage prostitution, to disseminate venereal diseases—to do anything which is likely to cause demoralization and weaken the power of the Party?"
> "Yes."
> "If, for example, it would somehow serve our interests to throw sulphuric acid in a child's face—are you prepared to do that?"
> "Yes."

The author of this cynical rot is quite a hero himself. He served for five years in the Indian Imperial Police, an excellent training center for dealing with the "proles." He was later associated with the Trotskyites in Spain, serving in the P.O.U.M. and he freely concedes that when this organization of treason to the Spanish Republic was "accused of profascist activities I defended them to the best of my ability." During World War II he busied himself with defamation of the Soviet Union.

And now, as Lionel Trilling approvingly notes in *The New Yorker*, Orwell "marks a turn in thought." What is the significance of this turn? The literary mouthpieces of imperialism have discovered that the crude anti-Sovietism of a Kravchenko* is not enough; the system of class oppression must be directly upheld and any belief in change and progress must be frightened out of people.

Like Trilling, the editorial writers of *Life* have shrewdly seized upon Orwell's generalized attack on the "welfare state" to attack not only the Soviet Union but [Henry] Wallace and the British Laborites. "Many readers in England," says *Life,* "will find that his book reinforces a growing suspicion that some of the British Laborites revel in austerity and would love to preserve it—just as the more fervent New Dealers in the U.S. often seemed to have the secret hope that the depression mentality of the '30's, source of their power and excuse for their experiments, would never end."

In short, Orwell's novel coincides perfectly with the propaganda of the National Association of Manufacturers, and it is being greeted for exactly the same reasons that Frederick Hayek's *The Road to Serfdom* was hailed a few years back.

The bourgeoisie, in its younger days, could find spokesmen who painted rosy visions of the future. In its decay, surrounded by burgeoning socialism, it is capable only of hate-filled, dehumanized anti-Utopias. Confidence has given way to the nihilistic literature of the graveyard. Now that Ezra Pound† has been given a government award and George Orwell has become a best-seller we would seem to have reached bottom. But there is a hideous ingenuity in the perversions of a dying capitalism, and it will keep probing for new depths of rottenness which the maggots will find "brilliant and morally invigorating."

1949

* Victor Kravchenko, an official of the Russian government, defected to the West and in 1946 published a book, *I Choose Freedom,* which was highly critical of the Stalin dictatorship.—Editor
† The American poet who during World War II broadcast pro-fascist and anti-Semitic speeches from Italy.—Editor

PART
SIX

Criticism

IRVING HOWE
The Fiction of Anti-Utopia

"I feel sometimes as though the whole modern world of capitalism and Communism and all were rushing toward some enormous efficient machine-made doom of the true values of life."

This sentence was written in 1922 by Max Eastman, then a prominent intellectual defender of the Russian Revolution. It contains the crux of what would later fill volumes of disenchantment, and the need to speak it constitutes one reason why the intellectual experience of our time has so notably been one of self-distrust and self-assault. For some decades there had already been present a tradition in which conservative thinkers assaulted the idea of utopia as an impious denial of the limitations of the human lot, or a symptom of political naïveté, or a fantasy both trivial and boring—this last view finding a curious echo in Wallace Stevens' dismissal of the utopia called heaven: "does ripe fruit never fall?" But the kind of fiction I have in mind and propose to call anti-utopian does not stem from the conservative tradition, even when wryly borrowing from it.

Eastman's sentence would not seem remarkable if spoken by G. K. Chesterton or Hilaire Belloc; its continuing power to shock depends upon our knowledge that it comes from a man of the left. And anti-utopian fiction, as it seeks to embody the sentiments expressed by Eastman, also comes primarily from men of the left. Eugene Zamiatin (*We*) is a dissident from Communism; George Orwell (*1984*) a heterodox socialist; Aldous Huxley (*Brave New World*) a scion of liberalism. The peculiar intensity of such fiction derives not so much from the horror aroused by a possible vision of the future, but from the writer's discovery that in facing the prospect of a future he had been trained to desire, he finds himself struck with horror. The work of these writers is a systematic release of trauma, a painful turning upon their own presuppositions. It is a fiction of urgent yet reluctant testimony, forced by profoundly serious men from their own resistance to fears they cannot evade.

What they fear is not, as liberals and radicals always have, that history will suffer a miscarriage; what they fear is that the long-awaited birth will prove to be a monster. Not many Americans are able to grasp this experience: few of us having ever cultivated the taste for utopia, fewer still have suffered the bitter aftertaste of anti-utopia. For Europeans, however, it all comes with the ferocity of shock. Behind the anti-utopian novel lies not merely the frightful vision of a totalitarian world, but something that seems still more alarming. To minds raised on the assumptions, whether liberal or Marxist, of 19th-Century philosophies of history—assumptions that the human enterprise has a purposive direction, or *telos,* and an upward rhythm, or progress—there is also the churning fear that history itself has proved to be a cheat. And a cheat not because it has turned away from our expectations, but because it betrays our hopes precisely through an inverted fulfillment of those expectations. Not progress denied but progress realized, is the nightmare haunting the anti-utopian novel. And behind this nightmare lies a crisis of thought quite as intense as that suffered by serious 19th Century minds when they discovered that far more painful than doubting the existence of God was questioning the validity of his creation.

Whether to distinguish literary genres or sub-genres through purely formal characteristics or to insist upon the crucial relevance of subject, theme and intellectual content, is something of a problem for theorists of criticism. It is all the more so in regard to fiction, which is less a genre than a menagerie of genres. I am inclined to think that in regard to prose fiction strictly formal characteristics will never suffice, even while remaining necessary, for proper description; and so I shall note here some of the main intellectual premises shaping anti-utopian fiction and then a few of those formal properties by which it may be distinguished from the familiar kinds of novel.

The first of the intellectual premises I have already remarked upon: what might be called the disenchantment with history, history both as experience and idea. The second is closely related to the first. It is the vision of a world anticipated by a character in Dostoevsky's *The Possessed* who declares his wish for a mode of existence in which "only the necessary is necessary." Zamiatin's *We,* the first and best of the anti-utopian novels, portrays a "glass paradise" in which all men live in principled unprivacy, without a self to hide or a mood to indulge. Zamiatin thus reflects, as Orwell later would in his "telescreen" and Charlie Chaplin in a sequence of *Modern Times,* the fear that the historical process, at breakneck-speed and regardless of our will, is taking us toward a *transparent universe* in which all categories are fixed, the problematic has been banished, unhappiness is treason and the gratuitous act beyond imagining. In *Brave New World* docile human creatures are produced in a hatchery: the ideal of man's self-determination, so important to Western liberalism, becomes a mocking rationale for procreation by norm. One of the "disturbed" characters in *We* remarks to one of the well-adjusted: "You want to encircle the infinite with a wall" and shifting from the metaphysical to the psychological, adds: "We are the happy arithmetical mean. As you would put it, the integration from zero to infinity, from imbeciles to Shakespeare."

This world of total integration is stripped of accident, contingency and myth; it permits no shelter for surprise, no margin for novelty, no hope for adventure. The rational raised to an irrational power becomes its god. Reality, writes Orwell in *1984,* "is not external. Reality exists in the human mind and nowhere else . . . whatever the Party holds to be truth *is* truth." Reality is not an objective fact to be acknowledged or transformed or resisted; it is the culminating fabrication produced by the *hubris* of rationalism.

But a certain kind of rationalism, I must hasten to add; since none of the anti-utopian novelists, at least in their novels, has anything to do with invoked mysticism. The sociologist Karl Mannheim distinguishes between two kinds of rationality, "substantial" and "functional." Substantial rationality is "an act of thought which reveals intelligent insight into the inter-relations of events in a given situation." Functional rationality, the parallel in conduct to the process of industrial rationalization, consists of

> . . . a series of actions . . . organized in such a way that it leads to a previously defined goal, every element in this series of actions receiving a functional position and role. . . . It is by no means characteristic, however, of functional organization that . . . the goal itself be considered rational. . . . One may strive to attain an irrational eschatological goal, such as salvation, by so organizing one's ascetic behavior that it will lead to this goal. . . .

And Mannheim remarks:

> The violent shocks of crises and revolutions have uncovered a tendency which has hitherto been working under the surface, namely the paralyzing effect of functional rationalization on the capacity for rational judgment.

In his abstract way Mannheim hits upon the nightmare-vision of the anti-utopian novelists: that what men do and what they are become unrelated; that a world is appearing in which technique and value have been split apart, so that technique spins forward with a mad fecundity while value becomes debased to a mere slogan of the state. This kind of "technicism," Spengler has remarked, is frequently visible in a society that has lost its self-assurance. And in his preface to *Brave New World* Huxley shows a keen awareness of the distinction between "substantial" and "functional rationality" when he remarks that "The people who govern the Brave New World may not be sane . . . but they are not madmen, and their aim is not anarchy but social stability." They live, that is, by the strict requirements of functional rationality.

All three of our writers have a lively appreciation of the need felt by modern men to drop the burden of freedom, that need crystallized in the remark of the 19th Century anarchist Michael Bakunin, "I do not want to be I, I want to be We." The schema of the anti-utopian novel requires that in one or two forlorn figures, sports from the perfection of adjustment, there arise once more the spontaneous appetite for individuality. In *Brave New World* it takes the form of historical nostalgia; in *1984,* a yearning for a personal relationship that will have no end other than its own fulfillment; and in *We,* a series of brilliant forays into self-consciousness. The narrator of *We* discloses the ethos of his world when he remarks that the half-forgotten Christians "knew that resignation is virtue and pride a vice; [and almost as if echoing Bakunin] that 'We' is from 'God,' and 'I' from the devil." But as a deviant from the deadening health of his society, he engages in a discovery of selfhood through a realization of how strange, how thoroughly artificial, the very notion of selfhood is:

> Evening. . . the sky is covered with a milky-golden tissue, and one cannot see what is there, beyond, on the heights. The ancients "knew" that the greatest, bored skeptic—their god—lived there. We know that crystalline, blue, naked, indecent Nothing is there. . . . I had firm faith in myself; I believed that I knew all about myself. But then . . . I look in the mirror. And for the first time in my life, yes, for the first time in my life, I see clearly, precisely, consciously and with surprise, I see myself as some "him!" I am "he." . . . And I know surely that "he" with his straight brows is a stranger. . . .

The idea of the personal self, which for us has become an indispensable assumption of existence, is seen by Zamiatin, Orwell and Huxley as a *cultural* idea. It is a fact within history, the product of the liberal era, and because it is susceptible to historical growth and decline, it may also be susceptible to historical destruction. All three of our anti-utopian novels are dominated by an overwhelming question: can human nature be manufactured? Not transformed or manipulated or debased, since these it obviously can be; but manufactured by will and decision.

When one speaks of the historical determinants of human nature, one tacitly assumes that there is a human nature, and that for all of its plasticity it retains some indestructible core. If Zamiatin, Orwell and Huxley wrote simply from the premise of psychological relativism, they would deprive themselves of whatever possibilities for drama their theme allows, for then the very idea of a limit to the malleability of human nature would be hard to maintain. They must assume that there are strivings in men toward candor, freedom, truth and love which cannot be suppressed indefinitely; yet they have no choice but to recognize that at any particular historical moment these strivings can be suppressed effectively, surviving for men of intelligence less as realities to be counted on than as potentialities to be nurtured. Furthermore, in modern technology there appears a whole new apparatus for violating human nature: brainwashing and torture in *1984,* artificial biological selection in *Brave New World,* and an operation similar to a lobotomy in *We.* And not only can desire be suppressed and impulse denied, they can be transformed into their very opposites, so that people sincerely take slavery to be freedom and learn, in *Brave New World,* that "the secret of happiness and virtue is liking what you've got to like."

Ultimately the anti-utopian novel keeps returning to the choice posed by Dostoevsky's legend of the Grand Inquisitor in *The Brothers Karamazov:* the misery of the human being who must bear his burden of independence against the contentment of the human creature at rest in his obedience. But what now gives this counterposition of freedom and happiness a particularly sharp edge is the fact that through the refinements of technology Dostoevsky's speculation can be realized in social practice. In a number of intellectual and literary respects *Brave New World* is inferior to *1984* and *We,* but in confronting this central question it is bolder and keener, for Huxley sees that the problem first raised by Dostoevsky—will the satisfaction of material wants quench the appetite for freedom?—relates not only to totalitarian dictatorships but to the whole of industrial society. Like so many other manifestations of our culture, the anti-utopian novel keeps rehearsing the problems of the 19th Century: in this instance, not merely Dostoevsky's prophetic speculation but also the quieter fear of Alexis de Tocqueville that "a kind of virtuous materialism may ultimately be established in the world which would not corrupt but enervate the soul, and noiselessly unbend its springs of action."

The main literary problem regarding anti-utopian fiction is to learn to read it according to its own premises and limits, which is to say, in ways somewhat different from those by which we read ordinary novels.

Strictly speaking, anti-utopian fictions are not novels at all. The literary critic Northrop Frye has usefully distinguished among kinds of fiction in order to remind us that we have lost in critical niceness by our habit of lumping all prose fiction under the heading of the novel. He is right of course, but I suspect that for common usage the effort to revive such distinctions is a lost cause, and that it may be better to teach readers to discriminate among kinds of novels. If, however, we do for the moment accept Frye's categories it becomes clear that books like *We, 1984,* and *Brave New World* are not really novels portraying a familiar social world but what he calls Menippean satire, a kind of fiction that

> ... deals less with people as such than with mental attitudes ... The Menippean satire thus resembles the confession in its ability to handle abstract ideas and theories, and differs from the novel in its characterization, which is stylized rather than naturalistic, and presents people as mouthpieces of the ideas they represent. ... At its most concentrated the Menippean satire presents us with a vision of the world in terms of a single intellectual pattern.

Accept this description and the usual complaints about the anti-utopian novel come to seem irrelevant. By its very nature the anti-utopian novel cannot satisfy the expectations we hold, often unreflectively, about the ordinary novel: expectations that are the heritage of 19th Century romanticism with its stress upon individual consciousness, psychological analysis and the scrutiny of intimate relations. When the English critic Raymond Williams complains that the anti-utopian novel lacks "a substantial society and correspondingly substantial persons," he is offering a description but intends it as a depreciation, quite as would a critic complaining that a sonnet lacks a complex dramatic plot. For the very premise of anti-utopian fiction is that it projects a world in which such elements—"substantial society . . . substantial persons"—have largely been suppressed and must now be painfully recovered, if recovered at all.

One might even speculate that it would be a mistake for the author of an anti-utopian novel to provide the usual complement of three-dimensional characters such as we expect in ordinary fiction, or to venture an extended amount of psychological specification. For these books try to present a world in which individuality has become obsolete and personality a sign of subversion. The major figures of such books are necessarily grotesques: they resemble persons who have lost the power of speech and must struggle to regain it; Winston Smith and Julia in *1984* are finally engaged in an effort to salvage the idea of the human *as an idea,* which means to experiment with the possibilities of solitude and the risks of contemplation. The human relations which the ordinary novel takes as its premise, become the evoked possibilities toward which the anti-utopian novel strains. What in the ordinary novel appears as the tacit assumption of the opening page is now, in the anti-utopian novel, a wistful hope usually unrealized by the concluding page. That the writer of anti-utopian fiction must deal with a world in which man has been absorbed by his function and society by the state, surely places upon him a considerable quota of difficulties. But that is the task he sets himself, and there can be no point in complaining that he fails to do what in the nature of things he cannot do.

The anti-utopian novel lacks almost all the usual advantages of fiction: it must confine itself to a rudimentary kind of characterization, it cannot provide much in the way of psychological nuance, it hardly pretends to a large accumulation of suspense. Yet, as we can all testify, the anti-utopian novel achieves its impact, and this it does through a variety of formal means:

1) *It posits a "flaw" in the perfection of the perfect.* This "flaw," the weakness of the remembered or yearned-for human, functions dramatically in the anti-utopian novel quite as the assumption of original sin or a socially-induced tendency toward evil does in the ordinary novel. The "flaw" provides the possibility and particulars of the conflict, while it simultaneously insures that the outcome will be catastrophic. Since the

ending of the anti-utopian novel is predictable and contained, so to say, within its very beginning, the tension it creates depends less on a developed plot than on an overpowering conception. Leading to—

2) *It must be in the grip of an idea at once dramatically simple and historically complex: an idea that has become a commanding passion.* This idea consists, finally, in a catastrophic transmutation of values, a stoppage of history at the expense of its actors. In reading the anti-utopian novel we respond less to the world it projects than to the urgency of the projection. And since this involves the dangers of both monotony and monomania—

3) *It must be clever in the management of its substantiating detail.* Knowing all too well the inevitable direction of things, we can be surprised only by the ingenuity of local detail. And here arises a possible basis for comparative valuations among anti-utopian novels. Orwell's book is impressive for its motivating passion, less so for its local composition. Huxley's is notably clever, but too rationalistic and self-contained: he does not write like a man who feels himself imperilled by his own vision. Zamiatin is both passionate and brilliant, clever and driven. His style, an astonishing mosaic of violent imagery, sustains his vision throughout the book in a way that a mere linear unfolding of his fable never could. But since the anti-utopian novel must satisfy the conflicting requirements of both a highly-charged central idea and cleverness in the management of detail, it becomes involved with special problems of verisimilitude. That is—

4) *It must strain our sense of the probable while not violating our attachment to the plausible.* To stay too close to the probable means, for the anti-utopian novel, to lose the very reason for its existence; to appear merely implausible means to surrender its power to shock. Our writers meet this difficulty by employing what I would call the dramatic strategy and the narrative psychology of "one more step." Their projected total state is one step beyond our known reality—not so much a picture of modern totalitarian society as an extension, by just one and no more than one step, of the essential pattern of the total state.

5) *In presenting the nightmare of history undone, it must depend on the ability of its readers to engage in an act of historical recollection.* This means, above all, to remember the power that the idea of utopia has had in Western society. "The Golden Age," wrote Dostoevsky, "is the most unlikely of all the dreams that have been, but for it men have given up their life and all their strength . . . Without it the people will not live and cannot die." Still dependent on this vision of the Golden Age, the anti-utopian novel thus shares an essential quality of all modern literature: it can realize its values only through images of their violation. The enchanted dream has become a nightmare, but a nightmare projected with such power as to validate the continuing urgency of the dream.

1962

The two following essays appeared shortly after the publication of *Nineteen Eighty-Four;* they testify to the powerful impact the book made upon thoughtful American intellectuals. Both Philip Rahv and Isaac Rosenfeld were concerned not merely with the immediate political targets at which Orwell was aiming but also with the larger moral implications: What in modern experience made it possible for a society to appear that could so totally oppress human beings and quench the appetite for freedom? And what were the implications of this fact for liberal and socialist thought? Philip Rahv, an influential literary critic and editor of the magazine *Partisan Review,* spoke for a whole generation of American intellectuals that had been repelled by the brutalities of the Stalin dictatorship yet wished to retain a commitment to radical values. Isaac Rosenfeld, a young novelist and critic, wrote about *Nineteen Eighty-Four* in less explicitly political terms; he was concerned with the moral drama of Orwell's struggle to complete *Nineteen Eighty-Four* shortly before dying and, like many other intellectuals, he saw Orwell as a model for writers, a man who spoke for truth and conscience.

PHILIP RAHV
The Unfuture of Utopia

George Orwell has been able to maintain an exceptional position among the writers of our time seriously concerned with political problems. His work has grown in importance and relevance through the years, evincing a steadiness of purpose and uncommon qualities of character and integrity that set it quite apart from the typical products of the radical consciousness in this period of rout and retreat. A genuine humanist in his commitments, a friend, that is, not merely of mankind but of man (man as he is, not denatured by ideological abstractions), Orwell has gone through the school of the revolutionary movement without taking over its snappishly doctrinaire attitudes. His attachment to the primary traditions of the British empirical mind has apparently rendered him immune to dogmatism. Nor has the release from certitude lately experienced by the more alert radical intellectuals left him in the disoriented state in which many of his contemporaries now find themselves. . . . It can be said of Orwell that he is the best kind of witness, the most reliable and scrupulous. All the more appalling, then, is the vision not of the remote but of the very close future evoked in his new novel*—a vision entirely composed of images of loss, disaster, and unspeakable degradation.

This is far and away the best of Orwell's books. As a narrative it has tension and actuality to a terrifying degree; still it will not do to judge it

* *Nineteen Eighty-Four.*

primarily as a literary work of art. Like all Utopian literature, from Sir Thomas More and Campanella to William Morris, [Edward] Bellamy, and [Aldous] Huxley, its inspiration is scarcely such as to be aesthetically productive of ultimate or positive significance; this seems to be true of Utopian writings regardless of the viewpoint from which the author approaches his theme. *Nineteen Eighty-Four* chiefly appeals to us as a work of the political imagination, and the appeal is exercised with gravity and power. It documents the crisis of socialism with greater finality than [Arthur] Koestler's *Darkness at Noon,* to which it will be inevitably compared, since it belongs, on one side of it, to the same genre, the melancholy mid-century genre of lost illusions and Utopia betrayed.

While in Koestler's novel there are still lingering traces of nostalgia for the Soviet Utopia, at least in its early heroic phase, and fleeting tenderness for its protagonists, betrayers and betrayed—some are depicted as Promethean types wholly possessed by the revolutionary dogma and annihilated by the consequences of their own excess, the *hubris* of Bolshevism—in Orwell's narrative the further stage of terror that has been reached no longer permits even the slightest sympathy for the revolutionaries turned totalitarian. Here Utopia is presented, with the fearful simplicity of a trauma, as the abyss into which the future falls. The traditional notion of Utopia as the future good is thus turned inside out, inverted—nullified. It is now sheer mockery to speak of its future. Far more accurate it is to speak of its *unfuture.* (The addition of the negative affix "un" is a favorite usage of Newspeak, the official language of Ingsoc—English socialism—a language in which persons purged by the Ministry of Love, i.e., the secret police, are invariably described as *unpersons.* The principles of Newspeak are masterfully analyzed by Orwell in the appendix to his book. Newspeak is nothing less than a plot against human consciousness, for its sole aim is so to reduce the range of thought through the destruction of words as to make "*thoughtcrime* literally impossible because there will be no words in which to express it.")

The prospect of the future drawn in this novel can on no account be taken as a phantasy. If it inspires dread above all, that is precisely because its materials are taken from the real world as we know it, from conditions now prevailing in the totalitarian nations, in particular the Communist nations, and potentially among us too. Ingsoc, the system established in Oceania, the totalitarian super-State that unites the English-speaking peoples, is substantially little more than an extension into the near future of the present structure and policy of Stalinism, an extension as ingenious as it is logical, predicated upon conditions of permanent war and the development of the technical means of espionage and surveillance to the point of the complete extinction of private life. Big Brother, the supreme dictator of Oceania, is obviously modeled on Stalin, both in his physical features and in his literary style ("a style at once military and pedantic, and, because of a trick of asking questions and then promptly answering them . . . easy to imitate"). And who is Goldstein, the dissident leader of Ingsoc against whom Two Minute Hate Periods are conducted in all Party offices, if not Trotsky, the grand heresiarch and useful scapegoat, who is even now as indispensable to Stalin as Goldstein is shown to be to Big Brother? The inserted chapters from Goldstein's imaginary book on "The Theory and Practice of Oligarchical Collectivism," are a wonderfully realised imitation not only of Trotsky's characteristic rhetoric but also of his mode and manner as a Marxist theoretician. Moreover, the established pieties of Communism are at once recognizable in the approved spiritual regimen of the Ingsoc Party faithful: "A Party member is expected to have no private emotions and no respites from enthusiasm. He is supposed to live in a continuous frenzy of hatred of foreign enemies and internal traitors, triumph over victories, and self-abasement before the power and wisdom of the Party." One of Orwell's best strokes is his analysis of the technique of "doublethink," drilled into the Party members, which consists of the willingness to assert that black is white when the Party demands it, and even to believe that black is white, while at the same time knowing very well that nothing of the sort can be true. Now what is "doublethink," actually, if not the technique continually practiced by the Communists and their liberal collaborators, dupes, and apologists? . . . As for "the control of the past," of which so much is made in Oceania through the revision of all records and the manipulation of memory through force and fraud, that too is by no means unknown in Russia, where periodically not only political history but also the history of art and literature are revamped in accordance with the latest edicts of the regime. The one feature of Oceanic society that appears to be really new is the proscription of sexual pleasure. The fact is, however, that a tendency in that direction has long been evident in Russia, where a new kind of prudery, disgusting in its unctuousness and hypocrisy, is officially promoted. In Oceania "the only recognized purpose of marriage was to beget children for the service of the Party." The new Russian laws regulating sexual relations are manifestly designed with the same purpose in mind. It is plain that any society which imposes a ban on personal experience must sooner or later distort and inhibit the sexual instinct. The totalitarian State cannot tolerate attachments between men and women that fall outside the political sphere and that are in their very nature difficult to control from above.

The diagnosis of the totalitarian perversion of socialism that Orwell makes in this book is far more remarkable than the prognosis it contains. This is not to deny that the book is prophetic; but its importance is mainly in its powerful engagement with the present. Through the invention of a society of which he can be imaginatively in full command, Orwell is enabled all the more effectively to probe the consequences for the human soul of the system of oligarchic collectivism—the system already prevailing in a good part of the world, which millions of people even this side of the Iron Curtain believe to be true-blue socialism and which at this time constitutes the only formidable threat to free institutions. Hence to read this novel simply as a flat prediction of what is to come is to misread it. It is not a writ of fatalism to bind our wills. Orwell makes no attempt to persuade us, for instance, that the English-speaking nations will inevitably lose their freedom in spite of their vigorous democratic temper and libertarian traditions. "Wave of the future" notions are alien to Orwell. His intention, rather, is to prod the Western world into a more conscious and militant resistance to the totalitarian virus to which it is now exposed.

As in *Darkness at Noon,* so in *Nineteen Eighty-Four* one of the major themes is the psychology of capitulation. Winston Smith, the hero of the novel, is shown arming himself with ideas against the Party and defying it by forming a sexual relationship with Julia; but from the first we know that he will not escape the secret police, and after he is caught we see him undergoing a dreadful metamorphosis which burns out his human essence, leaving him a wreck who can go on living only by becoming one of "them." The closing sentences of the story are the most pitiful of all: "He had won a victory over himself. He loved Big Brother." The meaning of the horror of the last section of the novel, with its unbearable description of the torture of Smith by O'Brien, the Ingsoc Commissar, lies in its disclosure of a truth that the West still refuses to absorb. Hence the widespread mystifications produced by the Moscow Trials ("Why did they confess?")* and more recently, by the equally spectacular displays of confessional ardor in Russia's satellite states (Cardinal Mindszenty [of Hungary] and others). The truth is that the modern totalitarians have devised a methodology of terror that enables them to break human beings by getting inside them. They explode the human character from within, exhibiting the pieces as the irrefutable proof of their own might and virtue. Thus Winston Smith begins with the notion that even if nothing else in the world was his own, still there were a few cubic centimeters inside his skull that belonged to him alone. But O'Brien, with his torture instruments and ruthless dialectic of power, soon teaches him that even these few cubic centimeters can never belong to him, only to the Party. What is so implacable about the despotisms of the twentieth century is that they have abolished martyrdom. If all through history the capacity

* Mr. Rahv is here referring to the series of trials of Old Bolshevik leaders (Zinoviev, Kamenev, Bukharin, Radek, etc.) staged in Moscow during the mid-thirties by the Stalin dictatorship. At these trials the defendants "confessed" to being counterrevolutionaries, accomplices of Nazism and so on. In 1956 Premier Khrushchev, in his famous report to the Twenty-Second Congress of the Communist Party of the Soviet Union, indicated, and in later speeches he acknowledged, that these trials were indeed the frame-ups that liberal and socialist critics of the Stalin dictatorship had charged.—Editor

and willingness to suffer for one's convictions served at once as the test and demonstration of sincerity, valor, and heroic resistance to evil, now even that capacity and willingness have been rendered meaningless. In the prisons of the M.V.D.* or the Ministry of Love suffering has been converted into its opposite—into the ineluctable means of surrender. The victim crawls before his torturer, he identifies himself with him and grows to love him. That is the ultimate horror.

The dialectic of power is embodied in the figure of O'Brien, who simultaneously recalls and refutes the ideas of Dostoevsky's Grand Inquisitor. For a long time we thought that the legend of the Grand Inquisitor contained the innermost secrets of the power-mongering human mind. But no, modern experience has taught us that the last word is by no means to be found in Dostoevsky. For even the author of *The Brothers Karamazov,* who wrote that "man is a despot by nature and loves to be a torturer," was for all his crucial insights into evil nevertheless incapable of seeing the Grand Inquisitor as he really is. There are elements of the idealistic rationalization of power in the ideology of the Grand Inquisitor that we must overcome if we are to become fully aware of what the politics of totalitarianism come to in the end.

Clearly, that is what Orwell has in mind in the scene when Smith, while yielding more and more to O'Brien, voices the thoughts of the Grand Inquisitor only to suffer further pangs of pain for his persistence in error. Smith thinks that he will please O'Brien by explaining the Party's limitless desire for power along Dostoevskyean lines: "That the Party did not seek power for its own ends, but only for the good of the majority. That it sought power because men in the mass were frail, cowardly creatures who could not endure liberty or face the truth, and must be ruled over and systematically deceived by others stronger than themselves. That the choice for mankind lay between freedom and happiness, and that, for the great bulk of mankind, happiness was better. That the Party was the eternal guardian of the weak, a dedicated sect doing evil that good might come, sacrificing its own happiness to that of others." This is a fair summary of the Grand Inquisitor's ideology. O'Brien, however, has gone beyond even this last and most insidious rationalization of power. He forcibly instructs Smith in the plain truth that "the Party seeks power for its own sake. We are not interested in the good of others; we are interested solely in power. . . . Power is not a means; it is an end. One does not establish a dictatorship in order to safeguard a revolution; one makes a revolution in order to establish the dictatorship. The object of persecution is persecution. The object of torture is torture. The object of power is power. Now do you begin to understand me?" And how does one human being assert his power over another human being? By mak-

---

* The Soviet secret police, also known at various times as the GPU and NKVD.—Editor

ing him suffer, of course. For "obedience is not enough. Unless he is suffering, how can you be sure that he is obeying your will and not his own? Power is in inflicting pain and humiliation. Power is in tearing human minds to pieces and putting them together again in new shapes of your own choosing." That, precisely, is the lesson the West must learn if it is to comprehend the meaning of Communism. Otherwise we shall go on playing Winston Smith, falling sooner or later into the hands of the O'Briens of the East, who will break our bones until we scream with love for Big Brother.

But there is one aspect of the psychology of power in which Dostoevsky's insight strikes me as being more viable than Orwell's strict realism. It seems to me that Orwell fails to distinguish, in the behavior of O'Brien, between psychological and objective truth. Undoubtedly it is O'Brien, rather than Dostoevsky's Grand Inquisitor, who reveals the real nature of total power; yet that does not settle the question of O'Brien's personal psychology, the question, that is, of his ability to live with this naked truth as his sole support; nor is it conceivable that the party elite to which he belongs could live with this truth for very long. Evil, far more than good, is in need of the pseudo-religious justifications so readily provided by the ideologies of world-salvation and compulsory happiness, ideologies generated both by the Left and the Right. Power is its own end, to be sure, but even the Grand Inquisitors are compelled, now as always, to believe in the fiction that their power is a means to some other end, gratifying noble and supernal. Though O'Brien's realism is wholly convincing in social and political terms, its motivation in the psychological economy of the novel remains unclear.

Another aspect of Orwell's dreadful Utopia that might be called into question is the role he attributes to the proletariat, a role that puts it outside politics. In Oceania the workers, known as the Proles, are assigned to the task of production, deprived of all political rights, but unlike the Party members, are otherwise left alone and even permitted to lead private lives in accordance with their own choice. That is an idea that appears to me to run contrary to the basic tendencies of totalitarianism. All societies of our epoch, whether authoritarian or democratic in structure, are mass-societies; and an authoritarian state built on the foundations of a mass-society could scarcely afford the luxury of allowing any class or group to evade its demand for complete control. A totalitarian-collectivist state is rigidly organized along hierarchical lines, but that very fact, so damaging to its socialist claims, necessitates the domination of all citizens, of whatever class, in the attempt to "abolish" the contradiction between its theory and practice by means of boundless demagogy and violence.

These are minor faults, however. This novel is the best antidote to the totalitarian disease that any writer has so far produced. Everyone should read it; and I recommend it particularly to those liberals who still cannot get over the political superstition that while absolute power is bad when exercised by the Right, it is in its very nature good and a boon to humanity once the Left, that is to say "our own people," takes hold of it.

1949

ISAAC ROSENFELD
Decency and Death

In an article on Arthur Koestler, written in 1944, George Orwell complained that no Englishman had as yet published a worthwhile novel on the theme of totalitarian politics—nothing to equal *Darkness at Noon*— "Because there is almost no English writer to whom it has happened to see totalitarianism from the inside." Five years later, with the publication of *1984* he had become the one exception. He had not in the interval gained any more intimate an acquaintance with the subject; the year he spent fighting with the POUM* in the Spanish Civil War was his closest approach to it. The success of *1984* must therefore be attributed to his imagination. But this is precisely the quality in which all his previous work had been weakest.

Orwell was fair, honest, unassuming, and reliable in everything he wrote. These qualities, though desirable in every writer, are specifically the virtues of journalism; and Orwell, it seems to me, had always been at his best, not in the novels or political articles, but in casual pieces of the kind he wrote for the *London Tribune* in his column, "As I Please." He was a writer in a small way—a different matter from the minor writer, to whose virtuosity and finesse he never aspired. This lack of literary manner enabled him to give himself directly, if sometimes feebly, to the reader; he held back his feelings (even in his account of the Stalinists' responsibility for the Barcelona street fighting† in *Homage to Catalonia*, his anger does not rise above the note of "You don't do such things!") but only in the manner of restraint, and there was nothing hypocritical or false about him. He had all the traditional English virtues, of which he made the traditional compression into one: decency. When he died, I felt

---

* The POUM (Partido Obrero de Unificacion Marxist—Party of Marxist Unification) was a left-socialist, anti-Stalinist party, especially active in the Barcelona region, where Orwell encountered its leaders and members during his visit to Spain at the time of the Civil War in the late 1930s. The POUM suffered repressions at the hands of the Communists and their allies in Loyalist Spain. This matter is discussed further in the essay by Lionel Trilling, p. 217.—Editor

† For an account of this event, see the essay by Lionel Trilling, p. 217.

as many of his readers who never knew him must have done, that this was a friend gone.

Down and Out in Paris and London, one of his earlier books, is the steady Orwell who underwent no apparent development. Recorded here are some of the worst days of his life when he was unemployed, broke, and starving. But the tone is substantially the same as that of the article on boys' weeklies in *Dickens, Dali & Others.* The Eton graduate and former Burma policeman accepts dishwashers and tramps as his fellow men without condescension and with only a little squeamishness at the filth of his surroundings. He makes no effort to bend his prose to the sounding of lower depths, and he was to feel no need to make a special adjustment to the language and problems of political journalism when he returned to England to gain some recognition as a writer. Detached yet close observation, dryness, a stamping out of whatever may once have been the snob in him (yet never at the expense of the Englishman) and the correlated stubborn attachment to common sense, to which he sometimes sacrificed his insight—this made up his basic journalistic style, unchanged through the years.

In *Burmese Days,* first published a year later in 1934, there is considerable bitterness as Orwell expresses his disgust with the Indian Civil Service. This is hardly the same man writing. For once he is full of contempt, especially toward his hero, John Flory, though the latter happens to be the only "decent" character in the novel—he is not bigoted as the rest of the whites, he does not have the Imperial attitude, he is humane toward the natives. Yet he is a weakling, he gives way to alcoholism and the unrelieved colonial ennui, and he is incapable of withstanding the corrupt moral pressure of his colleagues; Orwell cannot forgive him this. His attitude toward this character—in whom there must have been a good deal of himself—is neither completely personal nor detached, and here Orwell betrays a fault which, until *1984,* was to remain his greatest as a novelist, a fault of imagination, in not knowing what to do with a character, once the main traits and the setting have been provided. (The Burmese jungle, the character of the natives, their attitude toward the swinish pukka sahibs, the dances and festivals, the pidgin and official English were all excellently reported.) Flory, for all the significance a socialist writer might have given such a characterization, falls into the useless, unimaginative category of the weak liberal—anybody's whipping boy. The only interesting thing in his treatment of him is that it is so thoroughly bad-mannered; the mild Orwell makes not the slightest effort to spare his contempt for the man and ends by having him commit suicide, and the masochistic suggestion which this carries links Flory, however vaguely, with the ultimate characterization of the political hero (Winston Smith) as he who undergoes infinite degradation. Otherwise one is still unprepared for *1984.*

Coming Up for Air, written in 1938, reverts to the journalistic style of ease and understatement, the disquietude of *Burmese Days* worked out of it. But this does not do the novel much good, as it fails to catch the anxiety of the prewar days. The hero, George Bowling, running out on his job and family for a breather before the war which he knows is coming, refers to himself as a typical middle-aged suburban bloke, and Orwell, for the greater part of the book, is satisfied to treat him at this level. But his concern with politics had apparently been getting ahead of his style. Where Orwell's sense of politics in *Burmese Days* was of little more than incidental value, in *Coming Up for Air* it has become the source of the whole book. This, together with the continuing weakness of the novelist's imagination, accounts for such passages as the one in which Bowling, inspecting the shot motor of his car, compares it to the Austro-Hungarian Empire. Moreover, Orwell's politics suddenly appears to be out of joint. (A pity that it had not been more so. It is sometimes an advantage for a political writer to lose his grasp of politics, for the unreality of his observations brings him so much nearer to experience. But this, too, had to wait till *1984.*) Bowling's holiday consists in a return to his boyhood village, which he finds unrecognizably overgrown with factories and ugly housing developments. The values of his youth, Bowling realizes, have vanished for good. But this feeling is presented in such strength, it subverts the politics to a conservative tone. The decency which Orwell had linked, at one level, with the Socialist movement, in which he saw its only chance of surviving, now seems to belong entirely to the laissez-faire days preceding the first World War with their unshaken social traditions, the slower pace, the less highly developed technology. This again may be merely a failure of imagination, Orwell at as great a loss to know what to do with a theme as with a character; but it also suggests that the failure came of a division deep in him. He was a radical in politics and a conservative in feeling.

Though he continued to write his political articles and casual pieces in the same informal and disarming style, as though nothing were happening, his feelings were getting the better of him. This, though I have no evidence for it, I must suppose to be the case on the strength of the fact that he was for many years a sick, and during the writing of *1984,* a dying, man. His style, the character of the man, did not allow conflicts to appear at the surface, which had to remain undisturbed. He kept on writing in the easy manner that disarmed the reader of any suspicion of conflict, remaining empirical and optimistic all the time that he was turning over a metaphysics of evil.

A dying man, one may expect, will find consistency his last concern. Death exempts him from his own habits as much as it does from responsibility to others. Life being what it is in our world, the onset of death is often the first taste a man gets of freedom. At last the imagination can come into its own, and as a man yields to it his emotions take on a surprising depth and intensity. The extreme situation in which Orwell found himself as the rapid downhill course of tuberculosis approached enabled him for the first time to go from one extreme to the other: from his own sickness to the world's. His imagination, set free, was able to confirm the identity of the two extremes, turning sickness into art.

The torture scenes in *1984* have been compared with [Dostoevsky's] The Legend of the Grand Inquisitor. The comparison seems to me forced; a better one, it applies to the novel as a whole, is with Ippolit's "Essential Explanation" in [Dostoevsky's] *The Idiot*. The torturer O'Brien's words to Winston Smith as he is re-educating him, "The objective of power is power," are the equivalent, in what they reveal to Smith of a politics stripped bare of morality, of Ippolit's nightmare of the monstrous insect, representing the world of nature without God. That the objective of power is power may long have been obvious to some men, but for the restrained writer who had muffled the terror and disgust politics produced in him, who had held onto a socialist rationale and let out his antipathies in an exaggerated idyll of the conservative past—for him such words had a deeper meaning. They mark the end of decency. Decency, meaning precisely the reserve of Orwell's own character, the constitutional intolerance of the extreme course, has failed him. Now he is dying. What good has this withholding done? He turns, like Ippolit, against himself, with the cry, not of glad tears of release, but of the jealousy of life, "I have been cheated!" And now the decent man, Winston Smith, is unremittingly punished for the loss. He is given neither an opportunity for redemption nor even the small comfort of dying with his inner life intact. His end must be beyond the last extreme, a species of pure diabolism: it is to the embrace of Big Brother that Orwell steers him, one of the most hideous moments of revenge in literature.

It is beside the point to argue that this revenge is the Party's, which will not allow its victims to die unrepentant, or that Orwell was merely following the "confessions" of the Stalinist trials. These arguments are true, but it is also true that Winston (named, if unconsciously, to honor his conservative principle) was too close to Orwell for his torturer to be an entire stranger. So close a vengeance is always taken on oneself.

The significant point is that Winston yields. The force to which he is subjected is overwhelming, any man would crack. Yet in novels all actions are willed; the force that seems to break the will is in reality the rationalization of its action. Winston's breakdown covers a multiple suicide. There is first of all Orwell's own suicide, committed, according to the reports one hears, in the course of writing the novel and in the year that followed, when he neglected his health and remained active, though with two best-sellers he must have had the means for a change of climate and complete rest. Winston's yielding is reminiscent also of Ippolit's suicide, which the consumptive bungled only that his death might occur as so much the greater an indignity. There is defiance in this indignity, deliberately sought. Both Winston and Ippolit rebel against a world in which everything is possible, in which 2 + 2 no longer equal 4—by yielding. The defiance is marked by the extent of the yielding. Though Winston hasn't even a squeak of defiance left, so much the more defiant is it, as though he were to say, "Take away my last shred of decency, will you? Then here—take everything. Here's lungs and liver, mind and heart and soul!" Everything goes, nothing is saved. "He loved Big Brother."

This is Orwell finally yielding up the lifelong image, the character and style and habits of reason and restraint. I cannot conceive of a greater despair, and if it falls short of the magnificent it is only because Orwell was not a genius. But the mild journalist had at last attained art, expressing the totalitarian agony out of his own, as no English writer had done. He encompassed the world's sickness in his own: in this way, too, it may happen to a man to see totalitarianism "from inside." Whether Orwell's vision was true or false, consistent or not, or even adequate to reality, is a separate question, and not, it seems to me, very important in his case. All that matters is the force of the passion with which the man, who began as a writer in a small way, at last come through. The force with which he ended is the one with which greatness begins. This force, it will be observed, was enough to kill a man.

1950

IRVING HOWE
1984: History as Nightmare

About some books we feel that our reluctance to return to them is the true measure of our admiration. It is hard to suppose that many people go back, from a spontaneous desire, to reread *1984:* there is neither reason nor need to, no one forgets it. The usual distinctions between forgotten details and a vivid general impression mean nothing here, for the book is written out of one passionate breath, each word is bent to a severe discipline of meaning, everything is stripped to the bareness of terror.

Kafka's *The Trial* is also a book of terror, but it is a paradigm and to some extent a puzzle, so that one may lose oneself in the rhythm of the paradigm and play with the parts of the puzzle. Kafka's novel persuades us that life is inescapably hazardous and problematic, but the very "universality" of this idea helps soften its impact: to apprehend the terrible on the plane of metaphysics is to lend it an almost soothing aura. And besides, *The Trial* absorbs one endlessly in its aspect of enigma.

Though not nearly so great a book, *1984* is in some ways more terrible. For it is not a paradigm and hardly a puzzle; whatever enigmas it raises concern not the imagination of the author but the life of our time. It does not take us away from, or beyond, our obsession with immediate social reality, and in reading the book we tend to say—the linguistic clumsiness conceals a deep truth—that the world of 1984 is "more real" than our own. The book appalls us because its terror, far from being inherent in the "human condition," is particular to our century; what haunts us is the sickening awareness that in *1984* Orwell has seized upon those elements of our public life that, given courage and intelligence, were avoidable.

How remarkable a book *1984* really is, can be discovered only after a second reading. It offers true testimony, it speaks for our time. And because it derives from a perception of how our time may end, the book trembles with an eschatological fury that is certain to create among its readers, even those who sincerely believe they admire it, the most powerful kinds of resistance. It already has. Openly in England, more cautiously in America, there has arisen a desire among intellectuals to belittle Orwell's achievement, often in the guise of celebrating his humanity and his "goodness." They feel embarrassed before the apocalyptic desperation of the book, they begin to wonder whether it may not be just a little overdrawn and humorless, they even suspect it is tinged with the hysteria of the death-bed. Nor can it be denied that all of us would feel more comfortable if the book could be cast out. It is a remarkable book.

Whether it is a remarkable novel or a novel at all, seems unimportant. It is not, I suppose, really a novel, or at least it does not satisfy those expectations we have come to have with regard to the novel—expectations that are mainly the heritage of nineteenth century romanticism with its stress upon individual consciousness, psychological analysis and the study of intimate relations. One American critic, a serious critic, reviewed the book under the heading, "Truth Maybe, Not Fiction," as if thereby to demonstrate the strictness with which he held to distinctions of literary genre. Actually, he was demonstrating a certain narrowness of modern taste, for such a response to *1984* is possible only when discriminations are no longer made between fiction and the novel, which is but one kind of fiction though the kind modern readers care for most.

A cultivated eighteenth century reader would never have said of *1984* that it may be true but isn't fiction, for it was then understood that fiction, like poetry, can have many modes and be open to many mixtures;

the novel had not yet established its popular tyranny. What is more, the style of *1984*, which many readers take to be drab or uninspired or "sweaty," would have been appreciated by someone like Defoe, since Defoe would have immediately understood how the pressures of Orwell's subject, like the pressures of his own, demand a gritty and hammering factuality. The style of *1984* is the style of a man whose commitment to a dreadful vision is at war with the nausea to which that vision reduces him. So acute is this conflict that delicacies of phrasing or displays of rhetoric come to seem frivolous—*he has no time, he must get it all down.* Those who fail to see this, I am convinced, have succumbed to the pleasant tyrannies of estheticism; they have allowed their fondness for a cultivated style to blind them to the urgencies of prophetic expression. The last thing Orwell cared about when he wrote *1984,* the last thing he should have cared about, was literature.

Another complaint one often hears is that there are no credible or "three-dimensional" characters in the book. Apart from its rather facile identification of credibility with a particular treatment of character, the complaint involves a failure to see that in some books an extended amount of psychological specification or even dramatic incident can be disastrous. In *1984* Orwell is trying to present the kind of world in which individuality has become obsolete and personality a crime. The whole idea of the self as something precious and inviolable is a *cultural* idea, and as we understand it, a product of the liberal era; but Orwell has imagined a world in which the self, whatever subterranean existence it manages to eke out, is no longer a significant value, not even a value to be violated.

Winston Smith and Julia come through as rudimentary figures because they are slowly learning, and at great peril to themselves, what it means to be human. Their experiment in the rediscovery of the human, which is primarily an experiment in the possibilities of solitude, leads them to cherish two things that are fundamentally hostile to the totalitarian outlook: a life of contemplativeness and the joy of "purposeless"— that is, free—sexual passion. But this experiment cannot go very far, as they themselves know; it is inevitable that they be caught and destroyed.

Partly, that is the meaning and the pathos of the book. Were it possible, in the world of 1984, to show human character in anything resembling genuine freedom, in its play of spontaneous desire and caprice—it would not be the world of 1984. So that in a slightly obtuse way the complaint that Orwell's characters seem thin testifies to the strength of the book, for it is a complaint directed not against his technique but against his primary assumptions.

The book cannot be understood, nor can it be properly valued, simply by resorting to the usual literary categories, for it posits a situation in which these categories are no longer significant. Everything has hardened into politics, the leviathan has swallowed man. About such a world it is, strictly speaking, impossible to write a novel, if only because the human relationships taken for granted in the novel are here suppressed.* The book must first be approached through politics, yet not as a political study or treatise. It is something else, at once a model and a vision—a model of the totalitarian state in its "pure" or "essential" form and a vision of what this state can do to human life. Yet the theme of the conflict between ideology and emotion, as at times their fusion and mutual reinforcement, is still to be found in *1984*, as a dim underground motif. Without this theme, there could be no dramatic conflict in a work of fiction dominated by politics. Winston Smith's effort to reconstruct the old tune about the bells of St. Clement is a token of his desire to regain the condition of humanness, which is here nothing more than a capacity for so "useless" a feeling as nostalgia. Between the tune and Oceania there can be no peace.

1984 projects a nightmare in which politics has displaced humanity and the state has stifled society. In a sense, it is a profoundly antipolitical book, full of hatred for the kind of world in which public claims destroy the possibilities for private life; and this conservative side of Orwell's outlook he suggests, perhaps unconsciously, through the first name of his hero. But if the image of Churchill is thus raised in order to celebrate, a little wryly, the memory of the bad (or as Winston Smith comes to feel, the good) old days, the opposing image of Trotsky is raised, a little skeptically, in order to discover the inner meanings of totalitarian society. When Winston Smith learns to think of Oceania as a problem—which is itself to commit a "crimethink"—he turns to the forbidden work of Emmanuel Goldstein, *The Theory and Practise of Oligarchical Collectivism,* clearly a replica of Trotsky's *The Revolution Betrayed.* The power and intelligence of *1984* partly derives from a tension between these images; even as Orwell understood the need for politics in the modern world, he felt a profound distaste for the ways of political life, and he was honest enough not to try to suppress one or another side of this struggle within himself.

---

* Some people have suggested that *1984* is primarily a symptom of Orwell's psychological condition, the nightmare of a disturbed man who suffered from paranoid fantasies, was greatly troubled by dirt and feared that sexual contact would bring down punishment from those in authority. Apart from its intolerable glibness, such an "explanation" explains either too much or too little. Almost everyone has nightmares and a great many people have ambiguous feelings about sex, but few manage to write books with the power of *1984*. Nightmare the book may be, and no doubt it is grounded, as are all books, in the psychological troubles of its author. But it is also grounded in his psychological health, otherwise it could not penetrate so deeply the social reality of our time. The private nightmare, if it is there, is profoundly related to, and helps us understand, public events.

II

No other book has succeeded so completely in rendering the essential quality of totalitarianism. *1984* is limited in scope; it does not pretend to investigate the genesis of the totalitarian state, nor the laws of its economy, nor the prospect for its survival; it simply evokes the "tone" of life in a totalitarian society. And since it is not a realistic novel, it can treat Oceania as an *extreme instance,* one that might never actually exist but which illuminates the nature of societies that do exist.*

Orwell's profoundest insight is that in a totalitarian world man's life is shorn of dynamic possibilities. The end of life is completely predictable in its beginning, the beginning merely a manipulated preparation for the end. There is no opening for surprise, for that spontaneous animation which is the token of and justification for freedom. Oceanic society may evolve through certain stages of economic development, but the life of its members is static, a given and measured quantity that can neither rise to tragedy nor tumble to comedy. Human personality, as we have come to grasp for it in a class society and hope for it in a classless society, is obliterated; man becomes a function of a process he is never allowed to understand or control. The fetishism of the state replaces the fetishism of commodities.

There have, of course, been unfree societies in the past, yet in most of them it was possible to find an oasis of freedom, if only because none had the resources to enforce total consent. But totalitarianism, which represents a decisive break from the Western tradition, aims to permit no such luxuries; it offers a total "solution" to the problems of the twentieth century, that is, a total distortion of what might be a solution. To be sure, no totalitarian state has been able to reach this degree of "perfection," which Orwell, like a physicist who in his experiment assumes the absence of friction, has assumed for Oceania. But the knowledge that friction can never actually be absent does not make the experiment any the less valuable.

To the degree that the totalitarian state approaches its "ideal" condition, it destroys the margin for unforeseen behavior; as a character in Dostoevsky's *The Possessed* remarks, "only the necessary is necessary." Nor is there a social crevice in which the recalcitrant or independent mind can seek shelter. The totalitarian state assumes that—given modern technology, complete political control, the means of terror and a rationalized contempt for moral tradition—anything is possible. Anything can be done with men, anything with their minds, with history and with

---

* "My novel *1984*," wrote Orwell shortly before his death, "is *not* intended as an attack on socialism, or on the British Labor Party, but as a show-up of the perversions to which a centralized economy is liable. . . . I do not believe that the kind of society I describe necessarily will arrive, but I believe . . . that something resembling it *could* arrive."

words. Reality is no longer something to be acknowledged or experienced or even transformed; it is fabricated according to the need and will of the state, sometimes in anticipation of the future, sometimes as a retrospective improvement upon the past.

But even as Orwell, overcoming the resistance of his own nausea, evoked the ethos of the totalitarian world, he used very little of what is ordinarily called "imagination" in order to show how this ethos stains every aspect of human life. Like most good writers, he understood that imagination is primarily the capacity for apprehending reality, for seeing both clearly and deeply whatever it is that exists. That is why his vision of social horror, if taken as a model rather than a portrait, strikes one as essentially credible, while the efforts of most writers to create utopias or anti-utopias founder precisely on their desire to be scientific or inventive. Orwell understood that social horror consists not in the prevalence of diabolical machines or in the invasion of Martian automatons flashing death rays from mechanical eyes, but in the persistence of inhuman relations among men.

And he understood, as well, the significance of what I can only call the psychology and politics of "one more step." From a bearable neurosis to a crippling psychosis, from a decayed society in which survival is still possible to a totalitarian state in which it is hardly desirable, there may be only "one step." To lay bare the logic of that social regression which leads to totalitarianism Orwell had merely to allow his imagination to take . . . one step.

Consider such typical aspects of Oceanic society as telescreens and the use of children as informers against their parents. There are no telescreens in Russia, but there could well be: nothing in Russian society contradicts the "principle" of telescreens. Informing against parents who are political heretics is not a common practice in the United States, but some people have been deprived of their jobs on the charge of having maintained "prolonged associations" with their parents. To capture the totalitarian spirit, Orwell had merely to allow certain tendencies in modern society to spin forward without the brake of sentiment or humaneness. He could thus make clear the relationship between his model of totalitarianism and the societies we know in our experience, and he could do this without resorting to the clap-trap of science fiction or the crude assumption that we already live in 1984. In imagining the world of 1984 he took only one step, and because he knew how long and terrible a step it was, he had no need to take another.

III

Through a struggle of the mind and an effort of the will that clearly left him exhausted, Orwell came to see—which is far more than simply to understand—what the inner spirit or ethos of totalitarianism is. But it was characteristic of Orwell as a writer that he felt uneasy with a general idea or a total vision; things took on reality for him only as they were particular and concrete. The world of 1984 seems to have had for him the hallucinatory immediacy that Yoknapatawpha County has for Faulkner or London had for Dickens, and even as he ruthlessly subordinated his descriptions to the dominating theme of the book, Orwell succeeded in noting the details of Oceanic society with a painstaking and sometimes uncanny accuracy.

There are first the incidental accuracies of mimicry. Take, as an example, Orwell's grasp of the role played by the scapegoat-enemy of the totalitarian world, the rituals of hate for which he is indispensable, and more appalling, the uncertainty as to whether he even exists or is a useful fabrication of the state. Among the best passages in the book are those in which Orwell imitates Trotsky's style in *The Theory and Practise of Oligarchical Collectivism.* Orwell caught the rhetorical sweep and grandeur of Trotsky's writing, particularly his fondness for using scientific references in non-scientific contexts: "Even after enormous upheavals and seemingly irrevocable changes, the same pattern has always reasserted itself, just as a gyroscope will always return to equilibrium, however far it is pushed one way or another." And in another sentence Orwell beautifully captured Trotsky's way of using a compressed paradox to sum up the absurdity of a whole society: "The fields are cultivated with horse plows while books are written by machinery."

Equally skillful was Orwell's evocation of the physical atmosphere of Oceania, the overwhelming gloomy shabbiness of its streets and houses, the tasteless sameness of the clothes its people wear, the unappetizing gray-pink stew they eat, that eternal bureaucratic stew which seems to go with all modern oppressive institutions. Orwell had not been taken in by the legend that totalitarianism is at least efficient; instead of the usual chromium-and-skyscraper vision of the future, he painted London in 1984 as a composite of the city in its dismal grayness during the last (Second) world war and of the modern Russian cities with their Victorian ostentation and rotting slums. In all of his books Orwell had shown himself only mildly gifted at visual description but remarkably keen at detecting loathsome and sickening odors. He had the best nose of his generation— his mind sometimes betrayed him, his nose never. In the world of 1984, he seems to be suggesting, all of the rubbish of the past, together with some that no one had quite been able to foresee, is brought together.

The rubbish survived, but what of the past itself, the past in which men had managed to live and sometimes with a little pleasure? One of the most poignant scenes in the book is that in which Winston Smith, trying to discover what life was like before the reign of Big Brother, talks to an old prole in a pub. The exchange is unsatisfactory to Smith, since the worker can remember only fragments of disconnected fact and is quite unable to generalize from his memories; but the scene itself is a fine bit of dramatic action, indicating that not only does totalitarian society destroy the past through the obliteration of objective records but that it destroys the memory of the past through a disintegration of individual consciousness. The worker with whom Smith talks remembers that the beer was better before Big Brother (a very important fact) but he cannot really understand Smith's question: "Do you feel that you have more freedom now than you had in those days?" To pose, let alone understand, such a question requires a degree of social continuity, as well as a set of complex assumptions, which Oceania is gradually destroying.

The destruction of social memory becomes a major industry in Oceania, and here of course Orwell was borrowing directly from Stalinism which, as the most "advanced" form of totalitarianism, was infinitely more adept at this job than was fascism. (Hitler burned books, Stalin had them rewritten.) In Oceania the embarrassing piece of paper slides down memory hole—and that is all.

Orwell is similarly acute in noticing the relationship between the totalitarian state and what passes for culture. Novels are produced by machine; the state anticipates all wants, from "cleansed" versions of Byron to pornographic magazines; that vast modern industry which we call "popular culture" has become an important state function. Meanwhile, the language is stripped of words that suggest refinements of attitude or gradations of sensibility.

And with feeling as with language. Oceania seeks to blot out spontaneous affection because it assumes, with good reason, that whatever is uncalculated is subversive. Smith thinks to himself:

> It would not have occurred to [his mother] that an action which is ineffectual thereby becomes meaningless. If you loved someone, you loved him, and when you had nothing else to give, you still gave him love. When the last of the chocolate was gone, his mother had clasped the children in her arms. It was no use, it changed nothing, it did not produce more chocolate, it did not avert the child's death or her own; but it seemed natural for her to do it.

IV

At only a few points can one question Orwell's vision of totalitarianism, and even these involve highly problematic matters. If they are errors at all, it is only to the extent that they drive valid observations too hard: Orwell's totalitarian society is at times more *total* than we can presently imagine.

One such problem has to do with the relation between the state and "human nature." Granted that human nature is itself a cultural concept with a history of change behind it; granted that the pressures of fear and force can produce extreme variations in human conduct. There yet remains the question: to what extent can a terrorist regime suppress or radically alter the fundamental impulses of man? Is there a constant in human nature which no amount of terror or propaganda can destroy?

In Oceania the sexual impulse, while not destroyed, has been remarkably weakened among the members of the Outer Party. For the faithful, sexual energy is transformed into political hysteria. There is a harrowing passage in which Smith remembers his sexual relations with his former wife, a loyal party member who would submit herself once a week, as if for an ordeal and resisting even while insisting, in order to procreate for the party. The only thing she did not feel was pleasure.

Orwell puts the matter with some care:

> The aim of the Party was not merely to prevent men and women from forming loyalties which it might not be able to control. Its real, undeclared purpose was to remove all pleasure from the sexual act. Not love so much as eroticism was the enemy, inside marriage as well as outside it . . . The only recognized purpose of marriage was to beget children for the service of the Party. Sexual intercourse was to be looked on as a slightly disgusting minor operation, like having an enema . . . The Party was trying to kill the sex instinct, or, if it could not be killed, then to distort it and dirty it . . . And so far as the women were concerned, the Party's efforts were largely successful.

That Orwell has here come upon an important tendency in modern life, that the totalitarian state is inherently an enemy of erotic freedom, seems to me indisputable. And we know from the past that the sexual impulse can be heavily suppressed. In Puritan communities, for example, sex was regarded with great suspicion, and it is not hard to imagine that even in marriage the act of love might bring the Puritans very little pleasure. But it should be remembered that in Puritan communities hostility toward sex was interwoven with a powerful faith: men mortified themselves in behalf of God. By contrast, Oceania looks upon faith not merely as suspect but downright dangerous, for its rulers prefer mechanical assent to intellectual fervor or zealous belief. (They have probably read enough history to know that in the Protestant era enthusiasm had a way of turning into individualism.)

Given these circumstances, is it plausible that the Outer Party members would be able to discard erotic pleasure so completely? Is this not cutting too close to the limit of indestructible human needs? I should think that in a society so pervaded by boredom and grayness as Oceania is, there would be a pressing hunger for erotic adventure, to say nothing of experiments in perversion.

A totalitarian society can force people to do many things that violate their social and physical desires; it may even teach them to receive pain with quiet resignation; but I doubt that it can break down the fundamental, if sometimes ambiguous, distinction between pleasure and pain. Man's biological make-up requires him to obtain food, and, with less regularity or insistence, sex; and while society can do a great deal—it has—to dim the pleasures of sex and reduce the desire for food, it seems reasonable to assume that even when consciousness has been blitzed, the "animal drives" of man cannot be violated as thoroughly as Orwell suggests. In the long run, these drives may prove to be one of the most enduring forces of resistance to the totalitarian state.

Does not Orwell imply something of the sort when he shows Winston Smith turning to individual reflection and Julia to private pleasure? What is the source of their rebellion if not the "innate" resistance of their minds and bodies to the destructive pressures of Oceania? It is clear that they are no more intelligent or sensitive—certainly no more heroic— than most Outer Party members. And if their needs as human beings force these two quite ordinary people to rebellion, may not the same thing happen to others?

A related problem concerns Orwell's treatment of the workers in Oceania. The proles, just because they are at the bottom of the heap and perform routine tasks of work, get off rather better than members of the Outer Party: they are granted more privacy, the telescreen does not bawl instructions at them nor watch their every motion, and the secret police seldom troubles them, except to wipe out a talented or independent worker. Presumably Orwell would justify this by saying that the state need no longer fear the workers, so demoralized have they become as individuals and so powerless as a class. That such a situation might arise in the future it would be foolhardy to deny, and in any case Orwell is deliberately pushing things to a dramatic extreme; but we should also notice that nothing of the kind has yet happened, neither the Nazis nor the Stalinists having ever relaxed their control or surveillance of the workers to any significant extent. Orwell has here made the mistake of taking more than "one step" and thereby breaking the tie between the world we know and the world he has imagined.

But his treatment of the proles can be questioned on more fundamental grounds. The totalitarian state can afford no luxury, allow no exception; it cannot tolerate the existence of any group beyond the perimeter of its control; it can never become so secure as to lapse into indifference. Scouring every corner of society for rebels it knows do not exist, the totalitarian state cannot come to rest for any prolonged period of time. To do so would be to risk disintegration. It must always tend toward a condition of self-agitation, shaking and reshaking its members, testing and retesting them in order to insure its power. And since, as Winston Smith concludes, the proles remain one of the few possible sources of revolt, it can hardly seem plausible that Oceania would permit them even the relative freedom Orwell describes.

Finally, there is Orwell's extremely interesting though questionable view of the dynamics of power in a totalitarian state. As he portrays the party oligarchy in Oceania, it is the first ruling class of modern times to dispense with ideology. It makes no claim to be ruling in behalf of humanity, the workers, the nation or anyone but itself; it rejects as naive the rationale of the Grand Inquisitor that he oppresses the ignorant to accomplish their salvation. O'Brien, the representative of the Inner Party, says: "The Party seeks power entirely for its own sake. We are not interested in the good of the others; we are interested solely in power." The Stalinists and Nazis, he adds, had approached this view of power, but only in Oceania has all pretense to serving humanity—that is, all ideology—been discarded.

Social classes have at least one thing in common: an appetite for power. The bourgeoisie sought power, not primarily as an end in itself (whatever that vague phrase might mean), but in order to be free to expand its economic and social activity. The ruling class of the new totalitarian society, especially in Russia, is different, however, from previous ruling classes of our time: it does not think of political power as a means toward a nonpolitical end, as to some extent the bourgeoisie did; it looks upon political power as its essential end. For in a society where there is no private property the distinction between economic and political power becomes invisible.

So far this would seem to bear out Orwell's view. But if the ruling class of the totalitarian state does not conceive of political power as primarily a channel to tangible economic privileges, what *does* political power mean to it?

At least in the West, no modern ruling class has yet been able to dispense with ideology. All have felt an overwhelming need to rationalize their power, to proclaim some admirable objective as a justification for detestable acts. Nor is this mere slyness or hypocrisy; the rulers of a modern society can hardly survive without a certain degree of sincere belief in their own claims. They cling to ideology not merely to win and hold followers, but to give themselves psychological and moral assurance.

Can one imagine a twentieth century ruling class capable of discarding these supports and acknowledging to itself the true nature of its motives? I doubt it. Many Russian bureaucrats, in the relaxation of private cynicism, may look upon their Marxist vocabulary as a useful sham; but they must still cling to some vague assumption that somehow their political conduct rests upon ultimate sanctions. Were this not so, the totalitarian ruling class would find it increasingly difficult, perhaps impossible, to sustain its morale. It would go soft, it would become corrupted in the obvious ways, it would lose the fanaticism that is essential to its survival.

But ideology aside, there remains the enigma of totalitarian power. And it *is* an enigma. Many writers have probed the origins of totalitarianism, the dynamics of its growth, the psychological basis of its appeal, the economic policies it employs when in power. But none of the theorists who study totalitarianism can tell us very much about the "ultimate purpose" of the Nazis or the Stalinists; in the end they come up against the same difficulties as does Winston Smith in *1984* when he says, "I understand HOW: I do not understand WHY."

Toward what end do the rulers of Oceania strive? They want power; they want to enjoy the sense of exercising their power, which means to test their ability to cause those below them to suffer. Yet the question remains, why do they kill millions of people, why do they find pleasure in torturing and humiliating people they know to be innocent? For that matter, why did the Nazis and Stalinists?* What is the image of the world they desire, the vision by which they live?

I doubt that such questions can presently be answered, and it may be that they are not even genuine problems. A movement in which terror and irrationality play so great a role may finally have no goal beyond terror and irrationality; to search for an ultimate end that can be significantly related to its immediate activity may itself be a rationalist fallacy.

Orwell has been criticized by Isaac Deutscher† for succumbing to a "mysticism of cruelty" in explaining the behavior of Oceania's rulers, which means, I suppose, that Orwell does not entirely accept any of the usual socioeconomic theories about the aims of totalitarianism. It happens, however, that neither Mr. Deutscher nor anyone else has yet been able to provide a satisfactory explanation for that systematic excess in destroying human values which is a central trait of totalitarianism. I do not say that the mystery need remain with us forever, since it is possible that in time we shall be able to dissolve it into a series of problems more easily manageable. Meanwhile, however, it seems absurd to attack a writer for acknowledging with rare honesty his sense of helplessness before the "ultimate" meaning of totalitarianism—especially if that writer happens to have given us the most graphic vision of totalitarianism that has yet been composed. For with *1984* we come to the heart of the matter, the whiteness of the whiteness.

V

Even while noting these possible objections to Orwell's book, I have been uneasily aware that they might well be irrelevant—as irrelevant, say, as the objection that no one can be so small as Swift's Lilliputians.

---

* The writers in this collection use the term "Stalinist" in a variety of ways. For some it seems to be little more than a rough synonym for "Communist." Others use it to refer to Stalin's personal terrorist dictatorship during the years between, say, 1927 and 1955. Still others have in mind what they regard as a bureaucratic counterrevolution, of which Stalin was the leader and symbol, against the regime of early Communism. As with many political terms, there is no automatic way of knowing exactly which stress a writer means: one must use one's intelligence and try to infer the appropriate meaning from the context.—Editor

† See Mr. Deutscher's essay, p. 332.

What is more, it is extremely important to note that the world of *1984* is *not* totalitarianism as we know it, but totalitarianism after its world triumph. Strictly speaking, the society of Oceania might be called post-totalitarian. But I have let my objections stand simply because it may help the reader see Orwell's book somewhat more clearly if he considers their possible value and decides whether to accept or reject them.

1984 brings us to the end of the line. Beyond this—one feels or hopes—it is impossible to go. In Orwell's book the political themes of the novels that have been discussed in earlier chapters reach their final and terrible flowering, not perhaps in the way that writers like Dostoevsky or Conrad expected but in ways that establish a continuity of vision and value between the nineteenth and twentieth century political novelists.

There are some writers who live most significantly for their own age; they are writers who help redeem their time by forcing it to accept the truth about itself and thereby saving it, perhaps, from the truth about itself. Such writers, it is possible, will not survive their time, for what makes them so valuable and so endearing to their contemporaries—that mixture of desperate topicality and desperate tenderness—is not likely to be a quality conducive to the greatest art. But it should not matter to us, this possibility that in the future Silone or Orwell will not seem as important as they do for many people in our time. We know what they do for us, and we know that no other writers, including far greater ones, can do it.

In later generations *1984* may have little more than "historic interest." If the world of *1984* does come to pass, no one will read it except perhaps the rulers who will reflect upon its extraordinary prescience. If the world of *1984* does not come to pass, people may well feel that this book was merely a symptom of private disturbance, a nightmare. But we know better: we know that the nightmare is ours.

1956

ISAAC DEUTSCHER
1984—The Mysticism of Cruelty

The author of the following essay is a political analyst and historian who specializes in problems concerning Communism; he is the author of biographies of Stalin and Trotsky, as well as several studies of recent Soviet developments. The point of view that he brings to his analysis of *Nineteen Eighty-Four* is that of an independent radical, Marxist in persuasion, critical of the Stalin dictatorship, but convinced that there still remain in Russia valuable social achievements that recent anti-Communist sentiment has tended to ignore. Deutscher charges Orwell with succumbing to a species of anti-Communist "mysticism" that fails to make any distinctions in modern history except those of a simple black-and-white sort.

Few novels written in this generation have obtained a popularity as great as that of George Orwell's *1984*. Few, if any, have made a similar impact on politics. The title of Orwell's book is a political by-word. The terms coined by him—'Newspeak', 'Oldspeak', 'Mutability of the Past', 'Big Brother', 'Ministry of Truth', 'Thought Police', 'Crimethink', 'Doublethink', 'Hateweek', etc.—have entered the political vocabulary; they occur in most newspaper articles and speeches denouncing Russia and communism. Television and the cinema have familiarized many millions of viewers on both sides of the Atlantic with the menacing face of Big Brother and the nightmare of a supposedly communist Oceania. The novel has served as a sort of an ideological super-weapon in the cold war. As in no other book or document, the convulsive fear of communism, which has swept the West since the end of the Second World War, has been reflected and focused in *1984*.

The cold war has created a 'social demand' for such an ideological weapon just as it creates the demand for physical super-weapons. But the super-weapons are genuine feats of technology and there can be no discrepancy between the uses to which they may be put and the intention of their producers: they are meant to spread death or at least to threaten utter destruction. A book like *1984* may be used without much regard for the author's intention. Some of its features may be torn out of their context, while others, which do not suit the political purpose which the book is made to serve, are ignored or virtually suppressed. Nor need a book like *1984* be a literary masterpiece or even an important and original work to make its impact. Indeed a work of great literary merit is usually too rich in its texture and too subtle in thought and form to lend itself to adventitious exploitation. As a rule, its symbols cannot easily be transformed into hypnotizing bogies, or its ideas turned into slogans. The words of a great poet when they enter the political vocabulary do so by a process of slow, almost imperceptible infiltration, not by a frantic incursion. The literary masterpiece influences the political mind by fertilizing and enriching it from the inside, not by stunning it.

1984 is the work of an intense and concentrated, but also fear-ridden and restricted imagination. A hostile critic has dismissed it as a 'political horror-comic'. This is not a fair description: there are in Orwell's novel certain layers of thought and feeling which raise it well above that level. But it is a fact that the symbolism of *1984* is crude; that its chief symbol, Big Brother, resembles the bogy-man of a rather inartistic nursery tale;

and that Orwell's story unfolds like the plot of a science-fiction film of the cheaper variety, with mechanical horror piling up upon mechanical horror so much that, in the end, Orwell's subtler ideas, his pity for his characters, and his satire on the society of his own days (not of 1984) may fail to communicate themselves to the reader. *1984* does not seem to justify the description of Orwell as the modern Swift, a description for which *Animal Farm* provides some justification. Orwell lacks the richness and subtlety of thought and the philosophical detachment of the great satirist. His imagination is ferocious and at times penetrating, but it lacks width, suppleness, and originality.

The lack of originality is illustrated by the fact that Orwell borrowed the idea of *1984,* the plot, the chief characters, the symbols, and the whole climate of his story from a Russian writer who has remained almost unknown in the West. That writer is Evgenii Zamiatin, and the title of the book which served Orwell as the model is *We.* Like *1984, We* is an 'anti-Utopia', a nightmare vision of the shape of things to come, and a Cassandra cry. Orwell's work is a thoroughly English variation on Zamiatin's theme; and it is perhaps only the thoroughness of Orwell's English approach that gives to his work the originality that it possesses.

A few words about Zamiatin may not be out of place here: there are some points of resemblance in the life stories of the two writers. Zamiatin belonged to an older generation: he was born in 1884 and died in 1937. His early writings, like some of Orwell's, were realistic descriptions of the lower middle class. In his experience the Russian revolution of 1905 played approximately the same role that the Spanish civil war played in Orwell's. He participated in the revolutionary movement, was a member of the Russian Social Democratic Party (to which Bolsheviks and Mensheviks then still belonged), and was persecuted by the Tsarist police. At the ebb of the revolution, he succumbed to a mood of 'cosmic pessimism'; and he severed his connection with the Socialist Party, a thing which Orwell, less consistent and to the end influenced by a lingering loyalty to socialism, did not do. In 1917 Zamiatin viewed the new revolution with cold and disillusioned eyes, convinced that nothing good would come out of it. After a brief imprisonment, he was allowed by the Bolshevik government to go abroad; and it was as an émigré in Paris that he wrote *We* in the early 1920's.

The assertion that Orwell borrowed the main elements of *1984* from Zamiatin is not the guess of a critic with a foible for tracing literary influences. Orwell knew Zamiatin's novel and was fascinated by it. He wrote an essay about it, which appeared in the left-socialist *Tribune,* of which Orwell was Literary Editor, on 4 January 1946, just after the publication of *Animal Farm* and before he began writing *1984.* The essay is remarkable not only as a conclusive piece of evidence, supplied by Orwell himself, on the origin of *1984,* but also as a commentary on the idea underlying both *We* and *1984.*

The essay begins with Orwell saying that after having for years looked in vain for Zamiatin's novel, he had at last obtained it in a French edition (under the title *Nous Autres*), and that he was surprised that it had not been published in England, although an American edition had appeared without arousing much interest. 'So far as I can judge', Orwell went on, 'it is not a book of the first order, but it is certainly an unusual one, and it is astonishing that no English publisher has been enterprising enough to re-issue it.' (He concluded the essay with the words: 'This is a book to look out for when an English version appears.')

Orwell noticed that Aldous Huxley's *Brave New World* 'must be partly derived' from Zamiatin's novel and wondered why this had 'never been pointed out'. Zamiatin's book was, in his view, much superior and more 'relevant to our own situation' than Huxley's. It dealt 'with the rebellion of the primitive human spirit against a rationalized, mechanized, pain-less world'.

'Painless' is not the right adjective: the world of Zamiatin's vision is as full of horrors as is that of *1984*. Orwell himself produced in his essay a succinct catalogue of those horrors so that his essay reads now like a synopsis of *1984*. The members of the society described by Zamiatin, says Orwell, 'have so completely lost their individuality as to be known only by numbers. They live in glass houses . . . which enables the political police, known as the "Guardians", to supervise them more easily. They all wear identical uniforms, and a human being is commonly referred to either as "a number" or a "unif" (uniform).' Orwell remarks in parenthesis that Zamiatin wrote 'before television was invented'. In *1984* this tech-nological refinement is brought in as well as the helicopters from which the police supervise the homes of the citizens of Oceania in the opening passages of the novel. The 'unifs' suggest the 'Proles'. In Zamiatin's soci-ety of the future as in *1984* love is forbidden: sexual intercourse is strictly rationed and permitted only as an unemotional act. 'The Single State is ruled over by a person known as the Benefactor', the obvious prototype of Big Brother.

'The guiding principle of the State is that happiness and freedom are incompatible . . . the Single State has restored his [man's] happiness by removing his freedom.' Orwell describes Zamiatin's chief character as 'a sort of Utopian Billy Brown of London Town' who is 'constantly horrified by the atavistic impulses which seize upon him'. In Orwell's novel that Utopian Billy Brown is christened Winston Smith, and his problem is the same.

For the main *motif* of his plot Orwell is similarly indebted to the Rus-sian writer. This is how Orwell defines it: 'In spite of education and the vigilance of the Guardians, many of the ancient human instincts are still there.' Zamiatin's chief character 'falls in love (this is a crime, of course) with a certain I-330' just as Winston Smith commits the crime of falling in love with Julia. In Zamiatin's as in Orwell's story the love affair is mixed up with the hero's participation in an 'underground resistance movement'. Zamiatin's rebels 'apart from plotting the overthrow of the State, even indulge, at the moment when their curtains are down, in such vices as smoking cigarettes and drinking alcohol'; Winston Smith and Julia indulge in drinking 'real coffee with real sugar' in their hideout over Mr. Charrington's shop. In both novels the crime and the conspiracy are, of course, discovered by the Guardians or the Thought Police; and in both the hero 'is ultimately saved from the consequences of his own folly'.

The combination of 'cure' and torture by which Zamiatin's and Orwell's rebels are 'freed' from the atavistic impulses, until they begin to love Benefactor or Big Brother, are very much the same. In Zamiatin: 'The authorities announce that they have discovered the cause of the recent disorders: it is that some human beings suffer from a disease called imagination. The nerve centre responsible for imagination has now been located, and the disease can be cured by X-ray treatment. D-503 undergoes the operation, after which it is easy for him to do what he has known all along that he ought to do—that is, betray his confederates to the police.' In both novels the act of confession and the betrayal of the woman the hero loves are the curative shocks.

Orwell quotes the following scene of torture from Zamiatin:

'She looked at me, her hands clasping the arms of the chair, until her eyes were completely shut. They took her out, brought her to herself by means of an electric shock, and put her under the bell again. This operation was repeated three times, and not a word issued from her lips.'

In Orwell's scenes of torture the 'electric shocks' and the 'arms of the chair' recur quite often, but Orwell is far more intense, masochistic--sadistic, in his descriptions of cruelty and pain. For instance:

'Without any warning except a slight movement of O'Brien's hand, a wave of pain flooded his body. It was a frightening pain, because he could not see what was happening, and he had the feeling that some mortal injury was being done to him. He did not know whether the thing was really happening, or whether the effect was electrically produced; but his body had been wrenched out of shape, the joints were being slowly torn apart. Although the pain had brought the sweat out on his forehead, the worst of all was the fear that his backbone was about to snap. He set his teeth and breathed hard through his nose, trying to keep silent as long as possible.'

The list of Orwell's borrowings is far from complete; but let us now turn from the plot of the two novels to their underlying idea. Taking up the comparison between Zamiatin and Huxley, Orwell says: 'It is this intuitive grasp of the irrational side of totalitarianism—human sacrifice, cruelty as an end in itself, the worship of a Leader who is credited with divine attributes—that makes Zamiatin's book superior to Huxley's.' It is this, we may add, that made of it Orwell's model. Criticizing

Huxley, Orwell writes that he could find no clear reason why the society of *Brave New World* should be so rigidly and elaborately stratified: 'The aim is not economic exploitation. . . . *There is no power-hunger, no sadism, no hardness of any kind.* Those at the top have no strong motive for staying on the top, and though everyone is happy in a vacuous way, life has become so pointless that it is difficult to believe that such a society could endure.' (My italics.) In contrast, the society of Zamiatin's anti-Utopia could endure, in Orwell's view, because in it the supreme motive of action and the reason for social stratification are not economic exploitation, for which there is no need, but precisely the 'power-hunger, sadism, and hardness' of those who 'stay at the top'. It is easy to recognize in this the *leitmotif* of *1984*.

In Oceania technological development has reached so high a level that society could well satisfy all its material needs and establish equality in its midst. But inequality and poverty are maintained in order to keep Big Brother in power. In the past, says Orwell, dictatorship safeguarded inequality, now inequality safeguards dictatorship. But what purpose does the dictatorship itself serve? 'The party seeks power entirely for its own sake. . . . Power is not a means, it is an end. One does not establish a dictatorship in order to safeguard a revolution; one makes the revolution in order to establish the dictatorship. The object of persecution is persecution. . . . The object of power is power.'

Orwell wondered whether Zamiatin did 'intend the Soviet régime to be the special target of his satire'. He was not sure of this: 'What Zamiatin seems to be aiming at is not any particular country but the implied aims of the industrial civilization. . . . It is evident from *We* that he had a strong leaning towards primitivism. . . . *We* is in effect a study of the Machine, the genie that man has thoughtlessly let out of its bottle and cannot put back again.' The same ambiguity of the author's aim is evident also in *1984*.

Orwell's guess about Zamiatin was correct. Though Zamiatin was opposed to the Soviet régime, it was not exclusively, or even mainly, that régime which he satirized. As Orwell rightly remarked, the early Soviet Russia had few features in common with the supermechanized State of Zamiatin's anti-Utopia. That writer's leaning towards primitivism was in line with a Russian tradition, with Slavophilism and hostility towards the bourgeois West, with the glorification of the *muzhik* and of the old patriarchal Russia, with Tolstoy and Dostoyevsky. Even as an émigré, Zamiatin was disillusioned with the West in the characteristically Russian fashion. At times he seemed half-reconciled with the Soviet régime when it was already producing its Benefactor in the person of Stalin. In so far as he directed the darts of his satire against Bolshevism, he did so on the ground that Bolshevism was bent on replacing the old primitive Russia by the modern, mechanized society. Curiously enough, he set his story in the year 2600; and he seemed to say to the Bolsheviks: this is what Russia will look like if you succeed in giving to your régime the background of Western technology. In Zamiatin, like in some other Russian intellectuals disillusioned with socialism, the hankering after the primitive modes of thought and life was in so far natural as primitivism was still strongly alive in the Russian background.

In Orwell there was and there could be no such authentic nostalgia after the pre-industrial society. Primitivism had no part in his experience and background, except during his stay in Burma, when he was hardly attracted by it. But he was terrified of the uses to which technology might be put by men determined to enslave society; and so he, too, came to question and satirize 'the implied aims of industrial civilization'.

Although his satire is more recognizably aimed at Soviet Russia than Zamiatin's, Orwell saw elements of Oceania in the England of his own days as well, not to speak of the United States. Indeed, the society of *1984* embodies all that he hated and disliked in his own surroundings: the drabness and monotony of the English industrial suburb, the 'filthy and grimy and smelly' ugliness of which he tried to match in his naturalistic, repetitive, and oppressive style; the food rationing and the government controls which he knew in war-time Britain; the 'rubbishy newspapers containing almost nothing except sport, crime, and astrology, sensational five-cent novelettes, films oozing with sex'; and so on. Orwell knew well that newspapers of this sort did not exist in Stalinist Russia, and that the faults of the Stalinist Press were of an altogether different kind. *Newspeak* is much less a satire on the Stalinist idiom than on Anglo-American journalistic 'cablese', which he loathed and with which, as a working journalist, he was well familiar.

It is easy to tell which features of the party of *1984* satirize the British Labour Party rather than the Soviet Communist Party. Big Brother and his followers make no attempt to indoctrinate the working class, an omission Orwell would have been the last to ascribe to Stalinism. His Proles 'vegetate': 'heavy work, petty quarrels, films, gambling . . . fill their mental horizon.' Like the rubbishy newspapers and the films oozing with sex, so gambling, the new opium of the people, does not belong to the Russian scene. The Ministry of Truth is a transparent caricature of London's war-time Ministry of Information. The monster of Orwell's vision is, like every nightmare, made up of all sorts of faces and features and shapes, familiar and unfamiliar. Orwell's talent and originality are evident in the domestic aspect of his satire. But in the vogue which *1984* has enjoyed that aspect has rarely been noticed.

1984 is a document of dark disillusionment not only with Stalinism but with every form and shade of socialism. It is a cry from the abyss of despair. What plunged Orwell into that abyss? It was without any doubt the spectacle of the Stalinist Great Purges of 1936–8, the repercussions of which he experienced in Catalonia. As a man of sensitivity and integrity, he could not react to the purges otherwise than with anger and horror. His conscience could not be soothed by the Stalinist justifications and sophisms which at the time did soothe the conscience of, for instance, Arthur Koestler, a writer of greater brilliance and sophistication but of less moral resolution. The Stalinist justifications and sophisms were both *beneath* and *above* Orwell's level of reasoning—they were beneath and above the common sense and the stubborn empiricism of Billy Brown of London Town, with whom Orwell identified himself even in his most rebellious or revolutionary moments. He was outraged, shocked, and shaken in his beliefs. He had never been a member of the Communist Party. But, as an adherent of the semi-Trotskyist P.O.U.M., he had, despite all his reservations, tacitly assumed a certain community of purpose and solidarity with the Soviet régime through all its vicissitudes and transformations, which were to him somewhat obscure and exotic.

The purges and their Spanish repercussions not only destroyed that community of purpose. Not only did he see the gulf between Stalinists and anti-Stalinists opening suddenly inside embattled Republican Spain. This, the immediate effect of the purges, was overshadowed by 'the irrational side of totalitarianism—human sacrifice, cruelty as an end in itself, the worship of a Leader', and 'the colour of the sinister slave-civilizations of the ancient world' spreading over contemporary society.

Like most British socialists, Orwell had never been a Marxist. The dialectical-materialist philosophy had always been too abstruse for him. From instinct rather than consciousness he had been a staunch rationalist. The distinction between the Marxist and the rationalist is of some importance. Contrary to an opinion widespread in Anglo-Saxon countries, Marxism is not at all rationalist in its philosophy: it does not assume that human beings are, as a rule, guided by rational motives and that they can be argued into socialism by reason. Marx himself begins *Das Kapital* with the elaborate philosophical and historical inquiry into the 'fetishistic' modes of thought and behaviour rooted in 'commodity production'—that is, in man's work for, and dependence on, a market. The class struggle, as Marx describes it, is anything but a rational process. This does not prevent the rationalists of socialism describing themselves sometimes as Marxists. But the authentic Marxist may claim to be mentally better prepared than the rationalist is for the manifestations of irrationality in human affairs, even for such manifestations as Stalin's Great Purges. He may feel upset or mortified by them but he need not feel shaken in his *Weltanschauung*, while the rationalist is lost and helpless when the irrationality of the human existence suddenly stares him in the face. If he clings to his rationalism, reality eludes him. If he pursues reality and tries to grasp it, he must part with his rationalism.

Orwell pursued reality and found himself bereft of his conscious and unconscious assumptions about life. In his thoughts he could not hence-forth get away from the Purges. Directly and indirectly, they supplied the subject matter for nearly all that he wrote after his Spanish experi-ence. This was an honourable obsession, the obsession of a mind not in-clined to cheat itself comfortably and to stop grappling with an alarming moral problem. But grappling with the Purges, his mind became infected by their irrationality. He found himself incapable of explaining what was happening in terms which were familiar to him, the terms of empirical common sense. Abandoning rationalism, he increasingly viewed reality through the dark glasses of a quasi-mystical pessimism.

It has been said that *1984* is the figment of the imagination of a dying man. There is some truth in this, but not the whole truth. It was indeed with the last feverish flicker of life in him that Orwell wrote this book. Hence the extraordinary, gloomy intensity of his vision and language, and the almost physical immediacy with which he suffered the tortures which his creative imagination was inflicting on his chief character. He identified his own withering physical existence with the decayed and shrunken body of Winston Smith, to whom he imparted and in whom he invested, as it were, his own dying pangs. He projected the last spasms of his own suffering into the last pages of his last book. But the main expla-nation of the inner logic of Orwell's disillusionment and pessimism lies not in the writer's death agonies, but in the experience and the thought of the living man and in his convulsive reaction from his defeated ration-alism.

'I understand HOW: I do not understand WHY' is the refrain of *1984*. Winston Smith knows how Oceania functions and how its elaborate mechanism of tyranny works, but he does not know what is its ultimate cause and ultimate purpose. He turns for the answer to the pages of '*the book*', the mysterious classic of *crimethink*, the authorship of which is attributed to Emmanuel Goldstein, the inspirer of the conspiratorial Brotherhood. But he manages to read through only those chapters of '*the book*' which deal with the HOW. The Thought Police descends upon him just when he is about to begin reading the chapters which promise to explain WHY; and so the question remains unanswered.

This was Orwell's own predicament. He asked the Why not so much about the Oceania of his vision as about Stalinism and the Great Purges. At one point he certainly turned for the answer to Trotsky: it was from Trotsky-Bronstein that he took the few sketchy biographical data and even the physiognomy and the Jewish name for Emmanuel Goldstein; and the fragments of '*the book*', which take up so many pages in *1984*, are an obvious, though not very successful, paraphrase of Trotsky's *The Rev-olution Betrayed*. Orwell was impressed by Trotsky's moral grandeur and at the same time he partly distrusted it and partly doubted its authentic-ity. The ambivalence of his view of Trotsky finds its counterpart in Win-

ston Smith's attitude towards Goldstein. To the end Smith cannot find
out whether Goldstein and the Brotherhood have ever existed in reality,
and whether '*the* book' was not concocted by the Thought Police. The
barrier between Trotsky's thought and himself, a barrier which Orwell
could never break down, was Marxism and dialectical materialism. He
found in Trotsky the answer to How, not to Why.

But Orwell could not content himself with historical agnosticism. He
was anything but a sceptic. His mental make-up was rather that of the
fanatic, determined to get an answer, a quick and a plain answer, to his
question. He was now tense with distrust and suspicion and on the look-
out for the dark conspiracies hatched by *them* against the decencies of
Billy Brown of London Town. *They* were the Nazis, the Stalinists, and—
Churchill and Roosevelt, and ultimately all who had any *raison d'état* to
defend, for at heart Orwell was a simple-minded anarchist and, in his
eyes, any political movement forfeited its *raison d'être* the moment it
acquired a *raison d'état*. To analyse a complicated social background, to
try and unravel tangles of political motives, calculations, fears and suspi-
cions, and to discern the compulsion of circumstances behind *their* action
was beyond him. Generalizations about social forces, social trends, and
historic inevitabilities made him bristle with suspicion. Yet, without
some such generalizations, properly and sparingly used, no realistic answer could be given to the question which preoccupied Orwell. His gaze
was fixed on the trees, or rather on a single tree, in front of him, and he
was almost blind to the wood. Yet his distrust of historical generalizations led him in the end to adopt and to cling to the oldest, the most
banal, the most abstract, the most metaphysical, and the most barren of
all generalizations: all *their* conspiracies and plots and purges and diplo-
matic deals had one source and one source only—'sadistic power-hunger'.
Thus he made his jump from workaday, rationalistic common sense to
the mysticism of cruelty which inspires *1984*.*

In *1984* man's mastery over the machine has reached so high a level
that society is in a position to produce plenty for everybody and put an
end to inequality. But poverty and inequality are maintained only to

---

* This opinion is based on personal reminiscences as well as on an analysis of Orwell's work.
During the last war Orwell seemed attracted by the critical, then somewhat unusual,
tenor of my commentaries on Russia which appeared in *The Economist*, *The Observer*, and
Tribune. (Later we were both *The Observer's* correspondents in Germany and occasionally
shared a room in a Press camp.) However, it took me little time to become aware of the
differences of approach behind our seeming agreement. I remember that I was taken
aback by the stubbornness with which Orwell dwelt on 'conspiracies', and that his political reasoning struck me as a Freudian sublimation of persecution mania. He was, for
instance, unshakably convinced that Stalin, Churchill, and Roosevelt consciously plotted
to divide the world, and to divide it for good, among themselves, and to subjugate it in
common. (I can trace the idea of Oceania, Eastasia, and Eurasia back to that time.) '*They*
are all power-hungry,' he used to repeat. When once I pointed out to him that underneath
the apparent solidarity of the Big Three one could discern clearly the conflict between

satisfy the sadistic urges of Big Brother. Yet we do not even know whether Big Brother really exists—he may be only a myth. It is the collective cruelty of the party (not necessarily of its individual members who may be intelligent and well-meaning people), that torments Oceania. Totalitarian society is ruled by a disembodied sadism. Orwell imagined that he had 'transcended' the familiar and, as he thought, increasingly irrelevant concepts of social class and class interest. But in these Marxist generalizations, the interest of a social class bears at least some specific relation to the individual interests and the social position of its members, even if the class interest does not represent a simple sum of the individual interests. In Orwell's party the whole bears no relation to the parts. The party is not a social body actuated by any interest or purpose. It is a phantom-like emanation of all that is foul in human nature. It is the metaphysical, mad and triumphant, Ghost of Evil.

Of course, Orwell intended *1984* as a warning. But the warning defeats itself because of its underlying boundless despair. Orwell saw totalitarianism as bringing history to a standstill. Big Brother is invincible: 'If you want a picture of the future, imagine a boot stamping on a human face—for ever.' He projected the spectacle of the Great Purges on to the future, and he saw it fixed there for ever, because he was not capable of grasping the events realistically, in their complex historical context. To be sure, the events were highly 'irrational'; but he who because of this treats them irrationally is very much like the psychiatrist whose mind becomes unhinged by dwelling too closely with insanity. *1984* is in effect not so much a warning as a piercing shriek announcing the advent of the Black Millennium, the Millennium of damnation.

The shriek, amplified by all the 'mass-media' of our time, has frightened millions of people. But it has not helped them to see more clearly the issues with which the world is grappling; it has not advanced their understanding. It has only increased and intensified the waves of panic and hate that run through the world and obfuscate innocent minds. *1984* has taught millions to look at the conflict between East and West in terms of black and white, and it has shown them a monster bogy and a monster scapegoat for all the ills that plague mankind.

At the onset of the atomic age, the world is living in a mood of Apocalyptic horror. That is why millions of people respond so passionately to the Apocalyptic vision of a novelist. The Apocalyptic atomic and hydro-

---

them, already coming to the surface, Orwell was so startled and incredulous that he at once related our conversation in his column in *Tribune*, and added that he saw no sign of the approach of the conflict of which I spoke. This was by the time of the Yalta conference, or shortly thereafter, when not much foresight was needed to see what was coming. What struck me in Orwell was his lack of historical sense and of psychological insight into political life coupled with an acute, though narrow, penetration into some aspects of politics and with an incorruptible firmness of conviction.

gen monsters, however, have not been let loose by Big Brother. The chief predicament of contemporary society is that it has not yet succeeded in adjusting its way of life and its social and political institutions to the prodigious advance of its technological knowledge. We do not know what has been the impact of the atomic and hydrogen bombs on the thoughts of millions in the East, where anguish and fear may be hidden behind the façade of a facile (or perhaps embarrassed?) official optimism. But it would be dangerous to blind ourselves to the fact that in the West millions of people may be inclined, in their anguish and fear, to flee from their own responsibility for mankind's destiny and to vent their anger and despair on the giant Bogy-cum-Scapegoat which Orwell's *1984* has done so much to place before their eyes. . . .

'Have you read this book? You must read it, sir. Then you will know why we must drop the atom bomb on the Bolshies!' With these words a blind, miserable news-vendor recommended to me *1984* in New York, a few weeks before Orwell's death.

Poor Orwell, could he ever imagine that his own book would become so prominent an item in the programme of Hate Week?

1954

LIONEL TRILLING
George Orwell and the Politics of Truth

The following essay is concerned less with *Nineteen Eighty-Four* itself than with the larger cultural and moral significance of Orwell's career. Written with an eye toward the liberal audience of the post-World War II era, Trilling's essay presents Orwell as an example of rectitude and candor that intellectuals ought to emulate. Orwell is seen as especially important because he did not hesitate to tell the truth about the Communists long before it became fashionable to do so.

Lionel Trilling, author of outstanding critical studies collected in such works as *The Liberal Imagination* (1950), *The Opposing Self* (1955), and *Sincerity and Authenticity* (1972), was for many years, until his death in 1975, professor of English at Columbia University and one of our outstanding literary critics. During the 1950s he was especially concerned with the problems faced by American liberals as they tried to work out a moral and political response to the totalitarianism of both left and right.

George Orwell's *Homage to Catalonia* is one of the important documents of our time. It is a very modest book—it seems to say the least that can be said on a subject of great magnitude. But in saying the least it says the most. Its manifest subject is a period of the Spanish Civil War, in which, for some months, until he was almost mortally wounded, its author fought as a soldier in the trenches. Everyone knows that the Spanish war was a decisive event of our epoch, everyone said so when it was being fought, and everyone was right. But the Spanish war lies a decade and a half behind us, and nowadays our sense of history is being destroyed by the nature of our history—our memory is short and it grows shorter under the rapidity of the assault of events. What once occupied all our minds and filled the musty meeting halls with the awareness of heroism and destiny has now become chiefly a matter for the historical scholar. George Orwell's book would make only a limited claim upon our attention if it were nothing more than a record of personal experiences in the Spanish war. But it is much more than this. It is a testimony to the nature of modern political life. It is also a demonstration on the part of its author of one of the right ways of confronting that life. Its importance is therefore of the present moment and for years to come.

A politics which is presumed to be available to everyone is a relatively new thing in the world. We do not yet know very much about it. Nor have most of us been especially eager to learn. In a politics presumed to be available to everyone, ideas and ideals play a great part. And those of us who set store by ideas and ideals have never been quite able to learn that, just because they do have power nowadays, there is a direct connection between their power and another kind of power, the old, unabashed, cynical power of force. We are always being surprised by this. The extent to which Communism made use of unregenerate force was perfectly clear years ago, but many of us found it impossible to acknowledge this fact because Communism spoke boldly to our love of ideas and ideals. We tried as hard as we could to believe that politics might be an idyl, only to discover that what we took to be a political pastoral was really a grim military campaign or a murderous betrayal of political allies, or that what we insisted on calling agrarianism was in actuality a new imperialism. And in the personal life what was undertaken by many good people as a moral commitment of the most disinterested kind turned out to be an engagement to an ultimate immorality. The evidence of this is to be found in a whole literary genre with which we have become familiar in the last decade, the personal confession of involvement and then of disillusionment with Communism.

Orwell's book, in one of its most significant aspects, is about disillusionment with Communism, but it is not a confession. I say this because it is one of the important positive things to say about *Homage to Catalonia*, but my saying it does not imply that I share the *a priori* antagonistic feelings of many people toward those books which, on the basis of experience, expose and denounce the Communist party. About such books people of liberal inclination often make uneasy and rather vindictive jokes.

The jokes seem to me unfair and in bad taste. There is nothing shameful
in the nature of these books. There is a good chance that the commitment
to Communism was made in the first place for generous reasons, and it is
certain that the revulsion was brought about by more than sufficient
causes. And clearly there is nothing wrong in wishing to record the painful experience and to draw conclusions from it. Nevertheless, human nature being what it is—and in the uneasy readers of such books as well as
in the unhappy writers of them—it is a fact that public confession does
often appear in an unfortunate light, that its moral tone is less simple
and true than we might wish it to be. But the moral tone of Orwell's book
is uniquely simple and true. Orwell's ascertaining of certain political
facts was not the occasion for a change of heart, or for a crisis of the soul.
What he learned from his experiences in Spain of course pained him very
much, and it led him to change his course of conduct. But it did not
destroy him; it did not, as people say, cut the ground from under him. It
did not shatter his faith in what he had previously believed, nor weaken
his political impulse, nor even change its direction. It produced not a
moment of guilt or self-recrimination.

Perhaps this should not seem so very remarkable. Yet who can doubt
that it constitutes in our time a genuine moral triumph? It suggests that
Orwell was an unusual kind of man, that he had a temper of mind and
heart which is now rare, although we still respond to it when we see it.

It happened by a curious chance that on the day I agreed to write this
essay as the introduction to the new edition of *Homage to Catalonia*, and
indeed at the very moment that I was reaching for the telephone to tell
the publisher that I would write it, a young man, a graduate student of
mine, came in to see me, the purpose of his visit being to ask what I
thought about his doing an essay on George Orwell. My answer, naturally, was ready, and when I had given it and we had been amused and
pleased by the coincidence, he settled down for a chat about our common
subject. But I asked him not to talk about Orwell. I didn't want to dissi-
pate in talk what ideas I had, and also I didn't want my ideas crossed with
his, which were sure to be very good. So for a while we merely exchanged
bibliographical information, asking each other which of Orwell's books
we had read and which we owned. But then, as if he could not resist
making at least one remark about Orwell himself, he said suddenly in a
very simple and matter-of-fact way, "He was a virtuous man." And we sat
there, agreeing at length about this statement, finding pleasure in talking about it.

It was an odd statement for a young man to make nowadays, and I
suppose that what we found so interesting about it was just this oddity—
its point was in its being an old-fashioned thing to say. It was archaic in
its bold commitment of sentiment, and it used an archaic word with an
archaic simplicity. Our pleasure was not merely literary, not just a re-

sponse to the remark's being so appropriate to Orwell, in whom there was indeed a quality of an earlier and simpler day. We were glad to be able to say it about anybody. One doesn't have the opportunity very often. Not that there are not many men who are good, but there are few men who, in addition to being good, have the simplicity and sturdiness and activity which allow us to say of them that they are virtuous men, for somehow to say that a man "is good," or even to speak of a man who "is virtuous," is not the same thing as saying, "He is a virtuous man." By some quirk of the spirit of the language the form of that sentence brings out the primitive meaning of the word virtuous, which is not merely moral goodness, but also fortitude and strength in goodness.

Orwell, by reason of the quality that permits us to say of him that he was a virtuous man, is a figure in our lives. He was not a genius, and this is one of the remarkable things about him. His not being a genius is an element of the quality that makes him what I am calling a figure.

It has been some time since we in America have had literary figures—that is, men who live their visions as well as write them, who *are* what they write, whom we think of as standing for something as men because of what they have written in their books. They preside, as it were, over certain ideas and attitudes. Mark Twain was in this sense a figure for us, and so was William James. So too were Thoreau, and Whitman, and Henry Adams, and Henry James, although posthumously and rather uncertainly. But when in our more recent literature the writer is anything but anonymous, he is likely to be ambiguous and unsatisfactory as a figure, like Sherwood Anderson, or Mencken, or Wolfe, or Dreiser. There is something about the American character that does not take to the idea of the figure as the English character does. In this regard, the English are closer to the French than to us. Whatever the legend to the contrary, the English character is more strongly marked than ours, less reserved, less ironic, more open in its expression of willfulness and eccentricity and cantankerousness. Its manners are cruder and bolder. It is a demonstrative character—it shows itself, even shows off. Santayana, when he visited England, quite gave up the common notion that Dickens' characters are caricatures. One can still meet an English snob so thunderingly shameless in his worship of the aristocracy, so explicit and demonstrative in his adoration, that a careful, modest, ironic American snob would be quite bewildered by him. And in modern English literature there have been many writers whose lives were demonstrations of the principles which shaped their writing. They lead us to be aware of the moral personalities that stand behind the work. The two Lawrences, different as they were, were alike in this: that they assumed the roles of their belief and acted them out on the stage of the world. In different ways this was true of Yeats, and of Shaw, and even of Wells. It is true of T. S. Eliot, for all that he has spoken against the claims of personality in literature. Even E. M. Forster, who makes so much of privacy, acts out in public the role of the private man, becoming for us the very spirit of the private life. He is not merely a writer, he is a figure.

Orwell takes his place with these men as a figure. In one degree or another they are geniuses, and he is not; if we ask what it is he stands for, what he is the figure of, the answer is: the virtue of not being a genius, of fronting the world with nothing more than one's simple, direct, undeceived intelligence, and a respect for the powers one does have, and the work one undertakes to do. We admire geniuses, we love them, but they discourage us. They are great concentrations of intellect and emotion, we feel that they have soaked up all the available power, monopolizing it and leaving none for us. We feel that if we cannot be as they, we can be nothing. Beside them we are so plain, so hopelessly threadbare. How they glitter, and with what an imperious way they seem to deal with circumstances, even when they are wrong! Lacking their patents of nobility, we might as well quit. This is what democracy has done to us, alas—told us that genius is available to anyone, that the grace of ultimate prestige may be had by anyone, that we may all be princes and potentates, or saints and visionaries and holy martyrs, of the heart and mind. And then when it turns out that we are no such thing, it permits us to think that we aren't much of anything at all. In contrast with this cozening trick of democracy, how pleasant seems the old, reactionary Anglican phrase that used to drive people of democratic leanings quite wild with rage—"my station and its duties."

Orwell would very likely have loathed that phrase, but in a way he exemplifies its meaning. And it is a great relief, a fine sight, to see him doing this. His novels are good, quite good, some better than others, some of them surprising us by being so very much better than their modesty leads us to suppose they can be, all of them worth reading; but they are clearly not the work of a great or even of a "born" novelist. In my opinion, his satire on Stalinism, *Animal Farm*, was overrated—I think people were carried away by someone's reviving systematic satire for serious political purposes. His critical essays are almost always very fine, but sometimes they do not fully meet the demands of their subject—as, for example, the essay on Dickens. And even when they are at their best, they seem to have become what they are chiefly by reason of the very plainness of Orwell's mind, his simple ability to look at things in a downright, undeceived way. He seems to be serving not some dashing daimon but the plain, solid Gods of the Copybook Maxims. He is not a genius— what a relief! What an encouragement. For he communicates to us the sense that what he has done any one of us could do.

Or could do if we but made up our mind to do it, if we but surrendered a little of the cant that comforts us, if for a few weeks we paid no attention to the little group with which we habitually exchange opinions, if we took our chance of being wrong or inadequate, if we looked at things simply and directly, having in mind only our intention of finding out what they really are, not the prestige of our great intellectual act of looking at them. He liberates us. He tells us that we can understand our political and social life merely by looking around us; he frees us from the need for the inside dope. He implies that our job is not to be intellectual, certainly not to be intellectual in this fashion or that, but merely to be intelligent according to our lights—he restores the old sense of the democracy of the mind, releasing us from the belief that the mind can work only in a technical, professional way and that it must work competitively. He has the effect of making us believe that we may become full members of the society of thinking men. That is why he is a figure for us.

In speaking thus of Orwell, I do not mean to imply that his birth was presided over only by the Gods of the Copybook Maxims and not at all by the good fairies, or that he had no daimon. The good fairies gave him very fine free gifts indeed. And he had a strong daimon, but it was of an old-fashioned kind and it constrained him to the paradox—for such it is in our time—of taking seriously the Gods of the Copybook Maxims and putting his gifts at their service. Orwell responded to truths of more than one kind, to the bitter, erudite truths of the modern time as well as to the older and simpler truths. He would have quite understood what Karl Jaspers means when he recommends the "decision to renounce the absolute claims of the European humanistic spirit, to think of it as a stage of development rather than the living content of faith." But he was not interested in this development. What concerned him was survival, which he connected with the old simple ideas that are often not ideas at all but beliefs, preferences, and prejudices. In the modern world these had for him the charm and audacity of newly discovered truths. Involved as so many of us are, at least in our literary lives, in a bitter metaphysics of human nature, it shocks and dismays us when Orwell speaks in praise of such things as responsibility, and orderliness in the personal life, and fair play, and physical courage—even of snobbery and hypocrisy because they sometimes help to shore up the crumbling ramparts of the moral life.

It is hard to find personalities in the contemporary world who are analogous to Orwell. We have to look for men who have considerable intellectual power but who are not happy in the institutionalized life of intellectuality; who have a feeling for an older and simpler time, and a guiding awareness of the ordinary life of the people, yet without any touch of the sentimental malice of populism; and a strong feeling for the commonplace; and a direct, unabashed sense of the nation, even a conscious love of it. This brings Péguy to mind, and also Chesterton, and I think that Orwell does have an affinity with these men—he was probably unaware of it—which tells us something about him. But Péguy has been dead for quite forty years, and Chesterton* (it is a pity) is at the moment rather dim for us, even for those of us who are Catholics. And of course Orwell's affinity with these men is limited by their Catholicism, for although Orwell admired some of the effects and attitudes of religion, he seems to have had no religious tendency in his nature, or none that went beyond what used to be called natural piety.

In some ways he seems more the contemporary of William Cobbett and William Hazlitt than of any man of our own century. Orwell's radicalism, like Cobbett's, refers to the past and to the soil. This is not uncommon nowadays in the social theory of literary men, but in Orwell's attitude there is none of the implied aspiration to aristocracy which so often marks literary agrarian ideas; his feeling for the land and the past simply served to give his radicalism a conservative—a conserving—cast, which is in itself attractive, and to protect his politics from the ravages of ideology. Like Cobbett, he does not dream of a new kind of man, he is content with the old kind, and what moves him is the desire that this old kind of man should have freedom, bacon, and proper work. He had the passion for the literal actuality of life as it is really lived which makes Cobbett's *Rural Rides* a classic, although a forgotten one; his own *The Road to Wigan Pier* and *Down and Out in Paris and London* are in its direct line. And it is not the least interesting detail in the similarity of the two men that both had a love affair with the English language. Cobbett, the self-educated agricultural laborer and sergeant major, was said by one of his enemies to handle the language better than anyone of his time, and he wrote a first-rate handbook of grammar and rhetoric; Orwell was obsessed by the deterioration of the English language in the hands of the journalists and pundits, and nothing in *Nineteen Eighty-Four* is more memorable than his creation of Newspeak.

Orwell's affinity with Hazlitt is, I suspect, of a more intimate temperamental kind, although I cannot go beyond the suspicion, for I know much less about Orwell as a person than about Hazlitt. But there is an unquestionable similarity in their intellectual temper which leads them to handle their political and literary opinions in much the same way. Hazlitt remained a Jacobin all his life, but his unshakable opinions never kept him from giving credit when it was deserved by a writer of the opposite persuasion, not merely out of chivalrous generosity but out of respect for the truth. He was the kind of passionate democrat who could question whether democracy could possibly produce great poetry, and his essays in praise of Scott and Coleridge, with whom he was in intense political disagreement, prepare us for Orwell on Yeats and Kipling.

---

* G. K. Chesterton (1874–1936) was an English man-of-letters who espoused Rom n Catholicism toward the end of his life. Charles Péguy (1873–1914) was a French writer who began as an independent socialist and in his later years turned to a personal version of Catholicism.—Editor

The old-fashionedness of Orwell's temperament can be partly explained by the nature of his relation to his class. This was by no means simple. He came from that part of the middle class whose sense of its status is disproportionate to its income, his father having been a subordinate officer in the Civil Service of India, where Orwell was born. (The family name was Blair, and Orwell was christened Eric Arthur; he changed his name, for rather complicated reasons, when he began to write.) As a scholarship boy he attended the expensive preparatory school of which Cyril Connolly has given an account in *Enemies of Promise*. Orwell appears there as a school "rebel" and "intellectual." He was later to write of the absolute misery of the poor boy at a snobbish school. He went to Eton on a scholarship, and from Eton to Burma, where he served in the police. He has spoken with singular honesty of the ambiguousness of his attitude in the imperialist situation. He disliked authority and the manner of its use, and he sympathized with the Burmese; yet at the same time he saw the need for authority and he used it, and he was often exasperated by the natives. When he returned to England on leave after five years of service, he could not bring himself to go back to Burma. It was at this time that, half voluntarily, he sank to the lower depths of poverty. This adventure in extreme privation was partly forced upon him, but partly it was undertaken to expiate the social guilt which he felt he had incurred in Burma. The experience seems to have done what was required of it. A year as a casual worker and vagrant had the effect of discharging Orwell's guilt, leaving him with an attitude toward the working class that was entirely affectionate and perfectly without sentimentality.

His experience of being declassed, and the effect which it had upon him, go far toward defining the intellectual quality of Orwell and the particular work he was to do. In the thirties the middle-class intellectuals made it a moral fashion to avow their guilt toward the lower classes and to repudiate their own class tradition. So far as this was nothing more than a moral fashion, it was a moral anomaly. And although no one can read history without being made aware of what were the grounds of this attitude, yet the personal claim to a historical guilt yields but an ambiguous principle of personal behavior, a still more ambiguous basis of thought. Orwell broke with much of what the English upper middle class was and admired. But his clear, uncanting mind saw that, although the morality of history might come to harsh conclusions about the middle class and although the practicality of history might say that its day was over, there yet remained the considerable residue of its genuine virtues. The love of personal privacy, of order, of manners, the ideal of fairness and responsibility—these are very simple virtues indeed and they scarcely constitute perfection of either the personal or the social life. Yet they still might serve to judge the present and to control the future.

Orwell could even admire the virtues of the lower middle class, which an intelligentsia always finds it easiest to despise. His remarkable novel, *Keep the Aspidistra Flying*, is a *summa* of all the criticisms of a commercial civilization that have ever been made, and it is a detailed demonstration of the bitter and virtually hopeless plight of the lower-middle-class man. Yet it insists that to live even in this plight is not without its stubborn joy. Péguy spoke of "fathers of families, those heroes of modern life"—Orwell's novel celebrates this biological-social heroism by leading its mediocre, middle-aging poet from the depths of splenetic negation to the acknowledgment of the happiness of fatherhood, thence to an awareness of the pleasures of marriage, and of an existence which, while it does not gratify his ideal conception of himself, is nevertheless his own. There is a dim, elegiac echo of Defoe and of the early days of the middle-class ascendancy as Orwell's sad young man learns to cherish the small personal gear of life, his own bed and chairs and saucepans—his own aspidistra, the ugly, stubborn, organic emblem of survival.

We may say that it was on his affirmation of the middle-class virtues that Orwell based his criticism of the liberal intelligentsia. The characteristic error of the middle-class intellectual of modern times is his tendency to abstractness and absoluteness, his reluctance to connect idea with fact, especially with personal fact. I cannot recall that Orwell ever related his criticism of the intelligentsia to the implications of *Keep the Aspidistra Flying*, but he might have done so, for the prototypical act of the modern intellectual is his abstracting himself from the life of the family. It is an act that has something about it of ritual thaumaturgy—at the beginning of our intellectual careers we are like nothing so much as those young members of Indian tribes who have had a vision or a dream which gives them power on condition that they withdraw from the ordinary life of the tribe. By intellectuality we are freed from the thralldom to the familial commonplace, from the materiality and concreteness by which it exists, the hardness of the cash and the hardness of getting it, the inelegance and intractability of family things. It gives us power over intangibles and imponderables, such as Beauty and Justice, and it permits us to escape the cosmic ridicule which in our youth we suppose is inevitably directed at those who take seriously the small concerns of the material quotidian world, which we know to be inadequate and doomed by the very fact that it is so absurdly *conditioned*—by things, habits, local and temporary customs, and the foolish errors and solemn absurdities of the men of the past.

The gist of Orwell's criticism of the liberal intelligentsia was that they refused to understand the conditioned nature of life. He never quite puts it in this way but this is what he means. He himself knew what war and revolution were really like, what government and administration were really like. From firsthand experience he knew what communism was.

He could truly imagine what nazism was. At a time when most intellectuals still thought of politics as a nightmare abstraction, pointing to the
fearfulness of the nightmare as evidence of their sense of reality, Orwell
was using the imagination of a man whose hands and eyes and whole
body were part of his thinking apparatus. Shaw had insisted upon remaining sublimely unaware of the Russian actuality; Wells had pooh-
poohed the threat of Hitler and had written off as anachronisms the very
forces that were at the moment shaping the world—racial pride, leader-
worship, religious belief, patriotism, love of war. These men had trained
the political intelligence of the intelligentsia, who now, in their love of
abstractions, in their wish to repudiate the anachronisms of their own
emotions, could not conceive of directing upon Russia anything like the
same stringency of criticism they used upon their own nation. Orwell
observed of them that their zeal for internationalism had led them to
constitute Russia their new fatherland. And he had the simple courage to
point out that the pacifists preached their doctrine under condition of the
protection of the British navy, and that, against Germany and Russia,
Gandhi's passive resistance would have been of no avail.

He never abated his anger against the established order. But a paradox
of history had made the old British order one of the still beneficent things
in the world, and it licensed the possibility of a social hope that was being
frustrated and betrayed almost everywhere else. And so Orwell clung
with a kind of wry, grim pride to the old ways of the last class that had
ruled the old order. He must sometimes have wondered how it came
about that he should be praising sportsmanship and gentlemanliness and
dutifulness and physical courage. He seems to have thought, and very
likely he was right, that they might come in handy as revolutionary
virtues—he remarks of Rubashov, the central character of Arthur
Koestler's novel *Darkness at Noon*, that he was firmer in loyalty to the
revolution than certain of his comrades because he had, and they had
not, a bourgeois past. Certainly the virtues he praised were those of survival, and they had fallen into disrepute in a disordered world.

Sometimes in his quarrel with the intelligentsia Orwell seems to sound
like a leader-writer for the *Times* in a routine wartime attack on the
highbrows.

> . . . The general weakening of imperialism, and to some extent of the whole
> British morale, that took place during the nineteen thirties, was partly the
> work of the left-wing intelligentsia, itself a kind of growth that sprouted from
> the stagnation of the Empire.
>
> The mentality of the English left-wing intelligentsia can be studied in half a
> dozen weekly and monthly papers. The immediately striking thing about all
> these papers is their generally negative querulous attitude, their complete lack
> at all times of any constructive suggestion. There is little in them except the
> irresponsible carping of people who have never been and never expect to be in
> a position of power.

During the past twenty years the negative faineant outlook which has been fashionable among the English left-wingers, the sniggering of the intellectuals at patriotism and physical courage, the persistent effort to chip away at English morale and spread a hedonistic, what-do-I-get-out-of-it attitude to life, has done nothing but harm.

But he was not a leader-writer for the *Times*. He had fought in Spain and nearly died there, and on Spanish affairs his position had been the truly revolutionary one. The passages I have quoted are from his pamphlet, *The Lion and the Unicorn*, a persuasive statement of the case for socialism in Britain.

Toward the end of his life Orwell discovered another reason for his admiration of the old middle-class virtues and his criticism of the intelligentsia. Walter Bagehot used to speak of the political advantages of *stupidity*, meaning by the word a concern for one's own private material interests as a political motive which was preferable to an intellectual, theoretical interest. Orwell, it may be said, came to respect the old bourgeois virtues because they were stupid—that is, because they resisted the power of abstract ideas. And he came to love things, material possessions, for the same reason. He did not in the least become what is called "anti-intellectual"—this was simply not within the range of possibility for him—but he began to fear that the commitment to abstract ideas could be far more maleficent than the commitment to the gross materiality of property had ever been. The very stupidity of things has something human about it, something meliorative, something even liberating. Together with the stupidity of the old unthinking virtues it stands against the ultimate and absolute power which the unconditioned idea can develop. The essential point of *Nineteen Eighty-Four* is just this, the danger of the ultimate and absolute power which mind can develop when it frees itself from conditions, from the bondage of things and history.

But this, as I say, is a late aspect of Orwell's criticism of intellectuality. Through the greater part of his literary career his criticism was simpler and less extreme. It was as simple as this: that the contemporary intellectual class did not think and did not really love the truth.

In 1937 Orwell went to Spain to observe the civil war and to write about it. He stayed to take part in it, joining the militia as a private. At that time each of the parties still had its own militia units, although these were in process of being absorbed into the People's Army. Because his letters of introduction were from people of a certain political group in England, the ILP,* which had connections with the POUM,† Orwell joined a unit of that party in Barcelona. He was not at the time sympathetic to the views of his comrades and their leaders. During the days of

* Independent Labour Party of Great Britain.
† See also the essay by Isaac Rosenfeld, p. 316.

interparty strife, the POUM was represented in Spain and abroad as being a Trotskyist party. In point of fact it was not, although it did join with the small Trotskyist party to oppose certain of the policies of the dominant Communist party. Orwell's own preference, at the time of his enlistment, was for the Communist party line, and because of this he looked forward to an eventual transfer to a Communist unit.

It was natural, I think, for Orwell to have been a partisan of the Communist program for the war. It recommended itself to most people on inspection by its apparent simple common sense. It proposed to fight the war without any reference to any particular political idea beyond a defense of democracy from a fascist enemy. When the war was won, the political and social problems would be solved, but until the war should be won, any debate over these problems was to be avoided as leading only to the weakening of the united front against Franco.

Eventually Orwell came to understand that this was not the practical policy he had at first thought it to be. His reasons need not be reiterated here—he gives them with characteristic cogency and modesty in the course of his book, and under the gloomy but probably correct awareness that, the economic and social condition of Spain being what it was, even the best policies must issue in some form of dictatorship. In sum, he believed that the war was revolutionary or nothing, and that the people of Spain would not fight and die for a democracy which was admittedly to be a bourgeois democracy.

But Orwell's disaffection from the Communist party was not the result of a difference of opinion over whether the revolution should be instituted during the war or after it. It was the result of his discovery that the Communist Party's real intention was to prevent the revolution from ever being instituted at all—"The thing for which the Communists were working was not to postpone the Spanish revolution till a more suitable time, but to make sure it never happened." The movement of events, led by the Communists, who had the prestige and the supplies of Russia, was always to the right, and all protest was quieted by the threat that the war would be lost if the ranks were broken, which in effect meant that Russian supplies would be withheld if the Communist lead was not followed. Meanwhile the war was being lost because the government more and more distrusted the non-Communist militia units, particularly those of the Anarchists. "I have described," Orwell writes, "how we were armed, or not armed, on the Aragon front. There is very little doubt that arms were deliberately withheld lest too many of them should get into the hands of the Anarchists, who would afterwards use them for a revolutionary purpose; consequently, the big Aragon offensive which would have made Franco draw back from Bilbao and possibly from Madrid, never happened."

At the end of April, after three months on the Aragon front, Orwell

was sent to Barcelona on furlough. He observed the change in morale
that had taken place since the days of his enlistment—Barcelona was no
longer the revolutionary city it had been. The heroic days were over. The
militia, which had done such splendid service at the beginning of the war,
was now being denigrated in favor of the People's Army, and its members
were being snubbed as seeming rather queer in their revolutionary ardor,
not to say dangerous. The tone of the black market and of privilege had
replaced the old idealistic puritanism of even three months earlier. Orwell observed this but drew no conclusions from it. He wanted to go to the
front at Madrid, and in order to do so he would have to be transferred to
the International Column, which was under the control of the Communists. He had no objection to serving in a Communist command and, indeed, had resolved to make the transfer. But he was tired and in poor
health and he waited to conclude the matter until another week of his
leave should be up. While he delayed, the fighting broke out in Barcelona.

In New York and in London the intelligentsia had no slightest doubt of
what had happened—could not, indeed, have conceived that anything
might have happened other than what they had been led to believe had
actually happened. The Anarchists, together with the "Trotskyist"
POUM—so it was said—had been secreting great stores of arms with a
view to an uprising that would force upon the government their premature desire for collectivization. And on the third of May their plans were
realized when they came out into the streets and captured the Telephone
Exchange, thus breaking the united front in an extreme manner and
endangering the progress of the war. But Orwell in Barcelona saw nothing like this. He was under the orders of the POUM, but he was not
committed to its line, and certainly not to the Anarchist line, and he was
sufficiently sympathetic to the Communists to wish to join one of their
units. What he saw he saw as objectively as a man might ever see anything. And what he records is now, I believe, accepted as the essential
truth by everyone whose judgment is worth regarding. There were no
great stores of arms cached by the Anarchists and the POUM—there
was an actual shortage of arms in their ranks. But the Communist-
controlled government had been building up the strength of the Civil
Guard, a gendarmerie which was called "nonpolitical" and from which
workers were excluded. That there had indeed been mounting tension
between the government and the dissident forces is beyond question, but
the actual fighting was touched off by acts of provocation committed by
the government itself—shows of military strength, the call to all private
persons to give up arms, attacks on Anarchist centers, and, as a climax,
the attempt to take over the Telephone Exchange, which since the beginning of the war had been run by the Anarchists.

It would have been very difficult to learn anything of this in New York

or London. The periodicals that guided the thought of left-liberal intellectuals knew nothing of it, and had no wish to learn. As for the aftermath
of the unhappy uprising, they appeared to have no knowledge of that at
all. When Barcelona was again quiet—some six thousand Assault Guards
were imported to quell the disturbance—Orwell returned to his old front.
There he was severely wounded, shot through the neck; the bullet just
missed the windpipe. After his grim hospitalization, of which he writes so
lightly, he was invalided to Barcelona. He returned to find the city in the
process of being purged. The POUM and the Anarchists had been suppressed; the power of the workers had been broken and the police hunt
was on. The jails were already full and daily becoming fuller—the most
devoted fighters for Spanish freedom, men who had given up everything
for the cause, were being imprisoned under the most dreadful conditions,
often held incommunicado, often never to be heard of again. Orwell himself was suspect and in danger because he had belonged to a POUM regiment, and he stayed in hiding until, with the help of the British consul,
he was able to escape to France. But if one searches the liberal periodicals, which have made the cause of civil liberties their own, one can find
no mention of this terror. Those members of the intellectual class who
prided themselves upon their political commitment were committed not
to the fact but to the abstraction.*

And to the abstraction they remained committed for a long time to
come. Many are still committed to it, or nostalgically wish they could be.
If only life were not so tangible, so concrete, so made up of facts that are
at variance with each other; if only the things that people say are good
things were really good; if only things that are pretty good were entirely
good and we were not put to the everlasting necessity of qualifying and
discriminating; if only politics were not a matter of power—*then* we
should be happy to put our minds to politics, *then* we should consent to
think!

But Orwell had never believed that the political life could be an intellectual idyl. He immediately put his mind to the politics he had experienced. He told the truth, and told it in an exemplary way, quietly, simply,
with due warning to the reader that it was only one man's truth. He used

---

* In looking through the files of *The Nation* and the *New Republic* for the period of the
Barcelona fighting, I have come upon only one serious contradiction of the interpretation
of events that constituted the editorial position of both periodicals. This was a long letter
contributed by Bertram Wolfe to the correspondence columns of *The Nation*. When this
essay first appeared, some of my friends took me to task for seeming to imply that there
were no liberal or radical intellectuals who did not accept the interpretations of *The
Nation* and the *New Republic*. There were indeed such liberal or radical intellectuals. But
they were relatively few in number and they were treated with great suspiciousness and
even hostility by the liberal and radical intellectuals as a class. It is as a class that Orwell
speaks of the intellectuals of the left in the thirties, and I follow him in this.

no political jargon, and he made no recriminations. He made no effort to show that his heart was in the right place, or the left place. He was not interested in where his heart might be thought to be, since he knew where it was. He was interested only in telling the truth. Not very much attention was paid to his truth—*Homage to Catalonia* sold poorly in England, it had to be remaindered, it was not published in America, and the people to whom it should have said most responded to it not at all.

Its particular truth refers to events now far in the past, as in these days we reckon our past. It does not matter the less for that—this particular truth implies a general truth which, as now we cannot fail to understand, must matter for a long time to come. And what matters most of all is our sense of the man who tells the truth.

1955

JOHN WAIN
George Orwell

John Wain, who has written fiction, criticism, and biography, is an English man-of-letters. In this essay he performs the useful function of distinguishing the *kind* of fiction that *Nineteen Eighty-Four* can reasonably be said to be, so that false or unreasonable expectations may be avoided.

It is impossible to criticise an author's work adequately until you have understood what kind of books he was writing; there was a time, in fact, when the art of criticism pivoted largely on the doctrine of the 'kinds'. A Renaissance critic saw literature as divided (by Nature, not by human interference) into 'kinds', and his idea of the function of criticism was to determine, in case of doubt, what 'kind' a work belonged to, and how it measured up to the standards of that kind. Thus, a work could be censured for having excellences which were not proper to its kind, as well as for not having the ones that were. If Orwell's work has been grotesquely misjudged, and I think it has, the explanation is simple: it lies in the complete withering-away of the notion of literary kinds—so complete that we have abandoned the very word, and now speak of *genres*, as the Duchess told Alice to speak in French if she couldn't think of the English for a thing.

The 'kind' to which Orwell's work belongs is the polemic. All of it, in whatever form—novels, essays, descriptive sketches, volumes of auto-

biography—has the same object: to implant in the reader's mind a point
of view, often about some definite, limited topic (the Spanish Civil War,
the treatment of tramps in casual wards, the element of reactionary
propaganda in boys' fiction) but in any case about an issue over which he
felt it was wrong not to take sides. A writer of polemic is always a man
who, having himself chosen what side to take, uses his work as an instrument for strengthening the support for that side. English literature is full
of polemic writing; some of it is direct exhortation, but mostly it belongs,
nominally, to some other kind such as fiction or poetry, and is often in
danger of being under-rated by the standards of that kind. G. K.
Chesterton's novels, for instance, are, considered simply as novels, beneath criticism; but as polemic they do add up to something—one has the
impression of a clever and high-spirited man who really believes in his
religion, and where they fail is where this impression ceases to come over,
or comes over falsely, rather than where they cease to be good as novels. I
believe that nine-tenths of the bad criticism one reads is traceable to the
neglect of this simple and ancient doctrine. And with that I leave the
topic of Orwell's stature as a man of letters. It can safely wait; indeed, by
comparison with the urgent task of exposing and clarifying his basic
ideas, it can safely be neglected altogether. It is by his ideas, rather than
by any particular skill in putting them over, that he will live. And if that
is an oversimplification, it is one that Orwell himself would have agreed
to. 'All art is propaganda', he said once; a half-truth, as we see if we ask
'What is *Hamlet* propaganda for?' But the fact that Orwell read other
people's books as polemic is a pointer to how we should read him.

If we consider Orwell as a writer of polemic, then, it will at least help to
guide us past the initial paradox—the fact that his work, with so many
and such crippling faults, contrives to be so valuable and interesting. He
was a novelist who never wrote a satisfactory novel, a literary critic who
never bothered to learn his trade properly, a social historian whose history was full of gaps. Yet he matters. For as *polemic* his work is never
anything less than magnificent; and the virtues which the polemic kind
demands—urgency, incisiveness, clarity and humour—he possessed in
exactly the right combination.

This method might also preserve us from the error that has beset the
most recent commentators on Orwell: namely, a tendency to refer everything back to his personal character. A man has a right to have his opinions criticised at the level of opinion, no matter how many embarrassing
anecdotes we can remember about him. Not that there is any point in
denying that Orwell's opinions were, to some extent, the almost automatic result of his upbringing and environment. Everyone's are. His hatred of sham and cant, for instance, was obviously due at least partly to
the fact of his springing from the underside of the *haute bourgeoisie*—
what he called 'the lower-upper-middle-class'. These were the people who

tended to cling to the myth of an ascendancy that, in hard practical terms, they had long since forfeited; consequently their lives were a network of evasions and petty half-deceptions. As he put it:

> You lived, so to speak, at two levels simultaneously. Theoretically you knew all about servants and how to tip them, although in practice you had one, or at most two, resident servants. Theoretically you knew how to wear your clothes and how to order a good dinner, although in practice you could never afford to go to a decent tailor or a decent restaurant. Theoretically you knew how to shoot and ride, although in practice you had no horses to ride and not an inch of ground to shoot over. (*The Road to Wigan Pier,* Chapter VIII.)

Most Englishmen of Orwell's generation who were brought up in that particular tradition rejected it pretty decisively, sooner or later; his renunciation was unusually spectacular, because his impatience with any kind of falsity was unusually urgent. His real name was Eric Blair, but after the very beginning of his career he rejected both Christian name and surname, though for different reasons; 'Eric' because it was redolent of public-school stories and would, he felt, identify its owner with the wrong kind of English tradition, the tradition of Talbot Baines Reed if not actually that of Dean Farrar; 'Blair' because it was a Scotch name, and he was irked by the mass confidence trick which the Scots had played on the English in getting themselves automatically deferred to as more industrious, honest, brave, capable.

But, while granting all this, we must be careful. There are some of Orwell's beliefs that are almost invariably dismissed as products of his personal situation, mere reflexes, hardly to be dignified with the term 'ideas' at all—and it is easy to make this dismissal too readily. His wish to identify himself with the working class is an example. Some of the quainter sides of his character certainly came out over this business; when the spirit moved him, and it often moved him, he would launch into a grotesque imitation of a working man in such details as pouring his tea into his saucer to cool it. He has very frankly told us, in the autobiographical passages of *The Road to Wigan Pier*, how a good deal of this feeling was traceable to the events of his life. Five years in the Indian Imperial Police had given him a hatred of oppression which amounted to a mania, and, when he returned in 1927 to an England in which the working class was already menaced by unemployment, he naturally transferred to them the feelings he had been having about the Burmese. 'I had reduced everything to the simple theory that the oppressed are always right and the oppressors are always wrong: a mistaken theory, but the natural result of being one of the oppressors yourself. I felt that I had got to escape not merely from imperialism but from every form of man's dominion over man.' Hence the emotional identification with the manual worker, which, as we know, he occasionally carried to comic lengths. As when, for instance, he begins an illustrative anecdote by saying, 'On the day when King George V's body passed through London on its way to Westminster, I happened to be caught for an hour or two in the crowd in Trafalgar Square.' It wouldn't do, you see, to admit that he had gone along out of a natural curiosity to see the funereal pomp. Yet it must have been a formidable crowd in which a physically active man could be 'caught', against his will, for 'an hour or two'! This kind of thing raises an indulgent smile. But—and this is where we must go carefully—it does not follow that we can dismiss Orwell's ideas about the working class as a mere idiosyncrasy, belonging to the sphere of biography rather than that of ideas. 'If there is hope,' thinks the desperate man trapped in the hell of 1984, 'it lies in the proles.' As usual, we turn to the nonfiction for a clear exposition of the theme, and we find it in the essay, *Looking Back on the Spanish War.*

> The intelligentsia are the people who squeal loudest against Fascism, and yet a respectable proportion of them collapse into defeatism when the pinch comes. They are far-sighted enough to see the odds against them, and moreover they can be bribed—for it is evident that the Nazis think it worthwhile to bribe intellectuals. With the working class it is the other way about. Too ignorant to see through the trick that is being played on them, they easily swallow the promises of Fascism, yet sooner or later they always take up the struggle again. They must do so, because in their own bodies they always discover that the promises of Fascism cannot be fulfilled. To win over the working class permanently, the Fascists would have to raise the general standard of living, which they are unable and probably unwilling to do. The struggle of the working class is like the growth of a plant. The plant is blind and stupid, but it knows enough to keep pushing upwards towards the light, and it will do this in the face of endless discouragements.

Substitute the more generalized 'totalitarian' for 'Fascist' in that passage, and you have the fundamental reason for Orwell's wish to line up with the working man. Not that his attitude is sentimental or optimistic. The working man is like a plant, and the plant is 'blind and stupid'. But that blindness and stupidity represent a last-ditch defence of human freedom. It is a characteristically Orwellian position: grim, realistic, even bleak. But at least it enables us to dispose of the charge that his attitude to 'the proles' was a piece of literary man's *naïveté*. And that should encourage us to make the attempt, unfashionable though it is to consider his ideas as ideas, his arguments as arguments, rather than tag along in the fashionable search for 'personal' explanations that will safely put his books in the freak-show along with his shooting-stick and his home-made cigarettes.

Of course Orwell was in no sense an abstruse thinker. His political ideas were of the simplest. They were, in character, undisguisedly ethical;

he believed in the necessity of being frank and honest, and he believed in freedom for everyone, with no authoritarian rule and no tyrannising, economic or otherwise. These were the twin pillars on which all his ideas rested, and, while it may be convenient to take them one at a time for the purposes of rough-and-ready analysis, it is not possible to separate them for long. In his eyes they were one and the same. With the direct clear-sightedness that was his greatest intellectual gift, he saw that modern tyranny works by means of dishonesty and evasion. And not only 'modern'; Charles II, the last English king who still cherished hopes of a strong-arm repressive rule over his people, is on record as having believed that government was 'a safer and easier thing where the authority was believed infallible and the faith and submission of the people were implicit'. *Homo sapiens* naturally wishes to be free to do as he likes, not enslaved, not caged. Very well, the dictators answer, we will destroy the appetite for freedom; no one will fight for something he is not aware of lacking. Hence the Ministry of Truth, hence Doublethink, Newspeak, and the other devices for preventing people from grasping what is happening to them. It is a curious fact that Orwell's picture of the future is not particularly terrifying from the material point of view. Although he lived to see the atom bomb, lived to see it dropped twice on defenceless people, his vision of 1984 does not include extinction weapons. Airstrip One is permanently at war, in a vague sort of way, and every now and then a guided missile comes over and kills a few people in the street, but it is a guided missile of the type familiar in 1944, the type that were exploding round him as he wrote the book. He is not interested in extinction weapons because, fundamentally, they do not frighten him as much as spiritual ones; the death of his body is a misfortune for a man, but is not as bad as the death of his spirit; Orwell approved of Gandhi's opinion that 'there must be a limit to what we will do in order to stay alive', even if he laughed at him for fixing that limit 'well on this side of chicken broth'. Besides, a tyrant who has people shot is a tyrant easy to recognize. Killing people is not likely to remain unnoticed, for their absence will sooner or later be remarked on; but killing their instinct for freedom, degrading their status as human beings, can remain unnoticed almost indefinitely. If this view is incorrect, it took the Hungarians to prove it—and Orwell can't be blamed for not foreseeing *that*. So he made it his business to point at the very heart of the situation—the power of a totalitarian state to erase the past, by tampering with the records, until any trace of dissent becomes as if it had never been. This is an important point, so he must be allowed to speak for himself; it is worth the tedium of a rather long quotation:

> In the past people deliberately lied, or they unconsciously coloured what they wrote, or they struggled after the truth, well knowing that they must make many mistakes; but in each case they believed that 'the facts' existed and

were more or less discoverable. And in practice there was always a considerable body of fact which would have been agreed to by almost everyone. If you look up the history of the last war in, for instance, the *Encyclopaedia Britannica*, you will find that a respectable amount of the material is drawn from German sources. A British and a German historian would disagree deeply on many things, even on fundamentals, but there would still be the body of, as it were, neutral fact on which neither would seriously challenge the other. It is just this common basis of agreement, with its implication that human beings are all of one species of animal, that totalitarianism destroys. Nazi theory indeed specifically denies that such a thing as 'the truth' exists. There is, for instance, no such thing as 'Science'. There is only 'German Science', 'Jewish Science', etc. The implied objective of this line of thought is a nightmare world in which the Leader, or some ruling clique, controls not only the future but *the past*. If the Leader says of such and such an event, 'It never happened'—well, it never happened. If he says that two and two are five—well, two and two are five. This prospect frightens me much more than bombs—and after our experiences of the last few years that is not a frivolous statement. *(Looking Back on the Spanish War)*

That, then, was the prospect that frightened him more than bombs, which accounts for the relative absence of bombs from his nightmare of the future. High explosive was unpopular already. He felt the need to indicate the more deadly danger, and to follow this up by pointing out how easily any of us might unconsciously help to increase that danger. Anyone who talked or wrote in vague, woolly language, for instance—language which tended to veil the issues it claimed to be discussing—he denounced as an enemy. The language of free men must, he held, be vivid, candid, *truthful*. Those who took refuge in vagueness did so because they had something to hide. Once more we must quote at some length.

In our time, political speech and writing are largely the defence of the indefensible. Things like the continuance of British rule in India, the Russian purges and deportations, the dropping of the atom bombs on Japan, can indeed be defended, but only by arguments which are too brutal for most people to face, and which do not square with the professed aims of political parties. Thus political language has to consist largely of euphemism, question-begging and sheer cloudy vagueness. Defenceless villages are bombarded from the air, the inhabitants driven out into the countryside, the cattle machine-gunned, the huts set on fire with incendiary bullets: this is called *pacification*. Millions of peasants are robbed of their farms and sent trudging along the roads with no more than they can carry: this is called *transfer of population or rectification of frontiers*. People are imprisoned for years without trial, or shot in the back of the neck or sent to die of scurvy in Arctic lumber camps: this is called *elimination of unreliable elements*. Such phraseology is needed if one wants to name things without calling up mental pictures of them. . . . The inflated style is

itself a kind of euphemism. A mass of Latin words falls upon the facts like soft
snow, blurring the outlines and covering up all the details. The great enemy of
clear language is insincerity. When there is a gap between one's real and one's
declared aims, one turns as it were instinctively to long words and exhausted
idioms, like a cuttlefish squirting out ink (*Politics and the English Language*).

The relationship between style and character, always familiar from
the adage *Le style, c'est l'homme même*, seemed to Orwell one of the most
important truths; and it all came circling back to his conviction that the
price of freedom is candour. Why is Orwell himself a model of English
prose style? *Because he was not frightened.* He had a relatively simple
subject-matter to express, it is true, and his famous clarity may be admitted to arise partly from that fact; but after all, the great majority of
people who write have no very complex subject-matter, and one rarely
finds clarity and forthrightness that would pass the Orwellian test. Saying straight out what you mean, even in a liberal democracy, will always
call for a certain moral effort; a little too much anxiety to stand well with
everyone, to be a good fellow all round, and your style is ruined—as we
see from any edition of any weekly paper. But Orwell carried the argument one stage further. He noticed that large numbers of modern people,
uneasy in a world that seemed to be drifting, had attached themselves to
the anchorage of some form of orthodoxy. It might be Roman Catholicism, it might be Communism, it might be anarchism or pacifism. For
most practical purposes he lumped them together. Any word ending with
'ism' was enough to draw his ridicule. Thus in *The Road to Wigan Pier* we
find him saying bluntly 'The Communist and the Catholic are not saying
the same thing, in a sense they are even saying opposite things, and each
would gladly boil the other in oil if circumstances permitted; but from the
point of view of an outsider they are very much alike.' And this opposition was not merely temperamental, not merely a product of his rôle as
the 'born rebel'. It was based on a number of firmly reasoned arguments.
One of the chief of these concerned the nature of the imagination. It is of
particular interest to those of us who write, but not by any means to them
alone, since 'where there is no vision the people perish'. Let us look at it
for a moment.

Orwell believed that an author who sacrificed his intellectual freedom
was finished as an author. The ability to create, to imagine story and
character, depended, in his view, on the free and wide-ranging use of the
mind. And this is exactly what an orthodoxy, of any kind, is designed to
prevent. Anyone who accepts a system of beliefs, who declares himself in
favour of this or that Ism, lock, stock and barrel, is bound to commit
himself to a certain amount of hypocrisy, conscious or otherwise. No intelligent person ever lived who could swallow *all* the details of some over-
arching dogma such as Marxism or Roman Catholicism. People who em-

brace these beliefs do so, in the main, for reasons which are not, strictly, intellectual. Many Christians, for example, believe that everything that is best and noblest in the European tradition is rooted in Christianity, that if Christianity goes it will not be long before all values, all sanctions, go too. Consequently they give their support to the Church because they feel that it is more important for the Church to survive than for them to be one hundred per cent clear of intellectual hypocrisy. Equally obviously, many Communists, particularly in the East, embrace their creed because they feel that with all its faults it will be a means of ridding them of the servility of their former way of life; they know, if they have any intelligence, that the intellectual dogmas of dialectical materialism are riddled with absurdities and shortcomings, but they accept the absurdities along with the rest. It is human, understandable and consistent that people should do this. And if they are grocers or gravediggers, there is not much harm done. They can still go about their work efficiently, even though they have accepted a certain amount of built-in censorship. But if they are writers, they are finished. That is Orwell's point, and I have never seen it refuted. The key essay in which he expressed this view is 'The Prevention of Literature', reprinted in *Shooting an Elephant*. Here is a snatch:

> The journalist is unfree, and is conscious of unfreedom, when he is forced to write lies or suppress what seems to him important news: the imaginative writer is unfree when he has to falsify his subjective feelings, which from his point of view are facts. He may distort and caricature reality in order to make his meaning clearer, but he cannot misrepresent the scenery of his own mind: he cannot say with any conviction that he likes what he dislikes, or believes what he disbelieves. If he is forced to do so, the only result is that his creative faculties dry up. Nor can he solve the problem by keeping away from controversial topics. There is no such thing as genuinely non-political literature, and least of all in an age like our own, when fears, hatreds, and loyalties of a directly political kind are near to the surface of everyone's consciousness. Even a single taboo can have an all-round crippling effect upon the mind, because there is always the danger that any thought which is freely followed up may lead to the forbidden thought.

This is the sort of thing we should remember when we make use of Orwell as an ally in the cold war. Of course he hated Soviet totalitarianism; of course he wrote a poignant animal-fable to express the tragic plight of the Russian people, caught in its grasp; but that does not mean that every smooth-talking window-dresser of his works, Conservative in politics, Roman Catholic in religion, can claim him as a supporter. Next time you read one of the books or essays put out by these gentlemen, remember Orwell's contemptuous remark about 'all the smelly little orthodoxies which are now contending for our souls'. In his nostrils, *every* orthodoxy smelt bad—and he gave his reasons clearly and openly.

That phrase about the orthodoxies comes from Orwell's essay on Dickens, and I should like to turn, next, to his work as a literary critic. Now, obviously this has serious faults. It is, in fact, 'amateur' in both the good and the bad senses. He thought of his literary criticism as merely an extension of his everyday activities. Reading is one of the normal activities of anyone interested in the world he is living in; if you read, you will come to prefer some books to others, or alternatively to detest some more than others; it is reasonable, in that case, to write articles about them. An article about a book doesn't differ, significantly, from an article about anything else. That was his attitude. Unfortunately, it is true that literary criticism is a trade you have to learn; it *is* specialised, just as the writing of history is specialised; and the reader of Orwell's soon learns that he must overlook flaws which are the result of not having thought deeply enough about the nature of criticism. His amateurism permitted him to talk only about what caught his attention, and brush the rest aside; he had the amateur's untroubled assumption that what matters about a work of art is what he thinks about it, rather than what it is. His essay on Tolstoy's criticism of *King Lear*, for instance, is in many ways superb; apart from the fact that it contains a number of acute remarks about both Shakespeare and Tolstoy, it serves as a vehicle for some of Orwell's most moving and impressive utterances about human life. It is worth a dozen tidily accurate essays with no loose ends or ragged edges. But, all the same, it does contain some mis-statements, even absurdities, which arise from his characteristic lack of care over literary *nuances*. He says, for instance, that Shakespeare has told the story rather clumsily: 'It is too drawn-out and has too many characters and sub-plots. . . . Indeed it would probably be a better play if Gloucester and both his sons were eliminated.' This innocent remark reveals, first, that he cannot have taken the slightest trouble to read what other critics have said about the play, and secondly that, for all his acuteness, he was incapable of the sort of attentive, close study that we expect of a real literary critic. How odd that he could have read, or seen, *King Lear* without realising that the thousand and one echoes and interpenetrations between the main plot and the sub-plot are the chief technical means that Shakespeare is using! Any undergraduate, who had done a little reading and been to a lecture or two, could have put him right: but then the undergraduate would have missed all the things Orwell has seen. What he has seen, as usual, is the broad general 'message' of the play, and how it meshes in with life: both life in general, and Tolstoy's own peculiar life in particular, hitting off so many features of the great Russian's own situation that in the end he turned and denounced it angrily. It is an essay that will keep its relevance as long as human beings have moral problems; but, as a strictly 'literary' essay, it was, in many ways, doomed before it started. Compare it, for instance, with the famous essay on *Boys' Weeklies*. Orwell's treatment of *King Lear* and his treatment of *The Magnet* (a boy's paper that ran for about thirty years) are both brilliant, but they are not different enough. He treats them both as documents, expressing a certain attitude of life; and while it is true that he rather admires the attitude to life he finds in *King Lear*, and doesn't think much of the one he finds in *The Magnet*, this doesn't set them sufficiently far apart. If all the texts of these works were lost, and we had nothing but Orwell's essay to go on, we should never be able to tell, from reading it, that Shakespeare was as far superior to the amiable author of *The Magnet* as, in fact, he is.

So it isn't for 'literary criticism', in the real sense, that one reads Orwell's essays on books, any more than one reads his novels as 'imaginative work' in the real sense. It is all the same thing; a blunt, honest presentation of the important issues as he saw them, usually with a strong 'practical' bias. But it must be said, before we leave his criticism, that in a few instances this limitation actually operates as a strength. The essay on Kipling is perhaps the best example. Kipling is not an author of subtle shades or recondite effects; his work presents no technical problems, even simple ones like that of the relationship of plot and sub-plot in *King Lear*; it was possible for Orwell to arrive at a valid estimate of him merely by being clear-sighted about his subject-matter. The result is the best defence that Kipling has ever had, because it stresses that, while often wrong and stupid, he was never merely silly.

> He identified himself with the ruling power and not with the opposition. In a gifted writer this seems to us strange and even disgusting, but it did have the advantage of giving Kipling a certain grip on reality. The ruling power is always faced with the question, 'In such and such circumstances, what would you do?', whereas the opposition is not obliged to take responsibility or make any real decisions. Where it is a permanent and pensioned opposition, as in England, the quality of its thought deteriorates accordingly.

It was characteristic of Orwell that he found at least that much to admire in Kipling. He saw that it didn't excuse Kipling's follies, or make him a more pleasing writer, but in his eyes a readiness to take decisions and *do* something was worth a great deal of subtlety. That remark about the 'permanent and pensioned opposition', for instance, touches on a theme he often returned to. It ceased to be true, of course, after the sweeping electoral victory of the opposition in 1945, but during more of Orwell's writing life it was true that the people he felt bound to support, the English Left, were a long way from the centres of power and tended to cultivate a sterile, nagging brand of criticism. With this he had no sympathy at all. All his life, one of his favourite butts was the 'progressive' who cares more that his ideas should be 'advanced' than that they should be realistic and workable. In his essay on Wells, for instance, he remarked:

What has kept England on its feet during the past year [1940–41]? In part, no doubt, some vague idea about a better future, but chiefly the atavistic emotion of patriotism, the ingrained feeling of the English-speaking peoples that they are superior to foreigners. For the last twenty years the main object of English left-wing intellectuals has been to break this feeling down, and if they had succeeded, we might be watching the S.S. men patrolling the London streets at this moment.

That is the characteristic tone: what interests him is not the theoretically tidy or impressive solution, but the one that *works*—and works here and now. And this brings us back to the point about his 'kind' as a polemic writer. All the strengths and weaknesses of his work come out of this centre. For instance, it will seem to some people staggering and even culpable that Orwell should have steadfastly refused to tackle, in his work, the problem that he constantly acknowledged to be the most urgent of all—that of faith. As early as *A Clergyman's Daughter*, there is a remarkable outburst on the futility of human life if it is not sustained by faith. And as late as the essay on Arthur Koestler (1944) we find him saying, 'The real problem is how to restore the religious attitude while accepting death as final'. If this was 'the real problem', some will ask, why didn't he address himself to it? Because—and we will give him his own voice again—'privation and brute labour have to be abolished before the real problems of humanity can be tackled. The major problem of our time is the decay of the belief in personal immortality, and it cannot be dealt with while the average human being is either drudging like an ox or shivering in fear of the secret police.' (*Looking Back on the Spanish War.*) So Orwell postponed the ultimate task and laboured at the one nearest at hand. And when we come to weigh up his achievements, it may be that we shall count this sacrifice as one of them. For, to a writer, it *is* a sacrifice to admit that so many other things matter more urgently than writing. Orwell put the claim of his fellow-man consistently before his own, and the paradox is that it is this spirit, rather than any specifically literary quality, that will keep his work alive.

1963

PART
SEVEN

Personal Responses

The following pieces are personal responses to *Nineteen Eighty-Four* and to George Orwell, written by some of the most famous literary men of the time. By their very nature these works offer something different from reviews and essays. They suggest the respect and admiration that fellow writers felt for Orwell.

It is important to remember that these pieces were written under a variety of circumstances. Aldous Huxley's letter to Orwell, for example, offers the opinion of another anti-utopian novelist on *Nineteen Eighty-Four*, while Arthur Koestler's short essay is an act of personal homage written after Orwell's death.

BERTRAND RUSSELL
George Orwell

Bertrand Russell was one of the outstanding philosophers of the twentieth century. He wrote a large number of books on subjects ranging from symbolic logic to modern politics. In 1920 he published one of the first critical studies of Bolshevism from a liberal point of view, and a good many of the points made in that book anticipate those which Orwell would dramatize in *Nineteen Eighty-Four*. Russell's comment on Orwell appeared in a now defunct English magazine, *World Review*, shortly after Orwell's death.

George Orwell was equally remarkable as a man and as a writer. His personal life was tragic, partly owing to illness, but still more owing to a love of humanity and an incapacity for comfortable illusion. In our time the kind of man who, in Victorian days, would have been a comfortable Radical, believing in the perfectibility of Man and ordered evolutionary progress, is compelled to face harsher facts than those that afforded our grandfathers golden opportunities for successful polemics. Like every young man of generous sympathies, Orwell was at first in revolt against the social system of his age and nation, and inspired with hope by the Russian Revolution. Admiration of Trotsky, and experience of the treatment meted out to Trotskyists by Stalinists in the Spanish Civil War, destroyed his hopes of Russia without giving him any other hopes to put in their place. This, combined with illness, led to the utter despair of *1984*.

Orwell was not by nature pessimistic or unduly obsessed by politics. He had wide interests, and would have been genial if he had lived at a less painful time. In an admirable essay on Dickens, he even allows himself to comment not unsympathetically upon Dickens's belief that all would be well if people would behave well, and that it is not the reform of institutions that is really important. Orwell had too much human sympathy to imprison himself in a creed. He sums up Dickens by describing him as 'laughing, with a touch of anger in his laughter, but no triumph, no malignity. It is the face of a man who is fighting against something, but who fights in the open and is not frightened, the face of a man who is *generously angry*—in other words, of a nineteenth-century liberal, a free intelligence, a type hated with equal hatred by all the smelly little orthodoxies which are now contending for our souls.'

But our age is dominated by politics, as the fourth century was dominated by theology, and it is by his political writings that Orwell will be remembered—especially by *Animal Farm*.

Animal Farm naturally suggests comparison with *Gulliver's Travels*, particularly with the part dealing with the Houyhnhnms. Orwell's animals, it is true, including even the noble horse, are not much like Swift's incarnations of frosty reason. But Orwell, like Swift after Queen Anne's death, belonged to a beaten party, and both men travelled through defeat to despair. Both embodied their despair in biting and masterly satire. But while Swift's satire expresses universal and indiscriminating hate, Orwell's has always an undercurrent of kindliness: he hates the enemies of those whom he loves, whereas Swift could only love (and that faintly) the enemies of those whom he hated. Swift's misanthropy, moreover, sprang mainly from thwarted ambition, while Orwell's sprang from the betrayal of generous ideals by their nominal advocates. In a penetrating essay on 'Gulliver', Orwell set forth justly and convincingly the pettiness of Swift's hopes and the stupidity of his ideals. In neither respect did Orwell share Swift's defeats.

There is a very interesting little essay by Orwell on 'Wells, Hitler and the World State', written in 1941, at the beginning of which year Wells, unwarned by his silliness of 1914, was maintaining that Hitler's offensive power was spent: 'his ebbing and dispersed military resources are now probably not so very much greater than the Italians before they were put to the test in Greece and Africa,' Wells is quoted as announcing. Countering Wells's propaganda for a World State, Orwell retorts: 'What is the use of pointing out that a World State is desirable? All sensible men for decades past have been substantially in agreement with what Mr. Wells says; but the sensible men have no power. Hitler is a criminal lunatic, and Hitler has an army of millions of men.' To the end of his days Wells could not face the fact that 'sensible men have no power.'

Orwell faced it, and lived, however bleakly and unhappily, in the actual world. Elderly Radicals, like Wells and myself, find the transition to a world of stark power difficult. I am grateful to men who, like Orwell, decorate Satan with the horns and hooves without which he remains an abstraction.

Our age calls for a greater energy of belief than was needed in the eighteenth and nineteenth centuries. Imagine Goethe, Shelley and Wells confined for years to Buchenwald; how would they emerge? Obviously not as they went in. Goethe would no longer be 'the Olympian', nor Shelley the 'ineffectual angel', and Wells would have lost his belief in the omnipotence of reason. All three would have acquired knowledge as to the actual world, but would they have gained in wisdom? That would depend upon their courage, their capacity to endure, and the strength of their intellectual convictions. Most philosophers have more breadth of outlook when adequately nourished than when driven mad by hunger, and it is by no means a general rule that intense suffering makes men wise.

The men of our day who resemble Goethe, Shelley or Wells in temperament and congenital capacity have mostly gone through, either personally or through imaginative sympathy, experiences more or less resembling imprisonment in Buchenwald. Orwell was one of these men. He preserved an impeccable love of truth, and allowed himself to learn even the most painful lessons. But he lost hope. This prevented him from being a prophet for our time. Perhaps it is impossible, in the world as it is, to combine hope with truth; if so, all prophets must be false prophets. For my part, I lived too long in a happier world to be able to accept so glowing a doctrine. I find in men like Orwell the half, but only the half, of what the world needs; the other half is still to seek.

1950

ALDOUS HUXLEY
Letter to George Orwell

Dear Mr. Orwell,

It was very kind of you to tell your publishers to send me a copy of your book. It arrived as I was in the midst of a piece of work that required much reading and consulting of references; and since poor sight makes it necessary for me to ration my reading, I had to wait a long time before being able to embark on *Nineteen Eighty-Four*. Agreeing with all that the critics have written of it, I need not tell you, yet once more, how fine and how profoundly important the book is. May I speak instead of the thing with which the book deals—the ultimate revolution? The first hints of a philosophy of the ultimate revolution—the revolution which lies beyond politics and economics, and which aims at the total subversion of the individual's psychology and physiology—are to be found in the Marquis de Sade, who regarded himself as the continuator, the consummator, of Robespierre and Babeuf. The philosophy of the ruling minority in *Nineteen Eighty-Four* is a sadism which has been carried to its logical conclusion by going beyond sex and denying it. Whether in actual fact the policy of the boot-on-the-face can go on indefinitely seems doubtful. My own belief is that the ruling oligarchy will find less arduous and wasteful ways of governing and of satisfying its lust for power, and that these ways will resemble those which I described in *Brave New World*. I have had occasion recently to look into the history of animal magnetism and hypnotism, and have been greatly struck by the way in which, for a hundred and fifty years, the world has refused to take serious cognizance of the discoveries of Mesmer, Braid, Esdaile and the rest. Partly because of the prevailing materialism and partly because of prevailing respectability, nineteenth-century philosophers and men of science were not willing to investigate the odder facts of psychology. Consequently there was no pure science of psychology for practical men, such as politicians, soldiers and policemen, to apply in the field of government. Thanks to the voluntary ignorance of our fathers, the advent of the ultimate revolution was delayed for five or six generations. Another lucky accident was Freud's inability to hypnotize successfully and his consequent disparagement of hypnotism. This delayed the general application of hypnotism to psychiatry for at least forty years. But now psycho-analysis is being combined with hypnosis; and hypnosis has been made easy and indefinitely extensible through the use of barbiturates, which induce a hypnoid and suggestible state in even the most recalcitrant subjects. Within the next generation I believe that the world's rulers will discover that infant conditioning and narco-hypnosis are more efficient, as instruments of government, than clubs and prisons, and that the lust for power can be just as completely satisfied by suggesting people into loving their servitude as by flogging and kicking them into obedience. In other words, I feel that the nightmare of *Nineteen Eighty-Four* is destined to modulate into the nightmare of a world having more resemblance to that which I imagined in *Brave New World*. The change will be brought about as a result of a felt need for increased efficiency. Meanwhile, of course, there may be a large-scale biological and atomic war—in which case we shall have nightmares of other and scarcely imaginable kinds.

Thank you once again for the book.

Yours sincerely,
Aldous Huxley
1949

ALDOUS HUXLEY
A Footnote About *1984*

Talking of *1984* and the future, I have been greatly interested recently to find that what I prophesied about 'Hypnopaedia' in *Brave New World* is now an accomplished fact. Pillow microphones attached to clock-controlled phonographs playing suitable recordings at intervals during the night are now being used quite extensively here by pediatricians who want to get rid of childish fears and bad habits, such as bed-wetting, or help backward children acquire larger vocabularies, and by students who want to learn foreign languages in a quarter of the time ordinarily required for the job. (This device was largely employed by the U.S. Army in training men to acquire a working knowledge of colloquial Chinese or Japanese in a month or six weeks.) It looks very much as though the systematic brutality described in *1984* will seem to the really intelligent dictators of the future altogether too inefficient, messy and wasteful. Hypnopaedic methods can be used to make the rubber truncheon and the concentration camp unnecessary; and the ecstasy of satisfied power-lust can be obtained just as effectively from the spectacle of men and women conditioned into loving their servitude as by that of men and women driven by fear into unwilling obedience.

1950

ARTHUR KOESTLER
A Rebel's Progress:
To George Orwell's Death

To meet one's favourite author in the flesh is mostly a disillusioning experience. George Orwell was one of the few writers who looked and behaved exactly as the reader of his books expected him to look and behave. This exceptional concordance between the man and his work was a measure of the exceptional unity and integrity of his character.

An English critic recently called him the most honest writer alive; his uncompromising intellectual honesty was such that it made him appear almost inhuman at times. There was an emanation of austere harshness around him which diminished only in proportion to distance, as it were: he was merciless toward himself, severe upon his friends, unresponsive to admirers, but full of understanding sympathy for those on the remote periphery, the "crowds in the big towns with their knobby faces, their bad teeth and gentle manners; the queues outside the Labour Exchanges, the old maids biking to Holy Communion through the mists of the autumn mornings . . ."

Thus, the greater the distance from intimacy and the wider the radius of the circle, the more warming became the radiations of this lonely man's great power of love. But he was incapable of self-love or self-pity. His ruthlessness towards himself was the key to his personality; it determined his attitude towards the enemy within, the disease which had raged in his chest since his adolescence.

His life was one consistent series of rebellions both against the condition of society in general and his own particular predicament; against humanity's drift towards 1984 and his own drift towards the final breakdown. Intermittent haemorrhages marked like milestones the rebel's progress as a sergeant in the Burma police, a dishwasher in Paris, a tramp in England, a soldier in Spain. Each should have acted as a warning, and each served as a challenge, answered by works of increasing weight and stature.

The last warning came three years ago. It became obvious that his life-span could only be prolonged by a sheltered existence under constant medical care. He chose to live instead on a lonely island in the Hebrides, with his adopted baby son, without even a charwoman to look after him.

Under these conditions he wrote his savage vision of 1984. Shortly after the book was completed he became bedridden, and never recovered. Yet had he followed the advice of doctors and friends, and lived in the self-indulgent atmosphere of a Swiss sanatorium, his masterpiece could not have been written—nor any of his former books. The greatness and tragedy of Orwell was his total rejection of compromise. . . .

Animal Farm and *1984* are Orwell's last works. No parable was written since *Gulliver's Travels* equal in profundity and mordant satire to *Animal Farm*, no fantasy since Kafka's *In the Penal Settlement* equal in logical horror to *1984*. I believe that future historians of literature will regard Orwell as a kind of missing link between Kafka and Swift. For, to quote Connolly again, it may well be true that "it is closing time in the gardens of the West, and from now on an artist will be judged only by the resonance of his solitude or the quality of his despair."

                                                                        1955

E. M. FORSTER
George Orwell

George Orwell's originality has been recognized in this country; his peculiar blend of gaiety and grimness has been appreciated, but there is still a tendency to shy away from him. This appeared in our reception of his most ambitious work, *1984*. America clasped it to her uneasy heart, but we, less anxious or less prescient, have eluded it for a variety of reasons. It is too bourgeois, we say, or too much to the left, or it has taken the wrong left turn, it is neither a novel nor a treatise, and so negligible, it is negligible because the author was tuberculous, like Keats; anyhow, we can't bear it. This last reason is certainly a respectable one. We all of us have the right to shirk unpleasantness, and we must sometimes exercise it. It may be our only defence against the right to nag. And that Orwell was a bit of a nagger cannot be denied. He found much to discomfort him in his world and desired to transmit it, and in *1984* he extended discomfort into agony. There is not a monster in that hateful apocalypse which does not exist in embryo today. Behind the United Nation lurks Oceania, one of his three world-states. Behind Stalin lurks Big Brother, which seems appropriate, but Big Brother also lurks behind Churchill, Truman, Gandhi, and any leader whom propaganda utilizes or invents. Behind the North Koreans, who are so wicked, and the South Koreans, who are such heroes, lurk the wicked South Koreans and the heroic North Koreans, into which, at a turn of the kaleidoscope, they may be transformed. Orwell spent his life in foreseeing transformations and in stamping upon embryos. His strength went that way. *1984* crowned his work, and it is understandably a crown of thorns.

While he stamped he looked around him, and tried to ameliorate a world which is bound to be unhappy. A true liberal, he hoped to help through small things. Programmes mean pogroms. Look to the rose or the toad or, if you think them more significant, look to art or literature. There, in the useless, lies our scrap of salvation.

1972

T. R. FYVEL
A Writer's Life

The following memoir of George Orwell was written in 1950, shortly after his death, by a personal friend; it has been slightly revised for its present publication. During the years of World War II Orwell served as literary editor of *Tribune,* a left-Socialist weekly published in London; he was succeeded by T. R. Fyvel. Mr. Fyvel has since pursued a career as a journalist in England.

'The savage pilgrimage'—the term has been applied to the life of D. H. Lawrence. It could equally be used for the life of George Orwell, who died of consumption, like Lawrence, and died at much the same age. It is too soon yet for any detailed life of Orwell; the following is an attempt to adumbrate its outline, based on personal contact over ten years, on fragments of information he let fall in his writings (especially in *The Road to Wigan Pier*), and on assumptions one could draw from both.

II

George Orwell died just after the century had passed its halfway mark, on 23 January, 1950. For some months previously he had been lying ill in the private ward of a hospital in the centre of London. In this private ward, a square pane of glass is let into the door of each private sickroom, through which patient and caller can see each other. I visited him fairly often during these months, and my first glimpse of him was always through this glass, and always a slight shock, at the sight of his thin, drawn face, looking ominously waxen and still against the white pillow. But then, as I knocked, a sudden smile would bring his features back to life as he saw that another visitor was calling. And as one entered, he would immediately launch into some practical suggestion, such as 'Hallo, T., would you like to help yourself to a drink? There should be some whisky on the sideboard,' or else, 'If you find it too cold in here, don't worry about closing the window and turning on the heater.' His need thus to plunge straight into conversation was more than ordinary shyness. It had something of the schoolboy about it. And to the last, even on his sick-bed, Orwell retained those boyish traits which were so marked in his character.

How ill was he? It was difficult to discuss this. Even while he talked freely and vigorously, his condition looked worrying. From hints he had occasionally let drop, I knew that during and after the war he had suffered from spells of utter exhaustion. In 1946 and 1947 he had managed with difficulty to carry on journalist work. Then, together with his adopted son, a small child, he had left for the island of Jura, in the Hebrides, in order to write. He wrote few letters: worrying reports came that he had caught a bad chill, that he had exhausted himself in struggling to complete *1984*, that he had collapsed and was in hospital in Glasgow. In the late autumn of 1949 he was transferred to London, already very weak. His one remaining lung, he said, was not much worse, but he had not responded well to streptomycin treatment; and his body looked painfully, frighteningly wasted. Indeed, once or twice when I looked at him, I felt that the grim scene in *1984* when the hero, Winston Smith, weeps in prison at his shrunken, tortured body, had been drawn from life—his own life in hospital; and that the relentless, intangible force which crushes Winston Smith in *1984* symbolised not even so much the totalitarian threat Orwell feared as the intangible illness in his own wasted body, foreshadowing his own death.

Yet he did not like talking about this. To the last, he kept his form. He read the newspapers carefully, watching out for journalist misuse of

words—one of his pet worries—and noting down instances. The last piece
of work he was contemplating was to be a study of Joseph Conrad. The
interaction of the Continental and the English mind held a special interest for him. He had re-read [Conrad's] *The Secret Agent* and *Under Western Eyes;* and was delving again into the story of the European anarchists. We talked a great deal of this and other things. For instance,
Jewish intellectuals—why were they so exaggeratedly sensitive? That
was another question he found of perpetual interest. Or there were the
alternatives for the future education of his son. Orwell thought he should
go to a good Public School, but characteristically hoped that, by that
time, exclusive Public Schools might be abolished. Again, *1984* was appearing in German, with great success, in *Der Monat,* the American
monthly in Berlin. He had only a sketchy knowledge of German, and yet
a surprising feeling for the language. I went over some German pages
with him, and he was pleased to learn what was new to him, that Goeb-
bels had systematically developed a German 'Newspeak'—he had
guessed right again. Or else—a favourite theme—he discussed the various ways of making tea; and would the Swiss sanatorium to which he was
to go provide him with the strong, dark brew of tea he liked. The clear
Alpine water, he thought, might be unsuitable.

On the last occasion I saw him, he seemed particularly cheerful. It was
a Friday; the following Tuesday he was due to leave for Switzerland by
special charter aircraft. Everything was arranged; the Swiss authorities
had agreed to facilitate all formalities. Up in the Alps, he hoped to be
allowed to work for an hour or two a day. We sat reminiscing about our
early schooldays—mine democratic, at one of the best State schools in
German Switzerland, his Imperialist, at an English snob-prep. school.
For the first time he talked to me about himself at Eton, relating harmless and amusing incidents. Before I left, he urged me again to visit him
in his Alpine sanatorium; I said I would come if I could manage it. The
next morning I received the news that he had died suddenly, within a
minute or so after a haemorrhage.

III

George Orwell was born in 1903; like quite a few distinguished Englishmen (and Scotsmen and Irishmen) of his generation he was born in Imperial India. His father was a member of the Indian Civil Service, employed
in a not particularly leading position in Bengal. Orwell's real name—and
this surprised some people when the obituaries were printed—was Eric
Arthur Blair. Indeed, his early writings were signed 'E. A. Blair', until he
decided to change his literary name at the age of twenty-seven or eight.
Much later, I once asked him why he decided to give up such a perfectly
sound name. His explanation was characteristically evasive. 'Eric', he
said—he didn't like the name because of its romantic Norse associations

with the sentimental schoolboy histories of his childhood. And 'Blair', he said, was a Scottish name (which in origin was true enough, though his own forebears had been English for many generations); and he himself had a prejudice against the Scots because at his prep. school the richer boys had boasted to him about their fashionable summer holidays in the Scottish Highlands, and also because he was taught at the same school—against all historical evidence—that the Scots were fiercer and better soldiers than the English. In short, he himself felt, and wanted to be, English. 'Orwell', that was the name of the English river on whose banks he had lived for a time. And what could be more English, in the best patriotic sense, than 'George'? A curious explanation, yet I think it was partly true for England, the country to which he came as a boy, was, and remained, his genuine love. Yet the explanation was also partly evasive: names are highly symbolical things, and, as he knew, his own change of *nom de guerre* surely also represented a deliberate act to cut loose from the past, from his childhood, from certain unresolved conflicts which he could never quite shake off.

Through the place of his birth, Orwell had been endowed with vivid early memories, those indelible childhood memories, of the colonial scene—of India, its glaring sun, the swarming brown people and the gap between them and oneself. It was a scene he never quite forgot, and which was to give a bright colour to his future writing. There were also two daughters in the Blair family, one older, one younger than himself, and in 1911, as was the general custom, his mother came with the children to England, when he was eight years old; and he was sent to a fashionable boys' preparatory school on the South Coast.

In later years, Orwell talked very seldom of his family or early childhood, at least not in personal terms. His reticence seemed to go very deep. But one point he liked to make clear, because it irritated him, was that he was *not,* as sometimes described, an 'upper-class rebel'. Though he went to Eton on a scholarship, he insisted always that he came, in fact, from an insecure middle-class family always struggling to keep its head above water. As he wrote in the autobiographical chapter in *The Road to Wigan Pier:*

> I was born into what you may describe as the lower-upper-middle class. The upper-middle class, which had its heyday in the 'eighties and 'nineties, with Kipling as its poet laureate, was a sort of mound of wreckage left behind when the tide of Victorian prosperity receded. Or perhaps it would be better to change the metaphor and describe it not as a mound but a layer—the layer of society lying between £2,000 and £300 a year: my own family was not far from the bottom.

Though he defined it thus in money terms, the essential point about the English class system, he went on, was that it was *not* entirely explicable in terms of money. The distinguishing traditions of the English upper-middle class were not to any extent commercial, but mainly military, official, and professional, and of course semi-aristocratic and gentlemanly. But the fact that this class extended down to people living on £300 to £400 a year, and trying to ignore the gulf between themselves and those on £2,000 a year was, he says:

> a queer business. You lived, so to speak, at two levels simultaneously. Theoretically, you knew all about servants and how to tip them, although in practice you had one or, at most, two servants. Theoretically you knew how to wear your clothes and how to order a dinner, although in practice you could never afford to go to a decent tailor or a decent restaurant. Theoretically you knew how to shoot and ride, although in practice you had no horses to ride and not an inch of ground to shoot over.

At their best, these pretensions had their snobbish absurdity. But because they belonged essentially to the nineteenth-century Imperial heyday of England, as the twentieth century progressed they became increasingly painful, or even grotesque. At least, here is Orwell, looking back at the age of thirty-three when writing *Wigan Pier:*

> In the kind of shabby-genteel family that I am talking about there is far more consciousness of poverty than in any working-class family above the level of the dole. Rent and clothes and school bills are an unending nightmare, and every luxury, even a glass of beer, is an unwarrantable extravagance. Practically the whole family income goes in keeping up appearances. It is obvious that people of this kind are in an anomalous position and one might be tempted to write them off as mere exceptions and therefore unimportant. Actually, however, they are or were fairly numerous.

Indeed they were; they were the shabby-genteel class which Orwell, unlike many of his friends, knew from the *inside,* and this enabled him to write so clearly about them. He knew that their King-and-Empire patriotism derived closely from the fact that in India or Malaya or Kenya a man could, thank God, still live like a gentleman, with cheap horses, shooting, and servants, and that this patriotism yet existed in its own right. He enumerated the hatreds of this class—for the working classes 'who stank', the shopkeepers who were no gentlemen, the colonial natives who were 'niggers'. But he knew equally that these prejudices were not merely contemptible, as most intellectual Socialists held, but were the prejudices of an ill-paid English middle-class, itself ground down by lack of money and, as he said, forced to live on two levels. But though he saw the class from which he sprung so clearly—most of the heroes of his books were of this lower-upper-middle class, even Winston Smith in *1984*—yet he could never shake himself quite free from its outlook. As late as the War years, when he was a Socialist, when he mixed with cosmopolitan, intellectual friends, and wrote for *Tribune,* his whole appearance and manner still seemed strangely that of a somewhat down-at-heel Sahib.*

IV

In 1911, when he was eight years old, Orwell went to board at a preparatory school in the South of England, where he remained till he was twelve. And here one may tentatively take the search for Orwell the artist one step further, for these years, during which he was growing into a talented, sensitive, introspective boy, were years during which, as he himself suggested, he underwent suffering such as only a child can experience, and which left him psychologically scarred for the rest of his life. As I write this, I remember that Flory, the chief character of *Burmese Days*, like all Orwell's heroes a partial self-portrait, was drawn with a disfiguring birthmark across the face. This mark, one may guess, was only the physical expression of Orwell's own sense of unhappiness, of guilt and failure which, from his own account, he carried away from his early days at school.

The choice of education was certainly unfortunate. The preparatory school on the South Coast seems to have been an expensive and snobbish establishment, even for its day, specialising in grooming wealthy boys for Eton, Harrow, and half a dozen other expensive schools. In addition, however, the school took in each year two or three bright boys at very much reduced fees, boys whose explicit task it was to cram hard and win entrance scholarships to Eton, Harrow, etc. By doing so, they naturally brought prestige and profit to the school. Nevertheless, the school atmosphere was such that these reduced-fee boys were constantly reminded that they were not 'the right type of boy' (like boys from titled families or whose fathers had grouse-shoots in Scotland) and should be eternally grateful for the privilege of attending the school.

Of these boys, George Orwell was one. He had other handicaps. He was already affected by his lung complaint (which was not discovered) and usually found compulsory football and athletics a bore, and at times a torture. In addition, there was X, the wife of the master in charge of him, a woman of decided views and personality who had established an unusual ascendancy over the boys. To be the right kind of boy, in terms of money, family background, athletic success and the correct King-and-Country patriotic views, was to enjoy the favour of X; to fail in these

---

* Orwell, as is a writer's privilege, exaggerated somewhat. His own antecedents were quite respectable. Four generations back, his ancestor Charles Blair married an earl's daughter, and their descendants travelled far afield. Orwell showed his family sense by giving his adopted son the traditional family names of 'Richard Horatio.' From all accounts, the outward life of his parents between the wars was also a perfectly ordinary middle-class life, not to be identified in detail with the gloomy fictitious background which recurs in his novels. Even so, Orwell knew his class and was never unaware of its disintegration and the gap between pretensions and reality.

qualities was to be cast into outer darkness. Orwell, as he related, was not only among those scorned and perpetually corrected by X; in addition, X seemed to single him out to impress on him that he was stupid and sullen, utterly the wrong type, and would obviously come to no good.

One can see, or at least one can guess, that X deepened the dualism in Orwell's character. While he rebelled against her censure, *somewhere* her voice upholding the right sort of views remained—he never quite lost a slight sense of emotional discomfort at being an intellectual Socialist. Or, conversely, when X told him that in spite of what had been done for him at the school, he would come to nothing because that was in him— did he not, as it were, 'act out' this part fifteen years later, when he spent a year living with Paris slum dwellers and casual English tramps as one of them? Or did he not, at least, have to go through this experience of being a social outcast in order to get it out of his system?

All this is speculation. Orwell, one may be sure, was also an exceptionally talented schoolboy. The deepened self-mistrust, the sense of guilt and failure, were only one side of his school life between eight and thirteen. He managed in the end to be excused from games; he roamed across the fields and woods, fished, collected butterflies and acquired that love of the soft, gentle Southern English landscape which is portrayed with such love in his books. And, since he had a first-class brain, he won, without much difficulty, not one but two scholarships, one of them to Eton. And so one may picture him at thirteen, a tall, ungainly boy, successful in his work but with his self-confidence partly destroyed, as he said good-bye in 1916 to the little school where he had suffered so much, and which he never revisited.

V

At Eton, Orwell liked to tell his friends, nothing much happened to him. The choice of Eton was fortunate, for here, in this genuinely upper-class atmosphere, he enjoyed much more privacy than he would have had at most other schools. But he formed no great attachment for Eton.

Yet, by contrast with the prison-like atmosphere at preparatory school, at Eton he felt 'relatively happy'. Now that the climax of cramming for his scholarship was over, he bothered little about working hard. He took classics, but at the age of thirty, he said, he could not even repeat the Greek alphabet any more. He was still handicapped through being always short of money, but he made valuable friends. Cyril Connolly, who had been with him at the preparatory school, was also with him at Eton; another friend was Richard (now Sir Richard) Rees who around 1930 edited *The Adelphi* and there published Orwell's first essays, and also some poems. Also a contemporary of Orwell's at Eton was John Strachey, whose political views Orwell was to attack bitterly in the nineteen-thirties.

An important point was that Orwell's senior years at Eton fell into the period immediately after 1918 when Eton, like other leading English schools, was probably more revolutionary and 'Bolshie' than ever before—or after. This mood was a reaction against the unbearable four years of slaughter in the trenches and of a wave of hatred among the young for the 'old men' who were held responsible. According to Orwell—and his account seems slightly exaggerated—in his day at Eton the O.T.C.* was derided, even the flag mocked. He relates that when in 1920 an English master set the question 'Who are the ten greatest living men?' fifteen boys out of sixteen included Lenin. (How times have changed!) Later Orwell tended to regard this ebullient juvenile Leftism as shallow; with one side of his character he would in any case have thought it wrong; I believe, for instance, that he himself rather enjoyed serving in the O.T.C.

After the period of pleasant unemotional relaxation at Eton, Orwell in 1922 went out to Burma into the Indian Imperial Police, when he was not quite twenty years old. Why did he not go on to Cambridge University on a scholarship, as would have been quite feasible? According to Orwell, it was because one of his masters at Eton had told him that at Cambridge, without money to spare, he would be still more 'out of his class'. There seems to be some rationalization here: the choice to return to his antecedents was probably more deliberate, and also decisive. For with this journey to the Imperial East we come to the beginnings of Orwell the writer. At preparatory school he had suffered shockingly at the hands of those in authority over him. So he did in Burma, but the situation was even worse: he now had not only superiors, but had himself to wield that evil thing, authority. The evidence is in his books. Though this is not the place to discuss them in detail (they are discussed in detail elsewhere in this volume), one must use them in any study of his life. For, in personal affairs, Orwell was always extraordinarily reticent, so shy as to be almost secretive. Though he seemed to like to deal in personal asides, e.g. 'When I was fourteen or fifteen I was an odious little snob', this was always in terms of social classification: the self-revelation is only apparent. In his novels, on the other hand, he himself stands out; for, if he had sharp power of insight, he had much less of invention. From Flory in his first novel, *Burmese Days,* to Winston Smith in *1984,* his last, all his heroes are Orwell himself, suitably transmuted.

He served as a policeman in Burma for five years, during 1922–7, from his twentieth to his twenty-fifth year. One may imagine him there, a tall, somewhat consumptive and sensitive young man, a very undecided young man, well able to act the Sahib, yet at heart a rebel, liking to shoot and also liking strange books, and with his innate sense of guilt magnified to unbearable intensity by the authority and power of punishment at

* Officers' Training Corps.—Editor

his disposal. What made it particularly difficult was his job as policeman. He had decided early on that white rule in the East was an unwarrantable tyranny about which one could say little except a cynical 'Of course we've no right in this blasted country at all, only now we're here, for God's sake let's stay here.' Still, British doctors, engineers or road-builders could outwardly play the rôle of benevolent despots; but he, as a policeman, was the actual instrument of naked despotism, forced to do the dirty work. And he himself, he felt, was the last person who ought to wield authority and inflict punishment: as he stated in a revealing sentence: 'I never went into a jail without feeling (most visitors to jails feel the same) that my place was really on the other side of the bars.' But at the same time, his sense of guilt was a complex one. He was no open rebel against authority. Outwardly he could, and did, act the part of a pukka Sahib. He himself tells of an occasion when he had sat up at night in a train with a colleague, damning the British Empire: 'In the haggard morning light when the train crawled into Mandalay, we parted as guiltily as any adulterous couple.'

Out of the spark of this conflict came his first novel, *Burmese Days,* written quite a few years later. It is a young man's book, a young man's sad book.

The Burma years also produced the short reportage essay *Shooting an Elephant* (later published in the first Penguin *New Writing*). Orwell had to shoot the elephant because it had run amok in a native quarter; his treatment of the action and his feelings were as if he had committed judicial murder. As an intense, passionate descriptive piece it is superb; V. S. Pritchett said of it that it showed 'Orwell had the first quality that marks the outstanding writer—the dilatory eye.'

But this essay was not published till many years later, and *Burmese Days,* too, only appeared seven years after Orwell's return from Burma.

VI

This return took place in 1927; he said of it later, in the section 'How I became a Socialist' in *Wigan Pier:*

> When I came home on leave in 1927 I was already half determined to throw up the job, and one sniff of English air decided me. I was not going back to be part of that evil despotism. But I wanted much more than merely to escape from my job.

What did he want? The next year or two were the strangest in Orwell's life. He, the intellectual, the old Etonian, the ex-Sahib, deliberately went slumming in the most real sense, doing menial work in France, and associating with English tramps as one of them. Why did he do this? In the same passage in *Wigan Pier* he gave his emotional reasons:

For five years I had been a part of an oppressive system, and it left me with a bad conscience. Innumerable remembered faces—faces of prisoners in the dock, of men waiting in the condemned cells, of subordinates I had bullied and aged peasants I had snubbed, of servants and coolies I had hit with my fist in moments of rage (nearly everyone does these things in the East, at least occasionally; Orientals can be very provoking)—haunted me intolerably. I was conscious of an immense weight of guilt that I had got to expiate.

He was young and politically inexperienced, he goes on; he still believed in the simple theory that the oppressed were always right. And so he went in search of the oppressed.

The frightful doom of a decent working man suddenly thrown on the streets after a lifetime of steady work, his agonised struggles against economic laws he does not understand, all this was outside the range of my experience. When I thought of poverty, I thought of it in terms of brute starvation. Therefore my mind turned immediately towards the extreme cases, the social outcasts: tramps, beggars, criminals, prostitutes. These were 'the lowest of the low', and these were the people with whom I wanted to get into contact. What I profoundly wanted, at that time, was to find some way of getting out of the respectable world altogether. I meditated upon it a great deal; I even planned parts of it in detail; how one could sell everything, etc. . . .

That was his explanation, ten years later. But from hints he let drop, one may perhaps hazard another motive, arising out of a deeper and earlier sense of guilt. Deep in his mind, perhaps, there was still the voice of X, the feminine tyrant of his preparatory school, still echoing in his mind, so that he had to fulfil the prediction that he would come to no good, to 'get out of the respectable world altogether' in actual experience before he could get the conflict out of his system. There was probably yet another reason for the decision. Many years later, when I tackled Orwell on the subject, he said that in actual fact he had found it difficult to find work on returning from Burma. He had little money, few social connections, and no special trade; it was a time of unemployment; a respectable job would have been difficult enough. But in any case, the fact remains that, after returning from Burma, Orwell spent several months as an ill-paid dishwasher and slum-dweller in Paris and later tramped from place to place through the Home Counties. The upshot of the experience was his first published work, *Down and Out in Paris and London*. This book of autobiographical reportage was published in 1933.

A new writer had arrived. But Orwell's first book did not sell well. Indeed, his first years as a writer in the early nineteen-thirties were for Orwell years of endless struggle against poverty. He was at the start anything but a facile journalist; his passion for integrity made him reject two-thirds of what he put on paper. To keep himself during these years he worked as a private tutor and an underpaid schoolmaster in private schools. He married; and, together with his wife, for a time he kept a village pub and a village general store (its income, he said later, worked out at a pound per week). His lungs intermittently gave trouble again. His second novel, *The Clergyman's Daughter,* appeared in 1934, followed by *Burmese Days.* Compton Mackenzie wrote after the latter book: 'No realistic writer during the last five years has produced three volumes which can compare in directness, vigour, courage, and vitality, with these volumes from the pen of Mr. George Orwell.'

Yet Orwell's success remained confined to increasing prestige among a few discerning critics. (Once, in 1940, he told me that he reckoned—he loved making such calculations—that his literary earnings over the decade 1930–40 worked out at not quite three pounds per week.) The theme of agonising middle-class poverty, of a ludicrous poverty, is one which seemed seared into Orwell's earlier works, especially in his novel *Keep the Aspidistra Flying,* with its painful rather than tragic picture of a young bookseller's assistant taking his girl out on a Sunday with—agonising knowledge—only six and tuppence in his pocket. In its way, it was a social document of the times, too: Orwell said that, after the novel appeared, all kinds of young men wrote to him and said this had been exactly their own experience. But while he was turning out these novels of which, incidentally, he was afterwards very critical, hypercritical, life in England was becoming increasingly 'political', even among writers. Orwell, too, had attempted to become active as a Socialist. In 1936–7 came his first chance of prominence when his publisher, Victor Gollancz, asked him to make a journey through a depressed industrial area and to write a personal report. This report, which appeared under the title of *The Road to Wigan Pier,* was a Left Book Club choice.

The offer had coincided with Orwell's own urge to learn more of the English industrial working class by direct contact. His earlier desire 'to get out of the respectable world' had by now gone. But it had been replaced by a strong attachment for the 'ordinary people' of England who were untouched by the taint of power, coupled with a dislike of middle-class intellectuals. From this sentiment sprang his studies of such popular social phenomena as comic picture postcards, or schoolboys' penny dreadfuls, as well as his interest in best-seller novelists such as Dickens and Kipling—interests which were to produce his most brilliant essays. An ominous aspect of the thirties which had caught his attention was the growing cult of power and brutality in the machine age which he saw expressed in the gangster novels of the type of *No Orchids for Miss Blandish.* By this time, 1936, he was also convinced that the day of his own class, the lower reaches of the embittered upper-middle class, was done: 'I never open one of Kipling's books or go into one of the huge dull shops which were once the favourite haunt of the upper-middle class, without thinking "Change and Decay in all around I see".' He wanted to know more of the British workers. His Socialist work might bring him in touch with the working class intelligentsia, 'but they hardly are more typical than tramps or burglars.' Hence his interest in Wigan.

The result of his impressionist tour was what he would have called a 'good-bad-book'. And yet his descriptions of the shocking working-class squalor he found were vivid, heartfelt, and the chapter in which, with gusto, he depicted the hatred felt by the British middle-class for the workers, aroused a fierce outcry.

By the time this got under way, however, he was gone, too. In 1936 Franco, supported by the Axis, had raised the banner of Fascist revolt against the Spanish Republic. As a Socialist engaged in a desperate search for honest identification of belief and action, Orwell had no hesitation. He joined up, on the Republican side.

There was always a touch of Don Quixote about all Orwell's knight-errantry. It was typical of his political individualism that, through accident, he joined not the International Brigade, but the so-called 'Trotsky-ist' P.O.U.M., a Spanish Left-Wing opposition party later suppressed by the Spanish Communists. It was typical, too, that he was wounded, not in action but on a quiet day, through sticking his head out of a trench. But he was wounded very badly (a bullet went through his neck and his life was saved only by a fraction of an inch) and by the time he came out of hospital the P.O.U.M. was proscribed as 'counter-revolutionary'. With a number of their British I.L.P. friends under arrest, Orwell and his wife had to flee for their lives into France. From his experience of civil war, of death, dirt, and military hospitals and prisons, Orwell returned with his faith in 'ordinary people' unimpaired, but with his eyes opened to one fact: Communist despotism could be far more ruthless than the earlier, milder tyranny which it overthrew. All this he expressed in *Homage to Catalonia* (1938), one of the most clear-headed books to come out of the Spanish Civil War, honestly and beautifully written, but which, partly because it was a book of the still unfashionable non-Communist Left, partly because this was Orwell's fate, sold only a few hundred copies over the next year or two.

Back in England, in 1939, there appeared his next novel, *Coming Up for Air*. Its theme was that of a middle-aged travelling salesman, married, not very successful, a most ordinary figure, bewildered by the 'stream-lined' new age with which he could not cope, fearful of a coming war which he could not understand, who set out to revisit the scenes of his childhood, with their lost happiness. And here Orwell was touching on one of his profound nostalgias, a longing for the peace and beauty of the English pre-1914 countryside (the 'golden country', he called it in *1984*), of those fields, woods, and streams, where he himself had found peace when escaping from the tyranny of prep-school. And for the first time— he was now thirty-six—one of his novels enjoyed a moderate popular success, and went into several editions. But before he could write its successor, the war came.

VII

I first met the Orwells early in 1940. During most of the thirties I had been abroad in remote places and from my reading had marked out Orwell as one of three English writers I would like to meet. It was probably my second or third encounter with him which remained in my memory. It was at his small mews-flat near Baker Street, in London, a rather poverty-stricken affair of one or two rather bare, austere rooms with second-hand furniture. I saw an extremely tall, thin man, looking more than his years, with gentle eyes and deep lines that hinted at suffering on his face. The word 'saint' was used by one of his friends and critics after his death, and—well—perhaps he had a touch of this quality. Certainly there was nothing of the fierce pamphleteer in his personal manner. He was awkward, almost excessively mild. Both about him and his wife (who was also not in very good health, and died under a minor operation in 1945) there was something strangely unphysical.

On his desk, I recall, I saw several letters which were obviously from the Income Tax authorities—unopened. He had left the letters lying there, Orwell said, because at the moment he simply had no money. I asked lightly why he did not open them, face the worst and suggest an arrangement to the Inspector of Taxes. Orwell's answer suggested that he felt it in some way almost dishonourable that he had temporarily no money to pay his tax. As I write this, I recall another incident: when I succeeded him for a time as literary editor of *Tribune,* I discovered a whole drawer full of manuscripts, mostly hopelessly unsuitable, which Orwell had nevertheless accepted. I asked him why he had done this. He agreed sadly that it was almost incredible how badly some people could write. But the bad writers—that was the trouble—did not know how wretched their work was. And, however fiercely he might polemicise against intellectuals in general, he had not the heart to tell any individual writer that his work was fit only for rejection. So the drawers of his desk at *Tribune* had remained full of unrejected rejects.

For a while we saw each other regularly. The year 1940—Dunkirk, Battle of Britain, beginning of the Blitz—was the new *annus mirabilis,* and our joint publisher suggested that Orwell and I should together edit a series of pamphlets in book form dealing with war aims. This we did, and for some months Orwell was very active in this work and seemed to enjoy it.

At this time, too, he was trying unsuccessfully to get past the doctors to join the Army (the efforts of some of his intellectual friends to avoid war service roused him to scorn). As next best thing, he joined the Home Guard, where he took his duties very seriously. At the end of 1941, I think, he joined the Indian Service of the B.B.C. I saw little of him there, because I was presently whisked abroad. But I knew he was unhappy— once again he was exposed to the authority of superior officials, and

worse, had to wield authority himself. I have a feeling—I am afraid I
have a feeling—that the harmless Overseas Branch of the B.B.C. in Ox-
ford Street, with its life of directives, conferences and canteen meals,
served as the model for the nightmare picture of the Ministry of Truth in
1984; the patriotic wartime propaganda line he had to put out, exaggerated a hundred times, became the totalitarian distortion and suppression
of news and fact in the 'Ingsoc' he imagined.

When I returned to England in 1945, I found Orwell's situation much
changed. No longer in the B.B.C., he had become a practiced regular
journalist, suddenly able to write to time-table and with quite an astonishing output. Week by week he wrote his incisive 'As I Please', for
Tribune; he also wrote for the *Observer,* for the American Left-Wing
Partisan Review and *New Leader,* and he was reviewing for the *Man-
chester Evening News.* He was well-known in political circles; he had been
literary editor of *Tribune* while Aneurin Bevan was its editor. Among his
close friends were Arthur Koestler, and David Astor, who was about to
take over the editorship of the *Observer.* And above all he had just published *Animal Farm,* that savage satire on the Soviet Union whose nostalgic descriptions of the English countryside made it a perfect tale in its
own right. For once his passions had been kept in check, and his sense of
construction had not failed him. *Animal Farm* had been an instantane-
ous success, especially in America, where it was the Book of the Month
choice. At forty-two, Orwell was for the first time in his life comparatively well off.

But I found him in character quite unchanged—and physically very
tired. His wife had died suddenly; he was left with a small adopted son
who for the rest of his life was to be his main love and interest. And in his
mind he was worrying as much as ever before. He was worrying about
the Communist totalitarian threat which he felt the West did not adequately realise, and must be made to realise; he worried about the atom
bomb and the political dangers inherent in the ascendancy of scientists;
he worried about the post-war exhaustion in England, and about the
adulteration of the English language by journalists, propagandists and
advertisers, a subject to which he devoted more and more attention. In
spite of his many new friendships, he remained a solitary and lonely
man. He wanted to get away from it all, he told me, and talked about his
little farm in the island of Jura, in the Hebrides, where he wanted to
make his new home. For another two years, however, he worked strenu-
ously as a polemical journalist; he came regularly to a weekly meeting at
Tribune, and wrote several long studies for an intelligent but short-lived
periodical, *Polemic,* on Gandhi, on Tolstoy, on Communism, on language.

Then, in 1947, he packed up suddenly and was gone to Jura. The reason
he gave was that he wanted to take his adopted son and himself, for the
years that remained him, away from possible atomic war. But this was

conversational rationalisation. The motives that took him away were two. First, he wanted time to write *1984,* a book he had had in mind for several years. Secondly, there was his growing tiredness, not only physical but mental: forty years of conflict had burnt him out.

About the rest there is little to say. His letters from Jura were sparse. And as for his uncomfortable life in the rough Atlantic climate—totally unsuitable for a consumptive—and the accidents through which his health finally broke down, it seemed to me at times as though some force in him were driving him to complete the drama. By an immense and intense effort, working sometimes in bed, he managed to complete *1984;* but, as he admitted, his ill-health was responsible for the shortcomings of the book and at least partly for its excessively pessimistic tone. In 1949 he came South again, now bed-ridden. But he still believed, at least in optimistic moments, that there were some years of work still ahead of him. He fell in love again, and he married for a second time. A short time afterwards, in January 1950, came the abrupt end. The passionate pilgrimage was over.

1950

PART
EIGHT

The Politics of
Totalitarianism

The two essays that follow do not deal directly with *Nineteen Eighty-Four;* they are studies in political theory, with special emphasis on the peculiar or unique features of modern totalitarian society. Their concerns parallel those of Orwell in *Nineteen Eighty-Four.* Both of them discuss the totalitarian state and movement by developing what sociologists call a "typology," an abstract model of a society. Their approaches are different, but each contributes important ideas and conclusions. Richard Lowenthal was active during his youth in the German Social-Democratic movement. He fled Germany after the rise of Hitler and has since gained distinction as a political journalist in England. At present, he teaches in the Free University of Berlin. Hannah Arendt, also a refugee from Hitler's Germany, was a writer who lived in the United States. Her book *The Origins of Totalitarianism* (1951) is an extremely influential study; the chapter reprinted in the following section first appeared in the paperback reprint of that book.

RICHARD LOWENTHAL
Our Peculiar Hell

If I had to select items of twentieth-century evidence to be found one day by future historians and archaeologists, the gas chambers of Auschwitz and the protocols of the Moscow trials would be high on my list. Twentieth-century man has brought forth his own peculiar hell—the modern one-party dictatorship, inhibited by no law or moral consideration in the exercise of its power, recognizing no private refuge of the individual in its effort to penetrate every sphere of life and to make every subject serve its purpose. Ours is the century in which novels about the future ceased to be Utopias and became nightmares—and not without reason.

There are still historians and other educated people who would deny the originality and uniqueness of what, for want of a shorter name, we call totalitarianism. They point to the age-old tradition of Asiatic despotism, to the Pharaohs who had their pyramids built by state slaves, or—more pertinently—to the pattern of plebeian revolution ending in *tyrannis* in ancient Greece or in the Italian Renaissance. They recall the link-up between an expanding empire and a fanatical faith during the conquering period of Islam or the European wars of religion, and they conclude that our contemporary horrors are just another instalment in the recurrent story of unrestrained power and blind intolerance. The most they are willing to concede is that modern communications technique, by creating more efficient media of mass propaganda, has placed an additional weapon into the hands of the despot; but this by itself would hardly entitle us to speak of a basically new political and social phenomenon. In that view, a passionate concern with the phenomenon of totalitarianism appears merely as proof of a parochial time-horizon—a deplorable lack of historical detachment.

In fact, however, twentieth-century totalitarianism shows essential features which are not to be found in any slave state, theocracy or revolutionary *tyrannis* of the past. It contains elements of all three, but combines them in a new context: the slave state is not static, but commands a modern industrial economy with rapidly changing technique; the official religion is secular; the *tyrannis* continues the revolutionary transformation of society. For one thing, totalitarian dictatorship is the product of the age of mass democracy; it does not aim at keeping its subjects politically quiet, but at forcing them into active support of its ever-new campaigns. For another, it aims at controlling *all* spheres of life of a highly complex and differentiated society, at extinguishing any remnant of independent forces, every germ of pluralism. To quote the closing words of Trotsky's unfinished biography of Stalin:

> 'L'Etat, c'est moi' is almost a liberal formula by comparison with the actualities of Stalin's totalitarian régime. Louis XIV identified himself only with the State. The Popes of Rome identified themselves with both the State and the Church—but only during the epoch of temporal power. The totalitarian state goes far beyond Caesaro-Papism, for it has encompassed the entire economy of the country as well. Stalin can justly say, unlike the Sun King, 'La Société, c'est moi!'

In recent years, this unique nature of modern totalitarianism in its various forms—nationalist-fascist and communist—has come to be recognized by a growing number of students of political science, particularly in the United States. They have studied the centralized structure of the totalitarian party, which enables its leaders to change their "social basis" at need and to rely on a shifting balance of classes, and the manner in which this party merges with the state machine after the seizure of power. They have described the institutional tools of the totalitarian state, such as its monopoly of mass organization and of information, which enable it to mobilize all social energies for its purposes, and have pointed out the contrast to the merely negative controls employed by traditional authoritarianism. They have discussed the dynamic nature of the totalitarian power-drive and of the ideologies in which it finds expression, and the resulting tendency both to limitless outward expansion and to the limitless internal transformation of the conquered society according to a preconceived pattern.

But both the political scientists and the historians who have studied the rise and fall of this or that particular dictatorship have been somewhat reluctant to ask the basic historical question about twentieth-century totalitarianism—the question of what are the fundamental forces that have brought it into being at this particular stage in the development of humanity. By contrast, attempts at such a general and fundamental interpretation have come from political philosophers and religious thinkers: totalitarianism, when it has been recognized at all as one of the crucial problems of our time, has been largely "explained" as an error of thought—as a spiritual heresy or a fallacious political doctrine.

The most widespread among these interpretations centers around the concept of "secular religion." Modern man, we are told, having lost his faith in God, has found the human condition intolerable. Taught by the humanists that he is master of his own fate, he has readily fallen for the Utopian belief that the state can abolish evil and suffering by creating a perfect society, if only the right people are given absolute power; or for the satanic belief that he can overcome his sense of guilt by proving in action that he belongs to the chosen élite who may commit any crime without fear of retaliation. In either case, man's attempt to rebel against God ends in his total enslavement to the state—his effort to create heaven on earth in the creation of hell on earth.

A separate, but related, explanation traces the origin of totalitarianism to the fallacy of revolutionary democracy—in fact, to Rousseau. Belief in the rule of "the people," in the abstraction of the *volonté générale,* is shown to rest on the illusion of the natural "goodness" of the common people and the harmony of their interests; and this doctrine implies that only a limited number of wicked oppressors stands between the people and the attainment of universal happiness by political means. Moreover, as the actual people are normally unwilling to sacrifice their actual, limited and conflicting interests to the single-minded pursuit of this ideal, the doctrine logically leads a self-appointed élite of doctrinaires to substitute their own will for the theoretically deduced will of "the people"— i.e., to establish a revolutionary dictatorship of the Jacobin type. A belief which identifies the will of the ruling minority with that of "the people," its aims with universal happiness and its opponents with Evil incarnate, naturally justifies the elimination of all safeguards for dissenting groups and individuals and finally leads to the rule of a single leader—a rule as absolute as ever that of any king, but free from the restraints imposed by tradition on the hereditary monarch. The modern one-party state is thus seen as but a successful development of the "totalitarian democracy" of the Jacobins.

There is some truth in both these interpretations; certainly the relation of our twentieth-century party dictatorships to such phenomena as the Anabaptist republic of Jan van Leyden on one side, to the rule of the Jacobins on the other, is more genuine and throws more light on their nature than the alleged "precedents" we have mentioned before. In every case, the dictatorial élite derives its sense of mission, its self-sacrificing energy and its utter ruthlessness against all opponents from a conviction that it is the chosen bearer of revealed truth, that its victory will usher in the millennium, and that its opponents are by definition the representatives of Evil who must be annihilated so that the state of universal harmony and happiness may be attained. In every case, whether consciously religious or not, these ideas derive from the isolation of the element of chiliastic prophecy in the Judaeo-Christian tradition of our civilization, which is appropriated by the self-appointed élite for its own purposes; in every case, the resulting distortion of the élite's vision of society and its own role in it amounts to a collective paranoid phantasy, as Prof. Norman Cohn in his recent study of the chiliastic medieval sects* has brilliantly shown.

* *The Pursuit of the Millennium.*

The uncovering of this "spiritual" factor in totalitarian movements—
or, if one prefers, of the paranoid element in them—is thus as legitimate
a part of the study of this phenomenon as is the analysis of totalitarian
political institutions. Yet it still fails to answer the historical question
why this recurrent heresy, or recurrent paranoia, should have attained
such enormous destructive power just in our century. For far from con-
firming the view that these aberrations are the consequence of the widespread loss of religious faith, the evidence shows that they arose again
and again within the religious universe of the Middle Ages and have
undergone no essential change by assuming a secular form in modern
times. The real problem remains why, while the terroristic rules of earlier messianic movements remained ephemeral and isolated—that of the
Jacobins no less than those of the Bohemian Taborites and the Muenster
Anabaptists—totalitarianism has become one of the dominating forces of
our age. That fact cannot be adequately explained merely by uncovering
the spiritual and intellectual roots of the ideas which animate the active
totalitarian minorities; it calls for an understanding of the special conditions which have made it possible to found powerful empires on these
ideas.

I believe that the key to the role of totalitarianism in our century is
that contemporary civilization has to cope with an unprecedented pace of
social change. I am thus proposing to reverse the problem; instead of
looking for the origin of totalitarian deviltry, I suggest that we should
consider the precariousness of a free society in present-day conditions.

The first thing to note here is that any free society is bound to produce
spontaneous, manifold and uncoordinated change. By "free society" I do
not mean in this context a particular political system, such as modern
parliamentary democracy; still less do I mean a society which would
guarantee an optimum of all-round freedom. I simply mean any society
which is "pluralistic" in the widest possible sense—any society, that is,
where political, economic and spiritual power are not concentrated at a
single point, where the social structure is not frozen in caste-like rigidity,
and where the individual enjoys a minimum of security under the rule of
law. Such a "minimum-definition" of a free society serves merely to distinguish it from totalitarian despotism on one side and from a traditional
authoritarian society bound by rigid rules on the other, but leaves room
for a wide variety of institutions.

"Free societies" in this sense have clearly existed during the main periods of the classical, Greco-Roman civilization, and—with the exception of
certain periods of crisis—during most of the history of our own "Western
Christian" civilization, and have to some extent spread with the latter
over large portions of the globe. It would be far more debatable if the
concept were applied to the later centuries of Roman Caesarism or to the

Eastern Christian empires of Byzantium and Muscovy, and certainly wrong to use it for any of the great indigenous civilizations of Asia. And it is striking at first sight that the Greco-Roman and Western societies have also been the great seedbeds of spontaneous social change—culminating in the modern era of worldwide technological and economic transformation.

It is, of course, no accident that this "acceleration of history" has started from the "free" west. A society which contains a multitude of autonomous units, feeling relatively secure in the pursuit of their particular goals, is apt to produce more innovation of all kinds than one that is governed by an all-powerful despot with a vested interest in keeping things as they are; and that will be doubly true if the citizens of a free society have as much chance to better their position by their independent efforts as the subjects of the despot might get by carrying out his will. But beyond this, we must bear in mind that the most dynamic free societies we have known have belonged to civilizations which *believed* in a social order founded on freedom and in the value of the effort of the individual; and that belief in itself has been a powerful agent of social change. The individual in a free society may always feel that he could in some sense do better than he is doing—by improving his personality in accordance with classical or purifying his soul in accordance with Christian ideals, by extending his knowledge or adapting his conduct to stricter moral demands, by bettering his station, increasing his power, accumulating wealth or making a greater contribution to the common good. And whenever a number of individuals are engaged in such endeavors, whether idealistic or material, altruistic or self-seeking, the aggregate result is spontaneous social change: changes in population, in production techniques, in tastes and needs and in social stratification.

Now the functioning of any society depends on a set of common beliefs and institutions which together characterize a civilization. As social change occurs, the institutions have to be adapted and the beliefs reformulated; but there must be continuity in the fundamental values underlying all the changing formulations and institutional forms if the civilization is to survive. A belief in representative government and individual rights might in the Middle Ages have been interpreted as a belief in corporative institutions—the Estates—and in the rights of each according to his station; by the end of the 18th century, it could be interpreted without absurdity only as a belief in parliamentary government and equal political and legal rights for all citizens; in our time, it has increasingly come to include the demand for democratic control over economic life and for equality of economic opportunity. It is obvious that these changes in popular beliefs and accepted institutions have been necessitated by the changes in the social structure of our Western civilization brought about by spontaneous economic growth, by the spread of universal literacy and by the new problems posed by capitalist industry; it is equally obvious that they are changes within a continuity of fundamental values.

But there is no guarantee that the necessary ideological and institutional adjustments will always be made in good time. For it is implied in the definition of a free society that there is no single center responsible for making these adjustments—that its over-all development is not "planned." Instead, the adjustments occur as a result of political and social struggles between different groups, and their outcome is not predetermined; according to the particular constellation of forces in a particular place and time, they may take different forms or may altogether fail to be accomplished.

It is in that sense that the survival of a free society is always precarious. For where the necessary adjustments fail to be made, the official institutions and beliefs cease to correspond to the evident facts of social life and thus lose their binding force—their hold over the minds of men. In that case, the continuity of civilization is broken, and the door is opened to barbarism—to political and spiritual chaos.

This danger to the continuity of a civilization is clearly greatest when the spontaneous social changes are of a kind that is in flagrant contradiction with the traditional view of what the social order ought to be and hence with the moral norms of behavior of large groups, or that destroys the functional status and material security and hence the self-esteem of such groups. This may occur most easily when a society which only recently seemed to vegetate quietly in the shelter of a traditional way of life, where changes were slow and imperceptible, is suddenly awakened by outside intrusion and exposed to the unwonted air of freedom and drastic change.

To this phenomenon, so familiar from the consequences of the recent worldwide spread of Western influence, the most nearly analogous event in earlier Western history is the great crisis of the Renaissance—a crisis which started in the 14th century and did not end until Reformation and Counter-Reformation had done their work. At that time, the medieval forms of social and political organization broke down in all the most advanced areas of Europe; the medieval moral norms proved grossly inadequate to the new commercial economy; while the Church, the authoritative guardian of these norms, visibly shared in the general demoralization. It is surely significant that it was only during this period that the chiliastic heresies, which had occurred for centuries before, acquired the form of political mass movements and thus became true precursors of modern totalitarianism; for as Prof. Cohn has pointed out, it was only then that large masses of people found themselves in a situation of helpless disorientation and material and spiritual insecurity which offered a fertile soil for paranoiac reactions. We may add that the same period also saw the outbreak of a non-chiliastic form of mass paranoia—the hunting of witches—and that both forms rapidly lost importance after Reformation and Counter-Reformation had succeeded in bringing moral norms into line with the new social realities, thus restoring the continuity of Western Christian civilization. The paranoiac reactions, including the precursors of modern totalitarianism, had been part of a profound crisis of that civilization—due to a failure of its beliefs and institutions to keep pace with the realities of spontaneous social change.

Let us now return to the special conditions of our century. The pace of technical change has constantly accelerated during the last 150 years, and has been even quicker in the late-comer countries than among the pioneers of industrialization. Population change, stimulated by the early stages of industrial growth and sustained by the development of modern medicine, has been equally stupendous. Whole social strata have been destroyed and new ones created in country after country. Entire continents of traditional societies have been "opened up" by the expanding West and forced into a lop-sided international division of labor, only to react within a few generations with a political and economic countermovement of autonomous modernization which expelled the intruders and forced them in turn to readjust their channels of trade.

It seems natural enough that in the face of such a total upheaval, the mechanism of self-adjustment of some of the younger industrial countries on the fringe of Western civilization and of some of the hitherto traditional societies now sucked into the whirlpool should have broken down. But such a breakdown in the continuity of development of a civilization inevitably gives a chance to the totalitarians—the spiritually disaffected minorities who are prepared to sacrifice the basic values of that civilization to the cult of absolute power for the sake of the accomplishment of a preconceived "perfect" social order. For it is only under the impact of catastrophic social change, and of the apparent impossibility to regain their lost personal dignity and material security within an order based on the old values, that millions of people are prepared to entrust their fate to the advocates of "total" revolution, to take flight from freedom and to seek salvation in the arms of the omnipotent state. (We are speaking, of course, of genuinely "homegrown" totalitarian revolutions, not of totalitarian Quisling regimes imposed by conquest, which are a secondary phenomenon.)

In other words, the spiritual or ideological "heresy" of the true totalitarians will only become historically effective when it merges with the material and psychological despair of the masses, owing to the failure of a social order to solve, in accordance with its own fundamental values, the concrete and urgent problems imposed on it by the uncontrolled processes of change. Bolshevism, for all its spiritual antecedents which the historians of the Russian intelligentsia have traced, would not have won power in 1917 if its opponents had been willing and able to end the war immediately and to distribute the land. Nazism, for all its roots in German history, would not have been victorious in 1933 if Keynesian full-employment policies had been developed and accepted at that time by the ruling parties of the Weimar Republic. Northern Viet-Nam would not be Communist to-day if France had granted independence to the Indo-China states at the same time and on similar terms as Britain did in India, Burma and Ceylon. An analysis which stresses the crucial importance of these humdrum political, economic and social problems for the victory or defeat of totalitarianism in a given situation may seem less profound than one that emphasizes man's loss of faith and his subsequent rebellion against the human condition as the ultimate cause; but in contrast to the latter it has the merit of focusing attention on those elements in the situation which it may be in our power to change.

Modern totalitarian parties, then, get the chance to win power owing to the failure of free—or of newly freed traditional—societies to respond adequately to the problems created by accelerated or even catastrophic social change, and to their consequent breakdown. Once in power, they benefit in comparison with their precursors from all the modern advances in the technique of centralized administration and of communications as well as in the applied psychology of propaganda and terror. Yet these technical advances in the apparatus of oppression and mass manipulation are not the decisive reason for the comparative durability of modern totalitarian regimes. That reason must be found in the fact that, in contrast to the more naive utopianism of their predecessors, the totalitarian movements of our time are armed with "scientific" doctrines for the transformation of the actual societies on which they operate—doctrines which claim to point the way to some kind of national or social Utopia, but which lead in their practical application to the concentration of ever-increasing power in the hands of the totalitarian élite.

The totalitarian regimes are thus not only the result of the problems created by accelerated social change—they are the creators of an alternative method of coping with these problems. If traditional societies are characterized by built-in resistance to change, and free societies by the production of spontaneous and uncoordinated change, totalitarianism may be described as an engine of centrally manipulated change.

This, precisely, is the strength of totalitarianism as an established system, and the justification it proffers for all its horrors. It extinguishes freedom and individual security; it denies the very ideas of truth and justice; it seeks to eliminate every vestige of independent development not in order to keep things static in the manner of traditional despotism, but in order to replace the risks of "anarchic" and unforeseeable change by the certainties of "orderly" change according to a preconceived pattern, based on the values of the totalitarian movement and its concept of the future and purpose of society. The state must be all-powerful, because the state has become the demiurgus of society; the party tends to perpetuate its rule by the very fact that it continues to distort the development of society into an artificial pattern by what we have called a "permanent revolution from above," so that the resulting structure would collapse without the support of the dictatorial power. In the history of Soviet Communism—the most long-lived totalitarianism within our experience—the forced collectivization of 1929–32 and the forced incorporation of the new industrial bureaucracy into the ruling party as a result of the blood purge of 1936–38 have been such artificial transformations of society in the interest of the preservation of totalitarian power; the ultimate removal of the right of the kolkhozes to dispose of their produce, envisaged in Stalin's last pamphlet as an essential feature of the transition to the higher stage of "Communism," would have been another similar "revolution from above"; Mr. Khrushchev's present reorganization of the Soviet government and its economic planning machinery, armed at establishing more direct administrative control by the party machine and breaking the independence of the economic and administrative experts which has tended to reassert itself even inside the party, looks like an attempt at yet another turn of the same screw.

Yet there are two limits to this self-perpetuating hell. One is given by the fact that even the most efficient totalitarian state is unable to foresee, prevent or canalize all the spontaneous changes that may arise in the lives and minds of its members; the other is that spontaneous social development continues outside its territorial boundaries, and may for all its groping nature prove in the long run superior to the preconceived pattern. Both ultimately reduce themselves to the limits of human foresight or, to put it positively, to the infinite productivity of history. In the short run, the demiurgus armed with an all-embracing theory of society is apt to prove more effective in his chosen direction—the concentration of power—than the uncoordinated efforts of free men; in the long run, his doctrine is likely to hamper his objective by its inevitable one-sidedness. The resources of the Nazi empire, however completely geared to war, proved insufficient to secure world domination; the Communist system fails to promote productivity at the required rate. If the ever-new revolutions imposed on Soviet society by its rulers bear witness to the ingenuity of the latter, they also prove their need to improvise in response to changes and pressures not foreseen in the doctrine: Stalin's plan for the "transition to Communism" has had to be shelved, while Khrushchev's reorganization, suddenly conceived as an act of self-preservation of the party regime, was as unforeshadowed by Communist theory as Stalin's blood purge itself. Nor is there any inherent guarantee that such improvisations must always fulfill their purpose of preserving the regime rather than undermining it; for the very need for them proves that something in the theoretical expectations about the direction of economic and social change has gone wrong. The saving grace remains that even the most perfect man-made hell is based on the necessarily imperfect calculations of men.

It may appear that in this article I have been mouthing the Platitudes of Progress. In fact, however, I have made no assumptions about progress towards a given ideal of perfection. I have merely stated the obvious fact that free societies tend to produce "material progress" in the sense of spontaneous technical and social change; and I have suggested that "political and ideological progress"—the adaptation of ideas and institutions to that spontaneous change—is required not in order to assure an approach to perfection, but to prevent a breakdown of civilization. Progress, in that view, becomes a necessary object of endeavor not in order to achieve heaven on earth, but simply in order to avoid hell on earth. It seems to me that its rehabilitation in that modest but vital role is long overdue.

In attempting that rehabilitation, I have sought to offer a corrective for a certain bias which seems to be implicit in the one-sided spiritual and ideological explanation of totalitarianism: a bias in favor of traditional authority and revealed religion. By deriving the Utopianism or satanism of the totalitarian movements from man's attempt to rely on himself alone, and the belief in revolutionary dictatorship from the illusions of revolutionary democracy, these interpretations tend to place the "guilt" for essentially anti-humanistic and anti-democratic movements on the humanistic and democratic ideas of the Enlightenment.

In our context, on the other hand, both the ideas of the Enlightenment and their totalitarian perversions appear as so many different attempts by members of our free society to adjust their beliefs to the facts of a changing world. From that angle, it seems plainly futile to say that the attempt ought not to have been made at all. The important difference is that the men of the Enlightenment tried to make their adjustment by a continuous development of the basic Western beliefs in the value of reason and the freedom of the human person, while the totalitarians have rejected one or both of these fundamental values.

Moreover, our analysis has tended to show that the victories of totalitarianism so far have been due to the failures of free societies to move forward in timely adjustment to the spontaneous changes they have produced. The danger of totalitarian revolution is greatest where the resistance of the ruling groups to ideological and institutional change is most rigid. Our peculiar hell is not, after all, simply the penalty of human hubris trying to achieve the impossible—it is at least as much the penalty of human failure to move forward as far as possible in a changing world. It is not simply the consequence of a refusal to accept the human condition, but at least as much the price of a complacent readiness to accept inhuman but man-made conditions as if they were unalterable and god-given.

The answer to the totalitarian challenge is not the acceptance of things as they are; it is a sober, non-Utopian, but active faith in our power and duty to preserve our free civilization in the only way it can be preserved—by the unending labor of progress.

1957

HANNAH ARENDT
Ideology and Terror: A Novel Form of Government

In the preceding chapters we emphasized repeatedly that the means of total domination are not only more drastic but that totalitarianism differs essentially from other forms of political oppression known to us, such as despotism, tyranny and dictatorship. Wherever it rose to power, it developed entirely new political institutions and destroyed all social, legal and political traditions of the country. No matter what the specifically national tradition or the particular spiritual source of its ideology, totalitarian government always transformed classes into masses, supplanted the party system, not by one-party dictatorships, but by a mass movement, shifted the center of power from the army to the police, and established a foreign policy openly directed toward world domination. Present totalitarian governments have developed from one-party systems; whenever these became truly totalitarian, they started to operate according to a system of values so radically different from all others, that none of our traditional legal, moral or common sense utilitarian categories could any longer help us to come to terms with, or judge, or predict their course of action.

If it is true that the elements of totalitarianism can be found by retracing the history and analyzing the political implications of what we usually call the crisis of our century, then the conclusion is unavoidable that this crisis is no mere threat from the outside, no mere result of some aggressive foreign policy of either Germany or Russia, and that it will no more disappear with the death of Stalin than it disappeared with the fall of Nazi Germany. It may even be that the true predicaments of our time

will assume their authentic form—though not necessarily the cruelest—
only when totalitarianism has become a thing of the past.

It is in the line of such reflections to raise the question whether totalitarian government, born of this crisis and at the same time its clearest
and only unequivocal symptom, is merely a makeshift arrangement,
which borrows its methods of intimidation, its means of organization and
its instruments of violence from the well-known political arsenal of tyranny, despotism and dictatorships, and owes its existence only to the
deplorable, but perhaps accidental failure of the traditional political
forces—liberal or conservative, national or socialist, republican or mon-
archist, authoritarian or democratic. Or whether, on the contrary, there
is such a thing as the *nature* of totalitarian government, whether it has
its own essence and can be compared with and defined like other forms of
government such as Western thought has known and recognized since
the times of ancient philosophy. If this is true, then the entirely new and
unprecedented forms of totalitarian organization and course of action
must rest on one of the few basic experiences which men can have whenever they live together, and are concerned with public affairs. If there is
a basic experience which finds its political expression in totalitarian domination, then, in view of the novelty of the totalitarian form of government, this must be an experience which, for whatever reason, has never
before served as the foundation of a body politic and whose general
mood—although it may be familiar in every other respect—never before
has pervaded, and directed the handling of, public affairs.

If we consider this in terms of the history of ideas, it seems extremely
unlikely. For the forms of government under which men live have been
very few; they were discovered early, classified by the Greeks and have
proved extraordinarily long-lived. If we apply these findings, whose fundamental idea, despite many variations, did not change in the two and a
half thousand years that separate Plato from Kant, we are tempted at
once to interpret totalitarianism as some modern form of tyranny, that is
a lawless government where power is wielded by one man. Arbitrary
power, unrestricted by law, wielded in the interest of the ruler and hostile to the interests of the governed, on one hand, fear as the principle of
action, namely fear of the people by the ruler and fear of the ruler by the
people, on the other—these have been the hallmarks of tyranny throughout our tradition.

Instead of saying that totalitarian government is unprecedented, we
could also say that it has exploded the very alternative on which all
definitions of the essence of governments have been based in political
philosophy, that is the alternative between lawful and lawless government, between arbitrary and legitimate power. That lawful government
and legitimate power, on one side, lawlessness and arbitrary power on
the other, belonged together and were inseparable has never been ques-

tioned. Yet, totalitarian rule confronts us with a totally different kind of government. It defies, it is true, all positive laws, even to the extreme of defying those which it has itself established (as in the case of the Soviet Constitution of 1936, to quote only the most outstanding example) or which it did not care to abolish (as in the case of the Weimar Constitution which the Nazi government never revoked). But it operates neither without guidance of law nor is it arbitrary, for it claims to obey strictly and unequivocally those laws of Nature or of History from which all positive laws always have been supposed to spring.

It is the monstrous, yet seemingly unanswerable claim of totalitarian rule that, far from being "lawless," it goes to the sources of authority from which positive laws received their ultimate legitimation, that far from being arbitrary it is more obedient to these suprahuman forces than any government ever was before, and that far from wielding its power in the interest of one man, it is quite prepared to sacrifice everybody's vital immediate interests to the execution of what it assumes to be the law of History or the law of Nature. Its defiance of positive laws claims to be a higher form of legitimacy which, since it is inspired by the sources themselves, can do away with petty legality. Totalitarian lawfulness pretends to have found a way to establish the rule of justice on earth—something which the legality of positive law admittedly could never attain. The discrepancy between legality and justice could never be bridged because the standards of right and wrong into which positive law translates its own source of authority—"natural law" governing the whole universe, or divine law revealed in human history, or customs and traditions expressing the law common to the sentiments of all men—are necessarily general and must be valid for a countless and unpredictable number of cases, so that each concrete individual case with its unrepeatable set of circumstances somehow escapes it.

Totalitarian lawfulness, defying legality and pretending to establish the direct reign of justice on earth, executes the law of History or of Nature without translating it into standards of right and wrong for individual behavior. It applies the law directly to mankind without bothering with the behavior of men. The law of Nature or the law of History, if properly executed, is expected to produce mankind as its end product; and this expectation lies behind the claim to global rule of all totalitarian governments. Totalitarian policy claims to transform the human species into an active unfailing carrier of a law to which human beings otherwise would only passively and reluctantly be subjected. If it is true that the link between totalitarian countries and the civilized world was broken through the monstrous crimes of totalitarian regimes, it is also true that this criminality was not due to simple aggressiveness, ruthlessness, warfare and treachery, but to a conscious break of that *consensus iuris* which, according to Cicero, constitutes a "people," and which, as international law, in modern times has constituted the civilized world insofar as it remains the foundation-stone of international relations even under the conditions of war. Both moral judgment and legal punishment presuppose this basic consent; the criminal can be judged justly only because he takes part in the *consensus iuris*, and even the revealed law of God can function among men only when they listen and consent to it.

At this point the fundamental difference between the totalitarian and all other concepts of law comes to light. Totalitarian policy does not replace one set of laws with another, does not establish its own *consensus iuris*, does not create, by one revolution, a new form of legality. Its defiance of all, even its own positive laws implies that it believes it can do without any *consensus iuris* whatever, and still not resign itself to the tyrannical state of lawlessness, arbitrariness and fear. It can do without the *consensus iuris* because it promises to release the fulfillment of law from all action and will of man; and it promises justice on earth because it claims to make mankind itself the embodiment of the law.

This identification of man and law, which seems to cancel the discrepancy between legality and justice that has plagued legal thought since ancient times, has nothing in common with the *lumen naturale* or the voice of conscience, by which Nature or Divinity as the sources of authority for the *ius naturale* or the historically revealed commands of God, are supposed to announce their authority in man himself. This never made man a walking embodiment of the law, but on the contrary remained distinct from him as the authority which demanded consent and obedience. Nature or Divinity as the source of authority for positive laws were thought of as permanent and eternal; positive laws were changing and changeable according to circumstances, but they possessed a relative permanence as compared with the much more rapidly changing actions of men; and they derived this permanence from the eternal presence of their source of authority. Positive laws, therefore, are primarily designed to function as stabilizing factors for the ever changing movements of men.

In the interpretation of totalitarianism, all laws have become laws of movement. When the Nazis talked about the law of nature and when the Bolsheviks talk about the law of history, neither nature nor history is any longer the stabilizing source of authority for the actions of mortal men; they are movements in themselves. Underlying the Nazis' belief in race laws as the expression of the law of nature in man, is Darwin's idea of man as the product of a natural development which does not necessarily stop with the present species of human beings, just as under the Bolsheviks' belief in class-struggle as the expression of the law of history lies Marx's notion of society as the product of a gigantic historical movement which races according to its own law of motion to the end of historical times when it will abolish itself.

The difference between Marx's historical and Darwin's naturalistic approach has frequently been pointed out, usually and rightly in favor of Marx. This has led us to forget the great and positive interest Marx took in Darwin's theories; Engels could not think of a greater compliment to Marx's scholarly achievements than to call him the "Darwin of history."* If one considers, not the actual achievement, but the basic philosophies of both men, it turns out that ultimately the movement of history and the movement of nature are one and the same. Darwin's introduction of the concept of development into nature, his insistence that, at least in the field of biology, natural movement is not circular but unilinear, moving in an infinitely progressing direction, means in fact that nature is, as it were, being swept into history, that natural life is considered to be historical. The "natural" law of the survival of the fittest is just as much a historical law and could be used as such by racism as Marx's law of the survival of the most progressive class. Marx's class struggle, on the other hand, as the driving force of history is only the outward expression of the development of productive forces which in turn have their origin in the "labor-power" of men. Labor, according to Marx, is not a historical but a natural-biological force— released through man's "metabolism with nature" by which he conserves his individual life and reproduces the species.† Engels saw the affinity between the basic convictions of the two men very clearly because he understood the decisive role which the concept of development played in both theories. The tremendous intellectual change which took place in the middle of the last century consisted in the refusal to view or accept anything "as it is" and in the consistent interpretation of everything as being only a stage of some further development. Whether the driving force of this development was called nature or history is relatively secondary. In these ideologies, the term "law" itself changed its meaning: from expressing the framework of stability within which human actions and motions can take place, it became the expression of the motion itself.

Totalitarian politics which proceeded to follow the recipes of ideologies has unmasked the true nature of these movements insofar as it clearly showed that there could be no end to this process. If it is the law of nature to eliminate everything that is harmful and unfit to live, it would mean the end of nature itself if new categories of the harmful and unfit-to-live

* In his funeral speech on Marx, Engels said: "Just as Darwin discovered the law of development of organic life, so Marx discovered the law of development of human history." A similar comment is found in Engels' introduction to the edition of the *Communist Manifesto* in 1890, and in his introduction to the *Ursprung der Familie,* he once more mentions "Darwin's theory of evolution" and "Marx's theory of surplus value" side by side.

† For Marx's labor concept as "an eternal nature-imposed necessity, without which there can be no metabolism between man and nature, and therefore no life," see *Capital*, Vol. I, Part I, ch. 1 and 5. The quoted passage is from ch. 1, section 2.

could not be found; if it is the law of history that in a class struggle certain classes "wither away," it would mean the end of human history itself if rudimentary new classes did not form, so that they in turn could "wither away" under the hands of totalitarian rulers. In other words, the law of killing by which totalitarian movements seize and exercise power would remain a law of the movement even if they ever succeeded in making all of humanity subject to their rule.

By lawful government we understand a body politic in which positive laws are needed to translate and realize the immutable *ius naturale* or the eternal commandments of God into standards of right and wrong. Only in these standards, in the body of positive laws of each country, do the *ius naturale* or the Commandments of God achieve their political reality. In the body politic of totalitarian government, this place of positive laws is taken by total terror, which is designed to translate into reality the law of movement of history or nature. Just as positive laws, though they define transgressions, are independent of them—the absence of crimes in any society does not render laws superfluous but, on the contrary, signifies their most perfect rule—so terror in totalitarian government has ceased to be a mere means for the suppression of opposition, though it is also used for such purposes. Terror becomes total when it becomes independent of all opposition; it rules supreme when nobody any longer stands in its way. If lawfulness is the essence of non-tyrannical government and lawlessness is the essence of tyranny, then terror is the essence of totalitarian domination.

Terror is the realization of the law of movement; its chief aim is to make it possible for the force of nature or of history to race freely through mankind, unhindered by any spontaneous human action. As such, terror seeks to "stabilize" men in order to liberate the forces of nature or history. It is this movement which singles out the foes of mankind against whom terror is let loose, and no free action of either opposition or sympathy can be permitted to interfere with the elimination of the "objective enemy" of History or Nature, of the class or the race. Guilt and innocence become senseless notions; "guilty" is he who stands in the way of the natural or historical process which has passed judgment over "inferior races," over individuals "unfit to live," or "dying classes and decadent peoples." Terror executes these judgments, and before its court, all concerned are subjectively innocent: the murdered because they did nothing against the system, and the murderers because they do not really murder but execute a death sentence pronounced by some higher tribunal. The rulers themselves do not claim to be just or wise, but only to execute historical or natural laws; they do not apply laws, but execute a movement in accordance with its inherent law. Terror is lawfulness, if law is the law of the movement of some suprahuman force, Nature or History.

Terror as the execution of a law of movement whose ultimate goal is not the welfare of men or the interest of one man but the fabrication of mankind, eliminates individuals for the sake of the species, sacrifices the "parts" for the sake of the "whole." The suprahuman force of Nature or History has its own beginning and its own end, so that it can be hindered only by the new beginning and the individual end which the life of each man actually is.

Positive laws in constitutional government are designed to erect boundaries and establish channels of communication between men whose community is continually endangered by the new men born into it. With each new birth, a new beginning is born into the world, a new world has potentially come into being. The stability of the laws corresponds to the constant motion of all human affairs, a motion which can never end as long as men are born and die. The laws hedge in each new beginning and at the same time assure its freedom of movement, the potentiality of something entirely new and unpredictable; the boundaries of positive laws are for the political existence of man what memory is for his historical existence: they guarantee the pre-existence of a common world, the reality of some continuity which transcends the individual life span of each generation, absorbs all new origins and is nourished by them.

Total terror is so easily mistaken for a symptom of tyrannical government because totalitarian government in its initial stages must behave like a tyranny and raze the boundaries of man-made law. But total terror leaves no arbitrary lawlessness behind it and does not rage for the sake of some arbitrary will or for the sake of despotic power of one man against all, least of all for the sake of a war of all against all. It substitutes for the boundaries and channels of communication between individual men a band of iron which holds them so tightly together that it is as though their plurality had disappeared into One Man of gigantic dimensions. To abolish the fences of laws between men—as tyranny does—means to take away man's liberties and destroy freedom as a living political reality; for the space between men as it is hedged in by laws, is the living space of freedom. Total terror uses this old instrument of tyranny but destroys at the same time also the lawless, fenceless wilderness of fear and suspicion which tyranny leaves behind. This desert, to be sure, is no longer a living space of freedom, but it still provides some room for the fear-guided movements and suspicion-ridden actions of its inhabitants.

By pressing men against each other, total terror destroys the space between them; compared to the condition within its iron band, even the desert of tyranny, insofar as it is still some kind of space, appears like a guarantee of freedom. Totalitarian government does not just curtail liberties or abolish essential freedoms; nor does it, at least to our limited knowledge, succeed in eradicating the love for freedom from the hearts of man. It destroys the one essential prerequisite of all freedom which is simply the capacity of motion which cannot exist without space.

Total terror, the essence of totalitarian government, exists neither for nor against men. It is supposed to provide the forces of nature or history with an incomparable instrument to accelerate their movement. This movement, proceeding according to its own law, cannot in the long run be hindered; eventually its force will always prove more powerful than the most powerful forces engendered by the actions and the will of men. But it can be slowed down and is slowed down almost inevitably by the freedom of man, which even totalitarian rulers cannot deny, for this freedom—irrelevant and arbitrary as they may deem it—is identical with the fact that men are being born and that therefore each of them *is* a new beginning, begins, in a sense, the world anew. From the totalitarian point of view, the fact that men are born and die can be only regarded as an annoying interference with higher forces. Terror, therefore, as the obedient servant of natural or historical movement has to eliminate from the process not only freedom in any specific sense, but the very source of freedom which is given with the fact of the birth of man and resides in his capacity to make a new beginning. In the iron band of terror, which destroys the plurality of men and makes out of many the One who unfailingly will act as though he himself were part of the course of history or nature, a device has been found not only to liberate the historical and natural forces, but to accelerate them to a speed they never would reach if left to themselves. Practically speaking, this means that terror executes on the spot the death sentences which Nature is supposed to have pronounced on races or individuals who are "unfit to live," or History on "dying classes," without waiting for the slower and less efficient processes of nature or history themselves.

In this concept, where the essence of government itself has become motion, a very old problem of political thought seems to have found a solution similar to the one already noted for the discrepancy between legality and justice. If the essence of government is defined as lawfulness, and if it is understood that laws are the stabilizing forces in the public affairs of men (as indeed it always has been since Plato invoked Zeus, the god of the boundaries, in his *Laws*), then the problem of movement of the body politic and the actions of its citizens arises. Lawfulness sets limitations to actions, but does not inspire them; the greatness, but also the perplexity of laws in free societies is that they only tell what one should not, but never what one should do. The necessary movement of a body politic can never be found in its essence if only because this essence— again since Plato—has always been defined with a view to its permanence. Duration seemed one of the surest yardsticks for the goodness of a government. It is still for Montesquieu the supreme proof for the badness of tyranny that only tyrannies are liable to be destroyed from within, to decline by themselves, whereas all other governments are destroyed through exterior circumstances. Therefore what the definition of governments always needed was what Montesquieu called a "principle of action" which, different in each form of government, would inspire government and citizens alike in their public activity and serve as a criterion, beyond the merely negative yardstick of lawfulness, for judging all action in public affairs. Such guiding principles and criteria of action are, according to Montesquieu, honor in a monarchy, virtue in a republic and fear in a tyranny.

In a perfect totalitarian government, where all men have become One Man, where all action aims at the acceleration of the movement of nature or history, where every single act is the execution of a death sentence which Nature or History has already pronounced, that is, under conditions where terror can be completely relied upon to keep the movement in constant motion, no principle of action separate from its essence would be needed at all. Yet as long as totalitarian rule has not conquered the earth and with the iron band of terror made each single man a part of one mankind, terror in its double function as essence of government and principle, not of action, but of motion, cannot be fully realized. Just as lawfulness in constitutional government is insufficient to inspire and guide men's actions, so terror in totalitarian government is not sufficient to inspire and guide human behavior.

While under present conditions totalitarian domination still shares with other forms of government the need for a guide for the behavior of its citizens in public affairs, it does not need and could not even use a principle of action strictly speaking, since it will eliminate precisely the capacity of man to act. Under conditions of total terror not even fear can any longer serve as an advisor of how to behave, because terror chooses its victims without reference to individual actions or thoughts, exclusively in accordance with the objective necessity of the natural or historical process. Under totalitarian conditions, fear probably is more widespread than ever before; but fear has lost its practical usefulness when actions guided by it can no longer help to avoid the dangers man fears. The same is true for sympathy or support of the regime; for total terror not only selects its victims according to objective standards; it chooses its executioners with as complete a disregard as possible for the candidate's conviction and sympathies. The consistent elimination of conviction as a motive for action has become a matter of record since the great purges in Soviet Russia and the satellite countries. The aim of totalitarian education has never been to instill convictions but to destroy the capacity to form any. The introduction of purely objective criteria into the selective system of the SS troops was Himmler's great organizational invention, he selected the candidates from photographs according to purely racial criteria. Nature itself decided, not only who was to be eliminated, but also who was to be trained as an executioner.

No guiding principle of behavior, taken itself from the realm of human action, such as virtue, honor, fear, is necessary or can be useful to set into

motion a body politic which no longer uses terror as a means of intimidation, but whose essence *is* terror. In its stead, it has introduced an entirely new principle into public affairs that dispenses with human will to
action altogether and appeals to the craving need for some insight into
the law of movement according to which the terror functions and upon
which, therefore, all private destinies depend.

The inhabitants of a totalitarian country are thrown into and caught
in the process of nature or history for the sake of accelerating its movement; as such, they can only be executioners or victims of its inherent
law. The process may decide that those who today eliminate races and
individuals or the members of dying classes and decadent peoples are
tomorrow those who must be sacrificed. What totalitarian rule needs to
guide the behavior of its subjects is a preparation to fit each of them
equally well for the role of executioner and the role of victim. This two-
sided preparation, the substitute for a principle of action, is the ideology.

Ideologies—isms which to the satisfaction of their adherents can explain everything and every occurrence by deducing it from a single
premise—are a very recent phenomenon and, for many decades, played a
negligible role in political life. Only with the wisdom of hindsight can we
discover in them certain elements which have made them so disturbingly
useful for totalitarian rule. Not before Hitler and Stalin were the great
political potentialities of the ideologies discovered.

Ideologies are known for their scientific character: they combine the
scientific approach with results of philosophical relevance and pretend to
be scientific philosophy. The word "ideology" seems to imply that an idea
can become the subject matter of a science just as animals are the subject
matter of zoology, and that the suffix *-logy* in ideology, as in zoology,
indicates nothing but the *logoi*, the scientific statements made on it. If
this were true, an ideology would indeed be a pseudo-science and a
pseudo-philosophy, transgressing at the same time the limitations of science and the limitations of philosophy. Deism, for example, would then
be the ideology which treats the idea of God, with which philosophy is
concerned, in the scientific manner of theology for which God is a revealed reality. (A theology which is not based on revelation as a given
reality but treats God as an idea would be as mad as a zoology which is no
longer sure of the physical, tangible existence of animals.) Yet we know
that this is only part of the truth. Deism, though it denies divine revelation, does not simply make "scientific" statements on a God which is only
an "idea," but uses the idea of God in order to explain the course of the
world. The "ideas" of isms—race in racism, God in deism, etc.—never
form the subject matter of the ideologies and the suffix *-logy* never indicates simply a body of "scientific" statements.

An ideology is quite literally what its name indicates: it is the logic of an idea. Its subject matter is history, to which the "idea" is applied; the result of this application is not a body of statements about something that *is*, but the unfolding of a process which is in constant change. The ideology treats the course of events as though it followed the same "law" as the logical exposition of its "idea." Ideologies pretend to know the mysteries of the whole historical process—the secrets of the past, the intricacies of the present, the uncertainties of the future—because of the logic inherent in their respective ideas.

Ideologies are never interested in the miracle of being. They are historical, concerned with becoming and perishing, with the rise and fall of cultures, even if they try to explain history by some "law of nature." The word "race" in racism does not signify any genuine curiosity about the human races as a field for scientific exploration, but is the "idea" by which the movement of history is explained as one consistent process.

The "idea" of an ideology is neither Plato's eternal essence grasped by the eyes of the mind nor Kant's regulative principle of reason but has become an instrument of explanation. To an ideology, history does not appear in the light of an idea (which would imply that history is seen *sub specie* of some ideal eternity which itself is beyond historical motion) but as something which can be calculated by it. What fits the "idea" into this new role is its own "logic," that is a movement which is the consequence of the "idea" itself and needs no outside factor to set it into motion. Racism is the belief that there is a motion inherent in the very idea of race, just as deism is the belief that a motion is inherent in the very notion of God.

The movement of history and the logical process of this notion are supposed to correspond to each other, so that whatever happens happens according to the logic of one "idea." However, the only possible movement in the realm of logic is the process of deduction from a premise. Dialectical logic, with its process from thesis through antithesis to synthesis which in turn becomes the thesis of the next dialectical movement, is not different in principle, once an ideology gets hold of it; the first thesis becomes the premise and its advantage for ideological explanation is that this dialectical device can explain away factual contradictions as stages of one identical, consistent movement.

As soon as logic as a movement of thought—and not as a necessary control of thinking—is applied to an idea, this idea is transformed into a premise. Ideological world explanations performed this operation long before it became so eminently fruitful for totalitarian reasoning. The purely negative coercion of logic, the prohibition of contradictions, became "productive" so that a whole line of thought could be initiated, and forced upon the mind, by drawing conclusions in the manner of mere argumentation. This argumentative process could be interrupted neither by a new idea (which would have been another premise with a different set of consequences) nor by a new experience. Ideologies always assume that one idea is sufficient to explain everything in the development from the premise, and that no experience can teach anything because everything is comprehended in this consistent process of logical deduction. The danger in exchanging the necessary insecurity of philosophical thought for the total explanation of an ideology and its *Weltanschauung*, is not even so much the risk of falling for some usually vulgar, always uncritical assumption as of exchanging the freedom inherent in man's capacity to think for the straightjacket of logic with which man can force himself almost as violently as he is forced by some outside power.

The *Weltanschauungen* and ideologies of the nineteenth century are not in themselves totalitarian, and although racism and communism have become the decisive ideologies of the twentieth century they were not, in principle, any "more totalitarian" than the others; it happened because the elements of experience on which they were originally based—the struggle between the races for world domination, and the struggle between the classes for political power in the respective countries—turned out to be politically more important than those of other ideologies. In this sense the ideological victory of racism and communism over all other isms was decided before the totalitarian movements took hold of precisely these ideologies. On the other hand, all ideologies contain totalitarian elements, but these are fully developed only by totalitarian movements, and this creates the deceptive impression that only racism and communism are totalitarian in character. The truth is, rather, that the real nature of all ideologies was revealed only in the role that the ideology plays in the apparatus of totalitarian domination. Seen from this aspect, there appear three specifically totalitarian elements that are peculiar to all ideological thinking.

First, in their claim to total explanation, ideologies have the tendency to explain not what is, but what becomes, what is born and passes away. They are in all cases concerned solely with the element of motion, that is, with history in the customary sense of the word. Ideologies are always oriented toward history, even when, as in the case of racism, they seemingly proceed from the premise of nature; here, nature serves merely to explain historical matters and reduce them to matters of nature. The claim to total explanation promises to explain all historical happenings, the total explanation of the past, the total knowledge of the present, and the reliable prediction of the future. Secondly, in this capacity ideological thinking becomes independent of all experience from which it cannot learn anything new even if it is a question of something that has just come to pass. Hence ideological thinking becomes emancipated from the reality that we perceive with our five senses, and insists on a "truer" reality concealed behind all perceptible things, dominating them from this place of concealment and requiring a sixth sense that enables us to become aware of it. The sixth sense is provided by precisely the ideology, that particular ideological indoctrination which is taught by the educational institutions, established exclusively for this purpose, to train the "political soldiers" in the *Ordensburgen* of the Nazis or the schools of the Comintern and the Cominform. The propaganda of the totalitarian movement also serves to emancipate thought from experience and reality; it always strives to inject a secret meaning into every public, tangible event and to suspect a secret intent behind every public political act. Once the movements have come to power, they proceed to change reality in accordance with their ideological claims. The concept of enmity is replaced by that of conspiracy, and this produces a mentality in which reality—real enmity or real friendship—is no longer experienced and understood in its own terms but is automatically assumed to signify something else.

Thirdly, since the ideologies have no power to transform reality, they achieve this emancipation of thought from experience through certain methods of demonstration. Ideological thinking orders facts into an absolutely logical procedure which starts from an axiomatically accepted premise, deducing everything else from it; that is, it proceeds with a consistency that exists nowhere in the realm of reality. The deducing may proceed logically or dialectically; in either case it involves a consistent process of argumentation which, because it thinks in terms of a process, is supposed to be able to comprehend the movement of the suprahuman, natural or historical processes. Comprehension is achieved by the mind's imitating, either logically or dialectically, the laws of "scientifically" established movements with which through the process of imitation it becomes integrated. Ideological argumentation, always a kind of logical deduction, corresponds to the two aforementioned elements of the ideologies—the element of movement and of emancipation from reality and experience—first, because its thought movement does not spring from experience but is self-generated, and, secondly, because it transforms the one and only point that is taken and accepted from experienced reality into an axiomatic premise, leaving from then on the subsequent argumentation process completely untouched from any further experience. Once it has established its premise, its point of departure, experiences no longer interfere with ideological thinking, nor can it be taught by reality.

The device both totalitarian rulers used to transform their respective ideologies into weapons with which each of their subjects could force himself into step with the terror movement was deceptively simple and inconspicuous: they took them dead seriously, took pride, the one in his supreme gift for "ice cold reasoning" (Hitler) and the other in the "mercilessness of his dialectics," and proceeded to drive ideological implications into extremes of logical consistency which, to the onlooker, looked preposterously "primitive" and absurd: a "dying class" consisted of people

condemned to death; races that are "unfit to live" were to be extermi-
nated. Whoever agreed that there are such things as "dying classes" and
did not draw the consequence of killing their members, or that the right
to live had something to do with race and did not draw the consequence of
killing "unfit races," was plainly either stupid or a coward. This stringent
logicality as a guide to action permeates the whole structure of totalitarian movements and governments. It is exclusively the work of Hitler and
Stalin who, although they did not add a single new thought to the ideas
and propaganda slogans of their movements, for this reason alone must
be considered ideologists of the greatest importance.

What distinguished these new totalitarian ideologists from their predecessors was that it was no longer primarily the "idea" of the ideology—
the struggle of classes and the exploitation of the workers or the struggle
of races and the care for Germanic peoples—which appealed to them,
but the logical process which could be developed from it. According to
Stalin, neither the idea nor the oratory but "the irresistible force of logic
thoroughly overpowered [Lenin's] audience." The power, which Marx
thought was born when the idea seized the masses, was discovered to
reside, not in the idea itself, but in its logical process which "like a mighty
tentacle seizes you on all sides as a vise and from whose grip you are
powerless to tear yourself away; you must either surrender or make up
your mind to utter defeat."* Only when the realization of the ideological
aims, the classless society or the master race, was at stake, could this
force show itself. In the process of realization, the original substance
upon which the ideologies based themselves as long as they had to appeal
to the masses—the exploitation of the workers or the national aspira-
tions of Germany—is gradually lost, devoured as it were by the process
itself: in perfect accordance with "ice cold reasoning" and the "irresistible force of logic," the workers lost under Bolshevik rule even those rights
they had been granted under Tsarist oppression and the German people
suffered a kind of warfare which did not pay the slightest regard to the
minimum requirements for survival of the German nation. It is in the
nature of ideological politics—and is not simply a betrayal committed for
the sake of self-interest or lust for power—that the real content of the
ideology (the working class or the Germanic peoples), which originally
had brought about the "idea" (the struggle of classes as the law of history
or the struggle of races as the law of nature), is devoured by the logic with
which the "idea" is carried out.

The preparation of victims and executioners which totalitarianism requires in place of Montesquieu's principle of action is not the ideology
itself—racism or dialectical materialism—but its inherent logicality.

* Stalin's speech of January 28, 1924; quoted from Lenin, *Selected Works*, Vol. I, p. 33,
Moscow, 1947.—It is interesting to note that Stalin's "logic" is among the few qualities
that Khrushchev praises in his devastating speech at the Twentieth Party Congress.

The most persuasive argument in this respect, an argument of which Hitler like Stalin was very fond, is: You can't say A without saying B and C and so on, down to the end of the murderous alphabet. Here, the coercive force of logicality seems to have its source; it springs from our fear of contradicting ourselves. To the extent that the Bolshevik purge succeeds in making its victims confess to crimes they never committed, it relies chiefly on this basic fear and argues as follows: We are all agreed on the premise that history is a struggle of classes and on the role of the Party in its conduct. You know therefore that, historically speaking, the Party is always right (in the words of Trotsky: "We can only be right with and by the Party, for history has provided no other way of being in the right."). At this historical moment, that is in accordance with the law of history, certain crimes are due to be committed which the Party, knowing the law of history, must punish. For these crimes, the Party needs criminals; it may be that the party, though knowing the crimes, does not quite know the criminals; more important than to be sure about the criminals is to punish the crimes, because without such punishment, History will not be advanced but may even be hindered in its course. You, therefore, either have committed the crimes or have been called by the Party to play the role of the criminal—in either case, you have objectively become an enemy of the Party. If you don't confess, you cease to help History through the Party, and have become a real enemy.—The coercive force of the argument is: if you refuse, you contradict yourself and, through this contradiction, render your whole life meaningless; the A which you said dominates your whole life through the consequences of B and C which it logically engenders.

Totalitarian rulers rely on the compulsion with which we can compel ourselves, for the limited mobilization of people which even they still need; this inner compulsion is the tyranny of logicality against which nothing stands but the great capacity of men to start something new. The tyranny of logicality begins with the mind's submission to logic as a never-ending process, on which man relies in order to engender his thoughts. By this submission, he surrenders his inner freedom as he surrenders his freedom of movement when he bows down to an outward tyranny. Freedom as an inner capacity of man is identical with the capacity to begin, just as freedom as a political reality is identical with a space of movement between men. Over the beginning, no logic, no cogent deduction can have any power, because its chain presupposes, in the form of a premise, the beginning. As terror is needed lest with the birth of each new human being a new beginning arise and raise its voice in the world, so the self-coercive force of logicality is mobilized lest anybody ever start thinking—which as the freest and purest of all human activities is the very opposite of the compulsory process of deduction. Totalitarian government can be safe only to the extent that it can mobilize man's own will power in order to force him into that gigantic movement of History or Nature which supposedly uses mankind as its material and knows neither birth nor death.

The compulsion of total terror on one side, which, with its iron band, presses masses of isolated men together *and* supports them in a world which has become a wilderness for them, and the self-coercive force of logical deduction on the other, which prepares each individual in his lonely isolation against all others, correspond to each other and need each other in order to set the terror-ruled movement into motion and keep it moving. Just as terror, even in its pre-total, merely tyrannical form ruins all relationships between men, so the self-compulsion of ideological thinking ruins all relationships with reality. The preparation has succeeded when people have lost contact with their fellow men as well as the reality around them; for together with these contacts, men lose the capacity of both experience and thought. The ideal subject of totalitarian rule is not the convinced Nazi or the convinced Communist, but people for whom the distinction between fact and fiction (*i.e.*, the reality of experience) and the distinction between true and false (*i.e.*, the standards of thought) no longer exist.

The question we raised at the start of these considerations and to which we now return is what kind of basic experience in the living-together of men permeates a form of government whose essence is terror and whose principle of action is the logicality of ideological thinking. That such a combination was never used before in the varied forms of political domination is obvious. Still, the basic experience on which it rests must be human and known to men, insofar as even this most "original" of all political bodies has been devised by, and is somehow answering the needs of, men.

It has frequently been observed that terror can rule absolutely only over men who are isolated against each other and that, therefore, one of the primary concerns of all tyrannical government is to bring this isolation about. Isolation may be the beginning of terror; it certainly is its most fertile ground; it always is its result. This isolation is, as it were, pretotalitarian; its hallmark is impotence insofar as power always comes from men acting together, "acting in concert" (Burke); isolated men are powerless by definition.

Isolation and impotence, that is the fundamental inability to act at all, have always been characteristic of tyrannies. Political contacts between men are severed in tyrannical government and the human capacities for action and power are frustrated. But not all contacts between men are broken and not all human capacities destroyed. The whole sphere of private life with the capacities for experience, fabrication and thought are left intact. We know that the iron band of total terror leaves no space for such private life and that the self-coercion of totalitarian logic destroys man's capacity for experience and thought just as certainly as his capacity for action.

What we call isolation in the political sphere, is called loneliness in the sphere of social intercourse. Isolation and loneliness are not the same. I can be isolated—that is in a situation in which I cannot act, because there is nobody who will act with me—without being lonely; and I can be lonely—that is in a situation in which I as a person feel myself deserted by all human companionship—without being isolated. Isolation is that impasse into which men are driven when the political sphere of their lives, where they act together in the pursuit of a common concern, is destroyed. Yet isolation, though destructive of power and the capacity for action, not only leaves intact but is required for all so-called productive activities of men. Man insofar as he is *homo faber* tends to isolate himself with his work, that is to leave temporarily the realm of politics. Fabrication (*poiesis*, the making of things), as distinguished from action (*praxis*) on one hand and sheer labor on the other, is always performed in a certain isolation from common concerns, no matter whether the result is a piece of craftsmanship or of art. In isolation, man remains in contact with the world as the human artifice; only when the most elementary form of human creativity, which is the capacity to add something of one's own to the common world, is destroyed, isolation becomes altogether unbearable. This can happen in a world whose chief values are dictated by labor, that is where all human activities have been transformed into laboring. Under such conditions, only the sheer effort of labor which is the effort to keep alive is left and the relationship with the world as a human artifice is broken. Isolated man who lost his place in the political realm of action is deserted by the world of things as well, if he is no longer recognized as *homo faber* but treated as an *animal laborans* whose necessary "metabolism with nature" is of concern to no one. Isolation then becomes loneliness. Tyranny based on isolation generally leaves the productive capacities of man intact; a tyranny over "laborers," however, as for instance the rule over slaves in antiquity, would automatically be a rule over lonely, not only isolated, men and tend to be totalitarian.

While isolation concerns only the political realm of life, loneliness concerns human life as a whole. Totalitarian government, like all tyrannies, certainly could not exist without destroying the public realm of life, that is, without destroying, by isolating men, their political capacities. But totalitarian domination as a form of government is new in that it is not content with this isolation and destroys private life as well. It bases itself on loneliness, on the experience of not belonging to the world at all, which is among the most radical and desperate experiences of man.

Loneliness, the common ground for terror, the essence of totalitarian government, and for ideology or logicality, the preparation of its execu-

tioners and victims, is closely connected with uprootedness and superfluousness which have been the curse of modern masses since the beginning of the industrial revolution and have become acute with the rise of
imperialism at the end of the last century and the breakdown of political
institutions and social traditions in our own time. To be uprooted means
to have no place in the world, recognized and guaranteed by others; to be
superfluous means not to belong to the world at all. Uprootedness can be
the preliminary condition for superfluousness, just as isolation can (but
must not) be the preliminary condition for loneliness. Taken in itself,
without consideration of its recent historical causes and its new role in
politics, loneliness is at the same time contrary to the basic requirements
of the human condition *and* one of the fundamental experiences of every
human life. Even the experience of the materially and sensually given
world depends upon my being in contact with other men, upon our
common sense which regulates and controls all other senses and without
which each of us would be enclosed in his own particularity of sense data
which in themselves are unreliable and treacherous. Only because we
have common sense, that is only because not one man, but men in the
plural inhabit the earth can we trust our immediate sensual experiences.
Yet, we have only to remind ourselves that one day we shall have to leave
this common world which will go on as before and for whose continuity
we are superfluous in order to realize loneliness, the experience of being
abandoned by everything and everybody.

Loneliness is not solitude. Solitude requires being alone whereas loneliness shows itself most sharply in company with others. Apart from a few
stray remarks—usually framed in a paradoxical mood like Cato's statement (reported by Cicero, *De Re Publica*, I, 17): *numquam minus solum
esse quam cum solus esset*, "never was he less alone than when he was
alone," or, rather, "never was he less lonely than when he was in solitude"—it seems that Epictetus, the emancipated slave philosopher of
Greek origin, was the first to distinguish between loneliness and solitude.
His discovery, in a way, was accidental, his chief interest being neither
solitude nor loneliness, but being alone (*monos*) in the sense of absolute
independence. As Epictetus sees it (*Dissertationes,* Book 3, ch. 13) the
lonely man (*eremos*) finds himself surrounded by others with whom he
cannot establish contact or to whose hostility he is exposed. The solitary
man, on the contrary, is alone and therefore "can be together with himself" since men have the capacity of "talking with themselves." In solitude, in other words, I am "by myself," together with my self, and therefore two-in-one, whereas in loneliness I am actually one, deserted by all
others. All thinking, strictly speaking, is done in solitude and is a dialogue between me and myself; but this dialogue of the two-in-one does not
lose contact with the world of my fellow-men because they are represented in the self with whom I lead the dialogue of thought. The problem

of solitude is that this two-in-one needs the others in order to become one again: one unchangeable individual whose identity can never be mistaken for that of any other. For the confirmation of my identity I depend entirely upon other people; and it is the great saving grace of companionship for solitary men that it makes them "whole" again, saves them from the dialogue of thought in which one remains always equivocal, restores the identity which makes them speak with the single voice of one unexchangeable person.

Solitude can become loneliness; this happens when all by myself I am deserted by my own self. Solitary men have always been in danger of loneliness, when they can no longer find the redeeming grace of companionship to save them from duality and equivocality and doubt. Historically, it seems as though this danger became sufficiently great to be noticed by others and recorded by history only in the nineteenth century. It showed itself clearly when philosophers, for whom alone solitude is a way of life and a condition of work, were no longer content with the fact that "philosophy is only for the few" and began to insist that nobody "understands" them. Characteristic in this respect is the anecdote reported from Hegel's deathbed which hardly could have been told of any great philosopher before him: "Nobody has understood me except one; and he also misunderstood." Conversely, there is always the chance that a lonely man finds himself and starts the thinking dialogue of solitude. This seems to have happened to Nietzsche in Sils Maria when he conceived *Zarathustra*. In two poems ("Sils Maria" and "Aus hohen Bergen") he tells of the empty expectation and the yearning waiting of the lonely until suddenly *"um Mittag war's, da wurde Eins zu Zwei . . . Nun feiern wir, vereinten Siegs gewiss,/das Fest der Feste;/Freund Zarathustra kam, der Gast der Gäste!"* ("Noon was, when One became Two . . . Certain of united victory we celebrate the feast of feasts; friend Zarathustra came, the guest of guests.")

What makes loneliness so unbearable is the loss of one's own self which can be realized in solitude, but confirmed in its identity only by the trusting and trustworthy company of my equals. In this situation, man loses trust in himself as the partner of his thoughts and that elementary confidence in the world which is necessary to make experiences at all. Self and world, capacity for thought and experience are lost at the same time.

The only capacity of the human mind which needs neither the self nor the other nor the world in order to function safely and which is as independent of experience as it is of thinking is the ability of logical reasoning whose premise is the self-evident. The elementary rules of cogent evidence, the truism that two and two equals four cannot be perverted even under the conditions of absolute loneliness. It is the only reliable "truth" human beings can fall back upon once they have lost the mutual guarantee, the common sense, men need in order to experience and live and know their way in a common world. But this "truth" is empty or rather no truth at all, because it does not reveal anything. (To define consistency as truth as some modern logicians do means to deny the existence of truth.) Under the conditions of loneliness, therefore, the self-evident is no longer just a means of the intellect and begins to be productive, to develop its own lines of "thought." That thought processes characterized by strict self-evident logicality, from which apparently there is no escape, have some connection with loneliness was once noticed by Luther (whose experiences in the phenomena of solitude and loneliness probably were second to no one's and who once dared to say that "there must be a God because man needs one being whom he can trust") in a little-known remark on the Bible text "it is not good that man should be alone": A lonely man, says Luther, "always deduces one thing from the other and thinks everything to the worst." The famous extremism of totalitarian movements, far from having anything to do with true radicalism, consists indeed in this "thinking everything to the worst," in this deducing process which always arrives at the worst possible conclusions.

What prepares men for totalitarian domination in the non-totalitarian world is the fact that loneliness, once a borderline experience usually suffered in certain marginal social conditions like old age, has become an everyday experience of the evergrowing masses of our century. The merciless process into which totalitarianism drives and organizes the masses looks like a suicidal escape from this reality. The "ice-cold reasoning" and the "mighty tentacle" of dialectics which "seizes you as in a vise" appears like a last support in a world where nobody is reliable and nothing can be relied upon. It is the inner coercion whose only content is the strict avoidance of contradictions that seems to confirm a man's identity outside all relationships with others. It fits him into the iron band of terror even when he is alone, and totalitarian domination tries never to leave him alone except in the extreme situation of solitary confinement. By destroying all space between men and pressing men against each other, even the productive potentialities of isolation are annihilated; by teaching and glorifying the logical reasoning of loneliness where man knows that he will be utterly lost if ever he lets go of the first premise from which the whole process is being started, even the slim chances that loneliness may be transformed into solitude and logic into thought are obliterated. If this practice is compared with that of tyranny, it seems as if a way had been found to set the desert itself in motion, to let loose a sand storm that could cover all parts of the inhabited earth.

The conditions under which we exist today in the field of politics are indeed threatened by these devastating sand storms. Their danger is not that they might establish a permanent world. Totalitarian domination, like tyranny, bears the germs of its own destruction. Just as fear and the impotence from which fear springs are antipolitical principles and throw men into a situation contrary to political action, so loneliness and the logical-ideological deducing the worst that comes from it represent an antisocial situation and harbor a principle destructive for all human living-together. Nevertheless, organized loneliness is considerably more dangerous than the unorganized impotence of all those who are ruled by the tyrannical and arbitrary will of a single man. Its danger is that it threatens to ravage the world as we know it—a world which everywhere seems to have come to an end—before a new beginning rising from this end has had time to assert itself.

Apart from such considerations—which as predictions are of little avail and less consolation—there remains the fact that the crisis of our time and its central experience have brought forth an entirely new form of government which as a potentiality and an everpresent danger is only too likely to stay with us from now on, just as other forms of government which came about at different historical moments and rested on different fundamental experiences have stayed with mankind regardless of temporary defeats—monarchies, and republics, tyrannies, dictatorships and despotism.

But there remains also the truth that every end in history necessarily contains a new beginning; this beginning is the promise, the only "message" which the end can ever produce. Beginning, before it becomes a historical event, is the supreme capacity of man; politically, it is identical with man's freedom. *Initium ut esset homo creatus est*—"that a beginning be made man was created" said Augustine.* This beginning is guaranteed by each new birth; it is indeed every man.

1958

* *De Civitate Dei*, Book 12, chapter 20.

PART
NINE

A Recent View of
Nineteen Eighty-Four

MICHAEL HARRINGTON
Nineteen Eighty-Four Revisited

How well does George Orwell's *Nineteen Eighty-Four* stand up, more than thirty years after it was written? Has the course of history since 1949 confirmed its insights into the totalitarian tendencies in the world?

Before turning to the substance of that question, it is necessary to outline the ground rules for an answer. Utopian novels—or anti-utopian novels like *Nineteen Eighty-Four*—are not the work of seers who predict the future. Their truth has to do with an understanding of their own time and place at least as much as with their intuitions about what will come in the future. And they are, of necessity, somewhat monochromatic. We must ask, then: Was the tendency that they exaggerated and simplified *an* important factor in the history of our time, and not whether it was *the* single dominating factor (which is what utopias often pretend is the case).

Once we clarify our question and the way it must be answered, we can proceed to *Nineteen Eighty-Four* itself. The response will be framed in terms of two of Orwell's most important hypotheses: that there is a global trend in the direction of the monstrous future that he imagined; and that 1984 would therefore see a certain convergence between two societies, the Soviet Union and Britain under the Labour government.

First, however, let us probe our method, questioning our question. How does one evaluate utopian imaginings in the light of the actual history that comes after them?

The nineteenth-century German philosopher G. W. F. Hegel might help us to answer this question. In his *Philosophy of Right* Hegel noted that Plato's *Republic,* "which is usually taken as the very model of an *empty ideal*, did nothing more than conceptualize the nature of Greek mores at the time." Plato, Hegel argued, was a conservative deeply concerned about the breakup of traditional Greek society because of the growth of individualism. He was unable to locate an actual, political movement in that society which was capable of countering the trends he feared. Therefore, he imagined a "solution" to the Greek crisis from the vantage point of his own alienation from it. The law and order depicted in Plato's *Republic*, Hegel held, was an inverted image of the impiety, the contempt for the old ways, that Plato saw all around him. *The Republic*'s fantastic version of the future was actually his anguished response to the present.

Then Hegel came to a surprising conclusion. Plato had not found a realistic way to deal with the developments that appalled him; his alternative came from "on high" and was the product of his wish rather than of any movement within the society—even though, at the same time, Plato had correctly focused upon "the principle around which the actual transformation of the world turned." *The Republic* dramatized the basic conflict of Greek society at that time, the struggle between the traditional, organic community and the individualism and materialism of a new order.

Hegel's point can be applied to the masterpiece of English literature that gave this genre its name: Thomas More's *Utopia*. More was quite specific with regard to the social unrest that led him to imagine an ideal alternative. He wrote, "Sheep . . . those placid creatures, which used to require so little food, have now apparently developed a raging appetite, and turned into man-eaters. Fields, houses, towns, everything goes down their throats." This is a clear reference to the Acts of Enclosure of the sixteenth century. These acts gave previously communal lands to large landowners, who drove off surplus tenant farmers and converted farm lands to sheep pastures to meet the increasing market demand for wool production. The social and economic upheavals caused by the Enclosure Acts led to the increase of a rootless and highly competitive labor force in English cities, which in turn helped prepare the way for capitalism. Whatever else More's futuristic book may be, it is also a meditation on ways of dealing with a *contemporary* problem.

We should treat *Nineteen Eighty-Four* as Hegel dealt with Plato's *Republic* and in the spirit of these few comments on More's *Utopia*. It is pointless to ask whether the future turned out exactly as Orwell described it in his book. Of course it didn't and the author, a man of literary as well as political culture, knew it wouldn't. He was not trying to be an oracle. We would do better to consider how well *Nineteen Eighty-Four*'s imaginary future helps us understand 1949's reality and see whether it offers insights into *an* important trend of the years that followed. For this book, like every other imaginative utopia or anti-utopia, is a purposive exaggeration, a useful simplification.

But how, it might be fairly asked, can exaggerations and simplifications be useful? In the natural sciences, they are a standard feature in the experimental method. When Galileo studied the motion of a projectile, he first assumed that the air did not resist, that there was no friction. Then, when he had made his computations on the basis of this contrary-to-fact assumption, he corrected them in order to introduce friction into his equation. To this very day, the "laboratory conditions" that are needed for many investigations in physics and chemistry are artificial constructs that hold almost all of the infinite variables of the real world constant in order to permit the precise observation of one, or several, variables thought to be of critical importance.

Something like that is also done in the social sciences. In Volume I of *Das Kapital*, for instance, Karl Marx imagined a society totally isolated from the world market, with products exchanged by independent producers in proportion to the socially necessary labor time they contained, where there were no inefficiencies, no cheating, and indeed no capitalists (the producers hired no labor). He then analyzed the dynamic of this "world" that never had existed and never could. That enabled him to develop some fundamental concepts that he then used as he dropped his simplifying assumptions and came closer to the real world. Had he started with reality before developing those concepts, he argued, he would have confronted an unruly, endless mass of data without any way of knowing where to focus.

Utopias and anti-utopias, in general, and *Nineteen Eighty-Four* in particular, follow a similar method. They usually begin with some relatively simple premise, such as all property is owned in common, or that people are in a "state of nature" that is prior to society and law. Or as in the case of Orwell, that there is a completely totalitarian state. They then develop in detail the consequences of that premise in the organization of society. As a result, utopias and anti-utopias tend, even when dramatized, to be somewhat one-dimensional. As we observed earlier, their value resides in exploring one crucial trend, and their worth depends on whether they have concentrated on a crucial determinant of their times and the years that follow.

Given the conception of utopia and anti-utopia I have just outlined, I will not ask whether the world in the year 1984 will resemble the world described in the novel *Nineteen Eighty-Four*. It will not, but then neither have Plato's *Republic* or More's *Utopia* ever turned out to be "true" in that literal sense of the word. Rather, I want to raise the question of whether the reality of our time is in any significant sense "Orwellian." I think so.

George Orwell's *Nineteen Eighty-Four* was, as we will discuss a little later on, a response to the reality of Stalin's Russia in 1949. But one of Orwell's most distinctive intuitions was that the totalitarianism then visible in Russia was actually a worldwide trend; that English socialism—Ingsoc in Newspeak—was a precursor of the new Leviathan, or total state, which was thus no longer a specifically Russian phenomenon. How does this perception square with the reality of our time?

If Orwell's vision is taken literally, then this aspect of *Nineteen Eighty-Four* is clearly a failure. "Oligarchic collectivism" has not triumphed on a global scale; English socialism has not become totalitarian; world politics are not characterized by war for war's sake among three empires based on power for power's sake. The Soviet Union still bears some striking resemblances to Orwell's anti-utopia and so does China (Orwell's "Eastasia"). But the West, including its working class, has a much higher living standard than in 1949 when Orwell published his book; the European Common Market has emerged as a force in its own right; and international politics are much more complex than Orwell's three-cornered model. How then can we argue that there is continuing relevance in Orwell's book?

That can only be done if one measures *Nineteen Eighty-Four* in the way indicated at the outset: as a useful exaggeration, a functional simplification, and not as a prediction. Within *that* framework, Orwell focused upon one of the critical trends of the 1980s and the 1990s: the inexorable trend toward the collectivization of every economy and society in the world. That process has not even begun to approximate, in the Western democracies, the totalitarian structure imagined by Orwell. And yet, such a development remains a genuine possibility, even if not in the stark and unrelieved sense of *Nineteen Eighty-Four*. Orwell's democratic socialism—which he reaffirmed even as he wrote his anti-utopia and whose values, as we will see, suffuse his image of its opposite—remains the other main option. And just as Hegel credited Plato with having placed one of the central issues of his age at the heart of the Republic, so Orwell must be praised for having seen that the relation between freedom and collectivism is a critical axis around which the modern world turns.

I suggested a moment ago that *Nineteen Eighty-Four* is not simply a book written by a socialist but a socialist book. But why in the world would a writer committed to a democratic and communitarian socialism produce such a horrible vision of oligarchic collectivism? In exploring that point, some of the nuances of *Nineteen Eighty-Four* will emerge.

The theory of *Nineteen Eighty-Four*, and much else, is developed in the long excerpt from Emmanuel Goldstein's *Theory and Practice of Oligarchical Collectivism*, the book that Winston Smith reads avidly and that puts Julia to sleep. Almost every critic has recognized the person of Leon Trotsky in Emmanuel Goldstein. The physical description of Goldstein ("a lean Jewish face, with a great fuzzy aureole of white hair and a small goatee beard") evokes the actual Trotsky. But there is an interesting, and very substantial, point that most of those who make the equation of Goldstein and Trotsky overlook. Orwell's Goldstein holds views that the real Trotsky not only rejected but fought against vigorously at the end of his life. For Trotsky, the Stalinists who ruled Russia were not a ruling class but merely a parasitic caste, a social stratum that had *temporarily* usurped the worker's power, which was still incarnate in the institutions of Soviet society, above all in its nationalized property. For that reason, Trotsky insisted that the anti-Stalinist revolution he advocated was merely "political," i.e., that it would change the ruling bureaucracy but not, as in a "social revolution," transform the very basis of the society.

Goldstein, by contrast, adopts a position of Trotsky's opponents. The rulers of the totalitarian societies of 1984 are a "new aristocracy" recruited from "the salaried middle class and the upper grades of the working class." "It had always been assumed," Goldstein writes, "that if the capitalist class were expropriated, Socialism must follow. . . . Ingsoc . . . has in fact carried out the main item in the Socialist program, *with the result, foreseen and intended beforehand, that economic inequality has been made permanent"* (emphasis added). Though Orwell's Goldstein may resemble Trotsky, and though Orwell cleverly mimics Trotsky's style, the opinions here put into Goldstein's mouth are diametrically opposed to those of Trotsky.

The notion that collectivism could be tyrannical rather than democratic has a considerable history. In 1899, Polish anarcho-syndicalist Waclaw Machajski published *The Evolution of Social Democracy*, a book that saw socialism as an agency for the class power of intellectuals rather than of workers. After the Bolsheviks took power in Russia in 1917, their Left critics—anarchists and libertarian communists—began to attack them for creating a bureaucratic dictatorship. That notion was put forward by dissidents in Stalin's prisons in the twenties and developed by an independent Italian Marxist, Bruno Rizzi, in a book titled *The Bureaucratization of the World* in 1939. In the early forties, it was put forward within the Trotskyist movement by three Americans—Max Shachtman, Joseph Carter, and James Burnham—and it was debated by German exiles of the anti-Stalin left at about the same time.

Trotsky, as I have said, rejected the theory. But, in an article at the very end of his life, he conceded that it might be true that the October Revolution had in fact become the agency of a new form of antisocialist tyranny and the Soviet bureaucracy a new ruling class.

Orwell responded to one of the Trotskyist critics who later became a leading American conservative, James Burnham. He did so in two long essays, "James Burnham and the Managerial Revolution" (1946) and "Burnham's View of the Contemporary World Struggle" (1947). The idea for *Nineteen Eighty-Four* had occurred to Orwell in 1943 and he completed the rough draft of it in 1947; so these essays are clearly a part of the intellectual process that culminated in the novel. But then, even if we did not have the dates so clearly established, the link between Orwell's reaction to Burnham and *Nineteen Eighty-Four* is obvious from the texts themselves.

"In the *Managerial Revolution*," Orwell wrote in 1947,

Burnham foretold the rise of three superstates which would be unable to conquer one another and would divide the world between them. Now the superstates have dwindled to two, and, thanks to atomic weapons, neither of them is invincible. In the *Managerial Revolution* it was implied that all the superstates would be very much alike. They would all be totalitarian in structure; they would be collectivist but not democratic, and would be ruled over by a caste of managers, scientists and bureaucrats who would destroy old-style capitalism and keep the working class permanently in subjection. In other words, something rather like 'Communism' would prevail everywhere. In *The Machiavellians*, Burnham somewhat toned down his theory but continued to insist that politics is only the struggle for power and that government has to be based on force and fraud. Democracy is unworkable, and in any case the masses do not want it and will not make sacrifices in defence of it.

Later, Orwell concluded, Burnham changed these views considerably. But couldn't one still say that *Nineteen Eighty-Four* is a fictionalized version of Burnham's earlier vision of the world?

Well, yes and no. Despite fundamental disagreements with Burnham, Orwell had a certain grudging respect for his analytic audacity, his willingness to think "unthinkable" thoughts. But—and this is crucial—even as he credited Burnham with some insights he attacked him most sharply. The author of the *Managerial Revolution*, Orwell says, is secretly enamored with the very power he denounces. That is one of the reasons why his predicted futures are simply the projected present, i.e., that he enormously overestimated the power and potential of Nazism simply because it had just won some notable military victories. And Orwell charges that Burnham does not realize that a third choice of economic security within political freedom—or democratic socialism—could be counterposed to both the warring camps.

Edward Thompson, a brilliant British historian who broke decisively with his Stalinist past, nevertheless still thinks that *Nineteen Eighty-Four* was an apology for the North Atlantic Treaty Organization (NATO), that is, for the Western side in the Cold War. But that is to overlook precisely what divides Orwell from Burnham. *Nineteen Eighty-Four*, with its prediction of the totalitarianizing of *English* socialism, is hardly one of those cheerleading books that contrasted the righteousness of the West with the evil of the East during the period of intense struggle between the two. On the contrary, Orwell sees in the West a potential for the growth of the Eastern social structure. *Nineteen Eighty-Four* is the *cri de coeur* of a socialist. It ends, of course, with the triumph of Big Brother, but it does not rule out further rebellion even if it does not imagine how that would take place.

So *Nineteen Eighty-Four* is based, in a very real sense, on a socialist self-criticism, on the sad, but brutally candid, knowledge that one's most cherished hopes might provide the basis for one's most feared nightmare. Socialists once thought that collectivism—the principle that government, representing all the people, should manage the economic affairs of the nation—was the royal road to freedom; but now, they must learn, precisely if they remain true to their socialism, that it can also be the route to totalitarianism. Not that it *must* be (which would end the socialist hope), but that it *can* be. Still, it has already been conceded that Orwell's fears were *not* fulfilled, at least not yet. What contemporary value, then, does the vision of Western "oligarchic collectivism" have, given the fact that it has not taken place?

One of the great facts of these times is that there is a profound collectivist tendency in all societies, the non- and anti-Communist as well as the Communist. That is clearly the case in the Third World where the state—often the one-party, dictatorial state—plays a critical role even in countries with capitalist ideologies. (Brazil, under the rule of anti-Communist generals, has nationalized practically all large enterprises not owned by multinational corporations.) In the United States itself, the exigencies of economic management and military control have enormously increased the federal government's sphere of activity. Indeed, military needs and economic management frequently overlap, as in the huge defense budget upon which a number of giant American corporations depend for their revenues. On a more pacific level, one example of this collectivist tendency is the guarantee by the US government of loans to the Chrysler Corporation; another is the tax exemptions granted to American oil companies on their foreign investments. Indeed, federal tax policy in the United States tends to subsidize business investors through such devices as tax deferrals, depreciation allowances, and entertainment expenses.

To be sure, these developments have not been accompanied by anything like the total assault on freedom imagined in *Nineteen Eighty-Four*. But there were the assaults on civil liberties during the McCarthy period; Nixon's enemies list; the secret decisions to escalate the Vietnam War made by both Lyndon Johnson and Nixon; the wiretapping of government employees; the Watergate scandal; and so on. At no point were American freedoms fundamentally threatened, but these events certainly point to the antilibertarian potential of the modern state, including state functions originally created for the best of reasons (the welfare state).

And if Orwell's image of a complete convergence of all societies into a single social-economic system has not come to pass, there certainly are tendencies which go partly in that direction. The conservative analyst John Lukacs talked in a history of the Cold War of how America was becoming more "Soviet" (collectivized) and Russia more "American" (particularly in the area of technology). The late Isaac Deutscher, a Marxist critical of Stalin's regime but sympathetic to the economic structure that it created, thought that such a convergence was the basis of peaceful coexistence; so did Andrei Sakharov, perhaps the most effective of the Soviet dissidents. And something like this theory is to be found in the analysis of "industrial" or "post-industrial" society made by writers like Daniel Bell and Clark Kerr.

So Orwell was right about *a* tendency, which he turned into the *only* tendency in his novel, simplified and projected to the nth degree. He did not predict the future—but he did grasp, and wrote large, one of its critical determinants. The year 1984 will not, in the West, simply look like the world of the novel *Nineteen Eighty-Four*; but that fictional world remains a real possibility in the year 2000, or 2050, or 2100.

But what about the "original" that provided the model for Orwell's conception of a world system of "oligarchic collectivism"? What about the Soviet Union?

There can be no question that Orwell had Russia in mind when he wrote his novel. "Big Brother" is described in the very first page of the book in physical terms that apply to Stalin and to his rhetorical style. " 'What lessons do we learn from this fact, comrades? The lesson—which is also one of the fundamental principles of Ingsoc—that,' etc., etc."—is a perfect parody of the repetitious catechisms favored by the Russian dictator. Moreover, as we have seen, the theory of "oligarchic collectivism" was developed by some Trotskyists and libertarian Communists to explain the social class nature of the Soviet Union.

Yet here, too, there is a difference. For the Communists of 1949, the killing and suppression were genuinely believed to be necessary for the creation of socialism. That this was a monstrous falsehood does not change its subjective character as a faith. But for Orwell, the official ideology of the Communist Party is pure sham and its conscious goal—at least in the inner circle—is power for power's sake. Now there is no question that there is enormous cynicism among the devotees of the official "Marxism" of Communist states. In 1963 when I was in Poland, I asked a Communist official why the philosopher Leszek Kolakowski, a determined critic of the regime (who later went into exile), was allowed to remain in the Communist Party (from which he was finally expelled in 1966). Because, I was told, Wladyslaw Gomulka, the head of the Party, "did not want to expel the only Marxist left in Poland from the Communist Party."

And yet I doubt—on general philosophic grounds that cannot be proved or disproved—that it is possible for individuals to live without any values other than a hunger for power. I think that even the worst villains of history—say, Hitler—believed in part of their minds that their crimes were committed in order to serve "higher" values. In the period after Orwell's death, Marxism in Eastern Europe did not simply provide the official rationale for totalitarian policies. In Poland, Hungary, and Czechoslovakia, it also became the vibrant intellectual instrument of *opponents* of the system who eventually mobilized masses in behalf of "socialism with a human face," as it was called in Czechoslovakia in 1968.

In the Eastern European countries where, with the exception of Yugoslavia, Communism was imposed upon the people by the Soviet army, totalitarianism has been anything but the seamless monolith imagined by Orwell in *Nineteen Eighty-Four*. In Yugoslavia, where Tito and his comrades took power at the head of a genuinely popular antifascist movement, national opposition to Russian dominance led to the first great split in the "Eurasian" Communist front. Moreover, in Yugoslavia the system has clearly evolved from totalitarianism to authoritarianism, i.e., from the repression of *all* forms of criticism to the repression of only those forms of criticism that the regime regards as politically dangerous.

In East Germany, within months of Stalin's death in 1953, the "proles" carried out a general strike that was put down only by the Soviet tanks. In Poland in 1956, there was a rebellion of intellectuals, students, and workers, including occupation of the factories, which effectively kept the Russians from intervening. In Hungary in that year, the same forces came together in a social revolution that toppled the Communist regime and was later itself crushed in blood by the Russians. And in 1967–68 in Czechoslovakia, a democratic socialist movement started within the Communist Party itself and embraced great masses of people. Therefore, it is fair to say that when "oligarchic collectivism" faces *both* social class *and* national opposition, it is far from the impregnable system imagined by Orwell/ Thus *Nineteen Eighty-Four* is based on the *Russian* reality of 1947–48, i.e., the period in which Stalin was engaged in an insane witch hunt that struck at anyone who even mildly deviated from the Party line. In his novel, Orwell was clearly describing that Russian moment.)

But then the Russian system itself evolved. It did not undergo the upheavals experienced in East Germany, Poland, Hungary, and Czechoslovakia—or, more precisely, it has not yet experienced them—but it was clearly necessary to reform some of the dictatorship's most outrageously totalitarian features. Thus a "thaw" began in the Soviet Union several years after Stalin's death, and in 1956 the head of the Communist Party, Nikita Khrushchev, in his speech at the Twentieth Party Congress of the Soviet Communist Party, admitted some of the truths about the past. In contrast to *Nineteen Eighty-Four*, there were unpersons, living and dead, who became persons once again. Solzhenitsyn's novel on the prison camps was published and there were "rehabilitations."

But there were limits. Leon Trotsky remains an "arch-fiend." Even Nikolai Bukharin—the veteran Bolshevik who led Stalin's "Right" opposition—has been denied posthumous rehabilitation. And after Khrushchev's fall, there were ambivalent moves toward re-Stalinization. If, then, Orwell was wrong on the details, he was, and is, right about a central fact of Soviet life that remains in force to this very day: *that the history of the past is dictated by the politics of the present.* If individuals can be brought back from the Gulag or from the outer darkness in which historians have consigned their memory, they can still have their lives systematically falsified as well.

On another count, recent Communist history is less in conformity with Orwell's vision. Particularly in Eastern Europe—and above all in Poland—the proletariat has not remained passive and accepting. More than a decade of workers' struggles in Poland, including massive strikes, have forced the regime to maintain the standard of living for the majority of people at a much higher level than the rulers would like. Moreover, the successful struggles of the Polish workers culminated in the creation of an independent union movement in 1980. But if this history runs counter to one of Orwell's insights, it confirms another: that "oligarchic collectivism" is a very inefficient, low-productivity system, and that this is not a totalitarianism of satisified human needs (as in Huxley's *Brave New World*) but of their denial.

That leads to the third of Orwell's major predictions: his perspective upon the development of English socialism, or Ingsoc. That, it will be remembered, rests very heavily upon the assumption of a depoliticized and passive working class in the West. But certainly one of the reasons why Orwell's worst fears were not realized in Europe and the United States is, precisely, the continuing combativity of working people. There is, as we will see in a moment, no need to be romantic about this, but the fact is there nevertheless.

In the sixties and seventies, there were tremendous surges of working-class militance in Europe and Britain. In 1968, for instance, there was a general strike in France and almost equally forceful activity in Italy. In the 1970s, the British labor movement brought down the Conservative government of Prime Minister Edward Heath. At the same time, cultural analysts like Raymond Williams and the sociologists who studied the "affluent worker" realized that at least some of the old socialist traditions were being eroded in England. Instead of the old hymn-singing, millennial enthusiasm, there was now an "instrumental collectivism" of people fighting together for private, individualistic goals, not for a new society. And among the working-class young, there were cultural signs of a certain decay of all values; in other words, violence over soccer games was sometimes more of a factor in working-class conflict than the class struggle.

This increase of individualism in England, and incidentally in the United States, has led to the atomization of the working class and a loss of class solidarity. As a result of this loss, many workers now tend to identify their interests more closely than in the past with those of the petty bourgeoisie and their customary opposition to costly welfare programs, to government regulation of business and the environment, to low tariffs permitting foreign competition (in England, this takes the form of opposition to the Common Market), and to many other elements of the programs usually associated with liberalism. The shift in identification of interests has in turn resulted, at least for the moment, in large segments of the working class abandoning their traditional political parties and supporting the Conservative leader in England, Margaret Thatcher, and the Republican Party in the United States led by Ronald Reagan.

However, it would be premature to write the obituary of the working-class movement in the English-speaking world, just as it would be on the continent of Europe. The interests of working people and the bourgeoisie are not in fact identical. The failure of Prime Minister Margaret Thatcher's policies, as in her inability to reduce unemployment, has already alienated workers and driven a wedge between them and the middle class. In the United States, the working class is watching carefully the policies of the Reagan administration in such areas as the minimum wage and unemployment compensation.

In continental Europe, working-class solidarity seems much more intact than in England and the United States. The Socialist and Communist parties of France, Germany, and Italy continue to have the loyalty of the majority of workers and can periodically mobilize them in opposition to their respective governments. In other parts of Europe, proletarian solidarity continues to exert political power, as in the election of the Social Democratic leader Bruno Kreisky to an unprecedented fourth term as Chancellor of Austria. Even in Communist countries, workers have occasionally joined in opposition to the state apparatus, as in the Soviet Union where 250,000 factory workers went on strike in 1980 for better food and improved working conditions, and as, most dramatically, in Poland where shipyard workers toppled one regime and forced important concessions from its successor.

It should be clear from these events that Orwell's picture of a depoliticized and passive working class has at best only a mixed connection to historical reality. Here, as in the case of his theory of the worldwide triumph of oligarchic collectivism, Orwell was onto *a* trend, not onto *the* trend of working-class relations to political power.

Will the year 1984 be Orwellian? Yes and no. The world imagined by Orwell will not exist when that year comes. Yet profound tendencies in the direction of *Nineteen Eighty-Four* will continue long after 1984 is past. And ironically, one of the reasons why some of Orwell's worst fears will not come to pass is to be found in . . . Orwell. His novel itself falsified its own predictions by alerting people to their possibility. And that is the critical point to remember about Orwell. In *Nineteen Eighty-Four*, he described one of the two basic possibilities he saw before humanity in an extreme, simplified but useful way. He did so precisely because he continued to stand for the *other* possibility—because, as one who stood for the best, he actively wanted to falsify his projections of the worst.

"There is [little] question now of avoiding collectivism," Orwell wrote in 1940. "The only question is whether it is to be founded on willing cooperation or on the machine gun." In *Nineteen Eighty-Four*, he described the collectivism of the machine gun—and much worse—because he did not want it to happen, because he believed in the collectivism of willing cooperation. It is in part because of his capacity to be brutally candid about the worst possibilities in his own dream that his nightmare has not come true. It is still a possibility; but it can still be prevented.

1981

SUGGESTIONS FOR WRITING

1. Write an essay describing the kind of novel, or prose fiction, that *Nineteen Eighty-Four* is. If you believe that the book differs significantly from the usual or conventional novel, specify clearly the nature and extent of the differences.

   a. Is there much, or any, kinship between *Nineteen Eighty-Four* and science fiction? Why didn't Orwell create robots or other mechanical wonders such as are often found in science fiction? If he had, how would that have affected the nature of his work?

   b. Is there an element of prophecy in *Nineteen Eighty-Four?* If so, what kind is it?

   c. The central figure of the book undergoes terrible sufferings. Does this, in your opinion, make him a *tragic* hero? Can *Nineteen Eighty-Four* be regarded as a tragedy?

2. To what extent would you say that the characterizations of *Nineteen Eighty-Four* are a major source of interest in the book? Is characterization as important here as in a traditional nineteenth-century novel?

   a. We often speak of characters in novels as being three-dimensional or "true to life," by which we may mean that they appear to resemble in both outer conduct and inner nature people whom we know. Would you say that the characters in *Nineteen Eighty-Four* satisfy this requirement, or that they are created on different principles? If so, which principles? And in what way can it be said that the special treatment of character in *Nineteen Eighty-Four* is necessary for this kind of book?

3. One of the most remarkable and troubling incidents in the novel concerns the response of Winston Smith to his torturer O'Brien. Here is a crucial passage:

> He opened his eyes and looked up gratefully at O'Brien. At sight of the heavy, lined face, so ugly and so intelligent, his heart seemed to turn over. If he could have moved he would have stretched out a hand and laid it on O'Brien's arm. He had never loved him so deeply as at this moment, and not merely because he had stopped the pain. The old feeling, that at bottom it did not matter whether O'Brien was a friend or an enemy, had come back. O'Brien was a person who could be talked to. Perhaps one did not want to be loved so much as to be understood. O'Brien had tortured him to the edge of lunacy, and in a little while, it was certain, he would send him to his death. It made no difference. In some sense that went deeper than friendship, they were intimates. . . .

How would you describe the personal and/or political psychology behind this feeling of Winston Smith. Do you know whether there are actual historical parallels to such feelings?

4. Remembering that Winston is the first name of a leading political figure in contemporary England and Smith one of the most common second names in the English language, discuss why Orwell gave this name to his leading character.

5. Both Winston and Julia rebel against the world of *Nineteen Eighty-Four*, but their modes of rebellion are radically different. How would you describe this difference, and what effect does it have on the course of the story? In setting up these two characters in relation to one another, is Orwell trying to suggest something about the nature of individual resistance in a totalitarian society?

6. Some critics have called *Nineteen Eighty-Four* a "negative utopia" or a "utopia in reverse." Do you believe that the aspects of Oceania that Orwell attacks most sharply are simply imaginary projections of a possible future, or that they already exist in modern-day societies?

    a. To what extent is *Nineteen Eighty-Four* to be taken as a picture of contemporary totalitarianism, and in which ways does it go beyond what we know of such a society?

    b. If a writer like Orwell, in a book like *Nineteen Eighty-Four* "exaggerates" or "overstates," is that a permissible technique?

    c. Do you believe that, in milder forms, there are some aspects of Oceania society that Orwell may have drawn from modern democratic societies?

    d. Are there some elements in the world of *Nineteen Eighty-Four* that seem to you so farfetched, so much the product of Orwell's fear and perhaps even hysteria, that they cannot be justified even as extreme versions of a historical possibility?

7. It is clear fom the beginning of the book that Winston cannot possibly succeed in his rebellion against the Party. Since the book lacks this element of suspense, how does Orwell nevertheless manage to hold the reader's attention?

8. Consider the physical descriptions in *Nineteen Eighty-Four*, especially Orwell's use of certain kinds of adjectives. What is the predominant quality of his imagery? How does it help establish a certain tone that reinforces Orwell's central idea?

9. The two men who dominate Oceania, Big Brother and Goldstein, may not even exist as actual persons. In what ways does each of them nevertheless maintain a hold over the people, and how does their shadowiness as political leaders contribute to this hold?

10. Why does the party look upon sexuality as a threat to its domination? How does it nevertheless exploit the natural sex drives of its citizens?

11. A major element in all human culture is a sense of the past, a respect for and concern with the experience of the generations that have come and gone. How has this feeling been changed in Oceania and to what extent can one say that the past no longer exists but is manufactured?

12. In his study of Nazism, *Behemoth* (1944), the political scientist Franz Neumann describes totalitarian society as essentially "lawless"—that is, while it has innumerable restrictions and regulations, while the life of its subjects is constantly threatened by the power of the state, there is not available a fixed and

knowable pattern of legality. Is the same thing true in Oceania? And wherein do you think would lie the special terror for the people, as also the special effectiveness for the rulers, in the absense of laws to be broken, of a regulated system of legality or illegality?

13. One of the most interestng contributions of *Nineteen Eighty-Four* is the concept of "doublethink." How exactly would you describe it? Is it simply telling lies? Does it have any relation to the kind of "rationality" that dominates Oceania?

14. A related phenomenon in Oceania is "Newspeak." What do you think Orwell is trying to suggest here concerning the relationship between politics and language? Do you see certain connections between the ideas he puts forward in his essay "Politics and the English Language" and the ideas in *Nineteen Eighty-Four* concerning "Newspeak?"

15. Slogans play a specially important part in modern political movements. In what way do the slogans of Oceania—WAR IS PEACE, FREEDOM IS SLAVERY, IGNORANCE IS STRENGTH—contribute to the power of its rulers? Do you think Orwell meant to suggest that any actual totalitarian movement would use slogans so entirely revealing of its inner nature or that he had something else in mind?

16. One of the most precious elements of Western society is often said to be the concept of the self, the sense of uniqueness and individuality that individual persons cherish. To what extent is this influenced or even produced by certain kinds of societies? What does Oceania try to do with the sense of self?

17. Explain the differences in treatment afforded in Oceania to members of the Inner Party, members of the Outer Party, and the proles. How does this presumably contribute to the stability of the state? Why does Winston feel that if there is any hope for destroying the Party dictatorship it lies with the proles? What major political tradition of our time is reflected in Winston's feeling?

18. A number of apparently trivial objects are used symbolically by Orwell—the diary, the coral paperweight, the old rhyme. What does he mean to suggest through them? How do they contribute to the pathos of the story?

19. Why does Winston continue to be tortured even when it becomes clear that he has nothing more to tell and is already doomed? Is this sheer vindictiveness or brutality? Does it reveal something of the purpose and character of the totalitarian state?

20. On the basis of this book, would you say that Orwell is entirely pessimistic about the future of mankind? Why did he write *Nineteen Eighty-Four* at all?

PAPERS BASED ON THE SOURCES AND THE CRITICAL ESSAYS

1. After having read the brief selections from Huxley, Zamiatin, and Connolly, consider the extent to which they anticipate Orwell's approach in *Nineteen Eighty-Four*. Are there passages in Orwell's book to which these selections may be compared?

2. A paper that would be worth writing is a fuller comparison between the Huxley and Zamiatin books, on the one hand, and *Nineteen Eighty-Four* on the other. This would require you to read the two former novels, both available in paperback editions, and then to see at which points Orwell borrows from them and at which points he goes off on his own.

3. In the essay "The Fiction of Anti-Utopia," Irving Howe concludes with a series of points that he says characterize "anti-utopian fiction" as a literary genre. Would you say that *Nineteen Eighty-Four* satisfies all these requirements? The "model" that Howe is creating in this essay could not, of course, apply to any particular novel entirely. In which respects does *Nineteen Eighty-Four* deviate from this model?

4. It would seem fair to describe Isaac Deutscher's essay as a serious intellectual attack on *Nineteen Eighty-Four*. From which point of view does Deutscher seem to be writing. Do you accept any of his arguments? Try to imagine Orwell still alive and reading Deutscher's essay: What do you think he would say in reply?

5. Deutscher speaks of the "underlying boundless despair" of *Nineteen Eighty-Four*. Do you believe that is a sound judgment? To what extent, and in which ways?

6. In the course of his essay, "*1984*: History as Nightmare," Irving Howe writes that the book raises certain problems of credence, even within its own chosen limits. These involve such matters as the role of ideology in a totalitarian state, the life of the proles, sexuality in Oceania, and so forth. A somewhat similar criticism appears in Philp Rahv's essay. Do you believe these to be justified?

7. The last sentence in Rahv's essay (p. 315) contains an important political observation concerning the value of *Nineteen Eighty-Four*. How would you contrast this sentence with the essential theme developed in Deutscher's essay?

8. Samuel Sillen's attack on *Nineteen Eighty-Four* is written from a Communist point of view. Would you say that its main purpose is to reassure faithful followers who may have been disturbed by reading about *Nineteen Eighty-Four* in the non-Communist press or to persuade non-Communist readers not to let themselves be influenced by Orwell's work? In which ways does the tone of Sillen's essay help you answer the question?

9. Lionel Trilling in his essay on Orwell attempts to present him as a model of a certain kind of intellectual. What kind would you say that is? What are the moral or political lessons that Trilling draws from Orwell's career?

10. The essays by Richard Lowenthal and Hannah Arendt try to describe what is historically unique in the phenomenon of totalitarianism. Could you, drawing both upon these essays and your understanding of the problem, make up a list of the attributes of totalitarian society that would distinguish it from traditional, "old-fashioned" dictatorships, democracies, monarchies, and other forms of society? Sociologists sometimes speak of creating a "model" for a social phenomenon: that is, trying to abstract its essential elements from those that are merely accidental and thereby presenting a picture of the "pure" phenomenon (e.g., "pure" totalitarianism). Could you, on the basis of the material in this book, draw up such a model?

11. Do you believe that Soviet experiences since the death of Stalin have called into question the views concerning totalitarianism that are expressed in *Nineteen Eighty-Four* as well as in some of the essays in this book.

12. As Michael Harrington makes clear in his essay, there is considerable tension between individualist and collectivist tendencies within Communist and non-Communist societies, despite the growing concentration of power in both systems. One cause of these tensions is the contradiction between practice and theory. For example, Karl Marx said in *The German Ideology*, "Conceiving, thinking, the mental intercourse of men, appear . . . as the direct [outcome] of their material behavior . . . but men, developing their material production and their material intercourse, alter . . . their thinking and the products of their thinking." And, in the *The Holy Family*, he observed that "man is . . . free not through the negative power to avoid this or that, but through the positive power to assert his true individuality . . . and [thus] must be given social scope for the vital manifestation of his being." Such statements, and others like them, have been contradicted by the totalitarian practices of Communist states, which tend to restrict change and control thought, and have led Marxist dissidents, such as the Polish philosopher Leszek Kolakowski, to claim that individuals must judge independently the programs, policies, and doctrines of the Communist Party and government. Unlike Communist states, democratic societies no longer have a single, coherent body of doctrines, yet these societies have also experienced internal contradictions. In your opinion, what are some of these contradictions? In what ways do they reinforce the vision of social organization represented in *Nineteen Eighty-Four* and in what ways do they prevent that vision from coming true? In particular, how does the tension between individualist and collectivist tendencies in democratic societies relate to the totally controlled society envisioned by Orwell?

SUGGESTIONS FOR FURTHER READING

The critical literature on Orwell and *Nineteen Eighty-Four* is enormous and continues to grow each year. There is, however, a useful and reliable guide to the literature: Jeffrey and Valerie Meyers, *George Orwell: An Annotated Bibliography* (New York: Garland Publishing, 1977). All of the following books contain some biographical material as well as critical discussions of varying usefulness and from different points of view:

Atkins, John. *George Orwell: A Literary Study*. London: Calder & Boyars, 1971.

Brander, Laurence. *George Orwell*. London: Longmans, Green, 1954.

Connolly, Cyril. *Enemies of Promise*. Boston: Atlantic Monthly Press, 1939.

Greenblatt, Stephen. *Three Modern Satirists: Waugh, Orwell and Huxley*. New Haven, Conn.: Yale University Press, 1965.

Gross, Miriam, ed. *The World of George Orwell*. New York: Simon & Schuster, 1972.

Heppenstall, Rayner. *Four Absentees*. London: Barrie & Rockliff, 1960.

Hollis, Christopher. *A Study of George Orwell: The Man and His Works*. London: Hollis & Carter, 1956.

Hopkinson, Tom. *George Orwell*. London: Longmans, Green, 1956.

Kubal, David. *Outside the Whale: George Orwell's Art and Politics*. Notre Dame, Ind.: University of Notre Dame Press, 1972.

Meyers, Jeffrey. *A Reader's Guide to George Orwell*. London: Thames & Hudson, 1975.

Modern Fiction Studies XXI (Spring 1975). Special issue on Orwell.

Rees, Sir Richard. *George Orwell: Fugitive from the Camp of Victory*. Carbondale, Ill.: Southern Illinois University Press, 1961.

Stansky, Peter and William Abrahams. *The Unknown Orwell*. New York: Knopf, 1972.

Stanksy, Peter and William Abrahams. *Orwell: The Transformation*. New York: Knopf, 1980.

Steinhoff, William. *George Orwell and the Literary Origins of 1984*. Ann Arbor, Mich.: University of Michigan Press, 1975.

Voorhees, Richard. *The Paradox of George Orwell*. Lafayette, Ind.: Purdue University Press, 1961.

Williams, Raymond, ed. *George Orwell: Twentieth Century Interpretations*. Englewood Cliffs, N.J.: Prentice-Hall, 1974.

Woodcock, George. *The Crystal Spirit: A Study of George Orwell*. Boston: Little Brown, 1966.

The World Review, a now defunct English magazine, published a special issue on Orwell in June 1950, which contains valuable material.

Zwerdling, Alex. *Orwell and the Left*. New Haven, Conn.: Yale University Press, 1974.

The literature on totalitarianism is by now also enormous, and the following books are suggested merely as a sampling:

Arendt, Hannah. *The Origins of Totalitarianism.* New York: Harcourt Brace Jovanovich, 1973.

Friedrich, Carl J. and Zbigniew K. Brzezinski. *Totalitarian Dictatorship and Autocracy.* Cambridge, Mass.: Harvard University Press, 1957.

Friedrich, Carl J., ed. *Totalitarianism* (Proceedings of a Conference Held at the American Academy of Arts and Sciences, March 1953). Cambridge, Mass., 1954.

Fromm, Erich. *Escape from Freedom.* New York: Farrar, Farrar & Rinehart, 1941.

Lederer, Emil. *State of the Masses.* New York: Norton, 1940.

Neumann, Franz L. *Behemoth,* 2nd ed. New York: Octagon, 1944.

Walsh, Chad. *From Utopia to Nightmare.* New York: Harper & Row, 1962.

Acknowledgments

Edward Arnold Publishers Ltd.   for "George Orwell" from *Two Cheers for Democracy* by E. M. Forster. © 1972 by Edward Arnold Publishers Ltd. Reprinted by permission of Edward Arnold Publishers Ltd.

Curtis Brown Ltd.   for "George Orwell's Utopia" from *Critical Occasions* by Julian Symons. Copyright © 1966 Julian Symons. Reprinted by permission of Curtis Brown Ltd. For "George Orwell" from *Essays on Literature and Ideas* by John Wain. Reprinted by kind permission of Curtis Brown Ltd. on behalf of John Wain.

Coward-McCann, Inc.   for "*1984*—The Mysticism of Cruelty," from *Russia in Transition* by Isaac Deutscher. © 1957 by Hamish Hamilton, Ltd. Reprinted by permission of Coward-McCann, Inc.

Dissent   for "Our Peculiar Hell" by Richard Lowenthal, Fall, 1957. Copyright 1957. Reprinted by permission of *Dissent* and Richard Lowenthal.

E. P. Dutton & Co., Inc.   for selections from the book *We* by Eugene Zamiatin, translated by Gregory Zilboorg. Copyright, 1924, by E. P. Dutton & Co., Inc. Renewal, 1952, by Gregory Zilboorg. Reprinted by permission of the publishers.

Harcourt Brace Jovanovich, Inc.   for "Politics and the English Language" from *Shooting an Elephant and Other Essays* by George Orwell. Copyright, 1945, 1946, 1949, 1950 by Sonia Brownell Orwell. For "Why I Write" from *Such, Such Were the Joys* by George Orwell. Copyright, 1945, 1952, 1953 by Sonia Brownell Orwell. For *Nineteen Eighty-Four* by George Orwell, copyright, 1949, by Harcourt Brace Jovanovich, Inc. For "Orwell on the Future" from *Speaking of Literature and Society* by Lionel Trilling. Copyright 1949, 1977 by Diana Trilling, as Executrix of the Estate of Lionel Trilling. "The Prevention of Literature" and other selections from *The Collected Essays, Journalism and Letters of George Orwell*, Volumes 2, 3, and 4. Copyright © 1968 by Sonia Brownell Orwell. All reprinted by permission of Harcourt Brace Jovanovich, Inc.

Harper & Row, Publishers, Inc.   for selections from *Brave New World* by Aldous Huxley. Copyright 1932 by Aldous Huxley. For "Letter to George Orwell (E. H. BLAIR), Wrightwood, Cal., 21 October, 1949" in *Letters of Aldous Huxley,* edited by Grover Smith. Copyright © 1969 by Laura Huxley. For "Decency and Death" (pp. 251–257) in *An Age of Enormity* by Isaac Rosenfeld, ed. Theodore Solotaroff (World Publishing Company). Copyright 1950 by Vasiliki Rosenfeld. Copyright © 1962 by Harper & Row, Publishers, Inc. All reprinted by permission of Harper & Row, Publishers, Inc.

Horizon Press, Inc.   for "Orwell: History as Nightmare" from *Politics and the Novel* by Irving Howe, reprinted below as "*1984:* History as Nightmare." © 1957 by Irving Howe. Reprinted by permission of Horizon Press, Inc.

Hulton Estates Administration   for "A Footnote About *1984*" by Aldous Huxley, "George Orwell" by Bertrand Russell, and "A Writer's Life" by T. R. Fyvel; from *World Review,* June, 1950. Reprinted by permission.

The Macmillan Company   for "Year Nine" by Cyril Connolly. Copyright 1946 by Cyril Connolly. Reprinted with permission of the publisher from *The Condemned Playground* by Cyril Connolly.

Mainstream   for "Maggot-of-the-Month" by Samuel Sillen, from *Masses & Mainstream,* II, 8, August, 1949. Copyright 1949. Reprinted by permission.

The New Republic   for "The Fiction of Anti-Utopia" by Irving Howe, from *The New Republic,* April 23, 1962. Copyright 1962. Reprinted by permission.

The New York Times Co.   for "An Indignant and Prophetic Novel" by Mark Schorer, from *The New York Times Book Review,* June 12, 1949. © 1949 by The New York Times Company. Reprinted by permission.

Partisan Review   for "The Unfuture of Utopia" by Philip Rahv, from *Partisan Review,* XVI, 7, July, 1949. Copyright 1949. Reprinted by permission of the author.

449

A. D. Peters & Co. Ltd.   for "A Rebel's Progress: To George Orwell's Death," from *The Trail of the Dinosaur and Other Essays* by Arthur Koestler. Reprinted by permission of A. D. Peters & Co. Ltd.

Pioneer Publishers   for selection from *The Revolution Betrayed* by Leon Trotsky. Copyright 1945 by Pioneer Publishers.

Statesman & Nation Publishing Co. Ltd.   for "Review of *1984*" by V. S. Pritchett, from *The New Statesman and Nation,* June 18, 1949. Copyright 1949. Reprinted by permission of the publisher.

Tribune   for "Freedom and Happiness" by George Orwell, from *Tribune* (London), January 4, 1946. Copyright 1946. Reprinted by permission.

The Viking Press, Inc.   for "George Orwell and the Politics of Truth" from *The Opposing Self* by Lionel Trilling. Copyright 1955 by Lionel Trilling. Reprinted by permission of The Viking Press.

The World Publishing Company   for "Ideology and Terror: A Novel Form of Government," from *The Origins of Totalitarianism* by Hannah Arendt. Copyright 1951 by Hannah Arendt. Second Enlarged Edition copyright 1958 by Hannah Arendt. Reprinted by permission of the author.